Penguin Books
Life at Blandings

Pelham Grenville Wodehouse was born in 1881 in Guildford, the son of a civil servant, and educated at Dulwich College. He spent a brief period working for the Hong Kong and Shanghai Bank before abandoning finance for writing, earning a living by journalism and selling stories to magazines.

An enormously popular and prolific writer, he produced about a hundred books, and was probably best known for creating Jeeves, the ever resourceful 'gentleman's personal gentleman', and the good-hearted young blunderer Bertie Wooster. However, Wodehouse created many other comic figures, perhaps most notably the inhabitants of, and regular visitors to, Blandings Castle and its environs. He wrote the many Blandings stories over the course of more than sixty years; the first, *Something Fresh*, appeared in 1915, while at the time of his death he was working on the posthumously published *Sunset at Blandings*. He was part-author and writer of fifteen straight plays and of 250 lyrics for some thirty musical comedies. *The Times* hailed him as a 'comic genius recognized in his lifetime as a classic and an old master of farce'.

P. G. Wodehouse said, 'I believe there are two ways of writing novels. One is mine, making a sort of musical comedy without music and ignoring real life altogether; the other is going right deep down into life and not caring a damn.'

Wodehouse married in 1914 and took American citizenship in 1955. He was created a Knight of the British Empire in the 1975 New Year's Honours List. In a BBC interview he said that he had no ambitions left now that he had been knighted and there was a waxwork of him in Madame Tussaud's. He died on St Valentine's Day, 1975, at the age of ninety-three.

P. G. Wodehouse published and forthcoming in Penguin

P. G. Wodehouse
Life at Blandings: An Omnibus

P.G.Wodehouse

Life
at
Blandings

An Omnibus

Something Fresh
Summer Lightning
Heavy Weather

PENGUIN BOOKS

PENGUIN BOOKS

Published by the Penguin Group
Penguin Books Ltd, 80 Strand, London WC2R 0RL, England
Penguin Putnam Inc., 375 Hudson Street, New York, New York 10014, USA
Penguin Books Australia Ltd, 250 Camberwell Road, Camberwell, Victoria 3124, Australia
Penguin Books Canada Ltd, 10 Alcorn Avenue, Toronto, Ontario, Canada M4V 3B2
Penguin Books India (P) Ltd, 11 Community Centre, Panchsheel Park, New Delhi – 110 017, India
Penguin Books (NZ) Ltd, Cnr Rosedale and Airborne Roads, Albany, Auckland, New Zealand
Penguin Books (South Africa) (Pty) Ltd, 24 Sturdee Avenue, Rosebank 2196, South Africa

Penguin Books Ltd, Registered Offices: 80 Strand, London WC2R 0RL, England

www.penguin.com

Something Fresh first published by Herbert Jenkins 1915
Published in Penguin Books 1979
Copyright by the Trustees of the Wodehouse Estate

Summer Lightning first published by Herbert Jenkins 1929
Published in Penguin Books 1954
Copyright by the Trustees of the Wodehouse Estate

Heavy Weather first published by Herbert Jenkins 1933
Published in Penguin Books 1966
Copyright by the Trustees of the Wodehouse Estate

This collection first published 1981

28

Set in 9/11pt Monotype Trump
Typeset by Rowland Phototypesetting Ltd,
Bury St Edmunds, Suffolk
Printed in England by Clays Ltd, St Ives plc

ISBN-13: 978-0-140-05903-8

Contents

Something Fresh

Preface

When this book was first published – fifty-three years ago – writers in America, where I had been living since 1909, were divided into two sharply defined classes – the Swells who contributed regularly to the *Saturday Evening Post* and the Cannail or Dregs who thought themselves lucky if they landed an occasional story with *Munsey's*, the *Popular* or one of the other pulp magazines. I had been a chartered member of the latter section for five years when I typed the first words of *Something Fresh*.

Half-way through it I got married (and have been ever since) to an angel in human form who had seventy-five dollars. As I had managed to save fifty, we were fairly well fixed financially, but we felt we could do with a bit more, and by what I have always looked on as a major miracle we got it. My agent, who must have been an optimist to end all optimists, sent the story to the *Saturday Evening Post* and George Horace Lorimer, its world-famous editor, bought it as a serial and paid me the stupefying sum of $3,500 for it, at that time the equivalent of seven hundred gleaming golden sovereigns. I was stunned. I had always known in a vague sort of way that there was money like $3,500 in the world, but I had never expected to touch it. If I was a hundred bucks ahead of the game in those days, I thought I was doing well.

I have always had the idea that Lorimer must have been put in a receptive mood the moment he saw the title page. My pulp magazine stories had been by 'P. G. Wodehouse', but *Something Fresh* was the work of:

3

PELHAM GRENVILLE WODEHOUSE, and I am
convinced that that was what put it over.

A writer in America at that time who went about
without three names was practically going around
naked. Those were the days of Richard Harding Davies,
of James Warner Bellah, of Margaret Culkin Banning, of
Earl Derr Biggers, of Charles Francis Coe, Norman Reilly
Raine, Mary Roberts Rinehart, Clarence Buddington
Kelland, and Orison Swett – yes, really, I'm not kidding
– Marden. Naturally a level-headed editor like Lorimer
was not going to let a Pelham Grenville Wodehouse get
away from him.

If you ask me to tell you frankly if I like the names
Pelham Grenville, I must confess that I do not. I have
my dark moods when they seem to me about as low as
you can get. At the font I remember protesting
vigorously when the clergyman uttered them, but he
stuck to his point. 'Be that as it may,' he said firmly,
having waited for a lull, 'I name thee Pelham Grenville.'

Apparently I was called that after a godfather, and not
a thing to show for it except a small silver mug which I
lost in 1897. I little knew how the frightful label was
going to pay off thirty-four years later. (One could do a
bit of moralizing about that if one wanted to, but better
not for the moment. Some other time, perhaps.)

Something Fresh was the first of what I might call –
in fact, I will call – the Blandings Castle Saga. Since then
I have written nine novels and a number of short stories
about that stately home of England. And I should like to
give a warning to any young littérateur who is planning
to go in for this Saga racket, and that is to be very careful
in the early stages how he commits himself to dates and
what is known as locale. When I wrote *Something Fresh*
I rashly placed Blandings Castle in Shropshire because
my happiest days as a boy were spent near Bridgnorth,
overlooking the fact that to get to the heart of
Shropshire by train takes four hours (or did in my time.

No doubt British Railways by now have cut it down a lot). This meant that my characters were barred from popping up to London and popping back the same afternoon, which is so essential to characters in the sort of stories I write. Kent or Sussex would have served me better.

And as to dates. I wrote *Something Fresh* in 1914, and not realizing that this was not an end but a beginning and wanting to make Lord Emsworth fairly elderly I stated that he had been at Eton in the Sixties. This becomes awkward nowadays, for while the ninth earl is not supposed to be in his first youth, I certainly do not intend to portray him as a centenarian.

People are always asking me . . . well, someone did the other day . . . if I draw my characters from living originals. I don't. I never have, except in the case of Psmith. He was based more or less faithfully on Rupert D'Oyly Carte, the son of the Savoy Theatre man. He was at school with a cousin of mine, and my cousin happened to tell me about his monocle, his immaculate clothes, and his habit, when asked by a master how he was, of replying, 'Sir, I grow thinnah and thinnah.' I instantly recognized that I had been handed a piece of cake and I bunged him down on paper (*circ.* 1908). But none of the Blandings circle owes his or her existence to anyone but me. I thought them all up, starting from scratch.

I have often felt that life at Blandings must have been a very pleasant affair, if not for Lord Emsworth and his pig, at any rate for visitors to the castle. Plenty of ridin', shootin', and fishin' for those sportively inclined, and the browsing and sluicing of course beyond criticism. I have always refrained from describing the meals there, not wishing to make my readers' mouths water excessively, but I can now divulge that they were of the best and rendered all the more toothsome by being presided over by butler Beach, who also never failed to bring the tray of beverages into the drawing-room at 9.30.

The one thing that might be considered to militate against the peace of life at Blandings was the constant incursion of impostors. Blandings had impostors the way other houses have mice. I have recorded so far the activities of six of them, and no doubt more to come.

I am not certain who is the Empress's pig man now that La Simmons has left. I may be wrong, but I have a sort of idea that he will turn out to be the latest of that long line of impostors. It is about time that another was coming along. Without at least one impostor on the premises, Blandings Castle is never itself.

P. G. WODEHOUSE

I

The sunshine of a fair Spring morning fell graciously upon London town. Out in Piccadilly its heartening warmth seemed to infuse into traffic and pedestrians alike a novel jauntiness, so that bus-drivers jested and even the lips of chauffeurs uncurled into not unkindly smiles. Policemen whistled at their posts, clerks on their way to work, beggars approached the task of trying to persuade perfect strangers to bear the burden of their maintenance with that optimistic vim which makes all the difference. It was one of those happy mornings.

At nine o'clock precisely the door of No. 7A, Arundell Street, Leicester Square, opened, and a young man stepped out.

Of all the spots in London which may fairly be described as backwaters, there is none that answers so completely to the description as Arundell Street, Leicester Square. Passing along the north pavement of the Square, just where it joins Piccadilly, you hardly notice the bottle-neck opening of the tiny *cul-de-sac*.

Day and night the human flood roars past, ignoring it. Arundell Street is less than forty yards in length, and, though there are two hotels in it, they are not fashionable hotels. It is just a back-water.

In shape Arundell Street is exactly like one of those flat stone jars in which Italian wine of the cheaper sort is stored. The narrow neck which leads off Leicester Square opens abruptly into a small court. Two sides of this hotels occupy; the third is at present given up to furnished lodgings for the impecunious. These are always just going to be pulled down in the name of

Progress, to make room for another hotel, but they never do meet with that fate, and as they stand now so will they, in all probability, stand for generations to come.

They provide single rooms of moderate size, the bed modestly hidden during the day behind a battered screen. They contain a table, an easy-chair, a hard chair, a bureau, and a round tin bath, which, like the bed, goes into hiding after its useful work is performed. And you may rent one of these rooms, with breakfast thrown in, for five dollars a week.

Ashe Marson had done so. He had rented the second-floor front of No. 7A.

Twenty-six years before this story opens there had been born to the Reverend Joseph Marson, minister, and Sarah his wife, of Much Middlefold, Salop, a son. This son, christened Ashe after a wealthy uncle who subsequently double-crossed them by leaving his money to charities, in due course proceeded to Oxford to read for the Church. So far as can be ascertained from contemporary records, he did not read a great deal for the Church, but he did succeed in running the mile in four and a half minutes and the half-mile at a correspondingly rapid speed, and his researches in the art of long-jumping won him the respect of all.

He secured his Blue for Athletics, and gladdened thousands by winning the mile and the half-mile two years in succession against Cambridge at Queen's Club. But, owing to the pressure of other engagements, he unfortunately omitted to do any work, and, when the hour of parting arrived, he was peculiarly unfitted for any of the learned professions. Having, however, managed to obtain a sort of degree, enough to enable him to call himself a Bachelor of Arts, and realizing that you can fool some of the people some of the time, he applied for and secured a series of private tutorships. Having saved a little money at this dreadful trade, Ashe came to London and tried newspaper work. After two years of moderate success, he got in touch with the Mammoth Publishing Company.

The Mammoth Publishing Company, which controls several important newspapers, a few weekly journals, and a number of other things, does not disdain the pennies of the office-boy and the junior clerk. One of its many profitable ventures is a series of paper-covered tales of crime and adventure. It was here that Ashe found his niche. Those 'Adventures of Gridley Quayle, Investigator', which are so popular with a certain section of the reading public, were his work. Until the advent of Ashe and Mr Quayle, the 'British Pluck Library' had been written by many hands and had included the adventures of many heroes; but in Gridley Quayle the proprietors held that the ideal had been reached, and Ashe received a commission to conduct the entire 'British Pluck Library' (monthly) himself. On the meagre salary paid him for these labours he had been supporting himself ever since.

That was how Ashe came to be in Arundell Street, Leicester Square, on this May morning.

He was a tall, well-built, fit-looking young man, with a clear eye and a strong chin; and he was dressed, as he closed the front door behind him, in a sweater, flannel trousers, and rubber-soled gymnasium shoes. In one hand he bore a pair of Indian clubs, in the other a skipping-rope.

Having drawn in and expelled the morning air in a measured and solemn fashion which the initiated observer would have recognized as that 'scientific deep breathing' which is so popular nowadays, he laid down his clubs, adjusted his rope, and began to skip.

When one considers how keenly London, like all large cities, resents physical exercise, unless taken with some practical and immediate utilitarian object in view, this young man's calm, as he did this peculiar thing, was amazing. The rules governing exercise in London are

clearly defined. You may run, if you are running after a
hat, or an omnibus; you may jump, if you do so with the
idea of avoiding a taxi-cab or because you have stepped
on a banana-skin. But, if you run because you wish to
develop your lungs or jump because jumping is good for
the liver, London punishes you with its mockery. It
rallies round and points the finger of scorn.

Yet this morning, Arundell Street bore the spectacle
absolutely unmoved. Due West, the proprietor of the
Hotel Previtali leaned against his hostelry, his mind an
obvious blank; due North, the proprietor of the Hotel
Mathis propped up his caravanserai, manifestly thinking
of nothing. In various windows of the two hotels the
upper portions of employees appeared, and not a single
employee ceased his task for a moment to fling a jibe.
Even the little children who infested the court forbore to
scoff, and the customary cat rubbing itself against the
railings rubbed on without a glance.

The whole thing affords a remarkable object-lesson of
what a young man can achieve with patience and
perseverance.

When he had taken the second-floor front of No. 7A
three months before, Ashe Marson had realized that he
must forget those morning exercises which had become
a second nature to him, or else defy London's unwritten
law and brave London's mockery. He had not hesitated
long. Physical fitness was his gospel. On the subject of
exercise he was confessedly a crank. He decided to defy
London.

The first time he appeared in Arundell Street in his
sweater and flannels, he had barely whirled his Indian
clubs once round his head before he had attracted the
following audience:

(*a*) two cabmen (one intoxicated);
(*b*) four waiters from the Hotel Mathis;
(*c*) six waiters from the Hotel Previtali;

(*d*) six chambermaids from the Hotel Mathis;
(*e*) five chambermaids from the Hotel Previtali;
(*f*) the proprietor of the Hotel Mathis;
(*g*) the proprietor of the Hotel Previtali;
(*h*) a street-cleaner;
(*i*) eleven nondescript loafers;
(*j*) twenty-seven children;
(*k*) a cat.

They all laughed, even the cat, and kept on laughing. The intoxicated cabman called Ashe 'Bill Bailey!' and Ashe kept on swinging his clubs.

A month later, such is the magic of perseverance, his audience had narrowed down to the twenty-seven children. They still laughed, but without that ringing conviction which the sympathetic support of their elders had lent them.

And now, after three months, the neighbourhood, having accepted Ashe and his morning exercises as a natural phenomenon, paid him no further attention.

On this particular morning, Ashe Marson skipped with even more than his usual vigour. This was because he wished to expel by means of physical fatigue a small devil of discontent of whose presence within him he had been aware ever since getting out of bed. It is in the Spring that the ache for the Larger Life comes upon us, and this was a particularly mellow Spring morning. It was the sort of morning when the air gives us a feeling of anticipation, a feeling that, on a day like this, things surely cannot go joggling along in the same dull old groove, a premonition that something romantic and exciting is about to happen to us. On such a morning you will see stout old gentlemen make sudden rollicking swings with their umbrellas; and a note of shrill optimism thrills in the errand-boy's whistle, as he sees life opening before him, large and splendid.

But the south-west wind of Spring brings also

remorse. We catch the vague spirit of unrest in the air, and we regret our misspent youth.

Ashe was doing this. Even as he skipped, he was conscious of a wish that he had worked harder at Oxford, and was now in a position to be doing something better than hack-work for a soulless publishing company. Never before had he been so completely certain that he was sick to death of the rut into which he had fallen. The thought that after breakfast he must sit down and hammer out another Gridley Quayle adventure numbed him like a blow from what the papers always call 'some blunt instrument'. The mere thought of Gridley Quayle was loathsome on a morning like this, with all creation shouting at him that Summer was on its way and that there were brave doings afoot just round the corner.

Skipping brought no balm. He threw down his rope, and took up the Indian clubs.

Indian clubs left him still unsatisfied. The thought came to him that it was a long time since he had done his Larsen Exercises. Perhaps they would heal him.

A gentleman named Lieutenant Larsen, of the Danish Army, as the result of much study of the human anatomy, some time ago evolved a series of Exercises. All over the world at the present moment his apostles are twisting themselves into knots in accordance with the dotted lines in the illustrative plates of his admirable book. From Peebles to Baffin's Bay arms and legs are being swung in daily thousands from point A to point B, and flaccid muscles are gaining the consistency of india-rubber. Larsen's Exercises are the last word in exercises. They bring into play every sinew of the body. They promote a brisk circulation. They enable you, if you persevere, to fell oxen, if desired, with a single blow.

But they are not dignified. Indeed, to one seeing them suddenly and without warning for the first time, they are markedly humorous. The only reason why King

Henry of England, whose son sank with the White Ship,
never smiled again, was because Lieutenant Larsen had
not then invented his admirable Exercises.

So complacent, so insolently unselfconscious had
Ashe become in the course of three months, owing to
his success in inducing the populace to look on anything
he did with the indulgent eye of understanding, that it
simply did not occur to him, when he abruptly twisted
his body into the shape of a cork-screw in accordance
with the directions in the Lieutenant's book for the
consummation of Exercise One, that he was doing
anything funny. And the behaviour of those present
seemed to justify his confidence. The proprietor of the
Hotel Mathis regarded him without a smile. The
proprietor of the Hotel Previtali might have been in a
trance for all the interest he displayed. The hotel
employees continued their tasks impassively. The
children were blind and dumb. The cat across the way
stropped its backbone against the railings unheeding.

But, even as he unscrambled himself and resumed a
normal posture, from his immediate rear there rent the
quiet morning air a clear and musical laugh. It floated
out upon the breeze, and hit him like a bullet.

Three months ago Ashe would have accepted the
laugh as inevitable, and would have refused to allow it
to embarrass him. But long immunity from ridicule had
sapped his resolution. He spun round with a jump,
flushed and self-conscious.

From the window of the first-floor front of No. 7A a
girl was leaning. The Spring sunshine played on her
golden hair and lit up her bright blue eyes, fixed on his
flannelled and sweatered person with a fascinated
amusement. Even as he turned, the laugh smote him
afresh.

For the space of perhaps two seconds they stared at
each other, eye to eye. Then she vanished into the room.

Ashe was beaten. Three months ago a million girls

could have laughed at his morning exercises without
turning him from his purpose. Today this one scoffer,
alone and unaided, was sufficient for his undoing. The
depression which exercise had begun to dispel surged
back upon him. He had no heart to continue. Sadly
gathering up his belongings, he returned to his room,
and found a cold bath tame and uninspiring.

The breakfasts (included in rent) provided by Mrs
Bell, the landlady at No. 7A, were not exhilarating
feasts. By the time Ashe had done his best with the
dishevelled fried egg, the chicory, blasphemously called
coffee, and the charred bacon, Misery had him firmly in
its grip. And when he forced himself to the table, and
began to try to concoct the latest of the adventures of
Gridley Quayle, Investigator, his spirit groaned within
him.

With that musical laugh ringing in his ears, he found
himself wishing that he had never thought of Gridley
Quayle, that the baser elements of the British reading
public had never taken him for their hero, and that he
personally was dead.

The unholy alliance had been in progress now for
more than two years, and it seemed to Ashe that Gridley
grew less human each month. He was so complacent
and so maddeningly blind to the fact that only the most
amazing luck enabled him to detect anything. To depend
on Gridley Quayle for one's income was like being
chained to some horrible monster.

This morning, as he sat and chewed his pen, his
loathing for Gridley seemed to have reached its climax.
It was his habit, in writing these stories, to think of a
good title first, and then fit an adventure to it.

And overnight, in a moment of inspiration, he had
jotted down on an envelope the words:

THE ADVENTURE OF THE WAND OF DEATH

It was with the sullen repulsion of a vegetarian who

finds a caterpillar in his salad that he now sat glaring at them.

The title had seemed so promising overnight, so full of strenuous possibilities. It was still speciously attractive, but, now that the moment had arrived for writing the story, its flaws became manifest.

What was a Wand of Death? It sounded good, but, coming down to hard facts, what *was* it? You cannot write a story about a wand of death without knowing what a wand of death is; and, conversely, if you have thought of such a splendid title, you cannot jettison it offhand.

Ashe rumpled his hair, and gnawed his pen.

There came a knock at the door.

Ashe spun round in his chair. This was the last straw. If he had told Mrs Bell once that he was never to be disturbed in the morning on any pretext whatsoever, he had told her twenty times. It was simply too infernal to be endured if his work-time was to be cut into like this. He ran over in his mind a few opening remarks.

'Come in,' he shouted, and braced himself for battle.

A girl walked in, the girl of the first-floor front, the girl with the blue eyes who had laughed at his Larsen Exercises.

II

Various circumstances contributed to the poorness of the figure which Ashe cut in the opening moments of this interview. In the first place, he was expecting to see his landlady, whose height was about four feet six, and the sudden entry of someone who was about five feet seven threw the universe temporarily out of focus. In the second place, in anticipation of Mrs Bell's entry, he had twisted his face into a forbidding scowl and it was no slight matter to change this on the spur of the moment into a pleasant smile. Finally a man who has been sitting for half an hour in front of a sheet of paper bearing the words:

THE ADVENTURE OF THE WAND OF DEATH

and trying to decide what a wand of death may be, has not his mind under proper control.

The net result of these things was that, for perhaps half a minute, Ashe behaved absurdly. He goggled and he yammered. A lunacy commissioner, had one been present, would have made up his mind about him without further investigation. It was not for an appreciable time that he thought of rising from his seat. When he did, the combined leap and twist which he executed practically amounted to a Larsen Exercise.

Nor was the girl unembarrassed. If Ashe had been calmer, he would have observed upon her cheek the flush that told that she too was finding the situation trying. But, women being ever better equipped with poise than men, it was she who spoke first.

'I'm afraid I'm disturbing you.'

'No, no,' said Ashe. 'Oh no, not at all, not at all, no, oh no, not at all, no,' and would have continued to play upon the theme indefinitely, had not the girl spoken again.

'I wanted to apologize,' she said, 'for my abominable rudeness in laughing at you just now. It was idiotic of me, and I don't know why I did it. I'm sorry.'

Science, with a thousand triumphs to her credit, has not yet succeeded in discovering the correct reply for a young man to make who finds himself in the appalling position of being apologized to by a pretty girl. If he says nothing, he seems sullen and unforgiving. If he says anything, he makes a fool of himself. Ashe, hesitating between these two courses, suddenly caught sight of the sheet of paper over which he had been poring so long.

'What is a wand of death?' he asked.

'I beg your pardon?'

'A wand of death.'

'I don't understand.'

The delirium of the conversation was too much for Ashe. He burst out laughing. A moment later the girl did the same. And simultaneously embarrassment ceased to be.

'I suppose you think I'm mad?' said Ashe.

'Certainly,' said the girl.

'Well, I should have been if you hadn't come in.'

'Why was that?'

'I was trying to write a detective story.'

'I was wondering if you were a writer.'

'Do *you* write?'

'Yes. Do you ever read *Home Gossip*?'

'Never.'

'I congratulate you. It's a horrid little paper, all brown-paper patterns and advice to the love-lorn. I do a short story for it every week, under various names. A duke or an earl goes with each story. I loathe it intensely.'

'I am sorry for your troubles,' said Ashe firmly, 'but we are wandering from the point. What is a wand of death?'

'A wand of death?'

'A wand of death.'

The girl frowned reflectively.

'Why, of course it's the sacred ebony stick stolen from the Indian temple which is supposed to bring death to whoever possesses it. The hero gets hold of it, and the priests dog him and send him threatening messages. What else could it be?'

Ashe could not restrain his admiration.

'This is genius!'

'Oh, no.'

'Absolute genius. I see it all. The hero calls in Gridley Quayle, and that patronizing ass, by the aid of a series of wicked coincidences, solves the mystery, and there am I with another month's work done.'

17

She looked at him with interest.

'Are you the author of "Gridley Quayle"?'

'Don't tell me you read him!'

'I do *not* read him. But he is published by the same firm that publishes *Home Gossip,* and I can't help seeing his cover sometimes while I am waiting in the waiting-room to see the editress.'

Ashe felt like one who meets a boyhood's chum on a desert island. Here was a real bond between them.

'Do the Mammoth publish you too? Why, we are comrades in misfortune – fellow-serfs. We should be friends. Shall we be friends?'

'I should be delighted.'

'Shall we shake hands, sit down, and talk about ourselves a little?'

'But I am keeping you from your work.'

'An errand of mercy.'

She sat down. It is a simple act, this of sitting down, but like everything else it may be an index to character. There was something wholly satisfactory to Ashe in the manner in which the girl did it. She neither seated herself on the extreme edge of the easy-chair, as one braced for instant flight; nor did she wallow in the easy-chair, as one come to stay for the week-end. She carried herself in an unconventional situation with an unstudied self-confidence which he could not sufficiently admire. Etiquette is not rigid in Arundell Street, but, nevertheless, a girl in a first-floor front may be excused for showing surprise and hesitation when invited to a confidential chat with a second-floor front young man whom she has only known five minutes. But there is a Free Masonry among those who live in large cities on small earnings.

'Shall we introduce ourselves?' said Ashe. 'Or did Mrs Bell tell you my name? By the way, you have not been here long, have you?'

'I took my room the day before yesterday. But your name, if you are the author of Gridley Quayle, is Felix Clovelly, isn't it?'

'Good Heavens, no! Surely you don't think anyone's name could really be Felix Clovelly? That is only the cloak under which I hide my shame. My real name is Marson. Ashe Marson. And yours?'

'Valentine. Joan Valentine.'

'Will you tell me the story of your life, or shall I tell mine first?'

'I don't know that I have any particular story.'

'Come, come!'

'Well, I haven't.'

'Think again. Let us thrash this thing out. You were born!'

'I was.'

'Where?'

'In London.'

'Now we seem to be started. I was born in Much Middleford.'

'I'm afraid I never heard of it.'

'Strange! I know your birth-place quite well. But I have not yet made Much Middleford famous. In fact, I doubt if I ever shall. I am beginning to realize that I am one of the failures.'

'How old are you?'

'Twenty-six.'

'You are twenty-six, and you call yourself a failure? I think that is a shameful thing to say.'

'What would you call a man of twenty-six whose only means of making a living was the writing of Gridley Quayle stories? An empire builder?'

'How do you know it's your only means of making a living? Why don't you try something new?'

'Such as – ?'

'How should I know? Anything that comes along.

Good gracious, Mr Marson, here you are in the biggest city in the world, with chances of adventure simply shrieking to you on every side –'

'I must be deaf. The only thing I have heard shrieking to me on every side has been Mrs Bell – for the week's rent.'

'Read the papers. Read the advertisement columns. I'm sure you will find something sooner or later. Don't get into a groove. Be an adventurer. Snatch at the next chance, whatever it is.'

Ashe nodded.

'Continue,' he said. 'Proceed. You are stimulating me.'

'But why should you want a girl like me to stimulate you? Surely London is enough to do it without my help? You can always find *something* new, surely? Listen. Mr Marson. I was thrown on my own resources about five years ago. Never mind how. Since then I have worked in a shop, done typewriting, been on the stage, had a position as governess, been a lady's maid?'

'A *what*? A lady's maid?'

'Why not? It was all experience, and I can assure you I would much rather be a lady's maid than a governess.'

'I think I know what you mean. I was a private tutor once. I suppose a governess is the female equivalent. I have often wondered what General Sherman would have said about private tutoring, if he expressed himself so breezily about mere War. Was it fun being a lady's maid?'

'It was pretty good fun, and it gave me an opportunity of studying the aristocracy in its native haunts, which has made me *Home Gossip*'s established authority on dukes and earls.'

Ashe drew a deep breath – not a scientific deep breath, but one of admiration.

'You are perfectly splendid!'

'Splendid?'

'I mean you have such pluck!'

'Oh well, I keep on trying. I'm twenty-three, and I haven't achieved anything much yet, but I certainly don't feel like sitting back and calling myself a failure.'

Ashe made a grimace.

'All right,' he said, 'I got it!'

'I meant you to,' said Joan placidly. 'I hope I haven't bored you with my autobiography, Mr Marson? I'm not setting myself up as a shining example, but I do like action and hate stagnation.'

'You are absolutely wonderful,' said Ashe. 'You are a human correspondence course in Efficiency – one of the ones you see in the back pages of the magazines, beginning, "Young man, are you earning enough?" with a picture showing the dead-beat gazing wistfully at the boss's chair. You would galvanize a jellyfish.'

'If I have really stimulated you –'

'I think,' said Ashe pensively, 'that that was another insult. Well, I deserve it. Yes, you *have* stimulated me. I feel a new man. It's queer that you should have come to me right on top of everything else. I don't remember when I have felt so restless and discontented as this morning.'

'It's the Spring.'

'I suppose it is. I feel like doing something big and adventurous.'

'Well, do it then. You have a *Morning Post* on the table. Have you read it yet?'

'I glanced at it.'

'But you haven't read the advertisement pages? Read them. They may contain just the opening you want.'

'Well, I'll do it, but my experience of advertisement pages is that they are monopolized by philanthropists who want to lend you any sum from ten to a hundred pounds on your note of hand only. However, I will scan them.'

Joan rose, and held out her hand.

'Good-bye, Mr Marson. You've got your detective

story to write, and I have to think out something with a duke in it by tonight, so I must be going.' She smiled. 'We have travelled a good way from the point we started at, but I may as well go back to it before I leave you. I'm sorry I laughed at you this morning.'

Ashe clasped her hand in a fervent grip.

'I'm not. Come and laugh at me whenever you feel like it. I like being laughed at. Why, when I started my morning exercises, half London used to come and roll about the pavements in convulsions. I'm not an attraction any longer, and it makes me feel lonely. There are twenty-nine of those Larsen Exercises and you only saw part of the first. You have done so much for me that, if I can be of any use to you in helping you to greet the day with a smile, I shall be only too proud. Exercise Six is funny without being vulgar. I'll start with it tomorrow morning. I can also recommend Exercise Eleven. Don't miss it.'

'Very well. Well, good-bye for the present.'

'Good-bye.'

She was gone; and Ashe, thrilling with new emotions, stared at the door which had been closed behind her. He felt as if he had been awakened from sleep by a powerful electric shock.

A wonderful girl . . . An astounding girl . . . An amazing girl . . .

Close behind the sheet of paper on which he had inscribed the now luminous and suggestive title of his new Gridley Quayle story lay the *Morning Post*, whose advertisement columns he had promised her to explore. The least he could do was to begin at once.

His spirits sank as he did so. It was the same old game. A Mr Brian MacNeill, though doing no business with minors, was willing, even anxious, to part with his vast fortune to anyone over the age of twenty-one whose means happened to be a trifle straitened. This good man required no security whatever. Nor did his rivals in generosity, the Messrs Angus Bruce, Duncan Macfarlane, Wallace Mackintosh, and Donald MacNab. They, too, showed a curious distaste for dealing with minors, but anyone of maturer years could simply come round to the office and help himself.

Beneath these was the heart-cry of Young Man (Christian) who wanted a thousand pounds at once to help him to complete his education with the Grand Tour.

Ashe threw the paper down wearily. He had known all along that it was no good. Romance was dead, and the Unexpected no longer happened.

He picked up his pen, and began to write the Adventure of the Wand of Death.

2

In a bedroom on the fourth floor of the Hotel Guelph in Piccadilly, the Hon. Frederick Threepwood sat in bed with his knees drawn up to his chin and glared at the day with a glare of mental anguish. He had very little mind, but what he had was suffering.

He had just remembered.

It is like that in this life. You wake up, feeling as fit as a fiddle; you look at the window and see the sun and thank Heaven for a fine day; you begin to plan a perfectly corking luncheon-party with some of the chappies you met last night at the National Sporting Club, and then – you remember.

'Oh, dash it!' said the Hon. Freddie. And after a moment's pause, 'And I was feeling so dashed happy!'

For the space of some minutes he remained plunged in sad meditation. Then, picking up the telephone on the table at his side, he asked for a number.

'Hullo?'

'Hullo?' responded a rich voice at the other end of the wire.

'Oh, I say, is that you, Dickie?'

'Who is that?'

'This is Freddie Threepwood. I say, Dickie, old top, I want to see you about something devilish important. Will you be in at twelve?'

'Certainly. What's the trouble?'

'I can't explain over the wire, but it's deuced serious.'

'Very well. By the way, Freddie, congratulations on the engagement.'

'Thanks, old man. Thanks very much, and so forth,

but you won't forget to be in at twelve, will you? Good-bye.'

He replaced the receiver quickly, and sprang out of bed, for he had heard the door-handle turn. When the door opened he was giving a correct representation of a young man wasting no time in beginning his toilet for the day.

An elderly, thin-faced, bald-headed, amiably vacant man entered. He regarded the Hon. Freddie with a certain disfavour.

'Are you only just getting up, Frederick?'

'Hullo, guv'nor. Good morning. I shan't be two ticks now.'

'You should have been out and about two hours ago. The day is glorious.'

'Shan't be more than a minute, guv'nor, now. Just got to have a tub and chuck on a few clothes.'

He disappeared into the bathroom. His father, taking a chair, placed the tips of his fingers together and in this attitude remained motionless, a figure of disapproval and suppressed annoyance.

Like many fathers in his rank of life, the Earl of Emsworth had suffered much through that problem which – with the exception of Mr Lloyd George – is practically the only fly in the British aristocratic amber – the problem of What To Do With The Younger Sons. It is useless to try to gloss over the fact, the Younger Son is not required. You might reason with a British peer by the hour – you might point out to him how, on the one hand, he is far better off than the male codfish, who may at any moment find itself in the distressing position of being called on to provide for a family of over a million; and remind him, on the other, that every additional child he acquires means a corresponding rise for him in the estimation of ex-President Roosevelt; but you would not cheer him up in the least. He does not want the Younger Son.

Apart, however, from the fact that he was a younger son, and, as such a nuisance in any case, the Honourable Freddie had always annoyed his father in a variety of ways. The Earl of Emsworth was so constituted that no man or thing really had the power to trouble him deeply, but Freddie had come nearer to doing it than anybody else in the world. There had been a consistency, a perseverance, about his irritating performances which had acted on the placid peer as dripping water on a stone. Isolated acts of annoyance would have been powerless to ruffle his calm; but Freddie had been exploding bombs under his nose since he went to Eton.

He had been expelled from Eton for breaking out at night and roaming the streets of Windsor in a false moustache. He had been sent down from Oxford for pouring ink from a second-storey window on to the Junior Dean of his college. He had spent two years at an expensive London crammer's and failed to pass into the Army. He had also accumulated an almost record series of racing debts, besides as shady a gang of friends, for the most part vaguely connected with the turf, as any young man of his age ever contrived to collect.

These things try the most placid of parents, and finally Lord Emsworth had put his foot down. It was the only occasion in his life when he had acted with decision, and he did it with the accumulated energy of years. He stopped his son's allowance, haled him home to Blandings Castle, and kept him there so relentlessly that, until the previous night, when they had come up together by an afternoon train, Freddie had not seen London for nearly a year.

It was possibly the reflection that, whatever his secret troubles, he was at any rate once more in his beloved metropolis that caused Freddie at this point to burst into discordant song. He splashed and warbled simultaneously.

Lord Emsworth's frown deepened, and he began to tap

his fingers together irritably. Then his brow cleared, and a pleased smile flickered over his face. He, too, had remembered.

What Lord Emsworth had remembered was this. Late in the previous autumn, the next estate to Blandings had been rented by an American, a Mr Peters, a man with many millions, chronic dyspepsia, and one fair daughter, Aline. The two families had met. Freddie and Aline had been thrown together. And, only a few days before, the engagement had been announced, and for Lord Emsworth the only flaw in this best of all possible worlds had been removed.

The singing in the bathroom was increasing in volume, but Lord Emsworth heard it now without wincing. It was amazing what a difference it made to a man's comfort, this fair prospect of getting his younger son off his hands. For nearly a year Freddie, a prisoner at Blandings, had afflicted his father's nerves with a never-failing discomfort. Blandings was a large house, but not so large that father and son did not occasionally meet; and on these occasions it had maddened Lord Emsworth to perceive the martyred aspect of the young man. To Lord Emsworth the park and gardens of Blandings were the nearest earthly approach to Paradise. Freddie, chafing at captivity, had mooned about them with an air of crushed gloom which would have caused comment in Siberia.

Yes, he was glad Freddie was engaged to be married to Aline Peters. He liked Aline. He liked Mr Peters. Such was the relief he experienced that he found himself feeling almost affectionate towards Freddie, who emerged from the bathroom at this moment clad in a pink bath-robe, to find the paternal wrath evaporated and all, so to speak, right with the world.

Nevertheless, he wasted no time about his dressing. He was always ill at ease in his father's presence, and he wished to be elsewhere with all possible speed. He sprang into his trousers with such energy that he nearly tripped himself up.

As he disentangled himself, he recollected something which had slipped his memory.

'By the way, guv'nor, I met an old pal of mine last night, and asked him down to Blandings this week. That's all right, isn't it, what?'

For a moment Lord Emsworth's geniality faltered. He had experience of Freddie's old pals.

'Who is he? Kindly remember that Mr Peters and Aline and nearly all your relations will be at Blandings this week. If he is one of –'

'Oh no, that's all right. Honour bright. He isn't one of the old crowd. He's a man named Emerson. Most respectable chap. Policeman or something in Hong-Kong. He knows Aline quite well, he says. Met her on the boat coming over.'

'I do not remember any friend of yours named Emerson.'

'Well, as a matter of fact I met him last night for the first time. But it's all right. He's a good chap, don't you know, and all that sort of rot.'

Lord Emsworth was feeling too benevolent to raise the objections which he would certainly have raised, had his mood been less sunny.

'Certainly, let him come, if he wishes.'

'Thanks, guv'nor.'

Freddie completed his toilet.

'Doing anything special this morning, guv'nor? I rather thought of getting a bit of breakfast and then strolling round a bit. Have you had breakfast?'

'Two hours ago. I trust that, in the course of your strolling, you will find time to call at Mr Peters' and see Aline. I shall be going there directly after lunch. Mr Peters wishes to show me his collection of – I think scarabs was the word he used.'

'Oh, I'll look in all right. Don't you worry. Or, if I

don't, I'll call the old boy up on the phone and pass the
time of day. Well, I rather think I'll be popping off now
and getting that bit of breakfast, what?'

Several comments on this speech suggested
themselves to Lord Emsworth. In the first place, he did
not approve of Freddie's allusion to one of America's
merchant-princes as 'the old boy'. Secondly, his son's
attitude did not strike him as the ideal attitude of a
young man towards his betrothed. There seemed a lack
of warmth. But, he reflected, possibly this was simply
another manifestation of the Modern Spirit, and in any
case it was not worth bothering about, so he offered no
criticism; and presently, Freddie having given his shoes a
flick with a silk handkerchief and thrust the latter
carefully up his sleeve, they passed out and down into
the main lobby of the hotel, where they parted, Freddie
to his bit of breakfast, his father to potter about the
streets and kill time till lunch. London was always a
trial to the Earl of Emsworth. His heart was in the
country, and the city held no fascinations for him.

II

On one of the floors in one of the buildings in one of the
streets which slope precipitously from the Strand to the
Thames Embankment, there is a door, which would be
all the better for a lick of paint, which bears what is
perhaps the most modest and unostentatious
announcement of its kind in London.

The grimy ground-glass displays the words:

R. JONES

simply that, and nothing more.

Situated between a door profusely illustrated with the
legend, 'Sarawak and New Guinea Rubber Estates
Exploitation Company. General Manager, Jno.
Bradbury-Eggleston' and a door belonging to the

Bhangaloo Ruby Mines Incorporated, it has a touch of
the woodland violet nestling among orchids.

R. JONES.

It is rugged in its simplicity. You wonder, as you look
at it, if you have time to look at and wonder about these
things, who this Jones may be and what is the business
which he conducts with such a coy reticence.

As a matter of fact, these speculations had passed
through suspicious minds at Scotland Yard, which had
for some time taken not a little interest in R. Jones. But,
beyond ascertaining that he bought and sold curios, did a
certain amount of bookmaking during the flat-racing
season, and had been known to lend money, Scotland
Yard did not find out much about Mr Jones, and
presently dismissed him from its thoughts. Not that
Scotland Yard was satisfied. To a certain extent, baffled
would be a better description of its attitude. The
suspicion that R. Jones was, among other things, a
receiver of stolen goods still lingered, but proof was not
forthcoming.

R. Jones saw to that. He did a great many things, for
he was one of the busiest men in London; but what he
did best was seeing to it that proof was not forthcoming.

On the theory, given to the world by my
brother-author, William Shakespeare, that it is the lean
and hungry-looking men who are dangerous and that the
fat, the sleek-headed men and such as sleep o' nights, are
harmless, R. Jones should have been above suspicion. He
was infinitely the fattest man in the west-central postal
district of London. He was a round ball of a man, who
wheezed when he walked upstairs, which was seldom,
and shook like a jelly if some tactless friend, wishing to
attract his attention, tapped him unexpectedly on the
shoulder. But this occurred still less frequently than his
walking upstairs, for in R. Jones' circle it was recognized
that nothing is a greater breach of etiquette and worse

30

form than to tap people unexpectedly on the shoulder. That, it was felt, should be left to those who are paid by the Government to do it.

R. Jones was about fifty years old, grey-haired, of a mauve complexion, jovial among his friends, and perhaps even more jovial with chance acquaintances. It was estimated by envious intimates that his joviality with chance acquaintances, especially with young men of the upper classes with large purses and small foreheads, was worth hundreds of pounds a year to him. There was something about his comfortable appearance and his jolly manner which irresistibly attracted a certain type of young man. It was his good fortune that this type of young man should be the type, financially, most worth attracting.

Freddie Threepwood had fallen under his spell during his short but crowded life in London. They had met for the first time at the Derby, but ever since R. Jones had held, in Freddie's estimation, that position of guide, philosopher, and friend, which he held in the estimation of so many young men of Freddie's type.

That was why, at twelve o'clock punctually on this Spring morning, he tapped with his cane on R. Jones' ground-glass, and showed such satisfaction and relief when the door was opened by the proprietor in person.

'Well, well, well!' said R. Jones, rollickingly. 'Whom have we here? The dashing bridegroom-to-be, and no other!'

R. Jones, like Lord Emsworth, was delighted that Freddie was about to marry a nice girl with plenty of money. The sudden turning-off of the tap from which Freddie's allowance had flowed had hit him hard. He had other sources of income, of course, but few so easy and unfailing as Freddie had been in the days of his prosperity.

'The prodigal son, by George! Creeping back into the fold after all this weary time! It seems years since I saw

you, Freddie. The old guv'nor put his foot down, didn't
he, and stopped the funds? Damned shame! I take it that
things have loosened up a bit since the engagement was
announced, eh?'

Freddie sat down, and chewed the knob of his cane
unhappily.

'Well, as a matter of fact, Dickie, old top,' he said, 'not
so that you could notice it, don't you know. Things are
still pretty much the same. I managed to get away from
Blandings for a night, because the governor had to come
to London, but I've got to go back with him on the three
o'clock train. And, as for money, I can't get a quid out of
him. As a matter of fact, I'm in the deuce of a hole, and
that's why I've come to you.'

Even fat, jovial men have their moments of
depression. R. Jones' face clouded, and jerky remarks
about the hardness of times and losses on the Stock
Exchange began to proceed from him. As Scotland Yard
had discovered, he lent money on occasion, but he did
not lend it to youths in Freddie's unfortunate position.

'Oh, I don't want to make a touch, you know,' Freddie
hastened to explain. 'It isn't that. As a matter of fact, I
managed to raise five hundred of the best this morning.
That ought to be enough.'

'Depends what you want it for,' said R. Jones,
magically genial once more. The thought entered his
mind, as it had so often done, that the world was full of
easy marks. He wished he could meet the money-lender
who had been rash enough to advance the Honourable
Freddie five hundred pounds. These philanthropists
cross our path too seldom.

Freddie felt in his pocket, produced a cigarette-case,
and from it extracted a newspaper-clipping.

'Did you read about poor old Percy in the papers? The
case, you know?'

'Percy?'

'Lord Stockheath, you know.'

'Oh, the Stockheath breach-of-promise case? I did more than that. I was in court all three days.' R. Jones emitted a cosy chuckle. 'Is he a pal of yours? A cousin, eh? I wish you had seen him in the witness-box, with Jellicoe-Smith cross-examining him! The funniest thing I ever heard. And his letters to the girl! They read them out in court, and of all the –'

'Don't, old man! Dickie, old top, please! I know all about it. I read the reports. They made poor old Percy look an absolute ass.'

'Well, Nature had done that already, but I'm bound to say they improved on Nature's work. I should think your cousin Percy must have felt like a plucked chicken.'

A spasm of pain passed over the Honourable Freddie's vacant face. He wriggled in his chair.

'Dickie, old man, I wish you wouldn't talk like that. It makes me feel ill.'

'Why, is he such a pal of yours as all that?'

'It's not that. It's – the fact is, Dickie, old top, I'm in exactly the same bally hole as poor old Percy was, myself.'

'What! You have been sued for breach of promise?'

'Not absolutely that – yet. Look here, I'll tell you the whole thing. Do you remember a show at the Piccadilly about a year ago, called, "The Girl from Dublin"? There was a girl in the chorus.'

'Several. I remember noticing.'

'No. I mean one particular girl – a girl called Joan Valentine. The rotten part is that I never met her.'

'Pull yourself together, Freddie. What exactly is the trouble?'

'Well, don't you see, I used to go to the show every other night, and I fell frightfully in love with this girl –'

'Without having met her?'

'Yes. You see, I was rather an ass in those days.'

'No, no,' said R. Jones, handsomely.

33

'I must have been, or I wouldn't have been such an
ass, don't you know. Well, as I was saying, I used to
write this girl letters, saying how much I was in love
with her, and – and –'

'Specifically proposing marriage?'

'Eh?'

'I say, specifically proposing marriage?'

'I can't remember. I expect I did. I was awfully in
love.'

'How was it that you never met her?'

'She wouldn't meet me. She wouldn't even come
out to lunch. She didn't even answer my letters – just
sent word down by the Johnnie at the stage-door. And
then –'

Freddie's voice died away. He thrust the knob of his
cane into his mouth in a sort of frenzy.

'What then?' inquired R. Jones.

A scarlet blush manifested itself on Freddie's young
face. His eyes wandered sideways. After a long pause a
single word escaped him, almost inaudible.

'Poetry!'

R. Jones trembled as if an electric current had been
passed through his plump frame. His little eyes sparkled
with merriment.

'You wrote her poetry!'

'Yards of it, old boy, yards of it!' groaned Freddie.

Panic filled him with speech.

'You see the frightful hole I'm in? This girl is bound to
have kept the letters. I don't remember if I actually
proposed to her or not, but anyway she's got enough
material to make it worth while to have a dash at an
action, especially after poor old Percy has just got soaked
for such a pile of money, and made breach-of-promise
cases the fashion, so to speak. And now that the
announcement of my engagement is out, she's certain to
get busy. Probably she has been waiting for something of
the sort. Don't you see that all the cards are in her

34

hands? We couldn't afford to let the thing come into court. That poetry would dish my marriage for a certainty. I'd have to emigrate or something! Goodness knows what would happen at home. My old governor would murder me. So you see what a frightful hole I'm in, don't you, Dickie, old man?'

'And what do you want me to do?'

'Why, to get hold of this girl, and get back the letters, don't you see? I can't do it myself, cooped up miles away in the country. And besides I shouldn't know how to handle a thing like that. It wants a chappie with a lot of sense and a persuasive sort of way with him.'

'Thanks for the compliment, Freddie, but I should imagine that something a little more solid than a persuasive way would be required in a case like this. You said something a while ago about five hundred pounds?'

'Here it is, old man, in notes. I brought it on purpose. Will you really take the thing on? Do you think you can work it for five hundred?'

'I can have a try.'

Freddie rose with an expression approximating to happiness on his face. Some men have the power of inspiring confidence in some of their fellows, while filling others with distrust. Scotland Yard might look askance at R. Jones, but to Freddie he was all that was helpful and reliable. He shook R. Jones' hand several times in his emotion.

'That's absolutely topping of you, old man,' he said. 'Then I'll leave the whole thing to you. Write me the moment you have done anything, won't you. Good-bye, old top, and thanks ever so much.'

The door closed. R. Jones remained where he sat, his fingers straying luxuriously among the crackling paper. A feeling of complete happiness warmed R. Jones' bosom. He was not certain whether or not his mission would be successful, and, to be truthful, he was not letting this worry him much. What he was certain of, was the fact that the Heavens had opened unexpectedly and dropped five hundred pounds into his lap.

3

The Earl of Emsworth stood in the doorway of the Senior Conservative Club's vast dining-room, and beamed with a vague sweetness upon the two hundred or so Senior Conservatives, who, with much clattering of knife and fork, were keeping body and soul together by means of the coffee-room luncheon. He might have been posing for a Statue of Amiability. His pale blue eyes shone with a friendly light through their protecting glasses; the smile of a man at peace with all men curved his weak mouth; his bald head, reflecting the sunlight, seemed almost to wear a halo.

Nobody appeared to notice him. He so seldom came to London these days that he was practically a stranger in the club; and in any case your Senior Conservative, when at lunch, has little leisure for observing anything not immediately on the table in front of him. To attract attention in the dining-room of the Senior Conservative Club between the hours of one and two-thirty, you have to be a mutton-chop, not an earl.

It is possible that, lacking the initiative to make his way down the long aisle and find a table for himself, he might have stood there indefinitely, but for the restless activity of Adams, the head steward. It was Adams' mission in life to flit to and fro, hauling would-be lunchers to their destinations, as a St Bernard dog hauls travellers out of Alpine snow-drifts.

He sighted Lord Emsworth, and secured him with a genteel pounce.

'A table, your lordship? This way, your lordship.'

Adams remembered him, of course. Adams remembered everybody.

Lord Emsworth followed him beamingly, and presently came to anchor at a table at the farther end of the room. Adams handed him the bill of fare, and stood brooding over him like a Providence.

'Don't often see your lordship in the club,' he opened chattily. It was his business to know the tastes and dispositions of all the five thousand or so members of the Senior Conservative Club and to suit his demeanour to them. To some he would hand the bill of fare swiftly, silently, almost brusquely, as one who realizes that there are moments in life too serious for talk. Others, he knew, liked conversation, and to these he introduced the subject of food almost as a sub-motive.

Lord Emsworth, having examined the bill of fare with a mild curiosity, laid it down and became conversational.

'No, Adams, I seldom visit London nowadays. London does not attract me. The country . . . the fields . . . the woods . . . the birds . . .'

Something across the room seemed to attract his attention, and his voice trailed off. He inspected this for some time with bland interest, then turned to Adams once more.

'What was I saying, Adams?'

'The birds, your lordship.'

'Birds? What birds? What about birds?'

'You were speaking of the attractions of life in the country, your lordship. You included the birds in your remarks.'

'Oh yes, yes, yes. Oh yes, yes. Oh yes, to be sure. Do you ever go to the country, Adams?'

'Generally to the seashore, your lordship, when I take my annual vacation.'

Whatever was the attraction across the room once more exercised its spell. His lordship concentrated himself upon it to the exclusion of all other mundane affairs. Presently he came out of his trance again.

'What were you saying, Adams?'

'I said that I generally went to the seashore, your lordship.'

'Eh? When?'

'For my annual vacation, your lordship.'

'Your what?'

'My annual vacation, your lordship.'

'What about it?'

Adams never smiled during business hours, unless professionally, as it were, when a member made a joke, but he was storing up in the recesses of his highly respectable body, a large laugh, to be shared with his wife when he reached home that night. Mrs Adams never wearied of hearing of the eccentricities of the members of the club. It occurred to Adams that he was in luck today. He was expecting a little party of friends to supper that night, and he was a man who loved an audience. You would never have thought it, to look at him when engaged on his professional duties, but Adams had built up a substantial reputation as a humorist in his circle by his imitations of certain members of the club, and it was a matter of regret to him that he got so few opportunities nowadays of studying the absent-minded Lord Emsworth. It was rare luck, his lordship coming in today evidently in his best form.

'Adams, who is the gentleman over by the window? The gentleman in the brown suit?'

'That is a Mr Simmonds, your lordship. He joined us last year.'

'I never saw a man take such large mouthfuls. Did *you* ever see a man take such large mouthfuls, Adams?'

Adams refrained from expressing an opinion, but inwardly he was thrilling with artistic fervour. Mr Simmonds, eating, was one of his best imitations, though Mrs Adams was inclined to object to it on the

39

score that it was a bad example for the children. To be privileged to witness Lord Emsworth watching and criticizing Mr Simmonds was to collect material for a double-barrelled character-study which would assuredly make the hit of the evening.

'That man,' went on Lord Emsworth, 'is digging his grave with his teeth. Digging his grave with his teeth, Adams. Do *you* take large mouthfuls, Adams?'

'No, your lordship.'

'Quite right. Very sensible of you, Adams. Very sensible of you. Very sen . . . What was I saying, Adams?'

'About my not taking large mouthfuls, your lordship.'

'Quite right. Quite right. Never take large mouthfuls, Adams. Never gobble. Have you any children, Adams?'

'Two, your lordship.'

'I hope you teach them not to gobble. They pay for it in later life. Americans gobble when young, and ruin their digestions. My American friend, Mr Peters, suffers terribly from his digestion.'

Adams lowered his voice to a confidential murmur.

'If you will pardon the liberty, your lordship – I saw it in the paper – '

'About Mr Peters' digestion?'

'About Miss Peters, your lordship, and the Honourable Frederick. May I be permitted to offer my congratulations?'

'Eh? Oh yes, the engagement. Yes, yes, yes. Yes, to be sure. Yes, very satisfactory in every respect. High time he settled down and got a little sense. I put it to him straight. I cut off his allowance, and made him stay at home. That made him think, lazy young devil. I – '

Lord Emsworth had his lucid moments, and in the one that occurred now it came home to him that he was not talking to himself, as he had imagined, but confiding intimate family secrets to the head steward of his club's dining-room. He checked himself abruptly, and with a slight decrease of amiability fixed his gaze on the bill of

fare, and ordered clear soup. For an instant he felt
resentful against Adams for luring him on to soliloquize,
but the next moment his whole mind was gripped by the
fascinating spectacle of Mr Simmonds dealing with a
wedge of Stilton cheese, and Adams was forgotten.

The clear soup had the effect of restoring his lordship
to complete amiability, and, when Adams in the course
of his wanderings again found himself at the table, he
was once more disposed for light conversation.

'So you saw the news of the engagement in the paper,
did you, Adams?'

'Yes, your lordship, in the *Mail*. It had quite a long
piece about it. And the Honourable Frederick's
photograph and the young lady's were in the *Mirror*. Mrs
Adams clipped them out and put them in an album
knowing that your lordship was a member of ours. If I
may say so, your lordship, a beautiful young lady.'

'Devilish attractive, Adams, and devilish rich. Mr
Peters is a millionaire, Adams.'

'So I read in the paper, your lordship.'

'Damme, they all seem millionaires in America. Wish
I knew how they managed it. Honestly, I hope. Mr
Peters is an honest man, but his digestion is bad. He
used to bolt his food. *You* don't bolt your food, I hope,
Adams?'

'No, your lordship, I am most careful.'

'The late Mr Gladstone used to chew each mouthful
thirty-three times. Deuced good notion, if you aren't in a
hurry. What cheese would you recommend, Adams?'

'The gentlemen are speaking well of the gorgonzola.'

'All right, bring me some. You know, Adams, what I
admire about Americans is their resource. Mr Peters
tells me that, as a boy of eleven, he earned twenty
dollars a week selling mint to saloon-keepers, as they
call publicans over there. Why they wanted mint I
cannot recollect. Mr Peters explained the reason to me,
and it seemed highly plausible at the time, but I have

forgotten it. Possibly for mint-sauce. It impressed me, Adams. Twenty dollars is four pounds. *I* never earned four pounds a week when I was a boy of eleven. In fact, I don't think I ever earned four pounds a week. His story impressed me, Adams. Every man ought to have an earning capacity . . . Tell me, Adams, have I eaten my cheese?'

'Not yet, your lordship. I was about to send the waiter for it.'

'Never mind. Tell him to bring the bill instead. I remember that I have an appointment. I must not be late.'

'Shall I take the fork, your lordship?'

'The fork?'

'Your lordship has inadvertently put a fork in your coat-pocket.'

Lord Emsworth felt in the pocket indicated, and, with the air of an inexpert conjuror whose trick has succeeded contrary to his expectations, produced a silver-plated fork. He regarded it with surprise, then he looked wonderingly at Adams.

'Adams, I'm getting absent-minded. Have you ever noticed any traces of absent-mindedness in me before?'

'Oh no, your lordship.'

'Well, it's deuced peculiar. I have no recollection whatsoever of placing that fork in my pocket . . . Adams, I want a taxi-cab.'

He glanced round the room, as if expecting to locate one by the fireplace.

'The hall-porter will whistle one for you, your lordship.'

'So he will, by George, so he will. Good day, Adams.'

'Good day, your lordship.'

The Earl of Emsworth ambled benevolently to the door, leaving Adams with the feeling that his day had not been ill-spent. He gazed almost with reverence after the slow-moving figure.

'What a nut!' said Adams to his immortal soul.

Wafted through the sun-lit streets in his taxi-cab, the Earl of Emsworth smiled benevolently upon London's teeming millions. He was as completely happy as only a fluffy-minded old man with excellent health and a large income can be. Other people worried about all sorts of things – strikes, wars, suffragettes, diminishing birth-rates, the growing materialism of the age, and a score of similar subjects. Worrying, indeed, seemed to be the twentieth century's speciality. Lord Emsworth never worried. Nature had equipped him with a mind so admirably constructed for withstanding the disagreeableness of life that, if an unpleasant thought entered it, it passed out again a moment later. Except for a few of Life's fundamental facts, such as that his cheque-book was in the right-hand top drawer of his desk, that the Honourable Freddie Threepwood was a young idiot who required perpetual restraint, and that, when in doubt about anything, he had merely to apply to his secretary, Rupert Baxter – except for these basic things, he never remembered anything for more than a few minutes.

At Eton, in the sixties, they had called him Fathead.

His was a life which lacked, perhaps, the sublimer emotions which raised Man to the level of the gods, but it was undeniably an extremely happy one. He never experienced the thrill of ambition fulfilled, but, on the other hand, he never knew the agony of ambition frustrated. His name, when he died, would not live for ever in England's annals; he was spared the pain of worrying about this by the fact that he had no desire to live for ever in England's annals. He was possibly as nearly contented as a human being can be in this century of alarms and excursions. Indeed, as he bowled along in his cab, and reflected that a really charming girl, not in the chorus of any West-end theatre, a girl with plenty of money and excellent breeding had – in a moment, doubtless, of mental aberration – become engaged to be married to the Honourable Freddie, he told himself that life was at last absolutely without a crumpled roseleaf.

The cab drew up before a house gay with flowered window-boxes. Lord Emsworth paid the driver, and stood on the sidewalk looking up at this cheerful house, trying to remember why on earth he had told the man to drive there.

A few moments' steady thought gave him the answer to the riddle. This was Mr Peters' town house, and he had come to it by invitation to look at Mr Peters' collection of scarabs.

To be sure. He remembered now. His collection of scarabs.

Or was it Arabs?

He smiled. Scarabs, of course. You couldn't collect Arabs. He wondered idly, as he rang the bell, what scarabs might be. But he was interested in a fluffy kind of way in all forms of collecting, and he was very pleased to have the opportunity of examining these objects, whatever they were.

He rather thought they were a kind of fish.

II

There are men in this world who cannot rest, who are so constituted that they can only take their leisure in the shape of a change of work. To this fairly numerous class belonged Mr J. Preston Peters, father of Freddie's Aline. And to this merit – or defect – is to be attributed his almost maniacal devotion to that rather unattractive species of curio – the Egyptian scarab.

Five years before, a nervous breakdown had sent Mr Peters to a New York specialist.

The specialist had grown rich on similar cases, and his advice was always the same. He insisted on Mr Peters taking up a hobby.

'What sort of a hobby?' inquired Mr Peters irritably. His digestion had just begun to trouble him at the time, and his temper was not of the best.

The very word hobby seemed futile and ridiculous to him. His hobby was avoiding hobbies and attending to business. Which, the specialist pointed out, was precisely the reason why he had just written a hundred-dollar cheque for his advice. This impressed Mr Peters. He disliked writing unnecessary cheques, and, if the only way to avoid doing so was to have a hobby, a hobby he must have.

'Any sort of hobby,' said the specialist. 'There must be something outside of business in which you are interested?'

Mr Peters could not think of anything. Even his meals were beginning to interest him less.

'Now my hobby,' said the specialist, 'is the collecting of scarabs. Why should you not collect scarabs?'

'Because,' said Mr Peters, 'I shouldn't know one if you brought it to me on a plate. What *are* scarabs?'

'Scarabs,' said the specialist, warming to his subject, 'are Egyptian hieroglyphs.'

'And what,' inquired Mr Peters, 'are Egyptian hieroglyphs?'

The specialist began to wonder whether it would not have been better to advise Mr Peters to collect postage stamps.

'A scarab,' he said, 'derived from the Latin *scarabeus*, is literally a beetle.'

'I will *not* collect beetles,' said Mr Peters definitely. 'I despise beetles. Beetles give me that pain.'

'Scarabs are Egyptian symbols in the form of beetles,' the specialist hurried on. 'The most common form of scarab is in the shape of a ring. Scarabs were used for

45

seals. They were also employed as beads or ornaments.
Some scarabei bear inscriptions having references to
places, as, for instance, "Memphis is mighty for ever".'

Mr Peters' scorn changed suddenly to active interest.

'Have you got one like that?'

'Like – ?'

'A scarab boosting Memphis. It's my home town.'

'I think it possible that some other Memphis was
alluded to.'

'There isn't any other except the one in Tennessee,'
said Mr Peters patriotically.

The specialist owed the fact that he was a nerve
doctor instead of a nerve patient to his habit of never
arguing with his visitors.

'Perhaps,' he said, 'you would care to glance at my
collection? It is in the next room.'

That was the beginning of Mr Peters' devotion to
scarabs. At first he did his collecting without any love
for it, partly because he had to collect something or
suffer, but principally because of a remark the specialist
made as he was leaving the room.

'How long would it take me to get together that
number of the things?' he inquired, when, having looked
his fill upon the dullest assortment of objects which he
remembered ever to have seen, he was preparing to take
his leave.

The specialist was proud of his collection.

'How long? To make a collection as large as mine?
Many years, Mr Peters. Oh, many, many, years.'

'I'll bet you a hundred dollars I do it in six months.'

And from that moment Mr Peters had brought to the
collecting of scarabs the same furious energy which had
given him so many dollars and so much indigestion. He
went after scarabs like a dog after rats. He scooped in
scarabs from all the four corners of the earth, until, at
the end of a year, he found himself possessed of what,
purely as regarded quantity, was a record collection.

This marked the end of the first phase of, so to speak, the scarabean side of his life. Collecting had become a habit with him, but he was not yet a real enthusiast. It occurred to him that the time had arrived for a certain amount of pruning and elimination. He called in an expert, and bade him go through the collection and weed out what he felicitously termed the 'dead ones'. The expert did his job thoroughly. When he had finished, the collection was reduced to a mere dozen specimens.

'The rest,' he explained, 'are practically valueless. If you are thinking of making a collection that will have any value in the eyes of archaeologists, I should advise you to throw them away. The remaining twelve are good.'

'How do you mean "Good"? Why is one of these things valuable and another so much junk? They all look alike to me.'

And then the expert had talked to Mr Peters for nearly two hours about the New Kingdom, the Middle Kingdom, Osiris, Ammon, Mut, Bubastis, Dynasties, Cheops, the Hyksos kings, cylinders, bezels, Amenophis III, Queen Taia, the Princess Gilukhipa of Mitanni, the Lake of Zarukhe, Naucratis, and the Book of the Dead. He did it with a relish. He liked doing it.

When he had finished, Mr Peters thanked him and went to the bathroom, where he bathed his temples with eau de Cologne.

That talk changed J. Preston Peters from a supercilious scooper-up of random scarabs to a genuine scarab-maniac. It does not matter what a man collects; if Nature has given him the collector's mind, he will become a fanatic on the subject of whatever collection he sets out to make. Mr Peters had collected dollars; he began to collect scarabs with precisely the same enthusiasm. He would have become just as enthusiastic about butterflies, or old china, if he had turned his thoughts to them, but it chanced that what he had taken up was the collecting of the scarab, and it gripped him more and more as the years went on. Gradually he came to love his scarabs with that love passing the love of women which only collectors know. He became an expert on these curious relics of a dead civilization. For a time they ran neck and neck in his thoughts with business. When he retired from business, he was free to make them the master passion of his life. He treasured each individual scarab in his collection as a miser treasures gold.

Collecting, as Mr Peters did it, resembles the drink habit. It begins as an amusement, and ends as an obsession.

He was gloating over his treasures when the maid announced Lord Emsworth.

A curious species of mutual toleration – it could hardly be dignified by the title of friendship – had sprung up between these two men, so opposite in practically every respect. Each regarded the other with that feeling of perpetual amazement with which we encounter those whose whole view-point and mode of life is foreign to our own. The American's force and nervous energy fascinated Lord Emsworth. In a purely detached way Lord Emsworth liked force and nervous energy. They interested him. He was glad he did not possess them himself, but he enjoyed them as a spectacle just as a man who would not like to be a purple cow may have no objection to seeing one. As for Mr Peters, nothing like the earl had ever happened to him before in a long and varied life. He had seen men and cities, but Lord Emsworth was something new. Each, in fact, was to the other a perpetual freak-show with no charge for admission. And, if anything had been needed to cement the alliance it would have been supplied by the fact that they were both collectors.

They differed in collecting as they did in everything else. Mr Peters' collecting, as has been shown, was keen,

furious, concentrated; Lord Emsworth's had the amiable
dodderingness which marked every branch of his life. In
the museum at Blandings Castle you might find every
manner of valuable and valueless curio. There was no
central motive, the place was simply an amateur
junk-shop. Side by side with a Gutenberg Bible for which
rival collectors would have bidden without a limit, you
would come upon a bullet from the field of Waterloo,
one of a consignment of ten thousand shipped there for
the use of tourists by a Birmingham firm. Each was
equally attractive to its owner.

'My dear Mr Peters,' said Lord Emsworth sunnily,
advancing into the room, 'I trust I am not unpunctual. I
have been lunching at my club.'

'I'd have asked you to lunch here,' said Mr Peters, 'but
you know how it is with me. I've promised the doctor
I'll give those nuts and grasses of his a fair trial, and I
can do it pretty well when I'm alone or with Aline. But
to have to sit by and see someone else eating real food
would be trying me too high.'

Lord Emsworth murmured sympathetically. The
other's digestive tribulations touched a ready chord. An
excellent trencherman himself, he understood what Mr
Peters must suffer.

'Too bad,' he said.

Mr Peters turned the conversation into other
channels.

'These are my scarabs,' he said.

Lord Emsworth adjusted his glasses, and the mild
smile disappeared from his face, to be succeeded by a set
look. A stage director of a moving-picture firm would
have recognized the look; Lord Emsworth was
'registering' interest – interest which, he perceived from
the first instant, would have to be completely simulated;
for instinct told him, as Mr Peters began to talk, that he
was about to be bored as he had seldom been bored in
his life.

We may say what we will against the aristocracy of England; we may wear red ties and attend Socialist meetings; but we cannot deny that in certain crises blood will tell. An English peer of the right sort can be bored nearer to the point where mortification sets in, without showing it, than anyone else in the world. From early youth he has been accustomed to staying at English country-houses, where, though horses bored him intensely, he has had to accompany his host round the stables every morning and pretend to enjoy it, and this Spartan upbringing stands him in good stead in after years.

It was pleasant, then, to see the resolute, if painful, politeness with which Lord Emsworth accepted the trying role of the man who listens to a monomaniac discoursing on his pet subject. His mind was elsewhere, but early in the proceedings he began to make use of a musical 'Ah!' which, emitted at regular intervals, seemed to be all that Mr Peters demanded of him.

Mr Peters, in his character of showman, threw himself into his work with even more than his customary energy. He was both exhaustive and exhausting. His flow of speech never faltered. He spoke of the New Kingdom, the Middle Kingdom, Osiris, and Ammon; waxed eloquent concerning Mut, Bubastis, Cheops, the Hyksos kings, cylinders, bezels, and Amenophis III; and became at times almost lyrical when touching on Queen Taia, the Princess Gilukhipa of Mitanni, the Lake of Zarukhe, and the Book of the Dead.

Time slid by . . .

'Take a look at this, Lord Emsworth.'

As one who, brooding on love or running over business projects in his mind, walks briskly into a lamp-post and comes back to the realities of life with a sense of jarring shock, Lord Emsworth started, blinked, and returned to consciousness. Far away his mind had been, seventy miles away, in the pleasant hothouses and shady garden-walks of Blandings Castle. He came back to London to find that his host, with a mingled air of pride and reverence, was extending towards him a small, dingy-looking something.

He took it and looked at it. That, apparently, was what he was meant to do. So far, all was well.

'Ah!' he said.

That blessed word, covering everything. He repeated it, pleased at its ready resource.

'A Cheops of the Fourth Dynasty,' said Mr Peters fervently.

'I beg your pardon?'

'A Cheops! Of the Fourth Dynasty!'

Lord Emsworth began to feel like a hunted stag. He could not go on saying 'Ah!' indefinitely, yet what else was there to say to this curious little beastly sort of a beetle kind of thing?

'Dear me! A Cheops!'

'Of the Fourth Dynasty!'

'Bless my soul! The Fourth Dynasty!'

'What do you think of that, eh?'

Strictly speaking, Lord Emsworth thought nothing of it, and he was wondering how to veil this opinion in diplomatic words, when the providence which looks after all good men saved him by causing a knock at the door to occur.

In response to Mr Peters' irritated cry, a maid entered.

'If you please, sir. Mr Threepwood wishes to speak to you on the telephone.'

Mr Peters turned to his guest.

'Excuse me for one moment.'

'Certainly,' said Lord Emsworth gratefully. 'Certainly, certainly, certainly. By all means.'

The door closed behind Mr Peters. Lord Emsworth was alone.

For some moments he stood where he had been left, a figure with small signs of alertness about it. But Mr

Peters did not return immediately. The booming of his voice came faintly from some distant region. Lord Emsworth strolled to the window and looked out.

The sun still shone brightly on the quiet street. Across the road were trees. Lord Emsworth was fond of trees; he looked at these approvingly. Then round the corner came a vagrant man, wheeling flowers in a barrow.

Flowers! Lord Emsworth's mind shot back to Blandings like a homing pigeon. Flowers! Had he or had he not given head-gardener Thorne adequate instructions as to what to do with those hydrangeas? Assuming that he had not, was Thorne to be depended on to do the right thing by them by the light of his own intelligence?

Lord Emsworth began to brood upon head-gardener Thorne.

He was aware of some curious little object in his hand; he accorded it a momentary inspection. It had no message for him. It was probably something, but he couldn't remember what.

He put it in his pocket, and returned to his meditations.

III

At about the hour when the Earl of Emsworth was driving to keep his appointment with Mr Peters, a party of two sat at a corner table at Simpson's Restaurant in the Strand. One of the two was a small, pretty, good-natured looking girl of about twenty, the other a sturdy young man with a small moustache, a wiry crop of red-brown hair, and an expression of mingled devotion and determination. The girl was Aline Peters, the young man's name was George Emerson. He was, as Freddie had said, a policeman or something in Hong-Kong. That is to say, he was second-in-command of the police force in that distant spot. At present, he was home on leave. He had a strong, square face, with a dogged and persevering chin.

There is every kind of restaurant in London, from the restaurant which makes you fancy you are in Paris to the restaurant which makes you wish you were. There are places in Piccadilly, quaint lethal chambers in Soho, and strange food factories in Oxford Street and the Tottenham Court Road. There are restaurants which specialize in ptomaine, and restaurants which specialize in sinister vegetable-messes. But there is only one Simpson's.

Simpson's in the Strand is unique. Here if he wishes, the Briton may, for the small sum of half a dollar, stupefy himself with food. The God of Fatted Plenty has the place under his protection. Its keynote is solid comfort. County clergymen, visiting London for the annual Clerical Congress, come here to get the one square meal which will last them till next year's Clerical Congress. Fathers and uncles with sons or nephews on their hands rally to Simpson's with silent blessings on the head of the genius who founded the place, for here only can the young boa-constrictor really fill himself at moderate expense. Militant suffragettes come to it to make up leeway after their last hunger-strike.

A pleasant, soothing, hearty place. A restful Temple of Food. No strident orchestra forces the diner to bolt beef in ragtime. No long, central aisle distracts his attention with its stream of new arrivals. There he sits, alone with his food, while white-robed priests, wheeling their smoking trucks, move to and fro, ever ready with fresh supplies.

All round the room, some at small tables, some at large tables, the worshippers sit, in their eyes that resolute, concentrated look which is the peculiar property of the British luncher, ex-President Roosevelt's man-eating fish, and the American army-worm.

Conversation does not flourish at Simpson's. Only two of all those present on this occasion showed any disposition towards chattiness. They were Aline Peters and her escort.

'The girl you ought to marry,' Aline was saying, 'is Joan Valentine.'

'The girl I am going to marry,' said George Emerson, 'is Aline Peters.'

For answer Aline picked up from the floor beside her an illustrated paper, and, having opened it at a page towards the end, handed it across the table.

George Emerson glanced at it disdainfully. There were two photographs on the page. One was of Aline, the other of a heavy, loutish-looking youth, who wore that peculiar expression of painted glassiness which Young England always adopts in the face of a camera.

Under one photograph were printed the words, 'Miss Aline Peters, who is to marry the Hon. Frederick Threepwood in June.' Under the other, 'The Hon. Frederick Threepwood, who is to marry Miss Aline Peters in June.' Above the photographs was the legend, 'Forthcoming International Wedding. Son of the Earl of Emsworth to marry American heiress.' In one corner of the picture a Cupid draped in the Stars and Stripes aimed his bow at the gentleman; in the other another Cupid, clad in a natty Union Jack, was drawing a bead on the lady.

The sub-editor had done his work well. He had not been ambiguous. What he intended to convey to the reader was that Miss Aline Peters of America was going to marry the Hon. Frederick Threepwood, son of the Earl of Emsworth; and that was exactly the impression the average reader got.

George Emerson, however, was not an average reader. The sub-editor's work did not impress him.

'You mustn't believe everything you see in the

papers,' he said. 'What are the stout children in the bathing-suits supposed to be doing?'

'Those are Cupids, George, aiming at us with their little bows – a pretty and original idea.'

'Why Cupids?'

'Cupid is the God of Love. I can see that *you* never went to night-school.'

'What has the God of Love got to do with it?'

Aline placidly devoured a fried potato.

'You're simply trying to make me angry,' she said, 'and I call it very mean of you. You know perfectly well how fatal it is to get angry at meals. It was eating while he was in a bad temper that ruined father's digestion. George, that nice, fat carver is wheeling his truck this way. Flag him, and make him give me some more of that mutton.'

George looked round him morosely.

'Why is it,' he said, 'that every one in London looks exactly the same as every one else? They used to tell me that I should find that all Chinamen looked alike. There isn't a Chinaman in Hong-Kong that I would have the least difficulty in recognizing. But these blighters – ' His eyes roamed about the room. It returned to a stout young man at a neighbouring table, who had been the original cause of this homily, owing to the fact that he had reminded him of the Hon. Freddie Threepwood. He scowled at this harmless youth, who was browsing contentedly on fish-pie. 'Do you see the fellow in the grey suit?' he said. 'Look at the stodgy face. Mark the glassy eye. If that man sandbagged your Freddie and tied him up somewhere and turned up at the church instead of him, can you honestly tell me that you would know the difference? Come now, wouldn't you simply say, "Why, Freddie, how natural you look," and go through the ceremony without a suspicion?'

'He isn't a bit like Freddie. And you oughtn't to speak of him as Freddie. You don't know him.'

'Yes, I do. And what is more he expressly asked me to call him Freddie. "Oh, dash it, old top, don't keep on calling me Threepwood. Freddie to pals." Those were his very words.'

'George, you're making this up.'

'Not at all. We met last night at the National Sporting Club. Porky Jones was going twenty rounds with Eddie Flynn. I offered to give three to one on Eddie. Freddie, who was sitting next to me, took me in fivers. And if you want any further proof of your young man's fat-headedness, mark that. A child could have seen that Eddie had him going. Afterwards Threepwood chummed up with me, and told me that to real pals like me he was Freddie. I was a real pal, as I understood it, because I would have to wait for my money. The fact was, he explained, that his old governor had cut off his bally allowance.'

'You're simply trying to poison my mind against him, and I don't think it's very nice of you, George.'

'What do you mean, poison your mind? I'm not poisoning your mind, I'm simply telling you a few things about him. You know perfectly well that you don't love him, and that you aren't going to marry him, and that you are going to marry me.'

'How do you know I don't love my Freddie?'

'If you can look me straight in the eyes and tell me that you do, I will drop the whole thing and put on a little page's dress and carry your train up the aisle! Now then?'

'And all the while you're talking you're letting my carver get away,' said Aline.

George signalled to the willing priest, who steered his truck towards them. Aline directed his dissection of the shoulder of mutton with word and gesture.

'Enjoy yourself,' said Emerson coldly.

'So I do, George, so I do. What excellent meat they have in England.'

'I wish you would be a bit more spiritual. I don't want to sit here discussing food-products.'

'If you were in my position, George, you wouldn't want to talk about anything else. It's doing him a world of good, poor dear, but there are times when I'm sorry father ever started this food-reform thing. You don't know what it means for a healthy young girl to try and support life on nuts and grasses.'

'And why should you?' broke out Emerson. 'I'll tell you what it is, Aline, you are perfectly absurd about your father. I don't want to say anything against him to you, naturally, but –'

'Go ahead, George. Why this diffidence? Say what you like.'

'Very well, then, I will. I'll give it to you straight. You know quite well that you let your father bully you. I don't say it is your fault or his fault or anybody's fault. I just state it as a fact. It's temperament, I suppose. You are yielding, and he is aggressive, and he has taken advantage of it. Take this food business, for a start. Your father's digestion has gone wrong, and as a result he has to live on nuts and bananas and things. Why should you let him make you do the same?'

'It isn't a question of making. He doesn't make me, I do it to encourage him, to show him that it can be done. If I weakened he would lose all his resolution in a moment, and rush out and start a regular debauch of *pâté de fois gras* and lobster. And then he would suffer agonies. What a terrible thing it is, George, that father should combine a schoolboy appetite with a Rockefeller digestion. Either by itself wouldn't be so bad, but the combination is awful.'

George, baffled, but determined, resumed the attack.

'All right, then, if you really are starving yourself of your own free will, there is no more to say.'

'But you are going to say it, aren't you, George?'

'We now come to this idiot Freddie marriage business.

Your father has forced you into that. It's all very well to say that you are a free agent, and that fathers don't coerce their daughters nowadays. The trouble is that your father does. You let him do what he likes with you. And you won't break away from this Freddie foolishness because you can't find the pluck. I'm going to help you find it. I'm coming down to Blandings Castle when you go there on Friday.'

'Coming to Blandings?'

'Freddie invited me last night. I think it was done by way of interest on the money he owed me, but he did it, and I accepted.'

'But, George, my dear, dear boy, do you *never* read the Etiquette Books and the hints in the papers on how to be the Perfect Gentleman? Don't you know that you can't be a man's guest and take advantage of his hospitality to try to steal his fiancée away from him?'

'Watch me!'

A dreamy look came into Aline's eyes.

'I wonder what it feels like being a countess,' she said.

'You will never know,' George looked at her pityingly. 'My poor girl,' he said, 'have you been lured into this engagement in the belief that Freddie, the Idiot Child, is going to be an earl some day? They were ragging you. Freddie is not the heir. His elder brother, Lord Bosham, is as fit as a prize-fighter and has three healthy sons. Freddie has about as much chance of getting the title as I have.'

'George, your education has been sadly neglected. Don't you know that the heir to the title always goes for a yachting cruise with his whole family and gets drowned, and the children too? It happens in every English novel you read.'

'Listen, Aline, let us get this thing straight. I have been in love with you ever since we met on the *Olympic*. I proposed to you twice on the voyage and once in the train on the way to London. That was eight months ago, and I have been proposing to you at intervals ever since. I go to Scotland for a few weeks to see my people, and when I come back, what do I find? I find you engaged to be married to this Freddie excrescence.'

'I like your chivalrous attitude towards Freddie. So many men in your position might say horrid things about him.'

'Oh, I've nothing against Freddie. He is practically an imbecile and I don't like his face, but apart from that he's all right. But you will be glad later that you did not marry him. You are much too real a person. What a wife you will make for a hard-working man!'

'What does Freddie work hard at?'

'I am alluding at the moment not to Freddie but to myself. I shall come home tired out. Things will have gone wrong at my office. I shall be fagged, disheartened. And then you will come with cool, white hands, and placing them gently on my forehead –'

Aline shook her head.

'It's no good, George. Really, you had better realize it. I'm very fond of you, but we are not suited.'

'Why not?'

'You are too overwhelming, too much like a bomb. I think you must be one of these Supermen one reads about. You would want your own way and nothing but your own way. I expect it's through having to be constantly moving people on out in Hong-Kong, and all that sort of thing. Now Freddie will roll through hoops and sham dead, and we shall be the happiest pair in the world. I am much too placid and mild to make you happy. You want someone who would stand up to you. Somebody like Joan Valentine.'

'That's the second time you have mentioned this Joan Valentine. Who *is* she?'

'She is a girl who was at school with me. I was at school in England, you know – Mother wanted me to get

59

the tone, or something. We were the greatest chums. At least, I worshipped her and would have done anything for her, and I think she liked me. Then I went back to America and we lost touch with one another. I met her on the street yesterday, and she is just the same. She has been through the most awful times. Her father was quite rich, and he died suddenly, and she found that he hadn't left a penny. He had been living right up to his income all the time. His life wasn't even insured. She came to London, and, as far as I could make out from the short talk we had, she had done pretty nearly everything since we last met. She worked in a shop and went on the stage, and all sorts of things. Isn't it awful, George?'

'Frightful,' said Emerson. He was but faintly interested in Miss Valentine.

'She is so plucky and full of life. She would stand up to you.'

'Thanks! My idea of marriage is not a perpetual fight. My notion of a wife is something cosy and sympathetic and soothing. That is why I love you. We shall be the happiest –'

Aline laughed.

'Dear old George! And now pay the bill, and get me a taxi. I've endless things to do at home. If Freddie is in town, I suppose he will be calling to see me. Who is Freddie, do you ask? Freddie is my fiancé, George. My betrothed. The young man I'm going to marry.'

Emerson shook his head resignedly.

'Curious how you cling to that Freddie idea. Never mind. I'll come down to Blandings on Friday, and we will see what happens. Bear in mind the broad fact that you and I are going to get married and that nothing on earth is going to stop us.'

IV

The reason why all we novelists with bulging foreheads and expensive educations are abandoning novels and taking to writing motion-picture scenarii is because the latter are so infinitely the more simple and pleasant.

If this narrative, for instance, were a film-drama, the operator at this point would flash on the screen the words:

MR PETERS DISCOVERS THE LOSS OF THE SCARAB

and for a brief moment the audience would see an interior set, in which a little angry man with a sharp face and starting eyes would register first, Discovery; next Dismay. The whole thing would be over in an instant.

The printed word demands a greater elaboration.

It was Aline who had to bear the brunt of her father's mental agony when he discovered, shortly after his guest had left him, that the gem of his collection of scarabs had done the same. It is always the innocent bystander who suffers.

'The darned old sneak-thief!' said Mr Peters.

'Father!'

'Don't just sit there saying "Father!" What's the use of saying "Father!"? Do you think it is going to help, your saying "Father!"? I'd rather the old pirate had taken the house and lot than that scarab. He knows what's what! Trust him to walk off with the pick of the whole bunch. I did think I could trust the father of the man who's going to marry my daughter for a second alone with the things. There's no morality among collectors, none. I'd trust a syndicate of Jesse James, Captain Kidd, and Dick Turpin sooner than I would a collector. My Cheops of the Fourth Dynasty! I wouldn't have lost it for five thousand dollars.'

'But, father, couldn't you write him a letter, asking for

it back? He's such a nice old man; I'm sure he didn't mean to steal the scarab.'

Mr Peters' overwrought soul blew off steam in the shape of a passionate snort.

'Didn't mean to steal it! What do you think he meant to do – take it away and keep it safe for me in case I should lose it? Didn't mean to steal it! I bet you he's well known in Society as a kleptomaniac. I bet you that, when his name is announced, his friends lock up their spoons and send in a hurry-call to police headquarters for a squad to come and see that he doesn't sneak the front door. Of course, he meant to steal it. He has a museum of his own down in the country. My Cheops is going to lend tone to that. I'd give five thousand dollars to get it back. If there's a burglar in this country with the spirit to break into the Castle and steal that scarab and hand it back to me, there's five thousand waiting for him right here, and, if he wants to, he can knock that old pirate on the head with a jemmy into the bargain.'

'But, father, why can't you simply go to him and say it's yours and that you must have it back?'

'And have him come back at me by calling off this engagement of yours! Not if I know it. You can't go about the place charging a man with theft and expect him to go on being willing to have his son marry your daughter, can you? The slightest suggestion that I thought he had stolen this scarab, and he would do the Proud Old English Aristocrat and end everything. He's in the strongest position a thief has ever been in. You can't get at him.'

'I didn't think of that.'

'You don't think at all. That's the trouble with you,' said Mr Peters.

You see now why we prefer writing motion-picture scenarii. It is painful to a refined and sensitive young novelist to have to set down such a scene between father and child. But what is one to do? Years of indigestion had made Mr Peters' temper, even when in a normal mood, perfectly impossible; in a crisis like this it ran amuck. He vented it on Aline because he had always vented his irritabilities on Aline, because the fact of her sweet, gentle disposition, combined with the fact of their relationship, made her the ideal person to receive the overflow of his black moods. While his wife had lived, he had bullied her. On her death, Aline had stepped into the vacant position.

Aline did not cry, because she was not a girl who was given to tears, but for all her placid good-temper, she was wounded. She was a girl who liked everything in the world to run smoothly and easily, and these scenes with her father always depressed her. She took advantage of a lull in Mr Peters' flow of words and slipped from the room.

Her cheerfulness had received a shock. She wanted sympathy. She wanted comforting. For a moment she considered George Emerson in the role of comforter. But there were objections to George in this character. Aline was accustomed to tease and chaff George, but at heart she was a little afraid of him, and instinct told her that, as comforter, he would be too volcanic and super-manly for a girl who was engaged to marry another man in June. George as comforter would be far too prone to trust to action rather than to the soothing power of the spoken word. George's idea of healing the wound, she felt, would be to push her into a cab and drive to the nearest registrar's.

No, she would not go to George; to whom, then?

The vision of Joan Valentine came to her – of Joan as she had seen her yesterday, strong, cheerful, self-reliant, bearing herself in spite of adversity with a valiant jauntiness. Yes, she would go and see Joan.

She put on her hat and stole from the house.

Curiously enough, only a quarter of an hour before, R. Jones had set out with exactly the same object in view.

V

How pleasant it is after assisting at a scene of violence
and recrimination, to be transferred to one of peace and
goodwill. It is with a sense of relief that I find that the
snipe-like flight of this story takes us next, far from Mr
Peters and his angry outpourings, to the cosy
smoking-room of Blandings Castle.

At almost exactly the hour when Aline Peters set off
to visit her friend Miss Valentine, three men sat in the
cosy smoking-room of Blandings Castle.

They were variously occupied. In the long chair
nearest the door, the Hon. Frederick Threepwood –
Freddie to pals – was reading. Next to him sat a young
man whose eyes, glittering through rimless spectacles,
were concentrated on the upturned faces of several neat
rows of playing-cards. (Rupert Baxter, Lord Emsworth's
invaluable secretary, had no vices, but he sometimes
relaxed his busy brain with a game of solitaire.) Beyond
Baxter, a cigar in his mouth and a weak high-ball at his
side, the Earl of Emsworth took his ease. After the scene
we have just been through it does one good merely to
contemplate such a picture.

The book which the Hon. Freddie was reading was a
small, paper-covered book. Its cover was decorated with
a colour-scheme in red, black, and yellow, depicting a
tense moment in the lives of a man with a black beard, a
man with a yellow beard, a man without any beard at
all, and a young woman, who, at first sight, appeared to
be all eyes and hair. The man with the black beard, to
gain some private end, had tied this young woman with
ropes to a complicated system of machinery, mostly
wheels and pulleys. The man with the yellow beard was
in the act of pushing or pulling a lever. The beardless
man, protruding through a trap-door in the floor, was
pointing a large revolver at the parties of the second part.

Beneath this picture were the words, 'Hands up, you

scoundrels!' Above it, in a meandering scroll across the page 'Gridley Quayle, Investigator. The Adventure of the Secret Six. By Felix Clovelly.'

The Hon. Freddie did not so much read as gulp the adventure of the Secret Six. His face was crimson with excitement; his hair was rumpled; his eyes bulged. He was absorbed.

This is peculiarly an age in which each one of us may, if he do but search diligently, find the literature suited to his mental powers. Grave and earnest men, at Eton and elsewhere, had tried Freddie Threepwood with Greek, with Latin, and with English, and the sheeplike stolidity with which he declined to be interested in the masterpieces of all three tongues had left them with conviction that he would never read anything.

And then, years afterwards, he had suddenly blossomed out as a student. Only, it is true, a student of the Adventures of Gridley Quayle, but still a student. His was a dull life, and Gridley Quayle was the only person who brought romance into it. Existence for the Hon. Freddie was simply a sort of desert punctuated with monthly oases in the shape of new Quayle adventures.

It was his ambition to meet the man who wrote them.

Lord Emsworth sat and smoked and sipped and smoked again, at peace with all the world. His mind was as nearly a blank as it is possible for the human mind to be.

The hand which had not the task of holding the cigar was at rest in his trouser-pocket. The fingers of it fumbled idly with a small, hard object.

Gradually it filtered into his lordship's mind that this small hard object was not familiar. It was something new – something that was neither his keys, his pencil, nor his small change.

He yielded to a growing curiosity, and drew it out.

He examined it.

It was a little something, rather like a fossilized beetle. It touched no chord in him. He looked at it with an amiable distaste.

'Now, how in the world did that get there?' he said.

The Hon. Freddie paid no attention to the remark. He was now at the very crest of his story, when every line intensified the thrill. Incident was succeeding incident. The Secret Six were here, there, and everywhere, like so many malignant June bugs. Annabel, the heroine, was having a perfectly rotten time, kidnapped and imprisoned every few minutes. Gridley Quayle, hot on the scent, was covering someone or other with his revolver almost continuously. The Hon. Freddie had no time for chatting with his father.

Not so Rupert Baxter. Chatting with Lord Emsworth was one of the things for which he received his salary. He looked up from his cards.

'Lord Emsworth?'

'I have found a curious object in my pocket, Baxter. I was wondering how it got there.'

He handed the thing to his secretary. Rupert Baxter's eyes lit up with a sudden enthusiasm. He gasped.

'Magnificent!' he cried. 'Superb!'

Lord Emsworth looked at him inquiringly.

'It is a scarab, Lord Emsworth, and, unless I am mistaken – and I think I may claim to be something of an expert – a Cheops of the Fourth Dynasty. A wonderful addition to your museum.'

'Is it, by gad! You don't say so, Baxter!'

'It is indeed. If it is not a rude question, how much did you give for it, Lord Emsworth? It must have been the gem of someone's collection. Was there a sale at Christie's this afternoon?'

Lord Emsworth shook his head.

'I did not get it at Christie's for I recollect that I had an important engagement which prevented my going to

Christie's. I had – to be sure, yes. I had promised to call on Mr Peters and examine his collection of – now I wonder what it was that Mr Peters said he collected?'

'Mr Peters is one of the best-known living collectors of scarabs.'

'Scarabs! You are quite right, Baxter. And now that I recall the episode, this is a scarab, and Mr Peters gave it to me.'

'*Gave* it to you, Lord Emsworth!'

'Yes. The whole scene comes back to me. Mr Peters, after telling me a great many exceedingly interesting things about scarabs, which I regret to say I cannot remember, gave me this. And you say it is really valuable, Baxter?'

'It is, from a collector's point of view, of extraordinary value.'

'Bless my soul!' Lord Emsworth beamed. 'This is extremely interesting, Baxter. One has heard so much of the princely hospitality of Americans. How exceedingly kind of Mr Peters. I shall certainly treasure it, though I must confess that, from a purely spectacular standpoint, it leaves me a little cold. However, I must not look a gift horse in the mouth, eh, Baxter?'

From afar came the silver booming of a gong. Lord Emsworth rose.

'Time to dress for dinner? I had no idea it was so late. Baxter, you will be going past the museum door. Will you be a good fellow and place this among the exhibits? You will know what to do with it better than I. I always think of you as the curator of my little collection, Baxter; ha, ha! Mind how you step when you are in the museum. I was painting a chair there yesterday, and I think I left the paint-pot on the floor.'

He cast a less amiable glance at his studious son.

'Get *up*, Frederick, and go and dress for dinner. What is that trash you are reading?'

The Hon. Freddie came out of his book much as a

sleepwalker awakes, with a sense of having been
violently assaulted. He looked up with a kind of stunned
plaintiveness.

'Eh? governor?'

'Make haste. Beach rang the gong five minutes ago.
What is that you are reading?'

'Oh, nothing, governor. Just a book.'

'I wonder how you can waste your time on such trash.
Make haste.'

He turned to the door, and the benevolent expression
once more wandered athwart his face.

'*Extremely* kind of Mr Peters!' he said. 'Really, there
is something almost oriental in the lavish generosity of
our American cousins.'

VI

It had taken R. Jones just six hours to discover Joan
Valentine's address. That it had not taken him longer is
a proof of his energy and of the excellence of his system
of obtaining information. But R. Jones, when he
considered it worth his while, could be extremely
energetic, and he was a past master at the art of finding
out things.

He poured himself out of his cab, and rang the bell of
No. 7A. A dishevelled maid answered the ring.

'Miss Valentine in?'

'Yes, sir.'

R. Jones produced his card.

'On important business, tell her. Half a minute, I'll
write it.'

He wrote the words on the card, and devoted the brief
period of waiting to a careful scrutiny of his
surroundings. He looked out into the court and he
looked as far as he could down the dingy passage, and
the conclusions he drew from what he saw were
complimentary to Miss Valentine.

'If this girl is the sort of girl who would hold up
Freddie's letters,' he mused, 'she wouldn't be living in a
place like this. If she were on the make, she would have
more money than she evidently possesses. Therefore,
she is not on the make, and I should be prepared to bet
that she destroyed the letters as fast as she got them.'

Those were, roughly, the thoughts of R. Jones, as he
stood in the doorway of No. 7A, and they were
important thoughts, inasmuch as they determined his
attitude towards Joan in the approaching interview. He
perceived that this matter must be handled delicately,
that he must be very much the gentleman. It would be a
strain, but he must do it.

The maid returned and directed him to Joan's room
with a brief word and a sweeping gesture.

'Eh?' said R. Jones. 'First floor?'

'Front,' said the maid.

R. Jones trudged laboriously up the short flight of
stairs. It was very dark on the stairs, and he stumbled.
Eventually, however, light came to him through an open
door. Looking in, he saw a girl standing at the table. She
had an air of expectation, so he deduced that he had
reached his journey's end.

'Miss Valentine?'

'Please come in.'

R. Jones waddled in.

'Not much light on your stairs.'

'No. Will you take a seat?'

'Thanks.'

One glance at the girl convinced R. Jones that he had
been right. Circumstances had made him a rapid judge of
character, for in the profession of living by one's wits in
a large city, the first principle of offence and defence is
to sum people up at first sight. This girl was not on the
make.

Joan Valentine was a tall girl, with wheat-gold hair
and eyes as brightly blue as a November sky when the

sun is shining on a frosty world. There was in them a
little of November's cold glitter, too, for Joan had been
through much in the last few years, and experience, even
if it does not harden, erects a defensive barrier between
its children and the world. Her eyes were eyes that
looked straight and challenged. They could thaw to the
satin blue of the Mediterranean Sea where it purrs about
the little villages of Southern France, but they did not
thaw for everyone. She looked what she was – a girl of
action, a girl whom Life had made both reckless and
wary, wary of friendly advances, reckless when there
was a venture afoot.

Her eyes, as they met R. Jones' now, were cold and
challenging. She, too, had learned the trick of swift
diagnosis of character, and what she saw of R. Jones in
that first glance did not impress her very favourably.

'You wished to see me on business?'

'Yes,' said R. Jones. 'Yes . . . Miss Valentine, may I
begin by begging you to realize that I have no intention
of insulting you?'

Joan's eyebrows rose. For an instant she did her
visitor the injustice of suspecting that he had been
dining too well.

'I don't quite understand.'

'Let me explain. I have come here,' R. Jones went on,
getting more gentlemanly every moment, 'on a very
distasteful errand, to oblige a friend. Will you bear
in mind that, whatever I say, is said entirely on his
behalf?'

By this time Joan had abandoned the idea that this
stout person was a life-insurance tout, and was inclining
to the view that he was collecting funds for a charity.

'I came here at the request of the Hon. Frederick
Threepwood.'

'I don't quite understand.'

'You never met him, Miss Valentine, but, when you
were in the chorus at the Piccadilly Theatre, I believe he

wrote you some very foolish letters. Possibly you have
forgotten them?'

'I certainly have.'

'You have probably destroyed them, eh?'

'Certainly. I don't often keep letters. Why do you ask?'

'Well, you see, Miss Valentine, the Hon. Frederick
Threepwood is about to be married, and he thought that
possibly, on the whole, it would be better that the letters
– and poetry – which he wrote you were non-existent.'

Not all R. Jones' gentlemanliness – and during this
speech he diffused it like a powerful scent in waves
about him – could hide the unpleasant meaning of the
words.

'He was afraid I might try and blackmail him?' said
Joan with formidable calm.

R. Jones raised and waved a fat hand deprecatingly.

'My dear Miss Valentine!'

Joan rose and R. Jones followed her example. The
interview was plainly at an end.

'Please tell Mr Threepwood to make his mind quite
easy. He is in no danger.'

'Exactly, exactly, precisely. I assured Threepwood that
my visit here would be a mere formality. I was quite
sure you had no intention whatever of worrying him. I
will tell him definitely then, that you have destroyed
the letters?'

'Yes. Good evening.'

'Good evening, Miss Valentine.'

The closing of the door behind him left him in total
darkness, but he hardly liked to return and ask Joan to
reopen it in order to light him on his way. He was glad
to be out of her presence. He was used to being looked at
in an unfriendly way by his fellows, but there had been
something in Joan's eyes which had curiously
discomfited him. He groped his way down, relieved that
all was over and had ended well. He believed what she
had told him, and he could conscientiously assure

71

Freddie that the prospect of his sharing the fate of poor
old Percy was non-existent. It is true that he proposed to
add in his report that the destruction of the letters had
been purchased with difficulty, at a cost of just five
hundred pounds, but that was a mere business formality.

He had almost reached the last step when there was a
ring at the front door. With what he was afterwards
wont to call an inspiration, he retreated with unusual
nimbleness till he had almost reached Joan's door again.
Then he leaned over the banisters and listened.

The dishevelled maid opened the door. A girl's voice
spoke.

'Is Miss Valentine in?'

'She's in, but she's engaged.'

'I wish you would go up and tell her that I want to see
her. Say it's Miss Peters. Miss Aline Peters.'

The banisters shook beneath R. Jones' sudden clutch.
For a moment he had felt almost faint. Then he began to
think swiftly. A great light had dawned upon him, and
the thought outstanding in his mind was that never
again would he trust a man or woman on the evidence of
his senses. He could have sworn that this Valentine girl
was on the level. He had been perfectly satisfied with
her statement that she had destroyed the letters. And all
the while she had been playing as deep a game as he had
ever come across in the whole course of his professional
career. He almost admired her. How she had taken him
in! It was obvious now what her game was. Previous to
his visit she had arranged a meeting with Freddie's
fiancée, with the view of opening negotiations for the
sale of the letters. She had held him, Jones, at arms'
length, because she was going to sell the letters to
whoever would pay the best price. But for the accident of
his happening to be here when Miss Peters arrived,
Freddie and his fiancée would have been bidding against
each other, and raising each other's price. He had
worked the same game himself a dozen times, and he

resented the entry of female competition into what he regarded as essentially a male field of enterprise.

As the maid stumped up the stairs, he continued his retreat. He heard Joan's door open, and the stream of light showed him the dishevelled maid standing in the doorway.

'Ow, I thought there was a gentleman with you, miss.'

'He left a moment ago. Why?'

'There's a lady wants to see you. Miss Peters her name is.'

'Will you ask her to come up?'

The dishevelled maid was no polished mistress of ceremonies. She leaned down into the void, and hailed Aline.

'She says, will you come up.'

Aline's feet became audible on the staircase. There were greetings.

'Whatever brings you here, Aline?'

'Am I interrupting you, Joan, dear?'

'No. Do come in. I was only surprised to see you so late. I didn't know you paid calls at this hour. Is anything wrong? Come in.'

The door closed, the maid retired to the depths, and R. Jones stole cautiously down again. He was feeling absolutely bewildered. Apparently his deductions, his second thoughts had been all wrong, and Joan was, after all, the honest person he had imagined at first sight. These two girls had talked to each other as if they were old friends, as if they had known each other all their lives. That was the thing that perplexed R. Jones.

With the tread of a Red Indian he approached the door, and put his ear to it . He found that he could hear quite comfortably.

Aline meanwhile, inside the room, had begun to draw comfort from Joan's very appearance. She looked so capable.

73

Joan's eyes had changed the expression they had contained during the recent interview. They were soft now, with a softness that was half compassionate, half contemptuous. It is the compensation which Life gives to those whom it has handled roughly that they shall be able to regard with a certain contempt the small troubles of the sheltered. Joan remembered Aline of old, and knew her for a perennial victim of small troubles. Even in their school days she had always needed to be looked after and comforted. Her sweet temper had seemed to invite the minor slings and arrows of fortune. Aline was a girl who inspired protectiveness in a certain type of her fellow human beings. It was this quality in her which kept George Emerson awake at nights; and it appealed to Joan now. Joan, for whom life was a constant struggle to keep the wolf within a reasonable distance from the door, and who counted that day happy on which she saw her way clear to paying her weekly rent and possibly having a trifle over for some coveted hat or pair of shoes, could not help feeling, as she looked at Aline, that her own troubles were as nothing, and that the immediate need of the moment was to pet and comfort her friend. Her knowledge of Aline told her that the probable tragedy was that she had lost a brooch or had been spoken to crossly by somebody, but it also told her that such tragedies bulked very large on Aline's horizon. Trouble, after all, like beauty, is in the eye of the beholder, and Aline was far less able to endure with fortitude the loss of a brooch than she herself the loss of a position whose emoluments meant the difference between having just enough to eat and starving.

'You're worried about something,' she said. 'Sit down and tell me about it.'

Aline sat down, and looked about her at the shabby room. By that curious process of the human mind which makes the spectacle of another's misfortune a palliative for one's own, she was feeling oddly comforted already.

Her thoughts were not definite, and she could not analyse them, but what they amounted to was that, while it was an unpleasant thing to be bullied by a dyspeptic father, the world manifestly held worse tribulations which her father's other outstanding quality besides dyspepsia – wealth, to wit – enabled her to avoid. It was at this point that the dim beginnings of a philosophy began to invade her mind. The thing resolved itself almost into an equation. If father had not had indigestion, he would not have bullied her. But, if father had not made a fortune, he would not have had indigestion. Therefore, if father had not made a fortune, he would not have bullied her. Practically, in fact, if father did not bully her, he would not be rich. And, if he were not rich . . . She took in the faded carpet, the stained wallpaper, and the soiled curtains, in a comprehensive glance . . . It certainly cut both ways. She began to be a little ashamed of her misery.

'It's nothing at all, really,' she said. 'I think I've been making rather a fuss about very little.'

Joan was relieved. The struggling life breeds moods of depression, and such a mood had come to her just before Aline's arrival. Life, at that moment, had seemed to stretch before her like a dusty, weary road, without hope. She was sick of fighting. She wanted money and ease and a surcease from this perpetual race with weekly bills. The mood had been the outcome partly of R. Jones' gentlemanly-veiled insinuations, but still more, though she did not realize it, of her yesterday's meeting with Aline. Mr Peters might be unguarded in his speech, when conversing with his daughter, he might play the tyrant towards her in many ways, but he did not stint her in the matter of dress allowance, and on the occasion when she met Joan, Aline had been wearing so Parisian a hat and a tailor-made suit of such obviously expensive simplicity that green-eyed envy had almost spoiled Joan's pleasure at meeting this friend of her opulent

75

days. She had suppressed the envy, and it had revenged itself by assaulting her afresh in the form of the worst fit of blues which she had had in two years. She had been loyally ready to sink her depression in order to alleviate Aline's, but it was a distinct relief to find that the feat would not be necessary.

'Never mind,' she said, 'tell me what the very little thing was.'

'It was only father,' said Aline simply.

'Was he angry with you about something?'

'Not exactly angry with me. But – well, I was there.'

Joan's depression lifted slightly. She had forgotten, in the stunning anguish of the sudden spectacle of that hat and that tailor-made suit, that Paris hats and twenty-five pounds suits not infrequently had their accompanying disadvantages. After all, she was independent. She might have to murder her beauty with hats and frocks which had never been nearer Paris than the Tottenham Court Road, but at least no one bullied her because she happened to be at hand when tempers were short.

'What a shame!' she said. 'Tell me all about it.'

With a prefatory remark that it was all so ridiculous really, Aline embarked upon the narrative of the afternoon's events.

Joan heard her out, checking a strong disposition to giggle. Her viewpoint was that of the Average Person, and the Average Person cannot see the importance of the scarab in the scheme of things. The opinion she formed of Mr Peters was of an eccentric old gentleman making a great to-do about nothing at all. Losses had to have a concrete value before they could impress Joan. It was beyond her to grasp that Mr Peters would sooner have lost a diamond necklace, if he had happened to possess one, than his Cheops of the Fourth Dynasty.

It was not until Aline, having concluded her tale, added one more strand to it that she found herself treating the matter seriously.

'Father says he would give a thousand pounds to anyone who would get it back for him.'

'What!'

The whole story took on a different complexion for Joan. Money talks. Mr Peters' words might have been merely the rhetorical outbursts of a heated moment, but, even discounting them, there seemed to remain a certain exciting substratum. A man who shouts that he will give a thousand pounds for a thing may very well mean that he will give a hundred, and Joan's finances were perpetually in a condition which makes a hundred pounds a sum to be gasped at.

'He wasn't serious, surely?'

'I think he was,' said Aline.

'But a thousand pounds!'

'It isn't really very much to father, you know. He gives away a hundred thousand dollars a year to a University.'

'But for a grubby little scarab!'

'You don't understand how father loves his scarabs. Since he retired from business, he has been simply wrapped up in them. You know, collectors are like that. You read in the papers about men giving all sorts of money for funny things.'

Outside the door, R. Jones, his ear close to the panel, drank in all these things greedily. He would have been willing to remain in that attitude indefinitely in return for this kind of special information, but, just as Aline said these words, a door opened on the floor above and somebody came out, whistling, and began to descend the stairs.

R. Jones stood not upon the order of his going. He was down in the hall and fumbling with the handle of the front door with an agility of which few casual observers of his dimensions would have deemed him capable.

The next moment he was out in the street, walking

calmly towards Leicester Square, pondering over what he had heard.

Much of R. Jones' substantial annual income was derived from pondering over what he had heard.

In the room, Joan was looking at Aline with the distended eyes of one who sees visions or has inspirations. She got up. There are occasions when one must speak standing.

'Then you mean to say that your father would really give a thousand pounds to anyone who got this thing back for him?'

'I am sure he would. But who could do it?'

'I could,' said Joan. 'And what is more, I'm going to.'

Aline stared at her helplessly. In their schooldays, Joan had always swept her off her feet. Then, she had always had the feeling that with Joan nothing was impossible. Heroine-worship, like hero-worship, dies hard. She looked at Joan now with the stricken sensation of one who had inadvertently set powerful machinery in motion.

'But, Joan!'

It was all she could say.

'My dear child, it's perfectly simple. This earl of yours has taken the thing off to his castle, like a brigand. You say you are going down there on Friday for a visit. All you have to do is to take me along with you.'

'But, Joan!'

'Where's the difficulty?'

'I don't see how I could take you down very well.'

'Why not?'

'Oh, I don't know.'

'But, what is your objection?'

'Well, don't you see . . . If you come down there as a friend of mine, and were caught stealing the scarab, there would be . . . just the trouble father wants to avoid. About my engagement, you see, and so on.'

It was an aspect of the matter which had escaped Joan. She frowned thoughtfully.

'I see. Yes, there is that. But there must be a way.'

'You mustn't, Joan, really. Don't think any more about it.'

'Not think any more about it! My child, do you even faintly realize what a thousand pounds, or a quarter of a thousand pounds means to me? I would do anything for it, *anything*. And there's the fun of it. I don't suppose you can realize that either. I want a change. I want something new. I've been grubbing away here on nothing a week for years, and it's time I had a vacation. There must be a way by which you could get me down . . . Why, of course! Why didn't I think of it before! You shall take me on Friday as your lady's maid!'

'But, Joan, I couldn't.'

'Why not?'

'I – I couldn't.'

'Why not?'

'Oh well!'

Joan advanced upon her where she sat, and grasped her firmly by the shoulders. Her face was inflexible.

'Aline, my pet, it's no good arguing. You might just as well argue with a wolf on the trail of a fat Russian peasant. I need that money. I need it in my business. I need it worse than anybody has ever needed anything. And I'm going to have it. From now on till further notice, I am your lady's maid. You can give your present one a holiday.'

Aline met her eyes waveringly. The spirit of the old schooldays, when nothing was impossible where Joan was concerned, had her in its grip. Moreover, the excitement of the scheme began to attract her.

'But, Joan,' she said, 'you know it's simply ridiculous. You could never pass as a lady's maid. The other servants would find you out. I expect there are all sorts of things a lady's maid has got to do and not do.'

'My dear Aline, I know them all. You can't stump me
on below-stairs etiquette. I have *been* a lady's maid!'

'Joan!'

'It's quite true. Three years ago, when I was more than
usually impecunious. The wolf was glued to the door
like a postage stamp, so I answered an advertisement
and became a lady's maid.'

'You seem to have done everything.'

'I have – pretty nearly. It's all right for you Idle Rich,
Aline, you can sit still and contemplate Life, but we of
the submerged tenth have got to work.'

Aline laughed.

'You know, you always could make me do anything
you wanted, in the old days, Joan. I suppose I have got to
look on this as quite settled now?'

'Absolutely settled. Oh, Aline, there's one thing you
must remember. Don't call me Joan when I'm down at
the Castle. You must call me Valentine.' She paused.
The recollection of the Hon. Freddie had come to her.
No, Valentine would not do. 'No, not Valentine,' she
went on. 'It's too jaunty. I used it three years ago, but it
never sounded just right. I want something more
respectable, more suited to my position. Can't you
suggest something?'

Aline pondered.

'Simpson?'

'Simpson! It's exactly right. You must practise it.
Simpson! Say it kindly and yet distantly, as if I were a
worm, but a worm for whom you felt a mild liking. Roll
it round your tongue.'

'Simpson.'

'Splendid! Now, once again – a little more haughtily.'

'Simpson . . . Simpson . . . Simpson . . .'

Joan regarded her with affectionate approval.

'It's wonderful,' she said. 'You might have been doing
it all your life.'

*

'What are you laughing at?' asked Aline.

'Nothing,' said Joan. 'I was just thinking of something. There's a young man who lives on the floor above this, and I was lecturing him yesterday on Enterprise. I told him to go and find something exciting to do. I wonder what he would say if he knew how thoroughly I am going to practise what I preach.'

4

On the morning following Aline's visit to Joan
Valentine, Ashe sat in his room, the *Morning Post* on
the table before him. The heady influence of Joan had
not yet ceased to work within him, and he proposed, in
pursuance of his promise to her, to go carefully through
the column of advertisements however pessimistic he
might feel concerning the utility of that action.

His first glance assured him that the vast fortunes of
the philanthropists whose acquaintance he had already
made in print were not yet exhausted. Brian MacNeill
still dangled his gold before the public. So did Angus
Bruce. So did Duncan Macfarlane. So, likewise, Wallace
Mackintosh and Donald MacNab. They still had the
money and they still wanted to give it away.

The young Christian still wanted that thousand . . .

He was reading listlessly down the column, when,
from the mass of advertisements, one of an unusual sort
detached itself:

WANTED – Young Man of Good Appearance, who is poor
and reckless, to undertake delicate and dangerous
enterprise. Good pay for the right man. Apply between the
hours of ten and twelve at offices of Mainprice, Mainprice
& Boole, 3 Denvers Street, Strand.

And, as he read it, half past ten struck on the little clock
on his mantelpiece.

It was probably this fact that decided Ashe. If he had
been compelled to postpone his visit to the offices of
Messrs Mainprice, Mainprice & Boole until the

afternoon, it is possible that barriers of laziness might have reared themselves in the path of adventure, for Ashe, an Adventurer at heart, was also uncommonly lazy. But as it was, he could make an immediate start.

Pausing but to put on his shoes, and having satisfied himself by a glance at the mirror that his appearance was reasonably good, he seized his hat, shot out of the narrow mouth of Arundell Street like a shell, and scrambled into a taxi-cab with the feeling that, short of murder, they couldn't make it too delicate and dangerous for him.

He was conscious of strange thrills. This, he told himself, was the only possible mode of life with Spring in the air. He had always been partial to those historical novels in which the characters are perpetually vaulting on to chargers and riding across country on perilous errands. This leaping into taxi-cabs to answer stimulating advertisements in the *Morning Post* was very much the same sort of thing. It was with a fine fervour animating him that he entered the gloomy offices of Mainprice, Mainprice & Boole. His brain was afire, and he felt ready for anything.

'I have come in answ –' he began to the diminutive office-boy, who seemed to be the nearest thing visible to a Mainprice or a Boole.

'Siddown. Gottatakeyerturn,' said the office-boy, and for the first time Ashe perceived that the ante-room in which he stood was crowded to overflowing.

This, in the circumstances, was something of a damper. He had pictured himself, during the ride in the cab, striding into the office and saying, 'The delicate and dangerous enterprise. Lead me to it.' He had not realized till now that he was not the only man in London who read the advertisement columns of the *Morning Post*, and for an instant his heart sank at the sight of all this competition.

A second and more comprehensive glance at his rivals gave him confidence.

The 'Wanted' column of the morning paper is a sort of dredger which churns up strange creatures from the mud of London's underworld. Only in response to the dredger's operations do they come to the surface in such numbers as to be noticeable, for as a rule they are of a solitary habit and shun company: but when they do come they bring with them something of the horror of the depths. It is the saddest spectacle in the world, that of the crowd collected by a 'Wanted' advertisement. They are so palpably not wanted by anyone for any purpose whatsoever: yet every time they gather together with a sort of hopeful hopelessness. What they were originally, the units of these collections, Heaven knows. Fate has battered out of them every trace of individuality. Each now is exactly like his neighbour, no worse, no better.

Ashe, as he sat and watched them, was filled with conflicting emotions. One half of him, thrilled with the glamour of adventure, was chafing at the delay and resentful of these poor creatures as of so many obstacles to the beginning of all the brisk and exciting things which lay behind the mysterious brevity of the advertisement. The other, pitifully alive to the tragedy of the occasion, was grateful for the delay. On the whole he was glad to feel that if one of these derelicts did not secure the 'good pay for the right man', it would not be his fault. He had been the last to arrive, and he would be the last to pass through that door which was the gateway of adventure, the door with 'Mr Boole' inscribed on its ground-glass, beyond which sat the author of the mysterious request for assistance, interviewing applicants. It would be through their own shortcomings, not because of his superior attractions, if they failed to please that unseen arbiter.

That they were so failing was plain. Scarcely had one

scarred victim of London's unkindness passed through, than the bell would ring, the office-boy who, in the intervals of frowning sternly on the throng as much as to say that he would stand no nonsense, would cry 'Next!' and another dull-eyed wreck would drift through, to be followed a moment later by yet another. The one fact at present ascertainable concerning the unknown searcher for reckless young men of good appearance was that he appeared to be possessed of considerable decision of character, a man who did not take long to make up his mind. He was rejecting applicants now at the rate of two a minute.

Expeditious as he was, however, he kept Ashe waiting for a considerable time. It was not till the hands of the fat clock over the door pointed to twenty minutes past eleven that the office-boy's 'Next!' found him the only survivor. He gave his clothes a hasty smack with the palm of his hand and his hair a fleeting dab, to accentuate his good appearance, and turned the handle of the door of fate.

The room assigned by the firm to their Mr Boole for his personal use was a small and dingy compartment, redolent of that atmosphere of desolation which lawyers alone know how to achieve. It gave the impression of not having been swept since the foundation of the firm in the year 1786. There was one small window, covered with grime. It was one of those windows which you see only in lawyer's offices. Possibly, some reckless Mainprice or hairbrained Boole had opened it, in a fit of mad excitement induced by the news of the Battle of Waterloo, in 1815, and had been instantly expelled from the firm. Since then no one had dared to tamper with it.

Looking out of this window, or rather, looking at it, for X-rays could hardly have succeeded in actually penetrating the alluvial deposits upon the glass, was a little man. As Ashe entered, he turned, and looked at him as if he hurt him rather badly in some tender spot.

Ashe was obliged to own to himself that he felt a little nervous. It is not every day that a young man of good appearance, who has led a quiet life, meets face to face one who is prepared to pay him well for doing something delicate and dangerous. To Ashe the sensation was entirely novel. The most delicate and dangerous act he had performed to date had been the daily mastication of Mrs Bell's breakfasts (included in rent). Yes, he had to admit it, he was nervous: and the fact that he was nervous made him hot and uncomfortable.

To judge him by his appearance, the man at the window was also hot and uncomfortable. He was a little, truculent-looking man, and his face at present was red with a flush which sat unnaturally on a normally leaden-coloured face. His eyes looked out from under thick grey eyebrows with an almost tortured expression. This was partly owing to the strain of interviewing Ashe's preposterous predecessors, but principally to the fact that the little man had suddenly become seized with acute indigestion, a malady to which he was peculiarly subject.

He removed from his mouth the black cigar which he was smoking inserted a digestive tabloid, and replaced the cigar. Then he concentrated his attention upon Ashe. As he did so, the hostile expression of his face become modified. He looked surprised and – grudgingly – pleased.

'Well, what do *you* want?' he said.

'I came in answer to –'

'In answer to my advertisement? I had given up hope of seeing anything part-human. I thought you must be one of the clerks. You're certainly more like what I advertised for. Of all the seedy bunches of dead-beats I ever struck, the aggregation I've just been interviewing was the seediest. When I spend good money advertising for a young man of good appearance, then I want a young man of good appearance, not a tramp of fifty-five.'

Ashe was sorry for his predecessors, but he was bound to admit that they certainly had corresponded somewhat faithfully to the description just given. The comparative cordiality of his own reception removed the slight nervousness which had been troubling him. He began to feel confident, almost jaunty.

'I'm through,' said the little man wearily. 'I've had enough of interviewing applicants. You're the last one I'll see. Are there any more hoodoos outside?'

'Not when I came in.'

'Then we'll get down to business. I'll tell you what I want done, and, if you are willing, you can do it: if you are not willing, you can leave it and go to the devil. Sit down.'

Ashe sat down. He resented the little man's tone, but this was not the moment for saying so.

His companion scrutinized him narrowly.

'As far as appearance goes,' he said, 'you are what I want.' Ashe felt inclined to bow.

'Whoever takes on this job has got to act as my valet, and you look like a valet.' Ashe felt less inclined to bow. 'You're tall and thin and ordinary-looking. Yes, as far as appearance goes, you fill the bill.'

It seemed to Ashe that it was time to correct an impression which the little man appeared to have formed.

'I am afraid,' he said, 'that, if all you want is a valet, you will have to look elsewhere. I got the idea from your advertisement that something rather more exciting than that was in the air. I can recommend you to several good employment agencies, if you wish.'

He rose. 'Good morning,' he said. He would have liked to fling the massive pewter ink-pot at this little creature who had so keenly disappointed him.

'Sit down!' snapped the other.

Ashe resumed his seat. The hope of adventure dies

hard on a Spring morning, when one is twenty-six, and he had the feeling that there was more to come.

'Don't be a damned fool,' said the little man. 'Of course I'm not asking you to be a valet and nothing else.'

'You would want me to do some cooking and plain sewing on the side, perhaps?'

Their eyes met in a hostile glare. The flush on the little man's face deepened.

'Are you trying to get gay with me?' he demanded dangerously.

'Yes,' said Ashe.

The answer seemed to disconcert his adversary. He was silent for a moment.

'Well,' he said at last, 'maybe it's all for the best. If you weren't full of gall, probably you wouldn't have come here at all, and whoever takes on this job of mine has got to have gall, if he has nothing else. I think we shall suit each other.'

'What is the job?'

The little man's face showed doubt and perplexity.

'It's awkward. If I'm to make the thing clear to you, I've got to trust you and I don't know a thing about you. I wish I had thought of that before I inserted the advertisement.'

Ashe appreciated the difficulty.

'Couldn't you make an A B case out of it?'

'Maybe I could, if I knew what an A B case was.'

'Call the people mixed up in it A and B.'

'And forget half-way through who was which! No, I guess I'll have to trust you.'

'I'll play square.'

The little man fastened his eyes on Ashe's in a piercing stare. Ashe met them smilingly. His spirits, always fairly cheerful, had risen high by now. There was something about the little man, in spite of his brusqueness and ill-temper, which made him feel flippant.

'Pure white,' he said.

'Eh?'

'My soul. And this' – he thumped the left section of his waistcoat – 'solid gold. Proceed.'

'I don't know where to begin.'

'Without presuming to dictate, why not at the beginning?'

'It's all so darned complicated that I don't rightly know which *is* the beginning. Well, see here. I collect scarabs. I'm crazy about scarabs. Ever since I quit business, you might say that I have practically lived for scarabs.'

'Though it sounds an unkind thing to say of anyone,' said Ashe, 'incidentally, what *are* scarabs?' He held up his hand. 'Wait! It all comes back to me. Expensive Classical education now bearing belated fruit. Scarabeus? Latin-noun, nominative – a beetle. Scarabeum, accusative, the beetle. Scarabei, of the beetle. Scarabeo, to or for the beetle. I remember now. Egypt – Rameses – Pyramids – sacred scarabs. Right!'

'Well, I guess I've gotten together the best collection of scarabs outside the British Museum, and some of them are worth what you like to me. I don't reckon money when it comes to a question of my scarabs. Do you understand?'

'I take you, laddie.'

Displeasure clouded the little man's face.

'Don't call me "laddie"!'

'I used the word figuratively, as it were.'

'Well, don't do it again. My name is J. Preston Peters, and "Mr Peters" will do as well as anything else when you want to attract my attention.'

'Mine is Marson. You were saying, Mr Peters?'

'Well, it's this way,' said the little man.

Shakespeare and Pope have both emphasized the tediousness of a twice-told tale, so the episode of the stolen scarab need not be repeated at this point, though it must be admitted that Mr Peters' version of it differed considerably from the calm, dispassionate description which the author, in his capacity of official historian, has given earlier in the story. In Mr Peters' version, the Earl of Emsworth appeared as a smooth and purposeful robber, a sort of elderly Raffles, worming his way into the homes of the innocent and only sparing that portion of their property which was too heavy for him to carry away. Mr Peters, indeed, specifically described the Earl of Emsworth as an oily old plug-ugly.

It took Ashe some little time to get a thorough grasp of the tangled situation, but he did it at last. Only one point perplexed him.

'You want to employ somebody to go to the castle and get this scarab back for you. I follow that. But why must he go as your valet?'

'That's simple enough. You don't think I'm asking him to buy a black mask and break in, do you? I'm making it as easy for him as possible. I can't take a secretary down to the Castle, for everybody knows that, now I've retired, I haven't got a secretary; and, if I engaged a new one and he was caught trying to steal my scarab from the Earl's collection, it would look suspicous. But a valet is different. Anyone can get fooled by a crook valet with bogus references.'

'I see. There's just one other point. Suppose your accomplice does get caught. What then?'

'That,' said Mr Peters, 'is the catch, and it's just because of that that I am offering good pay to my man. We'll suppose for the sake of argument that you accept the contract, and get caught. Well, if that happens, you've got to look after yourself. I couldn't say a word. If I did, it would all come out, and, as far as the breaking-off of my daughter's engagement to young Threepwood was concerned, it would be just as bad as if I had tried to get the thing back myself. You've got to bear that in mind. You've got to remember it if you forget everything else. I don't appear in this business in any way whatsoever. If you get caught, you take what's coming to you without a word. You don't turn round and say, "I am innocent. Mr Peters will explain all," because Mr Peters certainly won't. Mr Peters won't utter a syllable of protest if they want to hang you. No, if you go into this, young man, you go into it with your eyes open. You go into it with a full understanding of the risks, because you think the reward, if you are successful, makes the taking of those risks worth while. You and I know that what you are doing isn't really stealing; it's simply a tactful way of getting back my own property. But the judge and jury will have different views.'

'I am beginning to understand,' said Ashe thoughtfully, 'why you called the job "delicate and dangerous".'

Certainly it had been no over-statement. As a writer of detective-stories for the British office-boy, he had imagined in his time many undertakings which might be so described, but few to which the description was more admirably suited.

'It is,' said Mr Peters, 'and this is why I'm offering good pay. Whoever carries this job through gets five thousand dollars cash.'

Ashe started.

'Five thousand dollars! A thousand pounds?'

'Yes.'

'When do I begin?'

'You'll do it?'

'For a thousand pounds I certainly will.'

'With your eyes open?'

'Wide open.'

A look of positive geniality illuminated Mr Peters' pinched features. He even went so far as to pat Ashe on the shoulder.

'Good boy!' he said. 'Meet me at Paddington Station at four o'clock on Friday. And if there's anything more you want to know, come round to this address.'

II

There remained the telling of Joan Valentine. For it
was obviously impossible not to tell her. When you
have revolutionized your life at the bidding of another,
you cannot well conceal the fact, as if nothing had
happened.

Ashe had not the slightest desire to conceal the fact.
On the contrary, he was glad to have such a capital
excuse for renewing the acquaintance.

He could not tell her, of course, the secret details of
the thing. Naturally, those must remain hidden. No, he
would just go airily in and say, 'You know what you told
me about doing something new? Well, I've just got a job
as a valet.'

So he went airily in and said it.

'To whom?' said Joan.

'To a man named Peters. An American.'

Women are trained from infancy up to conceal their
feelings. Joan did not start or otherwise express emotion.

'Not Mr Preston Peters?'

'Yes. Do you know him? What a remarkable thing.'

'His daughter,' said Joan, 'has just engaged me as a
lady's maid.'

'What!'

'It will not be quite the same thing as three years ago,'
Joan explained. 'It is just a cheap way of getting a
holiday. I used to know Miss Peters very well, you see. It
will be more like travelling as her guest.'

Ashe had not yet overcome his amazement.

'But – ? but – '

'Yes?'

'But what an extraordinary coincidence.'

'Yes. By the way, how did you get the situation? And
what put it into your head to be a valet at all? It seems
such a curious thing for you to think of doing.'

Ashe was embarrassed.

'I – I – well, you see, the experience will be useful to me, of course, in my writing.'

'Oh! Are you now thinking of taking up my line of work, Dukes?'

'No, no. Not exactly that.'

'It seems so odd. How did you happen to get in touch with Mr Peters?'

'Oh, I answered an advertisement.'

'I see.'

Ashe was becoming conscious of an undercurrent of something not altogether agreeable in the conversation. It lacked the gay ease of their first interview. He was not apprehensive lest she might have guessed his secret. There was, he felt, no possible means by which she could have done that. Yet the fact remained that those keen blue eyes of hers were looking at him in a peculiar and penetrating manner. He felt dampened.

'It will be nice being together,' he said feebly.

'Very,' said Joan.

There was a pause.

'I thought I would come and tell you.'

'Quite so.'

There was another pause.

'It seems so funny that you should be going out as a lady's maid.'

'Yes?'

'But of course you have done it before.'

'Yes.'

'The really extraordinary thing is that we should be going to the same people.'

'Yes.'

'It – it's remarkable, isn't it?'

'Yes.'

Ashe reflected. No, he did not appear to have any further remarks to make.

'Good-bye for the present,' he said.

'Good-bye.'

93

Ashe drifted out. He was conscious of a wish that he understood girls. Girls, in his opinion, were odd.

When he had gone, Joan Valentine hurried to the door, and having opened it an inch, stood listening. When the sound of his door closing came to her, she ran down the stairs and out into Arundell Street.

She went to the Hotel Mathis.

'I wonder,' she said to the sad-eyed waiter, 'if you have a copy of the *Morning Post*?'

The waiter, a child of romantic Italy, was only too anxious to oblige Youth and Beauty. He disappeared, and presently returned with a crumpled copy. Joan thanked him with a bright smile.

Back in her room she turned to the advertisement page. She knew that life was full of what the unthinking call coincidences, but the miracle of Ashe having selected by chance the father of Aline Peters as an employer was too much of a coincidence for her. Suspicion furrowed her brow.

It did not take her long to discover the advertisement which had sent Ashe hurrying in a taxi-cab to the offices of Messrs Mainprice, Mainprice & Boole. She had been looking for something of the kind.

She read it through twice and smiled. Everything was very clear to her. She looked at the ceiling above her, and shook her head.

'You are quite a nice young man, Mr Marson,' she said softly, 'but you musn't try and jump my claim. I dare say you need that money too, but I'm afraid you must go without. I am going to have it, and nobody else.'

5

The four-fifteen express slid softly out of Paddington
Station, and Ashe settled himself in the corner seat of
his second-class compartment. Opposite him, Joan
Valentine had begun to read a magazine. Along the
corridor, in a first-class smoking compartment, Mr
Peters was lighting a big black cigar. Still farther along
the corridor, in a first-class, non-smoking compartment,
Aline Peters looked out of the window and thought of
many things.

Ashe was feeling remarkably light-hearted. He wished
that he had not bought Joan that magazine and thus
deprived himself temporarily of the pleasure of her
conversation: but that was the only flaw in his
happiness. With the starting of the train, which might be
considered the formal and official beginning of the
delicate and dangerous enterprise on which he had
embarked, he had definitely come to the conclusion that
the life adventurous was the life for him. He had
frequently suspected this to be the case, but it had
required the actual experiment to bring certainty.

Almost more than physical courage the ideal
adventurer needs a certain lively inquisitiveness, the
quality of not being content to mind his own affairs: and
in Ashe this quality was highly developed. From
boyhood up he had always been interested in things
which were none of his business. And it is just that
attribute which the modern young man, as a rule, so
sadly lacks.

The modern young man may do adventurous things if
they are thrust upon him, but, left to himself, he will

edge away uncomfortably and look in the other direction
when the Goddess of Adventure smiles at him. Training
and tradition alike pluck at his sleeve and urge him not
to risk making himself ridiculous. And from sheer
horror of laying himself open to the charge of not
minding his own business he falls into a stolid disregard
of all that is out of the ordinary and exciting. He tells
himself that the shriek from the lonely house he passed
just now was only the high note of some amateur
songstress, and that the maiden in distress whom he
saw pursued by the ruffian with a knife was merely
earning the salary paid her by some motion-picture firm.
And he proceeds on his way looking neither to left nor
right.

Ashe had none of this degenerate coyness towards
adventure. It is true that it had needed the eloquence of
Joan Valentine to stir him from his groove, but that was
because he was also lazy. He loved new sights and new
experiences.

Yes, he was happy. The rattle of the train shaped
itself into a lively march. He told himself that he had
found the right occupation for a young man in the
Spring.

Joan, meanwhile, entrenched behind her magazine,
was also busy with her thoughts. She was not reading
the magazine: she held it before her as a protection,
knowing that, if she laid it down, Ashe would begin
to talk. And just at present she had no desire for
conversation. She, like Ashe, was contemplating the
immediate future, but unlike him was not doing so with
much pleasure. She was regretting heartily that she had
not resisted the temptation to uplift this young man,
and wishing that she had left him to wallow in the
slothful peace in which she had found him. It is curious
how frequently in this world our attempts to stimulate
and uplift swoop back on us and smite us like
boomerangs. Ashe's presence was the direct outcome of

her lecture on Enterprise, and it added a complication to an already complicated venture.

She did her best to be fair to Ashe. It was not his fault that he was about to try to deprive her of five thousand dollars which she looked upon as her personal property. But, illogically, she found herself feeling a little hostile.

She glanced furtively at him over the magazine, choosing by ill chance a moment when he had just directed his gaze at her. Their eyes met, and there was nothing for it but to talk. So she tucked away her hostility in a corner of her mind where she could find it again when she wanted it, and prepared for the time being to be friendly. After all, except for the fact that he was her rival, this was a pleasant and amusing young man, and one for whom, till he made the announcement which had changed her whole attitude towards him, she had entertained a distinct feeling of friendship.

Nothing warmer. There was something about him which made her feel that she would have liked to stroke his hair in a motherly way and straighten his tie and have cosy chats with him in darkened rooms by the light of open fires, and make him tell her his inmost thoughts and stimulate him to do something really worth while with his life: but this, she held, was merely the instinct of a generous nature to be kind and helpful even to a comparative stranger.

'Well, Mr Marson,' she said. 'Here we are!'

'Exactly what I was thinking,' said Ashe.

He was conscious of a marked increase in the exhilaration which the starting of the expedition had brought to him. At the back of his mind, he realized, there had been all along a kind of wistful resentment at the change in this girl's manner towards him. During the brief conversation when he had told her of his having secured his present situation, and later, only a few minutes back, on the platform of Paddington Station, he had sensed a coldness, a certain hostility, so different from her pleasant friendliness at their first meeting.

She had returned now to her earlier manner, and he was surprised at the difference it made. He felt somehow younger, more alive. The lilt of the train's rattle changed to a gay ragtime.

This was curious, because Joan was nothing more than a friend. He was not in love with her. One does not fall in love with a girl whom one has met only three times. One is attracted, yes; but one does not fall in love.

A moment's reflection enabled him to diagnose his sensations correctly. This odd impulse to leap across the compartment and kiss Joan was not love. It was merely the natural desire of a good-hearted young man to be decently chummy with his species.

'Well, what do you think of it all, Mr Marson?' said Joan. 'Are you sorry or glad that you let me persuade you to do this perfectly mad thing? I feel responsible for you, you know. If it had not been for me, you would have been comfortably at Arundell Street, writing your "Wand of Death".'

'I'm glad.'

'You don't feel any misgivings now that you are actually committed to domestic service?'

'Not one.'

Joan, against her will, smiled approval on this uncompromising attitude. This young man might be her rival, but his demeanour on the eve of perilous times appealed to her. That was the spirit she liked and admired, that reckless acceptance of whatever might come. It was the spirit in which she herself had gone into the affair, and she was pleased to find that it animated Ashe also. Though, to be sure, it had its drawbacks. It made his rivalry the more dangerous.

This reflection injected a touch of the old hostility into her manner.

'I wonder if you will continue to feel so brave.'

98

'What do you mean?'

Joan perceived that she was in danger of going too far. She had no wish to unmask Ashe at the expense of revealing her own secret. She must resist the temptation to hint that she had discovered his.

'I meant,' she said quickly, 'that from what I have seen of him, Mr Peters seems likely to be a rather trying man to work for.'

Ashe's face cleared. For a moment he had almost suspected that she had guessed his errand.

'Yes. I imagine he will be. He is what you might call quick-tempered. He has dyspepsia, you know.'

'I know.'

'What he wants is plenty of fresh air and no cigars, and a regular course of those Larsen exercises which amused you so much.'

Joan laughed.

'Are you going to try and persuade Mr Peters to twist himself about like that? Do let me see it if you do.'

'I wish I could.'

'Do suggest it to him.'

'Don't you think he would resent it from a valet?'

'I keep forgetting that you are a valet. You look so unlike one.'

'Old Peters didn't think so. He rather complimented me on my appearance. He said I was ordinary looking.'

'I shouldn't have called you that. You look so very strong and fit.'

'Surely there are muscular valets?'

'Well yes, I suppose there are.'

Ashe looked at her. He was thinking that never in his life had he seen a girl so amazingly pretty. What it was that she had done to herself was beyond him, but something, some trick of dress, had given her a touch of the demure which made her irresistible. She was dressed in sober black, the ideal background for her fairness.

'While on the subject,' he said. 'I suppose you know

99

you don't look in the least like a lady's maid. You look like a disguised princess.'

She laughed.

'That's very nice of you, Mr Marson, but you're quite wrong. Anyone could tell I was a lady's maid a mile away. You aren't criticizing the dress, surely?'

'The dress is all right. It's the general effect. I don't think your expression is right. It's – it's – there's too much *attack* in it. You aren't meek enough.'

'*Meek!* Have you ever seen a lady's maid, Mr Marson?'

'Why, no, now that I come to think of it, I don't believe I have.'

'Well, let me tell you that meekness is her last quality. Why should she be meek? Doesn't she go in after the Groom of the Chambers?'

'Go in? Go in where?'

'Into dinner.'

She smiled at the sight of his bewildered face.

'I'm afraid you don't know much about the etiquette of the new world you have entered so rashly. Didn't you know that the rules of precedence among the servants of a big house are more rigid and complicated than in Society?'

'You're joking.'

'I'm not joking. You try going into dinner out of your proper place when we get to Blandings, and see what happens. A public rebuke from the butler is the least that you could expect.'

A bead of perspiration appeared on Ashe's forehead.

'My God!' he whispered. 'If a butler publicly rebuked me I think I should commit suicide. I couldn't survive it.'

He stared with fallen jaw into the abyss of horror into which he had leaped so light-heartedly. The Servant Problem, on this large scale, had been non-existent for him till now. In the days of his youth at Much Middleford, Salop, his needs had been ministered to by a muscular Irishwoman. Later, at Oxford, there had been his 'scout' and his bed-maker, harmless persons both, provided you locked up your whisky. And in London, his last phase, a succession of servitors of the type of the dishevelled maid at No. 7A, had tended him. That, dotted about the land, there were houses in which larger staffs of domestics were maintained, he had been vaguely aware. Indeed, in 'Gridley Quayle, Investigator, The Adventure of the Missing Marquess' (number four of the series) he had drawn a picture of the home-life of a Duke, in which a butler and two powdered footmen had played their parts. But he had had no idea that rigid and complicated rules of etiquette swayed the private lives of these individuals. If he had given the matter a thought, he had supposed that, when the dinner-hour arrived, the butler and the two footmen would troop into the kitchen and squash in at the table wherever they found room.

'Tell me,' he said, 'tell me all you know. I feel as if I had escaped a frightful disaster.'

'You probably have. I don't suppose there is anything so terrible as a snub from a butler.'

'If there is I can't think of it. When I was at Oxford, I used to go and stay with a friend of mine who had a butler who looked like a Roman emperor in swallow-tails. He terrified me. I used to grovel to the man. Please give me all the tips you can.'

'Well, as Mr Peters' valet, I suppose you will be rather a big man.'

'I shan't feel it.'

'However large the house-party is, Mr Peters is sure to be the principal guest, so your standing will be correspondingly magnificent. You come after the butler, the housekeeper, the groom of the chambers, Lord Emsworth's valet, Lady Ann Warblington's lady's maid –'

'Who is she?'

'Lady Ann? Lord Emsworth's sister. She has lived with him since his wife died. What was I saying? Oh yes. After them come the Hon. Frederick Threepwood's valet and myself, and then you.'

'I'm not so high up then, after all?'

'Yes, you are. There's a whole crowd who come after you. It all depends on how many other guests there are besides Mr Peters.'

'I suppose I charge in at the head of a drove of housemaids and scullery-maids?'

'My dear Mr Marson, if a housemaid or a scullery-maid tried to get into the Steward's Room and have her meals with us, she would be – '

'Rebuked by the butler?'

'Lynched, I should think. Kitchen-maids and scullery-maids eat in the kitchen. Chauffeurs, footmen, under-butler, pantry-boys, hall-boys, odd man, and steward's room footman take their meals in the Servants' Hall, waited on by the hall-boy. The still-room maids have breakfast and tea in the still-room and dinner and supper in the Hall. The housemaids and nursery-maids have breakfast and tea in the housemaids' sitting-room and dinner and supper in the Hall. The head-housemaid ranks next to the head still-room maid. The laundry-maids have a place of their own near the laundry, and the head laundry-maid ranks above the head housemaid. The chef has his meals in a room of his own near the kitchen . . . Is there anything else I can tell you, Mr Marson?'

Ashe was staring at her with vacant eyes. He shook his head dumbly.

'We stop at Swindon in half an hour,' said Joan softly. 'Don't you think you would be wise to get out there and go straight back to London, Mr Marson? Think of all you would avoid.'

Ashe found speech.

'It's a nightmare.'

'You would be far happier in Arundell Street. Why don't you get out at Swindon and go back?'

Ashe shook his head.

'I can't. There's – there's a reason.'

Joan picked up her magazine again. Hostility had come out from the corner into which she had tucked it away, and was once more filling her mind. She knew that it was illogical, but she could not help it. For a moment during her revelations of servants' Etiquette she had allowed herself to hope that she had frightened her rival out of the field, and the disappointment made her feel irritable. She buried herself in a short story, and countered Ashe's attempts at renewing the conversation with cold monosyllables, till he ceased his efforts and fell into a moody silence.

He was feeling hurt and angry. Her sudden coldness, following on the friendliness with which she had talked for so long, puzzled and infuriated him. He felt as if he had been snubbed, and for no reason.

He resented the defensive magazine, though he had bought it for her himself. He resented her attitude of having ceased to recognize his existence. A sadness, a filmy melancholy crept over him. He brooded on the unutterable silliness of humanity, especially the female portion of it, in erecting artificial barriers to friendship.

It was so unreasonable. At their first meeting, when she might have been excused for showing defensiveness, she had treated him with unaffected ease. When that meeting had ended, there was a tacit understanding between them that all the preliminary awkwardness of the first stages of acquaintanceship were to be considered as having been passed, and that when they met again, if they ever did, it would be as friends. And here she was, luring him on with apparent friendliness, and then withdrawing into herself as if he had presumed.

A rebellious spirit took possession of him. *He* didn't

care! Let her be cold and distant. He would show her
that she had no monopoly of those qualities. He would
not speak to her until she spoke to him, and when she
spoke to him, he would freeze her with his courteous
but bleakly aloof indifference . . .

The train rattled on, Joan read her magazine. Silence
reigned in the second-class compartment.

Swindon was reached and passed. Darkness fell on
the land. The journey began to seem interminable to
Ashe.

But presently there came a creaking of brakes, and the
train jerked itself to another stop.

A voice on the platform made itself heard, calling,
'Market Blandings. Market Blandings Station.'

II

The village of Market Blandings is one of those sleepy
hamlets which modern progress has failed to touch,
except by the addition of a railway station and a room
over the grocer's shop where moving-pictures are on
view on Tuesdays and Fridays. The church is Norman,
and the intelligence of the majority of the natives
palaeozoic. To alight at Market Blandings Station in the
dusk of a rather chilly Spring day, when the south-west
wind has shifted to due east, and the thrifty inhabitants
have not yet lit their windows, is to be smitten with the
feeling that one is at the edge of the world with no
friends near.

Ashe, as he stood beside Mr Peters' luggage and raked
the unsympathetic darkness with a dreary eye, gave
himself up to melancholy. Above him an oil lamp shed a
meagre light. Along the platform a small but sturdy
porter was juggling with a milk-can. The east wind
explored his system with chilly fingers.

Somewhere out in the darkness, into which Mr Peters
and Aline had already vanished in a large automobile,

lay the Castle with its butler, and its fearful code of
etiquette. Soon the cart which was to convey him and
the trunks thither would be arriving. He shivered.

Out of the gloom and into the feeble rays of the
oil-lamp came Joan Valentine. She had been away
tucking Aline into the car. She looked warm and
cheerful. She was smiling in the old friendly way.

If girls realized their responsibilities, they would be
so careful when they smiled that they would probably
abandon the practice altogether. There are moments in a
man's life when a girl's smile can have as important
results as an explosion of dynamite. In the course of
their brief acquaintance Joan had smiled at Ashe many
times, but the conditions governing those occasions had
not been such as to permit him to be seriously affected.
He had been pleased on such occasions; he had admired
her smile in a detached and critical spirit; but he had not
been overwhelmed by it. The frame of mind necessary
for that result had been lacking. But now, after five
minutes of solitude on the depressing platform of
Market Blandings Station, he was what the spiritualists
call a sensitive subject. He had reached that depth of
gloom and bodily discomfort when a sudden smile has
all the effect of strong liquor and good news
administered simultaneously, warming the blood and
comforting the soul and generally turning the world
from a bleak desert into a land flowing with milk and
honey.

It is not too much to say that he reeled before Joan's
smile. It was so entirely unexpected. He clutched Mr
Peters' steamer-trunk in his emotion.

All his resolutions to be cold and distant were swept
away. He had the feeling that in a friendless universe
here was someone who was fond of him and glad to see
him.

A smile of such importance demands analysis, and in
this case repays it; for many things lay behind this smile

of Joan Valentine's on the platform of Market Blandings Station.

In the first place, she had had another of her swift changes of mood, and had once again tucked away hostility into its corner. She had thought it over, and had come to the conclusion that as she had no logical grievance against Ashe for anything he had done, to be distant to him was the behaviour of a cat. Consequently, she resolved, when they should meet again, to resume her attitude of good-fellowship. That in itself would have been enough to make her smile.

But there was another reason, which had nothing to do with Ashe. While she had been tucking Aline into the automobile, she had met the eye of the driver of that vehicle and had perceived a curious look in it, a look of amazement and sheer terror. A moment later, when Aline called the driver Freddie, she had understood. No wonder the Hon. Freddie had looked as if he had seen a ghost. It would be a relief to the poor fellow when, as he undoubtedly would do in the course of the drive, he inquired of Aline the name of her maid and was told it was Simpson. He would mutter something about, 'Reminds me of a girl I used to know,' and would brood on the remarkable way in which Nature produces doubles. But he had had a bad moment, and it was partly at the recollection of his face that Joan smiled.

A third reason was that the sight of the Hon. Freddie had reminded her that R. Jones had said that he had written her poetry. That thought too had contributed towards the smile that so dazzled Ashe.

Ashe, not being miraculously intuitive, accepted the easier explanation that she smiled because she was glad to be in his company, and this thought, coming on top of his mood of despair and general dissatisfaction with everything mundane, acted on him like some powerful chemical.

In every man's life there is generally one moment to

which in later years he can look back and say, 'In this moment I fell in love.' Such a moment came to Ashe now.

> Betwixt the stirrup and the ground
> Mercy I asked, mercy I found.

So sings the poet, and so it was with Ashe.

In the almost incredibly brief time which it took the small but sturdy porter to roll a milk-can across the platform and bump it with a clang against other milk-cans similarly treated a moment before, Ashe fell in love.

The word is so loosely used to cover a thousand varying shades of emotion – from the volcanic passion of an Anthony for a Cleopatra to the tepid preference of a grocer's assistant for the housemaid at the second house in the High Street as opposed to the cook at the first house past the post-office – that the mere statement that Ashe fell in love is not a sufficient description of his feelings as he stood grasping Mr Peters' steamer-trunk. We must expand. We must analyse.

From his fourteenth year onward Ashe had been in love many times. His sensations in the case of Joan were neither the terrific upheaval which had caused him in his fifteenth year to collect twenty-eight photographs of the principal girl of the Theatre-Royal, Birmingham, pantomime, nor the milder flame which had caused him, when at Oxford, to give up smoking for a week and try to learn by heart the Sonnets from the Portuguese. His love was something that lay between these two poles. He did not wish the station platform of Market Blandings to become suddenly congested with Red Indians, so that he might save Joan's life, and he did not wish to give up anything at all. But he was conscious, to the very depths of his being, that a future in which Joan did not figure would be so insupportable as not to bear considering, and in the immediate present, he very strongly favoured the idea of clasping Joan in his arms and kissing her till further notice. Mingled with these feelings was an excited gratitude to her for coming to him like this with that electric smile on her face; a stunned realization that she was a thousand times prettier than he had ever imagined: and a humility which threatened to make him loose his clutch on the steamer-trunk and roll about at her feet, yapping like a dog.

Gratitude, as far as he could dissect his tangled emotions, was the predominating ingredient of his mood. Only once in his life had he felt so passionately grateful to any human being. On that occasion, too, the object of his gratitude had been feminine.

Years before, when a boy in his father's home in distant Much Middleford, Salop, those in authority had commanded that he, in his eleventh year and shy as one can be only at that interesting age, rise in the presence of a room full of strangers, adult guests, and recite, 'The Wreck of the Hesperus'.

He had risen. He had blushed. He had stammered. He had contrived to whisper, 'It was the schooner Hesperus.' And then, in a corner of the room, a little girl, for no properly explained reason, had burst out crying. She had yelled, she had bellowed, and would not be comforted, and in the ensuing confusion Ashe had escaped to the woodshed at the bottom of the garden, saved by a miracle.

All his life he had remembered the gratitude he had felt for that timely girl, and never till now had he experienced any other similar spasm.

But, as he looked at Joan, he found himself renewing that emotion of fifteen years ago.

She was about to speak. In a sort of trance he watched her lips part. He waited almost reverently for the first words which she should speak to him in her new role of the only authentic goddess.

'Isn't it a shame,' she said, 'I've just put a penny in the chocolate slot machine, and it's empty. I've a good mind to write to the company.'

Ashe felt as if he were listening to the strains of some grand, sweet anthem.

The small but sturdy porter, weary of his work among the milk-cans, or perhaps – let us not do him an injustice, even in thought – having finished it, approached them.

'The cart from the castle's here.'

In the gloom beyond him there gleamed a light which had not been there before. The meditative snort of a horse supported his statement. He began to deal as authoritatively with Mr Peters' steamer-trunk as he had dealt with the milk-cans.

'At last,' said Joan. 'I hope it's a covered cart. I'm frozen. Let's go and see.'

Ashe followed her with the rigid gait of an automaton.

III

Cold is the ogre which drives all beautiful things into hiding. Below the surface of a frost-bound garden there lurk hidden bulbs which are only biding their time to burst forth in a riot of laughing colour (unless the gardener has planted them upside down) but shivering Nature dare not put forth her flowers till the ogre has gone. Not otherwise does cold suppress love. A man in an open cart on an English Spring night may continue to be in love, but love is not the emotion uppermost in his bosom. It shrinks within him and waits for better times.

For the cart was not a covered cart. It was open to the four winds of heaven, of which the one at present active proceeded from the bleak east. To this fact may be attributed Ashe's swift recovery from the exalted mood into which Joan's smile had thrown him, his almost instant emergence from the trance. Deep down in him he was aware that his attitude towards Joan had not changed, but his conscious self was too fully occupied with the almost hopeless task of keeping his blood circulating to permit of thoughts of love. Before the cart had travelled twenty yards he was a mere chunk of frozen misery.

After an eternity of winding roads, darkened cottages, and black fields and hedges, the cart turned in at a massive iron gate which stood open, giving entrance to a smooth gravel drive. Here the way ran for nearly a mile through an open park of great trees, and was then swallowed in the darkness of dense shrubberies. Presently to the left appeared lights, at first in ones and twos, shining out and vanishing again, then as the shrubberies ended and the smooth lawns and terraces began, blazing down on the travellers from a score of windows with the heartening effect of fires on a winter night. Against the pale grey sky Blandings Castle stood out like a mountain.

It was a noble pile, of early Tudor building. Its history is recorded in England's history books and Viollet-le-duc has written of its architecture. It dominated the surrounding country.

The feature of it which impressed Ashe most at this moment, however, was the fact that it looked warm, and for the first time since the drive began he found himself in a mood that approximated to cheerfulness. It was a little early to begin feeling cheerful, he discovered, for the journey was by no means over. Arrived within sight of the Castle, the cart began a detour, which, ten minutes later, brought it under an arch and over cobble-stones to the rear of the buildings, where it eventually pulled up in front of a great door.

Ashe descended painfully, and beat his feet against the cobbles. He helped Joan to climb down. Joan was apparently in a gentle glow. Women seem impervious to cold.

The door opened. Warm, kitcheny scents came through it. Strong men hurried out to take down the trunks, while fair women, in the shape of two nervous scullery-maids, approached Joan and Ashe and bobbed curtseys. This, under more normal conditions, would have been enough to unman Ashe, but in his frozen state a mere curtseying scullery-maid expended herself harmlessly upon him. He even acknowledged the greeting with a kindly nod.

The scullery-maids, it seemed, were acting in much the same capacity as the *attachés* of Royalty. One was there to conduct Joan to the presence of Mrs Twemlow the housekeeper, the other to lead Ashe to where Beach the butler waited to do honour to the valet of the Castle's most important guest.

After a short walk down a stone-flagged passage, Joan and her escort turned to the right. Ashe's objective appeared to be located to the left. He parted from Joan with regret. Her moral support would have been welcome.

Presently his scullery-maid stopped at a door and tapped thereon. A fruity voice, like old tawny port made audible, said 'Come in.' Ashe's guide opened the door.

'The gentleman, Mr Beach,' said she, and scuttled away to the less rarefied atmosphere of the kitchen.

Ashe's first impression of Beach the butler was one of tension. Other people, confronted for the first time with Beach, had felt the same. He had that strained air of being on the very point of bursting which one sees in frogs and toy balloons. Nervous and imaginative men, meeting Beach, braced themselves involuntarily, stiffening their muscles for the explosion. Those who had the pleasure of more intimate acquaintance with him soon passed this stage, just as people whose homes are on the slopes of Mount Vesuvius become immune to fear of eruptions. As far back as they could remember, Beach had always looked as if an apoplectic fit were a matter of minutes, but he never had apoplexy, and in time they came to ignore the possibility of it. Ashe, however, approaching him with a fresh eye, had the feeling that this strain could not possibly continue, and that within a very short space of time the worst must happen. The prospect of this did much to arouse him from the coma into which he had been frozen by the rigours of the journey.

Butlers as a class seem to grow less and less like anything human in proportion to the magnificence of their surroundings. There is a type of butler, employed in the comparatively modest homes of small country gentlemen, who is practically a man and a brother, who hob-nobs with the local tradesmen, sings a good comic song at the village inn, and in times of crisis will even turn to and work the pump when the water supply suddenly fails. The greater the house, the more does the butler diverge from this type. Blandings Castle was one of the more important of England's show-places, and Beach, accordingly, had acquired a dignified inertia which almost qualified him for inclusion in the vegetable kingdom. He moved, when he moved at all, slowly. He distilled speech with the air of one measuring out drops of some precious drug. His heavy-lidded eyes had the fixed expression of a statue's.

With an almost imperceptible wave of a fat white hand he conveyed to Ashe that he desired him to sit down. With a stately movement of his other hand he picked up a kettle which simmered on the hob. With an inclination of his head he called Ashe's attention to a decanter on the table.

In another moment Ashe was sipping a whisky toddy

with the feeling that he had been privileged to assist at some mystic rite.

Mr Beach, posting himself before the fire and placing his hands behind his back, permitted speech to drip from him.

'I have not the advantage of your name, Mr –'

Ashe introduced himself. Beach acknowledged the information with a half bow.

'You must have had a cold ride, Mr Marson. The wind is in the east.'

Ashe said yes, the ride had been cold.

'When the wind is in the east,' continued Mr Beach, letting each syllable escape with apparent reluctance, 'I Suffer From My Feet.'

'I beg your pardon?'

'I Suffer From My Feet,' repeated the butler, measuring out the drops. 'You are a young man, Mr Marson. Probably you do not know what it is to Suffer From Your Feet.'

He surveyed Ashe, his whisky toddy, and the wall beyond with his heavy-lidded inscrutability.

'Corns,' he said.

Ashe said that he was sorry.

'I Suffer Extremely From My Feet. Not only corns. I have but recently recovered from an Ingrowing Toe-Nail. I Suffered Greatly From My Ingrowing Toe-Nail. I Suffer From Swollen Joints.'

Ashe regarded this martyr with increasing disfavour. It is the flaw in the character of many excessively healthy young men that, while kind-hearted enough in most respects, they listen with a regrettable feeling of impatience to the confessions of those less happily situated as regards the ills of the flesh. Rightly or wrongly they hold that these statements should be reserved for the ear of the medical profession and other and more general topics selected for conversations with laymen.

'I'm sorry,' he said hastily. 'You must have a bad time. Is there a large house-party here just now?'

'We are expecting,' said Mr Beach, 'a Number of Guests. We shall in all probability sit down thirty or more to dinner.'

'A responsibility for you,' said Ashe ingratiatingly, well pleased to be quit of the feet topic.

Mr Beach nodded.

'You are right, Mr Marson. Few persons realize the responsibilities of a man in my position. Sometimes, I can assure you, it preys upon my mind, and I Suffer From Nervous Headaches.'

Ashe began to feel like a man trying to put out a fire which, as fast as he checks it at one point, breaks out at another.

'Sometimes, when I come off duty, everything gets Blurred. The outlines of objects grow misty. I have to sit down in a chair. The Pain Is Excruciating.'

'But it helps you to forget the pain in your feet.'

'No. No. I Suffer From My Feet simultaneously.'

Ashe gave up the struggle.

'Tell me about your feet,' he said.

Mr Beach told him all about his feet.

The pleasantest functions must come to an end, and the moment arrived when the final word on the subject of swollen joints was spoken. Ashe, who had resigned himself to a permanent contemplation of the subject, could hardly believe that he heard correctly when, at the end of some ten minutes, his companion changed the conversation.

'You have been with Mr Peters some time, Mr Marson?'

'Eh? Oh! Oh no, only since last Wednesday.'

'Indeed! Might I inquire whom you assisted before that?'

For a moment Ashe did what he would not have believed himself capable of doing – regretted that the

topic of feet was no longer under discussion. The
question placed him in an awkward position. If he lied,
and credited himself with a lengthy experience as a
valet, he risked exposing himself. If he told the truth,
and confessed that this was his maiden effort in the
capacity of gentleman's gentleman, what would the
butler think? There were objections to each course, but
to tell the truth was the easier of the two, so he told it.

'Your first situation?' said Mr Beach. 'Indeed!'

'I was – er – doing something else before I met Mr
Peters,' said Ashe.

Mr Beach was too well bred to be inquisitive, but his
eyebrows were not.

'Ah!' he said.

'?', cried his eyebrows. '???'

Ashe ignored the eyebrows.

'Something different,' he said.

There was an awkward silence. Ashe appreciated its
awkwardness. He was conscious of a grievance against
Mr Peters. Why could not Mr Peters have brought him
down here as his secretary? To be sure, he had advanced
some objection to that course in their conversation at
the offices of Mainprice, Mainprice & Boole, but merely
some silly, far-fetched objection. He wished that he had
had the sense to fight the point while there was time;
but, at the moment when they were arranging plans, he
had been rather tickled by the thought of becoming a
valet. The notion had a pleasing musical-comedy touch
about it. Why had he not foreseen the complications
which must ensue? He could tell by the look on his face
that this confounded butler was waiting for him to give
a full explanation. What would he think if he withheld
it? He would probably suppose that Ashe had been in
prison.

Well, there was nothing to be done about it. If Beach
was suspicious, he must remain suspicious. Fortunately,
the suspicions of a butler do not matter much.

Mr Beach's eyebrows were still mutely urging him to
reveal all, but Ashe directed his gaze at that portion of
the room which Mr Beach did not fill. He was hanged if
he was going to let himself be hypnotized by a pair of
eyebrows into incriminating himself. He glared stolidly
at the pattern of the wall-paper, which represented a
number of birds of an unknown species seated on a
corresponding number of exotic shrubs.

The silence was growing oppressive. Somebody had to
break it soon. And, as Mr Beach was still confining
himself to the language of the eyebrow and apparently
intended to fight it out on these lines if it took all
summer, Ashe broke it himself.

It seemed to him, as he reconstructed the scene in
bed that night, that Providence must have suggested the
subject of Mr Peters' indigestion, for the mere mention
of his employer's sufferings acted like magic on the
butler.

'I might have had better luck, while I was looking for
a place,' said Ashe. 'I dare say you know how
bad-tempered Mr Peters is? He is dyspeptic.'

'So,' responded Mr Beach, 'I have been informed.' He
brooded for a space. 'I, too,' he proceeded, 'Suffer From
My Stomach. I have a Weak Stomach. The Lining Of My
Stomach is not what I could wish the Lining Of My
Stomach to be.'

'Tell me,' said Ashe gratefully, 'all about the lining of
your stomach.'

It was a quarter of an hour later that Mr Beach was
checked in his discourse by the chiming of the little
clock on the mantelpiece. He turned round and gazed at
it with surprise not unmixed with displeasure.

'So late!' he said. 'I shall have to be going about my
duties. And you also, Mr Marson, if I may make the
suggestion. No doubt Mr Peters will be wishing to have
your assistance in preparing for dinner. If you go along
the passage outside you will come to the door which

separates our portion of the house from the other. I must beg you to excuse me. I have to go to the cellar.'

Following his directions, Ashe came, after a walk of a few yards, to a green baize door, which, swinging at his push, gave him a view of what he took correctly to be the main hall of the Castle, a wide, comfortable space, ringed with settees and warmed by a log fire burning in a mammoth fireplace. To the right a broad staircase led to upper regions.

It was at this point that Ashe realized the incompleteness of Mr Beach's directions. Doubtless the broad staircase would take him to the floor on which were the bedrooms, but how was he to ascertain without the tedious process of knocking and inquiring at each door which was the one assigned to Mr Peters? It was too late to go back and ask the butler for further guidance. Already he was on his way to the cellar in quest of the evening's wine.

As he stood irresolute, a door across the hall opened, and a man of his own age came out. Through the door which the young man held open for an instant while he answered a question from someone still within, Ashe had a glimpse of glass-topped cases.

Could this be the museum, his goal? The next moment the door, opening another few inches, revealed the outlying portions of an Egyptian mummy, and brought certainty.

It flashed across Ashe's mind that the sooner he explored the museum and located Mr Peters' scarab the better. He decided to ask Beach to take him there as soon as he had leisure.

Meanwhile the young man had closed the museum door, and was crossing the hall. He was a wiry-haired, severe-looking young man, with a sharp nose and eyes that gleamed through rimless spectacles. None other, in fact, than Lord Emsworth's private secretary, the Efficient Baxter.

Ashe hailed him.

'I say, old man, would you mind telling me how I get to Mr Peters' room? I've lost my bearings.'

He did not reflect that this was hardly the way in which valets in the best society addressed the Upper Classes. That is the worst of adopting what might be called a 'character' part. One can manage the business well enough; it is the dialogue which provides the pitfalls.

Mr Baxter would have accorded a hearty agreement to the statement that this was not the way in which a valet should have spoken to him. But at the moment he was not aware that Ashe was a valet. From his easy mode of address he assumed that he was one of the numerous guests who had been arriving at the Castle all day. As he had asked for Mr Peters he fancied that Ashe must be the Hon. Freddie's friend, George Emerson, whom he had not yet met.

Consequently, he replied with much cordiality that Mr Peters' room was the second to the left on the second floor.

He said that Ashe couldn't miss it. Ashe said that he was much obliged.

'Awfully good of you,' said Ashe.

'Not at all,' said Mr Baxter.

'You lose your way in a place like this,' said Ashe.

'Yes, don't you!' said Mr Baxter.

And Ashe went on his upward path, and in a few moments was knocking at the door indicated.

And sure enough it was Mr Peters' voice that invited him to enter.

IV

Mr Peters, partially arrayed in the correct garb for gentlemen to dine, was standing in front of the mirror, wrestling with his evening tie. As Ashe entered, he

118

removed his fingers and anxiously examined his handiwork. It proved unsatisfactory. With a yelp and an oath he tore the offending linen from his neck.

'Damn the thing!'

It was plain to Ashe that his employer was in no sunny mood. There are few things less calculated to engender sunniness in a naturally bad-tempered man than a dress-tie which will not let itself be pulled and twisted into the right shape. Even when things went well, Mr Peters hated dressing for dinner. Words cannot describe his feelings when they went wrong.

There is something to be said in excuse for this impatience. It is a hollow mockery to be obliged to deck one's person as for a feast, when that feast is to consist of a little asparagus and a few nuts.

His eyes met Ashe's in the mirror.

'Oh, it's you, is it? Come in then. Don't stand staring. Close that door quick. Hustle! Don't scrape your feet on the floor. Try to look intelligent. Don't gape. Where have you been all this while? Why didn't you come before? Can you tie a tie? All right then, do it.'

Somewhat calmed by the snow-white butterfly-shaped creation which grew under Ashe's fingers he permitted himself to be helped into his coat. He picked up the remnant of a black cigar from the dressing-table and relit it.

'I've been thinking about you,' he said.

'Yes?' said Ashe.

'Have you located the scarab yet?'

'No.'

'What the devil have you been doing with yourself then? You've had time to grab it a dozen times.'

'I have been talking to the butler.'

'What the devil do you waste time talking to butlers for? I suppose you haven't even located the museum yet?'

'Yes, I've done that.'

'Oh, you have, have you? Well, that's something. And how do you propose setting about the job?'

'The best plan would be to go there very late at night.'

'Well, you didn't propose to stroll in in the afternoon, did you? How are you going to find the scarab when you do get in?'

Ashe had not thought of that. The deeper he went into this business, the more things did there seem to be in it of which he had not thought.

'I don't know,' he confessed.

'You don't know! Tell me, young man, are you considered pretty bright, as Englishmen go?'

'I really couldn't say.'

'Oh, you couldn't, couldn't you, you blanked bone-headed boob!' cried Mr Peters, frothing over quite unexpectedly and waving his arms in a sudden burst of fury. 'What's the matter with you? Why don't you show a little more enterprise? Why don't you put something over? Why do you loaf about the place as if you were supposed to be an ornament? I want results, and I want them quick! I'll tell you how you can recognize my scarab when you get into the museum. That shameless old crook who sneaked it away from me has had the impudence to put it all by itself with a notice as big as a circus-poster alongside it saying that it is a Cheops of the Fourth Dynasty, presented' – Mr Peters choked – '*presented* by J. Preston Peters, Esq. That's how you're going to recognize it.'

Ashe did not laugh, but he nearly dislocated a rib in his effort to abstain. To rob a man of his choicest possession and then thank him publicly for letting you have it appealed to Ashe as excellent comedy.

'The thing isn't even in a glass case,' continued Mr Peters. 'It's lying on an open tray on top of a cabinet of Roman coins. Anybody who was left alone for two minutes in the place could take it. It's criminal carelessness to leave a valuable scarab lying about like that. If he was going to steal my Cheops, he might at least have had the decency to treat it as if it was worth something.'

'But it makes it easier for me to get it,' said Ashe consolingly.

'It's got to be made easy if you are to get it,' snapped Mr Peters. 'Here's another thing. You are going to try for it late at night. Well, what are you going to say if anyone catches you prowling around at that time? Have you considered that?'

'No.'

'You would have to say something, wouldn't you? You wouldn't discuss the latest play? You would have to think up some mighty good reason for being out of bed at that time, wouldn't you?'

'I suppose so.'

'Oh, you do admit that, do you? Well, what you would say is this. You would explain that I had rung for you to come and read me to sleep. Do you understand?'

'You think that would be a satisfactory explanation of my being in the museum?'

'Idiot! I don't mean that you're to say it if you're caught actually in the museum. If you're caught in the museum, the best thing you can do is to say nothing and hope that the judge will let you off lightly because it's your first offence. You're to say it if you're found wandering about on your way there.'

'It sounds thin to me.'

'Does it! Well let me tell you that it isn't so thin as you suppose, for it's what you will actually have to do most nights. Two nights out of three I have to be read to sleep. My indigestion gives me insomnia.'

As if to push this fact home, Mr Peters suddenly bent double.

'Oof!' he said. 'Wow!'

He removed the cigar from his mouth, and inserted a digestive tabloid.

'The lining of my stomach is all wrong,' he added.

It is curious how trivial are the immediate causes which produce revolutions. If Mr Peters had worded his complaint differently, Ashe would, in all probability, have borne it without active protest. He had been growing more and more annoyed with this little person who buzzed and barked and bit at him, but the idea of definite revolt had not occurred to him. But his sufferings at the hands of Beach the butler had reduced him to a state where he could endure no further mention of stomachic linings. There comes a time when our capacity for listening to data about the linings of other people's stomachs is exhausted.

He looked at Mr Peters sternly. He had ceased to be intimidated by the fiery little man, and regarded him simply as a hypochondriac who needed to be told a few useful facts.

'How do you expect not to have indigestion? You take no exercise and you smoke all day long.'

The novel sensation of being criticized, and by a beardless youth at that, held Mr Peters silent. He started convulsively, but he did not speak.

Ashe, on his pet subject, became eloquent. In his opinion dyspeptics cumbered the earth. To his mind, they had the choice between health and sickness, and they deliberately chose the latter.

'Your sort of man makes me sick. I know your type inside out. You overwork and shirk exercise and let your temper run away with you and smoke strong cigars on an empty stomach, and when you get indigestion as a natural result, you look on yourself as a martyr, and make the lives of everybody you meet miserable. If you would put yourself into my hands for a month I would have you eating bricks and thriving on them. Up in the morning, Larsen exercises, cold bath, brisk rub down, sharp walk . . .'

'Who the devil asked your opinion, you impertinent young hound?' inquired Mr Peters.

'Don't interrupt, confound you,' shouted Ashe. 'Now you have made me forget what I was going to say.'

There was a tense silence. Then Mr Peters began to speak.

'You – infernal – impudent – '

'Don't talk to me like that.'

'I'll talk to you just how – '

Ashe took a step towards the door.

'Very well, then,' he said. 'I resign. I give notice. You can get somebody else to do this job of yours for you.'

The sudden sagging of Mr Peters' jaw, the look of consternation which flashed upon his face, told him that he had found the right weapon, that the game was in his hands. He continued with a feeling of confidence.

'If I had known what being your valet involved, I wouldn't have undertaken the thing for a hundred thousand pounds. Just because you had some idiotic prejudice against letting me come down here as your secretary, which would have been the simple and obvious thing, I find myself in a position where at any moment I may be publicly rebuked by the butler and have the head still-room maid looking at me as if I were something the cat had brought in.' His voice trembled with self-pity. 'Do you realize a fraction of the awful things you have let me in for? How on earth am I to remember whether I go in before the chef or after the third footman? I shan't have a peaceful minute while I'm in this place. I've got to sit and listen by the hour to a bore of a butler who seems to be a sort of walking hospital. I've got to steer my way through a complicated system of etiquette. And on top of all that you have the nerve, the insolence, to imagine that you can use me as a punching-bag to work your bad temper off! You have the immortal rind to suppose that I will stand being nagged and bullied by you whenever your suicidal way of living brings on an attack of indigestion! You have the supreme cheek to fancy that you can talk as you please to me! Very well! I've had enough of it. If you want this scarab of yours recovered, let somebody else do it. I've retired from business.'

He took another step towards the door. A shaking hand clutched at his sleeve.

'My boy, my dear boy, be reasonable!'

Ashe was intoxicated with his own oratory. The sensation of bully-ragging a genuine millionaire was new and exhilarating. He expanded his chest, and spread his feet like a Colossus.

'That's all very well,' he said, coldly disentangling himself from the hand. 'You can't get out of it like that. We have got to come to an understanding. The point is that, if I am to be subjected to your – your senile malevolence every time you have a twinge of indigestion, no amount of money could pay me to stop on.'

'My dear boy, it shall not occur again. I was hasty.'

Mr Peters with agitated fingers relit the stump of his cigar.

'Throw away that cigar!'

'My boy!'

'Throw it away! You say you were hasty. Of course you were hasty. And as long as you abuse your digestion you will go on being hasty. I want something better than apologies. If I am to stop here, we must get to the root of things. You must put yourself in my hands as if I were your doctor. No more cigars. Every morning regular exercises.'

'No, no.'

'Very well.'

'No, stop, stop! What sort of exercises?'

'I'll show you tomorrow morning. Brisk walks.'

'I hate walking.'

124

'Cold baths.'

'No, no.'

'Very well.'

'No, stop. A cold bath would kill me at my age.'

'It would put new life into you. Do you consent to cold baths? No? Very well.'

'Yes, yes, yes.'

'You promise?'

'Yes, yes.'

'All right, then.'

The distant sound of the dinner-gong floated in.

'We settled that just in time,' said Ashe.

Mr Peters regarded him fixedly.

'Young man,' he said slowly, 'if, after all this you fail to recover my Cheops for me, I'll – I'll – by George, I'll skin you.'

'Don't talk like that,' said Ashe. 'That's another thing you have got to remember. If my treatment is to be successful, you must not let yourself think in that way. You must exercise self-control mentally. You must think beautiful thoughts.'

'The idea of skinning you *is* a beautiful thought,' said Mr Peters wistfully.

V

In order that their gaiety might not be diminished and the food turned to ashes in their mouths by the absence from the festive board of Mr Beach, it was the custom for the upper servants at Blandings to postpone the start of their evening meal until dinner was nearly over above stairs. This enabled the butler to take his place at the head of the table, without fear of interruption except for a few moments when coffee was being served.

Every night, shortly before half past eight, at which hour Mr Beach felt that he might safely withdraw from the dining-room and leave Lord Emsworth and his guests

to the care of Merridew, the under-butler, and James and
Alfred, the footmen, returning only for a few minutes to
lend tone and distinction to the distribution of cigars
and liqueurs, those whose rank entitled them to do so
made their way to the Housekeeper's Room, to pass in
desultory conversation the interval before Mr Beach
should arrive and a kitchen-maid, with all the
appearance of one who has been straining at the leash
and has at last managed to get free, opened the door with
the announcement, 'Mr Beach, if you please, dinner is
served.' Upon which Mr Beach, extending a crooked
elbow towards the housekeeper, would say, 'Mrs
Twemlow,' and lead the way high and disposedly down
the passage, followed in order of rank by the rest of the
company in couples, to the Steward's Room. For
Blandings was not one of those houses – or shall we say
hovels? – where the upper servants are expected not only
to feed but to congregate before feeding in the Steward's
Room. Under the auspices of Mr Beach and of Mrs
Twemlow, who saw eye to eye with him in these
matters, things were done properly at the Castle, with
the right solemnity. To Mr Beach and to Mrs Twemlow
the suggestion that they and their peers should gather
together in the same room in which they were to dine
would have been as repellent as an announcement from
Lady Ann Warblington, the châtelaine, that the
house-party would eat in the drawing-room.

When Ashe, returning from his interview with Mr
Peters, was intercepted by a respectful small boy and
conducted to the Housekeeper's Room, he was
conscious of a sensation of shrinking inferiority akin to
his emotions on his first day at school. The room was
full and apparently on very cordial terms with itself.
Everybody seemed to know everybody, and conversation
was proceeding in the liveliest manner. As a matter of
fact, the house-party at Blandings being in the main a
gathering together of the Emsworth clan by way of

honour and as a means of introduction to Mr Peters and his daughter, the bride-of-the-house-to-be, most of the occupants of the Housekeeper's Room were old acquaintances, and were renewing interrupted friendships at the top of their voices.

A lull followed Ashe's arrival, and all eyes, to his great discomfort, were turned in his direction. His embarrassment was relieved by Mrs Twemlow, who advanced to do the honours. Of Mrs Twemlow little need be attempted in the way of pen-portraiture beyond the statement that she went as harmoniously with Mr Beach as one of a pair of vases or one of a brace of pheasants goes with its fellow. She had the same appearance of imminent apoplexy, the same air of belonging to some dignified and haughty branch of the vegetable kingdom.

'Mr Marson, welcome to Blandings Castle.'

Ashe had been waiting for somebody to say that, and had been a little surprised that Mr Beach had not done so. He was also surprised at the housekeeper's ready recognition of his identity, until he saw Joan in the throng and deduced that she must have been the source of information. He envied Joan. In some amazing way she contrived to look not out of place in this gathering. He himself, he felt, had impostor stamped in large characters all over him.

Mrs Twemlow began to make the introductions – a long and tedious process which she performed relentlessly, without haste and without scamping her work. With each member of the aristocracy of his new profession Ashe shook hands, and on each member he smiled, until his facial and dorsal muscles were like to crack under the strain. It was amazing that so many high-class domestics could be collected into one moderate-sized room.

'Miss Simpson you know,' said Mrs Twemlow, and Ashe was about to deny the charge when he perceived

that Joan was the individual referred to. 'Mr Judson, Mr
Marson. Mr Judson is the Honourable Frederick's
gentleman.'

'You have not the pleasure of our Freddie's
acquaintance as yet, I take it, Mr Marson?' observed Mr
Judson genially, a smooth-faced, lazy-looking young
man. 'Freddie repays inspection.'

'Mr Marson, permit me to introduce you to Mr Ferris,
Lord Stockheath's gentleman.'

Mr Ferris, a dark, cynical man with a high forehead,
shook Ashe by the hand.

'Happy to meet you, Mr Marson.'

'Miss Willoughby, this is Mr Marson, who will take
you in to dinner. Miss Willoughby is Lady Mildred
Mant's lady. As of course you are aware, Lady Mildred,
our eldest daughter, married Colonel Horace Mant.'

Ashe was not aware, and he was rather surprised that
Mrs Twemlow should have a daughter whose name was
Lady Mildred, but Reason, coming to his rescue,
suggested that by 'our' she meant the offspring of the
Earl of Emsworth and his late countess. Miss
Willoughby was a light-hearted damsel with a smiling
face and chestnut hair done low over her forehead. Since
Etiquette forbade that he should take Joan in to dinner,
Ashe was glad that at least an apparently pleasant
substitute had been provided. He had just been
introduced to an appallingly statuesque lady of the name
of Chester, Lady Ann Warblington's own maid, and his
somewhat hazy recollections of Joan's lecture on Below
Stairs precedence had left him with the impression that
this was his destined partner. He had frankly quailed at
the prospect of being linked to so much aristocratic
hauteur.

When the final introduction had been made,
conversation broke out again. It dealt almost
exclusively, as far as Ashe could follow it, with the
idiosyncrasies of the employers of those present. He

took it that this happened all down the social scale below stairs. Probably the lower servants in the Servants' Hall discussed the upper servants in the Steward's Room, and the still lower servants in the housemaids' sitting-room discussed their superiors of the Servants' Hall, and the still-room gossiped about the housemaids' sitting-room. He wondered which was the bottom circle of all, and came to the conclusion that it was probably represented by the small respectful boy who had acted as his guide a short while before. This boy, having nobody to discuss anybody with, presumably sat in solitary meditation, brooding on the odd-job man.

He thought of mentioning this theory to Miss Willoughby, but decided that it was too abstruse for her, and contented himself with speaking of some of the plays he had seen before leaving London. Miss Willoughby was an enthusiast on the drama, and, Colonel Mant's devotion to his various clubs keeping him much in town, she had had wide opportunities of indulging her tastes. Miss Willoughby did not like the country. She thought it dull.

'Don't you think the country dull, Mr Marson?'

'I shan't find it dull here,' said Ashe, and was surprised to discover through the medium of a pleased giggle that he was considered to have perpetrated a compliment.

Mr Beach appeared in due season, a little distrait as becomes a man who has just been engaged on important and responsible duties.

'Alfred spilled the 'ock!' Ashe heard him announce to Mrs Twemlow in a bitter undertone. 'Within 'alf an inch of 'is lordship's arm he spilled it.'

Mrs Twemlow muttered condolences. Mr Beach's set expression was that of one who is wondering how long the strain of existence can be supported.

'Mr Beach, if you please, dinner is served.'

The butler crushed down sad thoughts, and crooked his elbow.

'Mrs Twemlow.'

Ashe, miscalculating degrees of rank in spite of all his caution, was within a step of leaving the room out of his proper turn, but the startled pressure of Miss Willoughby's hand on his arm warned him in time. He stopped to allow the statuesque Miss Chester to sail out under escort of a wizened little man with a horseshoe pin in his tie, whose name, in company with nearly all the others which had been spoken to him since he came into the room, had escaped Ashe's memory.

'You *were* nearly making a bloomer,' said Miss Willoughby brightly. 'You must be absent-minded, Mr Marson, like his lordship.'

'Is Lord Emsworth absent-minded?'

Miss Willoughby laughed.

'Why, he forgets his own name sometimes. If it wasn't for Mr Baxter, goodness knows what would happen to him.'

'I don't think I know Mr Baxter.'

'You will if you stay here long. You can't get away from him if you're in the same house. Don't tell anyone I said so, but he's the real master here. His lordship's secretary he calls himself, but he's really everything rolled into one like the man in the play.'

Ashe, searching in his dramatic memories for such a person in a play, inquired if Miss Willoughby meant Pooh Bah in the *Mikado*, of which there had been a revival in London recently. Miss Willoughby did mean Pooh Bah.

'But Nosey Parker is what *I* call him,' she said. 'He minds everybody's business as well as his own.'

The last of the procession trickled into the Steward's Room. Mr Beach said grace somewhat patronizingly. The meal began.

'You've seen Miss Peters, of course, Mr Marson?'

said Miss Willoughby, resuming conversation with the soup.

'Just for a few minutes at Paddington.'

'Oh! You haven't been with Mr Peters long then?'

Ashe began to wonder if everybody he met was going to ask him this dangerous question.

'Only a day or so.'

'Where were you before that?'

Ashe was conscious of a prickly sensation. A little more of this and he might as well reveal his true mission at the Castle and have done with it.

'Oh, I was – that is to say –'

'How are you feeling after the journey, Mr Marson?' said a voice from the other side of the table, and Ashe, looking up gratefully, found Joan's eyes looking into his with a curiously amused expression. He was too grateful for the interruption to try to account for this. He replied that he was feeling very well, which was not the case. Miss Willoughby's interest was diverted to a discussion of the defects of the various railway systems of Great Britain.

At the head of the table, Mr Beach had started an intimate conversation with Mr Ferris, the valet of Lord Stockheath, the Hon. Freddie's 'poor old Percy' – a cousin, Ashe had gathered, of Aline Peters' husband-to-be. The butler spoke in more measured tones even than usual, for he was speaking of tragedy.

'We were all extremely sorry, Mr Ferris, to read of your misfortune.'

Ashe wondered what had been happening to Mr Ferris.

'Yes, Mr Beach,' replied the valet, 'it's a fact we made a pretty poor show.' He took a sip from his glass. 'There is no concealing the fact – I have never tried to conceal it – that poor Percy is *not* bright.'

Miss Chester entered the conversation.

'I couldn't see where the girl, what's her name, was so

very pretty. All the papers had pieces where it said that she was attractive and what not, but she didn't look anything special to *me* from her photograph in the *Daily Sketch*. What his lordship could see in her I can't understand.'

'The photo didn't quite do her justice, Miss Chester. I was present in court, and I must admit she was *svelte*, decidedly *svelte*. And you must recollect that Percy, from childhood up, has always been a highly susceptible young nut. I speak as one who knows him.'

Mr Beach turned to Joan.

'We are speaking of the Stockheath breach-of-promise case, Miss Simpson, of which you doubtless read in the newspapers. Lord Stockheath is a nephew of ours. I fancy his lordship was greatly shocked at the occurrence.'

'He was,' chimed in Mr Judson from down the table. 'I happened to overhear him speaking of it to young Freddie. It was in the library in the morning when the judge made his final summing up and slipped into Lord Stockheath so crisp. "If ever anything of this sort happens to you, you young scallywag," he says to Freddie –'

Mr Beach coughed.

'Mr Judson!'

'Oh, it's all right, Mr Beach, we're all in the family here, in a manner of speaking. It isn't as if I was telling it to a lot of outsiders. I'm sure none of these ladies or gentlemen will let it go beyond this room?'

The company murmured virtuous acquiescence.

'He says to Freddie, "You young scallywag, if ever anything of this sort happens to you, you can pack up and go off to Canada, for I'll have nothing more to do with you," or words to that effect. And Freddie says, "Oh, dash it all, guv'nor, you know, what!"'

However short Mr Judson's imitation of his master's voice may have fallen of histrionic perfection, it pleased the company. The room shook with mirth.

Mr Beach thought it expedient to deflect the conversation. By the unwritten laws of the room every individual had the right to speak as freely as he wished about his own personal employer, but Judson, in his opinion, sometimes went a trifle too far.

'Tell me, Mr Ferris,' he said, 'does his lordship seem to bear it well?'

'Oh, Percy is bearing it well enough.' Ashe noted as a curious fact that while the actual valet of any person under discussion spoke of him almost affectionately by his Christian name, the rest of the company used the greatest ceremony and gave him his title with all respect. Lord Stockheath was Percy to Mr Ferris, and the Hon. Frederick Threepwood was Freddie to Mr Judson; but to Ferris Mr Judson's Freddie was the Hon. Frederick, and to Judson Mr Ferris' Percy was Lord Stockheath. It was rather a pleasant form of etiquette, and struck Ashe as somehow vaguely feudal.

'Percy,' went on Mr Ferris, 'is bearing it like a little Briton. The damages not having come out of *his* pocket. It's his old father, who had to pay them, that's taking it to heart. You might say he's doing himself proud. He says it's brought on his gout again, and that's why he's gone to Droitwich instead of coming here. I dare say Percy isn't sorry.'

'It has been,' said Mr Beach, summing up, 'a Most Unfortunate Occurrence. The modern tendency of the Lower Classes to get above themselves is becoming more marked every day. The young female in this case was, I understand, a barmaid. It is Deplorable that our young men should allow themselves to get into Such Entanglements.'

'The wonder to me,' said the irrepressible Mr Judson, 'is that more of these young chaps don't get put through it. His lordship wasn't so wide of the mark when he spoke like that to Freddie in the library that time. I give you my word it's a mercy young Freddie *hasn't* been up against it. When we was in London, Freddie and I,' he went on, cutting through Mr Beach's disapproving cough, 'before what you might call the crash, when his lordship cut off supplies and had him come back and live here, Freddie was asking for it, believe me. Fell in love with a girl in the chorus of one of the theatres. Used to send me to the stage-door with notes and flowers every night as regular as clockwork for weeks. What was her name? It's on the tip of my tongue. Funny how you forget these things. Freddie was pretty far gone. I recollect once, happening to be looking round his room in his absence, coming on a poem he had written to her. It was hot stuff, very hot. If that girl has kept those letters, it's my belief we shall see Freddie following in Lord Stockheath's footsteps.'

There was a hush of delighted horror round the table.

'Goo!' said Miss Chester's escort, with unction. 'You don't say so, Mr Judson! It wouldn't half make them look silly if the Honourable Freddie was sued for breach just now with the wedding coming on.'

'There is no danger of that.'

It was Joan's voice, and she had spoken with such decision that she had the ear of the table immediately. All eyes looked in her direction. Ashe was struck with her expression. Her eyes were shining, as if she were angry, and there was a flush on her face. A phrase he had used in the train came back to him. She looked like a princess in disguise.

'What makes you say that, Miss Simpson?' inquired Judson, annoyed. He had been at pains to make the company's flesh creep, and it appeared to be Joan's aim to undo his work.

It seemed to Ashe that Joan made an effort of some sort, as if she were pulling herself together and remembering where she was.

'Well,' she said, almost lamely, 'I don't think it at all likely that he proposed marriage to this girl.'

'You never can tell,' said Judson. 'My impression is that Freddie did. It's my belief that there's something on his mind these days. Before he went to London with his lordship the other day, he was behaving very strange. And since he came back it's my belief that he has been brooding. And I happen to know that he followed the affair of Lord Stockheath pretty close, for he clipped the clippings out of the paper. I found them myself one day when I happened to be going through his things.'

Beach cleared his throat – his mode of indicating that he was about to monopolize the conversation.

'And in any case, Miss Simpson,' he said solemnly, 'with things come to the pass they have come to, and with juries – drawn from the lower classes – in the Nasty Mood they're in, it don't seem hardly necessary in these affairs for there to have been any definite promise of marriage. What with all this Socialism rampant, they seem so 'appy at the idea of being able to do one of Us an injury that they give 'eavy damages without it. A few ardent Expressions, and that's enough for them. You recollect the Havant case, and when young Lord Mount Anville was sued. What it comes to is that Anarchy is getting the Upper Hand, and the Lower Classes are getting above themselves. It's all these here cheap newspapers that does it. They tempt the Lower Classes to get Above Themselves. Only this morning, I had to speak severe to that young fellow James, the footman. He was a good fellow once, and did his work well, and 'ad a proper respect for people; but now he's gone all to pieces. And why? Because six months ago he had the rheumatism, and had the audacity to send his picture and a testimonial saying that it had cured him of Awful Agonies to Walkinshaw's Supreme Ointment, and they printed it in half a dozen papers, and it has been the ruin of James. He has got Above Himself and don't care for nobody.'

'Well, all I can say is,' resumed Judson, 'that I 'ope to

goodness nothing won't happen to Freddie of that kind, for it's not every girl that would have him.'

There was a murmur of assent to this truth.

'Now your Miss Peters,' said Judson, tolerantly, 'she seems a nice little thing.'

'She would be pleased to hear you say so,' said Joan.

'Joan Valentine!' cried Judson, bringing his hands down on the tablecloth with a bang. 'I've just remembered it. That was the name of the girl Freddie used to write the letters and poems to. And that's who it is I've been trying all along to think who you reminded me of, Miss Simpson. You're the living image of Freddie's Miss Joan Valentine.'

Ashe was not normally a young man of particularly ready wit, but on this occasion it may have been that the shock of this revelation, added to the fact that something must be done speedily if Joan's discomposure was not to become obvious to all present, quickened his intelligence. Joan, usually so sure of herself, so ready of resource, had gone temporarily to pieces. She was quite white, and her eyes met Ashe's with almost a hunted expression.

If the attention of the company was to be diverted, something drastic must be done. A mere verbal attempt to change the conversation would be useless.

Inspiration descended upon Ashe.

In the days of his childhood in Much Middlefold, Salop, he had played truant from Sunday School again and again in order to frequent the society of one Eddie Waffles, the official Bad Boy of the locality. It was not so much Eddie's charm of conversation that had attracted him – though that had been great – as the fact that Eddie, among his other accomplishments, could give a lifelike imitation of two cats fighting in a backyard, and Ashe felt he could never be happy until he had acquired this gift from the master. In course of time he had done so. It might be that his absences from Sunday School in

the cause of Art had left him in later years a trifle shaky
on the subject of the Kings of Judah, but his hard-won
accomplishment had made him in request at every
smoking-concert at Oxford, and it saved the situation
now.

'Have you ever heard two cats fighting in a backyard?'
he inquired casually of his neighbour Miss Willoughby.

The next moment the performance was in full swing.

Young Master Waffles, who had devoted considerable
study to his subject, had conceived the combat of his
imaginary cats in a broad, almost a Homeric vein. The
unpleasantness opened with a low gurgling sound,
answered by another a shade louder and possibly a little
more querulous. A momentary silence was followed by a
long-drawn note like rising wind cut off abruptly and
succeeded by a grumbling mutter. The response to this
was a couple of sharp howls. Both parties to the contest
then indulged in a discontented whining, growing louder
and louder till the air was full of electric menace. And
then, after another sharp silence, came War, noisy and
overwhelming. Standing at Master Waffles' side, you
could almost follow every movement of that intricate
fray, and mark how now one, now the other of the
battlers gained a short-lived advantage. It was a great
fight. Shrewd blows were taken and given, and in the eye
of the imagination you could see the air thick with
flying fur. Louder and louder grew the din, and then, at
its height, it ceased in one crescendo of tumult, and all
was still save for a faint, angry moaning.

Such was the cat fight of Master Eddie Waffles, and
Ashe, though falling short of the master, as a pupil must,
rendered it faithfully and with energy.

To say that the attention of the company was
diverted from Mr Judson and his remarks by the
extraordinary noises which proceeded from Ashe's lips
would be to offer a mere shadowy suggestion of the
sensation caused by his efforts. At first stunned surprise,

then consternation greeted him. Beach the butler was
staring as one watching a miracle, nearer apparently to
apoplexy than ever. On the faces of the others every
shade of emotion was to be seen. That this should be
happening in the Steward's Room at Blandings Castle
was scarcely less amazing than if it had taken place in a
cathedral. The upper servants, rigid in their seats, looked
at each other, like Cortes' soldiers, 'with a wild
surmise'.

The last faint moan of feline defiance died away, and
silence fell upon the room.

Ashe turned to Miss Willoughby.

'Just like that,' he said. 'I was telling Miss
Willoughby,' he added apologetically to Mrs Twemlow,
'about the cats in London. They were a great trial.'

For perhaps three seconds his social reputation
swayed to and fro in the balance, while the company
pondered on what he had done. It was new – but was it
humorous or was it vulgar? There is nothing your
upper servants so abhor as vulgarity. That was what the
Steward's Room was trying to make up its mind about.

And then Miss Willoughby threw her shapely head
back, and the squeal of her laughter smote the ceiling.
And at that the company made its decision. Everybody
laughed. Everybody urged Ashe to give an encore.
Everybody was his friend and admirer.

Everybody but Beach the butler. Beach the butler was
shocked to his very core. His heavy-lidded eyes rested on
Ashe with disapproval.

It seemed to Beach the butler that this young man
Marson had Got Above Himself.

Ashe found Joan at his side. Dinner was over, and the
diners were making for the Housekeeper's Room.

'Thank you, Mr Marson. That was very good of you,
and very clever.' Her eyes twinkled. 'But what a terrible
chance you took. You have made yourself a popular
success, but you might just as easily have become a

138

social outcast. As it is, I am afraid Mr Beach did not
approve.'

'I'm afraid he didn't. In a minute or so I'm going to
fawn upon him and make all well.'

Joan lowered her voice.

'It was quite true what that odious little man said. He
did write me letters. Of course I destroyed them long
ago.'

'But weren't you running the risk in coming here that
he might recognize you? Wouldn't that make it rather
unpleasant for you?'

'I never met him, you see. He only wrote to me. When
he came to the station to meet us this evening, he
looked startled to see me, so I suppose he remembers my
appearance. But Aline will have told him that my name
is Simpson.'

'That fellow Judson said that he was brooding. I think
you ought to put him out of his misery.'

'Mr Judson must have been letting his imagination
run away with him. He is out of his misery. He sent a
horrid fat man named Jones to see me in London about
the letters, and I told him that I had destroyed them. He
must have let him know that by this time.'

'I see.'

They went into the Housekeeper's Room. Mr Beach
was standing before the fire. Ashe went up to him.

It was not an easy matter to mollify Mr Beach. Ashe
tried the most tempting topics. He mentioned swollen
feet, he dangled the lining of Mr Beach's stomach
temptingly before his eyes, but the butler was not to be
softened. Only when Ashe turned the conversation to
the subject of the museum did a flicker of animation stir
him.

Mr Beach was fond and proud of the Blandings Castle
museum. It had been the means of getting him into print
for the first and only time in his life. A year ago a
representative of the *Intelligencer and Echo* from the

neighbouring town of Blatchford had come to visit the
Castle on behalf of his paper, and he had begun one
section of his article with the words: 'Under the auspices
of Mr Beach, my genial cicerone, I then visited his
lordship's museum . . .' Mr Beach treasured the clipping
in a special writing desk.

He responded almost amiably to Ashe's questions.
Yes, he had seen the scarab – he pronounced it 'scayrub'
– which Mr Peters had presented to 'is lordship. He
understood that 'is lordship thought very highly of Mr
Peters' scayrub. He had overheard Mr Baxter telling his
lordship that it was extremely valuable.

'Mr Beach,' said Ashe, 'I wonder if you would take me
to see Lord Emsworth's museum?'

Mr Beach regarded him heavily.

'I shall be pleased to take you to see 'is lordship's
museum,' he replied.

VI

One can only attribute to the nervous mental condition
following on the interview which he had had with Ashe
in his bedroom the rash act which Mr Peters attempted
shortly after dinner.

Mr Peters, shortly after dinner, was in a dangerous
and reckless mood. He had had a wretched time all
through the meal. The Blandings *chef* had extended
himself in honour of the house-party, and had produced
a succession of dishes which, in happier days, Mr Peters
would have devoured eagerly. To be compelled by
considerations of health to pass these by was enough to
damp the liveliest optimist. Mr Peters had suffered
terribly. Occasions of feasting and revelry like the
present were for him so many battlefields on which
Greed fought with Prudence.

All through dinner he brooded upon Ashe's defiance
and the horrors which were to result from that defiance.

One of Mr Peters' most painful memories was of a two weeks' visit which he had once paid to Mr William Muldoon at his celebrated health-restoring establishment at White Plains in the State of New York. He had been persuaded to go there by a brother-millionaire whom till then he had always regarded as a friend. The memory of Mr Muldoon's cold shower-baths and brisk system of physical exercise still lingered.

The thought that under Ashe's rule he was to go through privately very much what he had gone through in the company of a gang of other unfortunates at Muldoon's froze him with horror. He knew these health-cranks who believed that all mortal ailments could be cured by cold showers and brisk walks. They were all alike, and they nearly killed you. His worst nightmare was the one where he dreamed that he was back at Muldoon's leading his horse up that infernal hill outside the village, your only reward, when you reached the summit, being the distant prospect of Sing-Sing prison.

He wouldn't stand it. He would be hanged if he would stand it. He would defy Ashe.

But if he defied Ashe, Ashe would go away, and then whom could he find to recover his lost scarab?

Mr Peters began to appreciate the true meaning of the phrase about the horns of a dilemma.

The horns of this dilemma occupied his attention until the end of dinner. He shifted uneasily from one to the other and back again. He rose from the table in a thoroughly overwrought condition of mind.

And then, somehow, in the course of the evening, he found himself alone in the Hall, not a dozen feet from the unlocked museum door.

It was not immediately that he appreciated the significance of this fact. He had come to the Hall because its solitude suited his mood. It was only after he had finished a cigar – Ashe could not stop him smoking after dinner – that it suddenly flashed upon him that he had ready to hand a solution of all his troubles. A brief minute's resolute action, and the scarab would be his again and the menace of Ashe a thing of the past.

He glanced about him. Yes, he was alone.

Not once, since the removal of the scarab had begun to exercise his mind, had Mr Peters contemplated for an instant the possibility of recovering it for himself. The prospect of the unpleasantness which would ensue had been enough to make him regard such an action as out of the question. The risk was too great to be considered for a moment.

But here he was in a position where the risk was negligible. Like Ashe, he had always visualized the recovery of his scarab as a thing of the small hours, a daring act to be performed when sleep held the Castle in its grip. That an opportunity would be presented to him of walking in quite calmly and walking out again with the Cheops in his pocket had never occurred to him as a possibility.

Yet now this chance was presenting itself in all its simplicity, and all he had to do was to grasp it. The door of the museum was not even closed. He could see from where he stood that it was ajar.

He moved cautiously in its direction – not in a straight line, as one going to a museum, but circuitously, as one strolling without an aim. From time to time he glanced over his shoulder.

He reached the door, hesitated, and passed it. He turned, reached the door again, and again passed it. He stood for a moment darting his eyes about the Hall, then, in a burst of resolution, dashed for the door and shot in like a rabbit.

At the same moment the Efficient Baxter, who from the shelter of a pillar on the gallery that ran round two-thirds of the Hall had been eyeing the peculiar movements of the distinguished guest with considerable interest for some minutes, began to descend the stairs.

Rupert Baxter, the Earl of Emsworth's indefatigable private secretary, was one of those men whose chief characteristic is a vague suspicion of their fellow human beings. He did not suspect them of this or that definite crime: he simply suspected them. He prowled through life as we are told that the Hosts of Midian prowled. His powers in this respect were well known at Blandings Castle. The Earl of Emsworth said: 'Baxter is invaluable, positively invaluable.' The Hon. Freddie said: 'A chappie can't take a step in this bally house without stumbling over that damn feller Baxter.' The man-servant and the maid-servant within the gates, employing, like Miss Willoughby, that crisp gift for characterization which is the property of the English lower orders, described him as a Nosey Parker.

Peering over the railings of the balcony and observing the curious movements of Mr Peters, who, as a matter of fact, while making up his mind to approach the door, had been backing and filling about the Hall in a quaint serpentine manner like a man trying to invent a new variety of the Tango, the Efficient Baxter had found himself in some way – why, he did not know – of what, he could not say – but in some nebulous way, suspicious.

He had not definitely accused Mr Peters in his mind of any specific tort or malfeasance. He had merely felt that something fishy was toward.

He had a sixth sense in such matters.

But when Mr Peters, making up his mind, leaped into the museum, Baxter's suspicions lost their vagueness and became crystallized. Certainty descended on him like a bolt from the skies.

On oath, before a solicitor, the Efficient Baxter would have declared that J. Preston Peters was about to try to purloin the scarab.

Lest we should seem to be attributing too miraculous powers of intuition to Lord Emsworth's secretary, it should be explained that the mystery which hung about that curio had exercised his mind not a little since his employer had given it to him to place in the museum. He knew Lord Emsworth's powers of forgetting, and he did not believe his account of the transaction. Scarab-maniacs like Mr Peters did not give away specimens from their collections as presents. But he had not divined the truth of what had happened in London. The conclusion at which he had arrived was that Lord Emsworth had bought the scarab, and had forgotten all about it. To support this theory was the fact that the latter had taken his cheque-book to London with him. Baxter's long acquaintance with the earl had left him with the conviction that there was no saying what he might not do if let loose in London with a cheque-book.

As to Mr Peters' motive for entering the museum, that too seemed completely clear to the secretary. He was a curio enthusiast himself and he had served collectors in a secretarial capacity, and he knew both from experience and observation that strange madness which may at any moment afflict the collector, blotting out morality and the nice distinction between *meum* and *tuum* as with a sponge. He knew that collectors who would not steal a loaf if they were starving might, and did, fall before the temptation of a coveted curio.

He descended the stairs three at a time, and entered the museum at the very instant when Mr Peters' twitching fingers were about to close on his treasure.

He handled the delicate situation with eminent tact. Mr Peters, at the sound of his step, had executed a backward leap which was as good as a confession of guilt, and his face was rigid with dismay, but the Efficient Baxter affected not to notice these phenomena. His manner, when he spoke, was easy and unembarrassed.

144

'Ah! Taking a look at our little collection, Mr Peters? You will see that we have given the place of honour to your Cheops. It is certainly a fine specimen, a wonderfully fine specimen.'

Mr Peters was recovering slowly. Baxter talked on to give him time. He spoke of Mut and Bubastis, of Ammon and the Book of the Dead. He directed the other's attention to the Roman coins.

He was touching on some aspects of the Princess Gilukhipa of Mitanni, in whom his hearer could scarcely fail to be interested, when the door opened and Beach the butler came in, accompanied by Ashe. In the bustle of the interruption Mr Peters escaped, glad to be elsewhere and questioning for the first time in his life the dictum that, if you want a thing well done, you must do it yourself.

'I was not aware, sir,' said Beach the butler, 'that you were in occupation of the museum. I would not have intruded. But this young man expressed a desire to examine the exhibits, and I took the liberty of conducting him.'

'Come in, Beach, come in,' said Baxter.

The light fell on Ashe's face, and he recognized him as the cheerful young man who had inquired the way to Mr Peters' room before dinner, and who, he had by this time discovered, was not the Hon. Freddie's friend George Emerson, nor indeed any other of the guests of the house.

He felt suspicious.

'Oh, Beach.'

'Sir.'

'Just a moment.'

He drew the butler into the Hall out of earshot.

'Beach, who is that man?'

'Mr Peters' valet, sir.'

'Mr Peters' valet?'

'Yes, sir.'

'Has he been in service long?' asked Baxter, remembering that a mere menial had addressed him as 'old man'.

Beach lowered his voice. He and the Efficient Baxter were old allies, and it seemed right to Beach to confide in him.

'He has only just joined Mr Peters, sir, and he has never been in service before. He told me so himself, and I was unable to elicit from him any information as to his antecedents. His manner struck me, sir, as peculiar. It crossed my mind to wonder whether Mr Peters happened to be aware of this. I should dislike to do any young man an injury, but, if you think that Mr Peters should be informed . . . It might be anyone coming to a gentleman without a character like this young man. Mr Peters might have been Deceived, sir.'

The Efficient Baxter's manner became distrait. His mind was working rapidly.

'Should he be Informed, sir?'

'Eh? Who?'

'Mr Peters, sir. In case he should have been Deceived!'

'No, no. Mr Peters knows his own business.'

'Far from me be it to appear officious, sir, but . . .'

'Mr Peters probably knows all about him. Tell me, Beach, who was it suggested this visit to the museum? Did you?'

'It was at the young man's express desire that I conducted him, sir.'

The Efficient Baxter returned to the museum without a word. Ashe, standing in the middle of the room, was impressing the geography of the place on his memory. He was unaware of the piercing stare of suspicion which was being directed at him from behind.

He did not see Baxter. He was not even thinking of Baxter. But Baxter was on the alert. Baxter was on the war-path.

Baxter *knew*.

6

Among the compensations of advancing age is a
wholesome pessimism, which, while it takes the fine
edge off whatever triumphs may come to us, has the
admirable effect of preventing Fate from working off on
us any of those gold bricks, coins with strings attached,
and unhatched chickens at which Ardent Youth
snatches with such enthusiasm, to its subsequent
disappointment. As we emerge from the twenties we
grow into a habit of mind, which looks askance at Fate
bearing gifts. We miss, perhaps, the occasional prize, but
we also avoid leaping light-heartedly into traps.

Ashe Marson had yet to reach the age of tranquil
mistrust, and, when Fate seemed to be treating him
kindly, he was still young enough to accept such
kindnesses on their face value and rejoice at them.

As he sat on his bed, at the end of his first night at
Blandings Castle, he was conscious to a remarkable
degree that Fortune was treating him well. He had
survived, not merely without discredit, but with positive
triumph, the initiatory plunge into the
etiquette-maelstrom of life below stairs. So far from
doing the wrong thing and drawing down on himself the
just scorn of the Steward's Room, he had been the life
and soul of the party. Even if tomorrow, in an
absent-minded fit, he should anticipate the groom of the
chambers in the march to the table, it would be forgiven
him, for the humorist has his privileges.

So much for that. But that was only a part of
Fortune's kindnesses. To have discovered on the first
day of their association the correct method of handling

and reducing to subjection his irascible employer was an even greater boon. A prolonged association with Mr Peters on the lines of which their acquaintance had begun would have been extremely trying. Now, by virtue of a fortunate stand at the outset, he had spiked the millionaire's guns.

Thirdly, and most important of all, he had not only made himself familiar with the locality and surroundings of the scarab, but he had seen beyond the possibility of doubt that the removal of it and the earning of the thousand pounds would be the simplest possible task. Already he was spending the money in his mind, and to such lengths had optimism led him that, as he sat on his bed reviewing the events of the day, his only doubt was whether to get the scarab at once or to let it remain where it was until he had the opportunity of doing Mr Peters' interior good on the lines which he had mapped out in their conversation. For, of course, directly he had restored the scarab to its rightful owner and pocketed the reward, his position as healer and trainer to the millionaire would cease automatically.

He was sorry for that, for it troubled him to think that a sick man should not be made well. But, on the whole, looking at it from every aspect, it would be best to get the scarab as soon as possible and leave Mr Peters' digestion to look after itself.

Being twenty-six and an optimist, he had no suspicion that Fate might be playing with him, that Fate might have unpleasant surprises in store, that Fate even now was preparing to smite him in his hour of joy with that powerful weapon, the Efficient Baxter.

He looked at his watch. It was five minutes to one. He had no idea whether they kept early hours at Blandings Castle or not, but he deemed it prudent to give the household another hour in which to settle down. After which he would just trot down and collect the scarab.

The novel which he had brought down with him from
London fortunately proved interesting. Two o'clock
came before he was ready for it. He slipped the book in
his pocket, and opened the door.

All was still – still and uncommonly dark. Along the
corridor in which his room was situated the snores of
sleeping domestics exploded, growled, and twittered in
the air. Every menial on the list seemed to be snoring,
some in one key, some in another, some defiantly, some
plaintively; but the main fact was that they were all
snoring, somehow thus intimating that, as far as this
side of the house was concerned, the coast might be
considered clear and interruption of his plans a
negligible risk.

Researches made at an earlier hour had familiarized
him with the geography of the place. He found his way
to the green baize door without difficulty, and, stepping
through, was in the Hall, where the remains of the log
fire still glowed a fitful red. This, however, was the only
illumination, and it was fortunate that he did not
require light to guide him to the museum.

He knew the direction and had measured the
distance. It was precisely seventeen steps from where he
stood. Cautiously, and with avoidance of noise, he began
making the seventeen steps. He was beginning the
eleventh when he bumped into somebody.

Somebody soft.

Somebody whose hand, as it touched his, felt small
and feminine.

The fragment of a log fell on the ashes, and the fire
gave a dying spurt. Darkness succeeded the sudden glow.
The fire was out. That little flame had been its last effort
before expiring. But it had been enough to enable him to
recognize Joan Valentine.

'Good Lord!' he gasped.

His astonishment was short-lived. Next moment the
only thing that surprised him was the fact that he was

not more surprised. There was something about this girl
that made the most bizarre happenings seem right and
natural. Ever since he had met her his life had changed
from an orderly succession of uninteresting days to a
strange carnival of the unexpected, and use was
accustoming him to it. Life had taken on the quality of a
dream in which anything might happen, and in which
everything which did happen was to be accepted with
the calmness natural in dreams. It was strange that she
should be here in the pitch-dark Hall in the middle of
the night, but – after all – no stranger than that he
should be. In this dream-world in which he now moved
it had to be taken for granted that people did all sorts of
odd things from all sorts of odd motives.

'Hullo!' he said.

'Don't be alarmed.'

'No, no.'

'I think we are both here for the same reason.'

'You don't mean to say –'

'Yes, I have come to earn the thousand pounds too, Mr
Marson. We are rivals.'

In his present frame of mind it seemed so simple and
intelligible to Ashe that he wondered if he was really
hearing it for the first time. He had an odd feeling that
he had known this all along.

'You are here to get the scarab?'

'Exactly.'

Ashe was dimly conscious of some objection to this,
but at first it eluded him. Then he pinned it down.

'But you aren't a young man of good appearance,' he
said.

'I don't know what you mean. But Aline Peters is an
old friend of mine. She told me that her father would
give a large reward to whoever recovered the scarab, so
I –'

'Look out!' whispered Ashe. 'Run! There's someone
coming!'

There was a soft footfall on the stairs, a click, and above Ashe's head a light flashed out. He looked around. He was alone, and the green baize door was swaying gently to and fro.

'Who's that? Who's there?' said a voice.

The Efficient Baxter was coming down the broad staircase.

A general suspicion of mankind and a definite and particular suspicion of one individual made a bad opiate. For over an hour sleep had avoided the Efficient Baxter with an unconquerable coyness. He had tried all the known ways of wooing slumber, but they had failed him, from the counting of sheep downwards. The events of the night had whipped his mind to a restless activity. Try as he might to lose consciousness, the recollection of the plot which he had discovered surged up and kept him wakeful. It is the penalty of the suspicious type of mind that it suffers from its own activity. From the moment when he detected Mr Peters in the act of rifling the museum and marked down Ashe as an accomplice, Baxter's repose was doomed. Nor poppy nor mandragora nor all the drowsy syrups of the world could ever medicine him to that sweet sleep that he owned yesterday.

But it was the recollection that, on previous occasions of wakefulness, hot whisky and water had done the trick, which had now brought him from his bed and downstairs. His objective was the decanter on the table of the smoking-room, which was one of the rooms opening off the gallery which looked down on the Hall. Hot water he could achieve in his bedroom by means of his Etna stove.

So out of bed he had climbed, and downstairs he had gone, and here he was, to all appearances, just in time to foil the very plot on which he had been brooding. Mr Peters might be in bed, but there in the Hall below him stood the Accomplice, not ten paces from the museum door.

He arrived on the spot at racing speed, and confronted Ashe.

'What are you doing here?'

And then, from the Baxter viewpoint, things began to go wrong. By all the rules of the game Ashe, caught as it were red-handed, should have wilted, stammered, and confessed all. But Ashe was fortified by that philosophic calm which comes to us in dreams, and moreover he had his story ready.

'Mr Peters rang for me, sir.'

He had never expected to feel grateful to the little firebrand who employed him, but he had to admit that the millionaire, in their last conversation, had shown forethought. The thought struck him that, but for Mr Peters' advice, he might by now be in an extremely awkward position, for his was not a swiftly inventive mind.

'Rang for you? At half past two in the morning?'

'To read to him, sir.'

'To read to him at this hour?'

'Mr Peters suffers from insomnia, sir. He has a weak digestion, and the pain sometimes prevents him from sleeping. The lining of his stomach is not at all what it should be.'

'I don't believe a word of it.'

With that meekness which makes the good man wronged so impressive a spectacle, Ashe produced and exhibited his novel.

'Here is the book, which I was about to read to him. I think, sir, if you will excuse me, I had better be going to his room. Goodnight, sir.'

And he proceeded to mount the stairs. He was sorry for Mr Peters, so shortly about to be aroused from a refreshing slumber, but these were Life's tragedies and must be borne bravely.

The Efficient Baxter dogged him the whole way, springing silently in his wake, and dodging into the

shadows whenever the light of an occasional electric
bulb made it inadvisable to keep in the open. Then,
abruptly, he gave up the pursuit. For the first time his
comparative impotence in this silent conflict on which
he had embarked was made manifest to him, and he
perceived that on mere suspicion, however strong, he
could do nothing. To accuse Mr Peters of theft or to
accuse him of being accessory to a theft was out of the
question. Yet his whole being revolted at the thought of
allowing the sanctity of the museum to be violated.
Officially its contents belonged to Lord Emsworth, but
ever since his connection with the Castle he had been in
charge of them, and he had come to look on them as his
own property. If he was only a collector by proxy, he had
nevertheless the collector's devotion to his curios,
beside which the lioness's attachment to her cubs is
tepid, and he was prepared to do anything to retain in his
possession a scarab towards which he already
entertained the feelings of a life-proprietor.

No, not quite anything. He stopped short at the idea
of causing unpleasantness between the father of the
Hon. Freddie and the father of the Hon. Freddie's
fiancée. His secretarial position at the Castle was a
valuable one, and he was loth to jeopardize it.

There was only one way in which this delicate affair
could be brought to a satisfactory conclusion. It was
obvious, from what he had seen that night, that Mr
Peters' connection with the attempt on the scarab was
to be merely sympathetic, and that the actual theft was
to be accomplished by Ashe. His only course, then, was
to catch Ashe actually in the museum. Then Mr Peters
need not appear in the matter at all. Mr Peters' position
in those circumstances would be simply that of a man
who had happened to employ through no fault of his
own a valet who happened to be a thief.

He had made a mistake, he perceived, in locking the
door of the museum. In future he must leave it open, as

a trap is open. And he must stay up at nights and keep watch.

With these reflections, the Efficient Baxter returned to his room.

Ashe, meanwhile, had entered Mr Peters' bedroom and switched on the light. Mr Peters, who had just succeeded in dropping off to sleep, sat up with a start.

'I've come to read to you,' said Ashe.

Mr Peters emitted a stifled howl, in which wrath and self-pity were nicely blended.

'You fool, do you know that I have just managed to get to sleep!'

'And now you're awake again,' said Ashe soothingly. 'Such is life. A little rest, a little folding of the hands in sleep, and then, bing! off we go again. I hope you will like this novel. I dipped into it and it seems good.'

'What do you mean by coming in here at this time of night? Are you crazy?'

'It was your suggestion, and, by the way, I must thank you for it. I apologize for calling it thin. It worked like a charm. I don't think he believed it – in fact, I know he didn't – but it held him. I couldn't have thought up anything half so good in an emergency.'

Mr Peters' wrath changed to excitement.

'Did you get it? Have you been after my Cheops?'

'I have been after your Cheops, but I didn't get it. Bad men were abroad. That fellow with the spectacles who was in the museum when I met you there this evening swooped down from nowhere, and I had to tell him that you had rung for me to read to you. Fortunately I had this novel on me. I think he followed me upstairs to see that I really did come to your room.'

Mr Peters groaned miserably.

'Baxter,' he said. 'He's a man named Baxter, Lord Emsworth's private secretary, and he suspects us. He's the man we – I mean you – have got to look out for.'

'Well, never mind. Let's be happy while we can. Make

yourself comfortable, and I'll start reading. After all, what could be pleasanter than a little literature in the small hours? Shall I begin?'

II

Ashe found Joan in the stable-yard after breakfast next morning, playing with a retriever puppy.

'Can you spare me a moment of your valuable time?'

'Certainly, Mr Marson.'

'Shall we walk out into the open somewhere where we can't be overheard?'

'Perhaps it would be better.'

They moved off.

'Request your canine friend to withdraw,' said Ashe. 'He prevents me marshalling my thoughts.'

'I'm afraid he won't withdraw.'

'Never mind. I'll do my best in spite of him. Tell me, was I dreaming, or did I really meet you in the hall this morning at about twenty minutes after two?'

'You did.'

'And did you really tell me that you had come to the Castle to steal –'

'Recover.'

'Recover Mr Peters' scarab?'

'I did.'

'Then it's true?'

'It is.'

Ashe scraped the ground with a meditative toe.

'This,' he said, 'seems to me to complicate matters somewhat.'

'It complicates them abominably.'

'I suppose you were surprised when you found that I was on the same game as yourself?'

'Not in the least.'

'You weren't!'

'I knew directly I saw the advertisement in the

Morning Post. And I hunted up the *Morning Post*
directly you had told me that you had become Mr
Peters' valet.'

'You have known all along?'

'I have.'

Ashe regarded her admiringly.

'You're wonderful!'

'Because I saw through you?'

'Partly that. But chiefly because you had the pluck to
undertake a thing like this.'

'*You* undertook it.'

'But I'm a man.'

'And I'm a woman? And my theory is, Mr Marson,
that a woman can do nearly everything better than a
man. What a splendid test-case this would make to
settle the Votes for Women question once and for all!
Here we are, you and I, a man and a woman, each trying
for the same thing, and each starting with equal chances.
Suppose I beat you? How about the inferiority of women
then?'

'I never said that women were inferior.'

'You did with your eye.'

'Besides you're an exceptional woman.'

'You can't get out of it with a compliment. I'm a very
ordinary woman, and I'm going to beat a real man.'

Ashe frowned.

'I don't like to think of us working against each other.'

'Why not?'

'Because I like you.'

'I like you, Mr Marson, but we must not let sentiment
interfere with business. You want Mr Peters' thousand
pounds. So do I.'

'I hate the thought of being the instrument to prevent
you getting the money.'

'You won't be. I shall be the instrument to prevent
you getting it. I don't like that thought either, but one
has got to face it.'

'It makes me feel mean.'

'That's simply your old-fashioned masculine attitude towards the female, Mr Marson. You look on a woman as a weak creature to be shielded and petted. We aren't anything of the sort. We're terrors. You mustn't let my sex interfere with your trying to get this reward. Think of me as if I were another man. We're up against each other in a fair fight, and I don't want any special privileges. If you don't do your best from now onwards, I shall never forgive you. Do you understand?'

'I suppose so.'

'And we shall need to do our best. That little man with the glasses is on his guard. I was listening to you last night from behind the door. By the way, you shouldn't have told me to run away, and then have stayed yourself to be caught. That is an example of the sort of thing I mean. It was chivalry, not business.'

'I had a story ready to account for my being there. You had not.'

'And what a capital story it was! I shall borrow it for my own use. If I am caught, I shall say that I had to read Aline to sleep because she suffers from insomnia. And I shouldn't wonder if she did, poor girl. She doesn't get enough to eat. She is being starved, poor child. I heard one of the footmen say that she refused everything at dinner last night. And though she vows it isn't, my belief is that it's all because she is afraid to make a stand against her old father. It's a shame.'

'She is a weak creature to be shielded and petted,' said Ashe solemnly.

Joan laughed.

'Well, yes, you caught me there. I admit that poor Aline is not a shining example of the formidable modern woman, but –' She stopped. 'Oh, bother, I've just thought of what I ought to have said – the good repartee which would have crushed you. I suppose it's too late now?'

'Not at all. I'm like that myself. Only it is generally

next day that I hit the right answer. Shall we go back?
. . . She is a weak creature, to be shielded and petted.'

'Thank you so much,' said Joan gratefully. 'And why
is she a weak creature? Because she has *allowed* herself
to be shielded and petted. Because she has permitted
Man to give her special privileges and generally – No, it
isn't so good as I thought it was going to be.'

'It should be crisper,' said Ashe critically. 'It lacks the
punch.'

'But it brings me back to my point, which is that I am
not going to imitate her and forfeit my independence of
action in return for chivalry. Try to look at it from my
point of view, Mr Marson. I know that you need the
money just as much as I do. Well, don't you think that I
should feel a little mean if I thought you weren't trying
your hardest to get it, simply because you didn't think it
would be fair to try your hardest against a woman? It
would cripple me. I should not feel as if I had the right to
do anything. It's too important a matter for you to treat
me like a child and let me win to avoid disappointing
me. I want the money, but I don't want it handed to me.'

'Believe me,' said Ashe earnestly, 'it will not be
handed to you. I have studied the Baxter question more
deeply than you, and I can assure you that Baxter is a
menace. What has put him so firmly on the right scent I
don't know, but he seems to have divined the exact state
of affairs in its entirety. As far as I am concerned, that is
to say. Of course he has no idea that you are mixed up in
the business, but I am afraid that his suspicion of me
will hit you as well. What I mean is that for some time
to come I fancy that that man proposes to camp out on
the rug in front of the museum door. It would be madness
for either of us to attempt to go there at present.'

'It is being made very hard for us, isn't it? And I
thought it was going to be so simple!'

'I think we should give him at least a week to simmer
down.'

'Fully that.'

'Let us look on the bright side. We are in no hurry. Blandings Castle is quite as comfortable as No. 7A Arundell Street, and the commissariat department is a revelation to me. I had no idea that servants did themselves so well. And as for the social side, I love it. I revel in it. For the first time in my life I feel as if I were somebody. Did you observe my manner towards the kitchen-maid who waited on us at dinner last night? A touch of the old *noblesse* about it, I fancy? Dignified, but not unkind, I think? And I can keep it up. As far as I'm concerned let this life continue indefinitely.'

'But what about Mr Peters? Don't you think there is a danger that he may change his mind about that thousand pounds if we keep him waiting too long?'

'Not a chance of it. Being almost within touch of his scarab has had the worst effects on him. It has intensified the craving. By the way, have you seen the scarab?'

'Yes, I got Mrs Twemlow to take me to the museum while you were talking to the butler. It was dreadful to feel that it was lying there in the open, waiting for someone to take it, and not be able to do anything.'

'I felt exactly the same. It isn't much to look at, is it? If it hadn't been for the label, I wouldn't have believed that it was the thing for which Peters was offering a thousand pounds reward. But that's his affair. A thing is worth what somebody will give for it. Ours is not to reason why. Ours but to elude Baxter, and gather it in.'

' "Ours", indeed! You speak as if we were partners, instead of rivals.'

Ashe uttered an exclamation.

'You've hit it! Why not? Why any cut-throat competition? Why shouldn't we form a company? It would solve everything.'

Joan looked thoughtful.

'You mean, divide the reward?'

'Exactly. Into two equal parts.'

'And the labour?'

'The labour?'

'How shall we divide that?'

Ashe hesitated.

'My idea,' he said, 'was that I should do the – what I might call the *rough* work, and – '

'You mean that you should do the actual taking of the scarab?'

'Exactly. I would look after that end of it.'

'And what would *my* duties be?'

'Well, you – you would, as it were – how shall I put it? You would, so to speak, lend moral support.'

'By lying snugly in bed, fast asleep?'

Ashe avoided her eyes.

'Well, yes – er – something on those lines.'

'While you ran all the risks.'

'No, no. The risks are practically non-existent.'

'I thought you said just now that it would be madness for either of us to attempt to go to the museum at present?'

Joan laughed.

'It won't do, Mr Marson. You remind me of an old cat I once had. Whenever he killed a mouse, he would bring it into the drawing-room and lay it affectionately at my feet. I would reject the corpse with horror and turn him out, but back he would come with his loathsome gift. I simply couldn't make him understand that he was not doing me a kindness. He thought highly of his mouse, and it was beyond him to realize that I did not want it. You are just the same with your chivalry. It's very kind of you to keep offering me your dead mouse, but, honestly, I have no use for it. I *won't* take favours just because I happen to be a female. If we are going to form this partnership, I insist on doing my fair share of the work, and running my fair share of the risks – the "practically non-existent" risks.'

'You're very – resolute.'

'Say pig-headed. I shan't mind. Certainly I am. A girl has got to be, even nowadays, if she wants to play fair. Listen, Mr Marson, I will not have the dead mouse. I do not like dead mice. If you attempt to work off your dead mouse on me, this partnership ceases before it has begun. If we are to work together, we are going to make alternate attempts to get the scarab. No other arrangement will satisfy me.'

'Then I claim the right to make the first one.'

'You don't do anything of the sort. We toss for a first chance like little ladies and gentlemen. Have you a coin? I will spin, and you call.'

Ashe made a last stand.

'This is perfectly – '

'Mr Marson!'

Ashe gave in. He produced a coin, and handed it to her gloomily.

'Under protest,' he said.

'Heads or tails?' said Joan, unmoved.

Ashe watched the coin gyrating in the sunshine.

'Tails,' he cried.

The coin stopped rolling.

'Tails it is,' said Joan. 'What a nuisance! Well, never mind. I get my chance if you fail.'

'I shan't fail,' said Ashe fervently. 'If I have to pull the museum down, I won't fail. Thank Heaven there's no chance now of your doing anything foolish.'

'Don't be too sure. Well, good luck, Mr Marson.'

'Thank you, partner.'

They shook hands.

As they parted at the door Joan made one further remark:

'There's just one thing, Mr Marson.'

'Yes?'

'If I could have accepted the mouse from anyone, I would certainly have accepted it from you.'

7

It is worthy of record, in the light of after events, that at
the beginning of their visit, it was the general opinion of
the guests gathered together at Blandings Castle that the
place was dull. The house-party had that air of torpor
which one sees in the saloon passengers of an Atlantic
liner, that appearance of resignation to an enforced
idleness and a monotony only to be broken by meals.
Lord Emsworth's guests gave the impression,
collectively, of being just about to yawn and look at
their watches.

This was partly the fault of the time of year, for most
house-parties are dull if they happen to fall between the
hunting and the shooting seasons, but must be
attributed chiefly to Lord Emsworth's extremely sketchy
notions of the duties of a host.

A host has no right to intern a regiment of his
relations in his house unless he also invites lively and
agreeable outsiders to meet them. If he does commit this
solecism, the least he can do is to work himself to the
bone in the effort to invent amusements and diversions
for his victims. Lord Emsworth had failed badly in both
these matters. With the exception of Mr Peters, his
daughter Aline, and George Emerson, there was nobody
in the house who did not belong to the clan; and as for
his exerting himself to entertain, the company was
lucky if it caught a glimpse of its host at meals. Lord
Emsworth belonged to the people-like-to-be-left-alone-
to-amuse-themselves-when-they-come-to-a-place school
of hosts. He pottered about the garden in an old coat,
now uprooting a weed, now wrangling with the autocrat

from Scotland who was – theoretically – in his service as head-gardener; dreamily satisfied, when he thought of them at all, that his guests were as perfectly happy as he was. Apart from his son Freddie, whom he had long since dismissed as a youth of abnormal tastes from whom nothing reasonable was to be expected, he could not imagine anyone not being content merely to be at Blandings when the buds were bursting on the trees.

A resolute hostess might have saved the situation, but Lady Ann Warblington's abilities in that direction stopped short at leaving everything to Mrs Twemlow and writing letters in her bedroom. When Lady Ann Warblington was not writing letters in her bedroom – which was seldom, for she had an apparently inexhaustible correspondence – she was nursing sick headaches in it. She was one of those hostesses whom a guest never sees except when he goes into the library and espies the tail of her skirt vanishing through the other door.

As for the ordinary recreations of the country-house, the guests could frequent the billiard-room, where they were sure to find Lord Stockheath playing a hundred up with his cousin, Algernon Wooster – a spectacle of the liveliest interest; or they could, if fond of the game, console themselves for the absence of a links in the neighbourhood with the exhilarating pastime of clock-golf; or they could stroll about the terraces with such of their relations as they happened to be on speaking terms with at the moment and abuse their host and the rest of their relations.

This was the favourite amusement, and after breakfast on a morning ten days after Joan and Ashe had formed their compact the terraces were full of perambulating couples. Here, Colonel Horace Mant, walking with the Bishop of Godalming, was soothing that dignitary by clothing in soldierly words thoughts which the latter had not been able to crush down but

which his holy office scarcely permitted him to utter.
There, Lady Mildred Mant, linked to Mrs Jack Hale, of
the collateral branch of the family, was saying things
about her father in his capacity of host and entertainer
which were making her companion feel another woman.
Farther on, stopping occasionally to gesticulate, could be
seen other Emsworth relatives and connections. It was a
typical scene of quiet, peaceful English family life.

Leaning on the broad stone balustrade of the upper
terrace, Aline Peters and George Emerson surveyed the
malcontents.

Aline gave a little sigh, almost inaudible. But
George's hearing was good.

'I was wondering when you were going to admit it,' he
said, shifting his position so that he faced her.

'Admit what?'

'That you couldn't stand the prospect. That the idea of
being stuck for life with this crowd, like a fly on
fly-paper, was too much for you. That you were ready to
break off your engagement to Freddie and come away
and marry me and live happily ever after.'

'George!'

'Well, wasn't that what it meant? Be honest.'

'What what meant?'

'That sigh.'

'I didn't sigh. I was just breathing.'

'Then you *can* breathe in this atmosphere? You
surprise me.' He raked the terraces with hostile eyes.
'Look at them! Look at them crawling around like doped
beetles. My dear girl, it's no use your pretending that
this sort of thing wouldn't kill you. You're pining away
already. You're thinner and paler since you came here.
Heavens! How we shall look back at this and thank our
stars that we're out of it, when we're settled down
happily in Hong-Kong. You'll like Hong-Kong. It's a
most picturesque place. Something going on all the
time.'

'George, you mustn't, really!'

'Why mustn't I?'

'It's wrong. You can't talk like that when we are both enjoying the hospitality –'

A wild laugh, almost a howl, disturbed the talk of the more adjacent of the perambulating relatives. Colonel Horace Mant, checked in mid-sentence, looked up resentfully at the cause of the interruption.

'I wish someone would tell me whether it's that fellow Emerson or young Freddie who's supposed to be engaged to Miss Peters. Hanged if you ever see her and Freddie together, but she and Emerson are never to be found apart. If my respected father-in-law had any sense, I should have thought he would have had sense enough to stop that. If that girl isn't in love with Emerson I'll be – I'll eat my hat.'

'No, no,' said the Bishop. 'No, no. Surely not, Horace. What were you saying when you broke off?'

'I was saying that if a man wanted his relations never to speak to each other again for the rest of their lives, the best thing he could do would be to herd them all together in a dashed barrack of a house a hundred miles from anywhere and then go off and spend all his time prodding dashed flower-beds with a spud, dash it!'

'Just so, just so. So you were. Go on, Horace. I find a curious comfort in your words.'

On the terrace above them, Aline was looking at George with startled eyes.

'George!'

'I'm sorry. But you shouldn't spring these jokes on me so suddenly. You said *enjoying*. Yes. Revelling in it, aren't we?'

'It's a lovely old place,' said Aline, defensively.

'And when you've said that, you've said everything. You can't live on scenery and architecture for the rest of your life. There's the human element to be thought of. And you're beginning –'

'There goes father,' interrupted Aline. 'How fast he is walking. George, have you noticed a sort of difference in father these last few days?'

'I haven't. My speciality is keeping an eye on the rest of the Peters family.'

'He seems better somehow. He seems to have almost stopped smoking – and I'm very glad, for those cigars were awfully bad for him. The doctor expressly told him he must stop them, but he wouldn't pay any attention to him. And he seems to take so much more exercise. My bedroom is next to his, you know, and every morning I can hear things going on through the wall. Father dancing about and puffing a good deal. And one morning I met his valet going in with a pair of Indian clubs and some boxing-gloves. I believe father is really taking himself in hand at last.'

George Emerson exploded.

'And about time, too! How much longer are you to go on starving yourself to death just to give him the resolution to stick to his dieting? It maddens me to see you at dinner. And it's killing you. You're getting pale and thin. You can't go on like this.'

A wistful look came over Aline's face.

'I do get a little hungry sometimes. Late at night generally.'

'You want someone to take care of you and look after you. I'm the man. You may think you can deceive me, but I can tell. I *know*, I tell you. You're weakening. You're beginning to see that it won't do. One of these days you're going to come to me, and say, "George, you were right. Let's sneak off to the station without anybody knowing and leg it for London and get married at a registrar's." Oh, *I* know! I couldn't have loved you all this time and not know. You're weakening.'

The trouble with these Supermen is that they lack reticence. They do not know how to omit. They expand their chests and whoop. And a girl, even a girl like Aline

Peters, cannot help resenting the note of triumph. But
Supermen despise tact. As far as one can gather, that is
the chief difference between them and the ordinary man.

A little frown appeared on Aline's forehead, and she
set her mouth mutinously.

'I'm not weakening at all,' she said, and her voice was,
for her, quite acid. 'You – you take too much for
granted.'

George was contemplating the landscape with a
conqueror's eye.

'You are beginning to see that it is impossible, this
Freddie foolery.'

'It is not foolery,' said Aline pettishly, tears of
annoyance in her eyes. 'And I wish you wouldn't call
him Freddie.'

'He asked me to. He *asked* me to.'

Aline stamped her foot.

'Well, never mind. Please don't do it.'

'Very well, little girl,' said George softly. 'I wouldn't
do anything to hurt you.'

The fact that it never even occurred to George
Emerson that he was being offensively patronizing
shows the stern stuff of which these Supermen are
made.

II

The Efficient Baxter bicycled broodingly to Market
Blandings for tobacco. He brooded for several reasons.
He had just seen Aline Peters and George Emerson in
confidential talk on the upper terrace, and that was one
thing that exercised his mind, for he suspected George
Emerson. He suspected him nebulously as a snake in the
grass, as an influence working against the orderly
progress of events concerning the marriage which had
been arranged and would shortly take place between
Miss Peters and the Hon. Frederick Threepwood. It

would be too much to say that he had any idea that George was putting in such hard and consistant work in his serpentine role, indeed, if he could have overheard the conversation just recorded, it is probable that Rupert Baxter would have had heart-failure; but he had observed the intimacy between the two, as he observed most things in his immediate neighbourhood, and he disapproved of it. He blamed the Hon. Freddie. If the Hon. Freddie had been a more ardent lover, he would have spent his time with Aline, and George Emerson would have taken his proper place as one of the crowd at the back of the stage. But Freddie's view of the matter seemed to be that he had done all that could be expected of a chappie in getting engaged to the girl, and that now he might consider himself at liberty to drop her for a while.

So Baxter, as he bicycled to Market Blandings for tobacco, brooded on Freddie, Aline Peters, and George Emerson.

He also brooded on Mr Peters and Ashe Marson.

Finally he brooded in a general way because he had had very little sleep for the past week.

The spectacle of a young man doing his duty and enduring considerable discomforts while doing it is painful, but it affords so excellent a moral picture that I cannot omit a short description of the manner in which Rupert Baxter had spent the nine nights which had elapsed since his meeting with Ashe in the small hours in the Hall.

In the gallery which ran above the Hall, there was a large chair, situated a few paces from the great staircase. On this, in an overcoat – for the nights were chilly – and rubber-soled shoes, the efficient Baxter had sat, without missing a single night, from one in the morning till daybreak, waiting, waiting, waiting. It had been an ordeal to try the stoutest determination. Nature had never intended Baxter for a night-bird. He loved his bed.

He knew that doctors held insufficient sleep made a
man pale and sallow, and he had always aimed at the
peach-bloom complexion which comes from a sensible
eight hours between the sheets. One of the Georges – I
forget which – once said that a certain number of hours'
sleep each night – I cannot recall at the moment how
many – made a man something, which for the time
being has slipped my memory. Baxter agreed with him.
It went against all his instincts to sit up in this fashion,
but it was his duty and he did it.

It troubled him that, as night after night went by, and
Ashe, the suspect, did not walk into the trap so carefully
laid for him, he found an increasing difficulty in keeping
awake. The first two or three of his series of vigils he
had passed in an unimpeachable wakefulness, his chin
resting on the rail of the gallery and his ears alert for the
slightest sound. But he had not been able to maintain
this standard of excellence. On several occasions he had
caught himself in the act of dropping off, and last night
he had actually woken with a start to find it quite light.
As his last recollection before that was of an inky
darkness, impenetrable to the eye, dismay gripped him
with a sudden clutch, and he ran swiftly down to the
museum. His relief on finding that the scarab was still
there had been tempered by thoughts of what might
have been.

Baxter, then, as he bicycled to Market Blandings for
tobacco, had good reason to brood.

Having bought his tobacco and observed the life and
thought of the town for half an hour – it was market-day
and the normal stagnation of the place was temporarily
relieved and brightened by pigs that eluded their keepers
and a bull-calf which caught a stout farmer at the
psychological moment when he was tying his shoe-lace
and lifted him six feet – he made his way to the
Emsworth Arms, the most respectable of the eleven inns
which the citizens of Market Blandings contrived in

some miraculous way to support. In most English country towns, if the public-houses do not actually outnumber the inhabitants, they all do an excellent trade. It is only when they are two to one that hard times hit them and set the inn-keepers blaming the Government.

It was not the busy bar, full to overflowing with honest British yeomen, many of them in the same condition, that Baxter sought. His goal was the genteel dining-room on the first floor, where a bald and shuffling waiter, own cousin to a tortoise, served luncheon to those desiring it. Lack of sleep had reduced Baxter to a condition where the presence and chatter of the house-party were unsupportable. It was his purpose to lunch at the Emsworth Arms and take a nap in an armchair afterwards.

He had relied on having the room to himself, for Market Blandings did not lunch to a great extent; but to his annoyance and disappointment the room was already occupied by a man in brown tweeds.

Occupied is the correct word, for at first sight, this man seemed to fill the room. Never since almost forgotten days when he used to frequent circuses and side-shows had Baxter seen a fellow human being so extraordinarily obese.

He was a man about fifty years old, grey-haired, of a mauve complexion, and his general appearance suggested joviality.

To Baxter's chagrin this person engaged him in conversation directly he took his seat at the table. There was only one table in the room, and it had the disadvantage that it collected those seated at it into one party. It was impossible for Baxter to withdraw into himself and ignore this person's advances.

It is doubtful if he could have done, however, had they been separated by yards of floor, for the fat man was not only naturally talkative, but, as it appeared from his opening remarks, speech had been dammed up within him for some time by lack of a suitable victim.

'Morning,' he began. 'Nice day. Good for the farmers. I'll move up to your end of the table if I may, sir. Waiter, bring my beef to this gentleman's end of the table.'

He creaked into a chair at Baxter's side, and resumed.

'Infernally quiet place, this, sir. I haven't found a soul to speak to since I arrived yesterday afternoon except deaf and dumb rustics. Are you making a long stay here?'

'I live outside the town.'

'I pity you. Wouldn't care to do it myself. Had to come here on business, and shan't be sorry when it's finished. I give you my word I couldn't sleep a wink last night because of the quiet. I was just dropping off when a beast of a bird outside the window gave a chirrup, and it brought me up with a jerk as if somebody had fired a gun off. There's a damned cat somewhere near my room which mews. I lie in bed waiting for the next mew, all worked up. Heaven save me from the country. It may be all right for you, if you've got a comfortable home and a pal or two to chat with after dinner, but you've no conception what it's like in this infernal town – I suppose it calls itself a town. A man told me there was a moving-picture place here, and I hurried off to it, and found that it was the wrong day. Only open Tuesdays and Fridays. What a hole! There's a church down the street. I'm told it's Norman or something. Anyway it's old. I'm not much of a man for churches as a rule, but I went and took a look at it. And then somebody told me that there was a fine view from the end of the High Street. So I went and took a look at that, and now, as far as I can make out, I've done the sights and exhausted every possibility of entertainment the town has to provide. Unless there's another church. I'm so reduced that I'll go and see the Methodist chapel, if there is one.'

Fresh air, want of sleep, and the closeness of the

dining-room combined to make Baxter drowsy. He ate his lunch in a torpor, hardly replying to his companion's remarks, who, for his part, did not seem to wish for or to expect replies. It was enough for him to be talking.

'What do people *do* with themselves in a place like this? When they want amusement, I mean. I suppose it's different if you've been brought up to it. Like being born colour-blind or something. You don't notice it. It's the visitors who suffer. They've no enterprise in this sort of place. There's a bit of land just outside here which would make a sweet steeplechase course. Natural barriers. Everything. It hasn't occurred to them to do anything with it. It makes you despair of your species, that sort of thing. Now, if I – '

Baxter dozed. With his fork still impaling a piece of cold beef he dropped into that half-awake, half-asleep state which is Nature's daytime substitute for the true slumber of the night. The fat man, either not noticing or not caring, talked on. His voice was a steady drone, lulling Baxter to rest.

Suddenly there was a break. Baxter sat up, blinking. He had a curious impression that his companion had said, 'Hallo, Freddie!' and that the door had just opened and closed again.

'Eh?' he said.

'Yes?' said the fat man.

'What did you say?'

'I was speaking of – '

'I thought you said, "Hullo, Freddie!"'

His companion eyed him indulgently.

'I thought you were dropping off when I looked at you. You've been dreaming. What should I say, "Hullo, Freddie!" for?'

The conundrum was unanswerable. Baxter did not attempt to answer it. But there remained at the back of his mind a quaint idea that he had caught sight as he awoke of the Hon. Frederick Threepwood, his face warningly contorted, vanishing through the door.

Yet what would the Hon. Freddie be doing at the Emsworth Arms?

A solution of the difficulty occurred to him. He had dreamed that he had seen Freddie, and that had suggested the words which, Reason pointed out, his companion could hardly have spoken. Even if the Hon. Freddie should enter the room, this fat man, who was apparently a drummer of some kind, would certainly not know who he was, nor would he address him so familiarly. Yes, that must be the explanation. After all the quaintest things happened in dreams. Last night, when he had fallen asleep in his chair, he had dreamed that he was sitting in a glass case in the museum making faces at Lord Emsworth, Mr Peters, and Beach, the butler, who were trying to steal him under the impression that he was a scarab of the reign of the Cheops of the Fourth Dynasty – a thing which he would never have done when awake.

Yes, he must certainly have been dreaming.

In the bedroom into which he had dashed to hide himself on discovering that the dining-room was in the possession of the Efficient Baxter, the Hon. Freddie sat on a rickety chair, scowling.

He elaborated a favourite dictum of his.

'You can't take a step *anywhere* without stumbling over that damn feller Baxter!'

He wondered if Baxter had seen him. He wondered if Baxter had recognized him. He wondered if Baxter had heard R. Jones say, 'Hullo, Freddie!'

He wondered, if such should be the case, whether R. Jones' presence of mind and native resource would be equal to explaining away the remark.

8

' "Put the butter or dripping in a kettle on the range, and when hot add the onions and fry them; add the veal and cook till brown. Add the water, cover closely, and cook very slowly until the meat is tender, then add the seasonings and place the potatoes on top of the meat. Cover and cook until the potatoes are tender, but not falling to pieces." '

'Sure,' said Mr Peters. '*Not* falling to pieces. That's right. Go on.'

' "Then add the cream and cook five minutes longer," ' read Ashe.

'Is that all?'

'That's all of that one.'

Mr Peters settled himself more comfortably in bed.

'Read me the piece where it says about Curried Lobster.'

Ashe cleared his throat.

' "Curried Lobster," ' he read. ' "Materials: Two two-pound lobsters, two teaspoonfuls lemon juice, half teaspoonful curry powder, two tablespoonfuls butter, one tablespoonful flour, one cup scalded milk, one cup cracker crumbs, half teaspoonful salt, quarter teaspoonful pepper." '

'Go on.'

' "Way of Preparing: Cream the butter and flour and add the scalded milk, then add the lemon juice, curry powder, salt and pepper. Remove the lobster meat from the shells and cut into half-inch cubes." '

' "Half-inch cubes," ' sighed Mr Peters wistfully. 'Yes?'

' "Add the latter to the sauce." '

174

'You didn't say anything about the latter. Oh, I see, it means the half-inch cubes. Yes?'

' "Refill the lobster shells, cover with buttered crumbs, and bake until the crumbs are brown. This will serve six persons." '

'And make them feel an hour afterwards as if they had swallowed a live wild-cat,' said Mr Peters ruefully.

'Not necessarily,' said Ashe. 'I could eat two portions of that at this very minute and go off to bed and sleep like a little child.'

Mr Peters raised himself on his elbow, and stared at him. They were in the millionaire's bedroom, the time being one in the morning, and Mr Peters had expressed a wish that Ashe would read him to sleep. He had voted against Ashe's novel and produced from the recesses of his suitcase a much-thumbed cookery-book. He explained that since his digestive misfortune had come upon him, he had derived a certain solace from its perusal. It may be that to some men a sorrow's crown of sorrow is remembering happier things, but Mr Peters had not found that to be the case. In his hour of affliction it soothed him to read of Hungarian Goulash and Escalloped Brains and to remember that he, too, the nut-and-grass eater of today, had once dwelt in Arcadia.

The passage of the days, which had so sapped the stamina of the Efficient Baxter, had had the opposite effect on Mr Peters. His was one of those natures which cannot deal in half-measures. Whatever he did he did with the same driving energy. After the first passionate burst of resistance, he had settled down into a model pupil in Ashe's one-man school of physical culture. It had been the same, now that he came to look back on it, at Muldoon's. Now that he remembered, he had come away from White Plains, hoping indeed never to see the place again, but undeniably a different man physically. It is not the habit of Professor Muldoon to let his patients loaf, but Mr Peters, after the initial plunge, had needed no driving. He had worked hard at his cure then, because it was the job in hand. He worked hard now, under Ashe's guidance, because, once he had begun, the thing interested and gripped him. Ashe, who had expected continued reluctance, had been astonished and delighted at the way in which the millionaire had behaved. Nature had really intended Ashe for a trainer. He identified himself so thoroughly with his man and rejoiced at the least signs of improvement.

In Mr Peters' case there had been distinct improvement already. Miracles do not happen nowadays, and it was too much to expect one who had maltreated his body so consistently for so many years to become whole in a day, but to an optimist like Ashe signs were not wanting that in due season Mr Peters would rise on stepping-stones of his dead self to higher things, and while never soaring into the class which devours curried lobster and smiles after it, might yet prove himself a devil of a fellow among the mutton cutlets.

'You're a wonder,' said Mr Peters. 'You're sassy and you have no respect for your elders and betters, but you deliver the goods. That's the point. Why, I'm beginning to feel great. Say, do you know, I felt a new muscle in the small of my back this morning! They are coming out on me like a rash.'

'That's the Larsen exercises. They develop the whole body.'

'Well, you're a pretty good advertisement for them, if they need one. What were you before you came to me – a prize-fighter?'

'That's the question everybody I have met since I arrived here has asked me. I believe it made the butler think I was some sort of a crook when I couldn't answer it. I used to write stories, detective stories.'

'What you ought to be doing is running a place over

here in England like Muldoon has back home. But you will be able to write one more story out of this business here, if you want to. When are you going to have another try for my scarab?'

'Tonight.'

'Tonight? How about Baxter?'

'I shall have to risk Baxter.'

Mr Peters hesitated. He had fallen out of the habit of being magnanimous during the past few years, for dyspepsia brooks no divided allegiance and magnanimity has to take a back seat when it has its grip on a man.

'See here,' he said awkwardly, 'I've been thinking it over lately, and what's the use? It's a queer thing, and if anybody had told me a week ago that I should be saying it I wouldn't have believed them, but I am beginning to like you. I don't want to get you into trouble. Let the old scarab go. What's a scarab anyway? Forget about it, and stick on here as my private Muldoon. If it's the money that's worrying you, forget that too. I'll give it you as your fee.'

Ashe was astounded. That it could really be his peppery employer who spoke was almost unbelievable. Ashe's was a friendly nature, and he could never be long associated with anyone without trying to establish pleasant relations, but he had resigned himself in the present case to perpetual warfare.

He was touched, and if he had ever contemplated abandoning his venture, this, he felt, would have spurred him on to see it through. This sudden revelation of the human in Mr Peters was like a trumpet-call.

'I wouldn't think of it,' he said. 'It's great of you to suggest such a thing, but I know just how you feel about the thing, and I'm going to get it for you if I have to wring Baxter's neck. Probably Baxter will have given up waiting as a bad job by now, if he has been watching all this while. We've given him ten nights to cool off. I expect he is in bed, dreaming pleasant dreams. It's nearly two o'clock. I'll wait another ten minutes and then go down.'

He picked up the cookery book.

'Lie back, and make yourself comfortable, and I'll read you to sleep first.'

'You're a good boy,' said Mr Peters drowsily.

'Are you ready? "Pork Tenderloin Larded. Half pound fat pork." '

A faint smile curved Mr Peters' lips. His eyes were closed and he breathed softly. Ashe went on in a low voice.

'"Four large pork tenderloins, one cup cracker crumbs, one cup boiling water, two tablespoonfuls butter, one teaspoonful salt, half teaspoonful pepper, one teaspoonful poultry seasoning." '

A little sigh came from the bed.

'"Way of Preparing: Wipe the tenderloins with a damp cloth. With a sharp knife make a deep pocket lengthwise in each tenderloin. Cut your pork into long thin strips, and with a needle lard each tenderloin. Melt the butter in the water, add the seasoning and the cracker crumbs, combining all thoroughly. Now fill each pocket in the tenderloin with this stuffing, place the tenderloins –" '

A snore sounded from the pillows, punctuating the recital like a mark of exclamation. Ashe laid down the book and peered into the darkness beyond the rays of the bed-lamp. His employer slept.

Ashe switched off the light and crept to the door. Out in the passage he stopped and listened. All was still.

He stole downstairs.

II

George Emerson sat in his bedroom smoking a cigarette. A light of resolution was in his eyes. He glanced at the table beside his bed and at what was on that table, and the light of resolution flamed into a glare of fanatic determination. So might a medieval knight have looked on the eve of setting forth to rescue a maiden from a dragon.

His cigarette burned down. He looked at his watch, put it back, and lit another cigarette. His aspect was the aspect of one waiting for the appointed hour.

Smoking his second cigarette, he resumed his meditations. They had to do with Aline Peters.

George Emerson was troubled about Aline Peters. Watching over her as he did with a lover's eye, he had perceived that about her which distressed him. On the terrace that morning she had been abrupt to him – what, in a girl of a less angelic disposition, one might have called snappy. Yes, to be just, she had snapped at him. That meant something. It meant that Aline was not well. It meant what her pallor and tired eyes meant – that the life she was leading was doing her no good.

Eleven nights had George dined at Blandings Castle, and on each of the eleven nights he had been distressed to see the manner in which Aline, declining the baked meats, had restricted herself to the miserable vegetable messes which were all that doctor's orders permitted to her suffering father. George's pity had its limits. His heart did not bleed for Mr Peters. Mr Peters' diet was his own affair. But that Aline should starve herself in this fashion, purely by way of moral support of her parent, was another matter.

George was perhaps a shade material. Himself a robust young man and taking what might be called an out-size in meals, he attached perhaps too much importance to food as an adjunct to the perfect life. In his survey of Aline, he took a line through his own requirements, and, believing that eleven such dinners as he had seen Aline partake of would have killed him, he decided that his loved one was on the point of starvation. No human being, he held, could exist on

such Barmecide feasts. That Mr Peters continued to do
so did not occur to him as a flaw in his reasoning. He
looked on Mr Peters as a sort of machine. Successful
business men often give that impression to the young. If
George had been told that Mr Peters went along on
petrol like a motor-car, he would not have been much
surprised. But that Aline, his Aline, should have to deny
herself the exercise of that mastication of rich meats
which, together with the gift of speech, raises Man
above the beasts of the field! That was what tortured
George.

He had devoted the day to thinking out a solution of
the problem. Such was the overflowing goodness of
Aline's heart that not even he could persuade her to
withdraw her moral support from her father and devote
herself to the keeping up of her strength as she should
do. It was necessary to think of some other plan.

And then a speech of hers had come back to him.

She had said – poor child! – 'I do get a little hungry
sometimes. Late at night, generally.'

The problem was solved. Food should be brought to
her late at night.

On the table by his bed was a stout sheet of
packing-paper. On this lay, like one of those pictures in
still-life which one sees on suburban parlour-walls, a
tongue, some bread, a knife, a fork, salt, a corkscrew,
and a small bottle of white wine.

It is a pleasure, when one has been able hitherto to
portray George's devotion only through the medium of
his speeches, to produce these comestibles as Exhibit A
to show that he loved Aline with no common love. For
it had not been an easy task to get them there. In a
house of smaller dimensions he would have raided the
larder without shame, but at Blandings Castle there was
no saying where the larder might be. All he knew was
that it lay somewhere beyond that green-baize door
opening on the Hall, past which he was wont to go on

his way to bed. To prowl through the maze of the servants' quarters in search of it was impossible. The only thing to be done was to go to Market Blandings and buy the things.

Fortune had helped him at the start by arranging that the Hon. Freddie also should be going into Market Blandings in the little runabout which seated two. He had acquiesced in George's suggestion that he, George, should occupy the other seat, but with a certain lack, it seemed to George, of enthusiasm. He had not volunteered any reason why he was going to Market Blandings in the little runabout, and on arrival there had betrayed an unmistakable desire to get rid of George at the earliest opportunity. As this had suited George to perfection, he being desirous of getting rid of the Hon. Freddie at the earliest opportunity, he had not been inquisitive, and they had parted at the outskirts of the town without mutual confidences. George had then proceeded to the grocer's, and after that to another of the Market Blandings inns, not the Emsworth Arms, where he had bought the white wine. He did not believe in the white wine, for he was a young man with a palate and mistrusted country cellars, but he assumed that, whatever its quality, it would cheer Aline in the small hours.

He had then tramped the whole five miles back to the Castle with his purchases.

It was here that his real troubles began, and the quality of his love was tested. The walk, to a heavily-laden man, was bad enough, but as nothing compared with the ordeal of smuggling the cargo up to his bedroom. Superman as he was, George was alive to the delicacy of the situation. One cannot convey food and drink to one's room at a strange house without, if detected, seeming to cast a slur on the table of the host. It was as one who carries dispatches through an enemy's lines that George took cover, emerged from cover, dodged, ducked, and ran; and the moment when he sank down on his bed, the door locked behind him, was one of the happiest of his life.

The recollection of that ordeal made the one he proposed to embark on now seem light in comparison. All he had to do was to go to Aline's room, knock softly on the door till signs of wakefulness made themselves heard from within, and then dart away into the shadows whence he had come, and so back to bed. He gave Aline credit for the intelligence which would enable her on finding a tongue, some bread, a knife, a fork, salt, a corkscrew, and a bottle of white wine on the mat, to know what to do with them and, perhaps, to guess whose was the loving hand which had laid them there.

The second clause, however, was not important, for he proposed to tell her whose was the hand next morning. Other people might hide their light under a bushel, not George Emerson.

It only remained now to allow time to pass until the hour should be sufficiently advanced to ensure safety for the expedition. He looked at his watch again. It was nearly two. By this time the house must be asleep.

He gathered up the tongue, the bread, the knife, the fork, the salt, the corkscrew, and the bottle of white wine, and left the room.

All was still. He stole downstairs.

III

On his chair on the gallery that ran round the Hall, swathed in an overcoat and wearing rubber-soled shoes, the Efficient Baxter sat and gazed into the darkness. He had lost the first fine careless rapture, as it were, which had helped him to endure these vigils, and a great weariness was upon him. He found a difficulty in keeping his eyes open, and when they were open the darkness seemed to press upon them painfully. Take

him for all in all, the Efficient Baxter had had about
enough of it.

Time stood still.

Baxter's thoughts began to wander. He knew that this
was fatal, and exerted himself to drag them back. He
tried to concentrate his mind on one definite thing. He
selected the scarab as a suitable object, but it played him
false. He had hardly concentrated on the scarab before
his mind was straying off to ancient Egypt, to Mr Peters'
dyspepsia, and on a dozen other branch lines of thought.

He blamed the fat man at the inn for this. If the fat
man had not thrust his presence and conversation upon
him, he would have been able to enjoy a sound sleep in
the afternoon, and would have come fresh to his
nocturnal task. He began to muse upon the fat man.

And, by a curious coincidence, whom should he meet
a few moments later but this same man.

It happened in a somewhat singular manner, though
it all seemed perfectly logical and consecutive to Baxter.
He was climbing up the outer wall of Westminster
Abbey in his pyjamas and a tall hat, when the fat man,
suddenly thrusting his head out of a window which
Baxter had not noticed till that moment, said, 'Hullo,
Freddie!' Baxter was about to explain that his name was
not Freddie, when he found himself walking down
Piccadilly with Ashe Marson. Ashe said to him, 'Nobody
loves me!' and the pathos of it cut the Efficient Baxter
like a knife. He was on the point of replying, but Ashe
vanished and Baxter discovered that he was not in
Piccadilly, as he had supposed, but in an aeroplane with
Mr Peters, hovering over the Castle. Mr Peters had a
bomb in his hand, which he was fondling with loving
care. He explained to Baxter that he had stolen it from
the Earl of Emsworth's museum. 'I did it with a slice of
cold beef and a pickle,' he explained, and Baxter found
himself realizing that that was the only way.

'Now watch me drop it,' said Mr Peters, closing one

eye and taking aim at the Castle. 'I have to do this by
the doctor's orders.' He loosed the bomb, and
immediately Baxter was in bed watching it drop. He was
frightened, but the idea of moving did not occur to him.
The bomb fell slowly, dipping and fluttering like a
feather. It came closer and closer. Then it struck with a
roar and a sheet of flame . . .

Baxter awoke to a sound of tumult and crashing. For a
moment he hovered between dreaming and waking, and
then sleep passed from him, and he was aware that
something noisy and exciting was in progress in the Hall
below.

IV

Coming down to first causes, the only reason why
collisions of any kind occur is because two bodies defy
Nature's law that a given spot on a given plane shall at a
given moment of time be occupied by only one body.
There was a certain spot near the foot of the great
staircase which Ashe, coming downstairs, and George
Emerson, coming up, had to pass on their respective
routes. George reached it at one minute and three
seconds after 2 a.m., moving silently but swiftly, and
Ashe, also maintaining a good rate of speed, arrived
there at one minute and four seconds after the hour,
when he ceased to walk and began to fly, accompanied
by George Emerson, now going down. His arms were
round George's neck, and George was clinging to his
waist. In due season they reached the foot of the stairs
and a small table covered with occasional china and
photographs in frames which lay adjacent to the foot of
the stairs.

That, especially the occasional china, was what
Baxter had heard.

George Emerson thought it was a burglar. Ashe did
not know what it was, but he knew he wanted to shake

it off, so he insinuated a hand beneath George's chin and pushed upwards. George, by this time parted for ever from the tongue, the bread, the knife, the fork, the salt, the corkscrew, and the bottle of white wine, and having both hands free for the work of the moment, held Ashe with the left and punched him in the ribs with the right. Ashe, removing his left arm from George's neck, brought it up as a reinforcement to his right, and used both as a means of throttling George. This led George, now permanently underneath, to grasp Ashe's ears firmly and twist them, relieving the pressure on his throat and causing Ashe to utter the first vocal sound of the evening, other than the explosive '*Ugh*' which both had emitted at the instant of impact. Ashe dislodged George's hands from his ears, and hit George in the ribs with his elbow. George kicked Ashe on the left ankle. Ashe rediscovered George's throat and began to squeeze it afresh, and a pleasant time was being had by all, when the Efficient Baxter, whizzing down the stairs, tripped over Ashe's legs, shot forward, and cannoned into another table, also covered with occasional china and photographs in frames. The hall at Blandings Castle was more an extra drawing-room than a hall, and, when not nursing a sick headache in her bedroom, Lady Ann Warblington would dispense afternoon tea there to her guests. Consequently it was dotted pretty freely with small tables. There were, indeed, no fewer than five or more in various spots waiting to be bumped into and smashed.

But the bumping into and smashing of small tables is a task that calls for plenty of time, a leisured pursuit, and neither George nor Ashe, a third party having been added to their little affair, felt a desire to stay on and do the thing properly. Ashe was strongly opposed to being discovered and called upon to account for his presence there at that hour, and George, conscious of the tongue and its adjuncts now strewn about the hall, had a similar prejudice against the tedious explanations which detection must involve. As if by mutual consent each relaxed his grip. They stood panting for an instant, then, Ashe in the direction where he supposed the green-baize door of the servants' quarters to be, George to the staircase which led to his bedroom, they went away from that place.

They had hardly done so, when Baxter, having dissociated himself from the contents of the table which he had upset, began to grope his way towards the electric light switch, the same being situated near the foot of the main staircase. He went on all fours, as a safer method of locomotion, if slower, than the one which he had attempted before.

Noises began to make themselves heard on the floors above. Roused by the merry crackle of occasional china, the house-party was bestirring itself to investigate. Voices sounded, muffled and inquiring.

Baxter, meanwhile, crawled steadily on his hands and knees towards the light switch. He was in much the same condition as one White Hope of the ring is after he has put his chin in the way of the fist of a rival member of the Truck-drivers' Union. He knew that he was still alive. More he could not say. The mists of sleep which still shrouded his brain and the shaking-up he had had from his encounter with the table, a corner of which he had rammed with the top of his head, combined to produce a dream-like state.

And so the Efficient Baxter crawled on, and as he crawled his hand, advancing cautiously, fell on a Something – a something that was not alive, something clammy and icy-cold, the touch of which filled him with a nameless horror.

To say that Baxter's heart stood still would be medically inexact. The heart does not stand still. Whatever the emotions of its owner, it goes on beating. It would be more accurate to say that Baxter felt like a man taking his first ride in an express elevator who has outstripped his vital organs by several floors and sees no immediate prospect of their ever catching up with him again. There was a great cold void where the more intimate parts of his body should have been. His throat was dry and contracted. The flesh of his back crawled. For he knew what it was that he had touched.

Painful and absorbing as had been his encounter with the table, Baxter had never lost sight of the fact that close beside him a furious battle between unseen forces was in progress. He had heard the bumping and the thumping and the tense breathing even as he picked occasional china from his person. Such a combat, he had felt, could hardly fail to result in personal injury to either the party of the first part or the party of the second part, or both. He knew now that worse than mere injury had happened, and that he knelt in the presence of death.

There was no doubt that the man was dead. Insensibility alone could never have produced this icy chill.

He raised his head in the darkness, and cried aloud, to those approaching.

He meant to cry, 'Help! Murder!' but fear prevented clear articulation.

What he shouted was, 'Heh! Mer!'

Upon which, from the neighbourhood of the staircase, someone began to fire off a revolver.

The Earl of Emsworth had been sleeping a sound and peaceful sleep when the imbroglio began downstairs. He sat up and listened. Yes, undoubtedly burglars. He switched on his light and jumped out of bed. He took a pistol from the drawer, and thus armed, went to look into the matter. The dreamy peer was no poltroon.

It was quite dark when he arrived on the scene of conflict in the van of a mixed bevy of pyjamaed and dressing-gowned relations. He was in the van because

meeting those relations in the passage above, he had said
to them, 'Let me go first. I have a pistol.' And they had
let him go first. They were, indeed, awfully nice about
it, not thrusting themselves forward or jostling or
anything, but behaving in a modest and self-effacing
manner which was pretty to watch. When Lord
Emsworth said, 'Let me go first,' young Algernon
Wooster, who was on the very point of leaping to the
fore, said, 'Yes, by Jove, sound scheme, by Gad!' and
withdrew into the background, and the Bishop of
Godalming said, 'By all means, Clarence, undoubtedly,
most certainly precede us.'

When his sense of touch told him that he had reached
the foot of the stairs, Lord Emsworth paused. The Hall
was very dark, and the burglars seemed temporarily to
have suspended activities. And then one of them, a man
with a ruffianly grating voice, spoke. What it was he
said, Lord Emsworth could not understand. It sounded
like 'Heh! Mer!' Probably some secret signal to his
confederate. Lord Emsworth raised his revolver and
emptied it in the direction of the sound.

Extremely fortunate for him, the Efficient Baxter had
not changed his all-fours attitude. This undoubtedly
saved Lord Emsworth the worry of engaging a new
secretary. The shots sang above Baxter's head, one after
the other, six in all, and found themselves billets other
than his person. They disposed themselves as follows.
The first shot broke a window and whistled out into the
night. The second shot hit the dinner-gong and made a
perfectly extraordinary noise like the Last Trump. The
third, fourth, and fifth shots embedded themselves in
the wall. The sixth and final shot hit a life-size picture
of his lordship's maternal grandmother in the face and
improved it out of all knowledge. One thinks no worse
of Lord Emsworth's maternal grandmother because she
looked like George Robey, and had allowed herself to be
painted, after the heavy Classical manner of some of the

portraits of a hundred years ago, in the character of
Venus (suitably draped, of course) rising from the sea;
but it was beyond the possibility of denial that her
grandson's bullet permanently removed one of Blandings
Castle's most prominent eyesores.

Having emptied his revolver, Lord Emsworth said,
'Who is there? Speak!' in rather an aggrieved tone, as if
he felt he had done his part in breaking the ice and it
was now for the intruder to exert himself and bear his
share of the social amenities.

The Efficient Baxter did not reply. Nothing in the
world would have induced him to speak at that moment
or to make any sound whatsoever that might betray his
position to a dangerous maniac who might at any
instant reload his pistol and resume the fusillade.
Explanations, in his opinion, could be deferred till
somebody had the presence of mind to switch on the
lights. He flattened himself on the carpet, and hoped for
better things. His cheek touched the corpse beside him,
but, though he winced and shuddered, he made no
outcry. After those six shots he was through with
outcries.

A voice from above – the Bishop's voice – said, 'I
think you have killed him, Clarence.'

Another voice – that of Colonel Horace Mant – said,
'Switch on those dashed lights, why doesn't someone,
dash it?'

The whole strength of the company began to demand
light.

When the lights came it was from the other side of
the Hall. Six revolver shots, fired at a quarter-past two in
the morning, will rouse even sleeping domestics. The
servants' quarters were buzzing like a hive. Shrill
feminine screams were puncturing the air. Mr Beach, the
butler, in a suit of pink silk pyjamas of which no one
would have suspected him, was leading a party of
men-servants down the stairs, not so much because he

wanted to lead them as because they pushed him. The passage beyond the green-baize door became congested, and there were cries for Mr Beach to open it, and look through and see what was the matter, but Mr Beach was smarter than that, and wriggled back so that he no longer headed the procession.

This done, he shouted. 'Open the door there, open that door. Look and see what the matter is.'

Ashe opened the door. Since his escape from the Hall he had been lurking in the neighbourhood of the green baize, and had been engulfed by the swirling throng. Finding himself with elbow-room for the first time, he pushed through, swung the door open, and switched on the lights.

They shone on a collection of semi-dressed figures, crowding the staircase, on a hall littered with china and glass, on a dented dinner-gong, on an edited and improved portrait of the late Countess of Emsworth, and on the Efficient Baxter, in an overcoat and rubber-soled shoes, lying beside a cold tongue.

At no great distance lay a number of other objects – a knife, a fork, some bread, salt, a corkscrew, and a bottle of white wine.

Using the word in the sense of saying something coherent the Earl of Emsworth was the first to speak. He peered down at his recumbent secretary and said, 'Baxter! My dear fellow, what the devil?'

The feeling of the company was one of profound disappointment. They were disgusted at the anti-climax. For an instant, when the Efficient one did not move, hope began to stir, but as soon as it was seen that he was not even injured, gloom reigned. One of two things would have satisfied them – either a burglar or a corpse. A burglar would have been welcome, dead or alive, but if Baxter proposed to fill the part adequately, it was imperative that he be dead. He had disappointed them deeply by turning out to be the object of their quest.

That he should not have been even grazed was too much.

There was a cold silence as he slowly raised himself from the floor.

As his eyes fell on the tongue, he started, and remained gazing fixedly at it. Surprise paralysed him.

Lord Emsworth was also looking at the tongue, and he leaped to a not unreasonable conclusion. He spoke coldly and haughtily, for he was not only annoyed like the others at the anti-climax, but offended. He knew that he was not one of your energetic hosts who exert themselves unceasingly to supply their guests with entertainment, but there was one thing on which, as a host, he did pride himself. In the material matters of life he did his guests well. He kept an admirable table.

'My dear Baxter,' he said in the tones which usually he reserved for the correction of his son Freddie, 'if your hunger is so great that you are unable to wait for breakfast and have to raid my larder in the middle of the night, I wish to goodness you would contrive to make less noise about it, I do not grudge you the food – help yourself when you please but do remember that people who have not such keen appetites as yourself, like to sleep during the night. A far better plan, my dear fellow, would be to have sandwiches – or buns – whatever you consider most sustaining sent up to your bedroom.'

Not even the bullets had disordered Baxter's faculties so much as this monstrous accusation. Explanations pushed and jostled one another in his fermenting brain, but he could not utter them. On every side he met gravely reproachful eyes. George Emerson was looking at him in pained disgust. Ashe Marson's face was the face of one who could never have believed this had he not seen it with his own eyes. The scrutiny of the knife-and-shoe boy was unendurable.

He stammered. Words began to proceed from him, tripping and stumbling over each other.

Lord Emsworth's frigid disapproval did not relax.

'Pray do not apologize, Baxter. The desire for food is human. It is your boisterous mode of securing and conveying it that I deprecate. Let us all go to bed.'

'But, Lord Emsworth –!'

'To bed,' repeated his lordship firmly.

The company began to stream moodily upstairs. The lights were switched off. The Efficient Baxter dragged himself away.

From the darkness in the direction of the servants' door a voice spoke.

'Greedy pig!' said the voice scornfully.

It sounded like the fresh young voice of the knife-and-shoe boy, but Baxter was too broken to investigate. He continued his retreat without pausing.

'Stuffin' of 'isself at all hours!' said the voice.

There was a murmur of approval from the unseen throng of domestics.

9

As we grow older and realize more clearly the limitations of human happiness, we come to see that the only real and abiding pleasure in life is to give pleasure to other people. One must assume that the Efficient Baxter had not reached the age when this comes home to a man, for the fact that he had given genuine pleasure to some dozens of his fellow-men brought him no balm.

There was no doubt about the pleasure which he had given. Once they had got over their disappointment at finding that he was not a dead burglar, the house-party rejoiced whole-heartedly at the break in the monotony of life at Blandings Castle. Relations who had not been on speaking terms for years forgot their quarrels, and strolled about the grounds in perfect harmony, abusing Baxter. The general verdict was that he was insane.

'Don't tell me that young fellow's all there,' said Colonel Horace Mant, 'because I know better. Have you noticed his eye? Furtive! Shifty! Nasty gleam in it. Besides, dash it, did you happen to take a look at the Hall last night after he had been there? It was in ruins, my dear sir, absolute dashed ruins. It was positively littered with broken china and tables which had been bowled over. Don't tell me that was just an accidental collision in the dark. My dear sir, the man must have been thrashing about, absolutely *thrashing* about, like a dashed salmon on a dashed hook. He must have had a paroxysm of some kind. Some kind of a dashed fit. A doctor could give you the name for it. It's a well-known form of insanity. Paranoia – isn't that what they call it? Rush of blood to the head, followed by a general running amuck. I've heard fellows who have been in India talk of it. Natives get it. Don't know what they're doing, and charge through the streets taking cracks at people with dashed whacking great knives. Same with this young man, probably in a modified form at present. He ought to be in a Home. One of these nights, if the thing grows on him, he will be massacring Emsworth in his bed.'

'My dear Horace!'

The Bishop of Godalming's voice was properly horror-stricken, but there was a certain unctuous relish in it.

'Take my word for it. Though, mind you, I don't say they aren't well suited. Every one knows that Emsworth has been to all practical intents and purposes a dashed lunatic for years.'

'My dear Horace! Your father-in-law. The head of the family.'

'A dashed lunatic, my dear sir, head of the family or no head of the family. A man as absent-minded as he is has no right to call himself sane.'

The Efficient Baxter, who had just left his presence, was feeling much the same about his noble employer. After a sleepless night he had begun at an early hour to try and corner Lord Emsworth in order to explain to him the true inwardness of last night's happenings. Eventually he had tracked him to the museum where he had found him happily engaged in painting a cabinet of birds' eggs. He was seated on a small stool, a large pot of red paint on the floor beside him, dabbing at the cabinet with a dripping brush. He was absorbed, and made no attempt whatever to follow his secretary's remarks.

For ten minutes Baxter gave a vivid picture of his vigil and the manner in which it had been interrupted.

'Just so, just so, my dear fellow,' said the earl, when he had finished. 'I quite understand. All I say is, if you do require additional food in the night, let one of the servants bring it to your room, before bed-time, then there will be no danger of these disturbances. There is no possible objection to your eating a hundred meals a day, my good Baxter, provided you do not rouse the whole house over them. Some of us like to sleep during the night.'

'But Lord Emsworth! I have just explained . . . It was not . . . I was not . . . !'

'Never mind, my dear fellow, never mind. Why make such an important thing of it? Many people like a light snack before actually retiring. Doctors, I believe, sometimes recommend it. Tell me, Baxter, how do you think the museum looks now? A little brighter? Better for the dash of colour? I think so. Museums are generally such gloomy places.'

'Lord Emsworth, may I explain once again?'

The earl looked annoyed.

'My dear Baxter, I have told you that there is nothing to explain. You are getting a little tedious . . . What a deep, rich red this is, and how clean new paint smells! Do you know, Baxter, I have been longing to mess about with paint ever since I was a boy. I recollect my old father beating me with a walking-stick. That would be before your time, of course. By the way, if you see Freddie, will you tell him I want to speak to him? He is probably in the smoking-room. Send him to me here.'

It was an overwrought Baxter who delivered the message to the Hon. Freddie, who, as predicted, was in the smoking-room, lounging in a deep armchair.

There are times when Life presses hard upon a man, and it pressed hard on Baxter now. Fate had played him a sorry trick. It had put him in a position where he had to choose between two courses, each as disagreeable as the other. He must either face a possible fiasco like that of last night, or else he must abandon his post and cease to mount guard over his threatened treasure.

His imagination quailed at the thought of a repetition of last night's horrors. He had been badly shaken by his collision with the table and even more so by the events which had followed it. Those revolver shots still rang in his ears.

It was probably the memory of those shots which turned the scale. It was unlikely that he would again become entangled with a man bearing a tongue and the other things – he had given up in despair the attempt to unravel the mystery of the tongue; it completely baffled him; but it was by no means unlikely that, if he spent another night in the gallery looking on the Hall, he might again become a target for Lord Emsworth's irresponsible fire-arm. Nothing, in fact, was more likely, for in the disturbed state of the public mind the slightest sound after nightfall would be sufficient cause for a fusillade. He had actually overheard young Algernon Wooster telling Lord Stockheath that he had a jolly good mind to sit upon the stairs that night with a shot-gun, because it was his opinion that there was a jolly sight more in this business than there seemed to be, and that what he thought of the bally affair was that there was a gang of some kind at work and that that feller, what's-his-name, that feller Baxter, was some sort of an accomplice.

With these things in his mind, Baxter decided to remain that night in the security of his bedroom. He had lost his nerve.

He formed this decision with the utmost reluctance, for the thought of leaving the road to the museum clear for marauders was bitter in the extreme.

If he could have overheard a conversation between Joan Valentine and Ashe Marson, it is probable that he would have risked Lord Emsworth's revolver and the shot-gun of the Honourable Algernon Wooster.

Ashe, when he met Joan and recounted the events of the past night, at which Joan, who was a sound sleeper, had not been present, was inclined to blame himself as a

failure. True, fate had been against him but the fact
remained that he had achieved nothing.

Joan, however, was not of this opinion.

'You have done wonders,' she said. 'You have cleared
the way for me. That is my idea of real team-work. I'm
so glad now that we formed our partnership. It would
have been too bad if I had got all the advantage of your
work and had jumped in and deprived you of the reward.
As it is, I shall go down and finish the thing off tonight
with a clear conscience.'

'You can't mean that you dream of going down to the
museum tonight?'

'Of course I do.'

'But it's madness.'

'On the contrary, tonight is the one night when there
ought to be no risk at all.'

'After what happened last night?'

'Because of what happened last night. Do you imagine
that Mr Baxter will dare to stir from his bed after that? If
ever there was a chance of getting this thing finished, it
will be tonight.'

'You're quite right. I never looked at it in that way.
Baxter wouldn't risk a second disaster. I'll certainly
make a success of it this time.'

Joan raised her eyebrows.

'I don't quite understand you, Mr Marson. Do you
propose to try and get the scarab again tonight?'

'Yes. It will be as easy as –'

'Are you forgetting that, by the terms of our
agreement, it is my turn?'

'You surely don't intend to hold me to that?'

'Certainly I do.'

'But good heavens, consider my position! Do you
seriously expect me to lie in bed while you do all the
work, and then to take a half share in the reward?'

'I do.'

'It's ridiculous.'

'It's no more ridiculous than that I should do the same. Mr Marson, it's no use our going over all this again. We settled it long ago.'

And she refused to discuss the matter further, leaving Ashe in a condition of anxious misery comparable only to that which, as night began to draw near, gnawed the vitals of the Efficient Baxter.

II

Breakfast at Blandings Castle was an informal meal. There was food and drink in the long dining-hall for such as were energetic enough to come down and get it, but the majority of the house-party breakfasted in their rooms, Lord Emsworth, whom nothing in the world would have induced to begin the day in the company of a crowd of his relations, most of whom he disliked, setting them the example.

When, therefore, Baxter, yielding to Nature after having remained awake till the early morning, fell asleep at nine o'clock, nobody came to rouse him. He did not ring his bell, so he was not disturbed, and he slept on until half past eleven, by which time, it being Sunday morning and the house-party including one bishop and several of the minor clergy, most of the occupants of the place had gone off to church.

Baxter shaved and dressed hastily, for he was in a state of nervous apprehension. He blamed himself for having lain in bed so long. When every minute he was away might mean the loss of the scarab, he had passed several hours in dreamy sloth.

He had woken with a presentiment. Something told him that the scarab had been stolen in the night, and he wished now that he had risked all and kept guard.

The house was very quiet as he made his way rapidly to the Hall. As he passed a window, he perceived Lord

Emsworth, in an un-Sabbatarian suit of tweeds and
bearing a gardening-fork, which must have pained the
Bishop, bending earnestly over a flower-bed; but he was
the only occupant of the grounds, and indoors there was
a feeling of emptiness. The Hall had that Sunday
morning air of wanting to be left to itself and
disapproving of the entry of anything human till lunch
time, which can only be felt by a guest in a large house
who remains at home when his fellows have gone to
church.

The portraits on the walls, especially the one of the
late Countess of Emsworth in the character of Venus
rising from the sea, stared at Baxter, as he entered, with
cold reproof. The very chairs seemed distant and
unfriendly. But Baxter was in no mood to appreciate
their attitude. His conscience slept. His mind was
occupied, to the exclusion of all other things, by the
scarab and its probable fate. How disastrously remiss it
had been of him not to keep guard last night! Long
before he opened the museum door he was feeling the
absolute certainty that the worst had happened.

His premonition was correct. The museum was still
there; the card announcing that here was a scarab of the
reign of Cheops of the Fourth Dynasty, presented by Mr
J. Preston Peters, was still there; the mummies, birds'
eggs, tapestry, missals, and all the rest of Lord
Emsworth's treasures were still there.

But the scarab was gone.

III

For all that this was precisely what he had expected, it
was an appreciable time before the Efficient Baxter
rallied from the blow. He stood transfixed, goggling at
the empty place.

He was still goggling when the Earl of Emsworth
pottered in. The Earl of Emsworth was one of the

world's leading potterers, and Sunday morning was his
favourite time for pottering. Since breakfast he had
pottered about the garden, pottered round the stables,
and pottered about the library. He now pottered into the
museum.

'Lord Emsworth!'

By the time Baxter sighted him and gave tongue, the
earl had pottered to within a foot or so of where the
secretary stood. A whisper would have reached him, but
such was the Efficient Baxter's emotion that he emitted
the words in a sharp roar which would have been
noticeably stentorian in a sea-captain exchanging
remarks with one of his men who happened at the
moment to be working in the crow's-nest. Lord
Emsworth sprang six feet, and, having disentangled
himself from a piece of old tapestry, put one hand to his
ear and, massaging it tenderly, glared at his young
assistant.

'What do you mean by barking at me like that, Baxter?
Really, you exceed all bounds. You are becoming a
perfect pest.'

'Lord Emsworth, it has gone. The scarab has gone.'

'You have broken my ear-drum.'

'Somebody has stolen the scarab which Mr Peters gave
you, Lord Emsworth.'

The probable fate of his ear-drum ceased to grip the
earl's undivided attention. He followed the secretary's
pointing finger with a startled eye, and examined the
spot where the tragedy had occurred.

'Bless my soul. You're perfectly right, my dear fellow.
Somebody has stolen the scarab. This is extremely
annoying. Mr Peters may be offended. I should dislike
intensely to wound Mr Peters' feelings. He may think
that I ought to have taken more care of it. Now, who in
the world could have stolen that scarab?'

Baxter was about to reply, when there came from the
direction of the Hall, slightly muffled by the intervening

door and passageway, a sound like the delivery of a ton of coal. A heavy body bumped down the stairs, and a voice which both recognized as that of the Hon. Freddie Threepwood uttered an oath that lost itself in a final crash and a musical splintering sound which Baxter for one had no difficulty in diagnosing as the dissolution of occasional china.

Neither Lord Emsworth nor Baxter had any difficulty in deducing from the evidence what had happened. The Hon. Freddie had fallen downstairs.

With a little ingenuity this portion of the story of Mr Peters' scarab could be converted into an excellent tract, driving home the perils, even in this world, of absenting oneself from church on Sunday morning. If the Hon. Freddie had gone to church, he would not have been running down the great staircase of the Castle at this hour; and, if he had not been running down the great staircase of the Castle at that hour, he would not have encountered Muriel.

Muriel was a Persian cat belonging to Lady Ann Warblington. Lady Ann had breakfasted in her room and lain in bed late, as she rather fancied that she had one of her sick headaches coming on. Muriel had left the room in the wake of the breakfast tray, being anxious to be present at the obsequies of a fried sole which had formed Lady Ann's simple meal, and had followed the maid who bore it until she had reached the Hall. At this point, the maid, who disliked Muriel, stopped and made a noise like an exploding ginger-beer bottle, at the same time taking a little run in Muriel's direction and kicking at her with a menacing foot. Muriel, wounded and startled, turned in her tracks and sprinted back up the stairs, at the exact moment when the Hon. Freddie, who for some reason was in a great hurry, ran lightly down them.

There was an instant when Freddie could have saved himself at the expense of planting a number ten boot on Muriel's spine, but even in that crisis he bethought him that he hardly stood solid enough with the authorities to risk adding to his misdeeds the slaughter of his aunt's favourite cat, and he executed a rapid swerve. The scared cat proceeded on her journey upstairs, while Freddie, touching the staircase at intervals, went on down.

Having reached the bottom, he sat amidst the occasional china like Marius among the ruins of Carthage, and endeavoured to ascertain the extent of his injuries. He had a growing suspicion that he was irretrievably fractured in a dozen places.

When his father and the Efficient Baxter arrived, they found him being helped to his feet by Ashe Marson.

Ashe had been near at hand when the secretary made the discovery that the museum had been robbed in the night. He had, indeed, anticipated Baxter in that discovery by a matter of minutes. For some little time he had been in waiting behind the green-baize door, hoping for an opportunity of finding whether Joan had carried out her threat of stealing the scarab, and he had contrived to pop in and out of the museum while the Hall was empty. It was not until he heard Baxter's voice raised in anguish that he realized how nearly he had been discovered. He had waited in his place of hiding during the conversation between the secretary and Lord Emsworth, and, like them, had been drawn to the stairs by the noise of Freddie's downfall.

He gave the victim a tentative pull, but Freddie sat down again with a sharp howl. He was still seated when the others arrived. He gazed up at them with silent pathos.

'It was that bally cat of Aunt Ann's, guv'nor. It came legging it up the stairs. I think I've broken my ankle.'

'You certainly have broken everything else,' said his father unsympathetically. 'Between you and Baxter I wonder there's a stick of furniture standing in the house.'

'Thanks, old chap,' said Freddie, gratefully, as Ashe

once more assisted him to his feet. 'I wish you would give me a hand up to my room.'

'And Baxter, my dear fellow,' said Lord Emsworth, 'you might telephone to Doctor Bird in Market Blandings and ask him to be good enough to drive out. I am sorry, Freddie,' he added, 'that you should have met with this accident, but – but – everything is so disturbing nowadays that I feel – I feel most disturbed.'

Ashe and Freddie began to move across the Hall, Freddie hopping, Ashe advancing with a sort of polka-step. Baxter stood looking after them wistfully. The sight of Ashe, coming on top of the discovery of the loss of the scarab, made him feel more clearly than ever that he had been out-manoeuvred. He was quite certain in his mind that Ashe was the thief, and the impossibility of denouncing him made life for the moment very bitter.

There was a sound of wheels outside, and the vanguard of the party, returned from church, entered the house.

'It's all very well to give it out officially that Freddie fell downstairs and sprained his ankle,' said Colonel Mant, discussing the affair with the Bishop of Godalming later in the day, 'but it's my firm belief that that fellow Baxter did precisely as I said he would – ran amuck and inflicted dashed frightful injuries on young Freddie. When I got into the house, there was Freddie being helped up the stairs, while Baxter was looking after him with a sort of evil glare. The whole thing is dashed fishy and mysterious, and the sooner I can get Mildred safely out of the place, the better I shall be pleased. The fellow's as mad as a hatter.'

IV

When Lord Emsworth, sighting Mr Peters in the group of
returned churchgoers, drew him aside and broke the
news that the valuable scarab so kindly presented by
him to the Castle museum had been stolen in the night
by some person unknown, he thought that the
millionaire took it exceedingly well. Although the
stolen object no longer belonged to him, Mr Peters no
doubt still continued to take an affectionate interest in
it, and might have been excused had he shown
annoyance that his gift had been so carelessly guarded.

He was, however, thoroughly magnanimous about
the matter. He deprecated the notion that the earl could
possibly have prevented this unfortunate occurrence. He
quite understood. He was not in the least hurt. Nobody
could have foreseen such a calamity. These things
happened, and one had to accept them. He himself had
once suffered in much the same way, the gem of his
collection having been removed almost beneath his eyes
in the smoothest possible fashion. Altogether, he
relieved Lord Emsworth's mind very much; and, when
he had finished doing so, he departed swiftly and rang
for Ashe.

When Ashe arrived he bubbled over with enthusiasm.
He was lyrical in his praise. He went so far as to slap
Ashe on the back. It was only when the latter disclaimed
all credit for what had occurred that he checked the flow
of approbation.

'It wasn't you who got it? Who was it then?'

'It was Miss Peters' maid. It's a long story, but we
were working in partnership. I tried for the thing and
failed, and she succeeded.'

It was with mixed feelings that Ashe listened while
Mr Peters transferred his adjectives of commendation to
Joan. He admired Joan's courage, he was relieved that
her venture had ended without disaster, and he knew

that she deserved whatever anyone could find to say in praise of her enterprise; but at first, though he tried to crush it down, he could not help feeling a certain amount of chagrin that a girl should have succeeded where he, though having the advantage of first chance, had failed. The terms of his partnership with Joan had jarred on him from the beginning. A man may be in sympathy with the modern movement for the emancipation of Women, and yet feel aggrieved when a mere girl proves herself a more efficient thief than he. Woman is invading Man's sphere more successfully every day, but there are still certain fields in which Man may consider that he is rightfully entitled to a monopoly, and the purloining of scarabs in the watches of the night is surely one of them. Joan, in Ashe's opinion, should have played a meeker and less active part.

These unworthy emotions did not last long. Whatever his short-comings, Ashe possessed a just mind. By the time he had found Joan, after Mr Peters had said his say and dispatched him below stairs for that purpose, he had purged himself of petty regrets and was prepared to congratulate her whole-heartedly. He was, however, resolved that nothing should induce him to share in the reward. On that point, he resolved, he would refuse to be shaken.

'I have just left Mr Peters,' he began. 'All is well. His cheque-book lies before him on the table, and he is trying to make his fountain-pen work long enough to write a cheque. But there is just one thing I want to say.'

She interrupted him. To his surprise, she was eyeing him coldly and with disapproval.

'And there is just one thing I want to say,' she said. 'And that is that, if you imagine that I shall consent to accept a penny of the reward –'

'Exactly what I was going to say. Of course, I couldn't dream of taking any of it.'

'I don't understand you. You are certainly going to have it all. I told you when we made our agreement that I would only take my share if you let me do my share of the work. Now that you have broken that agreement, nothing would induce me to take it. I know you meant it kindly, Mr Marson, but I simply can't feel grateful. I told you that ours was a business contract, and that I wouldn't have any chivalry, and I thought that, after you had given me your promise – '

'One moment,' said Ashe bewildered. 'I can't follow this. What do you mean?'

'What do I mean? Why, that you went down to the museum last night before me and took the scarab, although you had promised to stay away and give me my chance.'

'But I didn't do anything of the sort.'

It was Joan's turn to look bewildered.

'But you have got the scarab, Mr Marson?'

'Why, you have got it.'

'No.'

'But – but it has gone.'

'I know. I went down to the museum last night, as we had arranged, and, when I got there, there was no scarab. It had disappeared.'

They looked at each other in consternation. Ashe was the first to speak.

'It was gone when you got to the museum?'

'There wasn't a trace of it. I took it for granted that you had been down before me. I was furious.'

'But this is ridiculous,' said Ashe. 'Who can have taken it? There was nobody beside ourselves who knew that Peters was offering the reward. What exactly happened last night?'

'I waited till one o'clock. Then I slipped down, got into the museum, struck a match, and looked for the scarab. It wasn't there. I couldn't believe it at first. I struck some more matches, quite a number, but it was no good. The scarab had gone, so I went back to bed, and thought hard thoughts about you. It was silly of me. I ought to have known that you would not break your word. But there didn't seem any other solution of the thing's disappearance. Well, somebody must have taken it, and the question is, What are we to do?' She laughed. 'It seems to me that we were a little premature in quarrelling about how we were to divide that reward. It looks as if there wasn't going to be any reward.'

'Meanwhile,' said Ashe gloomily, 'I suppose I have got to go back and tell Peters. I expect it will break his heart.'

IO

Blandings Castle dozed in the calm of Sunday afternoon.
All was peace. Freddie was in bed, with orders from the
doctor to stay there till further notice. Lord Emsworth
had returned to his gardening-fork. The rest of the
house-party strolled about the grounds or sat in them,
for the day was one of those late Spring days which are
warm with a premature suggestion of mid-summer.

Aline Peters was sitting at the open window of her
bedroom, which commanded an extensive view of the
terraces. A pile of letters lay on the table beside her. The
postman came late to the Castle on Sundays, and she
had not been able to read them until lunch was over.

Aline was puzzled. She was conscious of a fit of
depression, for which she could in no way account. As a
rule something had to go very definitely wrong to make
her depressed, for she was not a girl who brooded easily
on the vague undercurrent of sadness in Life. As a rule
she found nothing tragic in the fact that she was alive.
She liked being alive.

But this afternoon she had a feeling that all was not
well with the world, which was the more remarkable in
that she was usually keenly susceptible to weather
conditions and revelled in sunshine like a kitten. Yet
here was a day nearly as fine as an American day and she
found no solace in it.

She looked down on the terrace, and as she looked the
figure of George Emerson appeared, walking swiftly. And
at the sight of him something seemed to tell her that she
had found the key to her gloom.

There are many kinds of walk. George Emerson's was

the walk of mental unrest. His hands were clasped behind his back, his eyes stared straight in front of him from beneath lowering brows, and between his teeth was an unlighted cigar. No man holds an unlighted cigar in his mouth unless unpleasant meditations have caused him to forget that he has it there. Plainly, then, all was not well with George Emerson.

Aline had suspected as much at lunch, and, looking back, she realized that it was at lunch that her depression had begun. The discovery startled her a little. She had not been aware, or she had refused to admit to herself, that George's troubles bulked so large on her horizon. She had always told herself that she liked George, that George was a dear old friend, that George amused and stimulated her; but she would have denied that she was so wrapped up in George that the sight of him in trouble would be enough to spoil for her the finest day she had seen since she left America. There was something not only startling but shocking in the thought, for she was honest enough with herself to recognize that Freddie, her official loved one, might have paced the Castle grounds chewing an unlighted cigar by the hour without stirring any emotion in her at all.

And she was to marry Freddie next month. This was surely a matter that called for thought. She proceeded, gazing down the while to the perambulating George, to give it thought.

Aline's was not a deep nature. She had never pretended to herself that she loved the Hon. Freddie in the sense in which the word is used in books. She liked him, and she liked the idea of being connected with the Peerage, and her father liked the idea, and she liked her father, and the combination of these likings had caused her to reply, 'Yes' when, last Autumn, Freddie, swelling himself out like an embarrassed frog and gulping, had uttered that memorable speech, beginning, 'I say, you know, it's like this, don't you know,' and ending, 'What

I mean is, will you marry me, what?' She had looked
forward to being placidly happy as the Hon. Mrs
Frederick Threepwood. And then, George Emerson had
reappeared in her life, a disturbing element.

Until today she would have resented the suggestion
that she was in love with George. She liked to be with
him, partly because he was so easy to talk to, and partly
because it was exciting to be continually resisting the
will-power which he made no secret of trying to
exercise.

But today there was a difference. She had suspected it
at lunch, and she realized it now. As she looked down at
him from behind the curtain and marked his air of
gloom, she could no longer disguise it from herself.

She felt maternal, horribly maternal. George was in
trouble, and she wanted to comfort him.

Freddie too was in trouble. But did she want to
comfort Freddie? No. On the contrary, she was already
regretting her promise, so lightly given before lunch, to
come and sit with him that afternoon. A well-marked
feeling of annoyance that he should have been so silly as
to tumble downstairs and sprain his ankle was her chief
sentiment respecting Freddie.

George Emerson continued to perambulate, and Aline
continued to watch him. At last she could endure it no
longer. She gathered up her letters, stacked them in a
corner of the dressing-table, and left the room.

George had reached the end of the terrace and turned
when she began to descend the stone steps outside the
front door. He quickened his pace as he caught sight of
her. He halted before her and surveyed her morosely.

'I have been looking for you,' he said.

'And here I am. Cheer up, George. Whatever is the
matter? I've been sitting in my room looking at you, and
you have been simply prowling. What has gone wrong?'

'Everything.'

'How do you mean, everything?'

'Exactly what I say. I'm done for. Read this.'

Aline took the yellow slip of paper.

'A cable,' said George. 'I got it this morning, mailed on from my rooms in London. Read it.'

'I'm trying to. It doesn't seem to make sense.'

George laughed grimly.

'It makes sense all right.'

'I don't see how you can say that. "Meredith elephant kangaroo . . ."'

'Official cypher. I was forgetting. "Elephant" means "seriously ill and unable to attend to duty". Meredith is the man who was doing my work while I was on leave.'

'Oh, I'm so sorry. Do you think he is very bad? Are you very fond of Mr Meredith?'

'Meredith is a good fellow, and I like him, but if it was simply a matter of his being ill I'm afraid I could manage to bear up. Unfortunately "kangaroo" means "return without fail by the next boat".'

Aline looked at him, in her eyes slow-growing comprehension of the situation.

'Oh,' she said at length.

'I put it stronger than that,' said George.

'But . . . the next boat . . . when is that?'

'Wednesday morning. I shall have to leave here tomorrow.'

Aline's eyes were fixed on the blue hills across the valley, but she did not see them. There was a mist between. She was feeling crushed and ill-treated and lonely. It was as if George was already gone and she left alone in an alien land.

'But, George,' she said.

She could find no other words for her protest against the inevitable.

'It's bad luck,' said Emerson quietly. 'But I shouldn't wonder if it is not the best thing really that could have happened. It finishes me cleanly, instead of letting me drag on and make both of us miserable. If this cable

hadn't come, I suppose I should have gone on bothering
you up to the day of your wedding. I should have fancied
to the last moment that there was a chance for me. But
this ends me with one punch. Even I haven't the nerve
to imagine that I can work a miracle in the few hours
before the train leaves tomorrow. I must just make the
best of it. If we ever meet again, and I don't see why we
should, you will be married. My particular brand of
mental suggestion doesn't work at long range. I shan't
hope to influence you by telepathy.'

He leaned on the balustrade at her side, and spoke in
a low, level voice.

'This thing,' he said, 'coming as a shock, coming out
of the blue sky without warning – Meredith is the last
man in the world you would expect to crack up; he
looked as fit as a drayhorse last time I saw him –
somehow seems to have hammered a certain amount of
sense into me. Odd it never struck me before, but I
suppose I have been about the most bumptious,
conceited fool that ever happened. Why I should have
imagined that there was a sort of irresistible fascination
in me which was bound to make you break off your
engagement and upset the whole universe simply to win
the wonderful reward of marrying me, is more than I can
understand. I suppose it takes a shock to make a fellow
see exactly what he really amounts to. I couldn't think
any more of you than I do, but, if I could, the way you
have put up with my mouthing and swaggering and
posing as a sort of superman would make me do it. You
have been wonderful.'

Aline could not speak. She felt as if her whole world
had been turned upside down in the last quarter of an
hour. This was a new George Emerson, a George at
whom it was impossible to laugh, an insidiously
attractive George. Her heart beat quickly. Her mind was
not clear, but dimly she realized that he had pulled
down her chief barrier of defence, and that she was more

open to attack than she had ever been. Obstinacy, the automatic desire to resist the pressure of a will that attempted to overcome her own, had kept her cool and level-headed in the past. With masterfulness she had been able to cope. Humility was another thing altogether.

Soft-heartedness was Aline's weakness. She had never clearly recognized it, but it had been partly pity which had induced her to accept Freddie. He had seemed so downtrodden and sorry for himself during those Autumn days when they had first met. Prudence warned her that strange things might happen if once she allowed herself to pity George Emerson.

The silence lengthened. Aline could find nothing to say. In her present mood there was danger in speech.

'We have known each other so long,' said Emerson, 'and I have told you so often that I love you that we have come to make almost a joke of it, as if we were playing some game. It just happens that that is our way, to laugh at things. But I am going to say it once again, even if it has come to be a sort of catch-phrase. I love you. I'm reconciled to the fact that I am done for, out of the running, and that you are going to marry somebody else; but I am not going to stop loving you. It isn't a question of whether I should be happier if I forgot you. I can't do it. It's just an impossibility, and that's all there is to it. Whatever I may be to you, you are part of me, and you always will be part of me. I might just as well try to go on living without breathing as living without loving you.'

He stopped, and straightened himself.

'That's all. I don't want to spoil a perfectly good Spring afternoon for you by pulling out the tragic stop. I had to say all that, but it's the last time. It shan't occur again. There will be no tragedy when I step into the train tomorrow. Is there any chance that you might come and see me off?'

213

Aline nodded.

'You will? That will be splendid. Now I'll go and pack and break it to my host that I must leave him. I expect it will be news to him to learn that I am here. I doubt if he knows me by sight.'

Aline stood where he had left her, leaning on the balustrade.

In the fullness of time there came to her the recollection that she had promised Freddie that shortly after lunch she would come and sit with him.

The Hon. Freddie, draped in purple pyjamas and propped up with many pillows, was lying in bed, reading 'Gridley Quayle, Investigator'. Aline's entrance occurred at a peculiarly poignant moment in the story, and gave him a feeling of having been brought violently to earth from a flight in the clouds. It is not often that an author has the good fortune to grip a reader as the author of Gridley Quayle gripped Freddie.

One of the results of his absorbed mood was that he greeted Aline with a stare of an even glassier quality than usual. His eyes were by nature a trifle prominent, and to Aline, in the overstrung condition in which her talk with George Emerson had left her, they seemed to bulge at her like a snail's. A man seldom looks at his best in bed, and to Aline, seeing him for the first time at this disadvantage, the Hon. Freddie seemed quite repulsive. It was with a feeling of positive panic that she wondered whether he would want her to kiss him.

Freddie made no such demand. He was not one of your demonstrative lovers. He contented himself with rolling over in bed and dropping his lower jaw.

'Hullo, Aline.'

Aline sat down on the edge of the bed.

'Well, Freddie.'

Her betrothed improved his appearance a little by hitching up his lower jaw. As if feeling that that would be too extreme a measure, he did not close his mouth altogether, but he diminished the abyss. The Hon. Freddie belonged to the class of persons who move through life with their mouths always restfully open.

It seemed to Aline that on this particular afternoon a strange dumbness had descended upon her. She had been unable to speak to George, and now she could not think of anything to say to Freddie. She looked at him, and he looked at her, and the clock on the mantelpiece went on ticking.

'It was that bally cat of Aunt Ann's,' said Freddie at length, essaying light conversation. 'It came legging it up the stairs, and I took the most frightful toss. I hate cats. Do you hate cats? I knew a fellow in London who couldn't stand cats.'

Aline began to wonder if there was not something permanently wrong with her organs of speech. It should have been a simple matter to develop the cat theme, but she found herself unable to do so. Her mind was concentrated, to the exclusion of all else, on the repellent nature of the spectacle provided by her loved one in pyjamas.

Freddie resumed the conversation.

'I was just reading a corking book. Have you ever read these things? They come out every month, and they're corking. The fellow who writes them must be a corker. It beats me how he thinks of these things. They are about a detective, a chap called Gridley Quayle. Frightfully exciting.'

An obvious remedy for dumbness struck Aline.

'Shall I read to you, Freddie?'

'Right-ho! Good scheme. I've got to the top of this page.'

Aline took the paper-covered book.

' "Seven guns covered him with deadly precision." Did you get as far as that?'

'Yes, just beyond. It's a bit thick, don't you know. This chappie Quayle has been trapped in a lonely house,

thinking he was going to see a pal in distress, and
instead of the pal there pop out a whole squad of masked
blighters with guns. I don't see how he's going to get out
of it myself, but I bet he does. He's a corker.'

If anybody could have pitied Aline more than she
pitied herself, as she waded through the adventures of
Mr Quayle, it would have been Ashe Marson. He had
writhed as he wrote the words, and she writhed as she
read them. The Hon. Freddie also writhed, but with
intense excitement.

'What's the matter? Don't stop,' he cried, as Aline's
voice ceased.

'I'm getting hoarse, Freddie.'

Freddie hesitated. The desire to remain on the trail
with Gridley struggled with rudimentary politeness.

'How would it be . . . Would you mind if I just took a
look at the rest of it myself? We could talk afterwards,
don't you know. I shan't be long.'

'Of course. Do read if you want to. But do you really
like this sort of thing, Freddie?'

'Me! Rather. Why, don't you?'

'I don't know. It seems a little . . . I don't know.'

Freddie had become absorbed in his story. Aline did
not attempt further analysis of her attitude towards Mr
Quayle. She relapsed into silence.

It was a silence pregnant with thought. For the first
time in their relations, she was trying to visualize to
herself exactly what marriage with this young man
would mean. Hitherto, it struck her, she had really seen
so little of Freddie that she had scarcely had a chance of
examining him. In the crowded world outside he had
always seemed a tolerable enough person. Today,
somehow, he was different. Everything was different
today.

This, she took it, was a fair sample of what she might
expect after marriage. Marriage meant, to come to
essentials, that two people were very often and for

lengthy periods alone together, dependent on each other for mutual entertainment. What exactly would it be like being alone often for lengthy periods with Freddie?

Well, it would, she assumed, be like this.

'It's all right,' said Freddie without looking up. 'He *did* get out. He had a bomb on him, and he threatened to drop it and blow the place to pieces unless the blighters let him go. So they cheesed it. I knew he had something up his sleeve.'

Like this . . .

Aline drew a deep breath. It would be like this – for ever and ever and ever, till she died.

She bent forward, and stared at him.

'Freddie,' she said, 'do you love me?'

There was no reply.

'Freddie, do you love me? Am I a part of you? If you hadn't me, would it be like trying to go on living without breathing?'

The Hon. Freddie raised a flushed face, and gazed at her with an absent eye.

'Eh, what?' he said. 'Do I . . . ? Oh yes. Rather. I say, one of the blighters has just loosed a rattlesnake into Gridley Quayle's bedroom through the transom.'

Aline rose from her seat and left the room softly. The Hon. Freddie read on, unheeding.

II

Ashe had not fallen far short of the truth in his estimate of the probable effect on Mr Peters of the information that his precious scarab had once more been removed by alien hands and was now farther from his grasp than ever. A drawback to success in life is that failure, when it does come, acquires an exaggerated importance. Success had made Mr Peters, in certain aspects of his character, a spoiled child. At the moment when Ashe broke the news, he would have parted with half his

fortune to recover the scarab. Its recovery had become a
point of honour. He saw it as the prize of a contest
between his will and that of whatever malignant powers
there might be, ranged against him in the effort to show
him that there were limits to what he could achieve. He
felt as he had felt in the old days when people sneaked
up behind him in Wall Street and tried to loosen his grip
on a railway or a pet stock. He was suffering from that
form of paranoia which makes men multimillionaires.
Nobody would be foolish enough to become a
multimillionaire, if it were not for the desire to prove
himself irresistible.

He obtained a small relief for his feelings by doubling
the existing reward, and Ashe went off in search of Joan,
hoping that this new stimulus, acting on their joint
brains, might develop inspiration.

'Have any fresh ideas been vouchsafed to you?' he
asked. 'You may look on me as baffled.'

Joan shook her head.

'Don't give it up,' she urged. 'Think again. Try to
realize what this means, Mr Marson. Between us we
have lost ten thousand dollars, in a single night. I can't
afford it. It is like losing a legacy. I absolutely refuse to
give in without an effort and go back to writing
duke-and-earl stories for *Home Gossip*.'

'The prospect of tackling Gridley Quayle again –'

'Why, I was forgetting that you were a writer of
detective stories. You ought to be able to solve this
mystery in a moment. Ask yourself, what would Gridley
Quayle have done?'

'I can answer that. Gridley Quayle would have waited
helplessly for some coincidence to happen to help him
out.'

'Had he no methods?'

'He was full of methods. But they never led him
anywhere without a coincidence. However, we might try
to figure it out. What time did you get to the museum?'

'One o'clock.'

'And you found the scarab gone. What does that suggest to you?'

'Nothing. What does it suggest to you?'

'Absolutely nothing. Let us try again. Whoever took the scarab must have had special information that Peters was offering the reward.'

'Then why hasn't he been to Mr Peters and claimed it?'

'True. That would seem to be a flaw in the reasoning. Once again. Whoever took it must be in urgent and immediate need of money.'

'And how are we to find out who was in urgent and immediate need of money?'

'Exactly. How indeed?'

There was a pause.

'I should think your Mr Quayle must have been a great comfort to his clients, wasn't he?' said Joan.

'Inductive reasoning, I admit, seems to have fallen down to a certain extent,' said Ashe. 'We must wait for the coincidence. I have a feeling that it will come.' He paused. 'I am very fortunate in the way of coincidences.'

'Are you?'

Ashe looked about him, and was relieved to find that they appeared to be out of earshot of their species. It was not easy to achieve this position at the Castle, if you happened to be there as a domestic servant. The space provided for the ladies and gentlemen attached to the guests was limited, and it was rarely that you could enjoy a stroll without bumping into a maid, a valet, or a footman. But now they appeared to be alone. The drive leading to the back regions of the Castle was empty. As far as the eye could reach, there were no signs of servants, upper or lower.

Nevertheless, Ashe lowered his voice.

'Was it not a strange coincidence,' he said, 'that you should have come into my life at all?'

'Not very,' said Joan prosaically. 'It was quite likely that we should meet, sooner or later, as we lived on different floors of the same house.'

'It was a coincidence that you should have taken that room.'

'Why?'

Ashe felt damped. Logically, no doubt, she was right, but surely she might have helped him out a little in this difficult situation. Surely her woman's intuition might have told her that a man who has been speaking in a loud and cheerful voice does not lower it to a husky whisper without some reason. The hopelessness of his task began to weigh upon him. Ever since that evening at Market Blandings station, when he had realized that he had loved her, he had been trying to find an opportunity to tell her so; and every time they had met the talk had seemed to be drawn irresistibly into practical and unsentimental channels. And now, when he was doing his best to reason it out that they were twin souls who had been brought together by a destiny which it would be foolish to struggle against, when he was trying to convey the impression that fate had designed them for each other, she said, 'Why?' It was hard.

He was about to go deeper into the matter, when, from the direction of the Castle, he perceived the Hon. Freddie's valet, Mr Judson, approaching. That it was this repellent young man's object to break in upon them and rob him of his one small chance of inducing Joan to appreciate as he did the mysterious workings of Providence as they affected herself and him was obvious. There was no mistaking the valet's desire for conversation. He had the air of one brimming over with speech. His wonted indolence was cast aside, and as he drew nearer, he positively ran. He was talking before he reached them.

'Miss Simpson, Mr Marson, it's true. What I said that night. It's a fact.'

Ashe regarded this intruder with a malevolent eye. Never fond of Mr Judson, he looked on him now with positive loathing. It had not been easy for him to work himself up to the point where he could discuss with Joan the mysterious ways of Providence, for there was that about her which made it hard to achieve sentiment. That indefinable something in Joan Valentine which made for nocturnal raids on other people's museums also rendered her a somewhat difficult person to talk to about twin souls and destiny. The qualities that Ashe loved in her, her strength, her capability, her valiant self-sufficingness, were the very qualities which seemed to check him when he tried to tell her that he loved them.

Mr Judson was still babbling.

'It's true. There ain't a doubt of it now. It's been and happened just as I said that night.'

'What did you say – which night?' inquired Ashe.

'That night at dinner, the first night you two came here. Don't you remember me talking about Freddie and the girl he used to write letters to in London, the girl I said was so like you, Miss Simpson? What was her name again? Joan Valentine. That was it. The girl at the theatre that Freddie used to send me with letters to pretty nearly every evening. Well, she's been and done it, same as I told you all that night that she was jolly likely to go and do. She's sticking young Freddie up for his letters, just as he ought to have known she would do if he hadn't been a young fat-head. They're all alike these girls, every one of them.'

Mr Judson paused, subjected the surrounding scenery to a cautious scrutiny, and resumed.

'I took a suit of Freddie's clothes away to brush just now, and happening' – Mr Judson paused and gave a little cough – 'happening to glance at the contents of his pockets, I came across a letter. I took a sort of look at it before setting it aside, and it was from a fellow named Jones, and it said that this girl Valentine was sticking on to young Freddie's letters what he'd written her and would see him blowed if she parted with them under another thousand. And, as I made out, Freddie had already given her five hundred. Where he got it is more than I can understand, but that's what the letter said. The fellow Jones said that he had passed it to her with his own hands, but she wasn't satisfied, and if she didn't get the other thousand she was going to bring an action for breach. And now Freddie has given me a note to take to this Jones, who is stopping in Market Blandings.'

Joan had listened to this remarkable speech with a stunned amazement. At this point she made her first comment.

'But that can't be true.'

'Saw the letter with my own eyes, Miss Simpson.'

'But –'

She looked at Ashe helplessly. Their eyes met, hers wide with perplexity, his bright with the light of comprehension.

'It shows,' said Ashe slowly, 'that he was in immediate and urgent need of money.'

'You bet it does,' said Mr Judson with relish. 'It looks to me as if young Freddie had reached the end of his tether this time. My word, there won't half be a kick-up if she does sue him for breach. I'm off to tell Mr Beach and the rest. They'll jump out of their skins.' His face fell. 'Oh, Lord, I was forgetting this note. He told me to take it at once.'

'I'll take it for you,' said Ashe. 'I'm not doing anything.'

Mr Judson's gratitude was effusive.

'You're a good feller, Marson,' he said. 'I'll do as much for you another time. I couldn't hardly bear not to tell a bit of news like this right away. I should burst or something.'

And Mr Judson, with shining face, hurried off to the housekeeper's room.

'I simply can't understand it,' said Joan at length. 'My head's going round.'

'Can't understand it? Why, it's perfectly clear. This is the coincidence for which, in my capacity of Gridley Quayle, I was waiting. I can now resume inductive reasoning. Weighing the evidence, what do we find? That young sweep Freddie is the man. *He* has the scarab.'

'But it's all such a muddle. I'm not holding his letters.'

'For Jones' purposes you are. Let's get this Jones element in the affair straightened out. What do you know of him?'

'He was an enormously fat man who came to see me one night and said that he had been sent to get back some letters. I told him I had destroyed them ages ago, and he went away.'

'Well, that part of it is clear, then. He is working a simple but ingenious game on Freddie. It wouldn't succeed with every one, I suppose, but, from what I have seen and heard of him, Freddie isn't strong on intellect. He seems to have accepted the story without a murmur. What does he do? He has to raise a thousand pounds immediately, and the raising of the first five hundred has exhausted his credit. He gets the idea of stealing the scarab.'

'But why? Why should he have thought of the scarab at all? That is what I can't understand. He couldn't have meant to give it to Mr Peters and claim the reward. He couldn't have known that Mr Peters was offering a reward. He couldn't have known that Lord Emsworth had not got the scarab quite properly. He couldn't have known – he couldn't have known anything.'

Ashe's enthusiasm was a trifle damped.

'There's something in that. But – I have it. Jones must
have known about the scarab and told him.'

'But how could he have known?'

'Yes, there's something in that, too. How could Jones
have known?'

'He couldn't. He had gone by the time Aline came
that night.'

'I don't quite understand. What night?'

'It was the night of the day I first met you. I was
wondering for a moment whether he could by any
chance have overheard Aline telling me about the scarab
and the reward Mr Peters was offering for it.'

'Overheard! That word is like a bugle-blast to me.
Nine out of ten of Gridley Quayle's triumphs were due
to his having overheard something. I think we are now
on the right track.'

'I don't. How could he have overheard us? The door
was closed, and he was in the street by that time.'

'How do you know he was in the street? Did you see
him out?'

'No, but he went.'

'He might have waited on the stairs – you remember
how dark they were at No. 7A – and listened.'

'Why?'

Ashe reflected.

'Why? Why? What a beast of a word that is. The
detective's bugbear. I thought I had got it till you said –
Great Scott. I'll tell you why. I see it all. I have him
with the goods. His object in coming to you about the
letters was because Freddie wanted them back owing
to his approaching marriage with Miss Peters, wasn't
it?'

'Yes.'

'You tell him you have destroyed the letters. He goes
off. Am I right?'

'Yes.'

'Before he is out of the house Miss Peters is giving her

name at the front door. Put yourself in Jones' place. What does he think? He is suspicious. He thinks there is some game on. He skips upstairs again, waits till Miss Peters has gone into your room, then stands outside and listens. How about that?'

'I do believe you are right. He might quite easily have done that.'

'He did do exactly that. I know it as if I had been there. In fact, it is highly probable that I was there. You say all this happened on the night of the day we first met? I remember coming downstairs that night – I was going out to a music-hall – and hearing voices in your room. I remember it distinctly. In all probability I nearly ran into Jones.'

'It does all seem to fit in, doesn't it?'

'It's a clear case. There isn't a flaw in it. The only question is, can I, on the evidence, go to young Freddie and choke the scarab out of him? On the whole I think I had better take this note to Jones, as I promised Judson, and see if I can't work something through him. Yes, that's the best plan. I'll be starting at once.'

III

Perhaps the greatest hardship in being an invalid is the fact that people come and see you and keep your spirits up. The Hon. Freddie Threepwood suffered extremely from this. His was not a gregarious nature, and it fatigued his limited brainpowers to have to find conversation for his numerous visitors. All he wanted was to be left alone to read the Adventures of Gridley Quayle and when tired of doing that, to lie on his back, and look at the ceiling and think of nothing. It is your dynamic person, your energetic World's Worker, who chafes at being laid up with a sprained ankle. The Hon. Freddie enjoyed it. From boyhood up he had loved lying in bed, and now that fate had allowed him to do this without incurring rebuke, he objected to having his reveries broken in upon by officious relatives.

He spent his rare intervals of solitude in trying to decide in his mind which of his cousins, uncles, and aunts was, all things considered, the greatest nuisance. Sometimes he would give the palm to Colonel Horace Mant, who struck the soldierly note ('I recollect in a hill campaign in the Winter of the year '93 giving my ankle the deuce of a twist'); anon the more spiritual attitude of the Bishop of Godalming seemed to annoy him more keenly. Sometimes he would head the list with the name of his cousin Percy, Lord Stockheath, who refused to talk of anything except his late breach-of-promise case and the effect the verdict had had on his old governor. Freddie was in no mood just now to be sympathetic with others of their breach-of-promise cases.

As he lay in bed reading on the Monday morning, the only flaw in his enjoyment of this unaccustomed solitude was the thought that presently the door was bound to open, and some kind inquirer insinuate himself into the room.

His apprehensions proved well-founded. Scarcely had he got well into the details of an ingenious plot on the part of a secret society to eliminate Gridley Quayle by bribing his cook (a bad lot) to sprinkle chopped-up horse-hair in his chicken fricassee, when the handle turned, and Ashe Marson came in.

Freddie was not the only person who had found the influx of visitors into the sick-room a source of irritation. The fact that the invalid seemed unable to get a moment to himself had annoyed Ashe considerably. For some little time he had hung about the passage in which Freddie's room was situated, full of enterprise but unable to make a forward move owing to the throng of sympathizers. What he had to say to the sufferer could not be said in the presence of a third party.

Freddie's sensation, on perceiving him, was one of

relief. He had been half afraid that it was the Bishop. He recognized Ashe as the valet chappie who had helped him to bed on the occasion of his accident. It might be that he had come in a respectful way to make inquiries but he was not likely to stop long. He nodded, and went on reading.

And then, glancing up, he perceived Ashe standing beside the bed, fixing him with a piercing stare.

The Hon. Freddie hated piercing stares. One of the reasons why he objected to being left alone with his future father-in-law, Mr Preston Peters, was that Nature had given the millionaire a penetrating pair of eyes, and the stress of business life in New York had developed in him a habit of boring holes in people with them. A young man had to have a stronger nerve and a clearer conscience than the Hon. Freddie to enjoy a *tête-à-tête* with Mr Peters.

But, while he accepted Aline's father as a necessary evil and recognized that his position entitled him to look at people as sharply as he liked, whatever their feelings, he was hanged if he was going to extend this privilege to Mr Peters' valet. This man standing beside him was giving him a look which seemed to his sensitive imagination to have been fired red-hot from a gun; and this annoyed and exasperated Freddie.

'What do you want?' he said querulously. 'What are you staring at me like that for?'

Ashe sat down, leaned his elbows on the bed, and applied the look again, from a lower elevation.

'Ah!' he said.

Whatever may have been Ashe's defects as far as the handling of the inductive-reasoning side of Gridley Quayle's character was concerned, there was one scene in each of his stories in which he never failed. That was the scene in the last chapter where Quayle, confronting his quarry, unmasked him. Quayle might have floundered in the earlier part of the story, but in his big

227

scene he was exactly right. He was curt, brisk, and
mercilessly compelling. Ashe, rehearsing this interview
in the passage before his entry, had decided that he could
hardly do better than model himself on the detective. So
he began to be curt, crisp, and mercilessly compelling to
Freddie; and after the first few sentences he had that
youth gasping for air.

'I will tell you,' he said. 'If you can spare me a few
moments of your valuable time, I will put the facts
before you. Yes, press that bell, if you wish, and I will
put them before witnesses. Lord Emsworth will no
doubt be pleased to learn that his son, whom he trusted,
is – a thief.'

Freddie's hand fell limply. The bell remained
untouched. His mouth opened to its fullest extent. In
the midst of his panic he had a curious feeling that he
had heard or read that last sentence somewhere before.
Then he remembered. Those very words occurred in
'Gridley Quayle, Investigator. The Adventure of the Blue
Ruby'.

'What – what do you mean?' he stammered.

'I will tell you what I mean. On Saturday night a
valuable scarab was stolen from Lord Emsworth's
private museum. The case was put into my hands –'

'Great Scott! Are you a detective?'

'Ah!' said Ashe.

Life, as many a worthy writer has pointed out, is full
of ironies. It seemed to Freddie that here was a supreme
example of this fact. All these years he had wanted to
meet a detective, and now that his wish had been
gratified the detective was detecting *him*.

'The case,' continued Ashe severely, 'was placed in
my hands. I investigated it. I discovered that you were in
urgent and immediate need of money.'

'How on earth did you do that?'

'Ah!' said Ashe. 'I further discovered that you were in
communication with an individual named Jones.'

'Good lord! How?'

Ashe smiled quietly.

'Yesterday I had a talk with this man Jones, who is staying in Market Blandings. Why is he staying in Market Blandings? Because he had a reason for keeping in touch with you. Because you were about to transfer to his care something which you could get possession of but which only he could dispose of. The scarab.'

The Hon. Freddie was beyond speech. He made no comment on this statement. Ashe continued.

'I interviewed this man Jones. I said to him. "I am in the Hon. Frederick Threepwood's confidence. I know everything. Have you any instructions for me?" He replied, "What do you know?" I answered, "I know that the Hon. Frederick Threepwood has something which he wishes to hand to you, but which he has been unable to hand to you owing to having had an accident and being confined to his room." He then told me to tell you to let him have the scarab by messenger.'

Freddie pulled himself together with an effort. He was in sore straits, but he saw one last chance. His researches in detective fiction had given him the knowledge that detectives occasionally relaxed their austerity when dealing with a deserving case. Even Gridley Quayle could sometimes be softened by a pathetic story. Freddie could recall half a dozen times when a detected criminal had been spared by him because he had done it all from the best motives. He determined to throw himself on Ashe's mercy.

'I say, you know,' he said ingratiatingly, 'I think it's bally marvellous the way you've deduced everything and so forth.'

'Well?'

'But I believe you would chuck it, if you heard my side of the case.'

'I know your side of the case. You think you are being blackmailed by a Miss Valentine for some letters you

once wrote her. You are not. Miss Valentine has
destroyed the letters. She told the man Jones so when he
went to see her in London. He kept your five hundred
pounds, and is trying to get another thousand out of you
under false pretences!'

'What! You can't be right.'

'I am always right.'

'You must be mistaken.'

'I am never mistaken.'

'But how do you know?'

'I have my sources of information.'

'She isn't going to sue me for breach?'

'She never had any intention of doing so.'

The Hon. Frederick sank back on the pillows.

'Good egg!' he said with fervour. He beamed happily.
'This,' he observed, 'is a bit of all right.'

'Never mind that,' said Ashe. 'Give me the scarab.
Where is it?'

'What are you going to do with it?'

'Restore it to its rightful owner.'

'Are you going to give me away to the governor?'

'I am not.'

'It strikes me,' said Freddie gratefully, 'that you are a
dashed good sort. You seem to me to have the makings
of an absolute topper! It's under the mattress. I had it on
me when I fell downstairs, and I had to shove it in
there.'

Ashe drew it out. He stood looking at it, absorbed. He
could hardly believe that his quest was at an end, and
that a small fortune lay in the palm of his hand.

Freddie was eyeing him admiringly.

'You know,' he said, 'I've always wanted to meet a
detective. What beats me is how you chappies find out
things.'

'We have our methods.'

'I believe you. You're a blooming marvel! What first
put you on my track?'

'That,' said Ashe, 'would take too long to explain. Of course I had to do some tense inductive reasoning. But I could not trace every link in the chain for you. It would be tedious.'

'Not to me.'

'Some other time.'

'I say, I wonder if you've ever read any of these things, these Gridley Quayle stories? I know them by heart.'

With the scarab safely in his pocket, Ashe could contemplate the brightly-coloured volume which the other extended towards him without active repulsion. Already he was beginning to feel a sort of sentiment for the depressing Quayle, as for something that had once formed part of his life.

'Do you read these things?'

'I should say I did.'

'I write them.'

There are certain supreme moments which cannot be adequately described. Freddie's appreciation of the fact that such a moment had occurred in his life expressed itself in a startled cry and a convulsive movement of all his limbs. He shot up from the pillows and gaped at Ashe.

'You write them? You don't mean *write* them?'

'Yes.'

'Great Scott!'

He would have gone on, doubtless, to say more, but at this moment voices made themselves heard outside the door. There was a movement of feet. Then the door opened, and a small procession entered.

It was headed by the Earl of Emsworth. Following him, came Mr Peters. And in the wake of the millionaire Colonel Horace Mant and the Efficient Baxter. They filed into the room, and stood by the bedside. Ashe seized the opportunity to slip out.

Freddie glanced at the deputation without interest. His mind was occupied with other matters. He supposed that they had come to inquire after his ankle, and he was mildly thankful that they had come in a body instead of one by one. The deputation grouped itself about the bed, and shuffled its feet. There was an atmosphere of awkwardness.

'Er, Frederick,' said Lord Emsworth. 'Freddie, my boy.'

Mr Peters fiddled dumbly with the coverlet, Colonel Mant cleared his throat. The Efficient Baxter scowled.

'Er, Freddie, my dear boy, I fear that we have a painful – ah – duty to perform.'

The words struck straight home at the Hon. Freddie's guilty conscience. Had they too, tracked him down, and was he now to be accused of having stolen that infernal scarab! A wave of relief swept over him as he realized that he had got rid of the thing. A decent chappie like that detective would not give him away. All he had to do was to keep his head and stick to stout denial. That was the game. Stout denial.

'I don't know what you mean,' he said defensively.

'Of course you don't, dash it,' said Colonel Mant. 'We're coming to that. And I should like to begin by saying that, though in a sense it was my fault, I fail to see how I could have acted – '

'Horace.'

'Oh, very well. I was only trying to explain.'

Lord Emsworth adjusted his pince-nez, and sought inspiration from the wallpaper.

'Freddie, my boy,' he began, 'we have a somewhat unpleasant – a somewhat – ah – disturbing . . . We are compelled to break it to you . . . We are all most pained and astounded and . . .'

The Efficient Baxter spoke. It was plain that he was in a bad temper.

'Miss Peters,' he snapped, 'has eloped with your friend Emerson.'

Lord Emsworth breathed a sigh of relief.

'Exactly, Baxter. Precisely. You have put the thing in a

nut-shell. Really, my dear fellow, you are invaluable.'

All eyes searched Freddie's face for signs of uncontrollable emotion. The deputation waited anxiously for his first grief-stricken cry.

'Eh, what?' said Freddie.

'It is quite true, Freddie, my dear boy. She went to London with him on the ten-fifty.'

'And, if I had not been forcibly restrained,' said Baxter acidly, casting a vindictive look at Colonel Mant, 'I could have prevented it.'

Colonel Mant cleared his throat again, and put a hand to his moustache.

'I'm afraid that is true, Freddie. It was a most unfortunate misunderstanding. I'll tell you how it happened. I chanced to be at the station bookstall when the train came in. Mr Baxter was also in the station. The train pulled up, and this young fellow Emerson got in. Said good-bye to us, don't you know, and got in. Just as the train was about to start, Miss Peters, exclaiming, "George, dear, I'm coming with you, dash it," or some such speech, proceeded to go hell for leather for the door of young Emerson's compartment. Upon which – '

'Upon which,' interrupted Baxter, 'I made a spring to try and catch her. Apart from any other consideration, the train was already moving, and Miss Peters ran a considerable risk of injury. I hardly moved when I felt a violent jerk at my ankle and fell to the ground. After I had recovered from the shock, which was not immediately, I found – '

'The fact is, Freddie, my boy, I acted under a misapprehension. Nobody can be sorrier for the mistake than I, but recent events in this house had left me with the impression that Mr Baxter here was not quite responsible for his actions. Overwork or something, I imagined. I have seen it happen so often in India, don't you know, where fellows run amuck and kick up the deuce's own delight. I am bound to admit that I have

been watching Mr Baxter rather closely lately, in the
expectation that something of this very kind might
happen. Of course, I now realize my mistake, and I have
apologized – apologized humbly, dash it. But at the
moment I was firmly under the impression that our
friend here had had an attack of some kind, and was
about to inflict injuries on Miss Peters. If I've seen it
happen once in India, I've seen it happen a dozen times. I
recollect in the hot weather of the year '92 – or was it
'93? – I think '93 – one of my native bearers . . .
However, I sprang forward and caught the crook of my
walking-stick in Mr Baxter's ankle and brought him
down. And by the time the explanations were made, it
was too late. The train had gone, with Miss Peters in it.'

'And a telegram has just arrived,' said Lord Emsworth,
'to say that they are being married this afternoon at a
registrar's. The whole occurrence is most disturbing.'

'Bear it like a man, my boy,' urged Colonel Mant.

To all appearances, Freddie was bearing it
magnificently. Not a single exclamation, either of wrath
or pain, had escaped his lips. One would have said that
the shock had stunned him or that he had not heard, for
his face expressed no emotion whatsoever.

The fact was that the story had made very little
impression on the Hon. Freddie of any sort. His relief at
Ashe's news about Joan Valentine, the stunning joy of
having met in the flesh the author of the Adventures of
Gridley Quayle, the general feeling that all was now
right with the world – these things deprived him of the
ability to be greatly distressed.

And there was a distinct feeling of relief, actual relief,
that now it would not be necessary for him to get
married. He had liked Aline, but, whenever he had really
thought of it, the prospect of getting married had rather
appalled him. A chappie looked such an ass getting
married . . .

It appeared, however, that some verbal comment on

the state of affairs was required of him. He searched in
his mind for something adequate.

'You mean to say Aline has bolted with Emerson?'

The deputation nodded painful nods. Freddie searched
in his mind again. The deputation held its breath.

'Well, I'm blowed,' said Freddie. 'Fancy that!'

IV

Mr Peters walked heavily into his room. Ashe Marson
was waiting for him there. He eyed Ashe dully.

'Pack,' he said.

'Pack?'

'Pack. We're getting out of here by the afternoon
train.'

'Has anything happened?'

'My daughter has eloped with Emerson.'

'What!'

'Don't stand there saying "What!" Pack.'

Ashe put his hand in his pocket.

'Where shall I put this?' he asked.

For a moment Mr Peters looked without
comprehension at what he was holding out, then his
whole demeanour altered. His eyes lit up. He uttered a
howl of pure rapture.

'You got it!'

'I got it.'

'Where was it? Who had taken it? How did you choke
it out of them? How did you find it? Who had it?'

'I don't know whether I ought to say. I don't want to
start anything. You won't tell anyone?'

'Tell anyone? What do you take me for? Do you think
I am going about advertising this? If I can sneak out
without that fellow Baxter jumping on my back, I shall
be satisfied. You can take it from me that there won't be
any sensational exposures if I can help it. Who had it?'

'Young Threepwood.'

235

'Threepwood? What did he want it for?'

'He needed money, and he was going to raise it on this.'
Mr Peters exploded.

'And I have been kicking because Aline can't marry
him, and has gone off with a regular fellow like young
Emerson. He's a good boy, young Emerson. He'll make a
name for himself one of these days. He's got get-up in
him. And I have been wanting to shoot him because he
has taken Aline away from that goggle-eyed chump up
in bed there. Why, if she had married Threepwood, I
should have had grandchildren who would have sneaked
my watch while I was dancing them on my knee. There
is a taint of some sort in the whole family. Father sneaks
my Cheops, and sonny sneaks it from father. What a
gang! And the best blood in England. If that's England's
idea of good blood, give me Kalamazoo. This settles it, I
was a chump ever to come to a country like this
Property isn't safe over here. I'm going back to America
on the next boat.

'Where's my cheque-book? I'm going to write you out
that cheque right away. You've earned it. Listen, young
man, I don't know what your ideas are, but if you aren't
chained to this country, I'd make it worth your while to
stay on with me. They say no one's indispensable, but
you come mighty near it. If I had you at my elbow for a
few years, I'd get right back into shape. I'm feeling better
now than I have felt in years, and you've only just
started in on me. How about it? You can call yourself
what you like – secretary or trainer or whatever suits
you best. What you will be is the fellow who makes me
take exercise and stop smoking cigars and generally
looks after me. How do you feel about it?'

It was a proposition which appealed both to Ashe's
commercial and to his missionary instincts. His only
regret had been that, the scarab recovered, he and Mr
Peters would now, he supposed, part company. He had
not liked the idea of sending the millionaire back to the

world a half-cured man. Already he had begun to look upon him in the light of a piece of creative work, to which he had just set his hand.

But the thought of Joan gave him pause. If this meant separation from Joan, it was not to be considered.

'Let me think it over,' he said.

'Well, think quick,' said Mr Peters.

V

It is said by those who have been through fires, earthquakes, and shipwrecks, that in such times of stress the social barriers are temporarily broken down, and the spectacle may be seen of persons of the highest social standing speaking quite freely to persons who are not in Society at all, and of quite nice people addressing others to whom they have never been introduced. The news of Aline Peters' elopement with George Emerson, carried beyond the green-baize door by Slingsby, the chauffeur, produced very much the same state of affairs in the servants' quarters at Blandings Castle.

It was not only that Slingsby was permitted to penetrate into the housekeeper's room and tell his story to his social superiors there, though that was an absolutely unprecedented occurrence; what was really extraordinary was that mere menials discussed the affair with the personal ladies and gentlemen of the Castle guests, and were allowed to do so uncrushed. James, the footman, that pushing individual, actually shoved his way into the Room, and was heard by witnesses to remark to no less a person than Mr Beach that it was a bit thick. And it is on record that his fellow-footman, Alfred, meeting the Groom of the Chambers in the passage outside, positively prodded him in the lower ribs, winked, and said, 'What a day we're having.' One has to go back to the worst excesses of the French Revolution to parallel these outrages.

It was held by Mr Beach and Mrs Twemlow afterwards that the social fabric of the Castle never fully recovered from this upheaval. It may be that they took an extreme view of the matter, but it cannot be denied that it wrought changes. The rise of Slingsby is a case in point. Until this affair took place, the chauffeur's standing had never been satisfactorily settled. Mr Beach and Mrs Twemlow led the party which considered that he was merely a species of coachman, but there was another smaller group which, dazzled by Slingsby's personality, openly declared that it was not right that he should take his meals in the Servants' Hall with such admitted plebeians as the odd man and the Steward's Room footman. The Aline–George elopement settled the point once and for all. Slingsby had carried George's bag to the train. Slingsby had been standing a few yards from the spot where Aline began her dash for the carriage door. Slingsby was able to exhibit the actual half-sovereign which George had tipped him, only five minutes before the great event. To send such a public man back to the Servants' Hall was impossible. By unspoken consent the chauffeur dined that night in the Steward's Room, from which he was never again dislodged.

Mr Judson alone stood apart from the throng which clustered about the chauffeur. He was suffering the bitterness of the supplanted. A brief while before, and he had been the central figure with his story of the letter which he had found in the Hon. Freddie's coat pocket. Now the importance of his story had been engulfed in that of this later and greater sensation, and Mr Judson was learning for the first time on what unstable foundations popularity stands.

Joan was nowhere to be seen. In none of the spots where she might have been expected to be at such a time was she to be found. Ashe had almost given up the search when, going to the back door and looking out as a last chance, he perceived her walking slowly on the gravel drive.

She greeted Ashe with a smile, but something was plainly troubling her. She did not speak for a moment, and they walked side by side.

'What is it?' said Ashe at length. 'What is the matter?'

She looked at him gravely.

'Gloom,' she said. 'Despondency, Mr Marson. A sort of flat feeling. Don't you hate things happening?'

'I don't quite understand!'

'Well, this affair of Aline, for instance. It's so big. It makes you feel as if the whole world had altered. I should like nothing to happen, ever, and life just to jog peacefully along. That's not the gospel I preached to you in Arundell Street, is it! I thought I was an advanced apostle of action. But I seem to have changed. I'm afraid I should never be able to make it clear what I do mean. I only know that I feel as if I had grown suddenly old. These things are such milestones. Already I am beginning to look on the time before Aline behaved so sensationally as terribly remote. Tomorrow it will be worse, and the day after that worse still. I can see that you don't in the least understand what I mean.'

'Yes, I do. Or I think I do. What it comes to, in a few words, is that somebody you were fond of has gone out of your life. Is that it?'

Joan nodded.

'Yes. At least, that is partly it. I didn't really know Aline particularly well, beyond having been at school with her, but you're right. It's not so much what has happened as what it represents that matters. This elopement has marked the end of a phase of my life. I think I have it now. My life has been such a series of jerks. I dash along, then something happens which stops that bit of my life with a jerk, and then I have to start over again – a new bit. I think I'm getting tired of jerks. I want something stodgy and continuous. I'm like one of the old bus horses who could go on for ever if people got off without making them stop. It's the having to get the bus moving again that wears one out. This little section of my life since we came here is over, and it is finished for good. I've got to start the bus going again on a new road and with a new set of passengers. I wonder if the old horses used to be sorry when they dropped one set of passengers and took on a lot of strangers?'

A sudden dryness invaded Ashe's throat. He tried to speak, but found no words. Joan went on.

'Do you ever get moods when life seems absolutely meaningless? It's a badly-constructed story, with all sorts of characters moving in and out who have nothing to do with the plot. And, when somebody comes along who you think really has something to do with the plot, he suddenly drops out. After a while you begin to wonder what the story is about, and you feel that it's about nothing – just a jumble.'

'There is one thing,' said Ashe, 'that knits it together.'

'What is that?'

'The love interest.'

Their eyes met, and suddenly there descended upon Ashe confidence. He felt cool and alert, sure of himself, as in the old days he had felt when he ran races and, the nerve-racking hours of waiting past, he listened for the starter's gun. Subconsciously he was aware that he had always been a little afraid of Joan, and that now he was no longer afraid.

'Joan, will you marry me?'

Her eyes wandered from his face. He waited.

'I wonder,' she said softly. 'You think that is the solution?'

'Yes.'

'How can you tell?' she broke out. 'We scarcely know each other. I shan't always be in this mood. I may get restless again. I may find that it is the jerks that I really like.'

'You won't.'

'You're very confident.'

'I am absolutely confident.'

' "She travels the fastest who travels alone," '
misquoted Joan.

'What is the good,' said Ashe, 'of travelling fast if
you're going round in a circle? I know how you feel. I've
felt the same myself. You are an individualist. You think
that there is something tremendous just round the
corner, and that you can get it if you try hard enough.
There isn't. Or, if there is, it isn't worth getting. Life is
nothing but a mutual aid association. I am going to help
old Peters; you are going to help me; I am going to help
you.'

'Help me to do what?'

'Make life coherent instead of a jumble.'

'Mr Marson –'

'Don't call me Mr Marson.'

'Ashe, you don't know what you are doing. You don't
know me. I've been knocking about the world for five
years, and I'm hard – hard right through. I should make
you wretched.'

'You are not in the least hard, and you know it. Listen
to me, Joan. Where's your sense of fairness? You crash
into my life, turn it upside down, dig me out of my quiet
groove, revolutionize my whole existence, and now you
propose to drop me and pay no further attention to me.
Is it fair?'

'But I don't. We shall always be the best of friends.'

'We shall. But we will get married first.'

'You are determined?'

'I am.'

Joan laughed happily.

'How perfectly splendid. I was terrified lest I might
have made you change your mind. I had to say all I did,
to preserve my self-respect after proposing to you. Yes, I
did. But strange it is that men never seem to understand

a woman, however plainly she talks. You don't think I was really worrying because I had lost Aline, do you? I thought I was going to lose you, and it made me miserable. You couldn't expect me to say so in so many words, but I thought you guessed. I practically said it. Ashe! What are you doing?'

Ashe paused for a moment to reply.

'I am kissing you,' he said.

'But you mustn't. There's a scullery-maid or something looking out of the kitchen window. She will see us.'

Ashe drew her to him.

'Scullery-maids have few pleasures,' he said. 'Theirs is a dull life. Let her see us.'

The Earl of Emsworth sat by the sick-bed, and regarded the Hon. Freddie almost tenderly.

'Oh, what? Yes, rather. Deuce of a shock, governor.'

'I have been thinking it over, my boy, and perhaps I have been a little hard on you. When your ankle is better, I have decided to renew your allowance, and you may return to London, as you do not seem happy in the country. Though how any reasonable being can prefer – '

The Hon. Freddie started, pop-eyed, to a sitting posture.

'My word! Not really?'

His father nodded.

'Yes. But, Freddie, my boy,' he added not without pathos, 'I *do* wish that this time you would endeavour, for my sake, not to make a fool of yourself.'

He eyed his offspring wistfully.

'I'll have a jolly good stab at it, governor,' said the Hon. Freddie.

Summer Lightning

Preface

A Certain critic – for such men, I regret to say, do exist – made the nasty remark about my last novel that it contained 'all the old Wodehouse characters under different names'. He has probably by now been eaten by bears, like the children who made mock of the prophet Elisha: but if he still survives he will not be able to make a similar charge against *Summer Lightning*. With my superior intelligence, I have outgeneralled the man this time by putting in all the old Wodehouse characters under the same names. Pretty silly it will make him feel, I rather fancy.

This story is a sort of Old Home Week for my – if I may coin a phrase – puppets. Hugo Carmody and Ronnie Fish appeared in *Money for Nothing*. Pilbeam was in *Bill the Conqueror*. And the rest of them, Lord Emsworth, the Efficient Baxter, Butler Beach, and the others have all done their bit before in *Something Fresh* and *Leave it to Psmith*. Even Empress of Blandings, that pre-eminent pig, is coming up for the second time, having made her debut in a short story called 'Pig-hoo-oo-ey!', which, with other Blandings Castle stories too fascinating to mention, will eventually appear in volume form.

The fact is, I cannot tear myself away from Blandings Castle. The place exercises a sort of spell over me. I am always popping down to Shropshire and looking in there to hear the latest news, and there always seems to be something to interest me. It is in the hope that it will also interest My Public that I have jotted down the bit of gossip from the old spot which I have called *Summer Lightning*.

A word about the title. It is related of Thackeray that, hitting upon *Vanity Fair* after retiring to rest one night, he leaped out of bed and ran seven times round the room, shouting at the top of his voice. Oddly enough, I behaved in exactly the same way when I thought of *Summer Lightning*. I recognized it immediately as the ideal title for a novel. My exuberance has been a little diminished since by the discovery that I am not the only one who thinks highly of it. Already I have been informed that two novels with the same name have been published in England, and my agent in America cables to say that three have recently been placed on the market in the United States. As my story has appeared in serial form under its present label, it is too late to alter it now. I can only express the modest hope that this story will be considered worthy of inclusion in the list of the Hundred Best Books Called Summer Lightning.

P.G. WODEHOUSE

1 — Trouble Brewing at Blandings

Blandings Castle slept in the sunshine. Dancing little ripples of heat-mist played across its smooth lawns and stone-flagged terraces. The air was full of the lulling drone of insects. It was that gracious hour of a summer afternoon, midway between luncheon and tea, when Nature seems to unbutton its waistcoat and put its feet up.

In the shade of a laurel bush outside the back premises of this stately home of England, Beach, butler to Clarence, ninth Earl of Emsworth, its proprietor, sat sipping the contents of a long glass and reading a weekly paper devoted to the doings of Society and the Stage. His attention had just been arrested by a photograph in an oval border on one of the inner pages: and for perhaps a minute he scrutinized this in a slow, thorough, pop-eyed way, absorbing its every detail. Then, with a fruity chuckle, he took a penknife from his pocket, cut out the photograph, and placed it in the recesses of his costume.

At this moment, the laurel bush, which had hitherto not spoken, said 'Psst!'

The butler started violently. A spasm ran through his ample frame.

'Beach!' said the bush.

Something was now peering out of it. This might have been a wood-nymph, but the butler rather thought not, and he was right. It was a tall young man with light hair. He recognized his employer's secretary, Mr Hugo Carmody, and rose with pained reproach. His heart was still jumping, and he had bitten his tongue.

'Startle you, Beach?'

249

'Extremely, sir.'

'I'm sorry. Excellent for the liver, though. Beach, do you want to earn a quid?'

The butler's austerity softened. The hard look died out of his eyes.

'Yes, sir.'

'Can you get hold of Miss Millicent alone?'

'Certainly, sir.'

'Then give her this note, and don't let anyone see you do it. Especially – and this is where I want you to follow me very closely, Beach – Lady Constance Keeble.'

'I will attend to the matter immediately, sir.'

He smiled a paternal smile. Hugo smiled back. A perfect understanding prevailed between these two. Beach understood that he ought not to be giving his employer's niece surreptitious notes: and Hugo understood that he ought not to be urging a good man to place such a weight upon his conscience.

'Perhaps you are not aware, sir,' said the butler, having trousered the wages of sin, 'that her ladyship went up to London on the three-thirty train?'

Hugo uttered an exclamation of chagrin.

'You mean that all this Red Indian stuff – creeping from bush to bush and not letting a single twig snap beneath my feet – has simply been a waste of time?' He emerged, dusting his clothes. 'I wish I'd known that before,' he said. 'I've severely injured a good suit, and it's a very moot question whether I haven't got some kind of a beetle down my back. However, nobody ever took a toss through being careful.'

'Very true, sir.'

Relieved by the information that the X-ray eye of the aunt of the girl he loved was operating elsewhere, Mr Carmody became conversational.

'Nice day, Beach.'

'Yes, sir.'

'You know, Beach, life's rummy. I mean to say, you

never can tell what the future holds in store. Here I am at Blandings Castle, loving it. Sing of joy, sing of bliss, home was never like this. And yet, when the project of my coming here was first placed on the agenda, I don't mind telling you the heart was rather bowed down with weight of woe.'

'Indeed, sir?'

'Yes. Noticeably bowed down. If you knew the circumstances, you would understand why.'

Beach did know the circumstances. There were few facts concerning the dwellers in Blandings Castle of which he remained in ignorance for long. He was aware that young Mr Carmody had been, until a few weeks back, co-proprietor with Mr Ronald Fish, Lord Emsworth's nephew, of a night-club called the Hot Spot, situated just off Bond Street in the heart of London's pleasure-seeking area; that, despite this favoured position, it had proved a financial failure; that Mr Ronald had gone off with his mother, Lady Julia Fish, to recuperate at Biarritz; and that Hugo, on the insistence of Ronnie that unless some niche was found for his boyhood friend he would not stir a step towards Biarritz or any other blighted place, had come to Blandings as Lord Emsworth's private secretary.

'No doubt you were reluctant to leave London, sir?'

'Exactly. But now, Beach, believe me or believe me not, as far as I am concerned, anyone who likes can have London. Mark you, I'm not saying that just one brief night in the Piccadilly neighbourhood would come amiss. But to dwell in, give me Blandings Castle. What a spot, Beach!'

'Yes, sir.'

'A Garden of Eden, shall I call it?'

'Certainly, sir, if you wish.'

'And now that old Ronnie's coming here, joy, as you might say, will be unconfined.'

'Is Mr Ronald expected, sir?'

'Coming either tomorrow or the day after. I had a letter from him this morning. Which reminds me. He sends his regards to you, and asks me to tell you to put your shirt on Baby Bones for the Medbury Selling Plate.'

The butler pursed his lips dubiously.

'A long shot, sir. Not generally fancied.'

'Rank outsider. Leave it alone, is my verdict.'

'And yet Mr Ronald is usually very reliable. It is many years now since he first began to advise me in these matters, and I have done remarkably well by following him. Even as a lad at Eton he was always singularly fortunate in his information.'

'Well, suit yourself,' said Hugo, indifferently. 'What was that thing you were cutting out of the paper just now?'

'A photograph of Mr Galahad, sir. I keep an album in which I paste items of interest relating to the Family.'

'What that album needs is an eye-witness's description of Lady Constance Keeble falling out of a window and breaking her neck.'

A nice sense of the proprieties prevented Beach from endorsing this view verbally, but he sighed a little wistfully. He had frequently felt much the same about the chatelaine of Blandings.

'If you would care to see the clipping, sir? There is a reference to Mr Galahad's literary work.'

Most of the photographs in the weekly paper over which Beach had been relaxing were of peeresses trying to look like chorus-girls and chorus-girls trying to look like peeresses: but this one showed the perky features of a dapper little gentleman in the late fifties. Beneath it, in large letters, was the single word:

GALLY

Under this ran a caption in smaller print.

The Hon. Galahad Threepwood, brother of the Earl of

Emsworth. A little bird tells us that 'Gally' is at Blandings
Castle, Shropshire, the ancestral seat of the family, busily
engaged in writing his Reminiscences. As every member
of the Old Brigade will testify, they ought to be as warm
as the weather, if not warmer.

Hugo scanned the exhibit thoughtfully, and handed it
back, to be placed in the archives.

'Yes,' he observed, 'I should say that about summed it
up. That old bird must have been pretty hot stuff, I
imagine, back in the days of Edward the Confessor.'

'Mr Galahad was somewhat wild as a young man,'
agreed the butler with a sort of feudal pride in his voice.
It was the opinion of the Servants' Hall that the Hon.
Galahad shed lustre on Blandings Castle.

'Has it ever occurred to you, Beach, that that book of
his is going to make no small stir when it comes out?'

'Frequently, sir.'

'Well, I'm saving up for my copy. By the way, I knew
there was something I wanted to ask you. Can you give
me any information on the subject of a bloke named
Baxter?'

'Mr Baxter, sir? He used to be private secretary to his
lordship.'

'Yes, so I gathered. Lady Constance was speaking to
me about him this morning. She happened upon me as I
was taking the air in riding kit and didn't seem
overpleased. "You appear to enjoy a great deal of leisure,
Mr Carmody," she said. "Mr Baxter," she continued,
giving me the meaning eye, "never seemed to find time
to go riding when he was Lord Emsworth's secretary. Mr
Baxter was always so hard at work. But, then, Mr
Baxter," she added, the old lamp becoming more
meaning than ever, "loved his work. Mr Baxter took a
real interest in his duties. Dear me! What a very
conscientious man Mr Baxter was, to be sure!" Or words
to that effect. I may be wrong, but I classed it as a dirty

dig. And what I want to know is, if Baxter was such a world-beater, why did they ever let him go?'

The butler gazed about him cautiously.

'I fancy, sir, there was some Trouble.'

'Pinched the spoons, eh? Always the way with these zealous workers.'

'I never succeeded in learning the full details, sir, but there was something about some flower-pots.'

'He pinched the flower-pots?'

'Threw them at his lordship, I was given to understand.'

Hugo looked injured. He was a high-spirited young man who chafed at injustice.

'Well, I'm dashed if I see then,' he said, 'where this Baxter can claim to rank so jolly high above me as a secretary. I may be leisurely, I may forget to answer letters, I may occasionally on warm afternoons go in to some extent for the folding of the hands in sleep, but at least I don't throw flower-pots at people. Not so much as a pen-wiper have I ever bunged at Lord Emsworth. Well, I must be getting about my duties. That ride this morning and a slight slumber after lunch have set the schedule back a bit. You won't forget that note, will you?'

'No, sir.'

Hugo reflected.

'On second thoughts,' he said, 'perhaps you'd better hand it back to me. Safer not to have too much written matter circulating about the place. Just tell Miss Millicent that she will find me in the rose-garden at six sharp.'

'In the rose-garden . . .'

'At six sharp.'

'Very good, sir. I will see that she receives the information.'

II

For two hours after this absolutely nothing happened in the grounds of Blandings Castle. At the end of that period there sounded through the mellow, drowsy stillness a drowsy, mellow chiming. It was the clock over the stables striking five. Simultaneously, a small but noteworthy procession filed out of the house and made its way across the sun-bathed lawn to where the big cedar cast a grateful shade. It was headed by James, a footman, bearing a laden tray. Following him came Thomas, another footman, with a gate-leg table. The rear was brought up by Beach, who carried nothing, but merely lent a tone.

The instinct which warns all good Englishmen when tea is ready immediately began to perform its silent duty. Even as Thomas set gateleg table to earth there appeared, as if answering a cue, an elderly gentleman in stained tweeds and a hat he should have been ashamed of. Clarence, ninth Earl of Emsworth, in person. He was a long, lean, stringy man of about sixty, slightly speckled at the moment with mud, for he had spent most of the afternoon pottering round pig-sties. He surveyed the preparations for the meal with vague amiability through rimless pince-nez.

'Tea?'

'Yes, your lordship.'

'Oh?' said Lord Emsworth. 'Ah? Tea, eh? Tea? Yes. Tea. Quite so. To be sure, tea. Capital.'

One gathered from his remarks that he realized that the tea-hour had arrived and was glad of it. He proceeded to impart his discovery to his niece, Millicent, who, lured by that same silent call, had just appeared at his side.

'Tea, Millicent.'

'Yes.'

'Er – tea,' said Lord Emsworth, driving home his point.

255

Millicent sat down, and busied herself with the pot.
She was a tall, fair girl with soft blue eyes and a face like
the Soul's Awakening. Her whole appearance radiated
wholesome innocence. Not even an expert could have
told that she had just received a whispered message from
a bribed butler and was proposing at six sharp to go and
meet a quite ineligible young man among the
rose-bushes.

'Been down seeing the Empress, Uncle Clarence?'

'Eh? Oh, yes. Yes, my dear. I have been with her all
the afternoon.'

Lord Emsworth's mild eyes beamed. They always did
when that noble animal, Empress of Blandings, was
mentioned. The ninth Earl was a man of few and simple
ambitions. He had never desired to mould the destinies
of the State, to frame its laws and make speeches in the
House of Lords that would bring all the peers and
bishops to their feet, whooping and waving their hats.
All he yearned to do, by way of ensuring admittance to
England's Hall of Fame, was to tend his prize sow,
Empress of Blandings, so sedulously that for the second
time in two consecutive years he would win the silver
medal in the Fat Pigs class at the Shropshire Agricultural
Show. And every day, it seemed to him, the glittering
prize was coming more and more within his grasp.

Earlier in the summer there had been one breathless
sickening moment of suspense, and disaster had seemed
to loom. This was when his neighbour, Sir Gregory
Parsloe-Parsloe, of Matchingham Hall, had basely lured
away his pig-man, the superbly gifted George Cyril
Wellbeloved, by the promise of higher wages. For a while
Lord Emsworth had feared lest the Empress, mourning
for her old friend and valet, might refuse food and fall
from her high standard of obesity. But his apprehensions
had proved groundless. The Empress had taken to
Pirbright, George Cyril's successor, from the first, and
was tucking away her meals with all the old abandon.

The Right triumphs in this world far more often than we realize.

'What do you do to her?' asked Millicent, curiously. 'Read her bedtime stories?'

Lord Emsworth pursed his lips. He had a reverent mind, and disliked jesting on serious subjects.

'Whatever I do, my dear, it seems to effect its purpose. She is in wonderful shape.'

'I didn't know she had a shape. She hadn't when I last saw her.'

This time Lord Emsworth smiled indulgently. Gibes at the Empress's rotundity had no sting for him. He did not desire for her that school-girl slimness which is so fashionable nowadays.

'She has never fed more heartily,' he said. 'It is a treat to watch her.'

'I'm so glad. Mr Carmody,' said Millicent, stooping to tickle a spaniel which had wandered up to take pot-luck, 'told me he had never seen a finer animal in his life.'

'I like that young man,' said Lord Emsworth emphatically. 'He is sound on pigs. He has his head screwed on the right way.'

'Yes, he's an improvement on Baxter, isn't he?'

'Baxter!' His lordship choked over his cup.

'You didn't like Baxter much, did you, Uncle Clarence?'

'Hadn't a peaceful moment while he was in the place. Dreadful feller! Always fussing. Always wanting me to *do* things. Always coming round corners with his infernal spectacles gleaming and making me sign papers when I wanted to be out in the garden. Besides he was off his head. Thank goodness I've seen the last of Baxter.'

'But have you?'

'What do you mean?'

'If you ask me,' said Millicent, 'Aunt Constance hasn't given up the idea of getting him back.'

Lord Emsworth started with such violence that his

pince-nez fell off. She had touched on his favourite
nightmare. Sometimes he would wake trembling in the
night, fancying that his late secretary had returned to
the castle. And though on these occasions he always
dropped off to sleep again with a happy smile of relief, he
had never ceased to be haunted by the fear that his sister
Constance, in her infernal managing way, was scheming
to restore the fellow to office.

'Good God! Has she said anything to you?'

'No. But I have a feeling. I know she doesn't like Mr
Carmody.'

Lord Emsworth exploded.

'Perfect nonsense! Utter, absolute, dashed nonsense.
What on earth does she find to object to in young
Carmody? Most capable, intelligent boy. Leaves me
alone. Doesn't fuss me. I wish to heaven she would . . .'

He broke off, and stared blankly at a handsome
woman of middle age who had come out of the house
and was crossing the lawn.

'Why, here she is!' said Millicent, equally and just as
disagreeably surprised. 'I thought you had gone up to
London, Aunt Constance.'

Lady Constance Keeble had arrived at the table.
Declining, with a distrait shake of the head, her niece's
offer of the seat of honour by the tea-pot, she sank into a
chair. She was a woman of still remarkable beauty, with
features cast in a commanding mould and fine eyes.
These eyes were at the moment dull and brooding.

'I missed my train,' she explained. 'However, I can do
all I have to do in London tomorrow. I shall go up by the
eleven-fifteen. In a way, it will be more convenient, for
Ronald will be able to motor me back. I will look in at
Norfolk Street and pick him up there before he starts.'

'What made you miss your train?'

'Yes,' said Lord Emsworth, complainingly. 'You
started in good time.'

The brooding look in his sister's eyes deepened.

'I met Sir Gregory Parsloe.' Lord Emsworth stiffened at the name. 'He kept me talking. He is extremely worried.' Lord Emsworth looked pleased. 'He tells me he used to know Galahad very well a number of years ago, and he is very much alarmed about this book of his.'

'And I bet he isn't the only one,' murmured Millicent.

She was right. Once a man of the Hon. Galahad Threepwood's antecedents starts taking pen in hand and being reminded of amusing incidents that happened to my dear old friend So-and-So, you never know where he will stop; and all over England, among the more elderly of the nobility and gentry, something like a panic had been raging ever since the news of his literary activities had got about. From Sir Gregory Parsloe-Parsloe, of Matchingham Hall, to grey-headed pillars of Society in distant Cumberland and Kent, whole droves of respectable men who in their younger days had been rash enough to chum with the Hon. Galahad were recalling past follies committed in his company and speculating agitatedly as to how good the old pest's memory was.

For Galahad in his day had been a notable lad about town. A *beau sabreur* of Romano's. A Pink 'Un. A Pelican. A crony of Hughie Drummond and Fatty Coleman; a brother-in-arms of the Shifter, the Pitcher, Peter Blobbs and the rest of an interesting but not strait-laced circle. Bookmakers had called him by his pet name, barmaids had simpered beneath his gallant chaff. He had heard the chimes at midnight. And when he had looked in at the old Gardenia, commissionaires had fought for the privilege of throwing him out. A man, in a word, who should never have been taught to write and who, if unhappily gifted with that ability, should have been restrained by Act of Parliament from writing Reminiscences.

So thought Lady Constance, his sister. So thought Sir Gregory Parsloe-Parsloe, his neighbour. And so thought the pillars of society in distant Cumberland and Kent. Widely as they differed on many points, they were unanimous on this.

'He wanted me to try to find out if Galahad was putting anything about him into it.'

'Better ask him now,' said Millicent. 'He's just come out of the house and seems to be heading in this direction.'

Lady Constance turned sharply and, following her niece's pointing finger, winced. The mere sight of her deplorable brother was generally enough to make her wince. When he began to talk and she had to listen, the wince became a shudder. His conversation had the effect of making her feel as if she had suddenly swallowed something acid.

'It always makes me laugh,' said Millicent, 'when I think what a frightfully bad shot Uncle Gally's godfathers and godmothers made when they christened him.'

She regarded her approaching relative with that tolerant – indeed, admiring – affection which the young of her sex, even when they have Madonna-like faces, are only too prone to lavish on such of their seniors as have had interesting pasts.

'Doesn't he look marvellous?' she said. 'It really is an extraordinary thing that anyone who has had as good a time as he has can be so amazingly healthy. Everywhere you look, you see men leading model lives and pegging out in their prime, while good old Uncle Gally, who apparently never went to bed till he was fifty, is still breezing along as fit and rosy as ever.'

'All our family have had excellent constitutions,' said Lord Emsworth.

'And I'll bet Uncle Gally needed every ounce of his,' said Millicent.

The Author, ambling briskly across the lawn, had now joined the little group at the tea-table. As his photograph had indicated, he was a short, trim, dapper little man of the type one associates automatically in one's mind with checked suits, tight trousers, white bowler hats, pink carnations, and race-glasses bumping against the left hip. Though bare-headed at the moment and in his shirt-sleeves, and displaying on the tip of his nose the ink-spot of the literary life, he still seemed out of place away from a paddock or an American bar. His bright eyes, puckered at the corners, peered before him as though watching horses rounding into the straight. His neatly-shod foot had about it a suggestion of pawing in search of a brass rail. A jaunty little gentleman, and, as Millicent had said, quite astonishingly fit and rosy. A thoroughly misspent life had left the Hon. Galahad Threepwood, contrary to the most elementary justice, in what appeared to be perfect, even exuberantly perfect physical condition. How a man who ought to have had the liver of the century could look and behave as he did was a constant mystery to his associates. His eye was not dimmed nor his natural force abated. And when, skipping blithely across the turf, he tripped over the spaniel, so graceful was the agility with which he recovered his balance that he did not spill a drop of the whisky-and-soda in his hand. He continued to bear the glass aloft like some brave banner beneath which he had often fought and won. Instead of the blot on the proud family, he might have been a teetotal acrobat.

Having disentangled himself from the spaniel and soothed the animal's wounded feelings by permitting it to sniff the whisky-and-soda, the Hon. Galahad produced a black-rimmed monocle, and, screwing it into his eye, surveyed the table with a frown of distaste.

'Tea?'

Millicent reached for a cup.

'Cream and sugar, Uncle Gally?'

He stopped her with a gesture of shocked loathing.

'You know I never drink tea. Too much respect for my

inside. Don't tell me you are ruining your inside with that poison.'

'Sorry, Uncle Gally. I like it.'

'You be careful,' urged the Hon. Galahad, who was fond of his niece and did not like to see her falling into bad habits. 'You be very careful how you fool about with that stuff. Did I ever tell you about poor Buffy Struggles back in 'ninety-three? Some misguided person lured poor old Buffy into one of those temperance lectures illustrated with coloured slides, and he called on me next day ashen, poor old chap – ashen. "Gally," he said. "What would you say the procedure was when a fellow wants to buy tea? How would a fellow set about it?" "Tea?" I said. "What do you want tea for?" "To drink," said Buffy. "Pull yourself together, dear boy," I said. "You're talking wildly. You can't drink tea. Have a brandy-and-soda." "No more alcohol for me," said Buffy. "Look what it does to the common earthworm." "But you're not a common earthworm," I said, putting my finger on the flaw in his argument right away. "I dashed soon shall be if I go on drinking alcohol," said Buffy. Well, I begged him with tears in my eyes not to do anything rash, but I couldn't move him. He ordered in ten pounds of the muck and was dead inside the year.'

'Good heavens! Really?'

The Hon. Galahad nodded impressively.

'Dead as a door-nail. Got run over by a hansom cab, poor dear old chap, as he was crossing Piccadilly. You'll find the story in my book.'

'How's the book coming along?'

'Magnificently, my dear. Splendidly. I had no notion writing was so easy. The stuff just pours out. Clarence, I wanted to ask you about a date. What year was it there was that terrible row between young Gregory Parsloe and Lord Burper, when Parsloe stole the old chap's false teeth, and pawned them at a shop in the Edgware Road? '96? I should have said later than that – '97 or '98.

Perhaps you're right, though. I'll pencil in '96
tentatively.'

Lady Constance uttered a sharp cry. The sunlight had
now gone quite definitely out of her life. She felt, as she
so often felt in her brother Galahad's society, as if foxes
were gnawing her vitals. Not even the thought that she
could now give Sir Gregory Parsloe-Parsloe the inside
information for which he had asked was able to comfort
her.

'Galahad! You are not proposing to print libellous
stories like that about our nearest neighbour?'

'Certainly I am.' The Hon. Galahad snorted
militantly. 'And, as for libel, let him bring an action if
he wants to. I'll fight him to the House of Lords. It's the
best documented story in my book. Well, if you insist it
was '96, Clarence . . . I'll tell you what,' said the Hon.
Galahad, inspired. 'I'll say "towards the end of the
nineties". After all, the exact date isn't so important. It's
the facts that matter.'

And, leaping lightly over the spaniel, he flitted away
across the lawn.

Lady Constance sat rigid in her chair. Her fine eyes
were now protruding slightly, and her face was drawn.
This and not the Mona Lisa's, you would have said,
looking at her, was the head on which all the sorrows of
the world had fallen.

'Clarence!'

'My dear?'

'What are you going to do about this?'

'Do?'

'Can't you see that something must be done? Do you
realize that if this awful book of Galahad's is published
it will alienate half our friends? They will think we are
to blame. They will say we ought to have stopped him
somehow. Imagine Sir Gregory's feelings when he reads
that appalling story!'

Lord Emsworth's amiable face darkened.

'I am not worrying about Parsloe's feelings. Besides, he did steal Burper's false teeth. I remember him showing them to me. He had them packed up in cotton-wool in a small cigar-box.'

The gesture known as wringing the hands is one that is seldom seen in real life, but Lady Constance Keeble at this point did something with hers which might by a liberal interpretation have been described as wringing.

'Oh, if Mr Baxter were only here!' she moaned.

Lord Emsworth started with such violence that his pince-nez fell off and he dropped a slice of seed-cake.

'What on earth do you want that awful feller here for?'

'He would find a way out of this dreadful business. He was always so efficient.'

'Baxter's off his head.'

Lady Constance uttered a sharp exclamation.

'Clarence, you really can be the most irritating person in the world. You get an idea and you cling to it in spite of whatever anybody says. Mr Baxter was the most wonderfully capable man I ever met.'

'Yes, capable of anything,' retorted Lord Emsworth with spirit. 'Threw flower-pots at me in the middle of the night. I woke up in the small hours and found flower-pots streaming in at my bedroom window and looked out and there was this feller Baxter standing on the terrace in lemon-coloured pyjamas, hurling the dashed things as if he thought he was a machine-gun, or something. I suppose he's in an asylum by this time.'

Lady Constance had turned a bright scarlet. Even in their nursery days she had never felt quite so hostile towards the head of the family as now.

'You know perfectly well that there was a quite simple explanation. My diamond necklace had been stolen, and Mr Baxter thought the thief had hidden it in one of the flower-pots. He went to look for it and got locked out and tried to attract attention by . . .'

264

'Well, I prefer to think the man was crazy, and that's the line that Galahad takes in his book.'

'His . . . ! Galahad is not putting that story in his book?'

'Of course he's putting it in his book. Do you think he's going to waste excellent material like that? And, as I say, the line Galahad takes – and he's a clear-thinking, level-headed man – is that Baxter was a raving, roaring lunatic. Well, I'm going to have another look at the Empress.'

He pottered off pigwards.

III

For some moments after he had gone, there was silence at the tea-table. Millicent lay back in her chair, Lady Constance sat stiffly upright in hers. A little breeze that brought with it a scent of wall-flowers began whispering the first tidings that the cool of evening was on its way.

'Why are you so anxious to get Mr Baxter back, Aunt Constance?' asked Millicent.

Lady Constance's rigidity had relaxed. She was looking her calm, masterful self again. She had the air of a woman who has just solved a difficult problem.

'I think his presence here essential,' she said.

'Uncle Clarence doesn't seem to agree with you.'

'Your Uncle Clarence has always been completely blind to his best interests. He ought never to have dismissed the only secretary he has ever had who was capable of looking after his affairs.'

'Isn't Mr Carmody any good?'

'No. He is not. And I shall never feel easy in my mind until Mr Baxter is back in his old place.'

'What's wrong with Mr Carmody?'

'He is grossly inefficient. And,' said Lady Constance, unmasking her batteries, 'I consider that he spends far too much of his time mooning around you, my dear. He

appears to imagine that he is at Blandings Castle simply
to dance attendance on you.'

The charge struck Millicent as unjust. She thought of
pointing out that she and Hugo only met occasionally
and then on the sly, but it occurred to her that the plea
might be injudicious. She bent over the spaniel. A keen
observer might have noted a defensiveness in her
manner. She looked like a girl preparing to cope with an
aunt.

'Do you find him an entertaining companion?'
Millicent yawned.

'Mr Carmody? No, not particularly.'

'A dull young man, I should have thought.'

'Deadly.'

'Vapid.'

'Vap to a degree.'

'And yet you went riding with him last Tuesday.'

'Anything's better than riding alone.'

'You play tennis with him, too.'

'Well, tennis is a game I defy you to play by yourself.'
Lady Constance's lips tightened.

'I wish Ronald had never persuaded your uncle to
employ him. Clarence should have seen by the mere
look of him that he was impossible.' She paused.

'It will be nice having Ronald here,' she said.

'Yes.'

'You must try to see something of him. If,' said Lady
Constance, in the manner which her intimates found
rather less pleasant than some of her other manners, 'Mr
Carmody can spare you for a moment from time to
time.'

She eyed her niece narrowly. But Millicent was a
match for any number of narrow glances, and had been
from her sixteenth birthday. She was also a girl who
believed that the best form of defence is attack.

'Do you think I'm in love with Mr Carmody, Aunt
Constance?'

Lady Constance was not a woman who relished the direct methods of the younger generation. She coloured.

'Such a thought never entered my head.'

'That's fine. I was afraid it had.'

'A sensible girl like you would naturally see the utter impossibility of marriage with a man in his position. He has no money and very little prospects. And, of course, your uncle holds your own money in trust for you and would never dream of releasing it if you wished to make an unsuitable marriage.'

'So it does seem lucky I'm not in love with him, doesn't it?'

'Extremely fortunate.'

Lady Constance paused for a moment, then introduced a topic on which she had frequently touched before. Millicent had seen it coming by the look in her eyes.

'Why you won't marry Ronald, I can't think. It would be so suitable in every way. You have been fond of one another since you were children.'

'Oh, I like old Ronnie a lot.'

'It has been a great disappointment to your Aunt Julia.'

'She must cheer up. She'll get him off all right, if she sticks at it.'

Lady Constance bridled.

'It is not a question of . . . If you will forgive my saying so, my dear, I think you have allowed yourself to fall into a way of taking Ronald far too much for granted. I am afraid you have the impression that he will always be there, ready and waiting for you when you at last decide to make up your mind. I don't think you realize what a very attractive young man he is.'

'The longer I wait, the more fascinating it will give him time to become.'

At a moment less tense, Lady Constance would have

taken time off to rebuke this flippancy; but she felt it would be unwise to depart from her main theme.

'He is just the sort of young man that girls are drawn to. In fact, I have been meaning to tell you. I had a letter from your Aunt Julia, saying that during their stay at Biarritz they met a most charming American girl, a Miss Schoonmaker, whose father, it seems, used to be a friend of your Uncle Galahad. She appeared to be quite taken with Ronald, and he with her. He travelled back to Paris with her and left her there.'

'How fickle men are!' sighed Millicent.

'She had some shopping to do,' said Lady Constance sharply. 'By this time she is probably in London. Julia invited her to stay at Blandings, and she accepted. She may be here any day now. And I do think, my dear,' proceeded Lady Constance earnestly, 'that, before she arrives, you ought to consider very carefully what your feelings towards Ronald really are.'

'You mean, if I don't watch my step, Miss Doopenhacker may steal my Ronnie away from me?'

It was not quite how Lady Constance would have put it herself, but it conveyed her meaning.

'Exactly.'

Millicent laughed. It was plain that her flesh declined to creep at the prospect.

'Good luck to her,' she said. 'She can count on a fish-slice from me, and I'll be a bridesmaid, too, if wanted. Can't you understand, Aunt Constance, that I haven't the slightest desire to marry Ronnie. We're great pals, and all that, but he's not my style. Too short, for one thing.'

'Short?'

'I'm inches taller than he is. When we went up the aisle, I should look like someone taking her little brother for a walk.'

Lady Constance would undoubtedly have commented on this remark, but before she could do so the procession reappeared, playing an unexpected return date. Footman James bore a dish of fruit, Footman Thomas a salver with a cream-jug on it. Beach, as before, confined himself to a straight ornamental role.

'Oo!' said Millicent welcomingly. And the spaniel, who liked anything involving cream, gave a silent nod of approval.

'Well,' said Lady Constance, as the procession withdrew, giving up the lost cause, 'if you won't marry Ronald, I suppose you won't.'

'That's about it,' agreed Millicent, pouring cream.

'At any rate, I am relieved to hear that there is no nonsense going on between you and this Mr Carmody. That I could not have endured.'

'He's only moderately popular with you, isn't he?'

'I dislike him extremely.'

'I wonder why. I should have thought he was fairly all right, as young men go. Uncle Clarence likes him. So does Uncle Gally.'

Lady Constance had a high, arched nose, admirably adapted for sniffing. She used it now to the limits of its power.

'Mr Carmody,' she said, 'is just the sort of young man your Uncle Galahad would like. No doubt he reminds him of the horrible men he used to go about London with in his young days.'

'Mr Carmody isn't a bit like that.'

'Indeed?' Lady Constance sniffed again. 'Well, I dislike mentioning it to you, Millicent, for I am old-fashioned enough to think that young girls should be shielded from a knowledge of the world, but I happen to know that Mr Carmody is not at all a nice young man. I have it on the most excellent authority that he is entangled with some impossible chorus-girl.'

It is not easy to sit suddenly bolt-upright in a deep garden-chair, but Millicent managed the feat.

'What!'

'Lady Allardyce told me so.'

'And how does she know?'

'Her son Vernon told her. A girl of the name of Brown. Vernon Allardyce says that he used to see her repeatedly, lunching and dining and dancing with Mr Carmody.'

There was a long silence.

'Nice boy, Vernon,' said Millicent.

'He tells his mother everything.'

'That's what I meant. I think it's so sweet of him.'

Millicent rose. 'Well, I'm going to take a short stroll.'

She wandered off towards the rose-garden.

IV

A young man who has arranged to meet the girl he loves in the rose-garden at six sharp naturally goes there at five-twenty-five, so as not to be late. Hugo Carmody had done this, with the result that by three minutes to six he was feeling as if he had been marooned among roses since the beginning of the summer.

If anybody had told Hugo Carmody six months before that half-way through the following July he would be lurking in trysting-places like this, his whole being alert for the coming of a girl, he would have scoffed at the idea. He would have laughed lightly. Not that he had not been fond of girls. He had always liked girls. But they had been, as it were, the mere playthings, so to speak, of a financial giant's idle hour. Six months ago he had been the keen, iron-souled man of business, all his energies and thoughts devoted to the management of the Hot Spot.

But now he stood shuffling his feet and starting hopefully at every sound, while the leaden moments passed sluggishly on their way. Then his vigil was enlivened by a wasp, which stung him on the back of the hand. He was leaping to and fro, licking his wounds,

when he perceived the girl of his dreams coming down
the path.

'Ah!' cried Hugo.

He ceased to leap and, rushing forward, would have
clasped her in a fond embrace. Many people advocate the
old-fashioned blue-bag for wasp-stings, but Hugo
preferred this treatment.

To his astonishment she drew back. And she was not
a girl who usually drew back on these occasions.

'What's the matter?' he asked, pained. It seemed to
him that a spanner had been bunged into a holy
moment.

'Nothing.'

Hugo was concerned. He did not like the way she was
looking at him. Her soft blue eyes appeared to have been
turned into stone.

'I say,' he said, 'I've just been stung by a beastly great
wasp.'

'Good!' said Millicent.

The way she was talking seemed to him worse than
the way she was looking.

Hugo's concern increased.

'I say, what's up?'

The granite eye took on an added hardness.

'You want to know what's up?'

'Yes – what's up?'

'I'll tell you what's up.'

'Well, what's up?' asked Hugo.

He waited for enlightenment, but she had fallen into
a chilling silence.

'You know,' said Hugo, breaking it, 'I'm getting pretty
fed up with all this secrecy and general snakiness. Seeing
you for an occasional odd five minutes a day and having
to put on false whiskers and hide in bushes to manage
that. I know the Keeble looks on me as a sort of cross
between a leper and a nosegay of deadly nightshade, but

I'm strong with the old boy. I talk pig to him. You might almost say I play on him as on a stringed instrument. So what's wrong with going to him and telling him in a frank and manly way that we love each other and are going to get married?'

The marble of Millicent's face was disturbed by one of those quick, sharp, short, bitter smiles that do nobody any good.

'Why should we lie to Uncle Clarence?'

'Eh?'

'I say, why should we tell him something that isn't true?'

'I don't get your drift.'

'I will continue snowing,' said Millicent coldly. 'I am not quite sure if I am ever going to speak to you again in this world or the next. Much will depend on how good you are as an explainer. I have it on the most excellent authority that you are entangled with a chorus-girl. How about it?'

Hugo reeled. But then St Anthony himself would have reeled if a charge like that had suddenly been hurled at him. The best of men require time to overhaul their consciences on such occasions. A moment and he was himself again.

'It's a lie!'

'Name of Brown.'

'Not a word of truth in it. I haven't set eyes on Sue Brown since I first met you.'

'No. You've been down here all the time.'

'And when I *was* setting eyes on her – why, dash it, my attitude from start to finish was one of blameless, innocent, one hundred per cent brotherliness. A wholesome friendship. Brotherly. Nothing more. I liked dancing and she liked dancing and our steps fitted. So occasionally we would go out together and tread the measure. That's all there was to it. Pure brotherliness. Nothing more. I looked on myself as a sort of brother.'

'Brother, eh?'

'Absolutely a brother. Don't,' urged Hugo earnestly, 'go running away, my dear old thing, with any sort of silly notion that Sue Brown was something in the nature of a vamp. She's one of the nicest girls you would ever want to meet.'

'Nice, is she?'

'A sweet girl. A girl in a million. A real good sort. A sound egg.'

'Pretty, I suppose?'

The native good sense of the Carmodys asserted itself at the eleventh hour.

'Not pretty,' said Hugo decidedly. 'Not pretty, no. Not at all pretty. Far from pretty. Totally lacking in sex-appeal, poor girl. But nice. A good sort. No nonsense about her. Sisterly.'

Millicent pondered.

'H'm,' she said.

Nature paused, listening. Birds checked their song, insects their droning. It was as if it had got about that this young man's fate hung in the balance and the returns would be in shortly.

'Well, all right,' she said at length. 'I suppose I'll have to believe you.'

''At's the way to talk!'

'But just you bear this in mind, my lad. Any funny business from now on . . .'

'As if . . . !'

'One more attack of that brotherly urge . . .'

'As though . . . !'

'All right, then.'

Hugo inhaled vigorously. He felt like a man who has just dodged a wounded tigress.

'Banzai!' he said. 'Sweethearts still!'

V

Blandings Castle dozed in the twilight. Its various inmates were variously occupied. Clarence, ninth Earl of Emsworth, after many a longing, lingering look behind, had dragged himself away from the Empress's boudoir and was reading his well-thumbed copy of *British Pig*. The Hon. Galahad, having fixed up the Parsloe-Burper passage, was skimming through his day's output with an artist's complacent feeling that this was the stuff to give 'em. Butler Beach was pasting the Hon. Galahad's photograph into his album. Millicent, in her bedroom, was looking a little thoughtfully into her mirror. Hugo, in the billiard-room, was practising pensive cannons and thinking loving thoughts of his lady, coupled with an occasional reflection that a short, swift binge in London would be a great wheeze if he could wangle it.

And in her boudoir on the second floor, Lady Constance Keeble had taken pen in hand and was poising it over a sheet of notepaper.

'Dear Mr Baxter,' she wrote.

2 — The Course of True Love

The brilliant sunshine which so enhanced the attractions of life at Blandings Castle had brought less pleasure to those of England's workers whose duties compelled them to remain in London. In his offices on top of the Regal Theatre in Shaftesbury Avenue, Mr Mortimer Mason, the stout senior partner in the firm of Mason and Saxby, Theatrical Enterprises Ltd, was of opinion that what the country really needed was one of those wedge-shaped depressions off the Coast of Iceland. Apart from making him feel like a gaffed salmon, Flaming June was ruining business. Only last night, to cut down expenses, he had had to dismiss some of the chorus from the show downstairs, and he hated dismissing chorus-girls. He was a kind-hearted man, and, having been in the profession himself in his time, knew what it meant to get one's notice in the middle of the summer.

There was a tap on the door. The human watchdog who guarded the outer offices entered.

'Well?' said Mortimer Mason wearily.

'Can you see Miss Brown, sir?'

'Which Miss Brown? Sue?'

'Yes, sir.'

'Of course.' In spite of the heat, Mr Mason brightened. 'Is she outside?'

'Yes, sir.'

'Then pour her in.'

Mortimer Mason had always felt a fatherly fondness for this girl, Sue Brown. He liked her for her own sake, for her unvarying cheerfulness and the honest way she

worked. But what endeared her more particularly to him
was the fact that she was Dolly Henderson's daughter.
London was full of elderly gentlemen who became
pleasantly maudlin when they thought of Dolly
Henderson and the dear old days when the heart was
young and they had had waists. He heaved himself from
his chair: then fell back again, filled with a sense of
intolerable injury.

'My God!' he cried. 'Don't look so cool.'

The rebuke was not undeserved. On an afternoon
when the asphalt is bubbling in the roadway and
theatrical managers melting where they sit, no girl has a
right to resemble a dewy rose plucked from some
old-world garden. And that, Mr Mason considered, was
just what this girl was deliberately resembling. She was
a tiny thing, mostly large eyes and a wide, happy smile.
She had a dancer's figure and in every movement of her
there was Youth.

'Sorry, Pa.' She laughed, and Mr Mason moaned
faintly. Her laugh had reminded him, for his was a
nature not without its poetical side, of ice tinkling in a
jug of beer. 'Try not looking at me.'

'Well, Sue, what's on your mind? Come to tell me
you're going to be married?'

'Not at the moment, I'm afraid.'

'Hasn't that young man of yours got back from
Biarritz yet?'

'He arrived this morning. I had a note during the
matinée. I suppose he's outside now, waiting for me.
Want to have a look at him?'

'Does it mean walking downstairs?' asked Mr Mason,
guardedly.

'No. He'll be in his car. You can see him from the
window.'

Mr Mason was equal to getting to the window. He
peered down at the rakish sports-model two-seater in the
little street below. Its occupant was lying on his spine,

smoking a cigarette in a long holder and looking
austerely at certain children of the neighbourhood
whom he seemed to suspect of being about to scratch
his paint.

'They're making fiancés very small this season,' said
Mr Mason, concluding his inspection.

'He is small, isn't he? He's sensitive about it, poor
darling. Still, I'm small, too, so that's all right.'

'Fond of him?'

'Frightfully.'

'Who is he, anyway? Yes, I know his name's Fish, and
it doesn't mean a thing to me. Any money?'

'I believe he's got quite a lot, only his uncle keeps it
all. Lord Emsworth. He's Ronnie's trustee, or
something.'

'Emsworth? I knew his brother years ago.' Mr Mason
chuckled reminiscently. 'Old Gally! What a lad! I've got
a scheme I'd like to interest old Gally in. I wonder where
he is now.'

'The *Prattler* this week said he was down at Blandings
Castle. That's Lord Emsworth's place in Shropshire.
Ronnie's going down there this evening.'

'Deserting you so soon?' Mortimer Mason shook his
head. 'I don't like this.'

Sue laughed.

'Well, I don't,' said Mr Mason. 'You be careful. These
lads will all bear watching.'

'Don't worry, Pa. He means to do right by our Nell.'

'Well, don't say I didn't warn you. So old Gally is at
Blandings, is he? I must remember that. I'd like to get in
touch with him. And now, what was it you wanted to
see me about?'

Sue became grave.

'I've come to ask you a favour.'

'Go ahead. You know me.'

'It's about those girls you're getting rid of.'

Mr Mason's genial face took on a managerial look.

'Got to get rid of them.'

'I know. But one of them's Sally Field.'

'Meaning what?'

'Well, Sally's awfully hard up, Pa. And what I came to ask,' said Sue breathlessly, 'was, will you keep her on and let me go instead?'

Utter amazement caused Mortimer Mason momentarily to forget the heat. He sat up, gaping.

'Do what?'

'Let me go instead.'

'Let you go instead?'

'Yes.'

'You're crazy.'

'No, I'm not. Come on, Pa. Be a dear.'

'Is she a great friend of yours?'

'Not particularly. I'm sorry for her.'

'I won't do it.'

'You must. She's down to her last bean.'

'But I need you in the show.'

'What nonsense! As if I made the slightest difference.'

'You do. You've got – I don't know – ' Mr Mason twiddled his fingers. 'Something. Your mother used to have it. Did you know I was the second juvenile in the first company she was ever in?'

'Yes, you told me. And haven't you got on! There's enough of you now to make two second juveniles. Well, you will do it, won't you?'

Mr Mason reflected.

'I suppose I'll have to, if you insist,' he said at length. 'If I don't, you'll just hand your notice in anyway. I know you. You're a sportsman, Sue. Your mother was just the same. But are you sure you'll manage all right? I shan't be casting the new show till the end of August, but I may be able to fix you up somewhere if I look round.'

'I don't see how you could look any rounder if you tried, you poor darling. Do you realize, Pa, that if you got up early every morning and did half an hour's Swedish exercises . . .'

'If you don't want to be murdered, stop!'

'It would do you all the good in the world, you know. Well, it's awfully sweet of you to bother about me, Pa, but you mustn't. You've got enough to worry you already. I shall be all right. Good-bye. You've been an angel about Sally. It'll save her life.'

'If she's that cross-eyed girl at the end of the second row who's always out of step, I'm not sure I want to save her life.'

'Well, you're going to do it, anyway. Good-bye.'

'Don't run away.'

'I must. Ronnie's waiting. He's going to take me to tea somewhere. Up the river, I hope. Think how nice it will be there, under the trees, with the water rippling . . .'

'The only thing that stops me hitting you with this ruler,' said Mr Mason, 'is the thought that I shall soon be getting out of this Turkish Bath myself. I've a show opening at Blackpool next week. Think how nice and cool it will be on the sands there, with the waves splashing . . .'

'. . . And you with your little spade and bucket, paddling! Oh, Pa, do send me a photograph. Well, I can't stand here all day, chatting over your vacation plans. My poor Ronnie must be getting slowly fried.'

II

The process of getting slowly fried, especially when you are chafing for a sight of the girl you love after six weeks of exile from her society, is never an agreeable one. After enduring it for some time, the pink-faced young man with the long cigarette-holder had left his seat in the car and had gone for shade and comparative coolness to the shelter of the stage entrance, where he now stood reading the notices on the call-board. He read them moodily. The thought that, after having been away from Sue for all these weeks, he was now compelled to leave her again and go to Blandings Castle was weighing on Ronald Overbury Fish's mind sorely.

Mac, the guardian of the stage door, leaned out of his hutch. The matinée over, he had begun to experience that solemn joy which comes to camels approaching an oasis and stage-door men who will soon be at liberty to pop round the corner. He endeavoured to communicate his happiness to Ronnie.

'Won't be long now, Mr Fish.'

'Eh?'

'Won't be long now, sir.'

'Ah,' said Ronnie.

Mac was concerned at his companion's gloom. He liked smiling faces about him. Reflecting, he fancied he could diagnose its cause.

'I was sorry to hear about that, Mr Fish.'

'Eh?'

'I say I was sorry to hear about that, sir.'

'About what?'

'About the Hot Spot, sir. That night-club of yours. Busting up that way. Going West so prompt.'

Ronnie Fish winced. He presumed the man meant well, but there are certain subjects one does not want mentioned. When you have contrived with infinite pains to wheedle a portion of your capital out of a reluctant trustee and have gone and started a night-club with it and seen that night-club flash into the receiver's hands like some frail egg-shell engulfed by a whirlpool, silence is best.

'Ah,' he said briefly, to indicate this.

Mac had many admirable qualities, but not tact. He was the sort of man who would have tried to cheer Napoleon up by talking about the Winter Sports at Moscow.

'When I heard that you and Mr Carmody was starting

one of those places, I said to the fireman "I give it two
months," I said. And it was six weeks, wasn't it, sir?'

'Seven.'

'Six or seven. Immaterial which. Point is I'm usually
pretty right. I said to the fireman "It takes brains to run
a night-club," I said. "Brains and a certain
what-shall-I-say." Won me half-a-dollar, that did.'

He searched in his mind for other topics to interest
and amuse.

'Seen Mr Carmody lately, sir?'

'No. I've been in Biarritz. He's down in Shropshire.
He's got a job as secretary to an uncle of mine.'

'And I shouldn't wonder,' said Mac cordially, 'if he
wouldn't make a mess of *that*.'

He began to feel that the conversation was now going
with a swing.

'Used to see a lot of Mr Carmody round here at one
time.'

The advance guard of the company appeared, in the
shape of a flock of musicians. They passed out of the
stage door, first a couple of thirsty-looking flutes, then a
group of violins, finally an oboe by himself with a scowl
on his face. Oboes are always savage in captivity.

'Yes, sir. Came here a lot, Mr Carmody did. Asking for
Miss Brown. Great friends those two was.'

'Oh?' said Ronnie thickly.

'Used to make me laugh to see them together.'

Ronnie appeared to swallow something large and
jagged.

'Why?'

'Well, him so tall and her so small. But there,' said
Mac philosophically, 'they say it's opposites that get on
best. I know I weigh seventeen stone and my missus
looks like a ninepenny rabbit, and yet we're as happy as
can be.'

Ronnie's interest in the poundage of the stage-door
keeper's domestic circle was slight.

'Ah,' he said.

Mac, having got on to the subject of Sue Brown, stayed there.

'You see the flowers arrived all right, sir.'

'Eh?'

'The flowers you sent Miss Brown, sir,' said Mac, indicating with a stubby thumb a bouquet on the shelf behind him. 'I haven't given her them yet. Thought she'd rather have them after the performance.'

It was a handsome bouquet, but Ronnie Fish stared at it with a sort of dumb horror. His pink face had grown pinker, and his eyes were glassy.

'Give me those flowers, Mac,' he said in a strangled voice.

'Right, sir. Here you are, sir. Now you look just like a bridegroom, sir,' said the stage-door keeper, chuckling the sort of chuckle that goes with seventeen stone and a fat head.

This thought had struck Ronnie, also. It was driven home a moment later by the displeasing behaviour of two of the chorus-girls who came flitting past. Both looked at him in a way painful to a sensitive young man, and one of them giggled. Ronnie turned to the door.

'When Miss Brown comes, tell her I'm waiting outside in my car.'

'Right, sir. You'll be in again, I suppose, sir?'

'No.' The sombre expression deepened on Ronnie's face. 'I've got to go down to Shropshire this evening.'

'Be away long?'

'Yes. Quite a time.'

'Sorry to hear that, sir. Well, good-bye, sir. Thank you, sir.'

Ronnie, clutching the bouquet, walked with leaden steps to the two-seater. There was a card attached to the flowers. He read it, frowned darkly, and threw the bouquet into the car.

Girls were passing now in shoals. They meant

nothing to Ronnie Fish. He eyed them sourly,
marvelling why the papers talked about 'beauty
choruses'. And then, at last, there appeared one at the
sight of whom his heart, parting from its moorings,
began to behave like a jumping bean. It had reached his
mouth when she ran up with both hands extended.

'Ronnie, you precious angel lambkin!'

'Sue!'

To a young man in love, however great the burden of
sorrows beneath which he may be groaning, the
spectacle of the only girl in the world, smiling up at
him, seldom fails to bring a temporary balm. For the
moment, Ronnie's gloom ceased to be. He forgot that he
had recently lost several hundred pounds in a disastrous
commercial venture. He forgot that he was going off that
evening to live in exile. He even forgot that this girl had
just been sent a handsome bouquet by a ghastly bargee
named P. Frobisher Pilbeam, belonging to the Junior
Constitutional Club. These thoughts would return, but
for the time being the one that occupied his mind to the
exclusion of all others was the thought that after six
long weeks of separation he was once more looking upon
Sue Brown.

'I'm so sorry I kept you waiting, precious. I had to see
Mr Mason.'

Ronnie started.

'What about?'

A student of the motion-pictures, he knew what
theatrical managers were.

'Just business.'

'Did he ask you to lunch, or anything?'

'No. He just fired me.'

'Fired you!'

'Yes, I've lost my job,' said Sue happily.

Ronnie quivered.

'I'll go and break his neck.'

'No, you won't. It isn't his fault. It's the weather.

283

They have to cut down expenses when there's a heat-wave. It's all the fault of people like you for going abroad instead of staying in London and coming to the theatre.' She saw the flowers and uttered a delighted squeal. 'For me?'

A moment before, Ronnie had been all chivalrous concern – a knight prepared to battle to the death for lady-love. He now froze.

'Apparently,' he said coldly.

'How do you mean, apparently?'

'I mean they are.'

'You pet!'

'Leap in.'

Ronnie's gloom was now dense and foglike once more. He gestured fiercely at the clustering children and trod on the self-starter. The car moved smoothly round the corner into Shaftesbury Avenue.

Opposite the Monico, there was a traffic-block, and he unloaded his soul.

'In re those blooms.'

'They're lovely.'

'Yes, but I didn't send them.'

'You brought them. Much nicer.'

'What I'm driving at,' said Ronnie heavily, 'is that they aren't from me at all. They're from a blighter named P. Frobisher Pilbeam.'

Sue's smile had faded. She knew her Ronald's jealousy so well. It was the one thing about him which she could have wished changed.

'Oh?' she said dismally.

The crust of calm detachment from all human emotion, built up by years of Eton and Cambridge, cracked abruptly and there peeped forth a primitive Ronald Overbury Fish.

'Who is this Pilbeam?' he demanded. 'Pretty much the Boy Friend, I take it, what?'

'I've never even met him!'

'But he sends you flowers.'

'I know he does,' wailed Sue, mourning for a golden afternoon now probably spoiled beyond repair. 'He keeps sending me his beastly flowers and writing me his beastly letters . . .'

Ronnie gritted his teeth.

'And I tell you I've never set eyes on him in my life.'

'You don't know who he is?'

'One of the girls told me that he used to edit that paper *Society Spice*. I don't know what he does now.'

'When he isn't sending you flowers, you mean?'

'I can't help him sending me flowers.'

'I don't suppose you want to.'

Sue's eyes flickered. Realizing, however, that her Ronnie in certain moods resembled a child of six, she made a pathetic attempt to lighten the atmosphere.

'It's not my fault if I get persecuted with loathsome addresses, is it? I suppose, when you go to the movies, you blame Lilian Gish for being pursued by the heavy.'

Ronnie was not to be diverted.

'Sometimes I ask myself,' he said darkly, 'if you really care a hang for me.'

'Oh, Ronnie!'

'Yes, I do – repeatedly. I look at you and I look at myself and that's what I ask myself. What on earth is there about me to make a girl like you fond of a fellow? I'm a failure. Can't even run a night-club. No brains. No looks.'

'You've got a lovely complexion.'

'Too pink. Much too pink. And I'm so damned short.'

'You're not a bit too short.'

'I am. My Uncle Gally once told me I looked like the protoplasm of a minor jockey.'

'He ought to have been ashamed of himself.'

'Why the dickens,' said Ronnie, laying bare his secret dreams, 'I couldn't have been born a decent height, like Hugo . . .' He paused. His hand shook on the steering-wheel. 'That reminds me. That fellow Mac at the stage door was saying that you and Hugo used to be as thick as thieves. Always together, he said.'

Sue sighed. Things were being difficult today.

'That was before I met you,' she explained patiently. 'I used to like dancing with him. He's a beautiful dancer. You surely don't suppose for a minute that I could ever be in love with Hugo?'

'I don't see why not.'

'Hugo!' Sue laughed. There was something about Hugo Carmody that always made her want to laugh.

'Well, I don't see why not. He's better looking than I am. Taller. Not so pink. Plays the saxophone.'

'Will you stop being silly about Hugo.'

'Well, I fear that bird. He's my best pal and I know his work. He's practically handsome. And lissom, to boot.' A hideous thought smote Ronnie like a blow. 'Did he ever . . .' He choked. 'Did he ever hold your hand?'

'Which hand?'

'Either hand.'

'How can you suggest such a thing!' cried Sue, shocked.

'Well, will you swear there's nothing between him and you?'

'Of course there isn't.'

'And nothing between this fellow Pilbeam and you?'

'Of course not.'

'Ah!' said Ronnie. 'Then I can go ahead, as planned.'

His was a mercurial temperament, and it had lifted him in an instant from the depths to the heights. The cloud had passed from his face, the look of Byronic despair from his eyes. He beamed.

'Do you know why I'm going down to Blandings tonight?' he asked.

'No. I only wish you weren't.'

'Well, I'll tell you. I've got to get round my uncle.'

'Do what?'

'Make myself solid with my Uncle Clarence. If you've
ever had anything to do with trustees you'll know that
the one thing they bar like poison is parting with
money. And I've simply got to have another chunk of
my capital, and a good big one, too. Without money,
how on earth can I marry you? Let me get hold of funds,
and we'll dash off to the registrar's the moment you say
the word. So now you understand why I've got to get to
Blandings at the earliest possible moment and stay there
till further notice.'

'Yes. I see. And you're a darling. Tell me about
Blandings, Ronnie.'

'How do you mean?'

'Well, what sort of a place is it? I want to imagine you
there while you're away.'

Ronnie pondered. He was not at his best as a word
painter.

'Oh, you know the kind of thing. Parks and gardens
and terraces and immemorial elms and all that. All the
usual stuff.'

'Any girls there?'

'My cousin Millicent. She's my Uncle Lancelot's
daughter. He's dead. The family want Millicent and me
to get married.'

'To each other, you mean? What a perfectly horrible
idea!'

'Oh, it's all right. We're both against the scheme.'

'Well, that's some comfort. What other girls will there
be at Blandings?'

'Only one that I know of. My mother met a female
called Schoonmaker at Biarritz. American. Pots of
money, I believe. One of those beastly tall girls. Looked
like something left over from Dana Gibson. I couldn't
stand her myself, but my mother was all for her, and I
didn't at all like the way she seemed to be trying to
shove her off on to me. You know – "Why don't you ring

up Myra Schoonmaker, Ronnie? I'm sure she would like to go to the Casino tonight. And then you could dance afterwards." Sinister, it seemed to me.'

'And she's going to Blandings? H'm!'

'There's nothing to h'm about.'

'I'm not so sure. Oh, well, I suppose your family are quite right. I suppose you ought really to marry some nice girl in your own set.'

Ronnie uttered a wordless cry, and in his emotion allowed the mudguard of the two-seater to glide so closely past an Austin Seven that Sue gave a frightened squeak and the Austin Seven went on its way thinking black thoughts.

'Do be careful, Ronnie, you old chump!'

'Well, what do you want to go saying things like that for? I get enough of that from the family, without having *you* start.'

'Poor old Ronnie! I'm sorry. Still, you must admit that they'd be quite within their rights, objecting to me. I'm not so hot, you know. Only a chorus-girl. Just one of the Ensemble!'

Ronnie said something between his teeth that sounded like 'Juk!' What he meant was, Be her station never so humble, a pure, sweet girl is a fitting mate for the highest in the land.

'And my mother was a music-hall singer.'

'A what!'

'A music-hall singer. What they used to call a Serio. You know – Pink tights and rather risky songs.'

This time Ronnie did not say 'Juk!' He merely swallowed painfully. The information had come as a shock to him. Somehow or other, he had never thought of Sue as having encumbrances in the shape of relatives; and he could not hide from himself the fact that a pink-tighted Serio might stir the Family up quite a little. He pictured something with peroxide hair who would call his Uncle Clarence 'dearie'.

'English, do you mean? On the Halls here in London?'

'Yes. Her stage name was Dolly Henderson.'

'Never heard of her.'

'I daresay not. But she was the rage of London twenty years ago.'

'I always thought you were American,' said Ronnie, aggrieved. 'I distinctly recollect Hugo, when he introduced us, telling me that you had just come over from New York.'

'So I had. Father took me to America soon after mother died.'

'Oh, your mother is – er – no longer with us?'

'No.'

'Too bad,' said Ronnie, brightening.

'My father's name was Cotterleigh. He was in the Irish Guards.'

'What!'

Ronnie's ecstatic cry seriously inconvenienced a traffic policeman in the exercise of his duties.

'But this is fine! This is the goods! It doesn't matter to me, of course, one way or the other. I'd love you just the same if your father had sold jellied eels. But think what an enormous difference this will make to my blasted family!'

'I doubt it.'

'But it will. We must get him over at once and spring him on them. Or is he in London?'

Sue's brown eyes clouded.

'He's dead.'

'Eh? Oh? Sorry!' said Ronnie.

He was dashed for a moment.

'Well, at least let me tell the family about him,' he urged, recovering. 'Let me dangle him before their eyes a bit.'

'If you like. But they'll still object to me because I'm in the chorus.'

Ronnie scowled. He thought of his mother, he

thought of his Aunt Constance, and reason told him that her words were true.

'Dash all this rot people talk about chorus-girls!' he said. 'They seem to think that just because a girl works in the chorus she must be a sort of animated champagne-vat . . .'

'Ugh!'

'Spending her life dancing on supper-tables with tight stockbrokers . . .'

'And not a bad way of passing an evening,' said Sue meditatively. 'I must try it some time.'

'. . . with the result that when it's a question of her marrying anybody, the fellow's people look down their noses and kick like mules. It's happened in our family before. My Uncle Gally was in love with some girl on the stage back in the dark ages, and they formed a wedge and bust the thing up and shipped him off to South Africa or somewhere to forget her. And look at him! Drew three sober breaths in the year nineteen-hundred and then decided that was enough. I expect I shall be the same. If I don't take to drink, cooped up at Blandings a hundred miles away from you, I shall be vastly surprised. It's all a lot of silly nonsense. I haven't any patience with it. I've a jolly good mind to go to Uncle Clarence tonight and simply tell him that I'm in love with you and intend to marry you and that if the family don't like it they can lump it.'

'I wouldn't.'

Ronnie simmered down.

'Perhaps you're right.'

'I'm sure I am. If he hears about me, he certainly won't give you your money. Whereas, if he doesn't, he may. What sort of a man is he?'

'Uncle Clarence? Oh, a mild, dreamy old boy. Mad about gardening and all that. At the moment, I hear, he's wrapped up in his pig.'

'That sounds cosy.'

'I'd feel a lot easier in my mind, I can tell you, going down there to tackle him, if I were a pig. I'd expect a much warmer welcome.'

'You were rather a pig just now, weren't you?'

Ronnie quivered. Remorse gnawed the throbbing heart beneath his beautifully cut waistcoat.

'I'm sorry. I'm frightfully sorry. The fact is, I'm so crazy about you, I get jealous of everybody you meet. Do you know, Sue, if you ever let me down, I'd . . . I don't know what I'd do. Er – Sue!'

'Hullo?'

'Swear something.'

'What?'

'Swear that, while I'm at Blandings, you won't go out with a soul. Not even to dance.'

'Not even to dance?'

'No.'

'All right.'

'Especially this man Pilbeam.'

'I thought you were going to say Hugo.'

'I'm not worrying about Hugo. He's safe at Blandings.'

'Hugo at Blandings?'

'Yes. He's secretarying for my Uncle Clarence. I made my mother get him the job when the Hot Spot conked.'

'So you'll have him *and* Millicent *and* Miss Schoonmaker there to keep you company! How nice for you.'

'Millicent!'

'It's all very well to say "Millicent!" like that. If you ask me, I think she's a menace. She sounds coy and droopy. I can see her taking you for walks by moonlight under those immemorial elms and looking up at you with big, dreamy eyes . . .'

'Looking down at me, you mean. She's about a foot taller than I am. And, anyway, if you imagine there's a girl on earth who would extract so much as a kindly glance from me when I've got you to think about, you're very much mistaken. I give you my honest word . . .'

He became lyrical. Sue, leaning back, listened contentedly. The cloud had been a threatening cloud, blackening the skies for a while, but it had passed. The afternoon was being golden, after all.

III

'By the way,' said Ronnie, the flood of eloquence subsiding. 'A thought occurs. Have you any notion where we're headed for?'

'Heaven.'

'I mean at the moment.'

'I supposed you were taking me to tea somewhere.'

'But where? We've got right out of the tea zone. What with one thing and another, I've just been driving at random – to and fro, as it were – and we seem to have worked round to somewhere in the Swiss Cottage neighbourhood. We'd better switch back and set a course for the Carlton or some place. How do you feel about the Carlton?'

'All right.'

'Or the Ritz?'

'Whichever you like.'

'Or – Gosh!'

'What's the matter?'

'Sue! I've got an idea.'

'Beginner's luck.'

'Why not go to Norfolk Street?'

'To your home?'

'Yes. There's nobody there. And our butler is a staunch bird. He'd get us tea and say nothing.'

'I'd like to meet a staunch butler.'

'Then shall we?'

'I'd love it. You can show me all your little treasures and belongings and the photographs of you as a small boy.'

Ronnie shook his head. It irked him to discourage
her pretty enthusiasm, but a man cannot afford to take
risks.

'Not those. No love could stand up against the sight of
me in a sailor suit at the age of ten. I don't mind,' he
said, making a concession, 'letting you see the one of me
and Hugo, taken just before the Public Schools Rackets
Competition, my last year at school. We were the Eton
pair.'

'Did you win?'

'No. At a critical moment in the semi-final that ass
Hugo foozled a shot a one-armed cripple ought to have
taken with his eyes shut. It dished us.'

'Awful!' said Sue. 'Well, if I ever had any impulse to
love Hugo, that's killed it.' She looked about her. 'I don't
know this aristocratic neighbourhood at all. How far is it
to Norfolk Street?'

'Next turning.'

'You're sure there's nobody in the house? None of the
dear old Family?'

'Not a soul.'

He was right. Lady Constance Keeble was not
actually in the house. At the moment when he spoke
she had just closed the front door behind her. After
waiting half an hour in the hope of her nephew's return,
she had left a note for him on the hall table, and was
going to Claridge's to get a cup of tea.

It was not until he had drawn up immediately
opposite the house that Ronnie perceived what stood
upon the steps. Having done so, he blenched visibly.

'Oh, my sainted aunt!' he said.

And seldom can the familiar phrase have been used
with more appropriateness.

The sainted aunt was inspecting the two-seater and
its contents with a frozen stare. Her eyebrows were two
marks of interrogation. As she had told Millicent, she
was old-fashioned, and when she saw her flesh and blood

293

snuggled up to girls of attractive appearance in two-seaters, she suspected the worst.

'Good afternoon, Ronald.'

'Er – hullo, Aunt Constance.'

'Will you introduce me?'

There is no doubt that peril sharpens the intellect. His masters at school and his tutors at the University, having had to do with Ronald Overbury Fish almost entirely at times when his soul was at rest, had classed him among the less keen-witted of their charges. Had they seen him now in this crisis they would have pointed at him with pride. And, being the sportsmen and gentlemen that they were, they would have hastened to acknowledge that they had grossly underestimated his ingenuity and initiative.

For, after turning a rather pretty geranium tint and running a finger round the inside of his collar for an instant, as if he found it too tight, Ronnie Fish spoke the only two words in the language which could have averted disaster.

'Miss Schoonmaker,' he said, huskily.

Sue at his side, gave a little gasp. These were unsuspected depths.

'Miss Schoonmaker!'

Lady Constance's resemblance to Apollyon straddling right across the way had vanished abruptly. Remorse came upon her that she should have wronged her blameless nephew with unfounded suspicions.

'Miss Schoonmaker, my aunt, Lady Constance Keeble,' said Ronnie, going from strength to strength, and speaking now quite easily and articulately.

Sue was not the girl to sit dumbly by and fail a partner in his hour of need. She smiled brightly.

'How do you do, Lady Constance?' she said. She smiled again, if possible even more brightly than before. 'I feel I know you already. Lady Julia told me so much about you at Biarritz.'

A momentary qualm lest, in the endeavour to achieve an easy cordiality, she had made her manner a shade too patronizing, melted in the sunshine of the older woman's smile. Lady Constance had become charming, almost effusive. She had always hoped that Ronald and Millicent would make a match of it: but, failing that, this rich Miss Schoonmaker was certainly the next best thing. And driving chummily about London together like this must surely, she thought, mean something, even in these days when chummy driving is so prevalent between the sexes. At any rate, she hoped so.

'So here you are in London!'

'Yes.'

'You did not stay long in Paris.'

'No.'

'When can you come down to Blandings?'

'Oh, very soon, I hope.'

'I am going there this evening. I only ran up for the day. I want you to drive me back, Ronald.'

Ronnie nodded silently. The crisis passed, a weakness had come upon him. He preferred not to speak, if speech could be avoided.

'Do try to come soon. The gardens are looking delightful. My brother will be so glad to see you. I was just on my way to Claridge's for a cup of tea. Won't you come too?'

'I'd love to,' said Sue, 'but I really must be getting on. Ronnie was taking me shopping.'

'I thought you stayed in Paris to do your shopping.'

'Not all of it.'

'Well, I shall hope to see you soon.'

'Oh, yes.'

'At Blandings.'

'Thank you so much. Ronnie, I think we ought to be getting along.'

'Yes.' Ronnie's mind was blurred, but he was clear on that point. 'Yes, getting along. Pushing off.'

'Well, I'm so delighted to have seen you. My sister told me so much about you in her letters. After you have put your luggage on the car, Ronald, will you come and pick me up at Claridge's?'

'Right ho.'

'I would like to make an early start, if possible.'

'Right ho.'

'Well, good-bye for the present, then.'

'Right ho.'

'Good-bye, Lady Constance.'

'Good-bye.'

The two-seater moved off, and Ronnie, taking his right hand from the wheel as it turned the corner, groped for a handkerchief, found it, and passed it over his throbbing brow.

'So that was Aunt Constance!' said Sue.

Ronnie breathed deeply.

'Nice meeting one of whom I have heard so much.'

Ronnie replaced his hand on the wheel and twiddled it feebly to avoid a dog. Reaction had made him limp.

Sue was gazing at him almost reverently.

'What genius, Ronnie! What ready wit! What presence of mind! If I hadn't heard it with my own ears, I wouldn't have believed it. Why didn't you ever tell me you were one of those swift thinkers?'

'I didn't know it myself.'

'Of course, I'm afraid it has complicated things a little.'

'Eh?' Ronnie started. This aspect of the matter had not struck him. 'How do you mean?'

'When I was a child, they taught me a poem . . .'

Ronnie raised a suffering face to hers.

'Don't let's talk about your childhood now, old thing,' he pleaded. 'Feeling rather shaken. Any other time . . .'

'It's all right. I'm not wandering from the subject. I can only remember two lines of the poem. They were, "Oh, what a tangled web we weave when first we practise to deceive." You do see the web is a bit tangled, don't you, Ronnie, darling?'

'Eh? Why? Everything looks pretty smooth to me. Aunt Constance swallowed you without a yip.'

'And when the real Miss Schoonmaker arrives at Blandings with her jewels and her twenty-four trunks?' said Sue gently.

The two-seater swerved madly across Grosvenor Street.

'Gosh!' said Ronnie.

Sue's eyes were sparkling.

'There's only one thing to do,' she said. 'Now you're in, you'll have to go in deeper. You'll have to put her off.'

'How?'

'Send her a wire saying she mustn't come to Blandings, because scarlet fever or something has broken out.'

'I couldn't!'

'You must. Sign it in Lady Constance's name.'

'But suppose . . .'

'Well, suppose they do find out? You won't be in any worse hole than you will be if she comes sailing up to the front door, all ready to stay a couple of weeks. And she will unless you wire.'

'That's true.'

'What it means,' said Sue, 'is that instead of having plenty of time to get that money out of Lord Emsworth you'll have to work quick.' She touched his arm. 'Here's a post-office,' she said. 'Go in and send that wire before you weaken.'

Ronnie stopped the car.

'You will have to do the most rapid bit of trustee-touching in the history of the world, I should think,' said Sue reflectively. 'Do you think you can manage it?'

'I'll have a jolly good prod.'

'Remember what it means.'

'I'll do that all right. The only trouble is that in the matter of biting Uncle Clarence's ear I've nothing to rely on but my natural charm. And as far as I've been able to make out,' said Ronnie, 'he hasn't noticed yet that I have any.'

He strode into the post-office, thinking deeply.

3 — Sensational Theft of a Pig

It was the opinion of the poet Calverley, expressed in his immortal Ode To Tobacco, that there is no heaviness of the soul which will not vanish beneath the influence of a quiet smoke. Ronnie Fish would have disputed this theory. It was the third morning of his sojourn at Blandings Castle; and, taking with him a tennis-ball which he proposed to bounce before him in order to assist thought, he had wandered out into the grounds, smoking hard. And tobacco, though Turkish and costly, was not lightening his despondency at all. It seemed to Ronnie that the present was bleak and the future grey. Roaming through the sun-flooded park, he bounced his tennis-ball and groaned in spirit.

On the credit side of the ledger one single item could be inscribed. Hugo was at the castle. He had the consolation, therefore, of knowing that that tall and lissom young man was not in London, exercising his fatal fascination on Sue. But, when you had said this, you had said everything. After all, even eliminating Hugo, there still remained in the metropolis a vast population of adult males, all either acquainted with Sue or trying to make her acquaintance. The poison-sac Pilbeam, for instance. By now it might well be that that bacillus had succeeded in obtaining an introduction to her. A devastating thought.

And even supposing he hadn't, even supposing that Sue, as she had promised, was virtuously handing the mitten to all the young thugs who surged around her with invitations to lunch and supper; where did that get a chap? What, in other words, of the future?

In coming to Blandings Castle, Ronnie was only too well aware, he had embarked on an expedition, the success or failure of which would determine whether his life through the years was to be roses, roses all the way or a dreary desert. And so far, in his efforts to win the favour and esteem of his Uncle Clarence, he seemed to have made no progress whatsoever. On the occasions when he had found himself in Lord Emsworth's society, the latter had looked at him sometimes as if he did not know he was there, more often as if he wished he wasn't. It was only too plain that the collapse of the Hot Spot had left his stock in bad shape. There had been a general sagging of the market. Fish Preferred, taking the most sanguine estimate, could scarcely be quoted at more than about thirty to thirty-five.

Plunged in thought, and trying without any success to conjure up a picture of a benevolent uncle patting him on the head with one hand while writing cheques with the other, he had wandered some distance from the house and was passing a small spinney, when he observed in a little dell to his left a peculiar object.

It was a large yellow caravan. And what, he asked himself, was a caravan doing in the grounds of Blandings Castle?

To aid him in grappling with the problem, he flung the tennis-ball at it. Upon which, the door opened and a spectacled head appeared.

'Hullo!' said the head.

'Hullo!' said Ronnie.

'Hullo!'

'Hullo!'

The thing threatened to become a hunting-chorus. At this moment, however, the sun went behind a cloud and Ronnie was enabled to recognize the head's proprietor. Until now, the light, shining on the other's glasses, had dazzled him.

'Baxter!' he exclaimed.

The last person he would have expected to meet in the park of Blandings. He had heard all about that row a couple of years ago. He knew that, if his own stock with Lord Emsworth was low, that of the Efficient Baxter was down in the cellar, with no takers. Yet here the fellow was, shoving his head out of caravans as if nothing had ever happened.

'Ah, Fish!'

Rupert Baxter descended the steps, a swarthy-complexioned young man with a supercilious expression which had always been displeasing to Ronnie.

'What are you doing here?' asked Ronnie.

'I happened to be taking a caravan holiday in the neighbourhood. And, finding myself at Market Blandings last night, I thought I would pay a visit to the place where I had spent so many happy days.'

'I see.'

'Perhaps you could tell me where I could find Lady Constance?'

'I haven't seen her since breakfast. She's probably about somewhere.'

'I will go and inquire. If you meet her, perhaps you would not mind mentioning that I am here.'

The Efficient Baxter strode off, purposeful as ever; and Ronnie, having speculated for a moment as to how his Uncle Clarence would comport himself if he came suddenly round a corner and ran into this bit of the dead past, and having registered an idle hope that, when this happened, he might be present with a camera, inserted another cigarette in its holder and passed on his way.

II

Five minutes later, Lord Emsworth, leaning pensively out of the library window and sniffing the morning air, received an unpleasant shock. He could have sworn he had seen his late secretary, Rupert Baxter, cross the gravel and go in at the front door.

'Bless my soul!' said Lord Emsworth.

The only explanation that occurred to him was that Baxter, having met with some fatal accident, had come back to haunt the place. To suppose the fellow could be here in person was absurd. When you shoot a secretary out for throwing flower-pots at you in the small hours, he does not return to pay social calls. A frown furrowed his lordship's brow. The spectre of one of his ancestors he could have put up with, but the idea of a Blandings Castle haunted by Baxter he did not relish at all. He decided to visit his sister Constance in her boudoir and see what she had to say about it.

'Constance, my dear.'

Lady Constance looked up from the letter she was writing. She clicked her tongue, for it annoyed her to be interrupted at her correspondence.

'Well, Clarence?'

'I say, Constance, a most extraordinary thing happened just now. I was looking out of the library window and – you remember Baxter?'

'Of course I remember Mr Baxter.'

'Well, his ghost has just walked across the gravel.'

'What *are* you talking about, Clarence?'

'I'm telling you. I was looking out of the library window and I suddenly saw –'

'Mr Baxter,' announced Beach, flinging open the door.

'Mr Baxter!'

'Good morning, Lady Constance.'

Rupert Baxter advanced with joyous camaraderie glinting from both lenses. Then he perceived his former employer and his exuberance diminished. 'Er – good morning, Lord Emsworth,' he said, flashing his spectacles austerely upon him.

There was a pause. Lord Emsworth adjusted his

pince-nez and regarded the visitor dumbly. Of the relief
which was presumably flooding his soul at the discovery
that Rupert Baxter was still on this side of the veil, he
gave no outward sign.

Baxter was the first to break an uncomfortable
silence.

'I happened to be taking a caravan holiday in this
neighbourhood, Lady Constance, and finding myself
near Market Blandings last night, I thought I would . . .'

'Why, of course! We should never have forgiven you if
you had not come to see us. Should we, Clarence?'

'Eh?'

'I said, should we?'

'Should we what?' said Lord Emsworth, who was still
adjusting his mind.

Lady Constance's lips tightened, and a moment
passed during which it seemed always a fifty-fifty
chance that a handsome silver ink-pot would fly through
the air in the direction of her brother's head. But she was
a strong woman. She fought down the impulse.

'Did you say you were travelling in a caravan, Mr
Baxter?'

'In a caravan. I left it in the park.'

'Well, of course you must come and stay with us. The
castle,' she continued, raising her voice a little, to
compete with a sort of wordless bubbling which had
begun to proceed from her brother's lips, 'is almost
empty just now. We shall not be having our first big
house-party till the middle of next month. You must
make quite a long visit. I will send somebody over to
fetch your things.'

'It is exceedingly kind of you.'

'It will be delightful having you here again. Won't it,
Clarence?'

'Eh?'

'I said won't it?'

'Won't it what?'

Lady Constance's hand trembled above the ink-pot like a hovering butterfly. She withdrew it.

'Will it not be delightful,' she said, catching her brother's eye and holding it like a female Ancient Mariner, 'having Mr Baxter back at the castle again?'

'I'm going down to see my pig,' said Lord Emsworth.

A silence followed his departure, such as would have fallen had a coffin just been carried out. Then Lady Constance shook off gloom.

'Oh, Mr Baxter, I'm so glad you were able to come. And how clever of you to come in a caravan. It prevented your arrival seeming prearranged.'

'I thought of that.'

'You think of everything.'

Rupert Baxter stepped to the door, opened it, satisfied himself that no listeners lurked in the passage, and returned to his seat.

'Are you in any trouble, Lady Constance? Your letter seemed so very urgent.'

'I am in dreadful trouble, Mr Baxter.'

If Rupert Baxter had been a different type of man and Lady Constance Keeble a different type of woman he would probably at this point have patted her hand. As it was, he merely hitched his chair an inch closer to hers.

'If there is anything I can do?'

'There is nobody except you who can do anything. But I hardly like to ask you.'

'Ask me whatever you please. And if it is in my power . . .'

'Oh, it is.'

Rupert Baxter gave his chair another hitch.

'Tell me.'

Lady Constance hesitated.

'It seems such an impossible thing to ask of anyone.'

'Please!'

'Well . . . you know my brother?'

Baxter seemed puzzled. Then an explanation of the peculiar question presented itself.

'Oh, you mean Mr . . . ?'

'Yes, yes, yes. Of course I wasn't referring to Lord Emsworth. My brother Galahad.'

'I have never met him. Oddly enough, though he visited the castle twice during the period when I was Lord Emsworth's secretary, I was away both times on my holiday. Is he here now?'

'Yes. Finishing his Reminiscences.'

'I saw in some paper that he was writing the history of his life.'

'And if you know what a life his had been you will understand why I am distracted.'

'Certainly I have heard stories,' said Baxter guardedly.

Lady Constance performed that movement with her hands which came so close to wringing.

'The book is full from beginning to end of libellous anecdotes, Mr Baxter. About all our best friends. If it is published we shall not have a friend left. Galahad seems to have known everybody in England when they were young and foolish, and to remember everything particularly foolish and disgraceful that they did. So . . .'

'So you want me to get hold of the manuscript and destroy it?'

Lady Constance stared, stunned by this penetration. She told herself that she might have known that she would not have to make long explanations to Rupert Baxter. His mind was like a searchlight, darting hither and thither, lighting up whatever it touched.

'Yes,' she gasped. She hurried on. 'It does seem, I know, an extraordinary thing to . . .'

'Not at all.'

'. . . but Lord Emsworth refuses to do anything.'

'I see.'

'You know how he is in the face of any emergency.'

'Yes, I do, indeed.'

'So supine. So helpless. So vague and altogether incompetent.'

'Precisely.'

'Mr Baxter, you are my only hope.'

Baxter removed his spectacles, polished them, and put them back again.

'I shall be delighted, Lady Constance, to do anything to help you that lies in my power. And to obtain possession of this manuscript should be an easy task. But is there only one copy of it in existence?'

'Yes, yes, yes. I am sure of that. Galahad told me that he was waiting till it was finished before sending it to the typist.'

'Then you need have no further anxiety.'

It was a moment when Lady Constance Keeble would have given much for eloquence. She sought for words that should adequately express her feelings, but could find none.

'Oh, Mr Baxter!' she said.

III

Ronnie Fish's aimlessly wandering feet had taken him westward. It was not long, accordingly, before there came to his nostrils a familiar and penetrating odour, and he found that he was within a short distance of the detached residence employed by Empress of Blandings as a combined bedroom and restaurant. A few steps, and he was enabled to observe that celebrated animal in person. With her head tucked well down and her tail wiggling with pure *joie de vivre*, the Empress was hoisting in a spot of lunch.

Everybody likes to see somebody eating. Ronnie leaned over the rail, absorbed. He poised the tennis-ball and with an absent-minded flick of the wrist bounced it on the silver medallist's back. Finding the pleasant, ponging sound which resulted soothing to harassed

nerves, he did it again. The Empress made excellent
bouncing. She was not one of your razor-backs. She
presented a wide and resistant surface. For some
minutes, therefore, the pair carried on according to plan
– she eating, he bouncing, until presently Ronnie was
thrilled to discover that this outdoor sport of his was
assisting thought. Gradually – mistily at first, then
assuming shape, a plan of action was beginning to
emerge from the murk of his mind.

How would this be, for instance?

If there was one thing calculated to appeal to his
Uncle Clarence, to induce in his Uncle Clarence a really
melting mood, it was the announcement that somebody
desired to return to the Land. He loved to hear of people
returning to the Land. How, then, would this be? Go to
the old boy, state that one had seen the light and was in
complete agreement with him that England's future
depended on checking the Drift to the Towns, and then
ask for a good fat slice of capital with which to start a
farm.

The project of starting a farm was one which was
bound to . . . Half a minute. Another idea on the way.
Yes, here it came, and it was a pippin. Not merely just
an ordinary farm, but a pig-farm! Wouldn't Uncle
Clarence leap in the air and shower gold on anybody
who wanted to live in the country and breed pigs? You
bet your Sunday cuffs he would. And, once the money
was safely deposited to the account of Ronald Overbury
Fish in Cox's Bank, then ho! for the registrar's hand in
hand with Sue.

There was a musical *plonk* as Ronnie bounced the
ball for the last time on the Empress's complacent back.
Then, no longer with dragging steps but treading on air,
he wandered away to sketch out the last details of the
scheme before going indoors and springing it.

IV

Too often it happens that, when you get these
brain-waves, you take another look at them after a short
interval and suddenly detect some fatal flaw. No such
disappointment came to mar the happiness of Ronnie
Fish.

'I say, Uncle Clarence,' he said, prancing into the
library, some half-hour later.

Lord Emsworth was deep in the current issue of a
weekly paper of porcine interest. It seemed to Ronnie, as
he looked up, that his eye was not any too chummy.
This, however, did not disturb him. That eye, he was
confident, would melt anon. If, at the moment, Lord
Emsworth could hardly have sat for his portrait in the
role of a benevolent uncle, there would, Ronnie felt, be a
swift change of demeanour in the very near future.

'I say, Uncle Clarence, you know that capital of mine.'

'That what?'

'My capital. My money. The money you're trustee of.
And a jolly good trustee,' said Ronnie handsomely.
'Well, I've been thinking things over and I want you, if
you will, to disgorge a segment of it for a sort of venture
I've got in mind.'

He had not expected the eye to melt yet, and it did
not. Seen through the glass of his uncle's pince-nez, it
looked like an oyster in an aquarium.

'You wish to start another night-club?'

Lord Emsworth's voice was cold, and Ronnie
hastened to disabuse him of the idea.

'No, no. Nothing like that. Night-clubs are a mug's
game. I ought never to have touched them. As a matter
of fact, Uncle Clarence, London as a whole seems to me
a bit of a washout these days. I'm all for the country.
What I feel is that the drift to the towns should be
checked. What England wants is more blokes going back
to the land. That's the way it looks to me.'

Ronnie Fish began to experience the first definite twinges of uneasiness. This was the point at which he had been confident that the melting process would set in. Yet, watching the eye, he was dismayed to find it as oysterlike as ever. He felt like an actor who has been counting on a round of applause and goes off after his big speech without a hand. The idea occurred to him that his uncle might possibly have grown a little hard of hearing.

'To the Land,' he repeated, raising his voice. 'More blokes going back to the Land. So I want a dollop of capital to start a farm.'

He braced himself for the supreme revelation.

'I want to breed pigs,' he said reverently.

Something was wrong. There was no blinking the fact any longer. So far from leaping in the air and showering gold, his uncle merely stared at him in an increasingly unpleasant manner. Lord Emsworth had removed his pince-nez and was wiping them; and Ronnie thought that his eye looked rather less agreeable in the nude than it had done through glass.

'Pigs!' he cried, fighting against a growing alarm.

'Pigs?'

'Pigs.'

'You wish to breed pigs?'

'That's right,' bellowed Ronnie. 'Pigs!' And from somewhere in his system he contrived to dig up and fasten on his face an ingratiating smile.

Lord Emsworth replaced his pince-nez.

'And I suppose,' he said throatily, quivering from his bald head to his roomy shoes, 'that when you've got 'em you'll spend the whole day bouncing tennis-balls on their backs?'

Ronnie gulped. The shock had been severe. The ingratiating smile lingered on his lips, as if fastened there with pins, but his eyes were round and horrified.

'Eh?' he said feebly.

Lord Emsworth rose. So long as he insisted on wearing an old shooting jacket with holes in the elbows and letting his tie slip down and show the head of a brass stud, he could never hope to be completely satisfactory as a figure of outraged majesty; but he achieved as imposing an effect as his upholstery would permit. He drew himself up to his full height, which was considerable, and from this eminence glared balefully down on his nephew.

'I saw you! I was on my way to the piggery and I saw you there bouncing your infernal tennis-balls on my pig's back. Tennis-balls!' Fire seemed to stream from the pince-nez. 'Are you aware that Empress of Blandings is an excessively nervous, highly-strung animal, only too ready on the slightest provocation to refuse her meals? You might have undone the work of months with your idiotic tennis-ball.'

'I'm sorry . . .'

'What's the good of being sorry?'

'I never thought . . .'

'You never do. That's what's the trouble with you. Pig-farm!' said Lord Emsworth vehemently, his voice soaring into the upper register. 'You couldn't manage a pig-farm. You aren't fit to manage a pig-farm. You aren't worthy to manage a pig-farm. If I had to select somebody out of the whole world to manage a pig-farm, I would choose you last.'

Ronnie Fish groped his way to the table and supported himself on it. He had a sensation of dizziness. On one point he was reasonably clear, viz. that his Uncle Clarence did not consider him ideally fitted to manage a pig-farm, but apart from that his mind was in a whirl. He felt as if he had stepped on something and it had gone off with a bang.

'Here! What *is* all this?'

It was the Hon. Galahad who had spoken, and he had spoken peevishly. Working in the small library with the door ajar, he had found the babble of voices interfering with literary composition and, justifiably annoyed, had come to investigate.

'Can't you do your reciting some time when I'm not working, Clarence?' he said. 'What's all the trouble about?'

Lord Emsworth was still full of his grievance.

'He bounced tennis-balls on my pig!'

The Hon. Galahad was not impressed. He did not register horror.

'Do you mean to tell me,' he said sternly, 'that all this fuss, ruining my morning's work, was simply about that blasted pig of yours?'

'I refuse to allow you to call the Empress a blasted pig! Good heavens!' cried Lord Emsworth passionately. 'Can none of my family appreciate the fact that she is the most remarkable animal in Great Britain? No pig in the whole annals of the Shropshire Agricultural Show has ever won the silver medal two years in succession. And that, if only people will leave her alone and refrain from incessantly pelting her with tennis-balls, is what the Empress is quite certain to do. It is an unheard of feat.'

The Hon. Galahad frowned. He shook his head reprovingly. It was all very well, he felt, a stable being optimistic about its nominee, but he was a man who could face facts. In a long and chequered life he had seen so many good things unstuck. Besides, he had his superstitions, and one of them was that counting your chickens in advance brought bad luck.

'Don't you be too cocksure, my boy,' he said gravely. 'I looked in at the Emsworth Arms the other day for a glass of beer, and there was a fellow in there offering three to one on an animal called Pride of Matchingham. Offering it freely. Tall, red-haired fellow with a squint. Slightly bottled.'

Lord Emsworth forgot Ronnie, forgot tennis-balls, forgot, in the shock of this announcement, everything except that deeper wrong which so long had been poisoning his peace.

'Pride of Matchingham belongs to Sir Gregory Parsloe,' he said, 'and I have no doubt that the man offering such ridiculous odds was his pigman, Wellbeloved. As you know, the fellow used to be in my employment, but Parsloe lured him away from me by the promise of higher wages.' Lord Emsworth's expression had now become positively ferocious. The thought of George Cyril Wellbeloved, that perjured pigman, always made the iron enter into his soul. 'It was a most abominable and unneighbourly thing to do.'

The Hon. Galahad whistled.

'So that's it, is it? Parsloe's pig-man going about offering three to one – against the form-book, I take it?'

'Most decidedly. Pride of Matchingham was awarded second prize last year, but it is a quite inferior animal to the Empress.'

'Then you look after that pig of yours, Clarence.' The Hon. Galahad spoke earnestly. 'I see what this means. Parsloe's up to his old games, and intends to queer the Empress somehow.'

'Queer her?'

'Nobble her. Or, if he can't do that, steal her.'

'You don't mean that.'

'I do mean it. The man's as slippery as a greased eel. He would nobble his grandmother if it suited his book. Let me tell you I've known young Parsloe for thirty years and I solemnly state that if his grandmother was entered in a competition for fat pigs and his commitments made it desirable for him to get her out of the way, he would dope her branmash and acorns without a moment's hesitation.'

'God bless my soul!' said Lord Emsworth, deeply impressed.

'Let me tell you a little story about young Parsloe. One or two of us used to meet at the Black Footman in

Gossiter Street in the old days – they've pulled it down now – and match our dogs against rats in the room behind the bar. Well, I put my Towser, an admirable beast, up against young Parsloe's Banjo on one occasion for a hundred pounds a side. And when the night came and he was shown the rats, I'm dashed if he didn't just give a long yawn and roll over and go to sleep. I whistled him . . . called him . . . Towser, Towser . . . No good . . . Fast asleep. And my firm belief has always been that young Parsloe took him aside just before the contest was to start and gave him about six pounds of steak and onions. Couldn't prove anything, of course, but I sniffed the dog's breath and it was like opening the kitchen door of a Soho chophouse on a summer night. That's the sort of man young Parsloe is.'

'Galahad!'

'Fact. You'll find the story in my book.'

Lord Emsworth was tottering to the door.

'God bless my soul! I never realized . . . I must see Pirbright at once. I didn't suspect . . . It never occurred . . .'

The door closed behind him. The Hon. Galahad, preparing to return to his labours, was arrested by the voice of his nephew Ronald.

'Uncle Gally!'

The young man's pink face had flamed to a bright crimson. His eyes gleamed strangely.

'Well?'

'You don't really think Sir Gregory will try to steal the Empress?'

'I certainly do. Known him for thirty years, I tell you.'

'But how could he?'

'Go to her sty at night, of course, and take her away.'

'And hide her somewhere?'

'Yes.'

'But an animal that size. Rather like looking in at the Zoo and pocketing one of the elephants, what?'

'Don't talk like an idiot. She's got a ring through her nose, hasn't she?'

'You mean, Sir Gregory could catch hold of the ring and she would breeze along quite calmly?'

'Certainly. Puffy Benger and I stole old Wivenhoe's pig the night of the Bachelor's Ball at Hammer Easton in the year '95. We put it in Plug Basham's bedroom. There was no difficulty about the thing whatsoever. A little child could have led it.'

He withdrew into the small library, and Ronnie slid limply into the chair which Lord Emsworth had risen from so majestically. He felt the need of sitting. The inspiration which had just come to him had had a stunning effect. The brilliance of it almost frightened him. That idea about starting a pig-farm had shown that this was one of his bright mornings, but he had never foreseen that he would be as bright as this.

'Golly!' said Ronnie.

Could he . . . ?

Well, why not?

Suppose . . . ?

No, the thing was impossible.

Was it? Why? Why was it impossible? Suppose he had a stab at it. Suppose, following his Uncle Galahad's expert hints, he were to creep out tonight, abstract the Empress from her home, hide her somewhere for a day or two and then spectacularly restore her to her bereaved owner? What would be the result? Would Uncle Clarence sob on his neck, or would he not? Would he feel that no reward was too good for his benefactor or wouldn't he? Most decidedly he would. Fish Preferred would soar immediately. That little matter of the advance of capital would solve itself. Money would stream automatically from the Emsworth coffers.

But could it be done? Ronnie forced himself to examine the scheme dispassionately, with a mind alert for snags.

He could detect none. A suitable hiding place occurred to him immediately – that disused gamekeeper's cottage in the west wood. Nobody ever went there. It would be as good as a Safe Deposit.

Risk of Detection? Why should there be any risk of detection? Who would think of connecting Ronald Fish with the affair?

Feeding the animal . . . ?

Ronnie's face clouded. Yes, here at last was the snag. This did present difficulties. He was vague as to what pigs ate, but he knew that they needed a lot of whatever it was. It would be no use restoring to Lord Emsworth a skeleton Empress. The cuisine must be maintained at its existing level, or the thing might just as well be left undone.

For the first time he began to doubt the quality of his recent inspiration. Scanning the desk with knitted brows, he took from the book-rest the volume entitled *Pigs, and How To Make Them Pay*. A glance at page 61, and his misgivings were confirmed.

''Myes,' said Ronnie, having skimmed through all the stuff about barley meal and maize meal and linseed meal and potatoes and separated milk or buttermilk. This, he now saw clearly, was no one man job. It called not only for a dashing principal but a zealous assistant.

And what assistant?

Hugo?

No. In many respects the ideal accomplice for an undertaking of this nature, Hugo Carmody had certain defects which automatically disqualified him. To enrol Hugo as his lieutenant would mean revealing to him the motives that lay at the back of the venture. And if Hugo knew that he, Ronnie, was endeavouring to collect funds in order to get married, the thing would be all over Shropshire in a couple of days. Short of putting it on the front page of the *Daily Mail* or having it broadcast over the wireless, the surest way of obtaining publicity for anything you wanted kept dark was to confide it to Hugo Carmody. A splendid chap, but the real, genuine human colander. No, not Hugo.

Then who? . . .

Ah!

Ronnie Fish sprang from his chair, threw his head back and uttered a yodel of joy so loud and penetrating that the door of the small library flew open as if he had touched a spring.

A tousled literary man emerged.

'Stop that damned noise! How the devil can I write with a row like that going on?'

'Sorry, Uncle, I was just thinking of something.'

'Well, think of something else. How do you spell "intoxicated"?'

'One "x".'

'Thanks,' said the Hon. Galahad, and vanished again.

V

In his pantry, in shirt-sleeved ease, Beach, the butler, sat taking the well-earned rest of a man whose silver is all done and who has no further duties to perform till lunch-time. A bullfinch sang gaily in a cage on the window-sill, but it did not disturb him, for he was absorbed in the Racing Intelligence page of the *Morning Post*.

Suddenly he rose, palpitating. A sharp rap had sounded on the door, and he was a man who reacted nervously to sudden noises. There entered his employer's nephew, Mr Ronald Fish.

'Hullo, Beach.'

'Sir?'

'Busy?'

'No, sir.'

'Just thought I'd look in.'

'Yes, sir.'

'For a chat.'

'Very good, sir.'

Although the butler spoke with his usual smooth courtesy, he was far from feeling easy in his mind. He did not like Ronnie's looks. It seemed to him that his young visitor was feverish. The limbs twitched, the eyes gleamed, the blood-pressure appeared heightened, and there was a super-normal pinkness in the epidermis of the cheek.

'Long time since we had a real, cosy talk, Beach.'

'Yes, sir.'

'When I was a kid, I used to be in and out of this pantry of yours all day long.'

'Yes, sir.'

A mood of extreme sentimentality now appeared to grip the young man. He sighed like a centenarian recalling far off, happy things.

'Those were the days, Beach.'

'Yes, sir.'

'No problems then. No worries. And even if I had worries, I could always bring them to you, couldn't I?'

'Yes, sir.'

'Remember the time I hid in here when my Uncle Gally was after me with a whangee for putting tin-tacks on his chair?'

'Yes, sir.'

'It was a close call, but you saved me. You were staunch and true. A man in a million. I've always thought that if there were more people like you in the world, it would be a better place.'

'I do my best to give you satisfaction, sir.'

'And how you succeed! I shall never forget your kindness in those dear old days, Beach.'

'Extremely good of you to say so, sir.'

'Later, as the years went by, I did my best to repay you, by sharing with you such snips as came my way.

317

Remember the time I gave you Blackbird for the
Manchester November Handicap?'

'Yes, sir.'

'You collected a packet.'

'It did prove a remarkably sound investment, sir.'

'Yes. And so it went on. I look back through the years,
and I seem to see you and me standing side by side, each
helping each, each doing the square thing by the other.
You certainly always did the square thing by me.'

'I trust I shall always continue to do so, sir.'

'I know you will, Beach. It isn't in you to do
otherwise. And that,' said Ronnie, beaming on him
lovingly, 'is why I feel so sure that, when I have stolen
my uncle's pig, you will be there helping to feed it till I
give it back.'

The butler's was not a face that registered nimbly. It
took some time for a look of utter astonishment to cover
its full acreage. Such a look had spread to perhaps
two-thirds of its surface when Ronnie went on.

'You see, Beach, strictly between ourselves, I have
made up my mind to sneak the Empress away and keep
her hidden in that gamekeeper's cottage in the west
wood and then, when Uncle Clarence is sending out
SOS's and offering large rewards, I shall find it there and
return it, thus winning his undying gratitude and
putting him in the right frame of mind to yield up a bit
of my money that I want to dig out of him. You get the
idea?'

The butler blinked. He was plainly endeavouring to
conquer a suspicion that his mind was darkening.
Ronnie nodded kindly at him as he fought for speech.

'It's the scheme of a lifetime, you were going to say?
You're quite right. It is. But it's one of those schemes
that call for a sympathetic fellow-worker. You see, pigs
like the Empress, Beach, require large quantities of food
at frequent intervals. I can't possibly handle the entire
commissariat department myself. That's where you're

going to help me, like a splendid fellow you are and always have been.'

The butler had now begun to gargle slightly. He cast a look of agonized entreaty at the bullfinch, but the bird had no comfort to offer. It continued to chirp reflectively to itself, like a man trying to remember a tune in his bath.

'An enormous quantity of food they need,' proceeded Ronnie. 'You'd be surprised. Here it is in this book I took from my uncle's desk. At least six pounds of meal a day, not to mention milk or buttermilk and bran made sloppy with swill.'

Speech at last returned to the butler. It took the form at first of a faint sound like the cry of a frightened infant. Then words came.

'But, Mr Ronald . . . !'

Ronnie stared at him incredulously. He seemed to be wrestling with an unbelievable suspicion.

'Don't tell me you're thinking of throwing me down, Beach? You? My friend since I was so high?' He laughed. He could see now how ridiculous the idea was. 'Of course you aren't! You couldn't. Apart from wanting to do me a good turn, you've gathered by this time, with that quick intelligence of yours, that there's money in the thing. Ten quid down, Beach, the moment you give the nod. And nobody knows better than yourself that ten quid, invested on Baby Bones for the Medbury Selling Plate at the current odds, means considerably more than a hundred in your sock on settling-day.'

'But, sir . . . It's impossible . . . I couldn't dream . . . If ever it was found out . . . Really, I don't think you ought to ask me, Mr Ronald . . .'

'Beach!'

'Yes, but, really, sir . . .'

Ronnie fixed him with a compelling eye.

'Think well, Beach. Who gave you Creole Queen for the Lincolnshire?'

'But, Mr Ronald . . .'

'Who gave you Mazzawattee for the Jubilee Stakes, Beach? What a beauty!'

A tense silence fell upon the pantry. Even the bullfinch was hushed.

'And it may interest you to know,' said Ronnie, 'that just before I left London I heard of something really hot for the Goodwood Cup.'

A low gasp escaped Beach. All butlers are sportsmen, and Beach had been a butler for eighteen years. Mere gratitude for past favours might not have been enough in itself to turn the scale, but this was different. On the subject of form for the Goodwood Cup he had been quite unable to reach a satisfying decision. It had baffled him. For days he had been groping in the darkness.

'Jujube, sir?' he whispered.

'Not Jujube.'

'Ginger George?'

'Not Ginger George. It's no use your trying to guess, for you'll never do it. Only two touts and the stable-cat know this one. But you shall know it, Beach, the minute I give that pig back and claim my reward. And that pig needs to be fed. Beach, how about it?'

For a long minute the butler stared before him, silent. Then, as if he felt that some simple, symbolic act of the sort was what this moment demanded, he went to the bullfinch's cage and put a green-baize cloth over it.

'Tell me just what it is you wish me to do, Mr Ronald,' he said.

VI

The dawn of another day crept upon Blandings Castle. Hour by hour the light grew stronger till, piercing the curtains of Ronnie's bedroom, it woke him from a disturbed slumber. He turned sleepily on the pillow. He was dimly conscious of having had the most

extraordinary dream, all about stealing pigs. In this
dream . . .

He sat up with a jerk. Like cold water dashed in his
face had come the realization that it had been no dream.

'Gosh!' said Ronnie, blinking.

Few things have such a tonic effect on a young man
accustomed to be a little heavy on waking in the
morning as the discovery that he has stolen a prize pig
overnight. Usually, at this hour, Ronnie was more or
less of an inanimate mass till kindly hands brought him
his early cup of tea: but today he thrilled all down his
pyjama-clad form with a novel alertness. Not since he
had left school had he 'sprung out of bed', but he did so
now. Bed, generally so attractive to him, had lost its
fascination. He wanted to be up and about.

He had bathed, shaved, and was slipping into his
trousers when his toilet was interrupted by the arrival of
his old friend Hugo Carmody. On Hugo's face there was
an expression which it was impossible to misread. It
indicated as plainly as a label that he had come bearing
news, and Ronnie, guessing the nature of this news,
braced himself to be suitably startled.

'Ronnie!'

'Well?'

'Heard what's happened?'

'What?'

'You know that pig of your uncle's?'

'What about it?'

'It's gone.'

'Gone?'

'Gone!' said Hugo, rolling the word round his tongue.
'I met the old boy half a minute ago, and he told me. It
seems he went down to the pig-bin for a before-breakfast
look at the animal, and it wasn't there.'

'Wasn't there?'

'Wasn't there.'

'How do you mean, wasn't there?'

'Well, it wasn't. Wasn't there at all. It had gone.'

'Gone?'

'Gone! Its room was empty and its bed had not been slept in.'

'Well, I'm dashed!' said Ronnie.

He was feeling pleased with himself. He felt he had played his part well. Just the right incredulous amazement, changing just soon enough into stunned belief.

'You don't seem very surprised,' said Hugo.

Ronnie was stung. The charge was monstrous.

'Yes, I do,' he cried. 'I seem frightfully surprised. I *am* surprised. Why shouldn't I be surprised?'

'All right. Just as you say. Spring about a bit more, though, another time when I bring you these sensational items. Well, I'll tell you one thing,' said Hugo with satisfaction. 'Out of evil cometh good. It's an ill wind that has no turning. For me this startling occurrence has been a life-saver. I've got thirty-six hours' leave out of it. The old boy is sending me up to London to get a detective.'

'A what?'

'A detective.'

'A detective!'

Ronnie was conscious of a marked spasm of uneasiness. He had not bargained for detectives.

'From a place called the Argus Inquiry Agency.'

Ronnie's uneasiness increased. This thing was not going to be so simple after all. He had never actually met a detective, but he had read a lot about them. They nosed about and found clues. For all he knew, he might have left a hundred clues.

'Naturally I shall have to stay the night in town. And, much as I like this place,' said Hugo, 'there's no denying that a night in town won't hurt. I've got fidgety feet, and a spot of dancing will do me all the good in the world. Bring back the roses to my cheeks.'

'Whose idea was it, getting down this blighted detective?' demanded Ronnie. He knew he was not being nonchalant, but he was disturbed.

'Mine.'

'Yours, eh?'

'All mine. I suggested it.'

'You did, did you?' said Ronnie.

He directed at his companion a swift glance of a kind that no one should have directed at an old friend.

'Oh?' he said morosely. 'Well, buzz off. I want to dress.'

VII

A morning spent in solitary wrestling with a guilty conscience had left Ronnie Fish thoroughly unstrung. By the time the clock over the stable struck the hour of one, his mental condition had begun to resemble that of the late Eugene Aram. He paced the lower terrace with bent head, starting occasionally at the sudden chirp of a bird, and longed for Sue. Five minutes of Sue, he felt, would make him a new man.

It was perfectly foul, mused Ronnie, this being separated from the girl he loved. There was something about Sue . . . he couldn't describe it, but something that always seemed to act on a fellow's whole system like a powerful pick-me-up. She was the human equivalent of those pink drinks you went and got – or, rather, which you used to go and get before a good woman's love had made you give up all that sort of thing – at that chemist's at the top of the Haymarket after a wild night on the moors. It must have been with a girl like Sue in mind, he felt, that the poet had written those lines 'When something something something brow, a ministering angel thou!'

At this point in his meditations, a voice from immediately behind him spoke his name.

'I say, Ronnie.

It was only his cousin Millicent. He became calmer.
For an instant, so deep always is a criminal's need for a
confidant, he had a sort of idea of sharing his hideous
secret with this girl, between whom and himself there
had long existed a pleasant friendship. Then he
abandoned the notion. His secret was not one that could
be lightly shared. Momentary relief of mind was not
worth purchasing at the cost of endless anxiety.

'Ronnie, have you seen Mr Carmody anywhere?'

'Hugo? He went up to London on the ten-thirty.'

'Went up to London? What for?'

'He's gone to a place called the Argus Enquiry Agency
to get a detective.'

'What, to investigate this business of the Empress?'

'Yes.'

Millicent laughed. The idea tickled her.

'I'd like to be there to see old man Argus's face when
he finds that all he's wanted for is to track down missing
pigs. I should think he would beat Hugo over the head
with a blood-stain.'

Her laughter trailed away. There had come into her
face the look of one suddenly visited by a displeasing
thought.

'Ronnie!'

'Hullo?'

'Do you know what?'

'What?'

'This looks fishy to me.'

'How do you mean?'

'Well, I don't know how it strikes you, but this Argus
Enquiry Agency is presumably on the phone. Why didn't
Uncle Clarence just ring them up and ask them to send
down a man?'

'Probably didn't think of it.'

'Whose idea was it, anyway, getting down a man?'

'Hugo's.'

'He suggested that he should run up to town?'

'Yes.'

'I thought as much,' said Millicent darkly.

'What do you mean?'

Millicent's eyes narrowed. She kicked moodily at a passing worm.

'I don't like it,' she said. 'It's fishy. Too much zeal. It looked very much to me as if our Mr Carmody had a special reason for wanting to get up to London for the night. And I think I know what the reason was. Did you ever hear of a girl named Sue Brown?'

The start which Ronnie gave eclipsed in magnitude all the other starts he had given that morning. And they had been many and severe.

'It isn't true!'

'What isn't true?'

'That there's anything whatever between Hugo and Sue Brown.'

'Oh? Well, I had it from an authoritative source.'

It was not the worm's lucky morning. It had now reached Ronnie, and he kicked at it, too. The worm had the illusion that it had begun to rain shoes.

'I've got to go in and make a phone call,' said Millicent, abruptly.

Ronnie scarcely noticed her departure. He had supposed himself to have been doing some pretty tense thinking all the morning, but, compared with its activity now, his brain hitherto had been stagnant.

It couldn't be true, he told himself. Sue had said definitely that it wasn't, and she couldn't have been lying to him. Girls like Sue didn't lie. And yet . . .

The sound of the luncheon gong floated over the garden.

Well, one thing was certain. It was simply impossible to remain here at Blandings Castle, getting his mind poisoned with doubts and speculations which for the life of him he could not keep out of it. If he took the two-seater and drove off in it the moment this infernal meal was over, he could be in London before eight. He could call at Sue's flat; receive her assurance once more that Hugo Carmody, tall and lissom though he might be, expert on the saxophone though he admittedly was, meant nothing to her; take her out to dinner and, while dining, ease his mind of that which weighed upon it. Then, fortified with comfort and advice, he could pop into the car and be back at the castle by lunch-time on the following day.

It wasn't, of course, that he didn't trust her implicitly. Nevertheless . . .

Ronnie went in to lunch.

4 — Noticeable Behaviour of Ronald Fish

If you go up Beeston Street in the south-western postal division of London and follow the pavement on the right-hand side, you come to a blind alley called Hayling Court. If you enter the first building on the left of this blind alley and mount a flight of stairs, you find yourself facing a door, on the ground-glass of which is the legend:

ARGUS
ENQUIRY
AGENCY
LTD

and below it, to one side, the smaller legend

P. FROBISHER PILBEAM, MGR

And if, at about the hour when Ronnie Fish had stepped into his two-seater in the garage of Blandings Castle, you had opened this door and gone in and succeeded in convincing the gentlemanly office-boy that yours was a *bona fide* visit, having nothing to do with the sale of life insurance, proprietary medicines or handsomely bound sets of Dumas, you would have been admitted to the august presence of the Mgr himself. P. Frobisher Pilbeam was seated at his desk, reading a telegram which had arrived during his absence at lunch.

This is peculiarly an age of young men starting out in business for themselves; of rare, unfettered spirits chafing at the bonds of employment and refusing to spend their lives working forty-eight weeks in the year for a salary. Quite early in his career Pilbeam had seen where the big money lay, and decided to go after it.

As editor of that celebrated weekly scandal-sheet, *Society Spice*, Percy Pilbeam had had exceptional opportunities of discovering in good time the true bent of his genius: with the result that, after three years of nosing out people's discreditable secrets on behalf of the Mammoth Publishing Company, his employers, he had come to the conclusion that a man of his gifts would be doing far better for himself nosing out such secrets on his own behalf. Considerably to the indignation of Lord Tilbury, the Mammoth's guiding spirit, he had borrowed some capital, handed in his portfolio, and was now in an extremely agreeable financial position.

The telegram over which he sat brooding with wrinkled forehead was just the sort of telegram an Enquiry agent ought to have been delighted to receive, being thoroughly cryptic and consequently a pleasing challenge to his astuteness as a detective, but Percy Pilbeam, in his ten minutes' acquaintance with it, had come to dislike it heartily. He preferred his telegrams easier.

Be sure send best man investigate big robbery.

It was unsigned.

What made the thing particularly annoying was that it was so tantalizing. A big robbery probably meant jewels, with a correspondingly big fee attached to their recovery. But you cannot scour England at random, asking people if they have had a big robbery in their neighbourhood.

Reluctantly, he gave the problem up; and, producing a pocket mirror, began with the aid of a pen nib to curl his small and revolting moustache. His thoughts had drifted now to Sue. They were not altogether sunny thoughts, for the difficulty of making Sue's acquaintance was beginning to irk Percy Pilbeam. He had written her

notes. He had sent her flowers. And nothing had
happened. She ignored the notes, and what she did with
the flowers he did not know. She certainly never
thanked him for them.

Brooding upon these matters, he was interrupted by
the opening of the door. The gentlemanly office-boy
entered. Pilbeam looked up, annoyed.

'How many times have I told you not to come in here
without knocking?' he asked sternly.

The office-boy reflected.

'Seven,' he replied.

'What would you have done if I had been in
conference with an important client?'

'Gone out again,' said the office-boy. Working in a
Private Enquiry Agency, you drop into the knack of
solving problems.

'Well, go out now.'

'Very good sir. I merely wished to say that, while you
were absent at lunch, a gentleman called.'

'Eh? Who was he?'

The office-boy, who liked atmosphere, and hoped
some day to be promoted to the company of Mr Murphy
and Mr Jones, the two active assistants who had their
lair on the ground floor, thought for a moment of saying
that, beyond the obvious facts that the caller was a
Freemason, left-handed, a vegetarian and a traveller in
the East, he had made no deductions from his
appearance. He perceived, however, that his employer
was not in the vein for that sort of thing.

'A Mr Carmody, sir. Mr Hugo Carmody.'

'Ah!' Pilbeam displayed interest. 'Did he say he would
call again?'

'He mentioned the possibility, sir.'

'Well, if he does, inform Mr Murphy and tell him to
be ready when I ring.'

The office-boy retired, and Pilbeam returned to his
thoughts of Sue. He was quite certain now that he did

not like her attitude. Her attitude wounded him.
Another thing he deplored was the reluctance of
stage-door keepers to reveal the private addresses of the
personnel of the company. Really, there seemed to be no
way of getting to know the girl at all.

Eight respectful knocks sounded on the door. The
office-boy, though occasionally forgetful, was
conscientious. He had restored the average.

'Well?'

'Mr Carmody to see you, sir.'

Pilbeam once more relegated Sue to the hinterland of
his mind. Business was business.

'Show him in.'

'This way, sir,' said the office-boy with a graceful
courtliness which, even taking into account the fact that
he suffered from adenoids, had an old-world flavour, and
Hugo sauntered across the threshold.

Hugo felt, and was looking, quietly happy. He seemed
to bring the sunshine with him. Nobody could have
been more wholeheartedly attached than he to Blandings
Castle and the society of his Millicent, but he was
finding London, revisited, singularly attractive.

'And this, if I mistake not, Watson, is our client now,'
said Hugo genially.

Such was his feeling of universal benevolence that he
embraced with his good-will even the repellent-looking
young man who had risen from the desk. Percy
Pilbeam's eyes were too small and too close together and
he marcelled his hair in a manner distressing to right-
thinking people, but today he had to be lumped in with
the rest of the species as a man and a brother, so Hugo
bestowed a dazzling smile upon him. He still thought
Pilbeam should not have been wearing pimples with a
red tie. One or the other if he liked. But not both.
Nevertheless he smiled upon him.

'Fine day,' he said.

'Quite,' said Pilbeam.

'Very jolly, the smell of the asphalt and carbonic gas.'

'Quite.'

'Some people might call London a shade on the stuffy side on an afternoon like this. But not Hugo Carmody.'

'No?'

'No. H. Carmody finds it just what the doctor ordered.' He sat down. 'Well, sleuth,' he said, 'to business. I called before lunch, but you were out.'

'Yes.'

'But here I am again. And I suppose you want to know what I've come about?'

'When you're ready to get round to it,' said Pilbeam patiently.

Hugo stretched his long legs comfortably.

'Well, I know you detective blokes always want a fellow to begin at the beginning and omit no detail, for there is no saying how important some seemingly trivial fact may be. Omitting birth and early education then, I am at the moment private secretary to Lord Emsworth, at Blandings Castle, in Shropshire. And,' said Hugo, 'I maintain, a jolly good secretary. Others may think differently, but that is my view.'

'Blandings Castle?'

A thought had struck the proprietor of the Argus Enquiry Agency. He fumbled in his desk and produced the mysterious telegram. Yes, as he had fancied, it had been handed in at a place called Market Blandings.

'Do you know anything about this?' he asked, pushing it across the desk.

Hugo glanced at the document.

'The old boy must have sent that after I left,' he said. 'The absence of signature is, no doubt, due to mental stress. Lord Emsworth is greatly perturbed. A-twitter. Shaken to the core, you might say.'

'About this robbery?'

'Exactly. It has got right in amongst him.'

Pilbeam reached for pen and paper. There was a stern, set, bloodhound sort of look in his eyes.

'Kindly give me the details.'

Hugo pondered a moment.

'It was a dark and stormy night . . . No, I'm a liar. The moon was riding serenely in the sky . . .'

'This big robbery? Tell me about it.'

Hugo raised his eyebrows.

'Big?'

'The telegram says "big".'

'These telegraph-operators will try to make sense. You can't stop them editing. The word should be "pig". Lord Emsworth's pig has been stolen!'

'Pig!' cried Percy Pilbeam.

Hugo looked at him a little anxiously.

'You know what a pig is, surely? If not, I'm afraid there is a good deal of tedious spade work ahead of us.'

The roseate dreams which the proprietor of the Argus had had of missing jewels broke like bubbles. He was deeply affronted. A man of few ideals, the one deep love of his life was for this Enquiry Agency which he had created and nursed to prosperity through all the dangers and vicissitudes which beset Enquiry Agencies in their infancy. And the thought of being expected to apply its complex machinery to a search for lost pigs cut him, as Millicent had predicted, to the quick.

'Does Lord Emsworth seriously suppose that I have time to waste looking for stolen pigs?' he demanded shrilly. 'I never heard such nonsense in my life.'

'Almost the exact words which all the other Hawkshaws used. Finding you not at home,' explained Hugo, 'I spent the morning going round to other Agencies. I think I visited six in all, and every one of them took the attitude you do.'

'I am not surprised.'

'Nevertheless, it seemed to me that they, like you, lacked vision. This pig, you see, is a prize pig. Don't picture to yourself something with a kink in its tail sporting idly in the mud. Imagine, rather, a favourite daughter kidnapped from her ancestral home. This is heavy stuff, I assure you. Restore the animal in time for the Agricultural Show, and you may ask of Lord Emsworth what you will, even unto half his kingdom.'

Percy Pilbeam rose. He had heard enough.

'I will not trouble Lord Emsworth. The Argus Enquiry Agency . . .'

'. . . does not detect pigs? I feared as much. Well, well, so be it. And now,' said Hugo, affably, 'may I take advantage of the beautiful friendship which has sprung up between us to use your telephone?'

Without waiting for permission – for which, indeed, he would have had to wait some time – he drew the instrument to him and gave a number. He then began to chat again.

'You seem a knowledgeable sort of bloke,' he said. 'Perhaps you can tell me where the village swains go these days when they want to dance upon the green? I have been absent for some little time from the centre of the vortex, and I have become as a child in these matters. What is the best that London has to offer to a young man with his blood up and the vine leaves more or less in his hair?'

Pilbeam was a man of business. He had no wish to converse with this client who had disappointed him and wounded his finest feelings, but it so happened that he had recently bought shares in a rising restaurant.

'Mario's,' he replied promptly. 'It's the only place.'

Hugo sighed. Once he had dreamed that the answer to a question like that would have been 'The Hot Spot'. But where was the Hot Spot now? Gone like the flowers that wither in the first frost. The lion and the lizard kept the courts where Jamshyd gloried and – after hours, unfortunately, which had started all the trouble – drank deep. Ah well, life was pretty complex.

333

A voice from the other end of the wire broke in on his reverie. He recognized it as that of the porter of the block of flats where Sue had her tiny abode.

'Hullo? Bashford? Mr Carmody speaking. Will you make a long arm and haul Miss Brown to the instrument. Eh? Miss Sue Brown, of course. No other Browns are any use to me whatsoever. Right ho, I'll wait.'

The astute detective never permits himself to exhibit emotion. Pilbeam turned his start of surprise into a grave, distrait nod, as if he were thinking out deep problems. He took up his pen and drew three crosses and a squiggle on the blotting-paper. He was glad that no gentlemanly instinct had urged him to leave his visitor alone to do his telephoning.

'Mario's, eh?' said Hugo. 'What's the band like?'

'It's Leopold's.'

'Good enough for me,' said Hugo with enthusiasm. He hummed a bar or two, and slid his feet dreamily about the carpet. 'I'm shockingly out of practice, dash it. Well, that's that. Touching this other matter, you're sure you won't come to Blandings?'

'Quite.'

'Nice place. Gravel soil, spreading views, well laid-out pleasure grounds, Company's own water . . . I would strongly advise you to bring your magnifying-glass and spend the summer. However, if you really feel . . . Sue! Hullo-ullo-ullo! This is Hugo. Yes, just up in town for the night on a mission of extraordinary secrecy and delicacy which I am not empowered to reveal. Speaking from the Argus Enquiry Agency, by courtesy of proprietor. I was wondering if you would care to come out and help me restore my lost youth, starting at about eight-thirty. Eh?'

A silence had fallen at the other end of the wire. What was happening was that in the hall of the block of flats Sue's conscience was fighting a grim battle against heavy odds. Ranged in opposition to it were her loneliness, her love of dancing and her desire once more to see Hugo, who, though he was not a man one could take seriously, always cheered her up and made her laugh. And she had been needing a laugh for days.

Hugo thought he had been cut off.

'Hullo-ullo-ullo-ullo-ullo-ullo!' he barked peevishly.

'Don't yodel like that,' said Sue. 'You've nearly made me deaf.'

'Sorry, dear heart. I thought the machine had conked. Well, how do you react? Is it a bet?'

'I do want to see you again,' said Sue, hesitatingly.

'You shall. In person. Clean shirt, white waistcoat, the Carmody studs, and everything.'

'Well . . . !'

A psychically gifted bystander, standing in the hall of the block of flats, would have heard at this moment a faint moan. It was Sue's conscience collapsing beneath an unexpected flank attack. She had just remembered that if she went to dine with Hugo she would learn all the latest news about Ronnie. It put the whole thing in an entirely different light. Surely Ronnie himself could have no objection to the proposed feast if he knew that all she was going for was to talk about him? She might dance a little, of course, but purely by the way. Her real motive in accepting the invitation, she now realized quite clearly, was to hear all about Ronnie.

'All right,' she said. 'Where?'

'Mario's. They tell me it's the posh spot these days.'

'Mario's?'

'Yes. M for mange, A for asthma, R for rheumatism . . . oh, you've got it? All right, then. At eight-thirty.'

Hugo put the receiver back. Once more he allowed his dazzling smile to play upon the Argus' proprietor.

'Much obliged for use of instrument,' he said. 'Thank you.'

'Thank *you*,' said Pilbeam.

'Well, I'll be pushing along. Ring us up if you change your mind. Market Blandings 32X. If you don't take on the job no one will. I suppose there are other sleuths in London besides the bevy I've interviewed today, but I'm not going to see them. I consider that I have done my bit and am through.' He looked about him. 'Make a good thing out of this business?' he asked, for he was curious on these points and was never restrained by delicacy from seeking information.

'Quite.'

'What does the work consist of? I've often wondered. Measuring footprints and putting the tips of your fingers together, and all that, I suppose?'

'We are frequently asked to follow people and report on their movements.'

Hugo laughed amusedly.

'Well, don't go following me and reporting on my movements. Much trouble might ensue. Bung-ho.'

'Good-bye,' said Percy Pilbeam.

He pressed a bell on the desk, and moved to the door to show his visitor out.

II

Leopold's justly famous band, its cheeks puffed out and its eyeballs rolling, was playing a popular melody with lots of stomp in it, and for the first time since she had accepted Hugo's invitation to the dance, Sue, gliding round the floor, was conscious of a spiritual calm. Her conscience, quieted by the moaning of the saxophones, seemed to have retired from business. It realized, no doubt, the futility of trying to pretend that there was anything wrong in a girl enjoying this delightful exercise.

How absurd, she felt, Ronnie's objections were. It was, considered Sue, becoming analytical, as if she were to make a tremendous fuss because he played tennis and

golf with girls. Dancing was just a game like those two
pastimes, and it so happened that you had to have a man
with you or you couldn't play it. To get all jealous and
throaty just because one went out dancing was simply
ridiculous.

On the other hand, placid though her conscience now
was, she had to admit that it was a relief to feel that he
would never know of this little outing.

Men were such children when they were in love. Sue
found herself sighing over the opposite sex's
eccentricities. If they were only sensible, how simple life
would be. It amazed her that Ronnie could ever have any
possible doubt, however she might spend her leisure
hours, that her heart belonged to him alone. She
marvelled that he should suppose for a moment that
even if she danced all night with every other man in the
world it would make any difference to her feelings
towards him.

All the same, holding the peculiar views he did, he
must undoubtedly be humoured.

'You won't breathe a word to Ronnie about our
coming here, will you, Hugo?' she said, repeating an
injunction which had been her opening speech on
arriving at the restaurant.

'Not a syllable.'

'I can trust you?'

'Implicitly. Telegraphic address, Discretion, Market
Blandings.'

'Ronnie's funny, you see.'

'One long scream.'

'I mean, he wouldn't understand.'

'No. Great surprise it was to me,' said Hugo, doing
complicated things with his feet, 'to hear that you and
the old hound had decided to team up. You could have
knocked me down with a feather. Odd he never confided
in his boyhood friend.'

'Well, it wouldn't do for it to get about.'

'Are you suggesting that Hugo Carmody is a babbler?'

'You do like gossiping. You know you do.'

'I know nothing of the sort,' said Hugo with dignity.
'If I were asked to give my opinion, I should say that I
was essentially a strong, silent man.'

He made a complete circle of the floor in that
capacity. His taciturnity surprised Sue.

'What's the matter?' she asked.

'Dudgeon,' said Hugo.

'What?'

'I'm sulking. That remark of yours rankles. That
totally unfounded accusation that I cannot keep a secret.
It may interest you to know that I, too, am secretly
engaged and have never so much as mentioned it to a
soul.'

'Hugo!'

'Yes. Betrothed. And so at long last came a day when
Love wound his silken fetters about Hugo Carmody.'

'Who's the unfortunate girl?'

'There is no unfortunate girl. The lucky girl . . . Was
that your foot?'

'Yes.'

'Sorry, I haven't got the hang of these new steps yet.
The lucky girl, I was saying, is Miss Millicent
Threepwood.'

As if stunned by the momentousness of the
announcement, the band stopped playing; and, chancing
to be immediately opposite their table, the man who
never revealed secrets led his partner to her chair. She
was gazing at him ecstatically.

'You don't mean that?'

'I do mean that. What did you think I meant?'

'I never heard anything so wonderful in my life!'

'Good news?'

'I'm simply delighted.'

'I'm pleased, too,' said Hugo.

'I've been trying not to admit it to myself, but I was

338

very scared about Millicent. Ronnie told me the family
wanted him and her to marry, and you never know what
may happen when families throw their weight about.
And now it's all right!'

'Quite all right.'

The music had started again, but Sue remained in her
seat.

'Not?' said Hugo, astonished.

'Not just yet. I want to talk. You don't realize what
this means to me. Besides, your dancing's gone off,
Hugo. You're not the man you were.'

'I need practice.' He lit a cigarette and tapped a
philosophical vein of thought, eyeing the gyrating
couples meditatively. 'It's the way they're always
introducing new steps that bothers the man who has
been living out in the woods. I have become a rusty
rustic.'

'I don't mean you were bad. Only you used to be such
a marvel. Dancing with you was like floating on a pink
cloud above an ocean of bliss.'

'A very accurate description, I should imagine,' agreed
Hugo. 'But don't blame me. Blame these Amalgamated
Professors of the Dance, or whatever they call
themselves – the birds who get together every couple of
weeks or so to decide how they can make things more
difficult. Amazing thing that they won't leave well
alone.'

'You must have change.'

'I disagree with you,' said Hugo. 'No other walk in life
is afflicted by a gang of thugs who are perpetually
altering the rules of the game. When you learn to play
golf, the professional doesn't tell you to bring the club
up slowly and keep the head steady and roll the forearms
and bend the left knee and raise the left heel and keep
your eye on the ball and not sway back and a few more
things, and then, after you've sweated yourself to the
bone learning all that, suddenly add "Of course, you

339

understand that this is merely intended to see you
through till about three weeks from next Thursday.
After that the Supreme Grand Council of Consolidated
Divot-Shifters will scrap these methods and invent an
entirely new set!"'

'Is this more dudgeon?'

'No. Not dudgeon.'

'It sounds like dudgeon. I believe your little feelings
are hurt because I said your dancing wasn't as good as it
used to be.'

'Not at all. We welcome criticism.'

'Well, get your mind off it and tell me all about you
and Millicent and . . .'

'When I was about five,' resumed Hugo, removing his
cigarette from the holder and inserting another, 'I
attended my first dancing-school. I'm a bit shaky on
some of the incidents of the days when I was trailing
clouds of glory, but I do remember that dancing-school.
At great trouble and expense I was taught to throw up a
rubber ball with my left hand and catch it with my right,
keeping the small of the back rigid and generally
behaving in a graceful and attractive manner. It doesn't
sound a likely sort of thing to learn at a dancing-school,
but I swear to you that that's what the curriculum was.
Now, the point I am making . . .'

'Did you fall in love with Millicent right away, or was
it gradual?'

'The point I am making is this. I became very good at
throwing and catching that rubber ball. I dislike
boasting, but I stood out conspicuously among a pretty
hot bunch. People would nudge each other and say
"Who is he?" behind their hands. I don't suppose, when I
was feeling right, I missed the rubber ball more than
once in twenty goes. But what good does it do me now?
Absolutely none. Long before I got a chance of exhibiting
my accomplishment in public and having beautiful
women fawn on me for my skill, the Society of

Amalgamated Professors of the Dance decided that the
Rubber-Ball Glide, or whatever it was called, was out of
date.'

'Is she very pretty?'

'And what I say is that all this chopping and changing
handicaps a chap. I am perfectly prepared at this
moment to step out on that floor and heave a rubber ball
about, but it simply isn't being done nowadays. People
wouldn't understand what I was driving at. In other
words, all the time and money and trouble that I spent
on mastering the Rubber-Ball Shimmy is a dead loss. I
tell you, if the Amalgamated Professors want to make
people cynics, they're going the right way to work.'

'I wish you would tell me all about Millicent.'

'In a moment. Dancing, they taught me at school,
dates back to the early Egyptians, who ascribed the
invention to the god Thoth. The Phrygian Corybantes
danced in honour of somebody whose name I've
forgotten, and every time the festival of Rhea Silvia
came round the ancient Roman hoofers were there with
their hair in a braid. But what was good enough for the
god Thoth isn't good enough for these blighted
Amalgamated Professors! Oh no! And it's been the same
all through the ages. I don't suppose there has been a
moment in history when some poor, well-meaning devil,
with ambition at one end of him and two left feet at the
other, wasn't getting it in the neck.'

'And all this,' said Sue, 'because you trod on my foot
for just one half-second.'

'Hugo Carmody dislikes to tread on women's feet,
even for half a second. He has his pride. Ever hear of
Father Mariana?'

'No.'

'Mariana, George. Born twelve hundred and
something. Educated privately and at Leipzig University.
Hobbies, fishing, illuminating vellum and mangling the
wurzel. You must have heard of old Pop Mariana?'

'I haven't, and I don't want to. I want to hear about Millicent.'

'It was the opinion of Father Mariana that dancing was a deadly sin. He was particularly down, I may mention, on the saraband. He said the saraband did more harm than the Plague. I know just how he felt. I'll bet he had worked like a dog at twenty-five pazazas the complete course of twelve lessons, guaranteed to teach the fandango: and, just when his instructor had finally told him that he was fit to do it at the next Saturday Night Social, along came the Amalgamated Brothers with their newfangled saraband, and where was Pop? Leaning against the wall with the other foot-and-mouth diseasers, trying to pretend dancing bored him. Did I hear you say you wanted a few facts about Millicent?'

'You did.'

'Sweetest girl on earth.'

'Really?'

'Absolutely. It's well known. All over Shropshire.'

'And she really loves you?'

'Between you and me,' said Hugo confidentially, 'I don't wonder you speak in that amazed tone. If you saw her, you'd be still more surprised. I am a man who thinks before he speaks. I weigh my words. And I tell you solemnly that that girl is too good for me.'

'But you're a sweet darling precious pet.'

'I know I'm a sweet darling precious pet. Nevertheless, I still maintain that she is too good for me. She is the nearest thing to an angel that ever came glimmering through the laurels in the quiet evenfall in the garden by the turrets of the old manorial hall.'

'Hugo! I'd no idea you were so poetical.'

'Enough to make a chap poetical, loving a girl like that.'

'And you really do love her?'

Hugo took a feverish gulp of champagne and rolled

his eye-balls as if he had been a member of Leopold's justly famous band.

'Madly. Devotedly. And when I think how I have deceived her my soul sickens.'

'Have you deceived her?'

'Not yet. But I'm going to in about five minutes. I put in a phone call to Blandings just now, and when I get through I shall tell her I'm speaking from my hotel bedroom, where I am on the point of going to bed. You see,' said Hugo confidentially, 'Millicent, though practically perfect in every other respect, is one of those girls who might misunderstand this little night out of mine, did it but come to her ears. Speaking of which, you ought to see them. Like alabaster shells.'

'I know what you mean. Ronnie's like that.'

Hugo stared.

'Ronnie?'

'Yes.'

'You mean to sit there and tell me that Ronnie's ears are like alabaster shells?'

'No, I meant that he would be furious if he knew that I had come out dancing. And, oh, I do love dancing so,' sighed Sue.

'He must never know!'

'No. That's why I asked you just now not to tell him.'

'I won't. Secrecy and silence. Thank goodness there's nobody who could tell Millicent, even if they wanted to. Ah! this must be the bringer of glad tidings, come to say my call is through. All set?' he asked the page-boy who had threaded his way through the crowd to their table.

'Yes, sir.'

Hugo rose.

'Amuse yourself somehow till I return.'

'I shan't be dull,' said Sue.

She watched him disappear, then leaned back in her seat, watching the dancers. Her eyes were bright, and Hugo's news had brought a flush to her cheeks. Percy

Pilbeam, who had been hovering in the background, hoping for such an opportunity ever since his arrival at the restaurant, thought he had never seen her looking prettier. He edged between the tables and took Hugo's vacated chair. There are men who, approaching a member of the other sex, wait for permission before sitting down, and men who sit down without permission. Pilbeam was one of the latter.

'Good evening,' he said.

She turned, and was aware of a nasty-looking little man at her elbow. He seemed to have materialized from nowhere.

'May I introduce myself, Miss Brown?' said this blot. 'My name is Pilbeam.'

At the same moment there appeared in the doorway and stood there raking the restaurant with burning eyes the flannel-suited figure of Ronald Overbury Fish.

III

Ronnie Fish's estimate of the time necessary for reaching London from Blandings Castle in a sports-model two-seater had been thrown out of gear by two mishaps. Half-way down the drive the car had developed some mysterious engine-trouble, which had necessitated taking it back to the stables and having it overhauled by Lord Emsworth's chauffeur. It was not until nearly an hour later that he had been able to resume his journey, and a blowout near Oxford had delayed him still further. He arrived at Sue's flat just as Sue and Hugo were entering Mario's.

Ringing Sue's front-door bell produced no result. Ronnie regretted that in the stress of all the other matters that occupied his mind he had forgotten to send her a telegram. He was about to creep away and have a bite of dinner at the Drones Club – a prospect which pleased him not at all, for the Drones at dinner-time was always full of hearty eggs who talked much too loud for a worried man's nerves, and might even go so far as to throw bread at him, when, descending the stairs into the hall, he came upon Bashford, the porter.

Bashford, who knew Ronnie well, said "Ullo, Mr Fish,' and Ronnie said 'Hullo, Bashford,' and Bashford said the weather seemed to keep up, and Ronnie said 'Yes, that's right, it did,' and it was at this point that the porter uttered these memorable – and, as events proved, epoch-making words:

'If you're looking for Miss Brown, Mr Fish, I've an idea she's gone to a place called Mario's.'

He poured further details into Ronnie's throbbing ear. Mr Carmody had rung up on the phone, might have been ar-parse four, and he, Bashford, not listening but happening to hear, had thought he had caught something said about this place Mario's.

'Mario's?' said Ronnie. 'Thanks, Bashford. Mario's, eh? Right!'

The porter, for Eton and Cambridge train their sons well, found nothing in the way Mr Fish spoke to cause a thrill. Totally unaware that he had been conversing with Othello's younger brother, he went back to his den in the basement and sat down with a good appetite to steak and chips. And Ronnie, quivering from head to foot, started the car and drove off.

Jealousy, said Shakespeare, and he was about right, is the green-eyed monster which doth mock the meat he feeds on. By the time Ronald Overbury Fish pushed through the swinging-door that guards the revelry at Mario's from the gaze of the passer-by, he was, like the Othello he so much resembled, perplexed in the extreme. He felt hot all over, then cold all over, then hot again, and the waiter who stopped him on the threshold of the dining-room to inform him that evening dress was indispensable on the dancing-floor, and that flannel suits must go up to the balcony, was running a risk which would have caused his insurance company to purse its lips and shake its head.

Fortunately for him, Ronnie did not hear. He was scanning the crowd before him in an effort to find Sue.

'Plenty of room in the balcony, sir,' urged the waiter, continuing to play with fire.

This time Ronnie did become dimly aware that somebody was addressing him, and he was about to turn and give the man one look, when half-way down a grove of black coats and gaily-decorated frocks he suddenly saw what he was searching for. The next moment he was pushing a path through the throng, treading on the toes of brave men and causing fair women to murmur bitterly that this sort of thing ought to be prevented by the management.

Five yards from Sue's table, Ronnie Fish would have said that his cup was full and could not possibly be made any fuller. But when he had covered another two and pushed aside a fat man who was standing in the fairway, he realized his mistake. It was not Hugo who was Sue's companion, but a reptilian-looking squirt with narrow eyes and his hair done in ridges. And, as he saw him, something seemed to go off in Ronnie's brain like a released spring.

A waiter, pausing with a tray of glasses, pointed out to him that on the dancing-floor evening dress was indispensable.

Gentlemen in flannel suits, he added, could be accommodated in the balcony.

'Plenty of room in the balcony, sir,' said the waiter.

Ronnie reached the table. Pilbeam at the moment was saying that he had wanted for a long time to meet Sue. He hoped she had got his flowers all right.

It was perhaps a natural desire to look at anything but this odious and thrusting individual who had forced his society upon her, that caused Sue to raise her eyes.

Raising them, she met Ronnie's. And, as she saw

him, her conscience, which she had supposed lulled for the night, sprang to life more vociferous than ever. It had but been crouching, the better to spring.

'Ronnie!'

She started up. Pilbeam also rose. The waiter with the glasses pressed the edge of his tray against Ronnie's elbow in a firm but respectful manner and told him that on the dancing-floor evening dress was indispensable. Gentlemen in flannel suits, however, would find ample accommodation in the balcony.

Ronnie did not speak. And it would have been better if Sue had not done so. For, at this crisis, some subconscious instinct, of the kind which is always waiting to undo us at critical moments, suggested to her dazed mind that when two men who do not know each other are standing side by side in a restaurant one ought to introduce them.

'Mr Fish, Mr Pilbeam,' murmured Sue.

Only the ringing of the bell that heralds the first round of a heavyweight championship fight could have produced more instant and violent results. Through Ronnie's flannel-clad body a sort of galvanic shock seemed to pass. Pilbeam! He had come expecting Hugo, and Hugo would have been bad enough. But Pilbeam! The man she had said she didn't even know. The man she hadn't met. The man whose gifts of flowers she had professed to resent. In person! In the flesh! Hobnobbing with her in a restaurant! By Gad, he meant to say! By George! Good Gosh!

His fists clenched. Eton was forgotten, Cambridge not even a memory. He inhaled so sharply that a man at the next table who was eating a mousse of chicken stabbed himself in the chin with his fork. He turned on Pilbeam with a hungry look. And at this moment, the waiter, raising his voice a little, for he was beginning to think that Ronnie's hearing was slightly affected, mentioned as an interesting piece of information that the management of Mario's preferred to reserve the dancing-floor exclusively for clients in evening dress. But there was a bright side. Gentlemen in flannel suits could be accommodated in the balcony.

It was the waiter who saved Percy Pilbeam. Just as a mosquito may divert for an instant a hunter who is about to spring at and bite in the neck a tiger of the jungle, so did this importunate waiter divert Ronnie Fish. What it was all about, he was too overwrought to ascertain, but he knew that the man was annoying him, pestering him, trying to chat with him when he had business elsewhere. With all the force of a generous nature, sorely tried, he plugged the waiter in the stomach with his elbow. There was a crash which even Leopold's band could not drown. The man who had stabbed himself with the fork had his meal still further spoiled by the fact that it suddenly began to rain glass. And, as regards the other occupants of the restaurant, the word 'Sensation' about sums the situation up.

Ronnie and the management of Mario's now formed two sharply contrasted schools of thought. To Ronnie the only thing that seemed to matter was this Pilbeam – this creeping, slinking, cuckoo-in-the-nest Pilbeam, the Lothario who had lowered all speed records in underhand villainy by breaking up his home before he had got one. He concentrated all his faculties to the task of getting round the table, to the other side of which the object of his dislike had prudently withdrawn, and showing him in no uncertain manner where he got off.

To the management, on the other hand, the vital issue was all this broken glassware. The waiter had risen from the floor, but the glasses were still there, and scarcely one of them was in a condition ever to be used again for the refreshment of Mario's customers. The head-waiter, swooping down on the fray like some god in the Iliad descending from a cloud, was endeavouring to place this point of view before Ronnie. Assisting him

with word and gesture were two inferior waiters –
Waiter A and Waiter B.

Ronnie was in no mood for abstract debate. He hit the
head-waiter in the abdomen, Waiter A in the ribs, and
was just about to dispose of Waiter B, when his activities
were hampered by the sudden arrival of reinforcements.
From all parts of the room other waiters had assembled –
to name but a few, Waiters C, D, E, F, G, and H – and he
found himself hard pressed. It seemed to him that he had
dropped into a Waiters' Convention. As far as the eye
could reach, the arena was crammed with waiters, and
more coming. Pilbeam had disappeared altogether, and
so busy was Ronnie now that he did not even miss him.
He had reached that condition of mind which the old
Vikings used to call Berserk and which among modern
Malays is termed running amok.

Ronnie Fish in the course of his life had had many
ambitions. As a child, he had yearned some day to
become an engine-driver. At school, it had seemed to
him that the most attractive career the world had to
offer was that of the professional cricketer. Later, he had
hoped to run a prosperous night-club. But now, in his
twenty-sixth year, all these desires were cast aside and
forgotten. The only thing in life that seemed really
worth while was to massacre waiters; and to this task he
addressed himself with all the energy and strength at his
disposal.

Matters now began to move briskly. Waiter C, who
rashly clutched the sleeve of Ronnie's coat, reeled back
with a hand pressed to his right eye. Waiter D, a married
man, contented himself with standing on the outskirts
and talking Italian. But Waiter E, made of sterner stuff,
hit Ronnie rather hard with a dish containing *omelette
aux champignons*, and it was as the latter reeled beneath
this buffet that there suddenly appeared in the forefront
of the battle a figure wearing a gay uniform and almost
completely concealed behind a vast moustache, waxed

at the ends. It was the commissionaire from the street-door; and anybody who has ever been bounced from a restaurant knows that commissionaires are heavy metal.

This one, whose name was McTeague, and who had spent many lively years in the army before retiring to take up his present duties, had a grim face made of some hard kind of wood and the muscles of a village blacksmith. A man of action rather than words, he clove his way through the press in silence. Only when he reached the centre of the maelstrom did he speak. This was when Ronnie, leaping upon a chair the better to perform the operation, hit him on the nose. On receipt of this blow, he uttered the brief monosyllable 'Ho!' and then, without more delay, scooped Ronnie into an embrace of steel and bore him towards the door, through which was now moving a long, large, leisurely policeman.

IV

It was some few minutes later that Hugo Carmody, emerging from the telephone-booth on the lower floor where the cocktail bar is, sauntered back into the dancing-room and was interested to find waiters massaging bruised limbs, other waiters replacing fallen tables, and Leopold's band playing in a sort of hushed undertone like a band that has seen strange things.

'Hullo!' said Hugo. 'Anything up?'

He eyed Sue inquiringly. She looked to him like a girl who has had some sort of a shock. Not, or his eyes deceived him, at all her old bright self.

'What's up?' she asked.

'Take me home, Hugo!'

Hugo stared.

'Home? Already? With the night yet young?'

'Oh, Hugo, take me home, quick.'

'Just as you say,' assented Hugo agreeably. He was now pretty certain that something was up. 'One second to settle the bill, and then homeward ho. And on the way you shall tell me all about it. For I jolly well know,' said Hugo, who prided himself on his keenness of observation, 'that something is – or has been – up.'

5 — A Phone Call for Hugo

The Law of Great Britain is a remorseless machine, which, once set in motion, ignores first causes and takes into account only results. It will not accept shattered dreams as an excuse for shattering glassware: nor will you get far by pleading a broken heart in extenuation of your behaviour in breaking waiters. Haled on the morrow before the awful majesty of Justice at Bosher Street Police Court and charged with disorderly conduct in a public place – to wit, Mario's Restaurant, and resisting an officer – to wit, P. C. Murgatroyd, in the execution of his duties, Ronald Fish made no impassioned speeches. He did not raise clenched fists aloft and call upon Heaven to witness that he was a good man wronged. Experience, dearly bought in the days of his residence at the University, had taught him that when the Law gripped you with its talons the only thing to do was to give a false name, say nothing and hope for the best.

Shortly before noon, accordingly, on the day following the painful scene just described, Edwin Jones, of 7 Nasturtium Villas, Cricklewood, poorer by the sum of five pounds, was being conveyed in a swift taxi-cab to his friend Hugo Carmody's hotel, there to piece together his broken life and try to make a new start.

On the part of the man Jones himself during the ride there was a disposition towards silence. He gazed before him bleakly and gnawed his lower lip. Hugo Carmody, on the other hand, was inclined to be rather jubilant. It seemed to Hugo that after a rocky start things had panned out pretty well.

'A nice, smooth job,' he said approvingly. 'I was scanning the beak's face closely during the summing up and I couldn't help fearing for a moment that it was going to be a case of fourteen days without the option. As it is, here you are, a free man, and no chance of your name being in the papers. A moral victory, I call it.'

Ronnie released his lower lip in order to bare his teeth in a bitter sneer.

'I wouldn't care if my name were in every paper in London.'

'Oh, come, old loofah! The honoured name of Fish?'

'What do I care about anything now?'

Hugo was concerned. This morbid strain, he felt, was unworthy of a Nasturtium Villas Jones.

'Aren't you rather tending to make a bit too much heavy weather over this?'

'Heavy weather!'

'I think you are. After all, when you come right down to it, what has happened? You find poor little Sue . . .'

'Don't call her "poor little Sue"!'

'You find the party of the second part,' amended Hugo, 'at a dance place. Well, why not? What, if you follow me, of it? Where's the harm in her going out to dance?'

'With a man she swore she didn't know!'

'Well, at the time when you asked her, probably she didn't know him. Things move quickly in a great city. I wish I had a quid for every girl I've been out dancing with, whom I hadn't known from Eve a couple of days before.'

'She promised me she wouldn't go out with a soul.'

'Ah, but with a merry twinkle in her eye, no doubt? I mean to say, you can't expect a girl nowadays to treat a promise like that seriously. I mean, dash it, be reasonable!'

'And with that little worm of all people!'

353

Hugo cleared his throat. He was conscious of a slight embarrassment. He had not wished to touch on this aspect of the affair, but Ronnie's last words gave a Carmody and a gentleman no choice.

'As a matter of fact, Ronnie, old man,' he said, 'you are wrong in supposing that she went to Mario's with the above Pilbeam. She went with me. Blameless Hugo, what. I mean, more like a brother than anything.'

Ronnie declined to be comforted.

'I don't believe you.'

'My dear chap!'

'I suppose you think you're damned clever, trying to smooth things over. She was at Mario's with Pilbeam.'

'I took her there.'

'You may have taken her. But she was dining with Pilbeam.'

'Nothing of the kind.'

'Do you think I can't believe my own eyes? It's no use your saying anything, Hugo, I'm through with her. She's let me down. Less than a week I've been away,' said Ronnie, his voice trembling, 'and she lets me down. Well, it serves me right for being such a fool as to think she ever cared a curse for me.'

He relapsed into silence. And Hugo, after turning over in his mind a few specimen remarks, decided not to make them. The cab drew up before the hotel, and Ronnie, getting out, uttered a wordless exclamation.

'No, let me,' said Hugo considerately. A bit rough on a man, he felt, after coughing up five quid to the hell-hounds of the Law, to be expected to pay the cab. He produced money and turned to the driver. It was some moments before he turned back again, for the driver, by the rules of the taxi-chauffeurs' Union, kept his petty cash tucked into his underclothing. When he did so, he was considerably astonished to find that Ronnie, while his back was turned, had, in some unaccountable manner, become Sue. The changeling

was staring unhappily at him from the exact spot where
he had left his old friend.

'Hullo!' he said.

'Ronnie's gone,' said Sue.

'Gone?'

'Yes. He walked off as quick as he could round the
corner when he saw me. He . . .' Sue's voice broke. 'He
didn't say a word.'

'How did you get here?' asked Hugo. There were other
matters, of course, to be discussed later, but he felt he
must get this point cleared up first.

'I thought you would bring him back to your hotel,
and I thought that if I could see him I could . . . say
something.'

Hugo was alarmed. He was now practically certain
that this girl was going to cry, and if there was one thing
he disliked it was being with crying girls in a public
spot. He would not readily forget the time when a
female named Yvonne Something had given way to a
sudden twinge of neuralgia in his company not far from
Piccadilly Circus, and an old lady had stopped and said
that it was brutes like him who caused all the misery in
the world.

'Come inside,' he urged quickly. 'Come and have a
cocktail or a cup of tea or a bun or something. I say,' he
said, as he led the way into the hotel lobby and found
two seats in a distant corner, 'I'm frightfully sorry about
all this. I can't help feeling it's my fault.'

'Oh, no.'

'If I hadn't asked you to dinner . . .'

'It isn't that that's the trouble. Ronnie might have
been a little cross for a minute or two if he had found
you and me together, but he would soon have got over it.
It was finding me with that horrid little man Pilbeam.
You see, I told him – and it was quite true – that I didn't
know him.'

'Yes, so he was saying to me in the cab.'

'Did he – What did he say?'

'Well, he plainly resented the Pilbeam, I'm afraid. His manner, when touching on the Pilbeam, was austere. I tried to drive into his head that that was just an accidental meeting and that you had come to Mario's with me, but he would have none of it. I fear, old thing, there's nothing to be done but leave the whole binge to Time, the Great Healer.'

A page-boy was making a tour of the lobby. He seemed to be seeking a Mr Gregory.

'If only I could get hold of him and make him listen. I haven't been given a chance to explain.'

'You think you could explain, even if given a chance?'

'I could try. Surely he couldn't help seeing that I really loved him, if we had a real talk?'

'And the trouble is, you're here and he'll be back at Blandings in a few hours. Difficult,' said Hugo, shaking his head. 'Complex.'

'Mr Carmody,' chanted the page-boy, coming nearer. 'Mr Carmody.'

'Hi!' cried Hugo.

'Mr Carmody? Wanted on the telephone, sir.'

Hugo's face became devout and saint-like.

'Awfully sorry to leave you for an instant,' he said, 'but do you mind if I rush? It must be Millicent. She's the only person who knows I'm here.'

He sped away, and Sue, watching him, found herself choking with sudden tears. It seemed to emphasize her forlornness so, this untimely evidence of another love-story that had not gone awry. She seemed to be listening to that telephone-conversation, hearing Hugo's delighted yelps as the voice of the girl he loved floated to him over the wire.

She pulled herself together. Beastly of her to be jealous of Hugo just because he was happy . . .

Sue sat up abruptly. She had had an idea.

It was a breath-taking idea, but simple. It called for

courage, for audacity, for a reckless disregard of consequences, but nevertheless it was simple.

'Hugo,' she cried, as that lucky young man returned and dropped into the chair at her side. 'Hugo, listen!'

'I say,' said Hugo.

'I've suddenly thought . . .'

'I say,' said Hugo.

'Do listen!'

'I say,' said Hugo, 'that was Millicent on the phone.'

'Was it? How nice. Listen, Hugo . . .'

'Speaking from Blandings.'

'Yes. But . . .'

'And she has broken off the engagement!'

'What!'

'Broken off the bally engagement,' repeated Hugo. He signalled urgently to a passing waiter. 'Get me a brandy-and-soda, will you?' he said. His face was pale and set. 'A stiffish brandy-and-soda, please.'

'Brandy-and-soda, sir?'

'Yes,' said Hugo. 'Stiffish.'

6 — Sue has an Idea

Sue stared at him, bewildered.

'Broken off the engagement?'

'Broken off the engagement.'

In moments of stress, the foolish question is always the one that comes uppermost in the mind.

'Are you sure?'

Hugo emitted a sound which resembled the bursting of a paper bag. He would have said himself, if asked, that he was laughing mirthlessly.

'Sure? Not much doubt about it.'

'But why?'

'She knows all.'

'All what?'

'Everything, you poor fish,' said Hugo, forgetting in a strong man's agony the polish of the Carmodys. 'She's found out that I took you to dinner last night.'

'What!'

'She has.'

'But how?'

The paper bag exploded again. A look of intense bitterness came into Hugo's face.

'If ever I meet that slimy, slinking, marcelle-waved by-product Pilbeam again,' he said, 'let him commend his soul to God! If he has time,' he added.

He took the brandy-and-soda from the waiter, and eyed Sue dully.

'Anything on similar lines for you?'

'No, thanks.'

'Just as you like. It's not easy for a man in my position to realize,' said Hugo, drinking deeply, 'that refusing a brandy-and-soda is possible. I shouldn't have said, off-hand, that it could be done.'

Sue was a warm-hearted girl. In the tragedy of this announcement she had almost forgotten that she had troubles herself.

'Tell me all about it, Hugo.'

He put down the empty glass.

'I came up from Blandings yesterday,' he said, 'to interview the Argus Enquiry Agency on the subject of sending a man down to investigate the theft of Lord Emsworth's pig.'

Sue would have liked to hear more about this pig, but she knew that this was no time for questions.

'I went to the Argus and saw this wen Pilbeam, who runs it.'

Again Sue would have liked to speak. Once more she refrained. She felt as if she were at a sick-bed, hearing a dying man's last words. On such occasions one does not interrupt.

'Meanwhile,' proceeded Hugo tonelessly, 'Millicent, suspecting – and I am surprised at her having a mind like that. I always looked on her as a pure, white soul – suspecting that I might be up to something in London, got the Argus on the long-distance telephone and told them to follow my movements and report to her. And, apparently, just before she called me up, she had been talking to them on the wire and getting their statement. All this she revealed to me in short, burning sentences, and then she said that if I thought we were still engaged, I could have three more guesses. But, to save me trouble, she would tell me the answer – viz.: No wedding-bells for me. And to think,' said Hugo, picking up the glass and putting it down again, after inspection, with a hurt and disappointed look, 'that I actually rallied this growth Pilbeam on the subject of following people and reporting on their movements. Yes, I assure you. Rallied him blithely. Just as I was leaving his office, we kidded merrily back and forth. And then I went out into the world, happy and carefree, little knowing that my every step was dogged by a blasted bloodhound. Well, all I can say is that, if Ronnie wants this Pilbeam's gore, and I gather that he does, he will jolly well have to wait till I've helped myself.'

Sue, womanlike, blamed the woman.

'I don't think Millicent can be a very nice girl,' she said, primly.

'An angel,' said Hugo. 'Always was. Celebrated for it. I don't blame her.'

'I do.'

'I don't.'

'I do.'

'Well, have it your own way,' said Hugo handsomely. He beckoned to the waiter. 'Another of the same, please.'

'This settles it,' said Sue.

Her eyes were sparkling. Her chin a resolute tilt.

'Settles what?'

'While you were at the telephone, I had an idea.'

'I have had ideas in my time,' said Hugo. 'Many of them. At the moment I have but one. To get within arm's length of the yam Pilbeam and twist his greasy neck till it comes apart in my hands. "What do you do here?" I said. "Measure footprints?" "We follow people and report on their movements," said he. "Ha, ha!" I laughed carelessly. "Ha, ha!" laughed he. General mirth and jollity. And all the while . . .'

'Hugo, will you listen?'

'And this is the bitter thought that now strikes me. What chance have I of scooping out the man's inside with my bare hands? I've got to go back to Blandings on the two-fifteen, or I lose my job. Leaving him unscathed in his bally lair, chuckling over my downfall and following some other poor devil's movements.'

'Hugo!'

The broken man passed a weary hand over his forehead.

'You spoke?'

'I've been speaking for the last ten minutes, only you won't listen.'

'Say on,' said Hugo, listlessly starting on the second restorative.

'Have you ever heard of a Miss Schoonmaker?'

'I seem to know the name. Who is she?'

'Me.'

Hugo lowered his glass, pained.

'Don't talk drip to a broken-hearted man,' he begged. 'What do you mean?'

'When Ronnie was driving me in his car, we met Lady Constance Keeble.'

'A blister,' said Hugo. 'Always was. Generally admitted all over Shropshire.'

'She thought I was this Miss Schoonmaker.'

'Why?'

'Because Ronnie said I was.'

Hugo sighed hopelessly.

'Complex. Complex. My God! How complex.'

'It was quite simple and natural. Ronnie had just been telling me about this girl – how he had met her at Biarritz and that she was coming to Blandings and so on, and when he saw Lady Constance looking at me with frightful suspicion it suddenly occurred to him to say that I was her.'

'That you were Lady Constance?'

'No, idiot. Miss Schoonmaker. And now I'm going to wire her – Lady Constance, not Miss Schoonmaker, in case you were going to ask – saying that I'm coming to Blandings right away.'

'Pretending to be this Miss Schoonmaker?'

'Yes.'

Hugo shook his head.

'Imposs.'

'Why?'

'Absolutely out of the q.'

'Why? Lady Constance is expecting me. Do be sensible.'

'I'm being sensible all right. But somebody is gibbering and, naming no names, it's you. Don't you realize that, just as you reach the front door, this Miss Schoonmaker will arrive in person, dishing the whole thing?'

'No, she won't.'

'Why won't she?'

'Because Ronnie sent her a telegram, in Lady Constance's name, saying that there's scarlet fever or something at Blandings and she wasn't to come.'

Hugo's air of the superior critic fell from him like a garment. He sat up in his chair. So moved was he that he spilled his brandy-and-soda and did not give it so much as a look of regret. He let it soak into the carpet, unheeded.

'Sue!'

'Once I'm at Blandings, I shall be able to see Ronnie and make him be sensible.'

'That's right.'

'And then you'll be able to tell Millicent that there couldn't have been much harm in my being out with you last night, because I'm engaged to Ronnie.'

'That's right, too.'

'Can you see any flaws?'

'Not a flaw.'

'I suppose, as a matter of fact, you'll give the whole thing away in the first five minutes by calling me Sue.'

Hugo waved an arm buoyantly.

'Don't give the possibility another thought,' he said. 'If I do, I'll cover it up adroitly by saying I meant, "Schoo". Short for Schoonmaker. And now go and send her another telegram. Keep on sending telegrams. Leave nothing to chance. Send a dozen and pitch it strong. Say that Blandings Castle is ravaged with disease. Not merely scarlet fever. Scarlet fever *and* mumps. Not to mention housemaid's knee, diabetes, measles, shingles, and the botts. We're on to a big thing, my Susan. Let us push it along.'

7 — A Job for Percy Pilbeam

Sunshine, calling to all right-thinking men to come out and revel in its heartening warmth, poured in at the windows of the great library of Blandings Castle. But to Clarence, ninth Earl of Emsworth, much as he liked sunshine as a rule, it brought no cheer. His face drawn, his pince-nez askew, his tie drooping away from its stud like a languorous lily, he sat staring sightlessly before him. He looked like something that had just been prepared for stuffing by a taxidermist.

A moralist, watching Lord Emsworth in his travail, would have reflected smugly that it cuts both ways, this business of being a peer of the realm with large private means and a good digestion. Unalloyed prosperity, he would have pointed out in his offensive way, tends to enervate; and in this world of ours, full of alarms and uncertainties, where almost anything is apt to drop suddenly on top of your head without warning at almost any moment, what one needs is to be tough and alert.

When some outstanding disaster happens to the ordinary man, it finds him prepared. Years of missing the eight-forty-five, taking the dog for a run on rainy nights, endeavouring to abate smoky chimneys, and coming down to breakfast and discovering that they have burned the bacon again, have given his soul a protective hardness, so that by the time his wife's relations arrive for a long visit he is ready for them.

Lord Emsworth had had none of this salutary training. Fate, hitherto, had seemed to spend its time thinking up ways of pampering him. He ate well, slept

well, and had no money troubles. He grew the best roses
in Shropshire. He had won a first prize for Pumpkins at
that county's Agricultural Show, a thing no Earl of
Emsworth had ever done before. And, just previous to
the point at which this chronicle opens, his younger son,
Frederick, had married the daughter of an American
millionaire and had gone to live three thousand miles
away from Blandings Castle, with lots of good, deep
water in between him and it. He had come to look on
himself as Fate's spoiled darling.

Can we wonder, then, that in the agony of this
sudden, treacherous blow he felt stunned and looked
eviscerated? Is it surprising that the sunshine made no
appeal to him? May we not consider him justified, as he
sat there, in swallowing a lump in his throat like an
ostrich gulping down a brass door-knob?

The answer to these questions, in the order given, is
No, No, and Yes.

The door of the library opened, revealing the natty
person of his brother Galahad. Lord Emsworth
straightened his pince-nez and looked at him
apprehensively. Knowing how little reverence there was
in the Hon. Galahad's composition, and how tepid was
his interest in the honourable struggles for supremacy of
Fat Pigs, he feared that the other was about to wound
him in his bereavement with some jarring flippancy.
Then his gaze softened and he was conscious of a
soothing feeling of relief. There was no frivolity in his
brother's face, only a gravity which became him very
well. The Hon. Galahad sat down, hitched up the knees
of his trousers, cleared his throat, and spoke in a tone
that could not have been more sympathetic or in better
taste.

'Bad business, this, Clarence.'

'Appalling, my dear fellow.'

'What are you going to do about it?'

Lord Emsworth shrugged his shoulders hopelessly. He

generally did when people asked him what he was going to do about things.

'I am at a loss,' he confessed. 'I do not know how to act. What young Carmody tells me has completely upset all my plans.'

'Carmody?'

'I sent him to the Argus Enquiry Agency in London to engage the services of a detective. It is a firm that Sir Gregory Parsloe once mentioned to me, in the days when we were on better terms. He said, in rather a meaning way, I thought, that if ever I had any trouble of any sort that needed expert and tactful handling, these were the people to go to. I gathered that they had assisted him in some matter the details of which he did not confide to me, and had given complete satisfaction.'

'Parsloe!' said the Hon. Galahad, and sniffed.

'So I sent young Carmody to London to approach them about finding the Empress. And now he tells me that his errand proved fruitless. They were firm in their refusal to trace missing pigs.'

'Just as well.'

'What do you mean?'

'Save you a lot of unnecessary expense. There's no need for you to waste money employing detectives.'

'I thought that possibly the trained mind . . .'

'I can tell you who's got the Empress. I've known it all along.'

'What!'

'Certainly.'

'Galahad!'

'It's as plain as the nose on your face.'

Lord Emsworth felt his nose.

'Is it?' he said doubtfully.

'I've just been talking to Constance . . .'

'Constance?' Lord Emsworth opened his mouth feebly. 'She hasn't got my pig?'

'I've just been talking to Constance,' repeated the

Hon. Galahad, 'and she called me some very unpleasant names.'

'She does, sometimes. Even as a child, I remember . . .'

'Most unpleasant names. A senile mischief-maker, among others, and a meddling old penguin. And all because I told her that the man who had stolen Empress of Blandings was young Gregory Parsloe.'

'Parsloe!'

'Parsloe. Surely it's obvious? I should have thought it would have been clear to the meanest intelligence.'

From boyhood up, Lord Emsworth had possessed an intelligence about as mean as an intelligence can be without actually being placed under restraint. Nevertheless, he found his brother's theory incredible.

'Parsloe?'

'Don't keep saying "Parsloe".'

'But, my dear Galahad . . .'

'It stands to reason.'

'You don't really think so?'

'Of course I think so. Have you forgotten what I told you the other day?'

'Yes,' said Lord Emsworth. He always forgot what people told him the other day.

'About young Parsloe,' said the Hon. Galahad impatiently. 'About his nobbling my dog Towser.'

Lord Emsworth started. It all came back to him. A hard expression crept into the eyes behind the pince-nez, which emotion had just jerked crooked again.

'To be sure. Towser. Your dog. I remember.'

'He nobbled Towser, and he's nobbled the Empress. Dash it, Clarence, use your intelligence. Who else except young Parsloe had any interest in getting the Empress out of the way? And, if he hadn't known there was some dirty work being planned, would that pig-man of his, Brotherhood or whatever his name is, have been going about offering three to one on Pride of Matchingham? I told you at the time it was fishy.'

The evidence was damning, and yet Lord Emsworth found himself once more a prey to doubt. Of the blackness of Sir Gregory Parsloe-Parsloe's soul he had, of course, long been aware. But could the man actually be capable of the Crime of the Century? A fellow-landowner? A Justice of the Peace? A man who grew pumpkins? A Baronet?

'But Galahad . . . A man in Parsloe's position . . .'

'What do you mean a man in his position? Do you suppose a fellow changes his nature just because a cousin of his dies and he comes into a baronetcy? Haven't I told you a dozen times that I've known young Parsloe all his life? Known him intimately. He was always as hot as mustard and as wide as Leicester Square. Ask anybody who used to go around Town in those days. When they saw young Parsloe coming, strong men winced and hid their valuables. He hadn't a penny except what he could get by telling the tale, and he always did himself like a prince. When I knew him first, he was living down on the river at Shepperton. His old father, the Dean, had made an arrangement with the keeper of the pub there to give him breakfast and bed and nothing else. "If he wants dinner, he must earn it," the old boy said. And do you know how he used to earn it? He trained that mongrel of his, Banjo, to go and do tricks in front of parties that came to the place in steam-launches. And then he would stroll up and hope his dog was not annoying them and stand talking till they went in to dinner and then go in with them and pick up the wine-list, and before they knew what was happening he would be bursting with their champagne and cigars. That's the sort of fellow young Parsloe was.'

'But even so . . .'

'I remember him running up to me outside that pub one afternoon – the Jolly Miller it was called – his face shining with positive ecstasy. "Come in, quick!" he said. "There's a new barmaid, and she hasn't found out yet I'm not allowed credit." '

'But, Galahad . . .'

'And if young Parsloe thinks I've forgotten a certain incident that occurred in the early summer of the year '95, he's very much mistaken. He met me in the Haymarket and took me into the Two Goslings for a drink – there's a hat-shop now where it used to be – and after we'd had it he pulls a sort of dashed little top affair out of his pocket, a thing with numbers written round it. Said he'd found it in the street and wondered who thought of these ingenious little toys and insisted on our spinning it for half-crowns. "You take the odd numbers, I'll take the even," says young Parsloe. And before I could fight my way out into the fresh air, I was ten pounds seven and sixpence in the hole. And I discovered next morning that they make those beastly things so that if you push the stem through and spin them the wrong way up you're bound to get an even number. And when I asked him the following afternoon to show me the top again, he said he'd lost it. That's the sort of fellow young Parsloe was. And you expect me to believe that inheriting a baronetcy and settling down in the country has made him so dashed pure and high-minded that he wouldn't stoop to nobbling a pig.'

Lord Emsworth uncoiled himself. Cumulative evidence had done its work. His eyes glittered, and he breathed stertorously.

'The scoundrel!'

'Tough nut, always was.'

'What shall I do?'

'Do? Why, go to him right away and tax him.'

'Tax him?'

'Yes. Look him squarely in the eye and tax him with his crime.'

'I will! Immediately.'

'I'll come with you.'

'Look him squarely in the eye!'

'And tax him!'

'And tax him.' Lord Emsworth had reached the hall and was peering agitatedly to right and left. 'Where the devil's my hat? I can't find my hat. Somebody's always hiding my hat. I will not have my hats hidden.'

'You don't need a hat to tax a man with stealing a pig,' said the Hon. Galahad, who was well versed in the manners and rules of good society.

II

In his study at Matchingham Hall in the neighbouring village of Much Matchingham, Sir Gregory Parsloe-Parsloe sat gazing at the current number of a weekly paper. We have seen that weekly paper before. On that occasion it was in the plump hands of Beach. And, oddly enough, what had attracted Sir Gregory's attention was the very item which had interested the butler.

> The Hon. Galahad Threepwood, brother of the Earl of Emsworth. A little bird tells us that 'Gally' is at Blandings Castle, Shropshire, the ancestral seat of the family, busily engaged in writing his reminiscences. As every member of the Old Brigade will testify, they ought to be as warm as the weather, if not warmer!

But whereas Beach, perusing this, had chuckled, Sir Gregory Parsloe-Parsloe shivered, like one who on a country ramble suddenly perceives a snake in his path.

Sir Gregory Parsloe-Parsloe, of Matchingham Hall, seventh baronet of his line, was one of those men who start their lives well, skid for a while, and then slide back on to the strait and narrow path and stay there. This is to say, he had been up to the age of twenty a blameless boy and from the age of thirty-one, when he had succeeded to the title, a practically blameless Bart. So much so that now, in his fifty-second year, he was on the eve of being accepted by the local Unionist Committee as their accredited candidate for the forthcoming by-election in the Bridgeford and Shifley Parliamentary Division of Shropshire.

But there had been a decade in his life, that dangerous decade of the twenties, when he had accumulated a past so substantial that a less able man would have been compelled to spread it over a far longer period. It was an epoch in his life to which he did not enjoy looking back, and years of irreproachable Barthood had enabled him, as far as he personally was concerned, to bury the past. And now, it seemed, this pestilential companion of his youth was about to dig it up again.

The years had turned Sir Gregory into a man of portly habit; and, as portly men do in moments of stress, he puffed. But, puff he never so shrewdly, he could not blow away that paragraph. It was still there, looking up at him, when the door opened and the butler announced Lord Emsworth and Mr Galahad Threepwood.

Sir Gregory's first emotion on seeing the taxing party file into the room was one of pardonable surprise. Aware of the hard feelings which George Cyril Wellbeloved's transference of his allegiance had aroused in the bosom of that gifted pig-man's former employer, he had not expected to receive a morning call from the Earl of Emsworth. As for the Hon. Galahad, he had ceased to be on cordial terms with him as long ago as the winter of the year nineteen hundred and six.

Then, following quickly on the heels of surprise, came indignation. That the author of the Reminiscences should be writing scurrilous stories about him with one hand and strolling calmly into his private study with, so to speak, the other occasioned him the keenest resentment. He drew himself up and was in the very act of staring haughtily, when the Hon. Galahad broke the silence.

'Young Parsloe,' said the Hon. Galahad, speaking in a sharp, unpleasant voice, 'your sins have found you out!'

It had been the baronet's intention to inquire to what he was indebted for the pleasure of this visit, and to inquire it icily; but at this remarkable speech the words halted on his lips.

'Eh?' he said blankly.

The Hon. Galahad was regarding him through his monocle rather as a cook eyes a black-beetle on discovering it in the kitchen sink. It was a look which would have aroused pique in a slug, and once more the Squire of Matchingham's bewilderment gave way to wrath.

'What the devil do you mean?' he demanded.

'See his face?' asked the Hon. Galahad in a rasping aside.

'I'm looking at it now,' said Lord Emsworth.

'Guilt written upon it.'

'Plainly,' agreed Lord Emsworth.

The Hon. Galahad, who had folded his arms in a menacing manner, unfolded them and struck the desk a smart blow.

'Be very careful, Parsloe! Think before you speak. And, when you speak, speak the truth. I may say, by way of a start, that we know all.'

How low an estimate Sir Gregory Parsloe had formed of his visitors' collective sanity was revealed by the fact that it was actually to Lord Emsworth that he now turned as the more intelligent of the pair.

'Emsworth! Explain! What the deuce are you doing here? And what the devil is that old image talking about?'

Lord Emsworth had been watching his brother with growing admiration. The latter's spirited opening of the case for the prosecution had won his hearty approval.

'You know,' he said curtly.

'I should say he dashed well does know,' said the Hon. Galahad. 'Parsloe, produce that pig!'

Sir Gregory pushed his eyes back into their sockets a split second before they would have bulged out of his head beyond recovery. He did his best to think calm, soothing thoughts. He had just remembered that he was a man who had to be careful about his blood-pressure.

'Pig?'

'Pig.'

'Did you say pig?'

'Pig.'

'What pig?'

'He says "What pig?"'

'I heard him,' said Lord Emsworth.

Sir Gregory Parsloe again had trouble with his eyes.

'I don't know what you are talking about.'

The Hon. Galahad unfolded his arms again and smote the desk a blow that unshipped the cover of the ink-pot.

'Parsloe, you sheep-faced, shambling exile from Hell,' he cried. 'Disgorge that pig immediately!'

'My Empress,' added Lord Emsworth.

'Precisely. Empress of Blandings. The pig you stole last night.'

Sir Gregory Parsloe-Parsloe rose slowly from his chair. The Hon. Galahad pointed an imperious finger at him, but he ignored the gesture. His blood-pressure was now hovering around the hundred-and-fifty mark.

'Do you mean to tell me that you seriously accuse . . .'

'Parsloe, sit down!'

Sir Gregory choked.

'I always knew, Emsworth, that you were as mad as a coot.'

'As a what?' whispered his lordship.

'Coot,' said the Hon. Galahad curtly. 'Sort of duck.' He turned to the defendant again. 'Vituperation will do

you no good, young Parsloe. We *know* that you have
stolen that pig.'

'I haven't stolen any damned pig. What would I want
to steal a pig for?'

The Hon. Galahad snorted.

'What did you want to nobble my dog Towser for in
the back room of the Black Footman in the spring of the
year '97?' he said. 'To queer the favourite, that's why
you did it. And that's what you're after now, trying to
queer the favourite again. Oh, we can see through you
all right, young Parsloe. We read you like a book.'

Sir Gregory had stopped worrying about his
blood-pressure. No amount of calm, soothing thoughts
could do it any good now.

'You're crazy! Both of you. Stark, staring mad.'

'Parsloe, will you or will you not cough up that
pig?'

'I have not got your pig.'

'That is your last word, is it?'

'I haven't seen the creature.'

'Why a coot?' asked Lord Emsworth, who had been
brooding for some time in silence.

'Very well,' said the Hon. Galahad. 'If that is the
attitude you propose to adopt, there is no course before
me but to take steps. And I'll tell you the steps I'm going
to take, young Parsloe. I see now that I have been
foolishly indulgent. I have allowed my kind heart to get
the better of me. Often and often, when I've been sitting
at my desk, I've remembered a good story that simply
cried out to be put into my Reminiscences, and every
time I've said to myself, "No," I've said. "That would
wound young Parsloe. Good as it is, I can't use it. I must
respect young Parsloe's feelings." Well, from now on
there will be no more forbearance. Unless you restore
that pig, I shall insert in my book every dashed thing I
can remember about you – starting with our first
meeting, when I came into Romano's and was

introduced to you while you were walking round the
supper-table with a soup tureen on your head and a stick
of celery in your hand, saying that you were a sentry
outside Buckingham Palace. The world shall know you
for what you are – the only man who was ever thrown
out of the Café de l'Europe for trying to raise the price of
a bottle of champagne by raffling his trousers at the
main bar. And, what's more, I'll tell the full story of the
prawns.'

A sharp cry escaped Sir Gregory. His face had turned a
deep magenta. In these affluent days of his middle age,
he always looked rather like a Regency buck who has
done himself well for years among the flesh-pots. He
now resembled a Regency buck who, in addition to
being on the verge of apoplexy, has been stung in the leg
by a hornet.

'I will,' said the Hon. Galahad firmly. 'The full, true
and complete story of the prawns, omitting nothing.'

'What was the story of the prawns, my dear fellow?'
asked Lord Emsworth, interested.

'Never mind. I know. And young Parsloe knows. And
if Empress of Blandings is not back in her sty this
afternoon, you will find it in my book.'

'But I keep telling you,' cried the suffering baronet,
'that I know nothing whatever about your pig.'

'Ha!'

'I've not seen the animal since last year's Agricultural
Show.'

'Ho!'

'I didn't know it had disappeared till you told me.'

The Hon. Galahad stared fixedly at him through the
black-rimmed monocle. Then, with a gesture of
loathing, he turned to the door.

'Come, Clarence!' he said.

'Are we going?'

'Yes,' said the Hon. Galahad with quiet dignity.
'There is nothing more that we can do here. Let us get

away from this house before it is struck by a thunderbolt.'

III

The gentlemanly office-boy who sat in the outer room of the Argus Enquiry Agency read the card which the stout visitor had handed to him and gazed at the stout visitor with respect and admiration. A polished lad, he loved the aristocracy. He tapped on the door of the inner office.

'A gentleman to see me?' asked Percy Pilbeam.

'A *baronet* to see you, sir,' corrected the office-boy. 'Sir Gregory Parsloe-Parsloe, Matchingham Hall, Salop.'

'Show him in immediately,' said Pilbeam with enthusiasm.

He rose and pulled down the lapels of his coat. Things, he felt, were looking up. He remembered Sir Gregory Parsloe. One of his first cases. He had been able to recover for him some letters which had fallen into the wrong hands. He wondered, as he heard the footsteps outside, if his client had been indulging in correspondence again.

From the baronet's sandbagged expression, as he entered, such might well have been the case. It is the fate of Sir Gregory Parsloe-Parsloe to come into this chronicle puffing and looking purple. He puffed and looked purple now.

'I have called to see you, Mr Pilbeam,' he said, after the preliminary civilities had been exchanged and he had lowered his impressive bulk into a chair, 'because I am in a position of serious difficulty.'

'I am sorry to hear that, Sir Gregory.'

'And because I remember with what discretion and resource you once acted on my behalf.'

Pilbeam glanced at the door. It was closed. He was

now convinced that his visitor's little trouble was the same as on the previous occasion, and he looked at the indefatigable man with frank astonishment.

Didn't these old bucks, he was asking himself, ever stop writing compromising letters? You would have thought they would have got writer's cramp.

'If there is any way in which I can assist you, Sir Gregory . . . Perhaps you will tell me the facts from the beginning?'

'The beginning?' Sir Gregory pondered. 'Well, let me put it this way. At one time, Mr Pilbeam, I was younger than I am today.'

'Quite.'

'Poorer.'

'No doubt.'

'And less respectable. And during that period of my life I unfortunately went about a good deal with a man named Threepwood.'

'Galahad Threepwood?'

'You know him?' said Sir Gregory, surprised.

Pilbeam chuckled reminiscently.

'I know his name. I wrote an article about him once, when I was editing a paper called *Society Spice*. Number One of the Thriftless Aristocrats series. The snappiest thing I ever did in my life. They tell me he called twice at the office with a horsewhip, wanting to see me.'

Sir Gregory exhibited concern.

'You have met him, then?'

'I have not. You are probably not familiar with the inner workings of a paper like *Society Spice*, Sir Gregory, but I may tell you that it is foreign to the editorial policy ever to meet visitors who call with horse-whips.'

'Would he have heard your name?'

'No. There was a very strict rule in the *Spice* office that the names of the editorial staff were not to be divulged.'

'Ah!' said Sir Gregory, relieved.

His relief gave place to indignation. There was an inconsistency about the Hon. Galahad's behaviour which revolted him.

'He cut up rough, did he, because you wrote things about him in your paper? And yet he doesn't seem to mind writing things himself about other people, damn him. That's quite another matter. A different thing altogether. Oh yes!'

'Does he write? I didn't know.'

'He's writing his reminiscences at this very moment. He's down at Blandings Castle, finishing them now. And the book's going to be full of stories about me. That's why I've come to see you. Dashed, infernal, damaging stories, which'll ruin my reputation in the county. There's one about some prawns . . .'

Words failed Sir Gregory. He sat puffing. Pilbeam nodded gravely. He understood the position now. As to what his client expected him to do about it, however, he remained hazy.

'But if these stories you speak of are libellous . . .'

'What has that got to do with it? They're true.'

'The greater the truth, the greater the . . .'

'Oh, I know all about that,' interrupted Sir Gregory impatiently. 'And, a lot of help it's going to be to me. A jury could give me the heaviest damages on record and it wouldn't do me a bit of good. What about my reputation in the county? What about knowing that every damned fool I met was laughing at me behind my back? What about the Unionist Committee? I may tell you, Mr Pilbeam, apart from any other consideration, that I am on the point of being accepted by our local Unionist Committee as their candidate at the next election. And if that old pest's book is published, they will drop me like a hot coal. Now do you understand?'

Pilbeam picked up a pen, and with it scratched his chin thoughtfully. He liked to take an optimistic view with regard to his clients' affairs, but he could not conceal from himself that Sir Gregory appeared to be out of luck.

'He is determined to publish this book?'

'It's the only object he's got in life, the miserable old fossil.'

'And he is resolved to include the stories?'

'He called on me this morning expressly to tell me so. And I caught the next train to London to put the matter in your hands.'

Pilbeam scratched his left cheekbone.

'H'm!' he said. 'Well, in the circumstances, I really don't see what is to be done except . . .'

'. . . get hold of the manuscript and destroy it, you were about to say? Exactly. That's precisely what I've come to ask you to do for me.'

Pilbeam opened his mouth, startled. He had not been about to say anything of the kind. What he had been intending to remark was that, the situation being as described, there appeared no course to pursue but to fold the hands, set the teeth, and await the inevitable disaster like a man and a Briton. He gazed blankly at this lawless Bart. Baronets are proverbially bad, but surely, felt Percy Pilbeam, there was no excuse for them to be as bad as all that.

'Steal the manuscript?'

'Only possible way.'

'But that's rather a tall order, isn't it, Sir Gregory?'

'Not,' replied the baronet ingratiatingly, 'for a clever young fellow like you.'

The flattery left Pilbeam cold. His distant, unenthusiastic manner underwent no change. However clever a man is, he was thinking, he cannot very well abstract the manuscript of a book of Reminiscences from a house unless he is first able to enter that house.

'How could I get into the place?'

'I should have thought you would have found a dozen ways.'

379

'Not even one,' Pilbeam assured him.

'Look how you recovered those letters of mine.'

'That was easy.'

'You told them you had come to inspect the gas meter.'

'I could scarcely go to Blandings Castle and say I had come to inspect the gas meter and hope to be invited to make a long visit on the strength of it. You do not appear to realize, Sir Gregory, that the undertaking you suggest would not be a matter of a few minutes. I might have to remain in the house for quite a considerable time.'

Sir Gregory found his companion's attitude damping. He was a man who, since his accession to the baronetcy and its accompanying wealth, had grown accustomed to seeing people jump smartly to it when he issued instructions. He became peevish.

'Why couldn't you go there as a butler or something?'

Percy Pilbeam's only reply to this was a tolerant smile. He raised the pen and scratched his head with it.

'Scarcely feasible,' he said. And again that rather pitying smile flitted across his face.

The sight of it brought Sir Gregory to the boil. He felt an irresistible desire to say something to wipe it away. It reminded him of the smiles he had seen on the faces of bookmakers in his younger days when he had suggested backing horses with them on credit and in a spirit of mutual trust.

'Well, have it your own way,' he snapped. 'But it may interest you to know that to get that manuscript into my possession I am willing to pay a thousand pounds.'

It did, as he had foreseen, interest Pilbeam extremely. So much so that in his emotion he jerked the pen wildly, inflicting a nasty scalp wound.

'A thuth?' he stammered.

Sir Gregory, a prudent man in money matters,

380

perceived that he had allowed his sense of the dramatic
to carry him away.

'Well, five hundred pounds,' he said, rather quickly.
'And five hundred pounds is a lot of money, Mr
Pilbeam.'

The point was one which he had no need to stress.
Percy Pilbeam had grasped it without assistance, and his
face grew wan with thought. The day might come when
the proprietor of the Argus Enquiry Agency would
remain unmoved by the prospect of adding five hundred
pounds to his bank balance, but it had not come yet.

'A cheque for five hundred the moment that old
weasel's manuscript is in my hands,' said Sir Gregory,
insinuatingly.

Nature had so arranged it that in no circumstances
could Percy Pilbeam's face ever become really beautiful,
but at this moment there stole into it an expression
which did do something to relieve, to a certain extent,
its normal unpleasantness. It was an expression of
rapture, of joy, of almost beatific happiness – the look, in
short, of a man who sees his way clear to laying his
hands on five hundred pounds.

There is about the mention of any substantial sum of
money something that seems to exercise a quickening
effect on the human intelligence. A moment before,
Pilbeam's mind had been an inert mass. Now, abruptly,
it began to function like a dynamo.

Get into Blandings Castle? Why, of course he could
get into Blandings Castle. And not sneak in either, with
a trousers-seat itching in apprehension of the kick that
should send him out again, but bowl proudly up to the
front door in his two-seater and hand his suit-case to the
butler and be welcomed as the honoured guest. Until
now he had forgotten, for he had deliberately set himself
to forget, the outrageous suggestion of that young idiot
whose name escaped him that he should come to
Blandings and hunt about for lost pigs. It had wounded

his self-respect so deeply at the time that he had driven
it from his thoughts. When he found himself thinking
about Hugo, he had immediately pulled himself together
and started thinking about something else. Now it all
came back to him. And Hugo's parting words, he
recalled, had been that if ever he changed his mind the
commission would still be open.

'I will take this case, Sir Gregory,' he said.

'Woof?'

'You may rely on my being at Blandings Castle by
tomorrow evening at the latest. I have thought of a way
of getting there.'

He rose from his desk, and paced the room with
knitted brows. That agile brain had begun to work under
its own steam. He paused once to look in a distrait
manner out of the window; and when Sir Gregory
cleared his throat to speak, jerked an impatient shoulder
at him. He could not have baronets, even with hyphens
in their names, interrupting him at a moment like this.

'Sir Gregory,' he said at length. 'The great thing in
matters like this is to be prepared with a plan. I have a
plan.'

'Woof!' said Sir Gregory.

This time he meant that he had thought all along that
his companion would get one after pacing like that.

'When you arrive home, I want you to invite Mr
Galahad Threepwood to dinner tomorrow night.'

The baronet shook like a jelly. Wrath and amazement
fought within him. Ask the man to dinner? After what
had occurred?

'As many others of the Blandings Castle party as you
think fit, of course, but Mr Threepwood without fail.
Once he is out of the house, my path will be clear.'

Wrath and amazement died away. The baronet had
grasped the idea. The beauty and simplicity of the
stratagem stirred his admiration. But was it not, he felt,
a simpler matter to issue such an invitation than to get

it accepted? A vivid picture rose before his eyes of the
Hon. Galahad as he had last seen him.

Then there came to him the blessed, healing thought
of Lady Constance Keeble. He would send the invitation
to her and – yes, dash it! – he would tell her the full
facts, put his cards on the table and trust to her
sympathy and proper feeling to enlist her in the case. He
had been long aware that her attitude towards the
Reminiscences resembled his own. He could rely on her
to help him. He could also rely on her somehow – by
what strange feminine modes of coercion he, being a
bachelor, could only guess at – to deliver the Hon.
Galahad Threepwood at Matchingham Hall in time for
dinner. Women, he knew, had this strange power over
their near relations.

'Splendid!' he said. 'Excellent! Capital. Woof! I'll see
it's done.'

'Then you can leave the rest to me.'

'You think, if I can get him out of the house, you will
be able to secure the manuscript?'

'Certainly.'

Sir Gregory rose and extended a trembling hand.

'Mr Pilbeam,' he said, with deep feeling, 'coming to
see you was the wisest thing I ever did in my life.'

'Quite,' said Percy Pilbeam.

8 — The Storm Clouds Hover over Blandings

Having re-read the half-dozen pages which he had written since luncheon, the Hon. Galahad Threepwood attached them with a brass paper-fastener to the main body of his monumental work and placed the manuscript in its drawer – lovingly, like a young mother putting her first-born to bed. The day's work was done. Rising from the desk, he yawned and stretched himself.

He was ink-stained but cheerful. Happiness, as solid thinkers have often pointed out, comes from giving pleasure to others; and the little anecdote which he had just committed to paper would, he knew, give great pleasure to a considerable number of his fellow-men. All over England they would be rolling out of their seats when they read it. True, their enjoyment might possibly not be shared to its full extent by Sir Gregory Parsloe-Parsloe, of Matchingham Hall, for what the Hon. Galahad had just written was the story of the prawns: but the first lesson an author has to learn is that he cannot please everybody.

He left the small library which he had commandeered as a private study and, descending the broad staircase, observed Beach in the hall below. The butler was standing mountainously beside the tea-table, staring in a sort of trance at a plateful of anchovy sandwiches: and it struck the Hon. Galahad, not for the first time in the last few days, that he appeared to have something on his mind. A strained, haunted look he seemed to have, as if he had done a murder and was afraid somebody was going to find the body. A more practised physiognomist would have been able to interpret that look. It was the one that butlers always wear when they have allowed themselves to be persuaded against their better judgement into becoming accessories before the fact in the theft of their employers' pigs.

'Beach,' he said, speaking over the banisters, for he had just remembered there was a question he wanted to ask the man about the somewhat eccentric Major-General Magnus in whose employment he had once been.

'What's the matter with you?' he added with some irritation. For the butler, jerked from his reverie, had jumped a couple of inches and shaken all over in a manner that was most trying to watch. A butler, felt the Hon. Galahad, is a butler, and a startled fawn is a startled fawn. He disliked the blend of the two in a single body.

'I beg your pardon, sir?'

'Why on earth do you spring like that when anyone speaks to you? I've noticed it before. He leaps,' he said complainingly to his niece Millicent, who now came down the stairs with slow, listless steps. 'When addressed, he quivers like a harpooned whale.'

'Oh?' said Millicent dully. She had dropped into a chair and picked up a book. She looked like something that might have occurred to Ibsen in one of his less frivolous moments.

'I am extremely sorry, Mr Galahad.'

'No use being sorry. Thing is not to do it. If you are practising the Shimmy for the Servants' Ball, be advised by an old friend and give it up. You haven't the build.'

'I think I may have caught a chill, sir.'

'Take a stiff whisky toddy. Put you right in no time. What's the car doing out there?'

'Her ladyship ordered it, sir. I understand that she and Mr Baxter are going to Market Blandings to meet the train arriving at four-forty.'

385

'Somebody expected?'

'The American young lady, sir. Miss Schoonmaker.'

'Of course, yes. I remember. She arrives today, does she?'

'Yes, sir.'

The Hon. Galahad mused.

'Schoonmaker. I used to know old Johnny Schoonmaker well. A great fellow. Mixed the finest mint-juleps in America. Have you ever tasted a mint-julep, Beach?'

'Not to my recollection, sir.'

'Oh, you'd remember all right if you had. Insidious things. They creep up to you like a baby sister and slide their little hands into yours and the next thing you know the Judge is telling you to pay the clerk of the court fifty dollars. Seen Lord Emsworth anywhere?'

'His lordship is at the telephone, sir.'

'Don't do it, I tell you!' said the Hon. Galahad petulantly. For once again the butler had been affected by what appeared to be a kind of palsy.

'I beg your pardon, Mr Galahad. It was something I was suddenly reminded of. There was a gentleman just after luncheon who desired to communicate with you on the telephone. I understood him to say that he was speaking from Oxford, being on his way from London to Blackpool in his automobile. Knowing that you were occupied with your literary work, I refrained from disturbing you. And till I mentioned the word "telephone", the matter slipped my mind.'

'Who was he?'

'I did not get the gentleman's name, sir. The wire was faulty. But he desired me to inform you that his business had to do with a dramatic entertainment.'

'A play?'

'Yes, sir,' said Beach, plainly impressed by this happy way of putting it. 'I took the liberty of advising him that you might be able to see him later in the afternoon. He said that he would call after tea.'

The butler passed from the hall with heavy, haunted steps, and the Hon. Galahad turned to his niece.

'I know who it is,' he said. 'He wrote to me yesterday. It's a theatrical manager fellow I used to go about with years ago. Man named Mason. He's got a play, adapted from the French, and he's had the idea of changing it into the period of the nineties and getting me to put my name to it.'

'Oh?'

'On the strength of my book coming out at the same time. Not a bad notion, either. Galahad Threepwood's a name that's going to have box-office value pretty soon. The house'll be sold out for weeks to all the old buffers who'll come flocking up to London to see if I've put anything about them into it.'

'Oh?' said Millicent.

The Hon. Galahad frowned. He sensed a lack of interest and sympathy.

'What's the matter with you?' he demanded.

'Nothing.'

'Then why are you looking like that?'

'Like what?'

'Pale and tragic, as if you'd just gone into Tattersall's and met a bookie you owed money to.'

'I am perfectly happy.'

The Hon. Galahad snorted.

'Yes, radiant. I've seen fogs that were cheerier. What's that book you're reading?'

'It belongs to Aunt Constance.' Millicent glanced wanly at the cover. 'It seems to be about Theosophy.'

'Theosophy! Fancy a young girl in the spring-time of life . . . What the devil has happened to everybody in this house? There's some excuse, perhaps, for Clarence. If you admit the possibility of a sane man getting so

attached to a beastly pig, he has a right to be upset. But
what's wrong with all the rest of you? Ronald! Goes
about behaving like a bereaved tomato. Beach! Springs
up and down when you speak to him. And that young
fellow Carmody . . .'

'I am not interested in Mr Carmody.'

'This morning,' said the Hon. Galahad, aggrieved, 'I
told that boy one of the most humorous limericks I ever
heard in my life – about an Old Man of – however, that
is neither here nor there – and he just gaped at me with
his jaw dropping, like a spavined horse looking over a
fence. There are mysteries afoot in this house, and I
don't like 'em. The atmosphere of Blandings Castle has
changed all of a sudden from that of a normal, happy
English home into something Edgar Allan Poe might
have written on a rainy Sunday. It's getting on my
nerves. Let's hope this girl of Johnny Schoonmaker's will
cheer us up. If she's anything like her father, she ought
to be a nice, lively girl. But I suppose, when she arrives,
it'll turn out that she's in mourning for a great-aunt or
brooding over the situation in Russia or something. I
don't know what young people are coming to nowadays.
Gloomy. Introspective. The old gay spirit seems to have
died out altogether. In my young days a girl of your age
would have been upstairs making an apple-pie bed for
somebody instead of lolling on chairs reading books
about Theosophy.'

Snorting once more, the Hon. Galahad disappeared
into the smoking-room, and Millicent, tight-lipped,
returned to her book. She had been reading for some
minutes when she became aware of a long, limp,
drooping figure at her side.

'Hullo,' said Hugo, for this ruin of a fine young man
was he.

Millicent's ear twitched, but she did not reply.

'Reading?'

He had been standing on his left leg. With a sudden

change of policy, he now shifted, and stood on his right.

'Interesting book?'

Millicent looked up.

'I beg your pardon?'

'Only said – is that an interesting book?'

'Very,' said Millicent.

Hugo decided that his right leg was not a success. He stood on his left again.

'What's it about?'

'Transmigration of Souls.'

'A thing I'm not very well up on.'

'One of the many, I should imagine,' said the haughty girl. 'Every day you seem to know less and less about more and more.' She rose, and made for the stairs. Her manner suggested that she was disappointed in the hall of Blandings Castle. She had supposed it a nice place for a girl to sit and study the best literature, and now, it appeared, it was overrun by the Underworld. 'If you're really anxious to know what Transmigration means, it's simply that some people believe that when you die your soul goes into something else.'

'Rum idea,' said Hugo, becoming more buoyant. He began to draw hope from her chattiness. She had not said as many consecutive words as this to him for quite a time. 'Into something else, eh? Odd notion. What do you suppose made them think of that?'

'Yours, for instance, would probably go into a pig. And then I would come along and look into your sty and I'd say, "Good gracious! Why, there's Hugo Carmody. He hasn't changed a bit!"'

The spirit of the Carmodys had been a good deal crushed by recent happenings, but at this it flickered into feeble life.

'I call that a beastly thing to say.'

'Do you?'

'Yes, I do.'

'I oughtn't to have said it?'

389

'No, you oughtn't.'

'Well, I wouldn't have, if I could have thought of anything worse.'

'And when you let a little thing like what happened the other night rot up a great love like ours, I – well, I call it a bit rotten. You know perfectly well that you're the only girl in the world I ever . . .'

'Shall I tell you something?'

'What?'

'You make me sick.'

Hugo breathed passionately through his nose.

'So all is over, is it?'

'You can jolly well bet all is over. And if you're interested in my future plans, I may mention I intend to marry the first man who comes along and asks me. And you can be a page at the wedding if you like. You couldn't look any sillier than you do now, even in a frilly shirt and satin knickerbockers.'

Hugo laughed raspingly.

'Is that so?'

'It is.'

'And once you said there wasn't another man like me in the world.'

'Well, I should hate to think there was,' said Millicent. And as the celebrated James-Thomas-Beach procession had entered with cakes and gate-leg tables and her last word seemed about as good a last word as a girl might reasonably consider herself entitled to, she passed proudly up the stairs.

James withdrew. Thomas withdrew. Beach remained gazing with a hypnotized eye at the cake.

'Beach!' said Hugo.

'Sir?'

'Curse all women!'

'Very good, sir,' said Beach.

He watched the young man disappear through the open front door, heard his footsteps crunch on the gravel, and gave himself up to meditation again. How gladly, he was thinking, if it had not been for upsetting Mr Ronald's plans, would he have breathed in his employer's ear as he filled his glass at dinner, 'The pig is in the gamekeeper's cottage in the west wood, your lordship. Thank you, your lordship.' But it was not to be. His face twisted, as if with sudden pain, and he was aware of the Hon. Galahad emerging from the smoking-room.

'Just remembered something I wanted to ask you, Beach. You were with old General Magnus, weren't you, some years ago, before you came here?'

'Yes, Mr Galahad.'

'Then perhaps you can tell me the exact facts about that trouble in 1912. I know the old chap chased young Mandeville three times round the lawn in his pyjamas, but did he merely try to stab him with the bread-knife or did he actually get home?'

'I could not say, sir. He did not honour me with his confidence.'

'Infernal nuisance,' said the Hon. Galahad. 'I like to get these things right.'

He eyed the butler discontentedly as he returned. More than ever was he convinced that the fellow had something on his mind. The very way he walked showed it. He was about to return to the smoking-room when his brother Clarence came into the hall. And there was in Lord Emsworth's bearing so strange a gaiety that he stood transfixed. It seemed to the Hon. Galahad years since he had seen anyone looking cheerful in Blandings Castle.

'Good God, Clarence! What's happened?'

'What, my dear fellow?'

'You're wreathed in smiles, dash it, and skipping like the high hills. Found that pig under the drawing-room sofa or something?'

Lord Emsworth beamed.

'I have had the most cheering piece of news, Galahad. That detective – the one I sent young Carmody to see – the Argus man, you know – he has come after all. He drove down in his car and is at this moment in Market Blandings, at the Emsworth Arms. I have been speaking to him on the telephone. He rang up to ask if I still required his services.'

'Well, you don't.'

'Certainly I do, Galahad. I consider his presence vital.'

'He can't tell you any more than you know already. There's only one man who can have stolen that pig, and that's young Parsloe.'

'Precisely. Yes. Quite true. But this man will be able to collect evidence and bring the thing home and – er – bring it home. He has the trained mind. I consider it most important that the case should be in the hands of a man with a trained mind. We should be seeing him very shortly. He is having what he describes as a bit of a snack at the Emsworth Arms. When he has finished, he will drive over. I am delighted. Ah, Constance, my dear.'

Lady Constance Keeble, attended by the Efficient Baxter, had appeared at the foot of the stairs. His lordship eyed her a little warily. The châtelaine of Blandings was apt sometimes to react unpleasantly to the information that visitors not invited by herself were expected at the castle.

'Constance, my dear, a friend of mine is arriving this evening, to spend a few days. I forgot to tell you.'

'Well, we have plenty of room for him,' replied Lady Constance, with surprising amiability. 'There is something I forgot to tell you, too. We are dining at Matchingham tonight.'

'Matchingham?' Lord Emsworth was puzzled. He could think of no one who lived in the village of Matchingham except Sir Gregory Parsloe-Parsloe. 'With whom?'

'Sir Gregory, of course. Who else do you suppose it could be?'

'What!'

'I had a note from him after luncheon. It is short notice, of course, but that doesn't matter in the country. He took it for granted that we would not be engaged.'

'Constance!' Lord Emsworth swelled slightly. 'Constance, I will not – dash it, I will not – dine with that man. And that's final.'

Lady Constance smiled a sort of lion-tamer's smile. She had foreseen a reaction of this kind. She had expected sales-resistance, and was prepared to cope with it. Not readily, she knew, would her brother become Parsloe-conscious.

'Please do not be absurd, Clarence. I thought you would say that. I have already accepted for you, Galahad, myself, and Millicent. You may as well understand at once that I do not intend to be on bad terms with our nearest neighbour, even if a hundred of your pig-men leave you and go to him. Your attitude in the matter has been perfectly childish from the very start. If Sir Gregory realizes that there has been a coolness, and has most sensibly decided to make the first move towards a reconciliation, we cannot possibly refuse the overture.'

'Indeed? And what about my friend? Arriving this evening.'

'He can look after himself for a few hours, I should imagine.'

'Abominable rudeness he'll think it.' This line of attack had occurred to Lord Emsworth quite suddenly. He found it good. Almost an inspiration, it seemed to him. 'I invite my friend Pilbeam here to pay us a visit, and the moment he arrives we meet him at the front door, dash it, and say, "Ah, here you are, Pilbeam! Well, amuse yourself, Pilbeam. We're off." And this Miss – er – this American girl. What will she think?'

'Did you say Pilbeam?' asked the Hon. Galahad.

'It is no use talking, Clarence. Dinner is at eight. And please see that your dress clothes are nicely pressed. Ring for Beach and tell him now. Last night you looked like a scarecrow.'

'Once and for all, I tell you . . .'

At this moment an unexpected ally took the arena on Lady Constance's side.

'Of course we must go, Clarence,' said the Hon. Galahad, and Lord Emsworth, spinning round to face this flank attack, was surprised to see a swift, meaning wink come and go on his brother's face. 'Nothing gained by having unpleasantness with your neighbours in the country. Always a mistake. Never pays.'

'Exactly,' said Lady Constance, a little dazed at finding this Saul among the prophets, but glad of the helping hand. 'In the country one is quite dependent on one's neighbours.'

'And young Parsloe – not such a bad chap, Clarence. Lots of good in Parsloe. We shall have a pleasant evening.'

'I am relieved to find that you, at any rate, have sense, Galahad,' said Lady Constance handsomely. 'I will leave you to try and drive some of it into Clarence's head. Come, Mr Baxter, we shall be late.'

The sound of the car's engine had died away before Lord Emsworth's feelings found relief in speech.

'But, Galahad, my dear fellow!'

The Hon. Galahad patted his shoulder reassuringly.

'It's all right, Clarence, my boy. I know what I'm doing. I have the situation well in hand.'

'Dine with Parsloe after what has occurred? After what occurred yesterday? It's impossible. Why on earth the man is inviting us, I can't understand.'

'I suppose he thinks that if he gives us a dinner I shall relent and omit the prawn story. Oh, I see Parsloe's motive all right. A clever move. Not that it'll work.'

'But what do you want to go for?'

The Hon. Galahad raked the hall with a conspiratorial monocle. It appeared to be empty. Nevertheless, he looked under a settee and, going to the front door, swiftly scanned the gravel.

'Shall I tell you something, Clarence?' he said, coming back. 'Something that'll interest you?'

'Certainly, my dear fellow. Certainly. Most decidedly.'

'Something that'll bring the sparkle to your eyes?'

'By all means. I should enjoy it.'

'You know what we're going to do? Tonight? After dining with Parsloe and sending Constance back in the car?'

'No.'

The Hon. Galahad placed his lips to his brother's ear.

'We're going to steal his pig, my boy.'

'What!'

'It came to me in a flash while Constance was talking. Parsloe stole the Empress. Very well, we'll steal Pride of Matchingham. Then we'll be in a position to look young Parsloe squarely in the eye and say, "What about it?"'

Lord Emsworth swayed gently. His brain, never a strong one, had tottered perceptibly on its throne.

'Galahad!'

'Only thing to do. Reprisals. Recognized military manoeuvre.'

'But how? Galahad, how can it be done?'

'Easily. If young Parsloe stole the Empress, why should we have any difficulty in stealing his animal? You show me where he keeps it, my boy, and I'll do the rest. Puffy Benger and I stole old Wivenhoe's pig at Hammer's Easton in the year '95. We put it in Plug Basham's bedroom. And we'll put Parsloe's pig in a bedroom, too.'

'In a bedroom?'

'Well, a sort of bedroom. Where are we going to hide the animal – that's what you've been asking yourself, isn't it? I'll tell you. We're going to put it in that caravan that your flower-pot-throwing friend Baxter arrived in. Nobody's going to think of looking there. Then we'll be in a position to talk terms to young Parsloe, and I think he will very soon see the game is up.'

Lord Emsworth was looking at his brother almost devoutly. He had always known that Galahad's intelligence was superior to his own, but he had never realized it could soar to quite such lofty heights as this. It was, he supposed, the result of the life his brother had lived. He himself, sheltered through the peaceful, uneventful years at Blandings Castle, had allowed his brain to become comparatively atrophied. But Galahad, battling through these same years with hostile skittle-sharps and the sort of man that used to be a member of the old Pelican Club, had kept his clear and vigorous.

'You really think it would be feasible?'

'Trust me. By the way, Clarence, this man Pilbeam of yours. Do you know if he was ever anything except a detective?'

'I have no idea, my dear fellow. I know nothing of him. I have merely spoken to him on the telephone. Why?'

'Oh, nothing. I'll ask him when he arrives. Where are you going?'

'Into the garden.'

'It's raining.'

'I have my macintosh. I really – I feel I really must walk about after what you have told me. I am in a state of considerable excitement.'

'Well, work it off before you see Constance again. It won't do to have her start suspecting there's something up. If there's anything you want to ask me about, you'll find me in the smoking-room.'

For some twenty minutes the hall of Blandings Castle remained empty. Then Beach appeared. At the same moment, from the gravel outside there came the purring

of a high-powered car and the sound of voices. Beach
posed himself in the doorway, looking, as he always did
on these occasions, like the Spirit of Blandings
welcoming the lucky guest.

9 — Enter Sue

'Leave the door open, Beach,' said Lady Constance.

'Very good, your ladyship.'

'I think the smell of the wet earth and the flowers is so refreshing, don't you?'

The butler did not. He was not one of your fresh-air men. Rightly conjecturing, however, that the question had been addressed not to him but to the girl in the beige suit who had accompanied the speaker up the steps, he forbore to reply. He cast an appraising bulging-eyed look at this girl and decided that she met with his approval. Smaller and slighter than the type of woman he usually admired, he found her, nevertheless, even by his own exacting standards of criticism, noticeably attractive. He liked her face and he liked the way she was dressed. Her frock was right, her shoes were right, her stockings were right, and her hat was right. As far as Beach was concerned, Sue had passed the Censor.

Her demeanour pleased him, too. From the flush on her face to the sparkle in her eyes, she seemed to be taking her first entry into Blandings Castle in quite the proper spirit of reverential excitement. To be at Blandings plainly meant something to her, was an event in her life: and Beach, who after many years of residence within its walls had come to look on the Castle as a piece of personal property, felt flattered and gratified.

'I don't think this shower will last long,' said Lady Constance.

'No,' said Sue, smiling brightly.

'And now you must be wanting some tea after your journey.'

'Yes,' said Sue, smiling brightly.

It seemed as if she had been smiling brightly for centuries. The moment she had alighted from the train and found her formidable hostess and this strangely sinister Mr Baxter waiting to meet her on the platform, she had begun to smile brightly and had been doing it ever since.

'Usually we have tea on the lawn. It is so nice there.'

'It must be.'

'When the rain is over, Mr Baxter, you must show Miss Schoonmaker the rose-garden.'

'I shall be delighted,' said the Efficient Baxter.

He flashed gleaming spectacles in her direction, and a momentary panic gripped Sue. She feared that already this man had probed her secret. In his glance, it seemed to her, there shone suspicion.

Such, however, was not the case. It was only the combination of large spectacles and heavy eyebrows that had created the illusion. Although Rupert Baxter was a man who generally suspected everybody on principle, it so happened that he had accepted Sue without question. The glance was an admiring, almost a loving glance. It would be too much to say that Baxter had already fallen a victim to Sue's charms, but the good looks which he saw and the wealth which he had been told about were undeniably beginning to fan the hidden fire.

'My brother is a great rose-grower.'

'Yes, isn't he? I mean, I think roses are so lovely.' The spectacles were beginning to sap Sue's morale. They seemed to be eating into her soul like some sort of corrosive acid. 'How nice and old everything is here,' she went on hurriedly. 'What is that funny-looking gargoyle thing over there?'

What she actually referred to was a Japanese mask which hung from the wall, and it was unfortunate that the Hon. Galahad should have chosen this moment to

come out of the smoking-room. It made the question
seem personal.

'My brother Galahad,' said Lady Constance. Her voice
lost some of the kindly warmth of the hostess putting
the guest at her ease and took on the cold disapproval
which the author of the Reminiscences always induced
in her. 'Galahad, this is Miss Schoonmaker.'

'Really?' The Hon. Galahad trotted briskly up. 'Is it?
Bless my soul! Well, well, well!'

'How do you do?' said Sue, smiling brightly.

'How are you, my dear? I know your father
intimately.'

The bright smile faded. Sue had tried to plan this
venture of hers carefully, looking ahead for all possible
pitfalls, but that she would encounter people who
knew Mr Schoonmaker intimately she had not foreseen.

'Haven't seen him lately, of course. Let me see . . .
Must be twenty-five years since we met. Yes, quite
twenty-five years.'

A warm and lasting friendship was destined to spring
up between Sue and the Hon. Galahad Threepwood, but
never in the whole course of it did she experience again
quite the gush of whole-hearted affection which surged
over her at these words.

'I wasn't born then,' she said.

The Hon. Galahad was babbling on happily.

'A great fellow, old Johnny. You'll find some stories
about him in my book. I'm writing my Reminiscences,
you know. Fine sportsman, old Johnny. Great grief to
him, I remember, when he broke his leg and had to go
into a nursing-home in the middle of the racing season.
However, he made the best of it. Got the nurses
interested in current form, and used to make a book
with them in fruit and cigarettes and things. I recollect
coming to see him one day and finding him quite
worried. He was a most conscientious man, with a

horror of not settling up when he lost, and apparently one of the girls had had a suet dumpling on the winner of the three o'clock race at fifteen to eight, and he couldn't figure out what he had got to pay her.'

Sue, laughing gratefully, was aware of a drooping presence at her side.

'My niece Millicent,' said Lady Constance. 'Millicent, my dear, this is Miss Schoonmaker.'

'How do you do?' said Sue, smiling brightly.

'How do you do?' said Millicent, like the silent tomb breaking its silence.

Sue regarded her with interest. So this was Hugo's Millicent. The sight of her caused Sue to wonder at the ardent nature of that young man's devotion. Millicent was pretty, but she would have thought that one of Hugo's exuberant disposition would have preferred something a little livelier.

She was startled to observe in the girl's eye a look of surprise. In a situation as delicate as hers was, Sue had no wish to occasion surprise to anyone.

'Ronnie's friend?' asked Millicent. 'The Miss Schoonmaker Ronnie met at Biarritz?'

'Yes,' said Sue faintly.

'But I had the impression that you were very tall. I'm sure Ronnie told me so.'

'I suppose almost anyone seems tall to that boy,' said the Hon. Galahad.

Sue breathed again. She had had a return of the unpleasant feeling of being boneless which had come upon her when the Hon. Galahad had spoken of knowing Mr Schoonmaker intimately. But, though she breathed, she was still shaken. Life at Blandings Castle was plainly going to be a series of shocks. She sat back with a sensation of dizziness. Baxter's spectacles seemed to her to be glittering more suspiciously than ever.

'Have you seen Ronald anywhere, Millicent?' asked Lady Constance.

'Not since lunch. I suppose he's out in the grounds somewhere.'

'I saw him half an hour ago,' said the Hon. Galahad. 'He came mooning along under my window while I was polishing up some stuff I wrote this afternoon. I called to him, but he just grunted and wandered off.'

'He will be surprised to find you here,' said Lady Constance, turning to Sue. 'Your telegram did not arrive till after lunch, so he does not know that you were planning to come today. Unless you told him, Galahad.'

'I didn't tell him. Never occurred to me that he knew Miss Schoonmaker. Forgot you'd met him at Biarritz. What was he like then? Reasonably cheerful?'

'Yes, I think so.'

'Didn't scowl and jump and gasp and quiver all over the place?'

'No.'

'Then something must have happened when he went up to London. It was after he came back that I remember noticing that he seemed upset about something. Ah, the rain's stopped.'

Lady Constance looked over her shoulder.

'The sky still looks very threatening,' she said, 'but you might be able to get out for a few minutes. Mr Baxter,' she explained, 'is going to show Miss Schoonmaker the rose-garden.'

'No, he isn't,' said the Hon. Galahad, who had been scrutinizing Sue through his monocle with growing appreciation. 'I am. Old Johnny Schoonmaker's little girl . . . why, there are a hundred things I want to discuss.'

The last thing Sue desired was to be left alone with the intimidating Baxter. She rose quickly.

'I should love to come,' she said.

The prospect of discussing the intimate affairs of the Schoonmaker family was not an agreeable one, but anything was better than the society of the spectacles.

'Perhaps,' said the Hon. Galahad, as he led her to the

door, 'you'll be able to put me right about that business of old Johnny and the mysterious woman at the New Year's Eve party. As I got the story, Johnny suddenly found this female – a perfect stranger, mind you – with her arms round his neck, telling him in a confidential undertone that she had made up her mind to go straight back to Des Moines, Iowa, and stick a knife into Fred. What he had done to win her confidence and who Fred was and whether she ever did stick a knife into him, your father hadn't found out by the time I left for home.'

His voice died away, and a moment later the Efficient Baxter, starting as if a sudden thought had entered his powerful brain, rose abruptly and made quickly for the stairs.

10 — A Shock for Sue

The rose-garden of Blandings Castle was a famous beauty-spot. Most people who visited it considered it deserving of a long and leisurely inspection. Enthusiastic horticulturists frequently went pottering and sniffing about it for hours on end. The tour through its fragrant groves personally conducted by the Hon. Galahad Threepwood lasted some six minutes.

'Well, that's what it is, you see,' he said, as they emerged, waving a hand vaguely. 'Roses and – er – roses, and all that sort of thing. You get the idea. And now, if you don't mind, I ought to be getting back. I want to keep in touch with the house. It slipped my mind, but I'm expecting a man to call to see me at any moment on some rather important business.'

Sue was quite willing to return. She liked her companion, but she had found his company embarrassing. The subject of the Schoonmaker family history showed a tendency to bulk too largely in his conversation for comfort. Fortunately, his practice of asking a question and answering it himself and then rambling off into some anecdote of the person or persons involved had enabled her so far to avoid disaster: but there was no saying how long this happy state of things would last. She was glad of the opportunity of being alone.

Besides, Ronnie was somewhere out in these grounds. At any moment, if she went wandering through them, she might come upon him. And then, she told herself, all would be well. Surely he could not preserve his sullen hostility in the face of the fact that she had come all this way, pretending dangerously to be Miss Schoonmaker, of New York, simply in order to see him?

Her companion, she found, was still talking.

'He wants to see me about a play. This book of mine is going to make a stir, you see, and he thinks that if he can get me to put my name to the play . . .'

Sue's thoughts wandered again. She gathered that the caller he was expecting had to do with the theatrical industry, and wondered for a moment if it was anyone she had ever heard of. She was not sufficiently interested to make inquiries. She was too busy thinking of Ronnie.

'I shall be quite happy,' she said, as the voice beside her ceased. 'It's such a lovely place. I shall enjoy just wandering about by myself.'

The Hon. Galahad seemed shocked at the idea.

'Wouldn't dream of leaving you alone. Clarence will look after you, and I shall be back in a few minutes.'

The name seemed to Sue to strike a familiar chord. Then she remembered. Lord Emsworth. Ronnie's Uncle Clarence. The man who held Ronnie's destinies in the hollow of his hand.

'Hi! Clarence!' called the Hon. Galahad.

Sue perceived pottering towards them a long, stringy man of mild and benevolent aspect. She was conscious of something of a shock. In Ronnie's conversation, the Earl of Emsworth had always appeared in the light of a sort of latter-day ogre, a man at whom the stoutest nephew might well shudder. She saw nothing formidable in this newcomer.

'Is that Lord Emsworth?' she asked, surprised.

'Yes. Clarence, this is Miss Schoonmaker.'

His Lordship had pottered up and was beaming amiably.

'Is it, indeed? Oh, ah, yes, to be sure. Delighted. How are you? How are you? Miss Who?'

'Schoonmaker. Daughter of my old friend Johnny Schoonmaker. You knew she was arriving. Considering that you were in the hall when Constance went to meet her . . .'

'Oh, yes.' The cloud was passing from what, for want of a better word, must be called Lord Emsworth's mind. 'Yes, yes, yes. Yes, to be sure.'

'I've got to leave you to look after her for a few minutes, Clarence.'

'Certainly, certainly.'

'Take her about and show her things. I wouldn't go too far from the house, if I were you. There's a storm coming up.'

'Exactly. Precisely. Yes, I will take her about and show her things. Are you fond of pigs?'

Sue had never considered this point before. Hers had been an urban life, and she could not remember ever having come into contact with a pig on what might be termed a social footing. But, remembering that this was the man whom Ronnie had described as being wrapped up in one of these animals, she smiled her bright smile.

'Oh, yes. Very.'

'Mine has been stolen.'

'I'm so sorry.'

Lord Emsworth was visibly pleased at this womanly sympathy.

'But I now have strong hopes that she may be recovered. The trained mind is everything. What I always say . . .'

What it was that Lord Emsworth always said was unfortunately destined to remain unrevealed. It would probably have been something good, but the world was not to hear it; for at this moment, completely breaking his train of thought, there came from above, from the direction of the window of the small library, an odd, scrabbling sound. Something shot through the air. And the next instant there appeared in the middle of a flower-bed containing lobelias something that was so manifestly not a lobelia that he stared at it in stunned amazement, speech wiped from his lips as with a sponge.

It was the Efficient Baxter. He was on all fours, and seemed to be groping about for his spectacles, which had fallen off and got hidden in the undergrowth.

II

Properly considered, there is no such thing as an insoluble mystery. It may seem puzzling at first sight when ex-secretaries start falling as the gentle rain from heaven upon the lobelias beneath, but there is always a reason for it. That Baxter did not immediately give the reason was due to the fact that he had private and personal motives for not doing so.

We have called Rupert Baxter efficient, and efficient he was. The word, as we interpret it, implies not only a capacity for performing the ordinary tasks of life with a smooth firmness of touch but in addition a certain alertness of mind, a genius for opportunism, a gift for seeing clearly, thinking swiftly, and Doing It Now. With these qualities Rupert Baxter was pre-eminently equipped; and it had been with him the work of a moment to perceive, directly the Hon. Galahad had left the house with Sue, that here was his chance of popping upstairs, nipping in to the small library, and abstracting the manuscript of the Reminiscences. Having popped and nipped, as planned, he was in the very act of searching the desk when the sound of a footstep outside froze him from his spectacles to the soles of his feet. The next moment, fingers began to turn the door-handle.

You may freeze a Baxter's body, but you cannot numb his active brain. With one masterful, lightning-like flash of clear thinking he took in the situation and saw the only possible way out. To reach the door leading to the large library, he would have to circumnavigate the desk.

The window, on the other hand, was at his elbow. So he jumped out of it.

All these things Baxter could have explained in a few words. Refraining from doing so, he rose to his feet and began to brush the mould from his knees.

'Baxter! What on earth?'

The ex-secretary found the gaze of his late employer trying to nerves which had been considerably shaken by his fall. The occasions on which he disliked Lord Emsworth most intensely were just these occasions when the other gaped at him open-mouthed like a surprised halibut.

'I overbalanced,' he said curtly.

'Overbalanced?'

'Slipped.'

'Slipped?'

'Yes. Slipped.'

'How? Where?'

It now occurred to Baxter that by a most fortunate chance the window of the small library was not the only one that looked out on to this arena into which he had precipitated himself. He might equally well have descended from the larger library which adjoined it.

'I was leaning out of the library window . . .'

'Why?'

'Inhaling the air . . .'

'What for?'

'And I lost my balance.'

'Lost your balance?'

'I slipped.'

'Slipped?'

Baxter had the feeling – it was one which he had often had in the old days when conversing with Lord Emsworth – that an exchange of remarks had begun which might go on for ever. A keen desire swept over him to be – and that right speedily – in some other place. He did not care where it was. So long as Lord

Emsworth was not there, it would be Paradise
enow.

'I think I will go indoors and wash my hands,' he said.

'And face,' suggested the Hon. Galahad.

'My face, also,' said Rupert Baxter coldly.

He started to move round the angle of the house, but
long before he had got out of hearing Lord Emsworth's
high and penetrating tenor was dealing with the
situation. His lordship, as so often happened on these
occasions, was under the impression that he spoke in a
hushed whisper.

'Mad as a coot!' he said. And the words rang out
through the still summer air like a public oration.

They cut Baxter to the quick. They were not the sort
of words to which a man with an inch and a quarter of
skin off his left shinbone ought ever to have been called
upon to listen. With flushed ears and glowing spectacles,
the Efficient Baxter passed on his way. Statistics relating
to madness among coots are not to hand, but we may
safely doubt whether even in the ranks of these
notoriously unbalanced birds there could have been
found at this moment one who was feeling half as mad
as he did.

Lord Emsworth continued to gaze at the spot where
his late secretary had passed from sight.

'Mad as a coot,' he repeated.

In his brother Galahad he found a ready supporter.

'Madder,' said the Hon. Galahad.

'Upon my word, I think he's actually worse than he
was two years ago. Then, at least, he never fell out of
windows.'

'Why on earth do you have the fellow here?'

Lord Emsworth sighed.

'It's Constance, my dear Galahad. You know what she
is. She insisted on inviting him.'.

'Well, if you take my advice, you'll hide the
flower-pots. One of the things this fellow does when he

gets these attacks,' explained the Hon. Galahad, taking
Sue into the family confidence, 'is to go about hurling
flower-pots at people.'

'Really?'

'I assure you. Looking for me, Beach?'

The careworn figure of the butler had appeared,
walking as one pacing behind the coffin of an old friend.

'Yes, sir. The gentleman has arrived, Mr Galahad. I
looked in the small library, thinking that you might
possibly be there, but you were not.'

'No, I was out here.'

'Yes, sir.'

'That's why you couldn't find me. Show him up to the
small library, Beach, and tell him I'll be with him in a
moment.'

'Very good, sir.'

The Hon. Galahad's temporary delay in going to see
his visitor was due to his desire to linger long enough to
tell Sue, to whom he had taken a warm fancy and whom
he wished to shield as far as it was in his power from the
perils of life, what every girl ought to know about the
Efficient Baxter.

'Never let yourself be alone with that fellow in a
deserted spot, my dear,' he counselled. 'If he suggests a
walk in the woods, call for help. Been off his head for
years. Ask Clarence.'

Lord Emsworth nodded solemnly.

'And it looks to me,' went on the Hon. Galahad, 'as if
his mania had now taken a suicidal turn. Overbalanced,
indeed! How the deuce could he have overbalanced?
Flung himself out bodily, that's what he did. I couldn't
think who it was he reminded me of till this moment.
He's the living image of a man I used to know in the
nineties. The first intimation any of us had that this
chap had anything wrong with him was when he turned
up to supper at the house of a friend of mine – George
Pallant. You remember George, Clarence? – with a

couple of days' beard on him. And when Mrs George, who had known him all her life, asked him why he hadn't shaved – "Shaved?" says this fellow, surprised. Packleby, his name was. One of the Leicestershire Packlebys. "Shaved, dear lady?" he says. "Well, considering that they even hide the butter-knife when I come down to breakfast for fear I'll try to cut my throat with it, is it reasonable to suppose they'd trust me with a razor?" Quite stuffy about it, he was, and it spoiled the party. Look after Miss Schoonmaker, Clarence. I shan't be long.'

Lord Emsworth had little experience in the art of providing diversion for young girls. Left thus to his native inspiration, he pondered awhile. If the Empress had not been stolen, his task would, of course, have been simple. He could have given this Miss Schoonmaker a half-hour of sheer entertainment by taking her down to the piggeries to watch that superb animal feed. As it was, he was at something of a loss.

'Perhaps you would care to see the rose-garden?' he hazarded.

'I should love it,' said Sue.

'Are you fond of roses?'

'Tremendously.'

Lord Emsworth found himself warming to this girl. Her personality pleased him. He seemed dimly to recall something his sister Constance had said about her – something about wishing that her nephew Ronald would settle down with some nice girl with money like that Miss Schoonmaker whom Julia had met at Biarritz. Feeling so kindly towards her, it occurred to him that a word in season, opening her eyes to his nephew's true character, might prevent the girl making a mistake which she would regret for ever when it was too late.

'I think you know my nephew Ronald?' he said.

'Yes.'

Lord Emsworth paused to smell a rose. He gave Sue a brief biography of it before returning to the theme.

'That boy's an ass,' he said.

'Why?' said Sue sharply. She began to feel less amiable towards this stringy old man. A moment before, she had been thinking that it was rather charming, that funny, vague manner of his. Now she saw him clearly for what he was – a dodderer, and a Class A dodderer at that.

'Why?' His lordship considered the point. 'Well, heredity, probably, I should say. His father, old Miles Fish, was the biggest fool in the Brigade of Guards.' He looked at her impressively through slanting pince-nez, as if to call her attention to the fact that this was something of an achievement. 'The boy bounces tennis-balls on pigs,' he went on, getting down to the ghastly facts.

Sue was surprised. The words, if she had caught them correctly, seemed to present a side of Ronnie's character of which she had been unaware.

'Does what?'

'I saw him with my own eyes. He bounced a tennis-ball on Empress of Blandings. And not once but repeatedly.'

The motherly instinct which all girls feel towards the men they love urged Sue to say something in Ronnie's defence. But, apart from suggesting that the pig had probably started it, she could not think of anything. They left the rose-garden and began to walk back to the lawn, Lord Emsworth still exercised by the thought of his nephew's shortcomings. For one reason and another, Ronnie had always been a source of vague annoyance to him since boyhood. There had even been times when he had felt that he would almost have preferred the society of his younger son, Frederick.

'Aggravating boy,' he said. 'Most aggravating. Always up to something or other. Started a night-club the other day. Lost a lot of money over it. Just the sort of thing he would do. My brother Galahad started some kind of a club many years ago. It cost my old father nearly a thousand pounds, I recollect. There is something about Ronald that reminds me very much of Galahad at the same age.'

Although Sue had found much in the author of the Reminiscences to attract her, she was able to form a very fair estimate of the sort of young man he must have been in the middle twenties. This charge, accordingly, struck her as positively libellous.

'I don't agree with you, Lord Emsworth.'

'But you never knew my brother Galahad as a young man,' his lordship pointed out cleverly.

'What is the name of that hill over there?' asked Sue in a cold voice, changing the unpleasant subject.

'That hill? Oh, that one?' It was the only one in sight. 'It is called the Wrekin.'

'Oh?' said Sue.

'Yes,' said Lord Emsworth.

'Ah,' said Sue.

They had crossed the lawn and were on the broad terrace that looked out over the park. Sue leaned on the low stone wall that bordered it and gazed before her into the gathering dusk.

The castle had been built on a knoll of rising ground, and on this terrace one had the illusion of being perched up at a great height. From where she stood, Sue got a sweeping view of the park and of the dim, misty Vale of Blandings that dreamed beyond. In the park rabbits were scuttling to and fro. In the shrubberies birds called sleepily. From somewhere out across the fields there came the faint tinkling of sheep-bells. The lake shone like old silver, and there was a river in the distance, dull grey between the dull green of the trees.

It was a lovely sight, age-old, orderly and English, but it was spoiled by the sky. The sky was overcast and looked bruised. It seemed to be made of dough, and one

could fancy it pressing down on the world like a heavy
blanket. And it was muttering to itself. A single heavy
drop of rain splashed on the stone beside Sue, and there
was a low growl far away as if some powerful and
unfriendly beast had spied her.

She shivered. She had been gripped by a sudden
depression, a strange foreboding that chilled the spirit.
That muttering seemed to say that there was no
happiness anywhere and never could be any. The air
was growing close and clammy. Another drop of rain
fell, squashily like a toad, and spread itself over her
hand.

Lord Emsworth was finding his companion
unresponsive. His stream of prattle slackened and died
away. He began to wonder how he was to escape from a
girl who, though undeniably pleasing to the eye, was
proving singularly difficult to talk to. Raking the
horizon in search of aid, he perceived Beach approaching,
a silver salver in his hand. The salver had a card on it,
and an envelope.

'For me, Beach?'

'The card, your lordship. The gentleman is in the
hall.'

Lord Emsworth breathed a sigh of relief.

'You will excuse me, my dear? It is most important
that I should see this fellow immediately. My brother
Galahad will be back very shortly, I have no doubt. He
will entertain you. You don't mind?'

He bustled away, glad to go, and Sue became
conscious of the salver, thrust deferentially towards her.

'For you, miss.'

'For me?'

'Yes, miss,' moaned Beach, like a winter wind wailing
through dead trees.

He inclined his head sombrely, and was gone. Sue
tore open the envelope. For one breath-taking instant
she had thought it might be from Ronnie. But the

writing was not Ronnie's familiar scrawl. It was bold,
clear, decisive writing, the writing of an efficient man.

She looked at the last page.

> Yours sincerely,
> R. J. BAXTER

Sue's heart was beating faster as she turned back to
the beginning. When a girl in the position in which she
had placed herself has been stared at through
steel-rimmed spectacles in the way this R. J. Baxter had
stared at her through his spectacles, her initial reaction
to mysterious notes from the man behind the lenses
cannot but be a panic fear that all has been discovered.

The opening sentence dispelled her alarm. Purely
personal motives, it appeared, had caused Rupert Baxter
to write these few lines. The mere fact that the letter
began with the words,

> Dear Miss Schoonmaker,

was enough in itself to bring comfort.

> At the risk of annoying you by the intrusion of my
> private affairs (*wrote the Efficient Baxter*), I feel that I
> must give you an explanation of the incident which
> occurred in the garden in your presence this
> afternoon. From the observation – in the grossest
> taste – which Lord Emsworth let fall in my hearing, I
> fear you may have placed a wrong construction on
> what took place. (I allude to the expression 'Mad as a
> coot', which I distinctly heard Lord Emsworth utter
> as I moved away.)
>
> The facts were precisely as I stated. I was leaning
> out of the library window, and, chancing to lean too
> far, I lost my balance and fell. That I might have
> received serious injuries and was entitled to expect

sympathy, I overlook. But the words 'Mad as a coot' I resent extremely.

Had this incident not occurred, I would not have dreamed of saying anything to prejudice you against your host. As it is, I feel that in justice to myself I must tell you that Lord Emsworth is a man to whose utterances no attention should be paid. He is to all intents and purposes half-witted. Life in the country, with its lack of intellectual stimulus, has caused his natural feebleness of mind to reach a stage which borders closely on insanity. His relatives look on him as virtually an imbecile and have, in my opinion, every cause to do so.

In these circumstances, I think I may rely on you to attach no importance to his remarks this afternoon.

Yours sincerely

R. J. BAXTER

PS You will, of course, treat this as entirely confidential.

PPS If you are fond of chess and would care for a game after dinner, I am a good player.

PPSS Or Bezique.

Sue thought it a good letter, neat and well-expressed. Why it had been written, she could not imagine. It had not occurred to her that love – or, at any rate, a human desire to marry a wealthy heiress – had begun to burgeon in R. J. Baxter's bosom. With no particular emotions, other than the feeling that if he was counting on playing Bezique with her after dinner he was due for a disappointment, she put the letter in her pocket, and looked out over the park again.

The object of all good literature is to purge the soul of its petty troubles. This, she was pleased to discover, Baxter's letter had succeeded in doing. Recalling its

polished phrases, she found herself smiling
appreciatively.

That muttering sky did not look so menacing now.
Everything, she told herself, was going to be all right.
After all, she did not ask much from Fate – just an
uninterrupted five minutes with Ronnie. And if Fate so
far had denied her this very moderate demand . . .

'All alone?'

Sue turned, her heart beating quickly. The voice,
speaking close behind her, had had something of the
effect of a douche of iced water down her back. For,
restorative though Baxter's letter had been, it had not
left her in quite the frame of mind to enjoy anything so
sudden and jumpy as an unexpected voice.

It was the Hon. Galahad, back from his interview
with the gentleman, and the sight of him did nothing to
calm her agitation. He was eyeing her, she thought, with
a strange and sinister intentness. And though his
manner, as he planted himself beside her and began to
talk, seemed all that was cordial and friendly, she could
not rid herself of a feeling of uneasiness. That look still
lingered in her mind's eye. With the air all heavy and
woolly and the sky growling pessimistic prophecies, it
had been a look to alarm the bravest girl.

Chattering amiably, the Hon. Galahad spoke of this
and that; of scenery and the weather; of birds and
rabbits; of friends of his who had served in prison and of
other friends who, one would have said on the evidence,
had been lucky to escape. Then his monocle was up
again, and that look was back on his face.

The air was more breathless than ever.

'You know,' said the Hon. Galahad, 'it's been a great
treat to me, meeting you, my dear. I haven't seen any of
your people for a number of years, but your father and I
correspond pretty regularly. He tells me all the news.
Did you leave your family well?'

'Quite well.'

'How was your Aunt Edna?'

'Fine,' said Sue feebly.

'Ah,' said the Hon. Galahad. 'Then your father must have been mistaken when he told me she was dead. But perhaps you thought I meant your Aunt Edith?'

'Yes,' said Sue gratefully.

'She's all right, I hope?'

'Oh, yes.'

'What a lovely woman!'

'Yes.'

'You mean she still is?'

'Oh, yes.'

'Remarkable! She must be well over seventy by now. No doubt you mean beautiful considering she is over seventy?'

'Yes.'

'Pretty active?'

'Oh, yes.'

'When did you see her last?'

'Oh – just before I sailed.'

And you say she's active? Curious! I heard two years ago that she was paralysed. I suppose you mean active for a paralytic.'

The little puckers at the corners of his eyes deepened into wrinkles. The monocle gleamed like the eye of a dragon. He smiled genially.

'Confide in me, Miss Brown,' he said. 'What's the game?'

11 — More Shocks for Sue

Sue did not answer. When the solid world melts abruptly beneath the feet, one feels disinclined for speech. Avoiding the monocle, she stood looking with wide, blank eyes at a thrush which hopped fussily about the lawn. Behind her, the sky gave a low chuckle, as if this was what it had been waiting for.

'Up there,' proceeded the Hon. Galahad, pointing to the small library, 'is the room where I work. And sometimes, when I'm not working, I look out of the window. I was looking out a short while back when you were down here talking to my brother Clarence. There was a fellow with me. He looked out, too.' His voice sounded blurred and far-away. 'A theatrical manager fellow whom I used to know very well in the old days. A man named Mason.'

The thrush had flown away. Sue continued to gaze at the spot where it had been. Across the years, for the mind works oddly in times of stress, there had come to her a vivid recollection of herself at the age of ten, taken by her mother to the Isle of Man on her first steamer trip and just beginning to feel the motion of the vessel. There had been a moment then, just before the supreme catastrophe, when she had felt exactly as she was feeling now.

'We saw you, and he said "Why, there's Sue!" – I said "Sue? Sue Who?" "Sue Brown," said this fellow Mason. He said you were one of the girls at his theatre. He didn't seem particularly surprised to see you here. He said he took it that everything had been fixed up all right and he was glad, because you were one of the best. He wanted to come and have a chat with you, but I headed him off. I thought you might prefer to talk over this little matter of your being Miss Sue Brown alone with me. Which brings me back to my original question. What, Miss Brown, is the game?'

Sue felt dizzy, helpless, hopeless.

'I can't explain,' she said.

The Hon. Galahad tut-tutted protestingly.

'You don't mean to say you propose to leave the thing as just another of those historic mysteries? Don't you want me ever to get a good night's sleep again?'

'Oh, it's so long.'

'We have the evening before us. Take it bit by bit, a little at a time. To begin with, what did Mason mean by saying that everything was all right?'

'I had told him about Ronnie.'

'Ronnie? My nephew Ronald?'

'Yes. And, seeing me here, he naturally took it for granted that Lord Emsworth and the rest of you had consented to the engagement and invited me to the castle.'

'Engagement?'

'I used to be engaged to Ronnie.'

'What! That young Fish?'

'Yes.'

'Good God!' said the Hon. Galahad.

Suddenly Sue began to feel conscious of a slackening of the tension. Mysteriously, the conversation was seeming less difficult. In spite of the fact that Reason scoffed at the absurdity of such an idea, she felt just as if she were talking to a potential friend and ally. The thought had come to her at the moment when, looking up, she caught sight of her companion's face. It is an unpleasant thing to say of any man, but there is no denying that the Hon. Galahad's face, when he was listening to the confessions of those who had behaved as they ought not to have behaved, very frequently lacked

the austerity and disapproval which one likes to see in
faces on such occasions.

'But however did Pa Mason come to be here?' asked
Sue.

'He came to discuss some business in connection with
. . . Never mind about that,' said the Hon. Galahad,
calling the meeting to order. 'Kindly refrain from
wandering from the point. I'm beginning to see daylight.
You are engaged to Ronald, you say?'

'I was.'

'But you broke it off?'

'He broke it off.'

'He did?'

'Yes. That's why I came here. You see, Ronnie was
here and I was in London and you can't put things
properly in letters, so I thought that if I could get down
to Blandings I could see him and explain and put
everything right . . . and I'd met Lady Constance in
London one day when I was with Ronnie and he had
introduced me as Miss Schoonmaker, so that part of it
was all right . . . so . . . Well, so I came.'

If this chronicle has proved anything, it has proved by
now that the moral outlook of the Hon. Galahad
Threepwood was fundamentally unsound. A man to
shake the head at. A man to view with concern. So felt
his sister, Lady Constance Keeble, and she was
undoubtedly right. If final evidence were needed, his
next words supplied it.

'I never heard,' said the Hon. Galahad, beaming like
one listening to a tale of virtue triumphant, 'anything so
dashed sporting in my life.'

Sue's heart leaped. She had felt all along that Reason,
in denying the possibility that this man could ever
approve of what she had done, had been mistaken. These
pessimists always are.

'You mean,' she cried, 'you won't give me away?'

'Me?' said the Hon. Galahad, aghast at the idea. 'Of course I won't. What do you take me for?'

'I think you're an angel.'

The Hon. Galahad seemed pleased at the compliment, but it was plain that there was something that worried him. He frowned a little.

'What I can't make out,' he said, 'is why you want to marry my nephew Ronald.'

'I love him, bless his heart.'

'No, seriously!' protested the Hon. Galahad. 'Do you know that he once put tin-tacks on my chair?'

'And he bounces tennis-balls on pigs. All the same, I love him.'

'You can't!'

'I do.'

'How can you possibly love a fellow like that?'

'That's just what he always used to say,' said Sue softly. 'And I think that's why I love him.'

The Hon. Galahad sighed. Fifty years' experience had taught him that it was no use arguing with women on this particular point, but he had conceived a warm affection for this girl, and it shocked him to think of her madly throwing herself away.

'Don't you go doing anything in a hurry, my dear. Think it over carefully. I've seen enough of you to know that you're a very exceptional girl.'

'I don't believe you like Ronnie.'

'I don't dislike him. He's improved since he was a boy. I'll admit that. But he isn't worthy of you.'

'Why not?'

'Well, he isn't.'

She laughed.

'It's funny that you of all people should say that. Lord Emsworth was telling me just now that Ronnie is exactly like what you used to be at his age.'

'What!'

'That's what he said.'

The Hon. Galahad stared incredulously.

'That boy like me?' He spoke with indignation, for his pride had been sorely touched. 'Ronald like me? Why, I was twice the man he is. How many policemen do you think it used to take to shift me from the Alhambra to Vine Street when I was in my prime? Two! Sometimes three. And one walking behind carrying my hat. Clarence ought to be more careful what he says, dash it. It's just this kind of loose talk that makes trouble. The fact of the matter is, he's gone and got his brain so addled with pigs he doesn't know what he is saying half the time.'

He pulled himself together with a strong effort. He became calmer.

'What did you and that young poop quarrel about?' he asked.

'He is not a poop!'

'He is. It's astonishing to me that any one individual can be such a poop. You'd have thought it would have required a large syndicate. How long have you known him?'

'About nine months.'

'Well, I've known him all his life. And I say he's a poop. If he wasn't, he wouldn't have quarrelled with you. However, we won't split straws. What did you quarrel about?'

'He found me dancing.'

'What's wrong with that?'

'I had promised I wouldn't.'

'And is that all the trouble?'

'It's quite enough for me.'

The Hon. Galahad made light of the tragedy.

'I don't see what you're worrying about. If you can't smooth a little thing like that over, you're not the girl I take you for.'

'I thought I might be able to.'

'Of course you'll be able to. Girls were always doing

that sort of thing to me in my young days, and I never
held out for five minutes, once the crying started. Go
and sob on the boy's waistcoat. How are you as a
sobber?'

'Not very good, I'm afraid.'

'Well, there are all sorts of other tricks you can try.
Every girl knows a dozen. Falling on your knees,
fainting, laughing hysterically, going rigid all over . . .
scores of them.'

'I think it will be all right if I can just talk to him. The
difficulty is to get an opportunity.'

The Hon. Galahad waved a hand spaciously.

'Make an opportunity! Why, I knew a girl years ago –
she's a grandmother now – who had a quarrel with the
fellow she was engaged to, and a week or so later she
found herself staying at the same country-house with
him – Heron's Hill it was. The Matchelows' place in
Sussex – and she got him into her room one night and
locked the door and said she was going to keep him
there all night and ruin both their reputations unless he
handed back the ring and agreed that the engagement
was on again. And she'd have done it, too. Her name was
Frederica Something. Red-haired girl.'

'I suppose you have to have red hair to do a thing like
that. I was thinking of a quiet meeting in the rose-
garden.'

The Hon. Galahad seemed to consider this tame, but
he let it pass.

'Well, whatever you do, you'll have to be quick about
it, my dear. Suppose old Johnny Schoonmaker's girl
really turns up? She said she was going to.'

'Yes, but I made Ronnie send her a telegram, signed
with Lady Constance's name, saying that there was
scarlet fever at the castle and she wasn't to come.'

One dislikes the necessity of perpetually piling up the
evidence against the Hon. Galahad Threepwood, to show

ever more and more clearly how warped was his moral
outlook. Nevertheless the fact must be stated that at
these words he threw his head up and uttered a high,
piercing laugh that sent the thrush, which had just
returned to the lawn, starting back as if a bullet had hit
it. It was a laugh which, when it had rung out in days of
yore in London's more lively night-resorts, had caused
commissionaires to leap like war-horses at the note of
the bugle, to spit on their hands, feel their muscles and
prepare for action.

'It's the finest thing I ever heard!' cried the Hon.
Galahad. 'It restores my faith in the younger generation.
And a girl like you seriously contemplates marrying a
boy like . . . Oh, well!' he said resignedly, seeming to
brace himself to make the best of a distasteful state of
affairs, 'It's your business, I suppose. You know your
own mind best. After all, the great thing is to get you
into the family. A girl like you is what this family has
been needing for years.'

He patted her kindly on the shoulder, and they
started to walk towards the house. As they did so, two
men came out of it.

One was Lord Emsworth. The other was Percy
Pilbeam.

II

There is about a place like Blandings Castle something
which, if you are not in the habit of visiting
country-houses planned on the grand scale, tends to sap
the morale. At the moment when Sue caught sight of
him the proprietor of the Argus Enquiry Agency was not
feeling his brightest and best.

Beach, ushering him through the front door, had
started the trouble. He had merely let his eye rest upon
Pilbeam, but it had been enough. The butler's eye,

through years of insufficient exercise and too hearty feeding, had acquired in the process of time a sort of glaze which many people found trying when they saw it. In Pilbeam it created an inferiority complex of the severest kind.

He could not know that to this godlike man he was merely a blur. To Beach, tortured by the pangs of a guilty conscience, almost everything nowadays was merely a blur. Misinterpreting his gaze, Pilbeam had read into it a shocked contempt, a kind of wincing agony at the thought that things like himself should be creeping into Blandings Castle. He felt as if he had crawled out from under a flat stone.

And it was at this moment that somebody in the dimness of the hall had stepped forward and revealed himself as the young man, name unknown, who had showed such a lively disposition to murder him on the dancing-floor of Mario's restaurant. And from the violent start which he gave, it was plain that the young man's memory was as good as his own.

So far, things had not broken well for Percy Pilbeam. But now his luck turned. There had appeared in the nick of time an angel from heaven, effectively disguised in a shabby shooting-coat and an old hat. He had introduced himself as Lord Emsworth, and he had taken Pilbeam off with him into the garden. Looking back over his shoulder, Pilbeam saw that the young man was still standing there, staring after him – wistfully, it seemed to him; and he was glad, as he followed his host out into the fresh air, to be beyond the range of his eye. Between it and the eye of Beach, the butler, there seemed little to choose.

Relief, however, by the time he arrived on the terrace, had not completely restored his composure. That inferiority complex was still at work, and his surroundings intimidated him. At any moment, he felt, on a terrace like this, there might suddenly appear to confront him and complete his humiliation some

brilliant shattering creature indigenous to this strange
and disturbing world – a Duchess, perhaps – a haughty
hunting woman it might be – the dashing daughter of a
hundred Earls, possibly, who would look at him as Beach
had looked at him and, raising beautifully pencilled
eyebrows in aristocratic disdain, turn away with a
murmured 'Most extraordinary!' He was prepared for
almost anything.

One of the few things he was not prepared for was
Sue. And at the sight of her he leaped three clear inches
and nearly broke a collar stud.

'Gaw!' he said.

'I beg your pardon?' said Lord Emsworth. He had not
caught his companion's remark and hoped he would
repeat it. The lightest utterance of a detective with the
trained mind is something not to be missed. 'What did
you say, my dear fellow?'

He, too, perceived Sue; and with a prodigious effort of
the memory, working by swift stages through Schofield,
Maybury, Coolidge and Spooner, recalled her name.

'Mr Pilbeam, Miss Schoonmaker,' he said. 'Galahad,
this is Mr Pilbeam. Of the Argus, you remember.'

'Pilbeam?'

'How do you do?'

'Pilbeam?'

'My brother,' said Lord Emsworth, exerting himself to
complete the introduction. 'This is my brother Galahad.'

'Pilbeam?' said the Hon. Galahad, lookingly intently
at the proprietor of the Argus. 'Were you ever connected
with a paper called *Society Spice*, Mr Pilbeam?'

The gardens of Blandings Castle seemed to the
detective to rock gently. There had, he knew, been a
rigid rule in the office of that bright, but frequently
offensive, paper that the editor's name was never to be
revealed to callers: but it now appeared only too
sickeningly evident that a leakage had occurred.
Underlings, he realized too late, can be bribed.

He swallowed painfully. Force of habit had come within a hair's-breadth of making him say 'Quite.'

'Never,' he gasped. 'Certainly not. No! Never.'

'A fellow of your name used to edit it. Uncommon name, too.'

'Relation, perhaps. Distant.'

'Well, I'm sorry you're not the man,' said the Hon. Galahad regretfully. 'I've been wanting to meet him. He wrote a very offensive thing about me once. Most offensive thing.'

Lord Emsworth, who had been according the conversation the rather meagre interest which he gave to all conversations that did not deal with pigs, created a diversion.

'I wonder,' he said, 'if you would like to see some photographs?'

It seemed to Pilbeam, in his disordered state, strange that anyone should suppose that he was in a frame of mind to enjoy the Family Album, but he uttered a strangled sound which his host took for acquiescence.

'Of the Empress, I mean, of course. They will give you some idea of what a magnificent animal she is. They will . . .' He sought for the *mot juste*. '. . . stimulate you. I'll go to the library and get them out.'

The Hon. Galahad was now his old, affable self again.

'You doing anything after dinner?' he asked Sue.

'There was some talk,' said Sue, 'of a game of Bezique with Mr Baxter.'

'Don't dream of it,' said the Hon. Galahad vehemently. 'The fellow would probably try to brain you with the mallet. I was thinking that if I hadn't got to go out to dinner I'd like to read you some of my book. I think you would appreciate it. I wouldn't read it to anybody except you. I somehow feel you've got the right sort of outlook. I let my sister Constance see a couple of pages once, and she was too depressing for words. An

428

author can't work if people depress him. I'll tell you what I'll do. I'll give you the thing to read. Which is your room?'

'The Garden Room, I think it's called.'

'Oh yes. Well, I'll bring the manuscript to you before I leave.'

He sauntered off. There was a moment's pause. Then Sue turned to Pilbeam. Her chin was tilted. There was defiance in her eye.

'Well?' she said.

III

Percy Pilbeam breathed a sigh of relief. At the first moment of their meeting, all that he had ever read about doubles had raced through his mind. This question clarified the situation. It put matters on a firm basis. His head ceased to swim. It was Sue Brown and no other who stood before him.

'What on earth are you doing here?' he asked.

'Never mind.'

'What's the game?'

'Never mind.'

'There's no need to be so dashed unfriendly.'

'Well, if you must know, I came here to see Ronnie and try to explain about that night at Mario's.'

There was a pause.

'What was that name the old boy called you?'

'Schoonmaker.'

'Why did he call you that?'

'Because that's who he thinks I am.'

'What on earth made you choose a name like that?'

'Oh, don't keep on asking questions.'

'I don't believe there is such a name. And when it comes to asking questions,' said Pilbeam warmly, 'what do you expect me to do? I never got such a shock in my life as when I met you just now. I thought I was seeing

things. Do you mean to say you're here under a false
name, pretending to be somebody else?'

'Yes.'

'Well, I'm hanged! And as friendly as you please with
everybody.'

'Yes.'

'Everybody except me.'

'Why should I be friendly with you? You've done your
best to ruin my life.'

'Eh?'

'Oh, never mind,' said Sue impatiently.

There was another pause.

'Chatty!' said Pilbeam, wounded again.

He fidgeted his fingers along the wall.

'That Galahad fellow seems to look on you as a
daughter or something.'

'We are great friends.'

'So I see. And he's going to give you his book to read.'

'Yes.'

A keen, purposeful, Argus-Enquiry-Agent sort of look
shot into Pilbeam's face.

'Well, this is where you and I get together,' he said.

'What do you mean?'

'I'll tell you what I mean. Do you want to make some
money?'

'No,' said Sue.

'What! Of course you do. Everybody does. Now listen.
Do you know why I'm here?'

'I've stopped wondering why you're anywhere. You
just seem to pop up.'

She started to move away. A sudden, disturbing
thought had come to her. At any moment Ronnie might
appear on the terrace. If he found her here, closeted, so
to speak, with the abominable Pilbeam, what would he
think? What, rather, would he not think?

'Where are you going?'

'Into the house.'

'Come back,' said Pilbeam urgently.

'I'm going.'

'But I've got something important to say.'

'Well?'

She stopped.

'That's right,' said Pilbeam approvingly. 'Now listen. You'll admit that, if I liked, I could give you away and spoil whatever game it is that you're up to in this place?'

'Well?'

'But I'm not going to do it. If you'll be sensible.'

'Sensible?'

Pilbeam looked cautiously up and down the terrace.

'Now listen,' he said. 'I want your help. I'll tell you why I'm here. The old boy thinks I've come down to find his pig, but I haven't. I've come to get that book your friend Galahad is writing.'

'What!'

'I thought you'd be surprised. Yes, that's what I'm after. There's a man living near here who's scared stiff that there's going to be a lot of stories about him in that book, and he came to see me at my office yesterday and offered me . . .' He hesitated a moment. '. . . Offered me,' he went on, 'a hundred pounds if I'd get into the house somehow and snitch the manuscript. And you being friendly with the old buster has made everything simple.'

'You think so?'

'Easy,' he assured her. 'Especially now he's going to give you the thing to read. All you have to do is hand it over to me, and there's fifty quid for you. For doing practically nothing.'

Sue's eyes lit up. Pilbeam had expected that they would. He could not conceive of a girl whose eyes would not light up at such an offer.

'Oh?' said Sue.

'Fifty quid,' said Pilbeam. 'I'm going halves with you.'

'And if I don't do what you want I suppose you will tell them who I really am?'

'That's it,' said Pilbeam, pleased at her ready intelligence.

'Well, I'm not going to do anything of the kind.'

'What!'

'And if,' said Sue, 'you want to tell these people who I am, go ahead and tell them.'

'I will.'

'Do. But just bear in mind that the moment you do I shall tell Mr Threepwood that it was you who wrote that thing about him in *Society Spice*.'

Percy Pilbeam swayed like a sapling in the breeze. The blow had unmanned him. He found no words with which to reply.

'I will,' said Sue.

Pilbeam continued speechless. He was still trying to recover from this deadly thrust through an unexpected chink in his armour when the opportunity for speech passed. Millicent had appeared, and was walking along the terrace towards them. She wore her customary air of settled gloom. On reaching them, she paused.

'Hullo,' said Millicent, from the depths.

'Hullo,' said Sue.

The library window framed the head and shoulders of Lord Emsworth.

'Pilbeam, my dear fellow, will you come up to the library. I have found the photographs.'

Millicent eyed the detective's retreating back with a mournful curiosity.

'Who's he?'

'A man named Pilbeam.'

'Pill, I should say, is right. What makes him waddle like that?'

Sue was unable to supply a solution to this problem. Millicent came and stood beside her, and, leaning on the stone parapet, gazed disparagingly at the park. She gave

432

the impression of disliking all parks, but this one
particularly.

'Ever read Schopenhauer?' she asked, after a silence.

'No.'

'You should. Great stuff.'

She fell into a heavy silence again, her eyes peering
into the gathering gloom. Somewhere in the twilight
world a cow had begun to emit long, nerve-racking
bellows. The sound seemed to sum up and underline the
general sadness.

'Schopenhauer says that all the suffering in the world
can't be mere chance. Must be meant. He says life's a
mixture of suffering and boredom. You've got to have
one or the other. His stuff's full of snappy cracks like
that. You'd enjoy it. Well, I'm going for a walk. You
coming?'

'I don't think I will, thanks.'

'Just as you like. Schopenhauer says suicide's
absolutely OK. He says Hindoos do it instead of going to
church. They bung themselves into the Ganges and get
eaten by crocodiles and call it a well-spent day.'

'What a lot you seem to know about Schopenhauer.'

'I've been reading him up lately. Found a copy in the
library. Schopenhauer says we are like lambs in a field,
disporting themselves under the eye of the butcher, who
chooses first one and then another for his prey. Sure you
won't come for a walk?'

'No thanks, really. I think I'll go in.'

'Just as you like,' said Millicent. 'Liberty Hall.'

She moved off a few steps, then returned.

'Sorry if I seem loopy,' she said. 'Something on my
mind. Been giving it a spot of thought. The fact is, I've
just got engaged to be married to my cousin Ronnie.'

The trees that stood out against the banking clouds
seemed to swim before Sue's eyes. An unseen hand had
clutched her by the throat and was crushing the life out
of her.

433

'Ronnie!'

'Yes,' said Millicent, rather in the tone of voice which Schopenhauer would have used when announcing the discovery of a caterpillar in his salad. 'We fixed it up just now.'

She wandered away, and Sue clung to the terrace wall. That at least was solid in a world that rocked and crashed.

'I say!'

It was Hugo. She was looking at him through a mist, but there was never any mistaking Hugo Carmody.

'I say! Did she tell you?'

Sue nodded.

'She's engaged.'

Sue nodded.

'She's going to marry Ronnie.'

Sue nodded.

'Death, where is thy sting?' said Hugo, and vanished in the direction taken by Millicent.

12 — Activities of Beach the Butler

The firm and dignified note in which Rupert Baxter had expressed his considered opinion of the Earl of Emsworth had been written in the morning-room immediately upon the ex-secretary's return to the house and delivered into Beach's charge with hands still stained with garden-mould. Only when this urgent task had been performed did he start to go upstairs in quest of the wash and brush-up which he so greatly needed. He was mounting the stairs to his bedroom and had reached the first floor when a door opened and his progress was arrested by what in a lesser woman would have been a yelp. Proceeding, as it did, from the lips of Lady Constance Keeble, we must call it an exclamation of surprise.

'Mr Baxter!'

She was standing in the doorway of her boudoir, and she eyed his dishevelled form with such open-mouthed astonishment that for an instant the ex-secretary came near to including her with the head of the family in the impromptu Commination Service which was taking shape in his mind. He was in no mood for wide-eyed looks of wonder.

'May I come in?' he said curtly. He could explain all, but he did not wish to do so on the first floor landing of a house where almost anybody might be listening with flapping ears.

'But, Mr Baxter!' said Lady Constance.

He paused for a moment to grit his teeth, then closed the door.

435

'What *have* you being doing, Mr Baxter?'

'Jumping out of window.'

'Jumping out of *win*-dow?'

He gave a brief synopsis of the events which had led up to his spirited act. Lady Constance drew in her breath with a remorseful hiss.

'Oh, dear!' she said. 'How foolish of me. I should have told you.'

'I beg your pardon?'

Even though she was in the safe retirement of her boudoir Lady Constance Keeble looked cautiously over her shoulder. In the stirring and complicated state into which life had got itself at Blandings Castle, practically everybody in the place, except Lord Emsworth, had fallen into the habit nowadays of looking cautiously over his or her shoulder before he or she spoke.

'Sir Gregory Parsloe said in his note,' she explained, 'that this man Pilbeam who is coming here this evening is acting for him.'

'Acting for him?'

'Yes. Apparently Sir Gregory went to see him yesterday and has promised him a large sum of money if he will obtain possession of my brother Galahad's manuscript. That is why he has invited us to dinner tonight, to get Galahad out of the house. So there was no need for you to have troubled.'

There was a silence.

'So there was no need,' repeated the Efficient Baxter slowly, wiping from his eye the remains of a fragment of mould which had been causing him some inconvenience, 'for me to have troubled.'

'I am so sorry, Mr Baxter.'

'Pray do not mention it, Lady Constance.'

His eye, now that the mould was out of it, was able to work again with its customary keenness. His spectacles, as he surveyed the remorseful woman before him, had a cold, steely look.

'I see,' he said. 'Well, it might perhaps have spared me some little inconvenience had you informed me of this earlier, Lady Constance. I have bruised my left shin somewhat severely and, as you see, made myself rather dirty.'

'I am so sorry.'

'Furthermore, I gathered from the remark he let fall that the impression my actions have made upon Lord Emsworth is that I am insane.'

'Oh, dear.'

'He even specified the precise degree of insanity. As mad as a coot, were his words.'

He softened a little. He reminded himself that this woman before him, who was so nearly doing what is described as wringing her hands, had always been his friend, had always wished him well, had never slackened her efforts to restore him to the secretarial duties which he had once enjoyed.

'Well, it cannot be helped,' he said. 'The thing now is to think of some way of recovering the lost ground.'

'You mean, if you could find the Empress?'

'Exactly.'

'Oh, Mr Baxter, if you only could!'

'I can.'

Lady Constance stared at his dark, purposeful, efficient face in dumb admiration. To another man who had spoken those words she would have replied 'How?' or even 'How on earth?' But, as they had proceeded from Rupert Baxter, she merely waited silently for enlightenment.

'Have you given this matter any consideration, Lady Constance?'

'Yes.'

'To what conclusions have you come?'

Lady Constance felt dull and foolish. She felt like Doctor Watson – almost like a Scotland Yard Bungler.

'I don't think I have come to any,' she said, avoiding

the spectacles guiltily. 'Of course,' she added, 'I think it is absurd to suppose that Sir Gregory . . .'

Baxter waved aside the notion. It was not even worth a 'Tchah!'

'In any matter of this kind,' he said, 'the first thing to do is to seek a motive. Who is there in Blandings Castle who could have had a motive for stealing Lord Emsworth's pig?'

Lady Constance would have given a year's income to have been able to make some reasonably intelligent reply, but all she could do was look and listen. Baxter was not annoyed. He would not have had it otherwise. He preferred his audiences dumb and expectant.

'Carmody.'

'Mr Carmody?'

'Precisely. He is Lord Emsworth's secretary, and a most inefficient secretary, a secretary who stands hourly in danger of losing his position. He sees me arrive at the Castle, a man who formerly held the post he holds. He is alarmed. He suspects. He searches wildly about in his mind for means of consolidating himself in Lord Emsworth's regard. Then he has an idea, the sort of wild, motion-picture-bred idea which would come to a man of his stamp. He thinks to himself that if he removes the pig and conceals it somewhere and then pretends to have found it and restores it to its owner, Lord Emsworth's gratitude will be so intense that all danger of his dismissal will be at an end.'

He removed his spectacles and wiped them. Lady Constance uttered a low cry. In anybody else it would have been a squeak. Baxter replaced his spectacles.

'I have no doubt the pig is somewhere in the grounds at this moment,' he said.

'But, Mr Baxter . . . !'

The ex-secretary raised a compelling hand.

'But he would not have undertaken a thing like this single-handed. A secretary's time is not his own, and it would be necessary to feed the pig at regular intervals. He would require an accomplice. And I think I know who that accomplice is. Beach!'

This time not even the chronicler's desire to place Lady Constance's utterances in the best and most attractive light can hide the truth. She bleated.

'Be-ee-ee-ee-ech!'

The spectacles raked her keenly.

'Have you observed Beach closely of late?'

She shook her head. She was not a woman who observed butlers closely.

'He has something on his mind. He is nervous. Guilty. Conscience-stricken. He jumps when you speak to him.'

'Does he?'

'Jumps,' repeated the Efficient Baxter. 'Just now I gave him a – I happened to address him, and he sprang in the air.' He paused. 'I have half a mind to go and question him.'

'Oh, Mr Baxter! Would that be wise?'

Rupert Baxter's intention of interrogating the butler had been merely a nebulous one, a sort of idle dream, but these words crystallized it into a resolve. He was not going to have people asking him if things would be wise.

'A few searching questions should force him to reveal the truth.'

'But he'll give notice!'

This interview had been dotted with occasions on which Baxter might reasonably have said 'Tchah!' but, as we have seen, until this moment he had refrained. He now said it.

'Tchah!' said the Efficient Baxter. 'There are plenty of other butlers.'

And with this undeniable truth he stalked from the room. The wash and brush-up were still as necessary as they had been ten minutes before, but he was too intent on the chase to think about washes and brushes-up. He hurried down the stairs. He crossed the hall. He passed through the green-baize door that led to the quarters of the Blandings Castle staff. And he was making his way along the dim passage to the pantry where at this hour Beach might be supposed to be, when its door opened abruptly and a vast form emerged.

It was the butler. And from the fact that he was wearing a bowler hat it was plain that he was seeking the great outdoors.

Baxter stopped in mid-stride and remained on one leg, watching. Then, as his quarry disappeared in the direction of the back entrance he followed quickly.

Out in the open it was almost as dark as it had been in the passage. That grey, threatening sky had turned black by now. It was a swollen mass of inky clouds, heavy with the thunder, lightning and rain which so often come in the course of an English summer to remind the island race that they are hardy Nordics and must not be allowed to get their fibre all sapped by eternal sunshine like the less favoured dwellers in more southerly climes. It bayed at Baxter like a bloodhound.

But it took more than dirty weather to quell the Efficient Baxter when duty called. Like the character in Tennyson's poem who followed the gleam, he followed the butler. There was but one point about Beach which even remotely resembled a gleam, but it happened to be the only one which at this moment really mattered. He was easy to follow.

The shrubbery swallowed the butler. A few seconds later, it had swallowed the Efficient Baxter.

II

There are those who maintain – and make a nice income by doing so in the evening papers – that in these degenerate days the old, hardy spirit of the Briton has died out. They represent themselves as seeking vainly for evidence of the survival of those qualities of

toughness and endurance which once made Englishmen
what they were. To such, the spectacle of Rupert Baxter
braving the elements could not have failed to bring cheer
and consolation. They would have been further
stimulated by the conduct of Hugo Carmody.

It had not escaped Hugo's notice, as he left Sue on the
terrace and started out in the wake of Millicent, that the
weather was hotting up for a storm. He saw the clouds.
He heard the fast-approaching thunder. For neither did
he give a hoot. Let it rain, was Hugo's verdict. Let it jolly
well rain as much as it dashed well wanted to. As if
encouraged, the sky sent down a fat, wet drop which
insinuated itself just between his neck and collar.

He hardly noticed it. The information confided to
him by his friend Ronald Fish had numbed his senses so
thoroughly that water down the back of the neck was
merely an incident. He was feeling as he had not felt
since the evening some years ago when, boxing for his
University in the light-weight division, he had
incautiously placed the point of his jaw in the exact spot
at the moment occupied by his opponent's right fist.
When you have done this or – equally – when you have
just been told that the girl you love is definitely
betrothed to another, you begin to understand how
Anarchists must feel when the bomb goes off too soon.

In all the black days through which he had been
living recently, Hugo had never really lost hope. It had
been dim sometimes, but it had always been there. It
was his opinion that he knew women, just as it was
Sue's idea that she knew men. Like Sue, he had placed
his trust in the thought that true love conquers all
obstacles; that coldness melts; that sundered hearts may
at long last be brought together again by a little
judicious pleading and reasoning. Even the fact that
Millicent stared at him, when they met, with large,
scornful eyes that went through him like stilettos,
unpleasant though it was, had not caused him to despair.

He had looked forward to the moment when he should contrive to get her alone and do a bit of snappy talking along the right lines.

But this was final. This was the end. This put the tin hat on it. She was engaged to Ronnie. Soon she would be married to Ronnie. Like a gadfly the hideous thought sent Hugo Carmody reeling on through the gloom.

It was so dark now that he could scarcely see before him. And, looking about him, he discovered that the reason for this was that he had made his way into a wood of sorts. The West Wood, he deduced dully, taking into consideration the fact that there was no other in this particular part of the estate. Well, he might just as well be in the West Wood as anywhere. He trudged on.

The ground beneath his feet was spongy, and equipped with low-lying brambles which pricked through his thin flannels and would have caused him discomfort if he had been in the frame of mind to notice brambles. There were trees against which he bumped, and logs over which he tripped. And ahead of him, in a small clearing, there was a dilapidated-looking cottage. He noticed this because it seemed the sort of place where a man, now that a warm, gusty wind had sprung up, might shelter and light a cigarette. The need for tobacco had become imperative.

He was surprised to find that it was raining, and had apparently, from the state of his clothes, been raining for quite some time. It was also thundering. The storm had broken, and the boom of it seemed to be all round him. A flash of lightning reminded him that he was in just the kind of place, among all these trees, where blokes get struck. At dinner-time they are missed, and later on search-parties come out with lanterns. Somebody stumbles over something soft, and the rays of the lantern fall on a charred and blackened form. Here, quickly, we have found him! Where? Over here. Is *that* Hugo Carmody? Well, well! Pick him up, boys, and bring him along. He was a good chap once. Moody, though, of late. Some trouble about a girl, wasn't it? She will be sorry when she hears of this. Drove him to it, you might almost say. Steady with that stretcher. Now, when I say '*To* me.' Right!

There was something about this picture which quite cheered Hugo up. Ajax defied the lightning. Hugo Carmody rather encouraged it than otherwise. He looked approvingly at a more than usually vivid flash that seemed to dart among the tree-tops like a snake. All the same, he was forced to reflect, he was getting dashed wet. No sense, when you came right down to it, in getting dashed wet. After all, a man could be struck by lightning just as well in that cottage sort of place over there. Ho! for the cottage, felt Hugo, and headed for it at a gallop.

He had just reached the door, when it was flung open. There was a noise rather like that made by a rising pheasant, and the next moment something white had flung itself into his arms and was weeping emotionally on his chest.

'Hugo! Hugo, darling!'

Reason told Hugo it could scarcely be Millicent who was clinging to him like this and speaking to him like this. And yet Millicent it most certainly appeared to be. She continued to speak, still in the same friendly, even chatty strain.

'Hugo! Save me!'

'Right ho!'

'I wur-wur-went in thur-thur-there to shush-shush-shelter from the rain and it's all pitch dark.'

Hugo squeezed her fondly and with the sort of relief that comes to men who find themselves squeezing where they had not thought to squeeze. No need for that snappy bit of talking now. No need for arguments and explanations, for pleadings and entreaties. No need for anything but a good biceps.

He was bewildered. But mixed with his bewilderment had come a certain feeling of complacency. There was no denying that it was enjoyable, this exhibition of tremulous weakness in one who, if she had had the shadow of a fault, had always been inclined to matter-of-factness and the display of that rather hard, bright self-sufficiency which is so characteristic of the modern girl. If this melting mood was due to the fact that Millicent, while in the cottage, had seen a ghost, Hugo wanted to meet that ghost and shake its hand. Every man likes to be in a position to say 'There, there, little woman!' to the girl of his heart, particularly if for the last few days she has been treating him like a more than ordinarily unpleasant worm, and Hugo Carmody felt that he was in that position now.

'There, there!' he said, not quite feeling up to risking the 'little woman'. 'It's all right.'

'But it tut-tut-tut . . .'

'It what?' said Hugo puzzled.

'It tut-tut-tut-tisn't. There's a man in there!'

'A man?'

'Yes. I didn't know there was anyone there, and it was pitch dark and I heard something move and I said "Who's that?" and then he suddenly spoke to me in German.'

'In German?'

'Yes.'

Hugo released her gently. His face was determined.

'I'm going in to have a look.'

'Hugo! Stop! You'll be killed.'

She stood there, rigid. The rain lashed about her, but she did not heed it. The lightning gleamed. She paid it no attention. For the minute that lasts an hour she waited, straining her ears for sounds of the death-struggle. Then a dim form appeared.

'I say, Millicent.'

'Hugo! Are you all right?'

'Yes. I'm all right. I say, Millicent, do you know what?'

'No, what?'

A chuckle came to her through the darkness.

'It's the pig.'

'It's what?'

'The pig.'

'Who's a pig?'

'This is. Your friend in here. It's Empress of Blandings, as large as life. Come and have a look.'

III

Millicent had a look. She came to the door of the cottage and peered in. Yes, just as he had said, there was the Empress. In the feeble light of the match which Hugo was holding, the noble animal's attractive face was peering up at her – questioningly, as if wondering if she might be the bearer of the evening snack which would be so exceedingly welcome. The picture was one which would have set Lord Emsworth screaming with joy. Millicent merely gaped.

'How on earth did she get here?'

'That's what I'm going to find out,' said Hugo. 'One always knew she must be cached somewhere, of course. What is this place, anyway?'

'It used to be a gamekeeper's cottage, I believe.'

'Well, there seems to be a room up above,' said Hugo, striking another match. 'I'm going to go up there and wait. It's quite likely that somebody will be along to feed the animal, and I'm going to see who it is.'

'Yes, that's what we'll do. How clever of you!'

'Not you. You get back home.'

'I won't.'

There was a pause. A strong man would, no doubt, have asserted himself. But Hugo, though feeling better than he had done for days, was not feeling quite so strong as all that.

445

'Just as you like.' He shut the door. 'Well, come on. We'd better be making a move. The fellow may be here at any moment.'

They climbed the crazy stairs and lowered themselves cautiously to a floor which smelled of mice and mildew. Below, all was in darkness, but there were holes through which it would be possible to look when the time should come for looking. Millicent could feel one near her face.

'You don't think this floor will give way?' she asked rather nervously.

'I shouldn't think so. Why?'

'Well, I don't want to break my neck.'

'You don't, don't you? Well, I would jolly well like to break mine,' said Hugo, speaking tensely in the darkness. It had just occurred to him that now would be a good time for a heart-to-heart talk. 'If you suppose I'm keen on going on living with you and Ronnie doing the Wedding Glide all over the place, you're dashed well mistaken. I take it you're aware that you've broken my bally heart, what?'

'Oh, Hugo!' said Millicent.

Silence fell. Below, the Empress rustled. Aloft, something scuttered.

'Oo!' cried Millicent. 'Was that a rat?'

'I hope so.'

'What!'

'Rats gnaw you,' explained Hugo. 'They cluster round and chew you to the bone and put an end to your misery.'

There was silence again. Then Millicent spoke in a small voice.

'You're being beastly,' she said.

Remorse poured over Hugo in a flood.

'I'm frightfully sorry. Yes, I know I am, dash it. But, look here, you know . . . I mean, all this getting engaged to Ronnie. A bit thick, what? You don't expect me to give three hearty cheers, do you? Wouldn't want me to break into a few carefree dance-steps?'

'I can't believe it's really happened.'

'Well, how did it happen?'

'It sort of happened all of a sudden. I was feeling miserable and very angry with you and . . . and all that. And I met Ronnie and he took me for a stroll and we went down by the lake and started throwing little bits of stick at the swans, and suddenly Ronnie sort of grunted and said "I say!" and I said "Hullo?" and he said "Will you marry me?" and I said "All right," and he said "I ought to warn you, I despise all women," and I said "And I loathe all men" and he said "Right-ho, I think we shall be very happy."'

'I see.'

'I only did it to score off you.'

'You succeeded.'

A trace of spirit crept into Millicent's voice.

'You never really loved me,' she said. 'You know jolly well you didn't.'

'Is that so?'

'Well, what did you want to go sneaking off to London for, then, and stuffing that beastly girl of yours with food?'

'She isn't my girl. And she isn't beastly.'

'She is.'

'Well, you seem to get on with her all right. I saw you chatting on the terrace together as cosily as dammit.'

'What!'

'Miss Schoonmaker.'

'I don't know what you're talking about. What's Miss Schoonmaker got to do with it?'

'Miss Schoonmaker isn't Miss Schoonmaker. She's Sue Brown.'

For a moment it seemed to Millicent that the crack in her companion's heart had spread to his head. Futile though the action was, she stared in the direction from which his voice had proceeded. Then, suddenly, his words took on a meaning. She gasped.

'She's followed you down here!'

'She hasn't followed me down here. She's followed Ronnie down here. Can't you get it into your nut,' said Hugo with justifiable exasperation, 'that you've been making floaters and bloomers and getting everything mixed up all along? Sue Brown has never cared a curse for me, and I've never thought anything about her, except that she's a jolly girl and nice to dance with. That's absolutely and positively the only reason I went out with her. I hadn't had a dance for six weeks and my feet had begun to itch so that I couldn't sleep at night. So I went to London and took her out and Ronnie found her talking to that pestilence Pilbeam and thought he had taken her out and she had told him she didn't even know the man, which was quite true, but Ronnie cut up rough and said he was through with her and came down here and she wanted to get a word with him, so she came down here, pretending to be Miss Schoonmaker, and the moment she gets here she finds Ronnie is engaged to you. A nice surprise for the poor girl!'

Millicent's head had begun to swim long before the conclusion of this recital.

'But what is Pilbeam doing down here?'

'Pilbeam?'

'He was on the terrace talking to her.'

A low snarl came through the darkness.

'Pilbeam here? Ah! So he came, after all, did he? He's the fellow Lord Emsworth sent me to, about the Empress. He runs the Argus Enquiry Agency. It was Pilbeam's minions that dogged my steps that night, at your request. So he's here, is he? Well, let him enjoy himself while he can. Let him sniff the country air while the sniffing is good. A bitter reckoning awaits that bloke.'

From the disorder of Millicent's mind another point emerged insistently demanding explanation.

'You said she wasn't pretty!'

'Who?'

'Sue Brown.'

'Nor she is.'

'You don't call her pretty? She's fascinating.'

'Not to me,' said Hugo doggedly. 'There's only one girl in the world that I call pretty, and she's going to marry Ronnie.' He paused. 'If you haven't realized by this time that I love you, and always shall love you, and have never loved anybody else, and never shall love anybody else, you're a fathead. If you brought me Sue Brown or any other girl in the world on a plate with water-cress round her, I wouldn't so much as touch her hand.'

Another rat – unless it was an exceptionally large mouse – had begun to make its presence felt in the darkness. It seemed to be enjoying an early dinner off a piece of wood. Millicent did not even notice it. She had reached out, and her hand had touched Hugo's arm. Her fingers closed on it desperately.

'Oh, Hugo!' she said.

The arm became animated. It clutched her, drew her along the mouse-and-mildew scented floor. And time stood still.

Hugo was the first to break the silence.

'And to think that not so long ago I was wishing that a flash of lightning would strike me amidships!' he said.

The aroma of mouse and mildew had passed away. Violets seemed to be spreading their fragrance through the cottage. Violets and roses. The rat, a noisy feeder, had changed into an orchestra of harps, dulcimers and sackbuts that played soft music.

And then, jarring upon these sweet strains, there came the sound of the cottage door opening. And a moment later light shone through the holes in the floor.

Millicent gave Hugo's arm a warning pinch. They

449

looked down. On the floor below stood a lantern, and beside it a man of massive build who, from the golloping noises that floated upwards, appeared to be giving the Empress those calories and proteins which a pig of her dimensions requires so often and in such large quantities.

This Good Samaritan had been stooping. Now he straightened himself and looked about him with an apprehensive eye. He raised the lantern, and its light fell upon his face.

And, as she saw that face, Millicent, forgetting prudence, uttered in a high, startled voice a single word.

'Beach!' cried Millicent.

Down below, the butler stood congealed. It seemed to him that the Voice of Conscience had spoken.

IV

Conscience, besides having a musical voice, appeared also to be equipped with feet. Beach could hear them clattering down the stairs, and the volume of noise was so great that it seemed as if Conscience must be a centipede. But he did not stir. It would have required at that moment a derrick to move him, and there was no derrick in the gamekeeper's cottage in the West Wood. He was still standing like a statue when Hugo and Millicent arrived. Only when the identity of the newcomers impressed itself in his numbed senses did his limbs begin to twitch and show some signs of relaxing. For he looked on Hugo as a friend. Hugo, he felt, was one of the few people in his world who, finding him in his present questionable position, might be expected to take the broad and sympathetic view.

He nerved himself to speak.

'Good evening, sir. Good evening, miss.'

'What's all this?' said Hugo.

Years ago, in his hot and reckless youth, Beach had

once heard that question from the lips of a policeman. It had disconcerted him then. It disconcerted him now.

'Well, sir,' he replied.

Millicent was staring at the Empress, who, after one courteous look of inquiry at the intruders, had given a brief grunt of welcome and returned to the agenda.

'*You* stole her, Beach? *You!*'

The butler quivered. He had known this girl since her long hair and rompers days. She had sported in his pantry. He had cut elephants out of paper for her and taught her tricks with bits of string. The shocked note in her voice scared him like vitriol. To her, he felt, niece to the Earl of Emsworth and trained by his lordship from infancy in the best traditions of pig-worship, the theft of the Empress must seem the vilest of crimes. He burned to re-establish himself in her eyes.

There comes in the life of every conspirator a moment when loyalty to his accomplices wavers before the urge to make things right for himself. We can advance no more impressive proof of the nobility of the butler's soul than that he did not obey this impulse. Millicent's accusing eyes were piercing him, but he remained true to his trust. Mr Ronald had sworn him to secrecy: and even to square himself he could not betray him.

And, as if by way of a direct reward from Providence for this sterling conduct, inspiration descended upon Beach.

'Yes, miss,' he replied.

'Oh, Beach!'

'Yes, miss, it was I who stole the animal. I did it for your sake, miss.'

Hugo eyed him sternly.

'Beach,' he said. 'This is pure apple-sauce.'

'Sir?'

'Apple-sauce, I repeat. Why endeavour to swing the

lead, Beach? What do you mean, you stole the pig for her sake?'

'Yes,' said Millicent. 'Why for my sake?'

The butler was calm now. He had constructed his story, and he was going to stick to it.

'In order to remove the obstacles in your path, miss.'

'Obstacles?'

'Owing to the fact that you and Mr Carmody have frequently entrusted me with your – may I say surreptitious correspondence, I have long been cognizant of your sentiments towards one another, miss. I am aware that it is your desire to contract a union with Mr Carmody, and I knew that there would be objections raised on the part of certain members of the family.'

'So far,' said Hugo critically, 'this sounds to me like drivel of the purest water. But go on.'

'Thank you, sir. And then it occurred to me that, were his lordship's pig to disappear, his lordship would, on recovering the animal, be extremely grateful to whoever restored it. It was my intention to apprise you of the animal's whereabouts, and suggest that you should inform his lordship that you had discovered it. In his gratitude, I fancied, his lordship would consent to the union.'

There could never be complete silence in any spot where Empress of Blandings was partaking of food; but something as near silence as was possible followed this speech. In the rays of the lantern Hugo's eyes met Millicent's. In hers, as in his, there was a look of stunned awe. They had heard of faithful old servitors. They had read about faithful old servitors. They had seen faithful old servitors on the stage. But never had they dreamed that faithful old servitors could be as faithful as this.

'Oh, Beach!' said Millicent.

She had used the words before. But how different this 'Oh, Beach!' was from that other, earlier 'Oh, Beach!' On that occasion, the exclamation had been vibrant with reproach, pain, disillusionment. Now, it contained gratitude, admiration, an affection almost too deep for speech.

And the same may be said of Hugo's 'Gosh!'

'Beach,' cried Millicent, 'you're an angel!'

'Thank you, miss.'

'A topper!' agreed Hugo.

'Thank you, sir.'

'However did you get such a corking idea?'

'It came to me, miss.'

'I'll tell you what it is, Beach,' said Hugo earnestly. 'When you hand in your dinner-pail in due course of time – and may the moment be long distant! – you've got to leave your brain to the nation. You've simply got to. Have it pickled and put in the British Museum, because it's the outstanding brain of the century. I never heard of anything so brilliant in my puff. Of course the old boy will be all over us.'

'He'll do anything for us,' said Millicent.

'This is not merely a scheme. It is more. It is an egg. Pray silence for your chairman. I want to think.'

Outside, the storm had passed. Birds were singing. Far away, the thunder still rumbled. It might have been the sound of Hugo's thoughts, leaping and jostling one another.

'I've worked it all out,' said Hugo at length. 'Some people might say, Rush to the old boy now and tell him we've found his pig. I say, No. In my opinion we ought to hold this pig for a rising market. The longer we wait, the more grateful he will be. Give him another forty-eight hours, I suggest, and he will have reached the stage where he will deny us nothing.'

'But . . .'

'No! Act precipitately and we are undone. Don't forget that it is not merely a question of getting your uncle's consent to our union. We've got to break it to him that

453

you aren't going to marry Ronnie. And the family have
always been pretty keen on your marrying Ronnie. To
my mind, another forty-eight hours at the very least is
essential.'

'Perhaps you're right.'

'I know I'm right.'

'Then we'll simply leave the Empress here?'

'No,' said Hugo decidedly. 'This place doesn't strike
me as safe. If we found her here, anybody might. We
require a new safe-deposit, and I know the very one.
It's . . .'

Beach came out of the silence. His manner betrayed
agitation.

'If it is all the same to you, sir, I would much prefer
not to hear it.'

'Eh?'

'It would be a great relief to me, sir, to be able to
expunge the entire matter from my mind. I have been
under a considerable mental strain of late, sir, and I
really don't think I could bear any more of it. Besides,
supposing I were questioned, sir. It may be my
imagination, but I have rather fancied from the way he
has looked at me occasionally that Mr Baxter harbours
suspicions.'

'Baxter always harbours suspicions about something,'
said Millicent.

'Yes, miss. But in this case they are well-grounded,
and if it is all the same to you and Mr Carmody, I would
greatly prefer that he was not in a position to go on
harbouring them.'

'All right, Beach,' said Hugo. 'After what you have
done for us, your lightest wish is law. You can be out of
this, if you want to. Though I was going to suggest that,
if you cared to go on feeding the animal . . .'

'No, sir . . . really . . . if you please . . .'

'Right ho, then. Come along, Millicent. We must be
shifting.'

454

'Are you going to take her away now?'

'This very moment. I pass this handkerchief through
the handy ring which you observe in the nose and . . .
Ho! Allez-oop! Good-bye, Beach. It is a far, far better
thing that I do than I have ever done – I think.'

'Good-bye, Beach,' said Millicent. 'I can't tell you how
grateful we are.'

'I am glad to have given satisfaction, miss. I wish you
every success and happiness, sir.'

Left alone, the butler drew in his breath till he
swelled like a balloon, then poured it out again in a long,
sighing puff. He picked up the lantern and left the
cottage. His walk was the walk of a butler from whose
shoulders a great weight has rolled.

V

It is a fact not generally known, for a nice sense of the
dignity of his position restrained him from exercising it,
that Beach possessed a rather attractive singing-voice. It
was a mellow baritone, in timbre not unlike that which
might have proceeded from a cask of very old, dry
sherry, had it had vocal cords; and we cannot advance a
more striking proof of the lightness of heart which had
now come upon him than by mentioning that, as he
walked home through the wood, he broke his rigid rule
and definitely warbled.

'There's a light in thy bow-er'

sang Beach,

'A light in thy BOW-er . . .'

He felt more like a gay young second footman than a
butler of years' standing. He listened to the birds with an
uplifted heart. Upon the rabbits that sported about his

455

path he bestowed a series of indulgent smiles. The
shadow that had darkened his life had passed away. His
conscience was at rest.

So completely was this so that when, on reaching the
house, he was informed by Footman James that Lord
Emsworth had been inquiring for him and desired his
immediate presence in the library, he did not even
tremble. A brief hour ago, and what menace this
announcement would have seemed to him to hold. But
now it left him calm. It was with some little difficulty
that, as he mounted the stairs, he kept himself from
resuming his song.

'Er – Beach.'

'Your lordship?'

The butler now became aware that his employer was
not alone Dripping in an unpleasant manner on the
carpet, for he seemed somehow to have got himself
extremely wet, stood the Efficient Baxter. Beach
regarded him with a placid eye. What was Baxter to him
or he to Baxter now?

'Your lordship?' he said again, for Lord Emsworth
appeared to be experiencing some difficulty in
continuing the conversation.

'Eh? What? What? Oh, yes.'

The ninth Earl braced himself with a visible effort.

'Er – Beach.'

'Your lordship?'

'I – er – I sent for you, Beach . . .'

'Yes, your lordship?'

At this moment Lord Emsworth's eye fell on a
volume on the desk dealing with Diseases in Pigs. He
seemed to draw strength from it.

'Beach,' he said, in quite a crisp, masterful voice, 'I
sent for you because Mr Baxter has made a remarkable
charge against you. Most extraordinary.'

'I should be glad to be acquainted with the gravamen
of the accusation, your lordship.'

'The what?' asked Lord Emsworth, starting.

'If your lordship would be kind enough to inform me of the substance of Mr Baxter's charge?'

'Oh, the substance? Yes. You mean the substance? Precisely. Quite so. The substance. Yes, to be sure. Quite so. Quite so. Yes, Exactly. No doubt.'

It was plain to the butler that his employer had begun to dodder. Left to himself this human cuckoo-clock would go maundering on like this indefinitely. Respectfully, but with the necessary firmness, he called him to order.

'What is it that Mr Baxter says, your lordship?'

'Eh? Oh, tell him, Baxter. Yes, tell him, dash it.'

The Efficient Baxter moved a step closer and began to drip on another part of the carpet. His spectacles gleamed determinedly. Here was no stammering, embarrassed Peer of the Realm, but a man who knew his own mind and could speak it.

'I followed you to the gamekeeper's cottage in the West Wood just now, Beach.'

'Sir?'

'You heard what I said.'

'Undoubtedly, sir. But I fancied I must be mistaken. I have not been to the spot you mention, sir.'

'I saw you with my own eyes.'

'I can only repeat my asseveration, sir,' said the butler with a saintly meekness.

Lord Emsworth, who had taken another look at *Diseases in Pigs*, became brisk again.

'He says he peeped through the window, dash it.'

Beach raised a respectful eyebrow. It was as if he had said that it was not his place to comment on the pastimes of the Castle's guests, however childish. If Mr Baxter wished to go out into the woods in the rain and play solitary games of Peep-Bo, that, said the eyebrow, that was a matter that concerned Mr Baxter alone.

'And you were in there, he says, feeding the Empress.'

457

'Your lordship?'

'And you were in there . . . Dash it, you heard.'

'I beg your pardon, your lordship, but I really fail to comprehend.'

'Well, if you want it in a nutshell, Mr Baxter says it was you who stole my pig.'

There were few things in the world that the butler considered worth raising both eyebrows at. This was one of the few. He stood for a moment, exhibiting them to Lord Emsworth; then turned to Baxter, so that he could see them, too. This done, he lowered them and permitted about three-eighths of a smile to play for a moment about his lips.

'Might I speak frankly, your lordship?'

'Dash it, man, we want you to speak frankly. That's the whole idea. That's why I sent for you. We want a full confession and the name of your accomplice and all that sort of thing.'

'I hesitate only because what I should like to say may possibly give offence to Mr Baxter, your lordship, which would be the last thing I should desire.'

The prospect of offending the Efficient Baxter, which caused such concern to Beach, appeared to disturb his lordship not at all.

'Get on. Say what you like.'

'Well, then, your lordship, I think it possible that Mr Baxter, if he will pardon my saying so, may have been suffering from a hallucination.'

'Tchah!' said the Efficient Baxter.

'You mean he's potty?' said Lord Emsworth, struck with the idea. In the excitement of his late secretary's information, he had overlooked this simple explanation. Now there came surging back to him all the evidence that went to support such a theory. Those flower-pots . . . That leap from the library window. He looked at Baxter keenly. There *was* a sort of wild gleam in his eyes. The old coot glitter.

'Really, Lord Emsworth!'

'Oh, I'm not saying you are, my dear fellow. Only . . .'

'It is quite obvious to me,' said Baxter stiffly, 'that this man is lying. Wait!' he continued, raising a hand. 'Are you prepared to come with his lordship and me to the cottage now, at this very moment, and let his lordship see for himself?'

'No, sir.'

'Ha!'

'I should first,' said Beach, 'wish to go downstairs and get my hat.'

'Quite right,' agreed Lord Emsworth cordially. 'Very sensible. Might catch a nasty cold in the head. Certainly get your hat, Beach, and meet us at the front door.'

'Very good, your lordship.'

A bystander, observing the little party that was gathered some five minutes later on the gravel outside the great door of Blandings Castle, would have noticed about it a touch of chill, a certain restraint. None of its three members seemed really in the mood for a ramble through the woods. Beach, though courtly, was not cordial. The face under his bowler hat was the face of a good man misjudged. Baxter was eyeing the sullen sky as though he suspected it of something. As for Lord Emsworth, he had just become conscious that he was about to accompany through dark and deserted ways one who, though on this afternoon's evidence the trend of his tastes seemed to be towards suicide, might quite possibly become homicidal.

'One moment,' said Lord Emsworth.

He scuttled into the house again, and came out looking happier. He was carrying a stout walking-stick with an ivory knob on it.

13 — Cocktails Before Dinner

Blandings Castle basked in the afterglow of a golden summer evening. Only a memory now was the storm which, two hours since, had raged with such violence through its parks, pleasure grounds and messuages. It had passed, leaving behind it peace and bird-song and a sunset of pink and green and orange and opal and amethyst. The air was cool and sweet, and the earth sent up a healing fragrance. Little stars were peeping down from a rain-washed sky.

To Ronnie Fish, slumped in an armchair in his bedroom on the second floor, the improved weather conditions brought no spiritual uplift. He could see the sunset, but it left him cold. He could hear the thrushes calling in the shrubberies, but did not think much of them. It is, in short, in no sunny mood that we re-introduce Ronald Overbury Fish to the reader of this chronicle.

The meditations of a man who has recently proposed to and been accepted by a girl, some inches taller than himself, for whom he entertains no warmer sentiment than a casual feeling that, take her for all in all, she isn't a bad sort of egg, must of necessity tend towards the sombre: and the surroundings in which Ronnie had spent the latter part of the afternoon had not been of a kind to encourage optimism. At the moment when the skies suddenly burst asunder and the world became a shower-bath, he had been walking along the path that skirted the wall of the kitchen-garden: and the only shelter that offered itself was a gloomy cave or dug-out that led to the heating apparatus of the hothouses. Into this he had dived like a homing rabbit, and here, sitting on a heap of bricks, he had remained for the space of fifty minutes with no company but one small green frog and his thoughts.

The place was a sort of Sargasso Sea into which had drifted all the flotsam and jetsam of the kitchen-garden which it adjoined. There was a wheelbarrow, lacking its wheel and lying drunkenly on its side. There were broken pots in great profusion. There was a heap of withered flowers, a punctured watering-can, a rake with large gaps in its front teeth, some potatoes unfit for human consumption and half a dead blackbird. The whole effect was extraordinarily like Hell, and Ronnie's spirits, not high at the start, had sunk lower and lower.

Sobered by rain, wheelbarrows, watering-cans, rakes, potatoes, and dead blackbirds, not to mention the steady, supercilious eye of a frog which resembled that of a Bishop at the Athenaeum inspecting a shy new member, Ronnie had begun definitely to repent of the impulse which had led him to ask Millicent to be his wife. And now, in the cosier environment of his bedroom, he was regretting it more than ever.

Like most people who have made a defiant and dramatic gesture and then have leisure to reflect, he was oppressed by a feeling that he had gone considerably farther than was prudent. Samson, as he heard the pillars of the temple begin to crack, must have felt the same. Gestures are all very well while the intoxication lasts. The trouble is that it lasts such a very little while.

In asking Millicent to marry him, he had gone, he now definitely realized, too far. He had overdone it. It was not that he had any objection to Millicent as a wife. He had none whatever – provided she were somebody else's wife. What was so unpleasant was the prospect of being married to her himself.

He groaned in spirit, and became aware that he was no longer alone. The door had opened, and his friend

Hugo Carmody was in the room. He noted with a dull surprise that Hugo was in the conventional costume of the English gentleman about to dine. He had not supposed the hour so late.

'Hullo,' said Hugo. 'Not dressed? The gong's gone.'

It now became clear to Ronnie that he simply was not equal to facing his infernal family at the dinner-table. He supposed that Millicent had spread the news of their engagement by this time, and that meant discussion, wearisome congratulations, embraces from his Aunt Constance, chaff of the vintage of 1895 from his Uncle Galahad – in short, fuss and gabble. And he was in no mood for fuss and gabble. Pot-luck with a tableful of Trappist monks he might just have endured, but not a hearty feed with the family.

'I don't want any dinner.'

'No dinner?'

'No.'

'Ill or something?'

'No.'

'But you don't want any dinner? I see. Rummy! However, your affair, of course. It begins to look as if I should have to don the nose-bag alone. Beach tells me that Baxter also will be absent from the trough. He's upset about something, it seems, and has asked for a snort and sandwiches in the smoking-room. And as for the pustule Pilbeam,' said Hugo grimly, 'I propose to interview him at the earliest possible date. And after that he won't want any dinner, either.'

'Where are the rest of them?'

'Didn't you know?' said Hugo, surprised. 'They're dining over at old Parsloe's. Your aunt, Lord Emsworth, old Galahad, and Millicent.' He coughed. A moment of some slight embarrassment impended. 'I say, Ronnie, old man, while on the subject of Millicent.'

'Well?'

'You know that engagement of yours?'

462

'What about it?'

'It's off.'

'Off?'

'Right off. A wash-out. She's changed her mind.'

'What!'

'Yes. She's going to marry me. I may tell you we have been engaged for weeks – one of those secret betrothals – but we had a row. Row now over. Complete reconciliation. So she asked me to break it to you gently that in the circs. she proposes to return you to store.'

A thrill of ecstasy shot through Ronnie. He felt as men on the scaffold feel when the messenger bounds in with the reprieve.

'Well, that's the first bit of good news I've had for a long time,' he said.

'You mean you didn't want to marry Millicent?'

'Of course I didn't.'

'Not so much of the "of course", laddie,' said Hugo, offended.

'She's an awfully nice girl . . .'

'An angel. Shropshire's leading seraph.'

'. . . but I'm not in love with her any more than she's in love with me.'

'In that case,' said Hugo, with justifiable censure, 'why propose to her? A goofy proceeding, it seems to me.' He clicked his tongue. 'Of course! I see what happened. You grabbed Millicent to score off Sue, and she grabbed you to score off me. And now, I suppose, you've fixed it up with Sue again. Very sound. Couldn't have made a wiser move. She's obviously the girl for you.'

Ronnie winced. The words had touched a nerve. He had been trying not to think of Sue, but without success. Her picture insisted on rising before him. Not being able to exclude her from his thoughts, he had tried to think of her bitterly.

'I haven't,' he cried.

463

Extraordinary how difficult it was, even now, to think bitterly of Sue. Sue was Sue. That was the fundamental fact that hampered him. Try as he might to concentrate it on the tragedy of Mario's restaurant, his mind insisted on slipping back to earlier scenes of sunshine and happiness.

'You haven't?' said Hugo, damped.

That Ronnie could possibly be in ignorance of Sue's arrival at the castle never occurred to him. Long ere this, he took it for granted, they must have met. And he assumed, from the equanimity with which his friend had received the news of the loss of Millicent, that Sue and he must have had just such another heart-to-heart talk as had taken place in the room above the gamekeeper's cottage. The dour sullenness of Ronnie's face made his kindly heart sink.

'You mean you haven't fixed things up?'

'No.'

Ronnie writhed. Sue in his car. Sue up the river. Sue in his arms to the music of sweet saxophones. Sue laughing. Sue smiling. Sue in the springtime, with the little breezes ruffling her hair . . .

He forced his mind away from these weakening visions. Sue at Mario's . . . That was better . . . Sue letting him down . . . Sue hobnobbing with the blister Pilbeam . . . That was much better.

'I think you're being very hard on that poor little girl, Ronnie.'

'Don't call her a poor little girl.'

'I will call her a poor little girl,' said Hugo firmly. 'To me, she is a poor little girl, and I don't care who knows it. I don't mind telling you that my heart bleeds for her. Bleeds profusely. And I must say I should have thought . . .'

'I don't want to talk about her.'

'. . . after her doing what she has done . . .'

'I don't want to talk about her, I tell you.'

Hugo sighed. He gave it up. The situation was what they called an *impasse*. Too bad. His best friend and a dear little girl like that parted for ever. Two jolly good eggs sundered for all eternity. Oh, well, that was Life.

'If you want to talk about anything,' said Ronnie, 'you had much better talk about this engagement of yours.'

'Only too glad, old man. Was afraid it might bore you, or would have touched more freely on subject.'

'I suppose you realize the Family will squash it flat?'

'Oh, no, they won't.'

'You think my Aunt Constance is going to leap about and bang the cymbals?'

'The Keeble, I admit,' said Hugo, with a faint shiver, 'may make her presence felt to some extent. But I rely on the ninth earl's support and patronage. Before long, I shall be causing the ninth to look on me as a son.'

'How?'

For a moment Hugo almost yielded to the temptation to confide in this friend of his youth. Then he realized the unwisdom of such a course. By an odd coincidence, he was thinking exactly the same of Ronnie as Ronnie at an earlier stage of this history had thought of him. Ronnie, he considered, though a splendid chap, was not fitted to be a repository of secrets. A babbler. A sieve. The sort of fellow who would spread a secret hither and thither all over the place before nightfall.

'Never mind,' he said. 'I have my methods.'

'What are they?'

'Just methods,' said Hugo, 'and jolly good ones. Well, I'll be pushing off. I'm late. Sure you won't come down to dinner? Then I'll be going. It is imperative that I get hold of Pilbeam with all possible speed. Don't want the sun to go down on my wrath. All has ended happily in spite of him, but that's no reason why he shouldn't be massacred. I look on myself as a man with a public duty.'

For some minutes after the door had closed, Ronnie

remained humped up in the chair. Then, in spite of everything, there began to creep upon him a desire for food, too strong to be resisted. Perfect health and a tealess afternoon in the open had given him a compelling appetite. He still shrank from the thought of the dining-room. Fond as he was of Hugo, he simply could not stand his conversation tonight. A chop at the Emsworth Arms would meet the case. He could get down there in five minutes in his two-seater.

He rose. His mind, as he moved to the door, was not entirely occupied with thoughts of food. Hugo's parting words had turned it in the direction of Pilbeam again.

What had brought Pilbeam to the castle, he did not know. But, now that he was here, let him look out for himself! A couple of minutes alone with P. Frobisher Pilbeam was just the medicine his bruised soul required. Apparently, from what he had said, Hugo also entertained some grievance against the man. It could be nothing compared with his own.

Pilbeam! The cause of all his troubles. Pilbeam! The snake in the grass. Pilbeam . . . ! Yes . . . ! His heart might be broken, his life a wreck, but he could still enjoy the faint consolation of dealing faithfully with Pilbeam.

He went out into the corridor. And, as he did so, Percy Pilbeam came out of the room opposite.

II

Pilbeam had dressed for dinner with considerable care. Owing to the fact that Lord Emsworth, in his woollen-headed way, had completely forgotten to inform him of the exodus to Matchingham Hall, he was expecting to meet a gay and glittering company at the meal, and had prepared himself accordingly. Looking at the result in the mirror, he had felt a glow of contentment. This glow was still warming him as he passed into the corridor. As his eyes fell on Ronnie, it faded abruptly.

In the days of his editorship of *Society Spice*, that frank and fearless journal, P. Frobisher Pilbeam had once or twice had personal encounters with people having no cause to wish him well. They had not appealed to him. He was a man who found no pleasure in physical violence. And that physical violence threatened now was only too sickeningly plain. It was foreshadowed in the very manner in which this small but sturdy young man confronting him had begun to creep forward. Pilbeam, who was an FRZS, had seen leopards at the Zoo creep just like that.

Years of conducting a weekly scandal-sheet, followed by a long period of activity as a private enquiry agent, undoubtedly train a man well for the exhibition of presence-of-mind in sudden emergencies. One finds it difficult in the present instance to over-praise Percy Pilbeam's ready resource. Had a great military strategist been present, he would have nodded approval. With the grim menace of Ronnie Fish coming closer and closer, Percy Pilbeam did exactly what Napoleon, Hannibal, or the great Duke of Marlborough would have done. Reaching behind him for the handle and twisting it sharply, he slipped through the door of his bedroom, banged it, and was gone. Many an eel has disappeared into the mud with less smoothness and celerity.

If the leopard which he resembled had seen its prey vanish into the undergrowth just before dinner-time, it would probably have expressed its feelings in exactly the same kind of short, rasping cry as proceeded from Ronnie Fish, witnessing this masterly withdrawal. For an instant he was completely taken aback. Then he plunged for the door and plunged into the room.

He stood, baffled. Pilbeam had vanished. To Ronnie's astonished eyes the apartment appeared entirely free from detectives in any shape or form whatsoever. There

was the bed. There were the chairs. There were the
carpet, the dressing-table, and the book-shelf. But of
private enquiry agents there was a complete shortage.

How long this miracle would have continued to
afflict him one cannot say. His mind was still dealing
dazedly with it, when there came to his ears a sharp
click, as of a key being turned in the lock. It seemed to
proceed from a hanging-cupboard at the other side of the
room.

Old Miles Fish, Ronnie's father, might, as Lord
Emsworth had asserted, have been the biggest fool in the
Brigade of Guards, but his son could reason and deduce.
Springing forward, he tugged at the handle of the
cupboard door. The door stood fast.

At the same moment there filtered through it the
sound of muffled breathing.

Ronnie was already looking grim. He now looked
grimmer. He placed his lips to the panel.

'Come out of that!'

The breathing stopped.

'All right,' said Ronnie, with a hideous calm. 'Right
jolly ho! I can wait.'

For some moments there was silence. Then from the
beyond a voice spoke in reply.

'Be reasonable!' said the voice.

'Reasonable?' said Ronnie thickly. 'Reasonable, eh?'
He choked. 'Come out! I only want to pull your head
off,' he added, with a note of appeal.

The voice became conciliatory.

'I know what you're upset about,' it said.

'You do, eh?'

'Yes, I quite understand. But I can explain everything.'

'What?'

'I say I can explain everything.'

'You can, can you?'

'Quite,' said the voice.

Up till now Ronnie had been pulling. It now occurred

to him that pushing might possibly produce more satisfactory results. So he pushed. Nothing, however, happened. Blandings Castle was a house which rather prided itself on its solidity. Its walls were walls and its doors doors. No jimcrack work here. The cupboard creaked, but did not yield.

'I say!'

'Well?'

'I wish you'd listen. I tell you I can explain everything. About that night at Mario's, I mean. I know exactly how it is. You think Miss Brown is fond of me. I give you my solemn word she can't stand the sight of me. She told me so herself.'

A pleasing thought came to Ronnie.

'You can't stay in there all night,' he said.

'I don't want to stay in here all night.'

'Well, come on out, then.'

The voice became plaintive.

'I tell you she had never set eyes on me before that night at Mario's. She was dining with that fellow Carmody, and he went out and I came over and introduced myself. No harm in that, was there?'

Ronnie wondered if kicking would do any good. A tender feeling for his toes, coupled with the reflection that his Uncle Clarence might have something to say if he started breaking up cupboard doors, caused him to abandon the scheme. He stood, breathing tensely.

'Just a friendly word, that's all I came over to say. Why shouldn't a fellow introduce himself to a girl and say a friendly word?'

'I wish I'd got there earlier.'

'I'd have been glad to see you,' said Pilbeam courteously.

'Would you?'

'Quite.'

'I shall be glad to see *you*,' said Ronnie, 'when I can get this damned door open.'

469

Pilbeam began to fear asphyxiation. The air inside the cupboard was growing closer. Peril lent him the inspiration which it so often does.

'Look here,' he said, 'are you Ronnie?'

Ronnie turned pinker.

'I don't want any of your dashed cheek.'

'No, but listen. Is your name Ronnie?'

Silence without.

'Because, if it is,' said Pilbeam, 'you're the fellow she's come here to see.'

More silence.

'She told me so. In the garden this evening. She came here calling herself Miss Shoemaker or some such name, just to see you. That ought to show you that I'm not the man she's keen on.'

The silence was broken by a sharp exclamation.

'What's that?'

Pilbeam repeated his remark. A growing hopefulness lent an almost finicky clearness to his diction.

'Come out!' cried Ronnie.

'That's all very well, but . . .'

'Come out, I want to talk to you.'

'You are talking to me.'

'I don't want to bellow this through a door. Come on out. I swear I won't touch you.'

It was not so much Pilbeam's faith in the knightly word of the Fishes that caused him to obey the request as a feeling that, if he stayed cooped up in this cupboard much longer, he would get a rush of blood to the head. Already he was beginning to feel as if he were breathing a solution of dust and mothballs. He emerged. His hair was rumpled, and he regarded his companion warily. He had the air of a man who has taken his life in his hands. But the word of the Fishes held good. As far as Ronnie was concerned, the war appeared to be over.

'What did you say? She's here?'

'Quite.'

'What do you mean, quite?'

'Certainly. Quite. She got here just before I did. Haven't you seen her?'

'No.'

'Well, she's here. She's in the room they call the Garden Room. I heard her tell that old bird Galahad so. If you go there now,' said Pilbeam insinuatingly, 'you could have a quiet word with her before she goes down to dinner.'

'And she said she had come here to see me?'

'Yes. To explain about that night at Mario's. And what I say,' proceeded Pilbeam warmly, 'is, if a girl didn't love a fellow, would she come to a place like this, calling herself Miss Schoolbred or something, simply to see him? I ask you!' said Pilbeam.

Ronnie did not answer. His feelings held him speechless. He was too deep in a morass of remorse to be able to articulate. Indeed, he was in a frame of mind so abased that he almost asked Pilbeam to kick him. The thought of how he had wronged his blameless Sue was almost too bitter to be borne. It bit like a serpent and stung like an adder.

From the surge and riot of his reflections one thought now emerged clearly, shining like a beacon on a dark night. The Garden Room!

Turning without a word, he shot out of the door as quickly as Percy Pilbeam a short while ago had shot in. And Percy Pilbeam, with a deep sigh, went to the dressing-table, took up the brush, and started to restore his hair to a state fit for the eyes of the nobility and gentry. This done, he smoothed his moustache and went downstairs to the drawing-room.

III

The drawing-room was empty. And, to Pilbeam's surprise, it continued to be empty for quite a considerable time. He felt puzzled. He had expected to meet a reproachful host with an eye on the clock and a haughty hostess clicking her tongue. As the minutes crept by and his solitude remained unbroken, he began to grow restless.

He wandered about the room staring at the pictures, straightening his tie and examining the photographs on the little tables. The last of these was one of Lord Emsworth, taken apparently at about the age of thirty, in long whiskers and the uniform of the Shropshire Yeomanry. He was gazing at this with the fascinated horror which it induced in everyone who saw it suddenly for the first time, when the door at last opened; and with a sinking sensation of apprehension Pilbeam beheld the majestic form of Beach.

For an instant he stood eyeing the butler with that natural alarm which comes to all of us when in the presence of a man who a few short hours earlier has given us one look and made us feel like a condemned food product. Then his tension relaxed.

It has been well said that for every evil in this world Nature supplies an antidote. If butlers come, can cocktails be far behind? Beach was carrying a tray with glasses and a massive shaker on it; and Pilbeam, seeing these, found himself regarding their formidable bearer almost with equanimity.

'A cocktail, sir?'

'Thanks.'

He accepted a brimming glass. The darkness of its contents suggested a welcome strength. He drank. And instantaneously all through his system beacon-fires seemed to burst into being.

He drained the glass. His whole outlook on life was

now magically different. Quite suddenly he had begun to feel equal to a dozen butlers, however glazed their eyes might be.

And it might have been an illusion caused by gin and vermouth, but this butler seemed to have changed considerably for the better since their last meeting. His eye, though still glassy, had lost the old basilisk quality. There appeared now, in fact, to be something so positively lighthearted about Beach's whole demeanour that the proprietor of the Argus Enquiry Agency was emboldened to plunge into conversation.

'Nice evening.'

'Yes, sir.'

'Nice after the storm.'

'Yes, sir.'

'Came down a bit, didn't it?'

'The rain was undoubtedly extremely heavy, sir. Another cocktail?'

'Thanks.'

The re-lighting of the beacons had the effect of removing from Pilbeam the last trace of diffidence and shyness. He saw now that he had been entirely mistaken in this butler. Encountering him in the hall at the moment of his arrival, he had supposed him supercilious and hostile. He now perceived that he was a butler and a brother. More like Old King Cole, that jolly old soul, indeed, than anybody Pilbeam had met for months.

'I got caught in it,' he said affably.

'Indeed, sir?'

'Yes. Lord Emsworth had been showing me some photographs of that pig of his . . . By the way, in strict confidence . . . what's your name?'

'Beach, sir.'

'In strict confidence, Beach, I know something about that pig.'

'Indeed, sir?'

'Yes. Well, after I had seen the photographs, I went for

473

a walk in the park and the rain came on and I got pretty wet. In fact, I don't mind telling you I had to get under cover and take my trousers off to dry.'

He laughed merrily.

'Another cocktail, sir?'

'Making three in all?'

'Yes, sir.'

'Perhaps you're right,' said Pilbeam.

For some moments he sat, pensive and distrait, listening to the strains of a brass band which seemed to have started playing somewhere in the vicinity. Then his idly floating thoughts drifted back to the mystery which had been vexing him before this delightful butler's entry.

'I say, Beach, I've been waiting here hours and hours. Where's this dinner I heard you beating gongs about?'

'Dinner is ready, sir, but I put it back some little while, as gentlemen aren't punctual in the summertime.'

Pilbeam considered this statement. It sounded to him as if it would make rather a good song-title. Gentlemen aren't punctual in the summertime, in the summertime (I said, In the summertime), So take me back to that old Kentucky shack . . . He tried to fit it to the music which the brass band was playing, but it did not go very well and he gave it up.

'Where is everybody?' he asked.

'His lordship and her ladyship and Mr Galahad and Miss Threepwood are dining at Matchingham Hall.'

'What! With old Pop Parsloe?'

'With Sir Gregory Parsloe-Parsloe, yes, sir.'

Pilbeam chuckled.

'Well, well, well! Quick worker, old Parsloe. Don't you think so, Beach? I mean, you advise him to do a thing, to act in a certain way, to adopt a certain course of action, and he does it right away. You agree with me, Beach?'

'I fear my limited acquaintance with Sir Gregory scarcely entitles me to offer an opinion, sir.'

'Talking of old Parsloe, Beach . . . you did say your name was Beach?'

'Yes, sir.'

'With a capital B?'

'Yes, sir.'

'Well, talking of old Parsloe, Beach, I could tell you something about him. Something he's up to.'

'Indeed, sir?'

'But I'm not going to. Respect client's confidence. Lips sealed. Professional secret.'

'Yes, sir?'

'As you rightly say, yes. Any more of that stuff in the shaker, Beach?'

'A little, sir, if you consider it judicious.'

'That's just what I do consider it. Start pouring.'

The detective sipped luxuriously, fuller and fuller every moment of an uplifting sense of well-being. If the friendship which had sprung up between himself and the butler was possibly a little one-sided, on the one side on which it did exist it was warm, even fervent. It seemed to Pilbeam that for the first time since he had arrived at Blandings Castle he had found a real chum, a kindred soul in whom he might confide. And he was filled with an overwhelming desire to confide in somebody.

'As a matter of fact, Beach,' he said, 'I could tell you all sorts of things about all sorts of people. Practically everybody in this house I could tell you something about. What's the name of that chap with the light hair, for instance? The old boy's secretary?'

'Mr Carmody, sir.'

'Carmody! That's the name. I've been trying to remember it. Well, I could tell you something about Carmody.'

'Indeed, sir?'

'Yes. Something about Carmody that would interest

you very much. I saw Carmody this afternoon when
Carmody didn't see me.'

'Indeed, sir?'

'Yes. Where is Carmody?'

'I imagine he will be down shortly, sir. Mr Ronald
also.'

'Ronald!' Pilbeam drew in his breath sharply. 'There's
a tough baby, Beach. That Ronnie. Do you know what
he wanted to do just now? Murder me!'

In Beach's opinion, for he did not look on Percy
Pilbeam as a very necessary member of society, this
would have been a commendable act, and he regretted
that its consummation had been prevented. He was also
feeling that the conscientious butler he had always
prided himself on being would long ere this have
withdrawn and left this man to talk to himself. But even
the best of butlers have human emotions, and the magic
of Pilbeam's small-talk held Beach like a spell. It
reminded him of the Gossip page of *Society Spice*, a
paper to which he was a regular subscriber. He was
piqued and curious. So far, it was true, his companion
had merely hinted, but something seemed to tell him
that, if he lingered on, a really sensational news-item
would shortly emerge.

He had never been more right in his life. Pilbeam by
this time had finished the fourth cocktail, and the urge
to confide had become overpowering. He looked at
Beach, and it nearly made him cry to think that he was
holding anything back from such a splendid fellow.

'And do you know why he wanted to murder me,
Beach?'

It scarcely seemed to the butler that the action
required anything in the nature of a reasoned
explanation, but he murmured the necessary response.

'I could not say, sir.'

'Of course you couldn't. How could you? You don't
know. That's why I'm telling you. Well, listen. He's in

love with a girl in the chorus at the Regal, a girl named
Sue Brown, and he thought I had been taking her out to
dinner. That's why he wanted to murder me, Beach.'

'Indeed, sir?'

The butler spoke calmly, but he was deeply stirred.
He had always flattered himself that the inmates of
Blandings Castle kept few secrets from him, but this was
something new.

'Yes. That was why. I had the dickens of a job holding
him off, I can tell you. Do you know what saved me,
Beach?'

'No, sir.'

'Presence of mind. I put it to him – to Ronnie – I put it
to Ronnie as a reasonable man that, if this girl loved me,
would she have come to this place, pretending to be
Miss Shoemaker, simply so as to see him?'

'Sir!'

'Yes, that's who Miss Shoemaker is, Beach. She's a
chorus-girl called Sue Brown, and she's come here to see
Ronnie.'

Beach stood transfixed. His eyes swelled bulbously
from their sockets. He was incapable of even an 'Indeed,
sir?'

He was still endeavouring to assimilate this
extraordinary revelation when Hugo Carmody entered
the room.

'Ah!' said Hugo, his eye falling on Pilbeam. He
stiffened. He stood looking at the detective like
Schopenhauer's butcher at the selected lamb.

'Leave us, Beach,' he said, in a grave, deep voice.

The butler came out of his trance.

'Sir?'

'Pop off.'

'Very good, sir.'

The door closed.

'I've been looking for you, viper,' said Hugo.

'Have you, Carmody?' said Percy Pilbeam

effervescently. 'I've been looking for you, too. Got
something I want to talk to you about. Each looking for
each. Or am I thinking of a couple of other fellows?
Come right in, Carmody, and sit down. Good old
Carmody! Jolly old Carmody! Splendid old Carmody!
Well, well, well, well, well!'

If the lamb mentioned above had suddenly accosted
the above-mentioned butcher in a similar strain of
hearty camaraderie, it could have hardly disconcerted
him more than Pilbeam with these cheery words
disconcerted Hugo. His stern, set gaze became a gaping
stare.

Then he pulled himself together. What did words
matter? He had no time to bother about words. Action
was what he was after. Action!

'I don't know if you're aware of it, worm,' he said, 'but
you came jolly near to blighting my life.'

'Doing what, Carmody?'

'Blighting my life.'

'List to me while I tell you of the Spaniard who
blighted my life,' sang Percy Pilbeam, letting it go like a
lark in the springtime. He had never felt happier or in
more congenial society. 'How did I blight your life,
Carmody?'

'You didn't.'

'You said I did.'

'I said you tried to.'

'Make up your mind, Carmody.'

'Don't keep calling me Carmody.'

'But, Carmody,' protested Pilbeam, 'it's your name,
isn't it? Certainly it is. Then why try to hush it up,
Carmody? Be frank and open. I don't mind people
knowing my name. I glory in it. It's Pilbeam – Pilbeam –
Pilbeam – that's what it is – Pilbeam!'

'In about thirty seconds,' said Hugo, 'it will be Mud.'

It struck Percy Pilbeam for the first time that in his
companion's manner there was a certain peevishness.

478

'Something the matter?' he asked, concerned.

'I'll tell you what's the matter.'

'Do, Carmody, do,' said Pilbeam. 'Do, do, do. Confide in me. I like your face.'

He settled himself in a deep arm-chair, and putting the tips of his fingers together after a little preliminary difficulty in making them meet, leaned back, all readiness to listen to whatever trouble it was that was disturbing this new friend of his.

'Some days ago, insect . . .'

Pilbeam opened his eyes.

'Speak up, Carmody,' he said. 'Don't mumble.'

Hugo's fingers twitched. He regarded his companion with a burning eye, and wondered why he was wasting time talking instead of at once proceeding to the main business of the day and knocking the fellow's head off at the roots. What saved Pilbeam was the reclining position he had assumed. If you are a Carmody and a sportsman, you cannot attack even a viper, if it persists in lying back on its spine and keeping its eyes shut.

'Some days ago,' he began again, 'I called at your office. And after we had talked of this and that, I left. I discovered later that immediately upon my departure you had set your foul spies on my trail and had instructed them to take notes of my movements and report on them. The result being that I came jolly close to having my bally life ruined. And, if you want to know what I'm going to do, I'm going to haul you out of that chair and turn you round and kick you hard and go on kicking you till I kick you out of the house. And if you dare to shove your beastly little nose back inside the place, I'll disembowel you.'

Pilbeam unclosed his eyes.

'Nothing,' he said, 'could be fairer than that. Nevertheless, that's no reason why you should go about stealing pigs.'

Hugo had often read stories in which people reeled

and would have fallen, had they not clutched at
whatever it was that they clutched at. He had never
expected to undergo that experience himself. But it is
undoubtedly the fact that, if he had not at this moment
gripped the back of a chair, he would have been hard put
to it to remain perpendicular.

'Pig-pincher!' said Pilbeam austerely, and closed his
eyes again.

Hugo, having established his equilibrium by means of
the chair, had now moved away. He was making a strong
effort to recover his morale. He picked up the
photograph of Lord Emsworth in his Yeomanry uniform
and looked at it absently; then, as if it had just dawned
upon him, put it down with a shudder, like a man who
finds that he had been handling a snake.

'What do you mean?' he said thickly.

Pilbeam's eyes opened.

'What do I mean? What do you think I mean? I mean
you're a pig-pincher. That's what I mean. You go to and
fro, sneaking pigs and hiding them in caravans.'

Hugo took up Lord Emsworth's photograph again,
saw what he was doing, and dropped it quickly. Pilbeam
had closed his eyes once more, and, looking at him,
Hugo could not repress a reluctant thrill of awe. He had
often read about the superhuman intuition of detectives,
but he had never before been privileged to observe it in
operation. Then an idea occurred to him.

'Did you see me?'

'What say, Carmody?'

'Did you see me?'

'Yes, I see you, Carmody,' said Pilbeam playfully.
'Peep-bo!'

'Did you see me put that pig in the caravan?'

Pilbeam nodded eleven times in rapid succession.

'Certainly I saw you, Carmody. Why shouldn't I see
you, considering I'd been caught in the rain and taken
shelter in the caravan and was in there with my trousers

off, trying to dry them because I'm subject to lumbago?'

'I didn't see you.'

'No, Carmody, you did not. And I'll tell you why, Carmody. Because I heard a girl's voice outside saying "Be quick, or somebody will come along!" and I hid. You don't suppose I would let a sweet girl see me in knee-length mesh-knit underwear, do you? Not done, Carmody,' said Pilbeam, severely. 'Not cricket.'

Hugo was experiencing the bitterness which comes to all criminals who discover, too late, that they have undone themselves by trying to be clever. It had seemed at the time such a good idea to remove the Empress from the gamekeeper's cottage in the West Wood and place her in Baxter's caravan, where nobody would think of looking. How could he have anticipated that the caravan would be bulging with blighted detectives?

At this tense moment, the door opened and Beach appeared.

'I beg your pardon, sir, but do you propose to wait any longer for Mr Ronald?'

'Eh?'

'Certainly not,' said Pilbeam. 'Who the devil's Mr Ronald, I should like to know? I didn't come to this place to do a fast-cure. I want my dinner, and I want it now. And if Mr Ronald doesn't like it, he can do the other thing.' He strode in a dominating manner to the door. 'Come along, Carmody. Din-dins.'

Hugo had sunk into a chair.

'I don't want any dinner,' he said, dully.

'You don't want any dinner?'

'No.'

'No dinner?'

'No.'

Pilbeam shrugged his shoulders impatiently.

'The man's an ass,' he said.

He headed for the stairs. His manner seemed to indicate that he washed his hands of Hugo.

Beach lingered.

'Shall I bring you some sandwiches, sir?'

'No thanks. What's that?'

A loud crash had sounded. The butler went to the door and looked out.

'It is Mr Pilbeam, sir. He appears to have fallen downstairs.'

For an instant a look of hope crept into Hugo's careworn face.

'Has he broken his neck?'

'Apparently not, sir.'

'Ah,' said Hugo regretfully.

14 — Swift Thinking by the Efficient Baxter

The efficient Baxter had retired to the smoking-room
shortly before half-past seven. He desired silence and
solitude, and in this cosy haven he got both. For a few
minutes nothing broke the stillness but the slow ticking
of a clock on the mantelpiece. Then from the direction
of the hall there came a new sound, faint at first but
swelling and swelling to a frenzied blare, seeming to
throb through the air with a note of passionate appeal
like a woman wailing for her demon lover. It was that
tocsin of the soul, that müezzin of the country-house,
the dressing-for-dinner gong.

Baxter did not stir. The summons left him unmoved.
He had heard it, of course. Butler Beach was a man who
swung a pretty gong-stick. He had that quick fore-arm
flick and wristy follow-through which stamp the master.
If you were anywhere within a quarter of a mile or so,
you could not help hearing him. But the sound had no
appeal for Baxter. He did not propose to go in to dinner.
He wanted to be alone with his thoughts.

They were not the sort of thoughts with which most
men would have wished to be left alone, being both dark
and bitter. That expedition to the gamekeeper's cottage
in the West Wood had not proved a pleasure-trip for
Rupert Baxter. Reviewing it in his mind, he burned with
baffled rage.

And yet everybody had been very nice to him – very
nice and tactful. True, at the moment of the discovery
that the cottage contained no pig and appeared to have
been pigless from its foundation, there had been perhaps

just the slightest suspicion of constraint. Lord Emsworth had grasped his ivory-knobbed stick a little more tightly, and had edged behind Beach in a rather noticeable way, his manner saying more plainly than was agreeable, 'If he springs, be ready!' And there had come into the butler's face a look, hard to bear, which was a blend of censure and pity. But after that both of them had been charming.

Lord Emsworth had talked soothingly about light and shade effects. He had said – and Beach agreed with him – that in the darkness of a thunderstorm anybody might have been deceived into supposing that he had seen a butler feeding a pig in the gamekeeper's cottage. It was probably, said Lord Emsworth – and Beach thought so, too – a bit of wood sticking out of the wall or something. He went on to tell a longish story of how he himself, when a boy, had fancied he had seen a cat with flaming eyes. He had concluded by advising Baxter – and Beach said the suggestion was a good one – to hurry home and have a nice cup of hot tea and go to bed.

His attitude, in short, could not have been pleasanter or more considerate. Yet Baxter, as he sat in the smoking-room, burned, as stated, with baffled rage.

The door handle turned. Beach stood on the threshold.

'If you have changed your mind, sir, about taking dinner, the meal is quite ready.'

He spoke as friend to friend. There was nothing in his manner to suggest that the man he addressed had ever accused him of stealing pigs. As far as Beach was concerned, all was forgotten and forgiven.

But the milk of human kindness, of which the butler was so full, had not yet been delivered on Baxter's doorstep. The hostility in his eye, as he fixed it on his visitor, was so marked that a lesser man than Beach might have been disconcerted.

'I don't want any dinner.'

484

'Very good, sir.'

'Bring me that whisky-and-soda quick.'

'Yes, sir.'

The door closed as softly as it had opened, but not before a pang like a red-hot needle had pierced the ex-secretary's bosom. It was caused by the fact that he had distinctly heard the butler, as he withdrew, utter a pitying sigh.

It was the sort of sigh which a kind-hearted man would have given on peeping into a padded cell in which some old friend was confined, and Baxter resented it with all the force of an imperious nature. He had not ceased to wonder what, if anything, could be done about it when the refreshments arrived, carried by James the footman. James placed them gently on the table, shot a swift glance of respectful commiseration at the patient, and passed away.

The sigh had cut Baxter like a knife. The look stabbed him like a dagger. For a moment he thought of calling the man back and asking him what the devil he meant by staring at him like that, but wiser counsels prevailed. He contented himself with draining a glass of whisky-and-soda and swallowing two sandwiches.

This done, he felt a little – not much, but a little – better. Before, he would gladly have murdered Beach and James and danced on their graves. Now, he would have been satisfied with straight murder.

However, he was alone at last. That was some slight consolation. Beach had come and gone. Footman James had come and gone. Everybody else must by now be either at Matchingham Hall or assembled in the dining-room. On the solitude which he so greatly desired there could be no further intrusion. He resumed his meditations.

For a time these dealt exclusively with the recent past, and were, in consequence, of a morbid character. Then, as the grateful glow of the whisky began to make

itself felt, a softer mood came to Rupert Baxter. His
mind turned to thoughts of Sue.

Men as efficient as Rupert Baxter do not fall in love in
the generally accepted sense of the term. Their attitude
towards the tender passion is more restrained than that
of the ordinary feckless young man who loses his heart
at first sight with a whoop and a shiver. Baxter approved
of Sue. We cannot say more. But this approval, added to
the fact that he had been informed by Lady Constance
that the girl was the only daughter of a man who
possessed sixty million dollars, had been enough to
cause him to ear-mark her in his mind as the future Mrs
Baxter. In that capacity he had docketed her and filed her
away at the first moment of their meeting.

Naturally, therefore, the remarks which Lord
Emsworth had let fall in her hearing had caused him
grave concern. It hampers a man in his wooing if the girl
he has selected for his bride starts with the idea that he
is as mad as a coot. He congratulated himself on the
promptitude with which he had handled the situation.
That letter which he had written her could not fail to
put him right in her eyes.

Rupert Baxter was a man in whose lexicon there was
no such word as failure. An heiress like this Miss
Schoonmaker would not, he was aware, lack for suitors:
but he did not fear them. If only she were making a
reasonably long stay at the castle, he felt that he could
rely on his force of character to win the day. In fact, it
seemed to him that he could almost hear the wedding
bells ringing already. Then, coming out of his dreams, he
realized that it was the telephone.

He reached for the instrument with a frown, annoyed
at the interruption, and spoke with an irritated
sharpness.

'Hullo?'

A ghostly voice replied. The storm seemed to have
affected the wires.

'Speak up!' barked Baxter.

He banged the telephone violently on the table. The treatment, as is so often the case, proved effective.

'Blandings Castle?' said the voice, no longer ghostly.

'Yes.'

'Post Office, Market Blandings, speaking. Telegram for Lady Constance Keeble.'

'I will take it.'

The voice became faint again. Baxter went through the movements as before.

'Lady Constance Keeble, Blandings Castle, Market Blandings, Shropshire, England,' said the voice, recovering strength as if it had shaken off a wasting sickness. 'Handed in at Paris.'

'Where?'

'Paris, France.'

'Oh? Well?'

The voice gathered volume.

'"Terribly sorry hear news . . ."'

'What?'

'"News."'

'Yes?'

'"Terribly sorry hear news stop Quite understand stop So disappointed shall be unable come to you later as going back America at end of month stop. Do hope we shall be able arrange something when I return next year stop Regards stop!"'

'Yes?'

'Signed "Myra Schoonmaker."'

'Signed – *what*?'

'Myra Schoonmaker.'

Baxter's mouth had fallen open. The forehead above the spectacles was wrinkled, the eyes behind them staring blankly and with a growing horror.

'Shall I repeat?'

'What?'

'Do you wish the message repeated?'

487

'No,' said Baxter in a choking voice.

He hung up the receiver. There seemed to be something crawling down his back. His brain was numbed.

Myra Schoonmaker! Telegraphing from Paris!

Then who was this girl who was at the castle calling herself by that preposterous name? An impostor, an adventuress. She must be.

And if he made a move to expose her she would revenge herself by showing Lord Emsworth that letter of his.

In his agitation of the moment he had risen to his feet. He now sat down heavily.

That letter . . . !

He must recover it. He must recover it at once. As long as it remained in the girl's possession, it was a pistol pointed at his head. Once let Lord Emsworth become acquainted with those very frank criticisms of himself which it contained, and not even his ally, Lady Constance, would be able to restore him to his lost secretaryship. The ninth Earl was a mild man, accustomed to bowing to his sister's decrees, but there were limits beyond which he could not be pushed.

And Baxter yearned to be back at Blandings Castle in the position he had once enjoyed. Blandings was his spiritual home. He had held other secretaryships – he held one now, at a salary far higher than that which Lord Emsworth had paid him – but never had he succeeded in recapturing that fascinating sense of power, of importance, of being the man who directed the destinies of one of the largest houses in England.

At all costs he must recover that letter. And the present moment, he perceived, was ideal for the venture. The girl must have the thing in her room somewhere, and for the next hour at least she would be in the dining-room. He would have ample opportunity for a search.

He did not delay. Thirty seconds later he was mounting the stairs, his face set, his spectacles gleaming grimly. A minute later, he reached his destination. No good angel, aware of what the future held, stood on the threshold to bar his entry. The door was ajar. He pushed it open and went in.

II

Blandings Castle, like most places of its size and importance, contained bedrooms so magnificent that they were never used. With their four-poster beds and their superb but rather oppressive tapestries, they had remained untenanted since the time when Queen Elizabeth I, dodging from country-house to country-house in that restless, snipe-like way of hers, had last slept in them. Of the guest-rooms still in commission, the most luxurious was that which had been given to Sue.

At the moment when Baxter stole cautiously in, it was looking its best in the gentle evening light. But Baxter was not in sight-seeing mood. He ignored the carved bedstead, the cosy arm-chairs, the pictures, the decorations, and the soft carpet into which his feet sank. The beauty of the sky through the french windows that gave on to the balcony drew but a single brief glance from him. Without delay, he made for the writing-desk which stood against the wall near the bed. It seemed to him a good point of departure for his search.

There were several pigeon-holes in the desk. They contained single sheets of notepaper, double sheets of notepaper, postcards, envelopes, telegraph-forms, and even a little pad on which the room's occupant was presumably expected to jot down any stray thoughts and reflections on Life which might occur to him or her before turning in for the night. But not one of them contained the fatal letter.

489

He straightened himself and looked about the room. The drawer of the dressing-table now suggested itself as a possibility. He left the desk and made his way towards it.

The primary requisite of dressing-tables being a good supply of light, they are usually placed in a position to get as much of it as possible. This one was no exception. It stood so near to the open windows that the breeze was ruffling the tassels on its lamp-shades: and Baxter, arriving in front of it, was enabled for the first time to see the balcony in its entirety.

And, as he saw it, his heart seemed to side-slip. Leaning upon the parapet and looking out over the sea of gravel that swept up to the front door from the rhododendron-fringed drive, stood a girl. And not even the fact that her back was turned could prevent Baxter identifying her.

For an instant he remained frozen. Even the greatest men congeal beneath the chill breath of the totally unexpected. He had assumed as a matter of course that Sue was down in the dining-room, and it took him several seconds to adjust his mind to the unpleasing fact that she was up on her balcony. When he recovered his presence of mind sufficiently to draw noiselessly away from the line of vision, his first emotion was one of irritation. This chopping and changing, this eleventh hour alteration of plans, these sudden decisions to remain upstairs when they ought to be downstairs, were what made women as a sex so unsatisfactory.

To irritation succeeded a sense of defeat. There was nothing for it, he realized, but to give up his quest and go. He started to tip-toe silently to the door, agreeably conscious now of the softness and thickness of the Axminster pile that made it possible to move unheard, and had just reached it, when from the other side there came to his ears a sound of chinking and clattering – the sound, in fact, which is made by plates and dishes when they are carried on a tray to a guest who, after a long railway journey, has asked her hostess if she may take dinner in her room.

Practice makes perfect. This was the second time in the last three hours that Baxter had found himself trapped in a room in which it was vitally urgent that he should not be discovered: and he was getting the technique of the thing. On the previous occasion, in the small library, he had taken to himself wings like a bird and sailed out of the window. In the present crisis, such a course, he perceived immediately, was not feasible. The way of an eagle would profit him nothing. Soaring over the balcony, he would be observed by Sue and would, in addition, unquestionably break his neck. What was needed here was the way of a diving-duck.

And so, as the door-handle turned, Rupert Baxter, even in this black hour efficient, dropped on all-fours and slid under the bed as smoothly as if he had been practising for weeks.

III

Owing to the restricted nature of his position and the limited range of vision which he enjoys, virtually the only way in which a man who is hiding under a bed can entertain himself is by listening to what is going on outside. He may hear something of interest, or he may hear only the draught sighing along the floor: but, for better or for worse, that is all he is able to do.

The first sound that came to Rupert Baxter was that made by the placing of the tray on the table. Then, after a pause, a pair of squeaking shoes passed over the carpet and squeaked out of hearing. Baxter recognized them as those of Footman Thomas, a confirmed squeaker.

After this, somebody puffed, causing him to deduce the presence of Beach.

'Your dinner is quite ready, miss.'

'Oh, thank you.'

The girl had apparently come in from the balcony. A chair scraped to the table. A savoury scent floated to Baxter's nostrils, causing him acute discomfort. He had just begun to realize how extremely hungry he was and how rash he had been, firstly to attempt to dine off a couple of sandwiches, and secondly to undertake a mission like his present one without a square meal inside him.

'That is chicken, miss. *En casserole*.'

Baxter had deduced as much, and was trying not to let his mind dwell on it. He uttered a silent groan. In addition to the agony of having to smell food, he was beginning to be conscious of a growing cramp in his left leg. He turned on one side and did his best to emulate the easy nonchalance of those Indian fakirs who, doubtless from the best motives, spend the formative years of their lives lying on iron spikes.

'It looks very good.'

'I trust you will enjoy it, miss. Is there anything further that I can do for you?'

'No, thank you. Oh, yes. Would you mind fetching that manuscript from the balcony. I was reading it out there, and I left it on the chair. It's Mr Threepwood's book.'

'Indeed, miss? An exceedingly interesting compilation, I should imagine?'

'Yes, very.'

'I wonder if it would be taking a liberty, miss, to ask you to inform me later, at your leisure, if I make any appearance in its pages.'

'You?'

'Yes, miss. From what Mr Galahad has let fall from time to time, I fancy it was his intention to give me printed credit as his authority for certain of the stories which appear in the book.'

'Do you want to be in it?'

492

'Most decidedly, miss. I should consider it an honour. And it would please my mother.'

'Have you a mother?'

'Yes, miss. She lives at Eastbourne.'

The butler moved majestically on to the balcony, and Sue's mind had turned to speculation about his mother and whether she looked anything like him, when there was a sound of hurrying feet without, the door flew open, and Beach's mother passed from her mind like the unsubstantial fabric of a dream. With a little choking cry she rose to her feet. Ronnie was standing before her.

15 — Over the Telephone

And meanwhile, if we may borrow an expression from a sister art, what of Hugo Carmody?

It is a defect unfortunately inseparable from any such document as this faithful record of events in and about Blandings Castle that the chronicler, in order to give a square deal to each of the individuals whose fortunes he has undertaken to narrate, is compelled to flit abruptly from one to the other in the manner popularized by the chamois of the Alps leaping from crag to crag. The activities of the Efficient Baxter seeming to him to demand immediate attention, he was reluctantly compelled some little while back to leave Hugo in the very act of reeling beneath a crushing blow. The moment has now come to return to him.

The first effect on a young man of sensibility and gentle upbringing of the discovery that an unfriendly detective has seen him placing stolen pigs in caravans is to induce a stunned condition of mind, a sort of mental coma. The face lengthens. The limbs grow rigid. The tie slips sideways and the cuffs recede into the coat-sleeves. The subject becomes temporarily, in short, a total loss.

It is perhaps as well, therefore, that we did not waste valuable time watching Hugo in the process of digesting Percy Pilbeam's sensational announcement, for it would have been like looking at a statue. If the reader will endeavour to picture Rodin's Thinker in a dinner-jacket and trousers with braid down the sides, he will have got the general idea. At the instant when Hugo Carmody makes his reappearance, life has just begun to return to the stiffened frame.

And with life came the dawning of intelligence. This ghastly snag which had popped up in his path was too big, reflected Hugo, for any man to tackle. It called for a woman's keener wit. His first act on emerging from the depths, therefore, was to leave the drawing-room and totter downstairs to the telephone. He got the number of Matchingham Hall and, establishing communication with Sir Gregory Parsloe-Parsloe's butler, urged him to summon Miss Millicent Threepwood from the dinner-table. The butler said in rather a reproving way that Miss Threepwood was at the moment busy drinking soup. Hugo, with the first flash of spirit he had shown for a quarter of an hour, replied that he didn't care if she was bathing in it. Fetch her, said Hugo, and almost added the words 'You scurvy knave.' He then clung weakly to the receiver, waiting, and in a short while a sweet, but agitated, voice floated to him across the wire.

'Hugo?'

'Millicent?'

'Is that you?'

'Yes. Is that you?'

'Yes.'

Anything in the nature of misunderstanding was cleared away. It was both of them.

'What's up?'

'Everything's up.'

'How do you mean?'

'I'll tell you,' said Hugo, and did so. It was not a difficult story to tell. Its plot was so clear that a few whispered words sufficed.

'You don't mean that?' said Millicent, the tale concluded.

'I do mean that.'

'Oh, golly!' said Millicent.

Silence followed. Hugo waited palpitatingly. The outlook seemed to him black. He wondered if he had

placed too much reliance in woman's wit. That 'Golly!'
had not been hopeful.

'Hugo!'

'Hullo?'

'This is a bit thick.'

'Yes,' agreed Hugo. The thickness had not escaped
him.

'Well, there's only one thing to do.'

A faint thrill passed through Hugo Carmody. One
would be enough. Woman's wit was going to bring home
the bacon after all.

'Listen!'

'Well?'

'The only thing to do is for me to go back to the
dining-room and tell Uncle Clarence you've found the
Empress.'

'Eh?'

'Found her, fathead.'

'How do you mean?'

'Found her in the caravan.'

'But weren't you listening to what I was saying?'
There were tears in Hugo's voice. 'Pilbeam saw us
putting her there.'

'I know.'

'Well, what's our move when he says so?'

'Stout denial.'

'Eh?'

'We stoutly deny it,' said Millicent.

The thrill passed through Hugo again, stronger than
before. It might work. Yes, properly handled, it would
work. He poured broken words of love and praise into
the receiver.

'That's right,' he cried. 'I see daylight. I will go to
Pilbeam and tell him privily that if he opens his mouth
I'll strangle him.'

'Well, hold on. I'll go and tell Uncle Clarence. I expect
he'll be out in a moment to have a word with you.'

'Half a minute! Millicent!'

'Well?'

'When am I supposed to have found this ghastly pig?'

'Ten minutes ago, when you were taking a stroll before dinner. You happened to pass the caravan and you heard an odd noise inside, and you looked to see what it was, and there was the Empress and you raced back to the house to telephone.'

'But, Millicent! Half a minute!'

'Well?'

'The old boy will think Baxter stole her.'

'So he will! Isn't that splendid! Well, hold on.'

Hugo resumed his vigil. It was some moments later that a noise like the clucking of fowls broke out at the Matchingham Hall end of the wire. He deduced correctly that this was caused by the ninth Earl of Emsworth endeavouring to clothe his thoughts in speech.

'Kuk-kuk-kuk . . .'

'Yes, Lord Emsworth?'

'Kuk-Carmody!'

'Yes, Lord Emsworth?'

'Is this true?'

'Yes, Lord Emsworth.'

'You've found the Empress?'

'Yes, Lord Emsworth.'

'In that feller Baxter's caravan?'

'Yes, Lord Emsworth.'

'Well, I'll be damned!'

'Yes, Lord Emsworth.'

So far Hugo Carmody had found his share of the dialogue delightfully easy. On these lines he would have been prepared to continue it all night. But there was something else besides, 'Yes, Lord Emsworth' that he must now endeavour to say. There is a tide in the affairs of men which, taken at the flood, leads on to fortune: and that tide, he knew, would never rise higher than at

497

the present moment. He swallowed twice to unlimber
his vocal cords.

'Lord Emsworth,' he said, and, though his heart was
beating fast, his voice was steady, 'there is something I
would like to take this opportunity of saying. It will
come as a surprise to you, but I hope not as an
unpleasant surprise. I love your niece Millicent, and she
loves me, Lord Emsworth. We have loved each other for
many weeks and it is my hope that you will give your
consent to our marriage. I am not a rich man, Lord
Emsworth. In fact, strictly speaking, except for my
salary I haven't a bean in the world. But my Uncle Lester
owns Rudge Hall, in Worcestershire – I daresay you have
heard of the place? You turn to the left off the main road
to Birmingham and go about a couple of miles . . . well,
anyway, it's a biggish sort of place in Worcestershire and
my Uncle Lester owns it and the property is entailed and
I'm next in succession . . . I won't pretend that my Uncle
Lester shows any indications of passing in his checks, he
was extremely fit last time I saw him, but, after all, he's
getting on and all flesh is as grass and, as I say, I'm next
man in, so I shall eventually succeed to quite a fairish
bit of the stuff and a house and park and rentroll and all
that, so what I mean is, it isn't as if I wasn't in a position
to support Millicent later on, and if you realized, Lord
Emsworth, how we love one another I'm sure you would
see that it wouldn't be playing the game to put any
obstacles in the way of our happiness, so what I'm
driving at, if you follow me, is, may we charge ahead?'

There was dead silence at the other end of the wire. It
seemed as if the revelation of a good man's love had
struck Lord Emsworth dumb. It was only some
moments later, after he had said 'Hullo!' six times and 'I
say, are you there?' twice that it was borne in upon
Hugo that he had wasted two hundred and eighty words
of the finest eloquence on empty space.

His natural chagrin at this discovery was sensibly

diminished by the sudden sound of Millicent's voice in his ear.

'Hullo!'

'Hullo!'

'Hullo!'

'Hullo!'

'Hugo!'

'Hullo!'

'I say, Hugo!' She spoke with the joyous excitement of a girl who has just emerged from the centre of a family dog-fight. 'I say, Hugo, things are hotting up here properly. I sprung it on Uncle Clarence just now that I want to marry you!'

'So did I. Only he wasn't there.'

'I said "Uncle Clarence, aren't you grateful to Mr Carmody for finding the Empress?" and he said "Yes, yes, yes, yes, yes, to be sure. Capital boy! Capital boy! Always liked him." And I said "I suppose you wouldn't by any chance let me marry him?" and he said "Eh, what? Marry him?" "Yes," I said. "Marry him." And he said "Certainly, certainly, certainly, certainly, by all means." And then Aunt Constance had a fit, and Uncle Gally said she was a kill-joy and ought to be ashamed of herself for throwing the gaff into love's young dream, and Uncle Clarence kept on saying "Certainly, certainly, certainly." I don't know what old Parsloe thinks of it all. He's sitting in his chair, looking at the ceiling and drinking hock. The butler left at the end of round one. I'm going back to see how it's all coming out. Hold the line.'

A man for whom Happiness and Misery are swaying in the scales three miles away, and whose only medium of learning the result of the contest is a telephone wire, is not likely to ring off impatiently. Hugo sat tense and breathless, like one listening in on the radio to a championship fight in which he has a financial interest. It was only when a cheery voice spoke at his elbow that he realized that his solitude had been invaded, and by Percy Pilbeam at that.

Percy Pilbeam was looking rosy and replete. He swayed slightly and his smile was rather wider and more pebble-beached than a total abstainer's would have been.

'Hullo, Carmody,' said Percy Pilbeam. 'What ho, Carmody. So here you are, Carmody.'

It came to Hugo that he had something to say to this man.

'Here, you!' he cried.

'Yes, Carmody?'

'Do you want to be battered to a pulp?'

'No, Carmody.'

'Then listen. You didn't see me put that pig in the caravan. Understand?'

'But I did, Carmody.'

'You didn't – not if you want to go on living.'

Percy Pilbeam appeared to be in a mood not only of keen intelligence but of the utmost reasonableness and amiability.

'Say no more, Carmody,' he said agreeably. 'I take your point. You want me not to tell anybody I saw you put that caravan in the pig. Quite, Carmody, quite.'

'Well, bear it in mind.'

'I will, Carmody. Oh yes, Carmody, I will. I'm going for a stroll outside, Carmody. Care to join me?'

'Go to hell!'

'Quite,' said Percy Pilbeam.

He tacked unsteadily to the door, aimed himself at it and passed through. And a moment later Millicent's voice spoke.

'Hugo?'

'Hullo?'

'Oh, Hugo, darling, the battle's over. We've won. Uncle Clarence has said "Certainly" sixty-five times, and he's just told Aunt Constance that if she thinks she can bully him she's very much mistaken. It's a walkover. They're all coming back right away in the car. Uncle Clarence is an angel.'

'So are you.'

'Me?'

'Yes, you.'

'Not such an angel as you are.'

'Much more of an angel than I am,' said Hugo, in the voice of one trained to the appraising and classifying of angels.

'Well, anyway, you precious old thing, I'm going to give them the slip and walk home along the road. Get out Ronnie's two-seater and come and pick me up and we'll go for a drive together, miles and miles through the country. It's the most perfect evening.'

'You bet it is!' said Hugo fervently. 'What I call something like an evening. Give me two minutes to get the car out and five to make the trip and I'll be with you.'

''At-a-boy!' said Millicent.

''At-a-baby!' said Hugo.

16 — Lovers' Meeting

Sue stood staring, wide-eyed. This was the moment which she had tried to picture to herself a hundred times. And always her imagination had proved unequal to the task. Sometimes she had seen Ronnie in her mind's eye cold, aloof, hostile; sometimes gasping and tottering, dumb with amazement; sometimes pointing a finger at her like a character in a melodrama and denouncing her as an impostor. The one thing for which she had not been prepared was what happened now.

Eton and Cambridge train their sons well. Once they have grasped the fundamental fact of life that all exhibitions of emotions are bad form, bomb-shells cannot disturb their poise and earthquakes are lucky if they get so much as an 'Eh, what?' from them. But Cambridge has its limitations, and so has Eton. And remorse had goaded Ronnie Fish to a point where their iron discipline had ceased to operate. He was stirred to his depths, and his scarlet face, his rumpled hair, his starting eyes and his twitching fingers all proclaimed the fact.

'Ronnie!' cried Sue.

It was all she had time to say. The thought of what she had done for his sake; the thought that for love of him she had come to Blandings Castle under false colours – an impostor – faced at every turn by the risk of detection – liable at any moment to be ignominiously exposed and looked at through a lorgnette by his Aunt Constance; the thought of the shameful way he had treated her . . . all these thoughts were racking Ronald Fish with a searing anguish. They had brought the hot

blood of the Fishes to the boil, and now, face to face
with her, he did not hesitate.

He sprang forward, clasped her in his arms, hugged
her to him. To Baxter's revolted ears, though he tried not
to listen, there came in a husky cataract the sound of a
Fish's self-reproaches. Ronnie was saying what he
thought of himself, and his opinion appeared not to be
high. He said he was a beast, a brute, a swine, a cad, a
hound, and a worm. If he had been speaking of Percy
Pilbeam, he could scarcely have been less
complimentary.

Even up to this point, Baxter had not liked the
dialogue. It now became perfectly nauseating. Sue said it
had all been her fault. Ronnie said, No, his. No, hers,
said Sue. No, his, said Ronnie. No, hers, said Sue. No,
altogether his, said Ronnie. It must have been his, he
pointed out, because, as he had observed before, he was a
hound and a worm. He now went further. He revealed
himself as a blister, a tick, and a perishing outsider.

'You're not!'

'I am!'

'You're not!'

'I am!'

'Of course you're not!'

'I certainly am!'

'Well, I love you anyway.'

'You can't.'

'I do.'

'You can't.'

'I do.'

Baxter writhed in silent anguish.

'How long?' said Baxter to his immortal soul. 'How
long?'

The question was answered with a startling
promptitude. From the neighbourhood of the french
windows there sounded a discreet cough. The debaters
sprang apart, two minds with but a single thought.

'Your manuscript, miss,' said Beach sedately.

Sue looked at him. Ronnie looked at him. Sue until this moment had forgotten his existence. Ronnie had supposed him downstairs, busy about his butlerine duties. Neither seemed very glad to see him.

Ronnie was the first to speak.

'Oh – hullo, Beach!'

There being no answer to this except 'Hullo, sir!' which is a thing that butlers do not say, Beach contented himself with a benignant smile. It had the unfortunate effect of making Ronnie think that the man was laughing at him, and the Fishes were men at whom butlers may not lightly laugh. He was about to utter a heated speech, indicating this, when the injudiciousness of such a course presented itself to his mind. Beach must be placated. He forced his voice to a note of geniality.

'So there you are, Beach?'

'Yes, sir.'

'I suppose all this must seem tolerably rummy to you?'

'No, sir.'

'No?'

'I had already been informed, Mr Ronald, of the nature of your feelings towards this lady.'

'What!'

'Yes, sir.'

'Who told you?'

'Mr Pilbeam, sir.'

Ronnie uttered a gasp. Then he became calmer. He had suddenly remembered that this man was his ally, his accomplice, linked to him not only by a friendship dating back to his boyhood but by the even stronger bond of mutual crime. Between them there need be no reserves. Delicate though the situation was, he now felt equal to it.

'Beach,' he said. 'How much do you know?'

'All, sir.'

'All?'

'Yes, sir.'

'Such as – ?'

Beach coughed.

'I am aware that this lady is a Miss Sue Brown. And, according to my informant, she is employed in the chorus of the Regal Theatre.'

'Quite the Encyclopaedia, aren't you?'

'Yes, sir.'

'I want to marry Miss Brown, Beach.'

'I can readily appreciate such a desire on your part, Mr Ronald,' said the butler with a paternal smile.

Sue caught at the smile.

'Ronnie! He's all right. I believe he's a friend.'

'Of course he's a friend! Old Beach. One of my earliest and stoutest pals.'

'I mean, he isn't going to give us away.'

'Me, miss?' said Beach shocked. 'Certainly not.'

'Splendid fellow, Beach!'

'Thank you, sir.'

'Beach,' said Ronnie, 'the time has come to act. No more delay. I've got to make myself solid with Uncle Clarence at once. Directly he gets back tonight, I shall go to him and tell him that Empress of Blandings is in the gamekeeper's cottage in the West Wood, and then, while he's still weak, I shall spring on him the announcement of my engagement.'

'Unfortunately, Mr Ronald, the animal is no longer in the cottage.'

'You've moved it?'

'Not I, sir. Mr Carmody. By a most regrettable chance Mr Carmody found me feeding it this afternoon. He took it away and deposited it in some place of which I am not cognizant, sir.'

'But, good heavens, he'll dish the whole scheme. Where is he?'

'You wish me to find him, sir?'

'Of course I wish you to find him. Go at once and ask him where that pig is. Tell him it's vital.'

'Very good, sir.'

Sue had listened with bewilderment to this talk of pigs.

'I don't understand, Ronnie.'

Ronnie was pacing the room in agitation. Once he came so close to where Baxter lay in his snug harbour that the ex-secretary had a flashing glimpse of a sock with a lavender clock. It was the first object of beauty that he had seen for a long time, and he should have appreciated it more than he did.

'I can't explain now,' said Ronnie. 'It's too long. But I can tell you this. If we don't get that pig back, we're in the soup.'

'Ronnie!'

Ronnie had ceased to pace the room. He was standing in a listening attitude.

'What's that?'

He sprang quickly to the balcony, looked over the parapet and came softly back.

'Sue!'

'What!'

'It's that blighter Pilbeam,' said Ronnie in a guarded undertone. 'He's climbing up the water-spout!'

17 — Spirited Conduct of Lord Emsworth

From the moment when it left the door of Matchingham Hall and started on its journey back to Blandings Castle, a silence as of the tomb had reigned in the Antelope car which was bringing Lord Emsworth, his sister Lady Constance Keeble, and his brother, the Hon. Galahad Threepwood, home from their interrupted dinner-party. Not so much as a syllable proceeded from one of them.

In the light of what Millicent, an eyewitness at the Front, had told Hugo over the telephone of the family battle which had been raging at Sir Gregory Parsloe's table, this will appear strange. If ever three people with plenty to say to one another were assembled together in a small space, these three, one would have thought, were those three. Lady Constance alone might have been expected to provide enough conversation to keep the historian busy for hours.

The explanation, like all explanations, is simple. It is supplied by that one word Antelope.

Owing to the fact that some trifling internal ailment had removed from the active list the Hispano-Suiza in which Blandings Castle usually went out to dinner, Voules, the chauffeur, had had to fall back upon this secondary and inferior car; and anybody who has ever owned an Antelope is aware that there is no glass partition inside it shutting off the driver from the cash customers. He is right there in their midst, ready and eager to hear everything that is said and to hand it on in due course to the Servants' Hall.

In these circumstances, though the choice seemed

one between speech and spontaneous combustion, the little company kept their thoughts to themselves. They suffered, but they did it. It would be difficult to find a better illustration of all that is implied in the fine old phrase *Noblesse oblige*. At Lady Constance we point with particular pride. She was a woman, and silence weighed hardest on her.

There were times during the drive when even the sight of Voules' large, red ears, all pricked up to learn the reason for this sudden and sensational return, was scarcely sufficient to restrain Lady Constance Keeble from telling her brother Clarence just what she thought of him. From boyhood up, he had not once come near to being her ideal man; but never had he sunk so low in her estimation as at the moment when she heard him giving his consent to the union of her niece Millicent with a young man who, besides being penniless, had always afflicted her with a nervous complaint for which she could find no name, but which is known to Scientists as the heeby-jeebies.

Nor had he re-established himself in any way by his outspoken remarks on the subject of the Efficient Baxter. He had said things about Baxter which no admirer of that energetic man could forgive. The adjectives mad, crazy, insane, gibbering – and, worse, potty – had played in and out of his conversation like flashes of lightning. And from the look in his eye she gathered that he was still saying them all over again to himself.

Her surmise was correct. To Lord Emsworth the events of this day had come as a stunning revelation. On the strength of that flower-pot incident two years ago, he had always looked on Baxter as mentally unbalanced; but, being a fair-minded man, he had recognized the possibility that a quiet, regular life and freedom from worries might, in the interval which had elapsed since his late secretary's departure from the castle, have effected a cure. Certainly the man had appeared quite

normal on the day of his arrival. And now into the space
of a few hours he had crammed enough variegated
lunacy to equip all the March Hares in England and
leave some over for the Mad Hatters.

The ninth Earl of Emsworth was not a man who was
easily disturbed. His was a calm which, as a rule, only
his younger son Frederick could shatter. But it was not
proof against the sort of thing that had been going on
today. No matter how placid you may be, if you find
yourself in close juxtaposition with a man who, when he
is not hurling himself out of windows, is stealing pigs
and trying to make you believe they were stolen by your
butler, you begin to think a bit. Lord Emsworth was
thoroughly upset. As the car bowled up the drive, he
was saying to himself that nothing could surprise him
now.

And yet something did. As the car turned the corner
by the rhododendrons and wheeled into the broad strip
of gravel that faced the front door, he beheld a sight
which brought the first sound he had uttered since the
journey began bursting from his lips.

'Good God!'

The words were spoken in a high, penetrating tenor,
and they made Lady Constance jump as if they had been
pins running into her. This unexpected breaking of the
great silence was agony to her taut nerves.

'What *is* the matter?'

'Matter? Look! Look at that fellow!'

Voules took it upon himself to explain. Never having
met Lady Constance socially, as it were, he ought
perhaps not to have spoken. He considered, however,
that the importance of the occasion justified the
solecism.

'A man is climbing the water-spout, m'lady.'

'What! Where? I don't see him.'

'He has just got into the balcony outside one of the
bedrooms,' said the Hon. Galahad.

509

Lord Emsworth went straight to the heart of the matter.

'It's that fellow Baxter!' he exclaimed.

The summer day, for all the artificial aid lent by daylight saving, was now definitely over, and gathering night had spread its mantle of dusk over the world. The visibility, therefore, was not good: and the figure which had just vanished over the parapet of the balcony of the Garden Room had been unrecognizable except to the eye of intuition. This, however, was precisely the sort of eye that Lord Emsworth possessed.

He reasoned closely. There were, he knew, on the premises of Blandings Castle other male adults besides Rupert Baxter: but none of these would climb up water-spouts and disappear over balconies. To Baxter, on the other hand, such a pursuit would seem the normal, ordinary way of passing an evening. It would be his idea of wholesome relaxation. Soon, no doubt, he would come out on to the balcony again and throw himself to the ground. That was the sort of fellow Baxter was – a man of strange pleasures.

And so, going, as we say, straight to the heart of the matter, Lord Emsworth, jerking the pince-nez off his face in his emotion, exclaimed:

'It's that fellow Baxter!'

Not since a certain day in their mutual nursery many years ago had Lady Constance gone to the length of actually hauling off and smiting her elder brother on the head with the flat of an outraged hand: but she came very near to doing it now. Perhaps it was the presence of Voules that caused her to confine herself to words.

'Clarence, you're an idiot!'

Even Voules could not prevent her saying that. After all, she was revealing no secrets. The chauffeur had been in service at the Castle quite long enough to have formed the same impression for himself.

Lord Emsworth did not argue the point. The car had

drawn up now outside the front door. The front door was open, as always of a summer evening, and the ninth Earl, accompanied by his brother Galahad, hurried up the steps and entered the hall. And, as they did so, there came to their ears the sound of running feet. The next moment, the flying figure of Percy Pilbeam came into view, taking the stairs four at a time.

'God bless my soul!' said Lord Emsworth.

If Pilbeam heard the words or saw the speaker, he gave no sign of having done so. He was plainly in a hurry. He shot through the hall and, more like a startled gazelle than a private enquiry agent, vanished down the steps. His shirt-front was dark with dirt-stains, his collar had burst from its stud, and it seemed to Lord Emsworth, in the brief moment during which he was able to focus him, that he had a black eye. The next instant, there descended the stairs and flitted past with equal speed the form of Ronnie Fish.

Lord Emsworth got an entirely wrong conception of the affair. He had no means of knowing what had taken place in the Garden Room when Pilbeam, inspired by alcohol and flushed with the thought that now was the time to get into that apartment and possess himself of the manuscript of the Hon. Galahad's Reminiscences, had climbed the water-spout to put the plan into operation. He knew nothing of the detective's sharp dismay at finding himself unexpectedly confronted with the menacing form of Ronnie Fish. He was ignorant of the lively and promising mix-up which had been concluded by Pilbeam's tempestuous dash for life. All he saw was two men fleeing madly for the open spaces, and he placed the obvious interpretation upon this phenomenon.

Baxter, he assumed, had run amok and had done it with such uncompromising thoroughness that strong men ran panic-stricken before him.

Mild though the ninth earl was by nature, a lover of

rural peace and the quiet life, he had, like all Britain's aristocracy, the right stuff in him. It so chanced that during the years when he had held his commission in the Shropshire Yeomanry the motherland had not called to him to save her. But, had that call been made, Clarence, ninth Earl of Emsworth, would have answered it with as prompt a 'Bless my Soul! Of course. Certainly!' as any of his Crusader ancestors. And in his sixtieth year the ancient fire still lingered. The Hon. Galahad, who had turned to watch the procession through the front door with a surprised monocle, turned back and found that he was alone. Lord Emsworth had disappeared. He now beheld him coming back again. On his amiable face was a look of determination. In his hand was a gun.

'Eh? What?' said the Hon. Galahad, blinking.

The head of the family did not reply. He was moving towards the stairs. In just that same silent purposeful way had an Emsworth advanced on the foe at Agincourt.

A sound as of disturbed hens made the Hon. Galahad turn again.

'Galahad! What is all this? What is happening?'

The Hon. Galahad placed his sister in possession of the facts as known to himself.

'Clarence has just gone upstairs with a gun.'

'With a gun!'

'Yes. Looked like mine, too. I hope he takes care of it.'

He perceived that Lady Constance had also been seized with the urge to climb. She was making excellent time up the broad staircase. So nimbly did she move that she was on the second landing before he came up with her.

And, as they stood there, a voice made itself heard from a room down the corridor.

'Baxter! Come out! Come out, Baxter, my dear fellow, immediately.'

In the race for the room from which the words had

appeared to proceed, Lady Constance, getting off to a good start, beat her brother by a matter of two lengths. She was thus the first to see a sight unusual even at Blandings Castle, though strange things had happened there from time to time.

Her young guest, Miss Schoonmaker, was standing by the window, looking excited and alarmed. Her brother Clarence, pointing a gun expertly from the hip, was staring fixedly at the bed. And from under the bed, a little like a tortoise protruding from its shell, there was coming into view the spectacled head of the Efficient Baxter.

18 — Painful Scene in a Bedroom

A man who has been lying under a bed for a matter of some thirty minutes and, while there, has been compelled to listen to the sort of dialogue which accompanied a lovers' reconciliation seldom appears at his best or feels his brightest. There was fluff in Baxter's hair, dust on his clothes, and on Baxter's face a scowl of concentrated hatred of all humanity. Lord Emsworth, prepared for something pretty wild-looking, found his expectations exceeded. He tightened his grasp on the gun, and to ensure a more accurate aim raised the butt of it to his shoulder, closing one eye and allowing the other to gleam along the barrel.

'I have you covered, my dear fellow,' he said mildly.

Rupert Baxter had not yet begun to stick straws in his hair, but he seemed on the verge of that final piece of self-expression.

'Don't point that damned thing at me!'

'I shall point it at you,' replied Lord Emsworth with spirit. He was not a man to be dictated to in his own house. 'And at the slightest sign of violence . . .'

'Clarence!' It was Lady Constance who spoke. 'Put that gun down.'

'Certainly not.'

'Clarence!'

'Oh, all right.'

'And now, Mr Baxter,' said Lady Constance, proceeding to dominate the scene in her masterly way. 'I am sure you can explain.'

Her agitation had passed. It was not in this strong woman to remain agitated long. She had been badly

shaken, but her faith in her idol still held good.
Remarkable as his behaviour might appear, she was sure
that he could account for it in a perfectly satisfactory
manner.

Baxter did not speak. His silence gave Lord Emsworth
the opportunity of advancing his own views.

'Explain?' He spoke petulantly, for he resented the
way in which his sister had thrust him from the centre
of the stage. 'What on earth is there to explain? The
thing's obvious.'

'Can't say I've quite got to the bottom of it,'
murmured the Hon. Galahad. 'Fellow under bed. Why?
Why under bed? Why here at all?'

Lord Emsworth hesitated. He was a kind-hearted
man, and he felt that what he had to say would be better
said in Baxter's absence. However, there seemed no way
out of it, so he proceeded.

'My dear Galahad, think!'

'Eh?'

'That flower-pot affair. You remember?'

'Oh!' Understanding shone in the Hon. Galahad's
monocle. 'You mean . . . ?'

'Exactly.'

'Yes, yes. Of course. Subject to these attacks, you
mean?'

'Precisely.'

This was not the first time Lady Constance Keeble
had had the opportunity of hearing a theory ventilated
by her brothers which she found detestable. She flushed
brightly.

'Clarence!'

'My dear?'

'Kindly stop talking in that offensive way.'

'God bless my soul!' Lord Emsworth was stung. 'I like
that. What have I said that is offensive?'

'You know perfectly well.'

'If you mean that I was reminding Galahad in the

most delicate way that poor Baxter here is not quite . . .'

'Clarence!'

'All very well to say "Clarence!" like that. You know yourself he isn't right in the head. Didn't he throw flower-pots at me? Didn't he leap out of the window this very afternoon? Didn't he try to make me think that Beach . . .'

Baxter interrupted. There were certain matters on which he considered silence best, but this was one on which he could speak freely.

'Lord Emsworth!'

'Eh?'

'It has now come to my knowledge that Beach was not the prime mover in the theft of your pig. But I have ascertained that he was an accessory.'

'A what?'

'He helped,' said Baxter, grinding his teeth a little. 'The man who committed the actual theft was your nephew Ronald.'

Lord Emsworth turned to his sister with a triumphant gesture, like one who has been vindicated.

'There! Now perhaps you'll say he's not potty? It won't do, Baxter, my dear fellow,' he went on, waggling a reproachful gun at his late employee. 'You really mustn't excite yourself by making up these stories.'

'Bad for the blood-pressure,' agreed the Hon. Galahad.

'The Empress was found this evening in your caravan,' said Lord Emsworth.

'What!'

'In your caravan. Where you put her when you stole her. And, bless my soul,' said Lord Emsworth, with a start, 'I must be going and seeing that she is put back in her sty. I must find Pirbright. I must . . .'

'In my caravan?' Baxter passed a feverish hand across his dust-stained forehead. Illumination came to him. 'Then that's what that fellow Carmody did with the animal!'

Lord Emsworth had had enough of this. Empress of Blandings was waiting for him. Counting the minutes to that holy reunion, he chafed at having to stand here listening to these wild ravings.

'First Beach, then Ronald, then Carmody! You'll be saying I stole her next, or Galahad here, or my sister Constance. Baxter, my dear fellow, we aren't blaming you. Please don't think that. We quite see how it is. You will overwork yourself, and, of course, nature demands the penalty. I wish you would go quietly to your room, my dear fellow, and lie down. All this must be very bad for you.'

Lady Constance intervened. Her eye was aflame, and she spoke like Cleopatra telling an Ethiopian slave where he got off.

'Clarence, will you kindly use whatever slight intelligence you may possess? The theft of your pig is one of the most trivial and unimportant things that ever happened in this world, and I consider the fuss that has been made about it quite revolting. But whoever stole the wretched animal . . .'

Lord Emsworth blenched. He stared as if wondering if he had heard aright.

'. . . and wherever it has been found, it was certainly not Mr Baxter who stole it. It is, as Mr Baxter says, much more likely to have been a young man like Mr Carmody. There is a certain type of young man, I believe, to which Mr Carmody belongs, which considers practical joking amusing. Do ask yourself, Clarence, and try to answer the question as reasonably as is possible for a man of your mental calibre: What earthly motive would Mr Baxter have for coming to Blandings Castle and stealing pigs?'

It may have been the feel of the gun in his hand which awoke in Lord Emsworth old memories of dashing days with the Shropshire Yeomanry and lent him some of the hot spirit of his vanished youth. The

fact remains that he did not wilt beneath his sister's
dominating eye. He met it boldly, and boldly answered
back.

'And ask yourself, Constance,' he said, 'what earthly
motive Mr Baxter has for anything he does.'

'Yes,' said the Hon. Galahad loyally. 'What motive
had our friend Baxter for coming to Blandings Castle and
scaring girls stiff by hiding under beds?'

Lady Constance gulped. They had found the weak
spot in her defences. She turned to the man who she still
hoped could deal efficiently with this attack.

'Mr Baxter!' she said, as if she were calling on him for
an after-dinner speech.

But Rupert Baxter had had no dinner. And it was
perhaps this that turned the scale. Quite suddenly there
descended on him a frenzied desire to be out of this, cost
what it might. An hour before, half an hour before, even
five minutes before, his tongue had been tied by a still
lingering hope that he might yet find his way back to
Blandings Castle in the capacity of private secretary to
the Earl of Emsworth. Now, he felt that he would not
accept that post, were it offered to him on bended
knee.

A sudden overpowering hatred of Blandings Castle
and all it contained gripped the Efficient Baxter. He
marvelled that he had ever wanted to come back. He
held at the present moment the well-paid and
responsible position of secretary and adviser to J. Horace
Jevons, the American millionaire, a man who not only
treated him with an obsequiousness and respect which
were balm to his soul, but also gave him such sound
advice on the investment of money that already he had
trebled his savings. And it was this golden-hearted
Chicagoan whom he had been thinking of deserting,
purely to satisfy some obscure sentiment which urged
him to return to a house which, he now saw, he loathed

as few houses have been loathed since human beings left off living in caves.

His eyes flashed through their lenses. His mouth tightened.

'I will explain!'

'I knew you would have an explanation,' cried Lady Constance.

'I have. A very simple one.'

'And short, I hope?' asked Lord Emsworth, restless. He was aching to have done with all this talk and discussion and to be with his pig once more. To think of the Empress languishing in a beastly caravan was agony to him.

'Quite short,' said Rupert Baxter.

The only person in the room who so far had remained entirely outside this rather painful scene was Sue. She had looked on from her place by the window, an innocent bystander. She now found herself drawn abruptly into the maëlstrom of the debate. Baxter's spectacles were raking her from head to foot, and he had pointed at her with an accusing forefinger.

'I came to this room, he said, 'to try to recover a letter which I had written to this lady who calls herself Miss Schoonmaker.'

'Of course she calls herself Miss Schoonmaker,' said Lord Emsworth, reluctantly dragging his thoughts from the Empress. 'It's her name, my dear fellow. That,' he explained gently, 'is why she calls herself Miss Schoonmaker. God bless my soul!' he said, unable to restrain a sudden spurt of irritability. 'If a girl's name is Schoonmaker, naturally she calls herself Miss Schoon-maker.'

'Yes, if it is. But hers is not. It is Brown.'

'Listen, my dear fellow,' said Lord Emsworth soothingly. 'You are only exciting yourself by going on like this. Probably doing yourself a great deal of harm.

Now, what I suggest is, that you go to your room and put a cool compress on your forehead and lie down and take a good rest. I will send Beach up to you with some nice bread-and-milk.'

'Rum and milk,' amended the Hon. Galahad. 'It's the only thing. I knew a fellow in the year '97 who was subject to these spells – you probably remember him, Clarence. Bellamy. Barmy Bellamy we used to call him – and whenever . . .'

'Her name is Brown!' repeated Baxter, his voice soaring in a hysterical crescendo. 'Sue Brown. She is a chorus-girl at the Regal Theatre in London. And she is apparently engaged to be married to your nephew Ronald.'

Lady Constance uttered a cry. Lord Emsworth expressed his feelings with a couple of tuts. The Hon. Galahad alone was silent. He caught Sue's eye, and there was concern in his gaze.

'I overheard Beach saying so in this very room. He said he had had the information from Mr Pilbeam. I imagine it to be accurate. But in any case, I can tell you this much. Whoever she is, she is an impostor who has come here under a false name. While I was in the smoking-room some time back a telegram came through on the telephone from Market Blandings. It was signed Myra Schoonmaker, and it had been handed in in Paris this afternoon. That is all I have to say,' concluded Baxter. 'I will now leave you, and I sincerely hope I shall never set eyes on any of you again. Good evening!'

His spectacles glinting coldly, he strode from the room and in the doorway collided with Ronnie, who was entering.

'Can't you look where you're going?' he asked.

'Eh?' said Ronnie.

'Clumsy idiot!' said the Efficient Baxter, and was gone.

In the room he had left, Lady Constance Keeble had

become a stony figure of menace. She was not at ordinary times a particularly tall woman, but she seemed now to tower like something vast and awful: and Sue quailed before her.

'Ronnie!' cried Sue weakly.

It was the cry of the female in distress, calling to her mate. Just so in prehistoric days must Sue's cavewoman ancestress have cried to the man behind the club when suddenly cornered by the sabre-toothed tiger which Lady Constance Keeble so closely resembled.

'Ronnie!'

'What's all this?' asked the last of the Fishes.

He was breathing rather quickly, for the going had been fast. Pilbeam, once out in the open, had shown astonishing form at the short sprint. He had shaken off Ronnie's challenge twenty yards down the drive, and plunged into a convenient shrubbery, and Ronnie, giving up the pursuit, had come back to Sue's room to report. It occasioned him some surprise to find that in his absence it had become the scene of some sort of public meeting.

'What's all this?' he said, addressing that meeting.

Lady Constance wheeled round upon him.

'Ronald, who is this girl?'

'Eh?' Ronnie was conscious of a certain uneasiness, but he did his best. He did not like his aunt's looks, but then he never had. Something was evidently up, but it might be that airy nonchalance would save the day. 'You know her, don't you? Miss Schoonmaker? Met her with me in London.'

'Is her name Brown? And is she a chorus-girl?'

'Why, yes,' admitted Ronnie. It was a bombshell, but Eton and Cambridge stood it well. 'Why, yes,' he said, 'as a matter of fact, that's right.'

Words seemed to fail Lady Constance. Judging from the expression on her face this was just as well.

'I'd been meaning to tell you about that,' said Ronnie. 'We're engaged.'

Lady Constance recovered herself sufficiently to find one word.

'Clarence!'

'Eh?' said Lord Emsworth. His thoughts had been wandering.

'You heard?'

'Heard what?'

Beyond the stage of turbulent emotion, Lady Constance had become suddenly calm and icy.

'If you have not been sufficiently interested to listen,' she said, 'I may inform you that Ronald has just announced his intention of marrying a chorus-girl.'

'Oh, ah?' said Lord Emsworth. Would a man of Baxter's outstandingly unbalanced intellect, he was wondering, have remembered to feed the Empress regularly? The thought was like a spear quivering in his heart. He edged in agitation towards the door, and had reached it when he perceived that his sister had not yet finished talking to him.

'So that is all the comment you have to make, is it?'

'Eh? What about?'

'The point I have been endeavouring to make you understand,' went on Lady Constance, with laborious politeness, 'is that your nephew Ronald has announced his intention of marrying into the Regal Theatre chorus.'

'Who?'

'Ronald. This is Ronald. He is anxious to marry Miss Brown, a chorus-girl. This is Miss Brown.'

'How do you do?' said Lord Emsworth. He might be vague, but he had the manners of the old school.

Ronnie interposed. The time had come to play the ace of trumps.

'She isn't an ordinary chorus-girl.'

'From the fact of her coming to Blandings Castle under a false name,' said Lady Constance, 'I imagine not. It shows unusual enterprise.'

'What I mean,' continued Ronnie, 'is, I know what a

bally snob you are, Aunt Constance – no offence, but
you know what I mean – keen on birth and family and
all that sort of rot . . . well, what I'm driving at is that
Sue's father was in the Guards.'

'A private? Or a corporal?'

'Captain. A fellow named . . .'

'Cotterleigh,' said Sue in a small voice.

'Cotterleigh,' said Ronnie.

'Cotterleigh!'

It was the Hon. Galahad who had spoken. He was
staring at Sue open-mouthed.

'Cotterleigh? Not Jack Cotterleigh?'

'I don't know whether it was Jack Cotterleigh,' said
Ronnie. 'The point I'm making is that it was Cotterleigh
and that he was in the Irish Guards.'

The Hon. Galahad was still staring at Sue.

'My dear,' he cried, and there was an odd sharpness in
his voice, 'was your mother Dolly Henderson, who used
to be a Serio at the old Oxford and the Tivoli?'

Not for the first time Ronald Fish was conscious of a
feeling that his Uncle Galahad ought to be in some kind
of a home. He would drag in Dolly Henderson! He would
stress the Dolly Henderson note at just this point in the
proceedings! He would spoil the whole thing by calling
attention to the Dolly Henderson aspect of the matter,
just when it was vital to stick to the Cotterleigh, the
whole Cotterleigh, and nothing but the Cotterleigh.
Ronnie sighed wearily. Padded cells, he felt, had been
invented specially for the Uncle Galahads of this world,
and the Uncle Galahads, he considered, ought never to
be permitted to roam about outside them.

'Yes,' said Sue. 'She was.'

The Hon. Galahad was advancing on her with
outstretched hands. He looked like some father in
melodrama welcoming the prodigal daughter.

'Well, I'm dashed!' he said. He repeated three times
that he was in this condition. He seized Sue's limp paws

523

and squeezed them fondly. 'I've been trying to think all this while who it was that you reminded me of, my dear girl. Do you know that in the years '96, '97, and '98, I was madly in love with your mother myself? Do you know that if my infernal family hadn't shipped me off to South Africa I would certainly have married her? Fact, I assure you. But they got behind me and shoved me on to the boat, and when I came back I found that young Cotterleigh had cut me out. Well.'

It was a scene which some people would have considered touching. Lady Constance Keeble was not one of them.

'Never mind about that now, Galahad,' she said. 'The point is . . .'

'The point is,' retorted the Hon. Galahad warmly, 'that that young Fish there wants to marry Dolly Henderson's daughter, and I'm for it. And I hope, Clarence, that you'll have some sense for once in your life and back them up like a sportsman.'

'Eh?' said the ninth Earl. His thoughts had once more been wandering. Even assuming that Baxter had fed the Empress, would he have given her the right sort of food and enough of it?

'You see for yourself what a splendid girl she is.'

'Who?'

'This girl.'

'Charming,' agreed Lord Emsworth courteously, and returned to his meditations.

'Clarence!' cried Lady Constance, jerking him out of them.

'Eh?'

'You are not to consent to this marriage.'

'Who says so?'

'I say so. And think what Julia will say.'

She could not have advanced a more impressive argument. In this chronicle the Lady Julia Fish, relict of the late Major-General Sir Miles Fish, CBO of the

Brigade of Guards, has made no appearance. We, therefore, know nothing of her compelling eye, her dominant chin, her determined mouth, and her voice, which, at certain times – as, for example, when rebuking a brother – could raise blisters on a sensitive skin. Lord Emsworth was aware of all these things. He had had experience of them from boyhood. His idea of happiness was to be where Lady Julia Fish was not. And the thought of her coming down to Blandings Castle and tackling him in his library about this business froze him to the marrow. It had been his amiable intention until this moment to do whatever the majority of those present wanted him to do. But now he hesitated.

'You think Julia wouldn't like it?'

'Of course Julia would not like it.'

'Julia's an ass,' said the Hon. Galahad.

Lord Emsworth considered this statement, and was inclined to agree with it. But it did not alter the main point.

'You think she would make herself unpleasant about it?'

'I do.'

'In that case . . .' Lord Emsworth paused. Then a strange soft light came into his eyes. 'Well, see you all later,' he said. 'I'm going down to look at my pig.'

His departure was so abrupt that it took Lady Constance momentarily by surprise, and he was out of the room and well down the corridor before she could recover herself sufficiently to act. Then she, too, hurried out. They could hear her voice diminishing down the stairs. It was calling 'Clarence!'

The Hon. Galahad turned to Sue. His manner was brisk, yet soothing.

'A shame to inflict these fine old English family rows on a visitor,' he said, patting her shoulder as one who, if things had broken right and there had not been a regular service of boats to South Africa in the nineties, might

525

have been her father. 'What you need, my dear, is a little rest and quiet. Come along, Ronald, we'll leave you. The place to continue this discussion is somewhere outside this room. Cheer up, my dear. Everything may come out all right yet.'

Sue shook her head.

'It's no good,' she said hopelessly.

'Don't you be too sure,' said the Hon. Galahad.

'I'll jolly well tell you one thing,' said Ronnie. 'I'm going to marry you, whatever happens. And that's that. Good heavens! I can work, can't I?'

'What at?' asked the Hon. Galahad.

'What at? Why – er – why, at anything.'

'The market value of any member of this family,' said the Hon. Galahad, who harboured no illusions about his nearest and dearest, 'is about threepence-ha-penny per annum. No! What we've got to do is get round old Clarence somehow, and that means talk and argument, which had better take place elsewhere. Come along, my boy. You never know your luck. I've seen stickier things than this come out right in my time.'

19 — Gally Takes Matters in Hand

Sue stood on the balcony, looking out into the night.
Velvet darkness shrouded the world, and from the heart
of it came the murmur of rustling trees and the clean,
sweet smell of earth and flowers. A little breeze had
sprung up, stirring the ivy at her side. Somewhere in it a
bird was chirping drowsily, and in the distance sounded
the tinkle of running water.

She sighed. It was a night made for happiness. And
she was quite sure now that happiness was not for her.

A footstep sounded behind her, and she turned
eagerly.

'Ronnie?'

It was the voice of the Hon. Galahad Threepwood
that answered.

'Only me, I'm afraid, my dear. May I come on to your
balcony? God bless my soul, as Clarence would say,
what a wonderful night!'

'Yes,' said Sue doubtfully.

'You don't think so.'

'Oh, yes.'

'I bet you don't. I know I didn't, that night when my
old father put his foot down and told me I was leaving
for South Africa on the next boat. Just such a night as
this it was, I remember.' He rested his arms on the
parapet. 'I never saw your mother after she was married,'
he said.

'No?'

'No. She left the stage and . . . Oh, well, I was rather
busy at the time – lot of heavy drinking to do, and so
forth – and somehow we never met. The next thing I

heard – two or three years ago – was that she was dead.
You're very like her, my dear. Can't think why I didn't
spot the resemblance right away.'

He became silent. Sue did not speak. She slid her
hand under his arm. It was all that there seemed to do. A
corncrake began to call monotonously in the darkness.

'That means rain,' said the Hon. Galahad. 'Or not. I
forget which. Did you ever hear your mother sing that
song . . . ? No, you wouldn't. Before your time. About
young Ronald,' he said, abruptly.

'What about him?'

'Fond of him?'

'Yes.'

'I mean really fond?'

'Yes.'

'How fond?'

Sue leaned out over the parapet. At the foot of the
wall beneath her Percy Pilbeam, who had been peering
out of a bush, popped his head back again. For the
detective, possibly remembering with his subconscious
mind stories heard in childhood of Bruce and the spider,
had refused to admit defeat and had returned by devious
ways to the scene of his disaster. Five hundred pounds is
a lot of money, and Percy Pilbeam was not going to be
deterred from attempting to earn it by the fact that at his
last essay he had only just succeeded in escaping with
his life. The influence of his potations had worn off to
some extent, and he was his calm, keen self again. It was
his intention to lurk in these bushes till the small hours,
if need be, and then to attack the water-spout again in
the Garden Room where the manuscript of the Hon.
Galahad's Reminiscences lay. You cannot be a good
detective if you are easily discouraged.

'I can't put it into words,' said Sue.

'Try.'

'No. Everything you say straight out about the way
you feel about anybody always sounds silly. Besides, to

you Ronnie isn't the sort of man you could understand
anyone raving about. You look on him just as something
quite ordinary.'

'If that,' said the Hon. Galahad critically.

'Yes, if that. Whereas to me he's something . . . rather
special. In fact, if you really want to know how I feel
about Ronnie, he's the whole world to me. There! I told
you it would sound silly. It's like something out of a
song, isn't it? I've worked in the chorus of that sort of
song a hundred times. Two steps left, two steps right,
kick, smile, both hands on heart – because he's all the
wo-orld to me-ee! You can laugh if you like.'

There was a momentary pause.

'I'm not laughing,' said the Hon. Galahad. 'My dear, I
only wanted to find out if you really cared for that young
Fish . . .'

'I wish you wouldn't call him "that young Fish".'

'I'm sorry, my dear. It seems to describe him so
neatly. Well, I just wanted to be quite sure you really
were fond of him, because . . .'

'Well?'

'Well, because I've just fixed it all up.'

She clutched at the parapet.

'What!'

'Oh, yes,' said the Hon. Galahad. 'It's all settled. I
don't say that you can actually count on an
aunt-in-law's embrace from my sister Constance – in
fact, if I were you, I wouldn't risk it. She might bite you
– but, apart from that, everything's all right. The
wedding bells will ring out. Your young man's in the
garden somewhere. You had better go and find him and
tell him the news. He'll be interested.'

'But . . . but . . .'

Sue was clutching his arm. A wild impulse was upon
her to shout and sob. She had no doubts now as to the
beauty of the night.

'But . . . how? Why? What has happened?'

'Well . . . You'll admit I might have married your
mother?'

'Yes.'

'Which makes me a sort of honorary father to you.'

'Yes.'

'In which capacity, my dear, your interests are mine.
More than mine, in fact. So what I did was to make your
happiness the *Price of the Papers*. Ever see that play?
No, before your time. It ran at the Adelphi before you
were born. There was a scene where . . .'

'What do you mean?'

The Hon. Galahad hesitated a moment.

'Well, the fact of the matter is, my dear, knowing how
strongly my sister Constance has always felt on the
subject of those Reminiscences of mine, I went to her
and put it to her squarely. "Clarence," I said to her, "is
not the sort of man to make any objection to anyone
marrying anybody, so long as he isn't expected to attend
the wedding. You're the real obstacle," I said. "You and
Julia. And if you come round, you can talk Julia over in
five minutes. You know she relies on your judgement."
And then I said that, if she gave up acting like a
barbed-wire entanglement in the path of true love, I
would undertake not to publish the Reminiscences.'

Sue clung to his arm. She could find no words.

Percy Pilbeam, who, for the night was very still, had
heard all, could have found many. Nothing but the
delicate nature of his present situation kept him from
uttering them, and that only just. To Percy Pilbeam it
was as if he had seen five hundred pounds flutter from
his grasp like a vanishing blue bird. He raged dumbly. In
all London and the Home Counties there were few men
who liked five hundred pounds better than P. Frobisher
Pilbeam.

'Oh!' said Sue. Nothing more. Her feelings were too
deep. She hugged his arm. 'Oh!' she said, and again 'Oh!'

She found herself crying, and was not ashamed.

'Now, come!' said the Hon. Galahad protestingly. 'Nothing so very extraordinary in that, was there? Nothing so exceedingly remarkable in one pal helping another?'

'I don't know what to say.'

'Then don't say it,' said the Hon. Galahad, much relieved. 'Why, bless you, I don't care whether the damned things are published or not. At least . . . No, certainly I don't . . . Only cause a lot of unpleasantness. Besides, I'll leave the dashed book to the Nation and have it published in a hundred years and become the Pepys of the future, what? Best thing that could have happened. Homage of Posterity and all that.'

'Oh!' said Sue.

The Hon. Galahad chuckled.

'It is a shame, though, that the world will have to wait a hundred years before it hears the story of young Gregory Parsloe and the prawns. Did you get to that when you were reading the thing this evening?'

'I'm afraid I didn't read very much,' said Sue. 'I was thinking of Ronnie rather a lot.'

'Oh? Well, I can tell you. You needn't wait a hundred years. It was at Ascot, the year Martingale won the Gold Cup . . .'

Down below, Percy Pilbeam rose from his bush. He did not care now if he were seen. He was still a guest in this hole of a castle, and if a guest cannot pop in and out of bushes if he likes, where does British hospitality come in? It was his intention to shake the dust of Blandings off his feet, to pass the night at the Emsworth Arms, and on the morrow to return to London, where he was appreciated.

'Well, my dear, it was like this. Young Parsloe . . .'

Percy Pilbeam did not linger. The story of the prawns meant nothing to him. He turned away, and the summer night swallowed him. Somewhere in the darkness an owl hooted. It seemed to Pilbeam that there was derision in the sound. He frowned. His teeth came together with a click.

If he could have found it, he would have had a word with that owl.

Heavy Weather

I

Sunshine pierced the haze that enveloped London. It came down Fleet Street, turned to the right, stopped at the premises of the Mammoth Publishing Company, and, entering through an upper window, beamed pleasantly upon Lord Tilbury, founder and proprietor of that vast factory of popular literature, as he sat reading the batch of weekly papers which his secretary had placed on the desk for his inspection. Among the secrets of this great man's success was the fact that he kept a personal eye on all the firm's products.

Considering what a pleasant rarity sunshine in London is, one might have expected the man behind the Mammoth to beam back. Instead, he merely pressed the buzzer. His secretary appeared. He pointed silently. The secretary drew the shade, and the sunshine, having called without an appointment, was excluded.

'I beg your pardon, Lord Tilbury . . .'

'Well?'

'A Lady Julia Fish has just rung up on the telephone.'

'Well?'

'She says she would like to see you this morning.'

Lord Tilbury frowned. He remembered Lady Julia Fish as an agreeable hotel acquaintance during his recent holiday at Biarritz. But this was Tilbury House, and at Tilbury House he did not desire the company of hotel acquaintances, however agreeable.

'Did she say what she wanted?'

'No, Lord Tilbury.'

'All right.'

The secretary withdrew. Lord Tilbury returned to his reading.

The particular periodical which had happened to come to hand was the current number of that admirable children's paper, *Tiny Tots*, and for some moments he scanned its pages with an attempt at his usual conscientious thoroughness. But it was plain that his heart was not in his work. The Adventures of Pinky, Winky, and Pop in Slumberland made little impression upon him. He passed on to a thoughtful article by Laura J. Smedley on what a wee girlie can do to help mother, but it was evident that for once Laura J. had failed to grip. Presently with a grunt he threw the paper down and for the third time since it had arrived by the morning post picked up a letter which lay on the desk. He already knew it by heart, so there was no real necessity for him to read it again, but the human tendency to twist the knife in the wound is universal.

It was a brief letter. Its writer's eighteenth-century ancestors, who believed in filling their twelve sheets when they took pen in hand, would have winced at the sight of it. But for all its brevity it had ruined Lord Tilbury's day.

It ran as follows:

> Blandings Castle,
> Shropshire
> Dear Sir,
> Enclosed find cheque for the advance you paid me on those Reminiscences of mine.
> I have been thinking it over, and have decided not to publish them, after all.
> Yours truly,
> G. Threepwood

'Cor!' said Lord Tilbury, an ejaculation to which he was much addicted in times of mental stress.

He rose from his chair and began to pace the room. Always Napoleonic of aspect, being short and square and stumpy and about twenty-five pounds overweight, he looked now like a Napoleon taking his morning walk at St Helena.

And yet, oddly enough, there were men in England who would have whooped with joy at the sight of that letter. Some of them might even have gone to the length of lighting bonfires and roasting oxen whole for the tenantry about it. Those few words over that signature would have spread happiness in every county from Cumberland to Cornwall. So true is it that in this world everything depends on the point of view.

When, some months before, the news had got about that the Hon. Galahad Threepwood, brother of the Earl of Emsworth and as sprightly an old gentleman as was ever thrown out of a Victorian music-hall, was engaged in writing the recollections of his colourful career as a man about town in the nineties, the shock to the many now highly respectable members of the governing classes who in their hot youth had shared it was severe. All over the country decorous Dukes and steady Viscounts, who had once sown wild oats in the society of the young Galahad, sat quivering in their slippers at the thought of what long-cupboarded skeletons those Reminiscences might disclose.

They knew their Gally, and their imagination allowed them to picture with a crystal clearness the sort of book he would be likely to produce. It would, they felt in their ageing bones, be essentially one of those of which the critics say 'A veritable storehouse of diverting anecdote.' To not a few – Lord Emsworth's nearest neighbour, Sir Gregory Parsloe-Parsloe of Matchingham Hall, was one of them – it was as if the Recording Angel had suddenly decided to rush into print.

Lord Tilbury, however, had looked on the thing from

a different angle. He knew – no man better – what big money there was in this type of literature. The circulation of his nasty little paper, *Society Spice*, proved that. Even though Percy Pilbeam, its nasty little editor, had handed in his portfolio and gone off to start a Private Inquiry Agency, it was still a gold-mine. He had known Gally Threepwood in the old days – not intimately, but quite well enough to cause him now to hasten to acquire all rights to the story of his life, sight unseen. It seemed to him that the book could not fail to be the *succès de scandale* of the year.

Acute, therefore, as had been the consternation of the Dukes and Viscounts on learning that the dead past was about to be disinterred, it paled in comparison with that of Lord Tilbury on suddenly receiving this intimation that it was not. There is a tender spot in all great men. Achilles had his heel. With Lord Tilbury it was his pocket. He hated to see money get away from him, and out of this book of Gally Threepwood's he had been looking forward to making a small fortune.

Little wonder, then, that he mourned and was unable to concentrate on *Tiny Tots*. He was still mourning when his secretary entered bearing a slip of paper.

Name – Lady Julia Fish.   *Business* – Personal.

Lord Tilbury snorted irritably. At a time like this! 'Tell her I'm . . .'

And then there flashed into his mind a sudden recollection of something he had heard somebody say about this Lady Julia Fish. The words 'Blandings Castle' seemed to be connected with it. He turned to the desk and took up *Debrett's Peerage*, searching among the E's for 'Emsworth, Earl of'.

Yes, there it was. Lady Julia Fish had been born Lady Julia Threepwood. She was a sister of the perjured Galahad.

That altered things. Here, he perceived, was an admirable opportunity of working off some of his stored-up venom. His knowledge of life told him that the woman would not be calling unless she wanted to get something out of him. To inform her in person that she was most certainly not going to get it would be balm to his lacerated feelings.

'Ask her to come up,' he said.

Lady Julia Fish was a handsome middle-aged woman of the large blonde type, of a personality both breezy and commanding. She came into the room a few moments later like a galleon under sail, her resolute chin and her china-blue eyes proclaiming a supreme confidence in her ability to get anything she wanted out of anyone. And Lord Tilbury, having bowed stiffly, stood regarding her with a pop-eyed hostility. Even setting aside her loathsome family connections, there was a patronizing good humour about her manner which he resented. And certainly, if Lady Julia Fish's manner had a fault, it was that it resembled a little too closely that of the great lady of a village amusedly trying to make friends with the backward child of one of her tenants.

'Well, well, well,' she said, not actually patting Lord Tilbury on the head but conveying the impression that she might see fit to do so at any moment, 'you're looking very bonny. Biarritz did you good.'

Lord Tilbury, with the geniality of a trapped wolf, admitted to being in robust health.

'So this is where you get out all those jolly little papers of yours, is it? I must say I'm impressed. Quite awe-inspiring, all that ritual on the threshold. Admirals in the Swiss Navy making you fill up forms with your name and business, and small boys in buttons eyeing you as if anything you said might be used in evidence against you.'

'What *is* your business?' asked Lord Tilbury.

539

'The practical note!' said Lady Julia, with indulgent approval. 'How stimulating that is. Time is money, and all that. Quite. Well, cutting the preamble, I want a job for Ronnie.'

Lord Tilbury looked like a trapped wolf who had thought as much.

'Ronnie?' he said coldly.

'My son. Didn't you meet him at Biarritz? He was there. Small and pink.'

Lord Tilbury drew in breath for the delivery of the nasty blow.

'I regret . . .'

'I know what you're going to say. You're very crowded here. Fearful congestion, and so on. Well, Ronnie won't take up much room. And I shouldn't think he could do any actual harm to a solidly established concern like this. Surely you could let him mess about at *something*? Why, Sir Gregory Parsloe, our neighbour down in Shropshire, told me that you were employing his nephew, Monty. And while I would be the last woman to claim Ronnie is a mental giant, at least he's brighter than young Monty Bodkin.'

A quiver ran through Lord Tilbury's stocky form. This woman had unbared his secret shame. A man who prided himself on never letting himself be worked for jobs, he had had a few weeks before a brief moment of madness when, under the softening influence of a particularly good public dinner, he had yielded to the request of the banqueter on his left that he should find a place at Tilbury House for his nephew.

He had regretted the lapse next morning. He had regretted it more on seeing the nephew. And he had not ceased to regret it now.

'That,' he said tensely, 'has nothing to do with the case.'

'I don't see why. Swallowing camels and straining at gnats is what I should call it.'

'Nothing,' repeated Lord Tilbury, 'to do with the case.'

He was beginning to feel that this interview was not working out as he had anticipated. He had meant to be strong, brusque, decisive – the man of iron. And here this woman had got him arguing and explaining – almost in a position of defending himself. Like so many people who came into contact with her, he began to feel that there was something disagreeably hypnotic about Lady Julia Fish.

'But what do you want your son to work here *for*?' he asked, realizing as he spoke that a man of iron ought to have scorned to put such a question.

Lady Julia considered.

'Oh, a pittance. Whatever the dole is you give your slaves.'

Lord Tilbury made himself clearer.

'I mean, why? Has he shown any aptitude for journalism?' This seemed to amuse Lady Julia.

'My dear man,' she said, tickled by the quaint conceit, 'no member of my family has ever shown any aptitude for anything except eating and sleeping.'

'Then why do you want him to join my staff?'

'Well, primarily, to distract his mind.'

'What!'

'To distract his ... well, yes, I suppose in a loose way you could call it a mind.'

'I don't understand you.'

'Well, it's like this. The poor half-wit is trying to marry a chorus-girl, and it seemed to me that if he were safe at Tilbury House, inking his nose and getting bustled about by editors and people, it might take his mind off the tender passion.'

Lord Tilbury drew a long, deep, rasping breath. The weakness had passed. He could be strong now. This outrageous insult to the business he loved had shattered the spell which those china-blue eyes and that confident manner had been weaving about him. He spoke curtly, placing his thumbs in the armholes of his waistcoat to lend emphasis to his remarks.

'I fear you have mistaken the functions of Tilbury House, Lady Julia.'

'I beg your pardon?'

'We publish newspapers, magazines, weekly journals. We are not a Home for the Lovelorn.'

There was a brief silence.

'I see,' said Lady Julia. She looked at him inquiringly. 'You sound very stuffy,' she went on. 'Not your old merry Biarritz self at all. Did your breakfast disagree with you this morning?'

'Cor!'

'Something's the matter. Why, at Biarritz you were known as Sunny Jim.'

Lord Tilbury was ill attuned to badinage.

'Yes,' he said. 'Something is the matter. If you really wish to know, I am scarcely in a frame of mind today to go out of my way to oblige members of your family. After what has occurred.'

'What has occurred?'

'Your brother Galahad . . .' Lord Tilbury choked. 'Look at this,' he said.

He extended the letter rather in the manner of one anxious to rid himself of a snake which has somehow come into his possession. Lady Julia scrutinized it with languid interest.

'It's monstrous. Abominable. He accepted the contract, and he ought to fulfil it. At the very least, in common decency, he might have given his reasons for behaving in this utterly treacherous and unethical way. But does he? Not at all. Explanations? None. Apologies? Regrets? Oh dear, no. He merely "decides not to publish". In all my thirty years of . . .'

Lady Julia was never a very good listener.

'Odd,' she said, handing the letter back. 'My brother Galahad is a man who moves in a mysterious way his wonders to perform. A quite unaccountable mentality. I knew he was writing this book, of course, but have no notion whatever why he has had this sudden change of heart. Perhaps some Duke who doesn't want to see himself in the "Peers I Have Been Thrown Out Of Public-Houses With" chapter has been threatening to take him for a ride.'

'Cor!'

'Or some Earl with a guilty conscience. Or a Baronet. "Society Scribe Bumped Off By Baronets" – that would make a good headline for one of your papers.'

'This is not a joking matter.'

'Well, at any rate, my dear man, it's no good savaging *me*. I'm not responsible for Galahad's eccentricities. I'm simply an innocent widow-woman trying to wangle a cushy job for her only son. Coming back to which, I rather gather from what you said just now that you do not intend to set Ronnie punching the clock?'

Lord Tilbury shook from stem to stern. His eyes gleamed balefully. Nature in the raw is seldom mild.

'I absolutely and positively refuse to employ your son at Tilbury House in any capacity whatsoever.'

'Well, that's a fair answer to a fair question, and seems to close the discussion.'

Lady Julia rose.

'Too bad about Gally's little effort,' she said silkily. 'You'll lose a lot of money, won't you? There's a mint of it in a really indiscreet book of Reminiscences. They tell me that Lady Wensleydale's *Sixty Years Near The Knuckle In Mayfair*, or whatever it was called, sold a hundred thousand copies. And, knowing Gally, I'll bet he would have started remembering where old Jane Wensleydale left off. *Good* morning, Lord Tilbury. So nice to have seen you again.'

543

The door closed. The proprietor of the Mammoth sat staring before him, his agony too keen to permit him even to say 'Cor!'

2

The spasm passed. Presently life seemed to steal back to
that rigid form. It would be too much to say that Lord
Tilbury became himself, but at least he began to
function once more. Though pain and anguish rack the
brow, the world's work has to be done. Like a
convalescent reaching for his barley-water, he stretched
out a shaking hand and took up *Tiny Tots* again.

And here it would be agreeable to leave him – the
good man restoring his *morale* with refreshing draughts
at the fount of wholesome literature. But this happy
ending was not to be. Once more it was to be proved
that this was not Lord Tilbury's lucky morning. Scarcely
had he begun to read, when his eyes suddenly protruded
from their sockets, his stout body underwent a strong
convulsion, and from his parted lips there proceeded a
loud snort. It was as if a viper had sprung from between
the pages and bitten him on the chin.

And this was odd, because *Tiny Tots* is a journal not
as a rule provocative of violent expressions of feeling.
Ably edited by that well-known writer of tales for the
young, the Rev. Aubrey Sellick, it strives always to take
the sane middle course. Its editorial page, in particular,
is a model of non-partisan moderation. And yet,
amazingly, it was this same editorial page which had
just made Lord Tilbury's blood-pressure hit a new
high.

It occurred to him that mental strain might have
affected his eyesight. He blinked and took another look.

No, there it was, just as before.

UNCLE WOGGLY TO HIS CHICKS

Well, chickabiddies, how are you all? Minding what Nursie says and eating your spinach like good little men? That's right. I know the stuff tastes like a motorman's glove, but they say there's iron in it, and that's what puts hair on the chest.

Lord Tilbury, having taken time out to make a noise like a leaking siphon, resumed his reading.

Well, now let's get down to it. This week, my dear little souls, Uncle Woggly is going to put you on to a good thing. We all want to make a spot of easy money these hard times don't we? Well, here's the lowdown, straight from the horse's mouth. All you have to do is to get hold of some mug and lure him into betting that a quart whisky bottle holds a quart of whisky.

Sounds rummy, what? I mean, that's what you would naturally think it would hold. So does the mug. But it isn't. It's really more, and I'll tell you why.

First you fill the bottle. This gives you your quart. Then you shove the cork in. And then – follow me closely here – you turn the bottle upside down and you'll find there's a sort of bulging-in part at the bottom. Well, slosh some whisky into that, and there you are. Because the bot. is now holding more than a quart and you scoop the stakes.

I have to acknowledge a sweet little letter from Frankie Kendon (Hendon) about his canary which goes tweet-tweet-tweet. Also one from Muriel Poot (Stow-in-the-Wold), who is going to lose her shirt if she ever bets anyone she knows how to spell 'tortoise' . . .

Lord Tilbury had read enough. There was some good stuff further on about Willy Waters (Ponders End) and his cat Miggles, but he did not wait for it. He pressed the buzzer emotionally.

'*Tots!*' he cried, choking. '*Tiny Tots!* Who is editing *Tiny Tots* now?'

'Mr Sellick is the regular editor, Lord Tilbury,' replied his secretary, who knew everything and wore horn-rimmed spectacles to prove it, 'but he is away on his vacation. In his absence, the assistant editor is in charge of the paper, Mr Bodkin.'

'Bodkin!'

So loud was Lord Tilbury's voice and so sharply did his eyes bulge that the secretary recoiled a step, as if something had hit her.

'That popinjay!' said Lord Tilbury, in a strange, low, grating voice. 'I might have guessed it. I might have foreseen something like this. Send Mr Bodkin here at once.'

It was a judgement, he felt. This was what came of going to public dinners and allowing yourself to depart from the principles of a lifetime. One false step, one moment of weakness when there were wheedling snakes of Baronets at your elbow, and what a harvest, what a reckoning!

He leaned back in his chair, tapping the desk with a paper-knife. He had just broken this, when there was a knock at the door and his young subordinate entered.

'Good morning, good morning, good morning,' said the latter affably. 'Want to see me about something?'

Monty Bodkin was rather an attractive popinjay, as popinjays go. He was tall and slender and lissom, and many people considered him quite good-looking. But not Lord Tilbury. He had disapproved of his appearance from their first meeting, thinking him much too well dressed, much too carefully groomed, and much too much like what he actually was, a member in good standing of the Drones Club. The proprietor of the Mammoth Publishing Company could not have put into words his ideal of a young journalist, but it would have been something rather shaggy, preferably with spectacles,

certainly not wearing spats. And while Monty Bodkin
was not actually spatted at the moment, there did
undoubtedly hover about him a sort of spat aura.

'Ha!' said Lord Tilbury, sighting him.

He stared bleakly. His demeanour now was that of a
Napoleon who, suffering from toothache, sees his way to
taking it out on one of his minor Marshals.

'Come in,' he growled.

'Shut the door,' he grunted.

'And don't grin like that,' he snarled. 'What the devil
are you grinning for?'

The words were proof of the deeps of
misunderstanding which yawned between the assistant
editor of *Tiny Tots* and himself. Certainly something
was splitting Monty Bodkin's face in a rather noticeable
manner, but the latter could have taken his oath it was
an ingratiating smile. He had intended it for an
ingratiating smile, and unless something had gone
extremely wrong with the works in the process of
assembling it, that is what it should have come out
as.

However, being a sweet-tempered popinjay and
always anxious to oblige, he switched it off. He was
feeling a little puzzled. The atmosphere seemed to him
to lack chumminess, and he was at a loss to account for
it.

'Nice day,' he observed tentatively.

'Never mind the day.'

'Right ho. Heard from Uncle Gregory lately?'

'Never mind your Uncle Gregory.'

'Right ho.'

'And don't say "Right ho."'

'Right ho,' said Monty dutifully.

'Read this.'

Monty took the proffered copy of *Tots*.

'You want me to read aloud to you?' he said, feeling
that this was matier.

'You need not trouble. I have already seen the passage in question. Here, where I am pointing.'

'Oh, ah, yes. Uncle Woggly. Right ho.'

'Will you stop saying "Right ho"! . . . Well?'

'Eh?'

'You wrote that, I take it?'

'Oh, rather.'

'Cor!'

Monty was now definitely perplexed. He could conceal it from himself no longer that there was ill-will in the air. Lord Tilbury's had never been an elfin personality, but he had always been a good deal more winsome than this.

A possible solution of his employer's emotion occurred to him.

'You aren't worrying about it not being accurate, are you? Because that's quite all right. I had it on the highest authority – from an old boy called Galahad Threepwood. Lord Emsworth's brother. You wouldn't have heard of him, of course, but he was a great lad about the metropolis at one time, and you can rely absolutely on anything he says about whisky bottles.'

He broke off, puzzled once more. He could not understand what had caused his companion to strike the desk in that violent manner.

'What the devil do you mean, you wretched imbecile,' demanded Lord Tilbury, speaking a little indistinctly, for he was sucking his fist, 'by putting stuff of this sort in *Tiny Tots*?'

'You don't like it?' said Monty groping.

'How do you suppose the mothers who read that drivel to their children will feel?'

Monty was concerned. This opened up a new line of thought.

'Wrong tone, do you think?'

'Mugs . . . Betting . . . Whisky . . . You have probably lost us ten thousand subscribers.'

'I say, that never occurred to me. Yes, by Jove, I see what you mean now. Unfortunate slip, what? May quite easily cause alarm and despondency. Yes, yes, yes, to be sure. Oh, yes, indeed. Well, I can only say I'm sorry.'

'You can not only say you are sorry,' said Lord Tilbury, correcting this view, 'you can go to the cashier, draw a month's salary, get to blazes out of here, and never let me see your face in the building again.'

Monty's concern increased.

'But this sounds like the sack. Don't tell me that what you are hinting at is the sack?'

Speech failed Lord Tilbury. He jerked his thumb doorwards. And such was the magic of his personality that Monty found himself a moment later with his fingers on the handle. Its cold hardness seemed to wake him from a trance. He halted, making a sort of Custer's Last Stand.

'Reflect!' he said.

Lord Tilbury busied himself with his papers.

'Uncle Gregory won't like this,' said Monty reproachfully.

Lord Tilbury quivered for an instant as if somebody had stuck a bradawl into him, but preserved an aloof silence.

'Well, he won't, you know.' Monty had no wish to be severe, but he felt compelled to point this out. 'He takes all the trouble to get me a job, I mean to say, and now this happens. Oh, no, don't deceive yourself, Uncle Gregory will be vexed.'

'Get out,' said Lord Tilbury.

Monty fondled the door handle for a space, marshalling his thoughts. He had that to say which he rather fancied would melt the other's heart a goodish bit, but he was not quite sure how to begin.

'Haven't you gone?' said Lord Tilbury.

Monty reassured him.

'Not yet. The fact is, there's something I rather wanted to call to your attention. You don't know it, but for private and personal reasons I particularly want to hold this *Tiny Tots* job for a year. There are wheels within wheels. It's a sort of bet, as a matter of fact. Have you ever met a girl called Gertrude Butterwick? . . . However, it's a long story and I won't bother you with it now. But you can take it from me that there definitely are wheels within wheels and unless I continue in your employment, till somewhere around the middle of next June, my life will be a blank and all my hopes and dreams shattered. So how about it? Would you, on second thoughts, taking this into consideration, feel disposed to postpone the rash act till then? If you've any doubts as to my doing my bit, dismiss them. I would work like the dickens. First at the office, last to come away, and solid, selfless service all the time – no clock-watching, no folding of the hands in . . .'

'Get OUT!' said Lord Tilbury.

There was a silence.

'You will not reconsider?'

'No.'

'You are not to be moved?'

'No.'

Monty Bodkin drew himself up.

'Oh, right ho,' he said stiffly. 'Now we know where we are. Now we know where we stand. If that is the attitude you take, I suppose there is nothing to be done about it. Since you have no heart, no sympathy, no feeling, no bowels – of compassion, I mean – I have no alternative but to shove off. I have only two things to say to you, Lord Tilbury. One is that you have ruined a man's life. The other is Pip-pip.'

He passed from the room, erect and dignified, like some young aristocrat of the French Revolution stepping into the tumbril. Lord Tilbury's secretary removed her

ear from the door just in time to avoid a nasty
flesh-wound.

A month's salary in his pocket, chagrin in his heart, and
in his soul that urgent desire for a quick one which
comes to young men at times like this, Monty Bodkin
stood hesitating in the doorway of Tilbury House. And
Fate, watching him, found itself compelled to do a bit of
swift thinking.

'Now, shall I,' mused Fate, 'send this sufferer to have
his snort at the Bunch of Grapes round the corner? Or
shall I put him in a taxi and shoot him off to the Drones
Club, where he will meet his old friend, Hugo Carmody,
with momentous results?'

It was no light decision to have to make. Much
depended on it. It would affect the destinies of Ronald
Fish and his betrothed, Sue Brown; of Clarence, ninth
Earl of Emsworth, and his pig, Empress of Blandings; of
Lord Tilbury, of the Mammoth Publishing Company; of
Sir Gregory Parsloe-Parsloe, Bart, of Matchingham Hall;
and of that unpleasant little man, Percy Pilbeam, late
editor of *Society Spice* and now proprietor of the Argus
Private Inquiry Agency.

'H'm!' said Fate.

'Oh, dash it!' said Fate. 'Let's make it the Drones.'

And so it came about that Monty, some twenty
minutes later, was seated in the club smoking-room,
side by side with young Mr Carmody, sipping a Lizard's
Breath and relating the story of his shattered career.

'Turfed out!' he concluded, with a bitter laugh.
'Driven into the snow! Well, that's Life, I suppose.'

Hugo Carmody was not unsympathetic, but he had a
fair mind and privately considered that Lord Tilbury had
acted with great good sense. Obviously, felt Hugo, the
whole secret of success, if you were running a business
and had Monty Bodkin working for you, was to get rid of
him at the earliest possible moment.

'Tough,' he said. 'Still, what do you want with a job? You're rolling in the stuff.'

Monty admitted that he was not unblessed with this world's goods, but said that that was not the point.

'Money's got nothing to do with it. It was holding down the job that mattered. There are wheels within wheels. I'll tell you all about it, shall I?'

'No thanks.'

'Just as you like. Another spot? Waiter, two more spots.'

'Anyway,' said Hugo, with a kindly desire to point out the bright side. 'If you hadn't got fired now, you'd have been bound to have got fired sooner or later, what? I mean to say, I don't see how you could ever have been much good to a concern like the Mammoth, unless they had used you as a paperweight. And I'll bet you were all wrong about that whisky bottle.'

Monty's spirit had been a good deal reduced by recent happenings, but he could not let this pass.

'I'll bet I wasn't,' he said warmly. 'I had the information straight from an authoritative source. Lord Emsworth's brother, old Gally Threepwood. My Uncle Gregory's place in Shropshire is only about a couple of miles from Blandings, and when I was a kid I used to be popping in and out all the time, and one day old Gally drew me aside . . .'

Hugo was interested.

'Your Uncle Gregory? Would that be Sir Gregory Parsloe?'

'Yes.'

'Well, well. I never knew you were Parsloe's nephew.'

'Why, have you met him?'

'Of course I've met him. I've been down at Blandings all the summer.'

'Not really? Oh, but, of course, I was forgetting. You and Ronnie Fish have always been pals, haven't you? You were staying with him?'

'No. I was secretarying for old Emsworth. A nice, soft job. I've chucked it now.'

'I thought a fellow called Baxter was his secretary.'

'My dear chap, you aren't abreast. Baxter left ages ago.'

Monty sighed, as a young man will who is made to realize that time is passing.

'Yes,' he agreed, 'I've lost touch with Blandings a bit. It must be three years since I was there. Somehow, ever since this business of going to the South of France in the summer started, I've never seemed to be able to get down. How are they all? Is old Emsworth much about the same?'

'What was he like when you used to infest the place?'

'Oh, a mild, dreamy, absent-minded sort of old bird. Talked about nothing but roses and pumpkins.'

'Then he is much about the same, except that now he talks about nothing but pigs.'

'Pigs, eh?'

'His Empress of Blandings won the silver medal in the Fat Pigs' Class at last year's Shropshire Agricultural Show, and is confidently expected to repeat this year. This gives the ninth Earl's conversation a porcine trend.'

'How's old Gally?'

'Still going strong.'

'And Beach?'

'Buttling away as hard as ever.'

'Well, well, well,' said Monty sentimentally. 'The old spot certainly doesn't seem to have changed much since . . . Good Lord!' he exclaimed abruptly, spilling the remains of his cocktail over his trousers and in his emotion not noticing it. He had been electrified by a sudden idea.

Although since his arrival at the Drones we have seen Monty Bodkin relaxed, at his ease, chatting of this and that, he had never forgotten that he had just lost a job and that, owing to there being wheels within wheels, it

554

was imperative that he secure another. And a bright
light had just flashed upon him.

Minds like Monty Bodkin's may not always work at
express speed, but they are subject to the same
subconscious processes as those of more brain-burdened
men. Right from the moment when Hugo had
mentioned that he had been acting as secretary to the
Earl of Emsworth, he had had a sort of nebulous idea
that there was a big and important message wrapped up
in this information, if only he could locate it. His
subconscious mind had been having a go at the problem
ever since, and now it passed the solution up to
headquarters.

He quivered with excitement.

'Just a second,' he said. 'Let's get this straight. You say
you were old Emsworth's secretary.'

'Yes.'

'And you've been fired?'

'I have not been fired,' said Hugo Carmody with
justifiable annoyance, 'I've resigned. If you really want
to know, I'm engaged to Lord Emsworth's niece, and I'm
taking her down to Worcestershire in about half an hour
to meet the head of the clan.'

Monty was too preoccupied to offer felicitations.

'When did you leave?'

'Day before yesterday.'

'Anybody been engaged to take your place?'

'Not that I know of.'

'Hugo,' said Monty earnestly, 'I'm going to get that
job. I'm going to phone straight off to my uncle Gregory
to snaffle it for me without delay.'

Hugo looked at him commiseratingly. It was painful
to be in the position of having to throw spanners into an
old friend's daydreams, but he felt the poor chap ought
to be told the truth.

'I shouldn't count too much on Sir G. Parsloe getting
you jobs with old Emsworth,' he said. 'As I remarked

before, you aren't quite abreast of modern Blandings
history. Relations between Blandings Castle and
Matchingham Hall are a bit strained just at the moment.
Not long ago your uncle did the dirty on old Emsworth
by luring his pig-man away from him.'

'Oh, a little thing like that . . .'

'Well, try this one. Lord Emsworth has a fixed idea
that your uncle is plotting to nobble Empress of
Blandings.'

'What! Why?'

'He's got it all worked out. Your uncle owns a pig
called Pride of Matchingham, and with the Empress out
of the way it would probably cop the silver medal at the
Show. So when the Empress was stolen the other
day . . .'

'Stolen! Who stole her?'

'Ronnie.'

Monty's head, never strong, was beginning to swim.

'What Ronnie? Do you mean Ronnie Fish?'

'That's right. It's a complicated story. Ronnie's
engaged to a girl, and he can't marry her unless old
Emsworth coughs up his money.'

'He's Ronnie's trustee?'

'Yes.'

'Trustees are tough eggs,' said Monty thoughtfully. 'I
had one till I was twenty-five, and it used to take me
weeks of patient spadework to extract so much as a
tenner from the man.'

'So, in order to ingratiate himself with old Emsworth,
Ronnie pinched his pig.'

Once more Monty became conscious of that
swimming sensation. He could not follow this.

'But why –?'

'Quite simple. His idea was to kidnap the pig, hide it
somewhere for a day or two, and then pretend to find it
and so win the old boy's gratitude. After which, to have
put the bite on him would have been an easy task. It was

a very sound scheme indeed. Of course, it all went
wrong. Any scheme of Ronnie's would.'

'What went wrong?'

'Well, various unforeseen events occurred, and in the
end the animal was discovered in a caravan belonging to
Baxter. I told you it was a little complicated,' said Hugo
kindly, noting the strained expression on his friend's
face.

Monty agreed, but on one point he found himself
reasonably clear.

'Then old Emsworth must have known that my uncle
didn't steal the pig? I mean, if it was found in
Baxter's . . .'

'Not at all. He thinks Baxter was working for your
uncle. I tell you once more, as I was saying at the
beginning, that, taking it by and large, I don't think I'd
rely too much on Sir Gregory's pull, if I were you.'

Monty chewed his lip thoughtfully.

'There's no harm in trying.'

'Oh, have a shot, by all means. I'm only saying it isn't
one of those stone-cold certainties that old Emsworth
will engage you as his secretary purely out of love for Sir
G. Parsloe.' Hugo looked at the clock, and rose. 'I've got
to be going,' he said, 'if I don't want to miss that train.'

Monty accompanied him to the front steps, and Hugo
hailed a cab.

'It might work,' said Monty pensively.

'Oh, rather. Certainly.'

'They might have had a what-is-it – a reconciliation
by this time.'

'I didn't see any signs of it when I left. And now I
must really rush,' said Hugo, getting into the cab. 'Oh,
by the way,' he added, leaning out of the window,
'there's just one thing. If you do go to Blandings, you'll
find the second prettiest girl in England there. Keep well
away, is my advice.'

'Eh?'

'Ronnie's fiancée. They're both at the Castle, and if you exhibit too much enthusiasm about her he is extremely apt to strangle you with his bare hands. Personally,' said Hugo, 'I regard jealousy as a mug's game, my view being that where there is thingummy there should be what-d'you-call-it. Perfect love, ditto trust. But Ronnie belongs more to the Othello or green-eyed monster school of thought. He was so jealous of a fellow called Pilbeam that he went so far on one occasion as to wreck a restaurant when he found him apparently dining with Sue in it. Oh, yes, a bird of strong feelings and keen sensibilities, old Ronnie.'

'How do you mean apparently dining?'

'She was really dining with me. Blameless Hugo. But Ronnie didn't know that. He discovered Sue in conversation with this Pilbeam – you'll find him at the Castle too . . .'

'Sue?' said Monty.

'Her name's Sue. Sue Brown.'

'What!'

'Sue Brown.'

'Not Sue Brown? You don't mean a girl called Sue Brown who was in the chorus at the Regal?'

'That's the one. You seem to know her.'

'Know her? I should say I do know her. Certainly I know her. I haven't seen her for about a couple of years, but at one time . . . Dear old Sue! Good old Sue! One of the sweetest things on earth, old Sue. You don't often come across such a ripper. Why . . .'

Hugo shook his head deprecatingly.

'Precisely the spirit against which I am warning you. Just the very tone you would do well to avoid. I think we may say that it is an excellent thing that your chances of getting to Blandings Castle are so remote. I should hate to read in my morning paper that your swollen body had been found floating in the lake.'

For some moments after the cab had rolled away,

Monty remained in deep thought on the steps. The news that Sue Brown, of all people, was at Blandings Castle had certainly made the prospect of securing employment there additionally attractive. It would be great seeing old Sue again.

As for all that pig business, he refused to allow himself to be discouraged. Probably much exaggerated. An excellent fellow, Hugo Carmody, one of the best, but always inclined to make a good story out of everything.

Full of optimism, Monty Bodkin went along the passage to the telephone-room.

'I want a trunk call,' he said. 'Matchingham 8-3.'

3

Some twenty-four hours after Monty Bodkin had put in his long-distance call to Matchingham 8–3, an observant bird, winging its way over Blandings Castle and taking a bird's-eye view of its parks, gardens, and messuages, would have noticed a couple walking up and down the terrace which fronts the main entrance of that stately home of England. And narrowing its gaze and shading its eyes with a claw, for the morning sun was strong, it would have seen that one of the pair was a small, sturdy young man of pink complexion, the other an extremely pretty girl in a green linen dress with a Quaker collar. Ronald Overbury Fish was saying good-bye to this Sue preparatory to driving in to Market Blandings and taking the twelve-forty train east. He was going to Norfolk to be best man at the wedding of his cousin George.

He did not anticipate that the parting would be a long one, for he expected to return on the morrow. Nevertheless, he felt constrained to give Sue a few words of advice as to her deportment during his absence.

First and foremost, he urged, she must use every feminine wile to fascinate his Uncle Clarence.

'Right,' said Sue. She was a tiny girl, with an enchanting smile and big blue eyes. These last were now sparkling with ready intelligence. She followed his reasoning perfectly. Lord Emsworth, though he had promised Ronnie his money, had not yet given it to him and might conceivably change his mind. Obviously, therefore, he must be fascinated. The task, moreover, would not be a distasteful one. In the brief time during which she had had the pleasure of his acquaintance, she had grown very fond of that mild and dreamy peer.

'Right,' she said.

'Keep surging round him like glue.'

'Right,' said Sue.

'In fact, I think you had better go and talk pig to him the moment I've left.'

'Right,' said Sue.

'And about Aunt Constance . . .' said Ronnie.

He paused, frowning. He always frowned when he thought of his aunt, Lady Constance Keeble.

When Ronald Fish, the Last of the Fishes, only son of Lady Julia Fish, and nephew to Clarence, ninth Earl of Emsworth, had announced that a marriage had been arranged and would shortly take place between himself and a unit of the Regal Theatre chorus, he had had what might be called a mixed Press. Some of the notices were good, others not.

Beach, the Castle butler, who had fostered for eighteen years a semi-paternal attitude towards Ronnie and had fallen in love with Sue at first sight, liked the idea. So did the Hon. Galahad Threepwood, who when a dashing young man about town in the nineties had wanted to marry Sue's mother. As for Lord Emsworth himself, he had said 'Oh, ah?' in an absent voice on hearing the news and had gone on thinking about pigs.

It was, as so often happens on these occasions, from the female side of the family that the jarring note had proceeded. Women are seldom without their class prejudices. Their views on the importance of Rank diverge from those of the poet Burns. We have seen how Lady Julia felt about the match. The disapproval of her sister Constance was equally pronounced. She grieved over this blot which was about to be splashed upon the escutcheon of a proud family, and let the world see that she grieved. She sighed a good deal, and when she was not sighing kept her lips tightly pressed together.

So now when Ronnie mentioned her name, he frowned.

'About Aunt Constance . . .'

He was going on to add that, should his Aunt Constance have the nerve during his absence to put on dog and do any of that haughty County stuff to his betrothed, the latter would be well advised to kick her in the face; when there emerged from the house a young man with marcelled hair, a shifty expression, and a small and repellent moustache. He stood for an instant on the threshold, hesitated, caught Ronnie's eye, smiled weakly, and disappeared again. Ronnie stood gazing tensely at the spot where he had been.

'Little blighter!' he growled, grinding his teeth gently. The sight of P. Frobisher Pilbeam always tended to wake the fiend that slept in Ronald Fish. 'Looking for you, I suppose!'

Sue started nervously.

'Oh, I shouldn't think so. We've hardly spoken for days.'

'He doesn't ever bother you now?'

'Oh, no.'

'What's he doing here, anyway? I thought he'd left.'

'I suppose Lord Emsworth asked him to stay on. What *does* he matter?'

'He used to send you flowers!'

'I know, but . . .'

'He trailed you to that restaurant that night.'

'I know. But surely you aren't worried about him any longer?'

'Me?' said Ronnie. 'No! Of course not.'

He spoke a little gruffly, for he was embarrassed. It is always embarrassing for a young man of sensibility to realize that he is making a priceless ass of himself. He knew perfectly well that there was nothing between Sue and this Pilbeam perisher and never had been anything. And yet the sight of him about the place could make him flush and scowl and get all throaty.

Of course, the whole trouble with him was that where Sue was concerned he suffered from an inferiority complex. He found it so difficult to believe that a girl like her could really care for a bird so short and pink as himself. He was always afraid that one of these days it would suddenly dawn upon her what a mistake she had made in supposing herself to be in love with him and would race off and fall in love with somebody else. Not Pilbeam, of course, but suppose somebody tall and lissom came along . . .

Sue was pressing her point. She wanted this thing settled and out of the way. The only cloud on her happiness was that tendency of her Ronald's towards jealousy, to which Hugo Carmody had alluded so feelingly in his conversation with Monty Bodkin. Jealousy when two people had come together and knew that they loved one another always seemed to her silly and incomprehensible. She had the frank, uncomplicated mind of a child.

'You promise you won't worry about him again?'

'Absolutely not.'

'Nor about anybody else?'

'Positively not. Couldn't possibly happen again.' He paused. 'The only thing is,' he said broodingly, 'I *am* so dashed short!'

'You're just the right height.'

'And pink.'

'My favourite colour. You're a precious little pink cherub, and I love you.'

'You really do?'

'Of course I do.'

'But suppose you changed your mind?'

'You are a chump, Ronnie.'

'I know I'm a chump, but I still say – Suppose you changed your mind?'

'It's much more likely that you'll change yours.'

'What!'

'Suppose when your mother arrives she talks you over?'

'What absolute rot!'

'I don't imagine she will approve of me.'

'Of course she'll approve of you.'

'Lady Constance doesn't.'

Ronnie uttered a spirited cry.

'Aunt Constance! I was trying to think who it was we were talking about when that Pilbeam blister came to a head. Listen. If Aunt Constance tries to come the old aristocrat over you while I'm away, punch her in the eye. Don't put up for a moment with any pursed-lip-and-lorgnette stuff.'

'And what do I do when your mother reaches for her lorgnette?'

'Oh, you won't have anything of that sort from Mother.'

'Hasn't she got a lorgnette?'

'Mother's all right.'

'Not like Lady Constance?'

'A bit, to look at. But quite different, really. Aunt Constance is straight Queen Elizabeth. Mother's a cheery soul.'

'She'll try to talk you over, all the same.'

'She won't.'

'She will. "Ronald, my dear boy, really! This absurd infatuation. Most extraordinary!" I can feel it in my bones.'

'Mother couldn't talk like that if you paid her. I keep telling you she's a genial egg.'

'She won't like me.'

'Of course she'll like you. Don't be . . . what the dickens is that word?' Sue was biting her lip with her small, very white tooth. Her blue eyes had clouded.

'I wish you weren't going away, Ronnie.'

'It's only for tonight.'

'Have you really got to go?'

'Afraid so. Can't very well let poor old George down.

564

He's relying on me. Besides, I want to watch his work at the altar rails. Pick up some hints on technique which'll come in useful when you and I . . .'

'If ever we do.'

'Do stop talking like that,' begged Ronnie.

'I'm sorry. But I do wish you hadn't got to go away. I'm scared. It's this place. It's so big and old. It makes me feel like a puppy that's got into a cathedral.'

Ronnie turned and gave his boyhood home an appraising glance.

'I suppose it is a fairly decent-sized old shack,' he admitted, having run his eye up to the battlements and back again. 'I never really gave the thing much thought before, but, now you mention it, I have seen smaller places. But there's nothing about it to scare anybody.'

'There is – if you were born and brought up in a villa in the suburbs. I feel that at any moment all the ghosts of your ancestors will come popping out, pointing at me and shouting "What business have *you* here, you little rat?"'

'They'd better not let me catch them at it,' said Ronnie warmly. 'Don't be so . . . what on earth is that word? I know it begins with an *m*. You mustn't feel like that. You've gone like a breeze here. Uncle Clarence likes you. Uncle Gally likes you. Everybody likes you – except Aunt Constance. And a fat lot we care what Aunt Constance thinks, what?'

'I keep worrying about your mother.'

'And I keep telling you . . .'

'I know. But I've got that funny feeling you get sometimes that things are going to happen. Trouble, trouble. A dark lady coming over the water.'

'Mother's fair.'

'It doesn't make it any better. I've got that presentiment.'

'Well, I don't see why you should. Everything's gone without a hitch so far.'

'That's just what I mean. I've been so frightfully happy, and I feel that all the beastly things that spoil happiness are just biding their time. Waiting. They can't do nothin' till Martin gets here!'

'Eh?'

'I was thinking of a thing one of the girls used to play on her gramophone in the dressing-room, the last show I was in. It was about a Negro who goes to a haunted house, and demon cats keep coming in, each bigger and more horrible than the last, and as each one comes in it says to the others, "Shall we start on him now?" and they shake their heads and say, "Not yet. We can't do nothin' till Martin gets here." Well, I can't help feeling that Martin soon will be here.'

Ronnie had found the word for which he had been searching.

'Morbid. I knew it began with an *m*. Don't be so dashed morbid!'

Sue gave herself a little shake, like a dog coming out of a pond. She put her arm in Ronnie's and gave it a squeeze.

'I suppose it is morbid.'

'Of course it is.'

'Everything may be all right.'

'Everything's going to be fine. Mother will be crazy about you. She won't be able to help herself. Because of all the . . .'

On the verge of becoming lyrical, Ronnie broke off abruptly. The Castle car had just come round the corner from the stables with Voules, the chauffeur, at the helm.

'I didn't know it was as late as that,' said Ronnie discontentedly.

The car drew up beside them, and he eyed Voules with a touch of austerity. It was not that he disliked the chauffeur, a man whom he had known since his boyhood and one with whom he had many a time played village cricket. It was simply that there are moments when a fellow wishes to be free from observation, and one of these is when he is about to bid farewell to his affianced.

However, there was good stuff in Ronald Fish. Ignoring the chauffeur's eye, which betrayed a disposition to be roguish, he gathered his loved one to him and, his face now a pretty cerise, kissed her with all a Fish's passion. This done, he entered the car, leaned out of the window, waved, went on waving, and continued to wave till Sue was out of sight. Then, sitting down, he gazed straight before him, breathing a little heavily through the nostrils.

Sue, having lingered until the car had turned the corner of the drive and was hidden by a clump of rhododendrons, walked pensively back to the terrace.

The August sun was now blazing down in all its imperious majesty. Insects were chirping sleepily in the grass, and the hum of bees in the lavender borders united with the sun and the chirping to engender sloth. A little wistfully Sue looked past the shrubbery at the cedar-shaded lawn where the Hon. Galahad Threepwood, thoughtfully sipping a whisky and soda, lay back in a deep chair, cool and at his ease. There was another chair beside him, and she knew that he had placed it there for her.

But duty is duty, no matter how warm the sun and drowsy the drone of insects. Ronnie had asked her to go and talk pig to Lord Emsworth, and the task must be performed.

She descended the broad stone steps and, turning westward, made for the corner of the estate sacred to that noble Berkshire sow, Empress of Blandings.

The boudoir of the Empress was situated in a little meadow, dappled with buttercups and daisies, round two sides of which there flowed in a silver semicircle the stream which fed the lake. Lord Emsworth, as his custom was, had pottered off there directly after breakfast, and now, at half past twelve, he was still standing, in company with his pig-man Pirbright, draped bonelessly over the rail of the sty, his mild eyes beaming with the light of a holy devotion.

From time to time he sniffed sensuously. Elsewhere throughout this fair domain the air was fragrant with the myriad scents of high summer, but not where Lord Emsworth was doing his sniffing. Within a liberal radius of the Empress's headquarters other scents could not compete. This splendid animal diffused an aroma which was both distinctive and arresting. Attractive, too, if you liked that sort of thing, as Lord Emsworth did.

Between Empress of Blandings and these two human beings who ministered to her comfort there was a sharp contrast in physique. Lord Emsworth was tall and thin and scraggy, Pirbright tall and thin and scraggier. The Empress, on the other hand, could have passed in a dim light for a captive balloon, fully inflated and about to make its trial trip. The modern craze for slimming had found no votary in her. She liked her meals large and regular, and had never done a reducing exercise in her life. Watching her now as she tucked into a sort of hash of bran, acorns, potatoes, linseed, and swill, the ninth Earl of Emsworth felt his heart leap up in much the same way as that of the poet Wordsworth used to do when he beheld a rainbow in the sky.

'What a picture, Pirbright!' he said reverently.

'Ur, m'lord.'

'She's bound to win. Can't help herself.'

'Yur, m'lord.'

'Unless . . . We mustn't let her get stolen again, Pirbright.'

'Nur, m'lord.'

Lord Emsworth adjusted his pince-nez thoughtfully. The ecstatic pig-gleam had faded from his eyes. His face was darkened by a cloud of concern. He was thinking of that bad Baronet, Sir Gregory Parsloe.

The theft of the Empress and the subsequent discovery of her in his ex-secretary Baxter's caravan had at first mystified Lord Emsworth completely. Why Baxter, though a recognized eccentric, should have been going about Shropshire stealing pigs seemed to him a problem incapable of solution.

But calm reflection had brought the answer to the riddle. Obviously the fellow had been a minion in the pay of Sir Gregory, operating throughout under orders from the Big Shot. And what was disquieting him now was the conviction that the danger was not yet passed. Baffled once, the Baronet, he felt, was crouching for another spring. With two weeks still to pass before the Agricultural Show, there was ample time for his subtle brain to conceive another hideous plot. At any moment, in short, the bounder was liable to come sneaking in, mask on face and poison-needle in hand, intent on nobbling the favourite.

His eyes roamed the paddock. It was a lonely spot, far from human habitation. A pig, assaulted here by Baronets, might well cry for help unheard.

'Do you think she's safe in this sty, Pirbright?' he asked anxiously. 'I feel we ought to move her to that new one by the kitchen garden. It's near your cottage.'

What reply the Vice-President in charge of Pigs would have made to this suggestion – whether it would have been an 'Ur', a 'Yur', or a 'Nur' – will never be known. For at this moment there appeared a figure at the sight of whom he touched his forelock and receded respectfully into the background.

Lord Emsworth, whose pince-nez had fallen off, put them on again and peered mildly, like a sheep looking over a fence.

'Ah, Connie, my dear.'

There had been times when the sudden advent of his sister, Lady Constance Keeble, at a moment when he was drooping his long body over the rail of the Empress's sanctum would have caused him agitation and discomfort. She had a way of appearing from nowhere and upbraiding him for expending on pigs time which had better have been devoted to correspondence connected with the business of the estate. But for the last two days, since the departure of that young fellow Carmody, he had had no secretary; and a man can't be expected to attend to his correspondence without a secretary. His conscience, accordingly, was clear, and he spoke with none of that irritable defensiveness, as of some wild creature at bay, which he sometimes displayed on these occasions.

'Ah, Connie, my dear, you are just in time to give me your advice. I was saying to Pirbright . . .'

Lady Constance did not wait for the sentence to be completed. In her dealings with the head of the family she was always inclined to infuse into her manner a suggestion of a rather short-tempered nurse with a rather fat-headed child.

'Never mind what you were saying to Pirbright. Do you know what time it is?'

Lord Emsworth did not. He never did. Beyond a vague idea that when it got too dark for him to see the Empress at a range of four feet it was getting on for dinner-time, he took little account of the hours.

'It's nearly one, and we have people coming to lunch at half past.'

Lord Emsworth assimilated this.

'Lunch? Oh, ah, yes. Yes, of course. Lunch, to be sure. Yes, lunch. You think I ought to come in and wash my hands?'

'And your face. It's covered with mud. And change those clothes. And those shoes. And put on a clean collar. Really, Clarence, you're as much trouble as a baby. Why you want to waste your time staring at beastly pigs, I can't imagine.'

Lord Emsworth accompanied her across the paddock, but his face – there was hardly any mud on it at all, really, just a couple of splashes or so – was sullen and mutinous. This was not the first time his sister had alluded in this offensive manner to one whom he regarded as the supreme ornament of her sex and species. Beastly pigs, indeed! He pondered moodily on the curious inability of his immediate circle to appreciate the importance of the Empress in the scheme of things. Not one of them seemed to have the sagacity to realize her true worth.

Well, yes, one, perhaps. That little girl what-was-her-name, who was going to marry his nephew Ronald, had always displayed a pleasing interest in the silver medallist.

'Nice girl,' he said, following this train of thought to its conclusion.

'What *are* you talking about, Clarence?' asked Lady Constance wearily. 'Who is a nice girl?'

'That little girl of Ronald's. I've forgotten her name. Smith, is it?'

'Brown,' said Lady Constance shortly.

'That's right, Brown. Nice girl.'

'You are entitled to your opinion, I suppose,' said Lady Constance.

They walked on in silence for some moments.

'While we are on the subject of Miss Brown,' said Lady Constance, speaking the name as she always did with her teeth rather tightly clenched and a stony look in her eyes, 'I forgot to tell you that I had a letter from Julia this morning.'

'*Did* you?' said Lord Emsworth, giving the matter some two-fifty-sevenths of his attention. 'Capital, capital. Who,' he asked politely, 'is Julia?'

Lady Constance was within easy reach of his head

and could quite comfortably have hit it, but she refrained. *Noblesse oblige.*

'*Julia!*' she said, with a rising inflection. 'There's only one Julia in our family.'

'Oh, you mean Julia?' said Lord Emsworth, enlightened. 'And what had Julia got to say for herself? She's at Biarritz, isn't she?' he said, making a great mental effort. 'Having a good time, I hope?'

'She's in London.'

'Oh, yes?'

'And she is coming here tomorrow by the two forty-five.'

Lord Emsworth's vague detachment vanished. His sister Julia was not a woman to whose visits he looked forward with joyous enthusiasm.

'Why?' he asked, with a strong note of complaint in his voice.

'It is the only good train in the afternoon, and gets her here in plenty of time for dinner.'

'I mean, why is she coming?'

It would be too much to say that Lady Constance snorted. Women of her upbringing do not snort. But she certainly sniffed.

'Well, really!' she said. 'Does it strike you as so odd that a mother whose only son has announced his intention of marrying a ballet-girl should wish to see her?'

Lord Emsworth considered this.

'Not ballet-girl. Chorus-girl, I understood.'

'It's the same thing.'

'I don't think so,' said Lord Emsworth doubtfully. 'I must ask Galahad.'

A sudden idea struck him.

'Don't you like this Smith girl?'

'Brown.'

'Don't you like this Brown girl?'

'I do not.'

'Don't you want her to marry Ronald?'

'I should have thought I had made my views on that matter sufficiently clear. I think the whole thing deplorable. I am not a snob . . .'

'But you are,' said Lord Emsworth, cleverly putting his finger on the flaw in her reasoning.

Lady Constance bridled.

'Well, if it is snobbish to prefer your nephew to marry in his own class . . .'

'Galahad would have married her mother thirty years ago if he hadn't been shipped off to South Africa.'

'Galahad was – and is – capable of anything.'

'I can remember her mother,' said Lord Emsworth meditatively. 'Galahad took me to the Tivoli once, when she was singing there. Dolly Henderson. A little bit of a thing in pink tights, with the jolliest smile you ever saw. Made you think of spring mornings. The gallery joined in the chorus, I recollect. Bless my soul, how did it go? Tum tum tumpty tum . . . Or was it Umpty tiddly tiddly pum?'

'Never mind how it went,' said Lady Constance. One reminiscencer in the family, she considered, was quite enough. 'And we are not talking of the girl's mother. The only thing I have to say about Miss Brown's mother is that I wish she had never had a daughter.'

'Well, I like her,' said Lord Emsworth stoutly. 'A very sweet, pretty, nice-mannered little thing, and extremely sound on pigs. I was saying so to young Pilbeam only yesterday.'

'Pilbeam!' cried Lady Constance.

She spoke with feeling, for the name had reminded her of another grievance. She had been wanting to get to the bottom of this Pilbeam mystery for days. About that young man's presence at the Castle there seemed to her something almost uncanny. She had no recollection of his arrival. It was as if he had materialized out of thin air. And being a conventional hostess, with a

573

conventional hostess's dislike of the irregular, she objected to finding that visitors with horrible moustaches, certainly not invited by herself, had suddenly begun to pervade the home like an escape of gas.

'Who is that nasty little man?' she demanded.

'He's an investigator.'

'A *what*?'

'A private investigator. He investigates privately.' There was a touch of quiet pride in Lord Emsworth's voice. He was sixty years old, and this was the first time he had ever found himself in the romantic role of an employer of private investigators. 'He runs the something detective agency. The Argus. That's it. The Argus Private Inquiry Agency.'

Lady Constance breathed emotionally.

'Ballet-girls . . . Detectives . . . I wonder you don't invite a few skittle-sharps here.'

Lord Emsworth said he did not know any skittle-sharps.

'And is one permitted to ask what a private detective is doing as a guest at Blandings Castle?'

'I got him down to investigate that mystery of the Empress's disappearance.'

'Well, that idiotic pig of yours has been back in her sty for days. What possible reason can there be for this man staying on?'

'Ah, that was Galahad's idea. It was Galahad's suggestion that he should stay on till after the Agricultural Show. He thought it would be a good thing to have somebody like that handy in case Parsloe tried any more of his tricks.'

'Clarence!'

'And I consider,' went on Lord Emsworth firmly, 'that he was quite right. I know it was Baxter who actually stole my pig, and you will no doubt say that Baxter is notoriously potty. But Galahad feels – and I feel – that it was not primarily his pottiness that led him to steal the Empress. We both think that Parsloe was behind the whole thing. And Galahad maintains – and I agree with him – that it is only a question of time before he makes another attempt. So the more watchers we have on the place the better. Especially if they have trained minds and are used to mixing with criminals, like Pilbeam.'

'Clarence, you're insane!'

'No, I am not insane,' retorted Lord Emsworth warmly. 'I know Parsloe. And Galahad knows Parsloe. You should read some of the stories about him in Galahad's book – thoroughly well documented stories, he assures me, showing the sort of man he was when Galahad used to go about London with him in their young days. Are you aware that in the year 1894 Parsloe filled Galahad's dog Towser up with steak and onions just before the big Rat contest, so that his own terrier Banjo should win? A fellow who stuck at nothing to attain his ends. And he's just the same today. Hasn't changed a bit. Look at the way he stole that man Wellbeloved away from me – the chap who used to be my pigman before Pirbright. Fellow capable of that is capable of anything.'

Lady Constance spurned the grass with a frenzied foot. She would have preferred to kick her brother with it, but one has one's breeding.

'You are a perfect imbecile about Sir Gregory,' she cried. 'You ought to be ashamed of yourself. So ought Galahad, if it were possible for him to be ashamed of anything. You are behaving like a couple of half-witted children. I hate this idiotic quarrel. If there's one thing that's detestable in the country, it is being on bad terms with one's neighbours.'

'I don't care how bad terms I'm on with Parsloe.'

'Well, I do. And that is why I was so glad to oblige him when he rang up about his nephew.'

'Eh?'

'I was delighted to have the chance of proving to him that there was at least one sane person in Blandings Castle.'

'Nephew? What nephew?'

'Young Montague Bodkin. You ought to remember him. He was here often enough when he was a boy.'

'Bodkin? Bodkin? Bodkin?'

'Oh, for pity's sake, Clarence, don't keep saying "Bodkin" as if you were a parrot. If you have forgotten him, as you forget everything that happened more than ten minutes ago, it does not matter in the least. The point is that Sir Gregory asked me as a personal favour to engage him as your secretary . . .'

Lord Emsworth was a mild man, but he could be stirred.

'Well, I'm dashed! Well, I'm hanged! The man steals my pig-man and engineers the theft of my pig, and he has the nerve . . .'

'. . . and I said I should be delighted.'

'What!'

'I said I should be delighted.'

'You don't mean you've done it?'

'Certainly. It's all arranged.'

'You mean you're letting a nephew of Parsloe loose in Blandings Castle, with two weeks to go before the Agricultural Show?'

'He arrives tomorrow by the two-forty-five,' said Lady Constance.

And as she had thrown her bomb and seen it explode and had now reached the front door and had no wish to waste her time listening to futile protests, she swept into the house and left Lord Emsworth standing.

He remained standing for perhaps a minute. Then the imperative necessity of sharing this awful news with a cooler, wiser mind than his own stirred him to life and activity. His face drawn, his long legs trembling beneath

him, he hurried towards the lawn where his brother
Galahad, whisky and soda in hand, reclined in his
deckchair.

4

Cooled by the shade of the cedar, refreshed by the
contents of the amber glass in which ice tinkled so
musically when he lifted it to his lips, the Hon. Galahad,
at the moment of Lord Emsworth's arrival, had achieved
a Nirvana-like repose. Storms might be raging elsewhere
in the grounds of Blandings Castle, but there on the
lawn there was peace – the perfect unruffled peace
which in this world seems to come only to those who
have done nothing whatever to deserve it.

The Hon. Galahad Threepwood, in his fifty-seventh
year, was a dapper little gentleman on whose grey but
still thickly-covered head the weight of a consistently
misspent life rested lightly. His flannel suit sat jauntily
upon his wiry frame, a black-rimmed monocle gleamed
jauntily in his eye. Everything about this Musketeer of
the nineties was jaunty. It was a standing mystery to all
who knew him that one who had had such an
extraordinarily good time all his life should, in the
evening of that life, be so superbly robust. Wan
contemporaries who had once painted a gaslit London
red in his company and were now doomed to an
existence of dry toast, Vichy water, and German cure
resorts felt very strongly on this point. A man of his
antecedents, they considered, ought by rights to be
rounding off his career in a bath-chair instead of flitting
about the place, still chaffing head waiters as of old and
calling for the wine list without a tremor.

A little cock-sparrow of a man. One of the Old Guard
which dies but does not surrender. Sitting there under

the cedar, he looked as if he were just making ready to
go to some dance-hall of the days when dance-halls were
dance-halls, from which in the quiet dawn it would take
at least three waiters, two commissionaires and a
policeman to eject him.

In a world so full of beautiful things, where he felt we
should all be as happy as kings, the spectacle of his
agitated brother shocked the Hon. Galahad.

'Good God, Clarence! You look like a bereaved
tapeworm. What's the matter?'

Lord Emsworth fluttered for a moment, speechless.
Then he found words.

'Galahad, the worst has happened!'

'Eh?'

'Parsloe has struck!'

'Struck? You mean he's been biffing you?'

'No, no, no. I mean it has happened just as you
warned me. He has been too clever for us. He has got
round Connie and persuaded her to engage his nephew
as my new secretary.'

The Hon. Galahad removed his monocle, and began
to polish it thoughtfully. He could understand his
companion's concern now.

'She told me so only a moment ago. You see what this
means? He is determined to work a mischief on the
Empress, and now he has contrived to insinuate an
accomplice into the very heart of the home. I see it all,'
said Lord Emsworth, his voice soaring to the upper
register. 'He failed with Baxter, and now he is trying
again with this young Bodkin.'

'Bodkin? Young Monty Bodkin?'

'Yes. What are we to do, Galahad?' said Lord
Emsworth.

He trembled. It would have pained the immaculate
Monty, could he have known that his prospective
employer was picturing him at this moment as a furtive,

shifty-eyed, rat-like person of the gangster type, liable at
the first opportunity to sneak into the sties of innocent
pigs and plant pineapple bombs in their bran-mash.

The Hon. Galahad replaced his monocle.

'Monty Bodkin?' he said, refreshing himself with a sip
from his glass. 'I remember him well. Nice boy. Not at
all the sort of fellow who would nobble pigs. Wait a
minute, Clarence. This wants thinking over.'

He mused awhile.

'No,' he said, 'you can dismiss young Bodkin as a
hostile force altogether.'

'What!'

'Put him right out of your mind,' insisted the Hon.
Galahad. 'Parsloe isn't planning to strike through him at
all.'

'But, Galahad . . .'

'No. Take it from me. Can't you see for yourself that
the thing's much too obvious, much too straightforward,
not young Parsloe's proper form at all? Reason it out. He
must know that we would suspect a nephew of his.
Then why is it worth his while to get him into the
place? Shall I tell you, Clarence?'

'Do,' said Lord Emsworth feebly, gaping like a fish.

As the head of the family was standing up and he was
sitting down, it was impossible for the Hon. Galahad to
tap him meaningly on the shoulder. He prodded him
meaningly in the leg.

'Because,' he said, 'he *wants* us to suspect him.'

'Wants us to suspect him?'

'Wants us to,' said the Hon. Galahad. 'He hopes by
introducing Monty Bodkin into the place to get us
watching him, following his every movement, keeping
our eyes glued on to him, so that when the real
accomplice acts we shall be looking in the wrong
direction.'

'God bless my soul!' said Lord Emsworth, appalled.

'Oh, it's all right,' said the Hon. Galahad soothingly.

'A cunning scheme, but we're too smart to fall for it. We see through it and are prepared.' He gave Lord Emsworth's leg another significant prod. 'Shall I tell you what is going to happen, Clarence?'

'Do,' said Lord Emsworth.

'I can read Parsloe's mind like a book. A day or two after young Monty's arrival, there will be a mysterious stranger sneaking about the grounds in the vicinity of the Empress's sty. He will be there because Parsloe, taking it for granted that our attention will be riveted on young Monty, will imagine that the coast is clear.'

'God bless my soul!'

'And apparently the coast will be clear. We must arrange that. From now on, Clarence, you must not loaf about the Empress openly. You must conceal yourself in the background. And you must instruct Pirbright to conceal himself in the background. This fellow must be led to suppose that vigilance has been relaxed. By these means, we shall catch him red-handed.'

In Lord Emsworth's eye, as he gazed at his brother, there was the reverential look of a disciple at the feet of his master. He had always known, he told himself, that as a practical adviser in matters having to do with the seamier side of life the other was unsurpassed. It was the result, he supposed, of the environment in which he had spent his formative years. Membership of the old Pelican Club might not elevate a man socially, but there was no doubt about its educative properties. If it dulled the moral sense, it undoubtedly sharpened the intellect.

'You have taken a great weight off my mind, Galahad,' he said. 'I feel sure you are perfectly right. The only mistake I think you make is in supposing that this young Bodkin is harmless. I am convinced that he will require watching.'

'Well, watch him, then, if it will make you any happier.'

'It will,' said Lord Emsworth decidedly. 'And

meanwhile I will be giving Pirbright his instructions.'

'Tell him to lurk.'

'Exactly.'

'Some rude disguise such as a tree or a pail of potato-peel would help.'

Lord Emsworth reflected.

'I don't think Pirbright could disguise himself as a tree.'

'Nonsense. What do you pay him for?'

Lord Emsworth continued dubious. Only God, he seemed to be feeling, can make a tree.

'Well, at any rate, tell him to lurk.'

'Oh, he shall certainly lurk.'

'From now on . . .' began the Hon. Galahad, and broke off to wave at some object in his companion's rear. The latter turned.

'Ah, that nice little Smith girl,' he said.

Sue had appeared on the edge of the lawn. Lord Emsworth beamed vaguely in her direction.

'By the way, Galahad,' he said, 'is a chorus-girl the same as a ballet-girl?'

'Certainly not. Different thing altogether.'

'I thought so,' said Lord Emsworth. 'Connie's an ass.'

He pottered away, and Sue crossed the turf to where the Hon. Galahad sat.

The author of the Reminiscences scanned her affectionately through his monocle. Amazing, he was thinking, how like her mother she was. He noticed it more every day. Dolly's walk, and just that way of tilting her chin and smiling at you that Dolly had had. For an instant the years fell away from the Hon. Galahad Threepwood, and something that was not of this world went whispering through the garden.

Sue stood looking down at him. She placed a maternal finger on top of his head, and began to twist the grey hair round it.

'Well, young Gally.'

'Well, young Sue.'

'You look very comfortable.'

'I am comfortable.'

'You won't be long. The luncheon gong will be going in a minute.'

The Hon. Galahad sighed. There was always something, he reflected.

'What a curse meals are! Don't let's go in.'

'I'm going in, all right. My good child, I'm starving.'

'Pure imagination.'

'Do you mean to say you're not hungry, Gally?'

'Of course I'm not. No healthy person really needs food. If people would only stick to drinking, doctors would go out of business. I can state you a case that proves it. Old Freddie Potts in the year '98.'

'Old Freddie Potts in the year '98, did you say, Mister Bones?'

'Old Freddie Potts in the year '98,' repeated the Hon. Galahad firmly. 'He lived almost entirely on Scotch whisky, and in the year '98 this prudent habit saved him from an exceedingly unpleasant attack of hedgehog poisoning.'

'What poisoning?'

'Hedgehog poisoning. It was down in the south of France that it happened. Freddie had gone to stay with his brother Eustace at his villa at Grasse. Practically a teetotaller, this brother, and in consequence passionately addicted to food.'

'Still, I can't see why he wanted to eat hedgehogs.'

'He did not want to eat hedgehogs. Nothing was farther from his intentions. But on the second day of old Freddie's visit he gave his chef twenty francs to go to market and buy a chicken for dinner, and the chef, wandering along, happened to see a dead hedgehog lying in the road. It had been there some days, as a matter of fact, but this was the first time he had noticed it. So, feeling that here was where he pouched twenty francs . . .'

'I wish you wouldn't tell me stories like this just before lunch.'

'If it puts you off your food, so much the better. Bring the roses to your cheeks. Well, as I was saying, the chef, who was a thrifty sort of chap and knew that he could make a dainty dinner dish out of his old grandmother, if allowed to mess about with a few sauces, added the twenty francs to his savings and gave Freddie and Eustace the hedgehog next day *en casserole*. Mark the sequel. At two-thirty prompt, Eustace, the teetotaller, turned nile-green, started groaning like a lost soul, and continued to do so for the remainder of the week, when he was pronounced out of danger. Freddie, on the other hand, his system having been healthfully pickled in alcohol, throve on the dish and finished it up cold next day.'

'I call that the most disgusting story I ever heard.'

'The most moral story you ever heard. If I had my way, it would be carved up in letters of gold over the door of every school and college in the kingdom, as a warning to the young. Well, what have you been doing with yourself all the morning, my dear? I expected you earlier.'

'I was talking to my precious Ronnie most of the time. He went off to catch his train about half an hour ago.'

'Ah, yes, he's going to young George Fish's wedding, isn't he? I could tell you a good story about George Fish's father, the Bishop.'

'If it's like the one about old Freddie Potts, I don't want to hear it. Well, after that I went to look for Lord Emsworth, because I had promised Ronnie to talk pig to him. But I saw Lady Constance with him, so I kept away. And then I came to see you, and found you talking together. You seemed to be having a very earnest conversation about something.'

The Hon. Galahad chuckled.

'Clarence has got the wind up, poor chap. About that

pig of his. He thinks Parsloe is trying to put it on the spot or kidnap it.'

Sue looked round cautiously.

'You know who stole it that first time, don't you, Gally?'

'Baxter, wasn't it? The thing was found in his caravan.'

'It was Ronnie.'

'What!' This was news to the Hon. Galahad. 'That young Fish?'

She gave his hair a tug.

'You are not to call him "that young Fish".'

'I apologize. But what on earth did he do it for?'

'He was going to find it and bring it back. So as to make Lord Emsworth grateful, you see.'

'You don't mean that young cloth-head had the intelligence to think up a scheme like that?' said the Hon. Galahad, amazed.

'And I won't have you calling my darling Ronnie a cloth-head either. He's very clever. As a matter of fact, though, he says he got the idea from you.'

'From me?'

'He says you told him you once stole a pig.'

'That's right,' said the Hon. Galahad. 'Puffy Benger and I stole old Wivenhoe's pig the night of the Bachelors' Ball at Hammer's Easton in the year '95. We put it in Plug Basham's bedroom. I never heard what happened when Plug met it. No doubt they found some formula. Wivenhoe, I remember, was rather annoyed about the affair. He was a good deal like Clarence in that respect. Worshipped his pig.'

'What makes Lord Emsworth think that Sir Gregory is going to hurt the Empress?'

'Apparently Connie has gone and engaged his nephew as Clarence's secretary, and he thinks it's a plot. So do I. But personally, as I told Clarence, I feel that Parsloe is using young Monty Bodkin purely as a cat's paw.'

'Monty Bodkin!'

'The nephew. I'm convinced, from what I remember of him, that he isn't at all the sort of fellow . . .'

'Oh, Gally!' cried Sue.

'Eh?'

'Monty Bodkin coming here?' Sue stared in dismay. 'Oh, Gally, what a mess! Oh, I knew something was going to happen. I told Ronnie so, I've been feeling it for days.'

'My dear child, what's the matter with you? What's wrong with young Bodkin coming here?'

'I used to be engaged to him!' said Sue.

It seemed to the Hon. Galahad that advancing years and the comparative abstinence of his later life must have dulled his once keen quickness at the uptake. Sue's face had lost its colour, and anxiety and alarm were clouding her pretty eyes, and he could make nothing of it.

'Were you?' he said. 'When was that?'

'Two years ago . . . Two and a half . . . Three . . . I can't remember. Before I met Ronnie. But what does that matter? I tell you I used to be engaged to him.'

The Hon. Galahad was still fogged.

'But what's your trouble? What's all the agitation about? Why does it upset you so much, the idea of meeting him again? Painful associations, do you mean? Embarrassing? Don't want to awake agonizing memories in the fellow's bosom?'

'Of course not. It isn't that. It's Ronnie.'

'Why Ronnie?'

'He's so jealous. You know how jealous he is.'

The Hon. Galahad began to understand.

'He can't help it, poor darling. It's just the way he is. He makes himself miserable about nothing. So what *will* he do when Monty arrives? I know Monty so well. He won't mean any harm, but he'll come bounding in, all hearty and bubbling, and start talking of old times. "Do you remember – ?" "I say, Sue, old girl, I wonder if you've forgotten – ?" . . . Ugh! It will drive poor Ronnie crazy.'

The Hon. Galahad nodded.

'I see what you mean. That touch of Auld Lang Syne *is* disturbing.'

'Why, he tries to pretend he isn't, but Ronnie's jealous even of Pilbeam.'

Once more the Hon. Galahad nodded. A grave nod. He quite realized that a man who could be jealous of the proprietor of the Argus Inquiry Agency was not a man lightly to be introduced to former fiancés, especially of the type of Monty Bodkin.

'We must give this matter a little earnest consideration,' he said thoughtfully. 'You wouldn't consider taking a firm line and telling Ronnie to go and boil his head and not make a young fool of himself, if he starts kicking up a fuss?'

'But you don't understand,' wailed Sue. 'He won't kick up a fuss. Ronnie isn't like that. He'll just get very stiff and cold and polite and suffer in a sort of awful Eton and Cambridge silence. And nothing I do will make him any better.'

An idea struck the Hon. Galahad.

'You're sure you really are in love with this young Fish?'

'I wish you wouldn't . . .'

'I'm sorry. I forgot. But you are?'

'Of course I am. There's nobody in the world for me but Ronnie. I've told you that before. I suppose what you're wondering is how I came to be engaged to Monty? Looking back, I can't think myself. He's a dear, of course, and when you're about seventeen, you're so flattered at finding that anyone wants to marry you that it seems wrong to refuse him. But it never amounted to anything. It only lasted a couple of weeks, anyhow. But Ronnie will imagine it was one of the world's great romances. He'll brood on it, and worry himself ill, wondering whether I'm still not pining for Monty. He's just like a kid in that way. It'll spoil everything.'

'And we may take it as pretty certain that Monty will let it out?'

'Of course he will. He's a babbler.'

'Yes, that's how I remember him. One of those fellows you can count on to say the wrong thing. Reminds me rather of a man I used to know in the old days called Bagshott. Boko Bagshott, we called him. Took a girl to supper once at the Garden. Supper scarcely concluded when angry old gentleman plunges into the room and starts shaking his fist in Boko's face. Boko rises with chivalrous gesture. "Have no fear, sir. I am a man of honour. I will marry your daughter." "Daughter?" says old gentleman, foaming a little at the mouth. "Damn it, that's my wife." Took all Boko's tact to pass it off, I believe.'

He pondered, staring thoughtfully through his black-rimmed monocle at a spider which was doing its trapeze act from an overhanging bough.

'Well, it's quite simple, of course.'

'Simple!'

'Presents no difficulties of any sort, now that one gives it one's full attention. Ronnie won't be back from that wedding till late tomorrow evening. You must run up to London first thing in the morning and warn young Monty how the land lies. Tell him that when he arrives here he must meet you as a stranger. Pitch it strong. Explain about Ronnie's unfortunate failing. Drive it well into his head that your whole happiness depends on him pretending he's never met you before, and I should think you would have no trouble whatever. I wouldn't call Monty Bodkin particularly bright, but he ought to be able to handle a thing like that, if you make it perfectly clear to him what he's got to do.'

She drew a deep breath.

'You're wonderful, Gally darling.'

'Experienced,' corrected the Hon. Galahad modestly.

'But can I do it? I mean, the trains.'

'On your head. Eight-fifty from Market Blandings gets you to London about noon. Interview Monty between then and two-thirty. Catch the two forty-five back, and you get to Market Blandings somewhere around a quarter to seven. Take the station taxi, stop it half-way up the drive, get out and walk the rest, and you'll be in your room with an hour to dress for dinner, and not a soul knowing a thing about it. No, even better than that, because I remember Connie telling me there's a dinner-party on tomorrow night, so I suppose you won't have to show up till nearly nine.'

'But lunch? Won't they wonder where I am if I'm not at lunch?'

'Connie's lunching out. You don't suppose Clarence will notice whether you're there or not. No, the only point we haven't covered is, can you find Monty? Do you know his address?'

'He's sure to be at the Drones.'

'Then all is well. Why on earth you worry about these things, when you know you've got an expert like me behind you, I can't imagine. It's a pity about young Ronnie, though. That disposition of his to make heavy weather. Silly to be jealous. He ought to realize by this time that you love him – goodness knows why.'

'I know why.'

'I don't. Fellow's a perfect ass.'

'He's not!'

'My dear child,' said the Hon. Galahad firmly, 'if a man who doesn't know that he can trust you isn't a perfect ass, what sort of ass is he?'

5

In supposing that she would be able to find her former
fiancé at the Drones, Sue had not erred. Telephoning
there from Paddington station shortly after twelve next
morning, she was rewarded almost immediately by a
series of sharp, hyena-like cries at the other end of the
wire. To judge from his remarks, this voice from the past
was music in Monty Bodkin's ears. Nothing, he gave her
to understand, could have given him more pleasure than
to get in touch after two years of separation with one
whom he esteemed so highly. At his suggestion, Sue had
got into a taxi, and now, across a table in the restaurant
of the Berkeley Hotel, she was looking at him and
congratulating herself on her wisdom in having arranged
this meeting. A Monty unprepared for the part he had to
play at Blandings Castle would, she felt, beyond a
question have crashed into poor darling Ronnie's
sensibilities like a high-powered shell. Over the
preliminary cocktails and right through the smoked
salmon he had been a sheer foaming torrent of 'Do you
remembers' and 'That reminds mes'.

It seemed to Sue that she had a difficult task before
her in trying to make clear to this exuberant old friend
that on his arrival at the Castle he must regard the dear
old days as a sealed book and herself as a complete
stranger. Yet when a toothsome *truite bleue* had induced
in him a sudden reverential silence and she was able at
length to give a brief exposition of the state of affairs,
she was surprised and pleased to gather from a series of
understanding nods that he appeared to be following her
remarks intelligently.

He finished the *truite bleue* and gave a final nod. It indicated a perfect grasp of the situation.

'My dear old soul,' he said reassuringly, 'say no more. I understand everything, understand it fully. As a matter of fact, Hugo Carmody had already tipped me off.'

'Oh, have you seen Hugo?'

'I met him at the club, and he warned me about Ronnie. I had the situation well in hand. On arriving at Blandings I was planning to treat you with distant civility.'

'Then I needn't have come up at all!'

'I wouldn't say that. If Ronnie's so apt to go off the deep end at the slightest provocation, we can't be too much on the safe side. Even distant civility might have hotted him up.'

Sue considered this.

'That's true,' she agreed.

'Better to be perfect strangers.'

'Yes.' Sue gave a little frown. 'How beastly it's all going to be, though.'

'That's all right. I shan't mind.'

'I wasn't thinking about you. It seems so rotten, deceiving Ronnie.'

'You've got to get used to that. Secret of a happy and successful married life. I thought you meant that it would be rather agony you and me just giving each other a distant bow when they introduced us and then shunning one another coldly. And it does seem darned silly, what? I mean, we were very close to each other once. Can one altogether forget those happy days?'

'I can. And so must you. For goodness sake, Monty, don't let's have any of what Gally calls that touch of Auld Lang Syne.'

'No, no. Quite.'

'I don't want Ronnie driven off his head.'

'Far from it.'

'Well, do remember to be careful.'

'Oh, I will. Rely on me.'

'Thanks, Monty darling . . . What's the matter?' asked Sue, as her host gave a sudden start.

A waiter had brought up a silver dish and uncovered it with the air of one doing a conjuring trick. Monty inspected it with the proper seriousness.

'Oh, nothing,' he said as the waiter retired. 'Just that "Monty darling." It brought back the old days.'

'For goodness' sake forget the old days!'

'Oh, quite. I will. Oh, rather. Most certainly. But it made me feel how rum life was. Life *is* rummy, you know. You can't get away from that.'

'I suppose it is.'

'Take a simple instance. Here are you and I, face to face across this table, lunching together like the dickens, precisely as in the dear old days, and all the time you are contemplating getting hitched up to R. Fish, while I am heart and soul in favour of an early union with Gertrude Butterwick.'

'What!'

'Butterwick. B for blister, U for ukelele . . .'

'Yes, I heard. But do you mean you're engaged, too, Monty?'

'Well, yes and no. Not absolutely. And yet not absolutely not. I am, as it were, on appro.'

'Can't she make up her mind?'

'Oh, her mind's made up all right. Oh, yes, yes, yes, indeed there's no doubt about good old Gertrude's mind, bless her. She loves me like billy-o. But there are wheels within wheels.'

'What do you mean?'

'It's an expression. It signifies . . . well, by Jove, now you bring up the point,' said Monty frankly, 'I'm dashed if I know just what it does signify. Wheels within wheels. Why wheels? What wheels? Still, there it is. I suppose the idea is to suggest that everything's pretty averagely complicated.'

'I understand what it means, of course. But why do you say it about yourself?'

'Because there's a snag sticking up in the course of true love. A very sizeable, jagged snag. Her blighted father, to wit, J. G. Butterwick, of Butterwick, Price, and Mandelbaum, export and import merchants.'

He swallowed a roast potato emotionally. Sue was touched. She had never ceased to congratulate herself on her sagacity in breaking off her engagement to this young man, but she was very fond of him.

'Oh, Monty, I'm so sorry. Poor darling. Doesn't he like you?'

Monty weighed this.

'Well, I wouldn't say that exactly. On two separate occasions he has said good morning to me, and once, round about Christmas time, I received a distinct impression that he was within an ace of offering me a cigar. But he's a queer bird. Years of exporting and importing have warped his mind a bit, with the result that for some reason I can't pretend to understand he appears to look on me as a sort of waster. The first thing he did when I ankled in and told him that subject to his approval I was about to marry his daughter was to ask me how I earned my living.'

'That must have been rather a shock.'

'It was. And a still worse one was when he went on to add that unless I got a job of some kind and held it down for a solid year, to show him that I wasn't a sort of waster, those wedding bells would never ring out.'

'You poor lamb. How perfectly awful!'

'Ghastly. I reeled. I stared. I couldn't believe the fellow was serious. When I found he was, I raced off to Gertrude and told her to jam her hat on and come round to the nearest registrar's. Only to discover, Sue, that she was one of those old-fashioned girls who won't dream of doing the dirty on Father. Solid middle-class stock, you understand. Backbone of England, and all that. So,

593

elopements being off, I had no alternative but to fall in with the man's extraordinary scheme. I got my Uncle Gregory to place me with the Mammoth Publishing Company in the capacity of assistant editor of *Tiny Tots*. And if only I could have contrived to remain an assistant editor, I should be there now. But my boss went off on a holiday, silly ass, leaving me in charge of the sheet and in a well-meant attempt to ginger the bally thing up a bit I made rather a bloomer in the Uncle Woggly department. The result being that a couple of days ago they formed a hollow square and drummed me out. And now I'm starting all over again at Blandings.'

'I see. I couldn't understand why you wanted to be Lord Emsworth's secretary. I was afraid you must have lost all your money.'

'Oh, no. I've got my money all right. And what,' demanded Monty, swinging an arm in a passionate gesture and hitting a waiter on the chest and saying 'Oh, sorry!' 'does money amount to? What *is* money? Fairy gold. That's what it is. Dead Sea fruit. Because it doesn't help me a damn towards scooping in Gertrude.'

'Is she an awfully nice girl?'

'An angel, Sue. No question about that. Quite the angel, absolutely.'

'Well, I do hope you will come out all right, Monty dear.'

'Thanks, old thing.'

'And I'm glad you didn't pine for me. I've felt guilty at times.'

'Oh, I pined. Oh, yes, certainly I *pined*. But you know how it is. One perks up and sees fresh faces. Tell me, Sue,' said Monty anxiously. 'I ought to be able to hold down that secretary job for a year, oughtn't I? I mean, people don't fire secretaries much, do they?'

'If Hugo could keep the place, I should think you ought to be able to. How are you on pigs?'

'Pigs?'

'Lord Emsworth . . .'

'Of course, yes, I remember now, Hugo told me. The old boy has gone porcine, has he not? You mean you would advise me to suck up to his pig, this what's-its-name of Blandings, to omit no word or act to conciliate it? Thanks for the tip. I'll bear it in mind.' He beamed affectionately at her across the table, and went so far as to take her hand in his. 'You've cheered me up, young Sue. You always did, I remember. You've got one of those sunny temperaments which look on the bright side and never fail to spot the blue bird. As you say, if a chap like Hugo could hold the job, it ought to be a snip for a man of my gifts, especially if I show myself pig-conscious. I anticipate a pleasant and successful year, with a wedding at the end of it. By which time, I take it, you will be an old married woman. When do you and Ronnie plan to leap off the dock?'

'As soon as ever Lord Emsworth lets him have his money. He wants to buy a partnership in a motor business.'

'Any opposish from the family?'

'Well, I don't think Lady Constance is frightfully pleased about it all.'

'Possibly it slipped out by some chance that you had been in the chorus?'

'It was mentioned.'

'Ah, that would account for it. But she's biting the bullet all right?'

'She seems resigned.'

'Then all is well.'

'I suppose so. And yet . . . Monty, do you ever get a feeling that something unpleasant is going to happen?'

'I got it two days ago, when my Lord Tilbury reached for the slack of my trousers and started to heave me out.'

'I've got it. I was saying so to Ronnie, and he told me not to be morbid.'

'Ronnie knows words like "morbid", does he? Two syllables and everything.'

'Monty, what is Ronnie's mother really like?'

Monty rubbed his chin.

'Haven't you met her yet?'

'No. She's been over in Biarritz.'

'But is returning?'

'I suppose so.'

"Myes. Post-haste, I should imagine. 'Myes!'

'For goodness' sake, don't say "'Myes". You're making my flesh creep. Is she such a terror?'

Monty scratched his right cheekbone.

'Well, I'll tell you. Many people would say she was a genial soul.'

'That's what Ronnie said.'

'The jovial hunting type. Lady Di. Bluff goodwill, the jolly smile for everyone, and slabs of soup at Christmas time for the deserving villagers. But I don't know. I'm not so sure. I'll tell you this much. When I was a kid I was far more scared of her than I was of Lady Constance.'

'Why?'

'Ah, there you have me. But I was. Still, don't let me take the joy out of your life. For all we know, she may at this very moment be practising "O Perfect Love" on the harmonium. And now, I don't want to hurry you, but the sands are running out a bit. My train goes at two forty-five . . .'

'What?'

'Two-four-five, pip emma.'

'You aren't going to Blandings today . . . by the two forty-five?'

'That's right.'

'But I'm going back on the two forty-five.'

'Well, that's fine. We'll travel together.'

'But we mustn't travel together.'

'Why not? Nobody's going to see us, and we can be as distant as the dickens on arrival. Pleasant chit-chat as far as Market Blandings, and cold aloofness from there on, is the programme as I see it. It's silly to overdo this perfect stranger business.'

Sue, thinking it over, was inclined to agree with him. She had had one solitary railway journey that day, and was not indisposed for pleasant company on the way back.

'And if you think, young Susan,' said Monty, who, though chivalrous, could stand up for his rights, 'that I intend to wait on and travel by something that stops and shunts at every station, you err. It's a four hours' journey even by express. We'll just nip round to my flat and pick up my things . . .'

'And miss the train. No, thank you. I can't take any chances. I'll meet you at the station.'

'Just as you like,' said Monty agreeably. 'I was only thinking that if you came to my flat, I could show you sixteen photographs of Gertrude.'

'You can describe them to me on the journey.'

'I will,' said Monty. 'Waiter, laddishiong.'

It was as the hands of the big clock at Paddington station were pointing to two-forty that Lady Julia Fish made her way through the crowd on the platform, her progress rendered impressive by the fact that her maid, two porters, and a boy who mistakenly supposed that he had found a customer for his oranges and nut-chocolate revolved about her like satellites around a sun.

Towards the turmoil in her immediate neighbourhood she displayed her usual good-humoured disdain. Where others ran she sauntered. Composedly she allowed one porter to open the door of an empty compartment, the other to place therein her bag, papers, novels, and magazines. She dismissed the maid, tipped the porters, and, settling herself in a corner seat, surveyed the bustle and stir without in an indulgent manner.

The ceremony of getting the two forty-five express off was now working up to a crescendo. Porters flitted to and fro. Guards shouted and poised green flags. The platform rang with the feet of belated travellers. And the train had just given a sort of shiver and began to move out of the station, when the door of the compartment was wrenched open and something that seemed to have six legs shot in, tripped over her, and collapsed into the seat opposite. It was a perspiring young man of the popinjay type, whose face, though twisted, was not so twisted that she was unable to recognize in him that Montague Bodkin who had once been so frequent a visitor at the home of her ancestors.

Monty had run it fine. What with hunting for a mislaid cigarette-case and getting held up in a traffic block in Praed Street, he had contrived this spectacular entry only by dint of sprinting the length of the platform at a rate of speed which he had not achieved since his university days.

But though warm and out of breath, he was still the *preux chevalier* who knew that when you have just barked the skin of a member of the other sex apologies must be made.

'It is quite all right, Mr Bodkin,' said Lady Julia as he made them. 'I am sorry I was in your way.'

Monty started violently.

'Gosh!' he exclaimed.

'I beg your pardon.'

'I mean – er – hullo, Lady Julia!'

'Hullo, Mr Bodkin.'

'Phew!' said Monty, dabbing agitatedly at his forehead with the handkerchief which so perfectly matched his tie and socks.

His distress was not caused entirely – or even to any great extent – by the reflection that he had just taken an

inch of skin off the daughter of a hundred earls. That, no
doubt, was regrettable, but what was really exercising
his mind was the thought that Sue being presumably on
the train and having presumably observed his rush down
the platform would be coming along at any moment to
see if he got aboard all right. It seemed to him that it
was going to require all his address to handle the
situation which her advent would create.

'Fancy running into you,' he said dismally.

' "Over me" would be a better way of putting it. I felt
like some unfortunate Hindu beneath the wheels of
Juggernaut. And where are you bound for, Mr Bodkin?'

'Eh? Oh, Market Blandings.'

'You are going to stay with your uncle at
Matchingham?'

'Oh, no. I'm booked for the Castle. Lord Emsworth
has taken me on as his secretary.'

'But how very odd. I thought you were working with
the Mammoth Publishing Company.'

'I've resigned.'

'Resigned?'

'Resigned,' said Monty firmly. He was not going to
reveal his Moscow to this woman.

'What made you resign?'

'Oh, various things. There are wheels within wheels.'

'How cosy!' said Lady Julia.

Monty decided to change the subject.

'I hear everything's much about the same at
Blandings.'

'Who told you that?'

'Fellow named Carmody, who has been secretarying
there. He said everything was much about the same.'

'What a very unobservant young man he must be!
Didn't he mention that there had been an earthquake
there, an upheaval, a social cataclysm?'

'I beg your . . . What was that?'

'Prepare yourself for a shock, Mr Bodkin. Ronnie is at

Blandings, and with him a chorus-girl of the name of
Brown, whom he proposes to marry.'

A little uncertain as to the judicious line to take,
Monty decided to be astounded.

'No!'

'I assure you.'

'A chorus-girl?'

'Named Sue Brown. You don't know her, by any
chance?'

'No. Oh, no. No.'

'I thought possibly you might.' Lady Julia looked out
of the window at the flying countryside. 'Very trying for
a parent. Don't you think so, Mr Bodkin?'

'Oh, most.'

'Still, I suppose it might have been worse. There is
rather a consoling ring about that simple name. I mean,
Sue Brown doesn't sound like a girl who will bring
breach of promise actions when the thing is broken off.'

'Broken off!'

'It might so easily have been Suzanne de Brune.'

'But – er – are you thinking of breaking it off?'

'Why, of course. You seem very concerned. Or is this
joy?'

'No – I – er – It just occurred to me that it might be a
bit difficult. I mean, Ronnie's a pretty determined sort of
chap.'

'He inherits it from his mother,' said Lady Julia.

It was during the silence which followed this remark
that Sue entered the compartment.

At the moment of her arrival Monty was staring out of
the window and Lady Julia had leaned back in her seat.
There was nothing, accordingly, to indicate any
connection between the two, and Sue was just about to
address to her old friend a cordial word of congratulation
on his abilities as a sprinter, when the sound of the
opening door caused him to turn. And so blank, so icy

was the stare of non-recognition which she encountered that she sank bewildered on the cushions with all the sensations of one who, after being cut by the county, walks into a brick wall.

It was not long, however, before enlightenment came. Monty was a young man who believed in taking no chances.

'Nice and green the country's looking, Lady Julia,' he observed. 'Isn't it, Lady Julia?'

His companion gave it a glance.

'Very, considering there has been no rain for such a long time.'

'I should think Ronnie must be enjoying it at Blandings, Lady Julia.'

'I beg your pardon?'

'I say,' said Monty, spacing his words carefully, 'that your son Ronnie must be enjoying the green of the countryside at Blandings Castle. He likes it green,' explained Monty. And with another frigid stare at Sue he leaned back and puffed his cheeks out.

There was a pause. Monty had not wrought in vain. An electric thrill seemed to pass through Sue's small body. Her heart was thumping.

'I beg your pardon,' she said breathlessly. 'Are you Lady Julia Fish?'

'I am.'

'My name's Sue Brown,' said Sue, wishing that she could have achieved a vocal delivery a little more impressive than that of a very young, startled mouse.

'Well, well, well!' said Lady Julia. 'Fancy that. Quite a coincidence, Mr Bodkin.'

'Oh, quite. Most.'

'We were just talking about you, Miss Brown.'

Sue nodded speechlessly.

'I am losing a son and gaining a daughter, and you're the daughter, eh?'

Sue continued to nod. Monty, personally, considered

that she was overdoing it. She ought, he felt, to be saying something. Something bright and snappy like . . . well, he couldn't on the spur of the moment think just what, but something bright and snappy.

'Yes,' said Lady Julia, 'I recognize you. Ronnie sent me a photograph of you, you know. I thought it charming. Well, you must come over here and tell me all about yourself. We will get rid of Mr Bodkin . . . By the way, you did tell me you had not met Miss Brown?'

'Definitely not. Certainly not. Far from it. Not at all.'

'Don't speak in that tone of horrified loathing, Mr Bodkin. I'm sure Miss Brown is a very nice girl, well worthy of your acquaintance. At any rate, you've met her now. Mr Bodkin, Miss Brown.'

'How do you do?' said Monty stiffly.

'How do you do?' said Sue with aloofness.

'Mr Bodkin is coming to Blandings as my brother's secretary.'

'Fancy!' said Sue.

'And now run along and look at the green countryside, Mr Bodkin. Miss Brown and I want to have a talk about all sorts of things.'

'I'll go and have a smoke,' said Monty, inspired.

'Do,' said Lady Julia.

Monty Bodkin sat in his smoking-compartment, well pleased with himself. It had been a near thing, and it had taken a man of affairs to avert disaster, but he had brought it off. Another half-second and young Sue would have spilled the beans. He was, as we say, pleased with himself, and he was also pleased with Sue. She had shown a swift grasp of the situation. There had been a moment when he had feared he was being too subtle, trying the female intelligence, notoriously so greatly inferior to the male, too high. But all had been well. Good old Sue had understood those guarded hints of his, and now everything looked pretty smooth.

He closed his eyes contentedly, and dropped off into a refreshing sleep.

From this he was aroused some half an hour later by the click of the door; and, opening his eyes and blinking once or twice, was enabled to perceive Sue standing before him.

'Ah! Interview over?'

Sue nodded and sat down. Her face was grave, like that of a puzzled child. Extraordinarily pretty it made her look, felt Monty, and for an instant there stole over him a faint regret for what might have been. Then he thought of Gertrude Butterwick and was strong again.

'I say, I did that distant aloofness stuff rather well, don't you think?'

'Oh, yes.'

'And pretty shrewd of me to grapple with a tricky situation so promptly and give you that instant pointer as to how matters stood?'

'Oh, yes.'

'What do you mean, Oh, yes? It was genius.' He looked at her with some intentness. 'You seem a shade below par. Didn't the interview go off well?'

'Oh, yes.'

'Don't keep saying "Oh, yes." What happened?'

'Oh, we talked.'

'Of course you talked, chump. What did you say?'

'I told her about myself, and – oh, you know, all that sort of thing.'

'And wasn't she chummy?'

She reflected, biting her lip.

'She was quite nice.'

'I know what that means – rotten.'

'No, she seemed perfectly friendly. Laughed a good deal and . . . well, just what you were saying. Lady Di. Bluff goodwill. But –'

'But you seemed to sense the velvet hand beneath the

iron glove? No, dash it, that's not right,' said Monty,
musing. 'The other way about it should be, shouldn't it?
You got the impression that she was simply waiting till
your back was turned to stick a knife in it?'

'A little. It's something about her eyes. She doesn't
smile with them. Of course, I may be all wrong.'

Monty looked dubious. He lit a cigarette and puffed at
it thoughtfully.

'No, I think you're right. I wish I didn't, but I do. I
don't mind telling you that a second before you came in
she was saying she was jolly well going to break the
whole thing off.'

'Oh?'

'Of course,' Monty hastened to add consolingly, 'she
hasn't got a dog's chance of doing it. There are few more
resolute birds than Ronnie. But she'll try her damnedest.
Tough eggs, that Blandings Castle female contingent.
Odd that they should be so much deadlier than the male.
Look at old Emsworth . . . old Gally . . . young Freddie
. . . you've never met Freddie, have you? . . . All jolly
good sorts. And against them you have this Julia, yonder
Constance, and a whole lot more, all snakes of the first
water. When you get to know that family better, you'll
realize that there are dozens of aunts you've not heard of
yet – far-flung aunts scattered all over England, and each
the leading blister of her particular county. It's a sort of
family taint. Still, as I say, old Ronnie is staunch.
Nobody could talk him out of prancing up the aisle with
the girl he loves.'

'No,' said Sue, her eyes dreamy.

'And now, pardon the suggestion, but wouldn't it be
as well if you shoved off? Suppose she happened to come
along and found us hobnobbing here like this?'

'I never thought of that.'

'Always think of everything,' said Monty paternally.

He closed his eyes again. The train rattled on towards
Market Blandings.

6

It was nearly an hour after the two forty-five had arrived at its destination that a slower, shabbier train crawled in and deposited Ronnie Fish on the platform of the little station of Market Blandings. The festivities connected with his cousin George's wedding and the intricacies of a railway journey across the breadth of England had combined to prevent an earlier return.

He was tired, but happy. The glow of sentiment which warms young men in love when they watch other people getting married still lingered. Mendelssohn's well-known march was on his lips as he gave up his ticket, and it was with a perceptible effort that he checked himself from saying to the driver of the station cab, 'Wilt thou, Robinson, take this Ronald to Blandings Castle?' Even when he reached his destination and found the hands of the grandfather clock in the hall pointing to ten to eight, his exuberance did not desert him. It was his pride that he could shave, bathe, and dress, always provided that nothing went wrong with the tie, in nine and a quarter minutes.

Tonight, all was well. The black strip of *crêpe-de-Chine* assumed the perfect butterfly shape of its own volition, and at eight precisely he was standing in the combination drawing-room and picture-gallery in which Blandings Castle was wont to assemble long before the evening meal.

He was surprised to find himself alone. And it was not long before surprise gave way to a stronger emotion. For some minutes he wandered to and fro, gazing at the portraits of his ancestors on the walls; but to a man who has just come from a long and dusty train journey ancestral portraits are a poor substitute for the old familiar juice. He pressed the bell, and presently Beach the butler appeared.

'Oh, hullo, Beach. I say, Beach, what about the cocktails?'

The butler seemed surprised.

'I was planning to serve them when the guests arrived, Mr Ronald.'

'Guests? There aren't people coming to dinner, are there?'

'Yes, sir. We shall sit down twenty-four.'

'Good Lord! A binge?'

'Yes, sir.'

'I must go and put on a white tie.'

'There is plenty of time, Mr Ronald. Dinner will not be served till nine o'clock. Perhaps you would prefer me to bring you an aperitif in advance of the formal cocktails?'

'I certainly would. I'm dying by inches.'

'I will attend to the matter immediately.'

The butler of Blandings Castle was not a man who when he said 'immediately' meant 'somewhere in the distant future'. Like a heavyweight jinn, stirred to activity by the rubbing of a lamp, he vanished and reappeared; and it was only a few minutes later that Ronnie was blossoming like a flower in the gentle rain of summer and finding himself disposed for leisurely chat.

'Twenty-four?' he said. 'Golly, we're going gay. Who's coming?'

The butler's eyes took on a glaze similar to that seen in those of policemen giving evidence.

'His lordship the Bishop of Poole, Sir Herbert and Lady Musker, Sir Gregory Parsloe-Parsloe . . .'

'What!'

'Yes, sir.'

'Who invited *him*?'

'Her ladyship, I should imagine, sir.'

'And he's coming? Well, I suppose he knows his own business,' said Ronnie dubiously. 'Better keep a close eye on Uncle Clarence, Beach. If you see him toying with a knife, remove it.'

'Very good, sir.'

'Who else?'

'Colonel and Mrs Mauleverer and daughter, the Honourable Major and Lady Augusta Lindsay-Todd and niece . . .'

'All right. You needn't go on. I get the general idea. Eighteen local nibs, plus the gang of six in residence.'

'Eight, Mr Ronald.'

'Eight?'

'His lordship, her ladyship, Mr Galahad, yourself, Miss Brown, Mr . . .' The butler's voice shook a little. '. . . Pilbeam . . .'

'Exactly. Six, you old ass.'

'There is also Mr Bodkin, sir.'

'Bodkin?'

'Sir Gregory Parsloe's nephew, Mr Ronald. Mr Montague Bodkin. You may recall him as a somewhat frequent visitor to the Castle during his school days.'

'Of course I remember old Monty. But you've got muddled. You've counted him in among the resident patients, when he's really one of the outside crowd.'

'No, sir. Mr Bodkin is assuming Mr Carmody's duties as his lordship's secretary.'

'Not really?'

'Yes, sir. I understand the appointment was ratified two days ago.'

'But that's odd. What does Monty want, sweating as a secretary? He's got about fifteen thousand a year of his own.'

'Indeed, sir?'

'Well, he had. Somehow or other we've not happened

607

to run into each other much these last two years. Do
you think he's lost it?'

'Very possibly, sir. A great many people have become
fiscally crippled of late.'

'Rummy,' said Ronnie.

Then speculation on this mystery was borne away on
a flood of sober pride. With a pardonable feeling of
smugness, Ronnie Fish realized that his soul had
achieved such heights of nobility that the prospect of a
Monty Bodkin buzzing about the Castle premises in
daily contact with Sue was causing him no pang of
apprehension or jealousy.

Not so very long ago, such a thought would have been
a dagger in his bosom. It was just the Monty type of chap
– tall, lissom, good-looking, and not pink – that he had
always feared. And now he could contemplate his
coming without a tremor. Pretty good, felt Ronnie.

'Well, come along with your eight,' he said. 'That's
only seven, so far.'

The butler coughed.

'I was assuming, Mr Ronald, that you were aware that
her ladyship, your mother, arrived this evening on the
two forty-five train.'

'What!'

'Yes, sir.'

'Good Lord!'

Beach regarded him solicitously, but did not develop
the theme. He had a nice sense of the proprieties.
Between himself and this young man there had existed
for eighteen years a warm friendship. Ronnie as a child
had played bears in his pantry. Ronnie as a boy had gone
fishing with him on the lake. Ronnie as a freshman at
Cambridge had borrowed five-pound notes from him to
see him through to his next allowance. Ronnie, grown to
man's estate, had given him many a sound tip on the
races, from which his savings bank account had profited
largely. He knew the last detail of Ronnie's romance,

sympathized with his aims and objects, was aware that
an interview of extreme delicacy faced him; and, had
they been sitting in his pantry now, would not have
hesitated to offer sympathy and advice.

But because this was the drawing-room, his lips were
sealed. A mere professional gesture was all he could
allow himself.

'Another cocktail, Mr Ronald?'

'Thanks.'

Ronnie, sipping thoughtfully, found his equanimity
returning. For a moment, he could not deny it, there had
been a slight sinking of the heart; but now he was telling
himself that his mother had always been a cheery soul,
one of the best, and that there was no earthly reason to
suppose that she was likely to make any serious trouble
now. True, there might be a little stiffness at first, but
that would soon wear off.

'Where is she, Beach?'

'In the Garden Room, Mr Ronald.'

'I ought to go there, I suppose. And yet . . . No,' said
Ronnie, on second thoughts. 'Might be a little rash,
what? There she would be with her hair-brush handy,
and the temptation to put me across her knee and . . .
No. I think you'd better send a maid or someone to
inform her that I await her here.'

'I will do so immediately, Mr Ronald.'

With a quiver of the left eyebrow intended to indicate
that, had such a thing been possible to a man in his
position, he would gladly have remained and lent moral
support, the butler left the room. And presently the door
reopened, and Lady Julia Fish came sailing in.

Ronnie straightened his tie, pulled down his
waistcoat, and advanced to meet her.

The emotions of a young man on encountering his
maternal parent, when in the interval since they last
saw one another he has announced his betrothal to a

member of the chorus, are necessarily mixed. Filial love cannot but be tempered with apprehension. On the whole, however, Ronnie was feeling reasonably debonair. He and his mother had laughed together at a good many things in their time, and he was optimistic enough to hope that with a little adroitness on his part the coming scene could be kept on the lighter plane. As he had said to Sue, Lady Julia Fish was not Lady Constance Keeble.

Nevertheless, as he kissed her, he was aware of something of the feeling which he had had in his boxing days when shaking hands with an unpleasant-looking opponent.

'Hullo, mother.'

'Well, Ronnie.'

'Here you are, what?'

'Yes.'

'Nice journey?'

'Quite.'

'Not rough, crossing over?'

'Not at all.'

'Good,' said Ronnie. 'Good.'

He began to feel easier.

'Well,' he proceeded chattily, 'we got old George off all right.'

'George?'

'Cousin George. I've just been best-manning at his wedding.'

'Ah, yes. I had forgotten. It was today, was it not?'

'That's right. I only got back half an hour ago.'

'Did everything go off well?'

'Splendidly. Not a hitch.'

'Family pleased, I suppose?'

'Oh, delighted.'

'They would be, wouldn't they? Seeing that George was marrying a girl of excellent position with ten thousand a year of her own.'

'H'r'rmph,' said Ronnie.

'Yes,' said Lady Julia, 'you'd better say "H'r'rmph!"'

There was a pause. Ronnie, who had just straightened his tie again, pulled it crooked and began straightening it once more. Lady Julia watched these manifestations of unrest with a grim blue stare. Ronnie, looking up and meeting it, diverted his gaze towards a portrait of the second Earl which hung on the wall beside him.

'Amazing beards those blokes used to wear,' he said nonchalantly.

'I wonder you can look your ancestors in the face.'

'I can't, as a matter of fact. They're an ugly crowd. The only decent one is Daredevil Dick Threepwood who married the actress.'

'You would bring up Daredevil Dick, wouldn't you?'

'That's right, mother. Let's see the old smile.'

'I'm not smiling. What you observed was a twitch of pain. Really, Ronnie, you ought to be certified.'

'Now, mother . . .'

'Ronnie,' said Lady Julia, 'if you dare to lift up your finger and say "Tweet-tweet, shush-shush, come-come," I'll hit you. It's no good grinning in that sickening way. It simply confirms my opinion that you are a raving lunatic, an utter imbecile, and that you ought to have been placed under restraint years ago.'

'Oh, dash it.'

'It's no good saying "Oh, dash it."'

'Well, I do say "Oh, dash it." Be reasonable. Naturally I don't expect you to start dancing round and strewing roses out of a hat, but you might preserve the decencies of debate. Highly offensive, that last crack.'

Lady Julia sighed.

'Why *do* all you young fools want to marry chorus-girls?'

'Read any good books lately, mother?' asked Ronnie, pacifically.

Lady Julia refused to be diverted.

611

'It's too amazing. It's a disease. It really is. Just like measles or whooping-cough. All young men apparently have to go through it. It seems only the other day that my poor father was shipping your Uncle Galahad off to Africa to ensure a cure.'

'I'll tell you something interesting about that, mother. The girl Uncle Gally was in love with . . .'

'I was a child at the time, but I can recall it so distinctly. Father thumping tables, mother weeping, and all that rather charming, old-world atmosphere of family curses. And now it's you! Well, well, one can only thank goodness that it never seems to last long. The fever takes its course, and the patient recovers. Ronnie, my poor half-wit, you can't really be serious about this?'

'Serious!'

'But, Ronnie, really! A chorus-girl.'

'There's a lot to be said for chorus-girls.'

'Not in my presence. I couldn't bear it. It's so *callow* of you, my dear boy. If this had happened when you were at Eton, I wouldn't have said a word. But when you're grown up and are supposed to have some sense. Look at the men who marry chorus-girls. A race apart. Young Datchet . . . That awful old Bellinger . . .'

'Ah, but you're overlooking something, my dear old parent. There are chorus-girls and chorus-girls.'

'This is your kind heart speaking.'

'And when you get one like Sue . . .'

'No, Ronnie. It's nice of you to try to cheer me up, but it can't be done. I regard the entire personnel of the ensembles of our musical comedy theatres as – if you will forgive me being Victorian for a moment – painted hussies.'

'They've got to paint.'

'Well, they needn't huss. And they needn't ensnare my son.'

'I'm not sure I like that word "ensnare" much.'

'You probably won't much like any of the words

you're going to get from me tonight. Honestly, Ronnie. I know it hurts your head to think, but try to just for a moment. It isn't simply a question of class. It's the whole thing . . . the different viewpoint . . . the different standards . . . everything. I take it that your idea when you marry is to settle down and lead a normal sort of life, and how are you going to have that with a chorus-girl? How are you going to trust a woman of that sort of upbringing, who has lived on excitement ever since she was old enough to kick her beastly legs up in front of an audience and sees nothing wrong in going off and having affairs with every man that takes her fancy? That sort of girl would be sneaking off round the corner the moment your back was turned.'

'Not Sue.'

'Yes, Sue.'

Ronnie smiled indulgently.

'Wait till you meet her!'

'I have met her, thanks.'

'What?'

'She was in the train, and introduced herself.'

'But what was she doing in the train?'

'Returning here from London.'

'I didn't know she had gone up to London.'

'So I imagine,' said Lady Julia.

Not many minutes had passed since Ronnie Fish had been urging his mother to smile. With these words she had done so, but the fulfilment of his wish brought him no pleasure. The pink of his face deepened. There had come a tightness about his mouth. He had changed his mind about the desirability of keeping the scene light.

'Do you mind if I just get this straight?' he said coldly. 'A moment ago you were talking about girls who ran off and had affairs . . . and now you tell me you have met Sue.'

'Exactly.'

'Then you . . . had Sue in mind?'

'Exactly.'

Ronnie laughed, unpleasantly.

'On the strength, apparently, of her having gone up to London for the day – to do some shopping or something, I suppose. I wouldn't call this your ripest form, mother.'

'On the strength, if you really wish to know, of seeing her and young Monty Bodkin lunching together at the Berkeley and finding them together on the train . . .'

'Monty Bodkin!'

'. . . where they had the effrontery to pretend they had never met before.'

'She was lunching with Monty?'

'Lunching with Monty and ogling Monty and holding hands with Monty! Oh, for heaven's sake, Ronnie, do use a little intelligence. Can't you see this girl is just like the rest of them? If you can't, you really must be a borderline case. Young Bodkin came here today to be your uncle's secretary. Two days ago he had some sort of employment with the Mammoth Publishing Company. He told me on the train that he had resigned. Why did he resign? And why is he coming here? Obviously because this girl wanted him here and put him up to it. And directly she hears it's settled, she takes advantage of your being away to sneak up to London and talk things over with him. If there was nothing underhand going on, why should they have pretended that they were perfect strangers? No, as you said just now, I am *not* dancing round and strewing roses out of a hat!'

She broke off. The door had opened. Lady Constance Keeble came in.

In the doorway Lady Constance paused. She looked from one to the other with speculation in her eyes. She was a veteran of too many fine old crusted family rows not to be able to detect a strained atmosphere when she saw one. Her sister Julia was clenching and unclenching her hands. Her nephew Ronald was staring straight before him, red-eyed. A thrill ran through Lady Constance, such as causes the war-horse to start at the sound of the bugle. It was possible, of course, that this was a private fight, but her battling instinct urged her to get into it.

But there was in Lady Constance Keeble an instinct even stronger than that of battle, and that was the one which impelled her to act as critic of the sartorial deficiencies of her nearest and dearest. Years of association with her brother Clarence, who, if you took your eye off him for a second, was apt to come down to dinner in flannel trousers and an old shooting-jacket, had made this action almost automatic with the chatelaine of Blandings.

So now, eager for the fray, it was as the critic rather than as the warrior queen that she spoke.

'My dear Ronald! That tie!'

Ronnie Fish gazed at her lingeringly. It needed, he felt, but this. Poison was running through his veins, his world was rocking, green-eyed devils were shrieking mockery in his ears, and along came blasted aunts babbling of ties. It was as if somebody had touched Othello on the arm as he poised the pillow and criticized the cut of his doublet.

'Don't you know we have a dinner-party tonight? Go and put on a white tie at once.'

Even in his misery the injustice of the thing cut Ronnie to the quick. Did his aunt suppose him ignorant of the merest decencies of life? Naturally, if he had known before he started dressing that there was a big binge on, he would have assumed the correct costume of the English gentleman for formal occasions. But considering that he had been told only about two minutes ago . . .

'And a tail-coat.'

It was the end. If this woman's words had any meaning at all, it was that she considered him capable of wearing a white tie with a dinner-jacket. Until this moment he had been intending to speak. The thing had now passed beyond speech. Directing at Lady Constance a look which no young man ought to have directed at an aunt, he strode silently from the room.

Lady Constance stood listening to the echoes of a well-slammed door.

'Ronald seems upset,' she observed.

'It runs in the family,' said Lady Julia.

'What was the trouble?'

'I have just been telling him that he is off his head.'

'I quite agree with you.'

'And I should like now,' said Lady Julia, 'to apply the same remark to you.'

She was breathing quickly. The china-blue of her eyes had an enamelled look. It was thirty-five years since she had scratched Lady Constance's face, but she seemed so much in the vein for some such demonstration that the latter involuntarily drew back.

'Really, Julia!'

'What do you mean, Constance, by inviting that girl to Blandings?'

'I did nothing of the sort.'

'You didn't invite her?'

'Certainly not.'

'She popped up out of a trap, eh?'

Lady Constance emitted that sniff of hers which came so near to being a snort.

'She wormed her way into the place under false pretences, which amounts to the same thing. You remember that Miss Schoonmaker, the American girl you met at Biarritz and wrote to me about? You gave me the impression that you hoped there might eventually be something between her and Ronald.'

'I really can't understand what you are talking about. Why need we discuss Myra Schoonmaker?'

'I am trying to explain to you how this Brown girl comes to be at the Castle. About ten days ago I was in

London, and I met Ronald in his car with a girl, and he introduced her to me as Miss Schoonmaker. I had no means of checking his statement. It never occurred to me to doubt it. I assumed that she really was Miss Schoonmaker, and naturally invited her to the Castle. She arrived, and she had not been here twenty-four hours when we discovered that she was not Miss Schoonmaker at all, but this chorus-girl of Ronald's. Presumably they had planned the thing between them in order to get her here.'

'And when you found out she was an impostor you asked her to stay on? I see.'

Lady Constance flushed brightly.

'I was compelled to allow her to stay on.'

'Why?'

'Because . . . Oh, Clarence!' said Lady Constance, with the exasperation which the sudden spectacle of the head of the family so often aroused in her. The ninth Earl had selected this tense moment to potter into the room.

'Eh?' he said.

'Go away!'

'Yes,' said Lord Emsworth, 'lovely.' As so frequently happened with him, he was in a gentle trance. He wandered to the piano, extended a long, lean finger, and stabbed absently at one of the treble notes.

The sharp, tinny sound seemed to affect his sister Constance like a pin in the leg.

'Clarence!'

'Eh?'

'Don't *do* that!'

'God bless my soul!' said Lord Emsworth querulously.

He turned from the piano, and Lady Constance was enabled to see him steadily and see him whole. The sight caused her to utter a stricken cry.

'Clarence!'

'Eh?'

'What – *what* is that thing in your shirt-front?'

The ninth Earl squinted down.

'It's a paper-fastener. One of those brass things you fasten papers with. I lost my stud.'

'You must have more than one stud.'

'Here's another, up here.'

'Have you only two studs?'

'Three,' said Lord Emsworth, a little proudly. 'For the front of the shirt, three. Dashed inconvenient things. The heads come off. You screw them off and then you put them in and then you screw them on.'

'Well, go straight up to your room and screw on the spare one.'

It was not often that Lord Emsworth found himself in the position of being able to score a debating point against his sister Constance. The fact that he was about to do so now filled him with justifiable complacency. It seemed to lend to his manner a strange, quiet dignity.

'I can't,' he said. 'I swallowed it.'

Lady Constance was not the woman to despair for long. A short, sharp spasm of agony and she had seen the way.

'Wait here,' she said. 'Mr Bodkin is sure to have dozens of spare studs. If you dare to move till I come back . . .'

She hurried from the room.

'Connie fusses so,' said Lord Emsworth equably.

He pottered back to the piano.

'Clarence,' said Lady Julia.

'Eh?'

'Leave that piano alone. Pull yourself together. Try to concentrate. And tell me about this Miss Brown.'

'Miss who?'

'Miss Brown.'

'Never heard of her,' said Lord Emsworth brightly, striking a D flat.

'Don't gibber, Clarence. Miss Brown.'

'Oh, Miss Brown? Yes. Yes, of course. Yes. Miss

Brown, to be sure. Yes. Nice girl. She's going to marry Ronald.'

'Is she? That's a debatable point.'

'Oh, yes, it's all settled. I'm giving the boy his money and he's going into the motor business, and they're going to get married.'

'I want to know how all this has happened. How is it that this chorus-girl . . .'

'You're quite right,' said Lord Emsworth cordially. 'I told Connie she was wrong, but she wouldn't believe me. A chorus-girl is quite different from a ballet-girl. Galahad assures me of this.'

'If you will kindly let me finish . . .'

'By all means, by all means. You were saying – ?'

'I was asking you how it has come about that everyone in this madhouse appears to have accepted it as quite natural and satisfactory that Ronnie should be marrying a girl like that. She seems to be an honoured guest at the Castle, and yet, apart from anything else, she came here under a false name . . .'

'Odd, that,' said Lord Emsworth. 'She told us her name was Schoolbred, and it turned out she was quite wrong. It wasn't Schoolbred at all. Silly mistake to make.'

'And when that turned out, may I ask why you didn't turn *her* out?'

'Why, we couldn't, of course.'

'Why not?'

'Well, naturally we couldn't. Galahad wouldn't have liked it.'

'Galahad?'

'That's right. Galahad.'

Lady Julia threw up her arms in a passionate gesture. 'Is everybody crazy?' she cried.

Lady Constance came hurrying back into the room. 'Clarence!'

'You all keep saying "Clarence!"' said Lord Emsworth

peevishly. ' "Clarence . . . Clarence" . . . One would
think I was a Pekingese or something. Well, what is it
now?'

'Listen, Clarence,' said Lady Constance, speaking in a
clear, even voice, 'and follow me carefully. Mr Bodkin is
in the North Room. You know where the North Room
is? On the first floor, down the passage to the right of
the landing. You know which your right hand is? Very
well. Then go immediately to the North Room, and
there you will find Mr Bodkin. He has studs and will fit
them into your shirt.'

'I'm dashed if I'm going to have my secretary dressing
me like a nursemaid!'

'If you think that with sixteen people coming to
dinner I am going to trust you to put in studs for
yourself . . .'

'Oh, all right,' said Lord Emsworth. 'All right, all
right, all right. Lots of fuss for nothing.'

The door closed. Lady Julia came out of the frozen
coma into which her brother's words had thrown her.

'Constance!'

'Well?'

'Just before you came in, Clarence told me that the
reason why this Brown girl was allowed to stay on at the
Castle was that Galahad wished it.'

'Yes.'

'And we must all respect Galahad's wishes, must we
not? I don't suppose,' said Lady Julia, mastering her
complex emotions with a strong effort, 'that there are
forty million people in England who think more highly
of Galahad than I do. Tell me,' she went on with
strained politeness, 'if it is not troubling you too much,
how exactly does he come into the thing at all? Why
Galahad? Why not Beach? Or Voules? Or the boy who
cleans the knives and boots? What earthly business is it
of Galahad's?'

Lady Constance was not by nature a patient woman,

but she could make allowances for a mother's grief.

'I know how you must be feeling, Julia, and you can't be more upset about it than I am. Galahad, unfortunately, is in a position to dictate.'

'I cannot conceive of any possible position Galahad could be in which would permit him to dictate to me, but no doubt you will explain what you mean later. What I would like to know first is why he wants to dictate. What is this girl to him that he should apparently have constituted himself a sort of guardian angel to her?'

'To explain that, I must ask you to throw your mind back.'

'Better not start me throwing things.'

'Do you remember, years ago, Galahad getting entangled with a woman named Henderson, a music-hall singer?'

'Certainly. Well?'

'This girl is her daughter.'

Lady Julia was silent for a moment.

'I see. Galahad's daughter, too?'

'I believe not. But that explains his interest in her.'

'Possibly. Yes, no doubt it does. Sentiment is the last thing of which I would have suspected Galahad, but if the old love has lingered down the years I suppose we must accept it. All right. Very touching, no doubt. But it still leaves unexplained the mystery of why everybody here seems to be treating Galahad as if his word was law. You said he was in a position to dictate. Why?'

'I was coming to that. The whole thing, you see, turns on whether Clarence lets Ronald have his money or not. If he does, Ronald can defy us all. Without it he is helpless. And in ordinary circumstances you and I know that we could easily reason with Clarence and make him do the sensible thing and refuse to release the money . . .'

'Well?'

'Well, Galahad was clever enough to see that, too. So he made a bargain. You know those abominable Reminiscences he has been writing. He said that if Ronald was given his money he would suppress them.'

'What!'

'Suppress them. Not publish them.'

'Is *that* what you meant when you said that he was in a position to dictate?'

'Yes. It is sheer blackmail, of course, but there is nothing to be done.'

Lady Julia was staring, bewildered. She flung her hands up to her carefully coiffured head, seemed to realize at the last moment that a touch would ruin it, and lowered them again.

'Am I mad?' she cried. 'Or is everybody else? You seriously mean that I am supposed to acquiesce in my son ruining his life simply in order to keep Galahad from publishing his Reminiscences?'

'But, Julia, you don't know what they're like. Think of the life Galahad led as a young man. He seems to have known everybody in England who is looked up to and respected today and to have shared the most disgraceful escapades with them. One case alone, for example – Sir Gregory Parsloe. I have not read the thing, of course, but he tells me that there is a story in Galahad's book about himself when he was a young man in London . . . something about some prawns – I don't know what . . . which would make him the laughing-stock of the county. The book is full of that kind of story, and every story about somebody who is looked on today as a model of propriety. If it is published, it will ruin the reputations of half the best people in England.'

Lady Julia laughed shortly.

'I'm afraid I don't share your reverence for the feelings of the British aristocracy, Connie. I agree that Galahad probably knows the shady secrets of two-thirds of the peerage, but I don't feel your shrinking horror at the thought of the public reading them in print. I haven't the slightest objection in the world to Galahad throwing bombshells. At any rate, whatever the effect of his literary efforts on the peace of mind of the governing classes, I certainly do not intend to buy him off at the price of having Ronnie marrying any Miss Browns.'

'You don't mean that you are going to try to stop this marriage?'

'I most certainly am.'

'But, Julia! This book of Galahad's. It will alienate every friend we've got. They will say we ought to have stopped him. You don't know . . .'

'I know this, that Galahad can publish Reminiscences till he is blue in the face, but I am not going to have my son making a fool of himself and doing something he'll regret for the rest of his life. And now, if you will excuse me, Connie, I propose to take a short stroll on the terrace in the faint hope of cooling off. I feel so incandescent that I'm apt to burst into spontaneous flame at any moment, like dry tinder.'

With which words Lady Julia Fish took her departure through the french windows. And Lady Constance, having remained for some few moments in anguished thought, moved to the fireplace and rang the bell.

Beach appeared.

'Beach,' said Lady Constance, 'please telephone at once to Sir Gregory Parsloe at Matchingham. Tell him I must see him immediately. Say it is of the utmost importance. Ask him to hurry over so as to get here before people begin to arrive. And when he comes show him into the library.'

'Very good, m'lady.'

The butler spoke with his official calm, but inwardly he was profoundly stirred. He was not a nimble-minded man, but he could put two and two together, and it seemed to him that in some mysterious way, beyond the power of his intellect to grasp, all these alarms and excursions must be connected with the love-story of his old friend, Mr Ronald, and his new – but very highly esteemed – friend, Sue Brown.

He had left Mr Ronald with his mother. Then Lady Constance had gone in. A short while later, Mr Ronald had come out and gone rushing upstairs with all the appearance of an overwrought soul. And now here was Lady Constance, after a conversation with Lady Julia, ringing bells and sending urgent telephone messages.

It must mean something. If Beach had been Monty Bodkin, he would have said that there were wheels within wheels. Heaving gently like a seaweed-covered sea, he withdrew to carry out his instructions.

The butler's telephone message found Sir Gregory Parsloe enjoying a restful cigarette in his bedroom. He had completed his toilet some little time before; but, being an experienced diner-out and knowing how sticky that anteprandial vigil in somebody else's drawing-room can be, he had not intended to set out for Blandings Castle for another twenty minutes or so. Like so many elderly, self-indulgent bachelors, he was inclined to shirk life's grimmer side.

But the information that Lady Constance Keeble wished to have urgent speech with him had him galloping down the stairs and lumbering into his car in what for a man of his build was practically tantamount to a trice. It must, he felt, be those infernal Reminiscences that she wanted to see him about: and, feeling nervous and apprehensive, he told the chauffeur to drive like the devil.

In the past two weeks, Sir Gregory Parsloe-Parsloe, of Matchingham Hall, seventh Baronet of his line, had run the gamut of the emotions. He had plumbed the depths of horror on learning that his old companion, the Hon. Galahad Threepwood, was planning to publish the story of his life. He had soared to dizzy heights of relief on learning that he had decided not to do so. But from that relief there had been a reaction. What, he had asked himself, was to prevent the old pest changing his mind again? And this telephone call seemed to suggest that he might have done so.

Of all the grey-haired pillars of Society who had winced and cried aloud at the news that the Hon. Galahad was about to unlock the doors of memory, it was probably Sir Gregory Parsloe who had winced most and cried loudest. His position was so particularly vulnerable. He had political ambitions, and was, indeed, on the eve of being accepted by the local Unionist committee as the party's candidate for the forthcoming by-election in the Bridgeford and Shifley Parliamentary Division of Shropshire. And no one knew better than himself that Unionist committees look askance at men with pasts.

Small wonder, then, that Sir Gregory Parsloe writhed in his car and, clumping up the stairs of Blandings Castle to the library in Beach's wake, sank into a chair and sat gazing at Lady Constance with apprehension on every feature of his massive face. Years of good living had given Sir Gregory something of the look of a buck of the Regency days. He resembled now a Regency buck about to embark on a difficult interview with the family lawyer.

Lady Constance made no humane attempt to break the bad news gently. She was far too agitated for that. Sir Gregory got it like a pail of water in the face, and sat spluttering as if it had actually been water she had poured over him.

'What shall we do?' lamented Lady Constance. 'I know Julia so well. She is entirely self-centred. So long as she can get what she wants, other people don't count. Julia is like that, and always has been. She will stop this marriage. I don't know how, but she will do it. And if the marriage is broken off, Galahad will have no reason for suppressing his abominable book. The manuscript will go to the publishers next day. What did you say?'

Sir Gregory had not spoken. He had merely uttered a wordless sound half-way between a grunt and a groan.

'Have you nothing to suggest?' said Lady Constance.

Before the baronet could reply, if he would have replied, there was an interruption. The door of the library opened and a head inserted itself. It was a small, brilliantined head, the eyes beneath the narrow forehead furtive, the moustache below the perky nose a nasty little moustache. Having smiled weakly, it withdrew.

It was a desire for solitude that had brought P. Frobisher Pilbeam to the library. A few moments before, he had been in the drawing-room and had found its atmosphere oppressive. Solid county gentlemen and their wives had begun to arrive, and the sense of being an alien in a community where everybody seemed extraordinarily intimate with everybody else had weighed upon him, inducing red ears and a general sensation of elephantiasis about the hands and feet.

Taking advantage, therefore, of the fact that the lady with the weather-beaten face who had just asked him what pack he hunted with had had her attention diverted elsewhere, he had stolen down to the library to be alone. And the first thing he saw there was Lady Constance Keeble. So, as we say, Percy Pilbeam smiled weakly and withdrew.

The actual time covered by his appearance and disappearance was not more than two or three seconds, but it had been enough for Lady Constance Keeble to give him one of the celebrated Keeble looks. Turning from this task and lowering the raised eyebrow and uncurling the curled lip, she was astonished to observe that Sir Gregory Parsloe was staring at the closed door with the aspect of one who had just seen a beautiful vision.

'What – what – what . . .'

'I beg your pardon?' said Lady Constance, perplexed.

'Good heavens! Was that *Pilbeam*?'

Lady Constance was shocked.

'Do you know Mr Pilbeam?' she asked in a tone which suggested that she would have expected something better than this from the seventh holder of a proud title.

Sir Gregory was not a man of the build that leaps from chairs, but he had levered himself out of the one he sat in with an animation that almost made the thing amount to a leap.

'Know him? Why, he's in the Castle because I know him! I engaged him to steal that infernal manuscript of your brother's.'

'What!'

'Certainly. A week or so ago. Emsworth called one morning with Threepwood to see me, and accused me of having stolen that dashed pig of his, and when I told him I knew nothing about it Threepwood got nasty and said he was going to make a special effort to remember all the discreditable things that had ever happened to me as a young man and put them in his book. So I ran up to London next day and went to see this fellow Pilbeam – he had acted for me before in a certain rather delicate matter – and found that Emsworth had asked him to come here to investigate the theft of his pig, and I offered him five hundred pounds if, when he was at the Castle, he would steal the manuscript.'

'Good gracious!'

'And then you told me the pig had been found and Threepwood was going to suppress the book, so I naturally assumed that the chap would have gone back to London. Why, if he's still here, the whole thing's simple. He must go ahead, as originally planned, and get hold of that manuscript and hand it over to us and we'll destroy it. Then it won't matter if this marriage you speak of takes place or not.' He paused. Animation gave place to concern. 'But suppose there are more copies than one?'

'There aren't.'

'You're sure? He may have had it typed.'

'No, I know he has not. He had never really finished the horrible thing. He keeps it in his desk and takes it out and adds bits to it.'

'Then we're all right.'

'If Mr Pilbeam can get possession of the manuscript.'

'Oh, he'll do that. You can rely on him. There isn't a smarter young fellow in London at that sort of thing. Why, he got hold of some letters of mine . . . but that is neither here nor there. I can assure you that if you engage Pilbeam to steal compromising papers, you will have them in the course of a day or two. It's what he's best at. You say Threepwood keeps the thing in a desk. Desks are nothing to Pilbeam. Those – er – those letters of mine . . . to which I alluded just now . . . those letters . . . perfectly innocent, you understand, but a wrong construction might have been placed upon one or two passages in them had they been published as the girl . . . as their recipient had threatened . . . Well, to cut a long story short, to secure them Pilbeam had to pretend to be the man come to inspect the gas meter and break into a safe. This will be child's play to him. If you will excuse me, I will go and find him at once. We must put the matter in hand without delay. What a pity he popped off like that. We could have had everything arranged by now.'

Sir Gregory hurried from the room, baying on the scent like one of his own hounds. And Lady Constance, drawing a deep breath, leaned back in her chair and closed her eyes. After all that had passed in the last twenty minutes, she felt the need to relax.

On her face, as she sat, there might have been observed not merely relief, but a sort of awed look, as of one who contemplates the inscrutable workings of Providence.

Providence, she now perceived, did not put even Pilbeams into the world without a purpose.

Sue stood leaning out over the battlements of Blandings
Castle, her chin cupped in her hands. Her eyes were
clouded, her mouth a thin red line of depression. A little
furrow of unhappiness had carved itself in the smooth
whiteness of her forehead.

It was an instinct for the high places, like that of a
small, nervous cat which fears vague perils on the lower
levels, that had sent her climbing to this eminence.
Wandering past the great gatehouse where a channel of
gravel divided the west wing of the castle from the
centre block, she had espied an open door, giving on to
mysterious stone steps; and, mounting these, had found
herself on the roof, with all Shropshire spread beneath
her.

The change of elevation had done nothing to alter her
mood. It was four o'clock of a sultry, overcast,
oppressive afternoon, and a sullen stillness had fallen on
the world. The heat wave which for the past two weeks
had been grilling England was in the uncomfortable
process of working up to a thunderstorm. Shropshire,
under a leaden sky, had taken on a sinister and a
brooding air. The flowers in the gardens drooped
forlornly. The lake was a grey smudge, and the river in
the valley below a thread of sickly, tarnished silver.
Gone, too, was the friendly charm of the Scotch fir
spinneys that dotted the park. They seemed now black
and haunted and menacing, as if witches lived in
crooked little cottages in the heart of them.

'Ugh!' said Sue, hating Shropshire.

Until this moment, except for a few cows with secret

sorrows, there had been no living creature to mitigate
the gloom of the grim prospect. It was as if life,
discouraged by the weather conditions, had died out
upon the earth. But as she spoke, shaking her head with
the flicker of a grimace, she perceived on the path below
a familiar form. It looked up, sighted her, waved, and
disappeared in the direction of the gatehouse. And
presently feet boomed hollowly on the stone stairs, and
there came into view the slouch-hatted head of Monty
Bodkin.

'Hullo, Sue. All alone?'

Monty, who seemed, like everything else, to be
affected by the weather, puffed, removed his hat, fanned
himself, and laid it down.

'Gosh, what a day!' he observed. 'You been up here long?'

'About an hour.'

'I've been closeted with that fellow Pilbeam in the
smoking-room. Went in to fill my cigarette-case and got
into conversation with him. He's been telling me all
about himself. Interesting chap.'

'I think he's a worm.'

'He is a worm,' agreed Monty. 'But even worms, don't
you think, are of more than passing interest when they
run private inquiry agencies? Did you know he was a
private detective?'

'Yes.'

'Now, there's a job I should like.'

'You would hate it, Monty. Sneaking about, spying on
people.'

'But with a magnifying-glass, remember,' urged
Monty. 'You don't feel that it makes a difference if you
do it with a magnifying-glass? No? Well, perhaps you're
right. In any case, I suppose it requires special gifts. I
wouldn't know a clue if you brought me one on a
skewer. I say, did you ever see such a day? I feel as if I
were in a frying-pan. Still, I suppose one's as well off up
here as anywhere.'

'I suppose so.'

Monty surveyed his surroundings with a sentimental eye.

'Must have been fifteen years since I was on this roof. As a kid you couldn't keep me off it. I smoked my first cigar behind that buttress. Slightly to the left is the spot where I was sick. You see that chimney-stack?'

Sue saw the chimney-stack.

'I once watched old Gally chase Ronnie twenty-seven times round that with a whangee. He had been putting tin-tacks on his chair. Ronnie had on Gally's chair, I mean, of course, not Gally on Ronnie's. Where is Ronnie by the way?'

'Lady Julia asked him to take her to Shrewsbury in his two-seater, to do some shopping.'

Sue's voice was flat, and Monty looked at her inquiringly.

'Well, why not?'

'Oh, I don't know,' said Sue. 'Only, considering that she was at Biarritz for three months and then in Paris and after that in London, it seems odd that she should wait to do her shopping till she got to Shrewsbury.'

Monty nodded sagely.

'I see what you mean. A ruse, you think? A cunning stratagem to keep him out of the way? I shouldn't wonder if you weren't right.'

Sue looked out over the grey world.

'She needn't have bothered,' she said, in a small voice. 'Ronnie seems quite capable of keeping out of my way without assistance.'

'What do you mean by that?'

'Haven't you noticed?'

'Well, I'll tell you,' said Monty apologetically. 'What with being a good deal exercised about my lord Emsworth's questionable attitude and musing in my spare time on good old Gertrude, I haven't been much in

the vein for noticing things. Has he been keeping out of
your way?'

'Ever since we got back.'

'Oh, rot.'

'It isn't rot.'

'A girlish fancy, child.'

'It's nothing of the kind. He's been avoiding me all the
time. He'll do anything to keep from being alone with
me. And if ever we do happen to be alone together he's
quite different.'

'How do you mean, different?'

'Polite. Horribly, disgustingly polite. All sort of stiff
and formal, as if I were a stranger. You know that way
he gets when he's with someone he doesn't like.'

Monty was concerned.

'I say, this wants thinking over. I confess that my
primary scheme, on spotting you leaning over the
ramparts, was to buzz up and pour out my troubles on
your neck. But if this is really so, you had better do the
pouring. As what's-his-name said to the stretcher-case,
"Your need is greater than mine." '

'Are you in trouble, too?'

'Trouble?' Monty held up a warning hand. 'Listen.
Don't tempt me. One more word of encouragement, and
I'll be monopolizing the conversation.'

'Go on. I can wait.'

'You're sure?'

'Quite.'

Monty sighed gratefully.

'Well, it'll be a relief, I must own,' he admitted. 'Sue,
old girl, I am becoming conscious of an impending
doom. The future is looking black. For some reason
which I am unable to fathom I don't seem to have made
a hit with my employer.'

'What makes you think that?'

'Signs, Sue. Signs and portents. The old blighter bites

at me. He clicks his tongue irritably. I look up and find his eyes fixed on me with an expression of loathing. You wouldn't think it possible that a man who could stick Hugo Carmody as a secretary for a matter of eleven weeks would be showing distress signs after a mere two days of me, but there it is. Why, I cannot say, but the ninth Earl obviously hates my insides.'

'Are you sure you aren't imagining all this?'

'Quite sure.'

'But it seems so unlike Lord Emsworth. I've always thought him such an old dear.'

'Precisely how I had remembered him from boyhood days. He used to tip me when I went back to school – tip me lavishly and with the kindest of smiles. But no longer. Not any more. He now views me with concern and dogs my footsteps.'

'Does *what*?'

'Dogs my footsteps. Tails me up, as they say at Scotland Yard. Do you recall that hymn about "See the hosts of Midian prowl and prowl around"? Well, that's what this extraordinary bloke does. For some strange reason of his own he has started watching me, as if he were suspecting me of nameless crimes. I'll give you an instance. Yesterday afternoon I had gone down to the pig-bin to chirrup to that pig of his in the hope of establishing cordial relations, as you advised, and as I approached the animal's lair I happened to glance round, and there he was peering out from behind a tree, his face alight with mistrust. Wouldn't you call that prowling?'

'It certainly seems like prowling.'

'It is prowling. Grade A prowling. And what, I am asking myself, will the harvest be? You may say, Oh, why worry? arguing that an Earl, on his own ground, has a perfect right to hide behind trees and glare at secretaries. But I go deeper than that. I look on the thing as a symptom, and a dangerous symptom. I contend that

634

the Earl who hides behind trees today is an Earl who
intends to apply the order of the boot tomorrow. And,
my gosh, Sue, I can't afford to go getting the boot twice
daily like this. If I don't stay put in some sort of job for a
year, I fail to gather in Gertrude, and how am I to get
another job if I lose this one? I'm not an easy man to
place. I have my limitations, and I know it.'

'Poor old Monty!'

' "Poor old Monty" sums up the thing extraordinarily
neatly,' agreed the haunted man. 'I'm sunk if this old
bird fires me. And what makes it so particularly foul is
that I haven't a notion what he's got against me. I've
made a point of being so fearfully alert and obsequious
and the perfect secretary generally. I've been simply
fascinating. The whole thing's a mystery.'

Sue reflected.

'I'll tell you what to do. Why not get hold of Ronnie
and ask him to ask Lord Emsworth tactfully . . .'

Monty shook his head.

'Not Ronnie. No. Not within the sphere of practical
politics. Now, there's another mystery, Sue. Old Ronnie.
Once one of my closest pals, and now frigid, aloof,
distant. Says "Oh, yes?" and "Really?" when I speak to
him, and turns away as if desirous of terminating the
conversation.'

'Really?'

'And "Oh, yes?" '

'I mean, does he really seem not to like you?'

'He's as sniffy as dammit. And I can't . . . Great Scott,
Sue,' cried Monty, struck with an idea, 'you don't
suppose that by any chance he Knows All?'

'That you and I were once engaged? How could he?'

'No, that's right. He couldn't, could he?'

'Nobody here can have told him, because nobody
knows. Except Gally, who wouldn't breathe a word.'

'True. It only occurred to me as a rather rummy
coincidence that he's upstage like this with both of us.

635

Why, if he does not Know All, should he be keeping out of your way, as you say he's doing?'

All Sue's pent-up misery found voice. She had not intended to confide in Monty, for she was a girl whom life had trained to keep her troubles to herself. But Ronnie had gone to Shrewsbury, and the heat was making her head ache, and the sky was looking like the under side of a dead fish, and she wished she were dead, so she poured out all the poison that was in her heart.

'I'll tell you why. Because his mother has been talking to him . . . never stopped since she got here . . . talking to him and nagging at him and telling him what a fool he is to think of marrying a girl like me, when there are dozens of girls in his own set . . . Oh, yes, she has. I know it just as if I had been there. I know exactly the sort of things she would say. And all quite true, too, I suppose. "My dear boy, a chorus-girl!" Well, so I am. You can't get away from that. Why should anyone want to marry me?'

Monty clicked his tongue. He could not subscribe to this.

'My dear old egg! Do it myself tomorrow, if not already ear-marked elsewhere. I consider Ronnie dashed lucky.'

'That's sweet of you, Monty, but I'm afraid Ronnie doesn't agree with you.'

'Oh, rot!'

'I wish I could think so.'

'Absolute rot. Ronnie's not the sort of chap to back out of marrying a girl he's asked to marry him.'

'Oh, I know that. His word is his bond. We men of honour! My poor old Monty, you don't really think I would marry a man who has stopped being fond of me, simply because he's too decent to break the engagement? If there's one person I despise in the world, it's the girl who clings to a man when she knows it's only politeness that keeps him from telling her for goodness' sake to go away and leave him in peace. If ever I really feel certain that Ronnie wants to be rid of me,' said Sue, staring dry-eyed at the menacing sky, 'I'll chuck it all up in a second, no matter how much it hurts.'

Monty shuffled uneasily.

'I think you're making too much of it all,' he said, but without conviction. 'If you boil it down, probably all that's happened is that the old chap's got a touch of liver. Enough to give anyone a touch of liver, weather like this.'

Sue did not reply. She had walked to the battlements and was looking down. Something in the aspect of her back seemed to tell Monty Bodkin that she was either crying or about to cry, and he did not know what to do for the best. The face of Gertrude Butterwick, floating between him and the sky, forbade the obvious move. A man with a Gertrude Butterwick on his books cannot lightly put his arms round other waists and murmur 'There, there,' into other ears.

He coughed and said, 'Er – well . . .'

Sue did not turn. He coughed again. Then, with a 'Well – I – er – ah . . .' he sidled to the stairs. The clang of the closing door came to Sue's ears as she dabbed at her eyes with the tiny fragment of lace which she called a handkerchief. She was relieved that he had gone. There are moments when a girl must be alone to wrestle single-handed with her own particular devils.

This she did, bravely and thoroughly. There was in her small body the spirit of an Amazon. She fought the devils and routed the devils, till presently a final sniff told that the battle had been won. Shropshire, which had been a thing of mist, became firmer in its outlines. She put away the handkerchief and stood blinking defiantly.

She was happier now. The determination to finish everything if she saw Ronnie wanted it finished had not weakened. It still lay rooted at the back of her mind. But

hope had dawned again. She was telling herself that she
understood Ronnie's odd behaviour. He was worried,
poor darling, as who would not be with a woman of Lady
Julia Fish's powerful personality going on at him all the
time. And when a man is worried, he naturally becomes
preoccupied.

The sound of a car drawing up on the other side of the
house broke in upon her meditations. She hurried across
the roof, her heart quickening.

She turned away, disappointed. It was not Ronnie,
back from Shrewsbury. It was only a short, stout man
who had driven up in the station taxi. A short, stout,
stumpy man of no importance whatever.

So thought Sue in her ignorance. The stout man, had
he known that he was being thus casually dismissed as
negligible, would have been not only offended, but
amazed.

For this visitor to Blandings Castle, for all that he
arrived without pomp, driven to his destination by
charioteer Robinson in that humble conveyance, the
Market Blandings station taxi, was none other than
George Alexander Pyke, first Viscount Tilbury, founder
and proprietor of the Mammoth Publishing Company of
Tilbury House, Tilbury Street, London.

There are men of the bulldog breed who do not readily
admit defeat. Crushed to earth, they rise again. To this
doughty band belonged George Alexander, Viscount
Tilbury. He had built up a very large fortune chiefly by
the simple method of never knowing when he was
beaten, and the fact that he was now ringing the doorbell
of Blandings Castle proved that the ancient spirit still
lingered. He had come to tackle the Hon. Galahad
Threepwood in person about those Reminiscences of his,
and he meant to stand no nonsense.

Many men in his position, informed that the Hon.
Galahad had decided to withhold his book from

publication, would have felt that there was nothing to be done about it. They would have accepted the situation as one beyond their power to change, and would have contented themselves with grieving over their monetary loss and thinking hard thoughts of the man responsible. Lord Tilbury was made of sterner stuff. He grieved – we have seen him grieving – and he thought hard thoughts: but it never occurred to him for an instant not to do something about it.

A busy man, he could not get away from his office immediately. Pressure of work had delayed the starting of the expedition until today. But at eleven-fifteen that morning he had taken the train for Market Blandings and, after establishing himself at the Emsworth Arms in that sleepy little town, had directed Robinson, of the station taxi, to take him on to the Castle.

His mood was one of stern self-confidence. The idea that he might fail in his mission did not strike him as even a remote possibility. He had only a dim recollection of the Hon. Galahad, for he had not met him for twenty-five years, and even in the old days had never been really an intimate of his, but he retained a sort of general impression of an amiable, easygoing man. Not at all the type of man to hold out against a forceful, straight from the shoulder talk such as he proposed to subject him to as soon as this door-bell was answered. Lord Tilbury had great faith in the magic of speech.

Beach answered the bell.

'Is Mr Threepwood in? Mr Galahad Threepwood?'

'Yes, sir. What name shall I say?'

'Lord Tilbury.'

'Very good, m'lord. If you will step this way. I fancy Mr Galahad is in the small library.'

The small library, however, proved empty. It contained evidence of the life literary in the shape of a paper-piled desk and a good deal of ink on the carpet and elsewhere, but it had no human occupant.

'Possibly Mr Galahad is on the lawn. He walks there sometimes,' said the butler indulgently, as one tolerant of the foibles of genius. 'If your lordship will take a seat . . .'

He withdrew, and began to descend the stairs with measured tread, but Lord Tilbury did not take a seat. He was staring, transfixed, at something that lay upon the desk. He drew closer – furtively, with a sidelong eye on the door.

Yes, his surmise had been correct. It was the manuscript of the Reminiscences that lay before him. Evidently its author had only just risen from the task of polishing it, for the ink was still wet on a paragraph where, searching like some Flaubert for the *mot juste*, he had run his pen through the word 'intoxicated' and substituted for it the more colourful 'pickled to the gills'.

Lord Tilbury's eyes, always prominent, bulged a trifle farther from their sockets. His breathing quickened.

Every man who by his own unaided efforts has succeeded in wresting a great fortune from a resistant world has something of the buccaneer in him, a touch of the practical, Do-It-Now pirate of the Spanish Main. In Lord Tilbury, as a younger man, there had been quite a good deal. And while prosperity and the diminishing necessity of giving trade rivals the elbow had tended to atrophy this quality, it had not died altogether. Standing there within arm's length of the manuscript, with the coast clear and a taxi waiting at the front door, he was seriously contemplating the quick snatch and the masterful dash for the open.

And it was perhaps fortunate, for sudden activity of the kind might have proved injurious to a man of his full habit, that before he could quite screw his courage to the sticking point his ear caught the sound of approaching footsteps. He drew back like a cat from a cream-jug, and when the Hon. Galahad arrived was looking out of the window, humming a careless barcarolle.

The Hon. Galahad paused in the doorway and stuck his black-rimmed monocle in his eye. Behind the glass the eye was bright and questioning. His forehead wrinkled with mental strain as he surveyed his visitor.

'Don't tell me,' he begged. 'Let me think. I pride myself on my memory. You're fatter and you've aged a lot, but you're someone I used to know quite well at one time. In some odd way I seem to associate you with a side of beef . . . Shorty Smith? . . . Stumpy Whiting? . . . No, I've got it, by gad! Stinker Pyke!' He beamed with honest satisfaction. 'Not bad, that, considering that it must be fully twenty-five years since I saw you last. Pyke. That's who you are. And we used to call you Stinker. Well, well, how are you, Stinker?'

Lord Tilbury's face had taken on an austere pinkness. He disliked the reference to his increased bulk, and advancing years, and it is never pleasant for an elderly man of substance to be addressed by a name which even in his youth was offensive to him. He said as much.

'Well, all right. Pyke, then,' said the Hon. Galahad agreeably. 'How are you, Pyke? Good Lord, this certainly puts the clock back. The last time I saw you must have been that night at Romano's when Plug Basham started throwing bread and got a little over-excited, and one thing led to another and in about two minutes there you were on the floor, laid out cold by a dashed great side of beef and all the undertakers present making bids for the body. I can see your face now,' said the Hon. Galahad, chuckling. 'Most amusing.'

He grew more serious. His smile vanished. He shook his head sadly.

'Poor old Plug!' he sighed. 'A fellow who never knew where to stop. His only fault, poor chap.'

Lord Tilbury had not come a hundred and fourteen

miles to talk about the late Major Wilfred Basham, a man who, even before the episode alluded to, had never been a favourite of his. He endeavoured to intimate this, but the Hon. Galahad when in reminiscent mood was not an easy man to divert.

'I took the whole thing up with him at the Pelican next day. I tried to reason with him. Throwing sides of beef about in restaurants wasn't done, I said. Not British. Bread, yes, I said. Sides of beef, no. I pointed out that all the trouble was caused by his fatal practice of always ordering a quart where other men began with pints. He saw it, too. "I know, I know," he said. "I'm a darned fool. In fact, between you and me, Gally, I suppose I'm one of those fellows my father always warned me against. But the Bashams have always ordered quarts. It's an old Basham family custom." Then the only way was, I said, to swear off altogether. He said he couldn't. A little something with his meals was an absolute necessity to him. So there I had to leave it. And then one day I met him again at a wedding reception at one of the hotels.'

'I . . .' said Lord Tilbury.

'A wedding reception,' proceeded the Hon. Galahad. 'And, by a curious coincidence, there was another wedding reception going on at the same hotel, and, oddly enough, their bride was some sort of connection of our bride. So pretty soon these two wedding parties began to mix and mingle, everybody happy and having a good time, and suddenly I felt something plucking at my elbow and there was old Plug, looking as white as a sheet. "Yes, Plug?" I said, surprised. The poor, dear fellow uttered a hollow groan. "Gally, old man," he said, "lead me away, old chap. The end has come. The stuff has begun to get me. I have had only the merest sip of champagne, and yet I assure you I can distinctly see two brides."'

'I . . .' said Lord Tilbury.

'A shock to the poor fellow, as you can readily imagine. I could have set his mind at rest, of course, but I saw that this was providential. Just the sort of jolt he had been needing. I drew him into a corner and talked to him like a Dutch uncle. And this time he gave me his solemn word that from that day onward he would never touch another drop. "Can you do it, Plug?" I said. "Have you the strength, the will-power?" "Yes, Gally," he replied bravely, "I can. Why, dash it," he said, "I've got to. I can't go through the rest of my life seeing two of everything. Imagine! Two bookies you owe money to . . . Two process-servers . . . Two Stinker Pykes . . ." Yes, old man, in that grim moment he thought of you . . . And he went off with a set, resolute look about his jaw which it did me good to see.'

'I . . .' said Lord Tilbury.

'And about two weeks later I came on him in the Strand, and he was bubbling over with quiet happiness. "It's all right, Gally," he said, "it's all right, old lad. I've done it. I've won the battle." "Amazing, Plug," I said. "Brave chap! Splendid fellow! Was it a terrific strain?" His eyes lit up. "It was at first," he said. "In fact, it was so tough that I didn't think I should be able to stick it out. And then I discovered a teetotal drink that is not only palatable but positively appetizing. Absinthe, they call it, and now I've got that I don't care if I never touch wine, spirits, or any other intoxicants again."'

'I am not interested,' said Lord Tilbury, 'in your friend Basham.'

The Hon. Galahad was remorseful.

'I'm sorry,' he said. 'Shouldn't have rattled on. An old failing of mine, I'm afraid. Probably you've come on some most important errand, and here have I been yarning away, wasting your time. Quite right to pull me up. Take a seat, and tell me why you've suddenly bobbed up like this after all these years, Stinker.'

'Don't call me Stinker!'

'Of course. I'm sorry. Forgot. Well, carry on, Pyke.'

'And don't call me Pyke. My name is Tilbury.'

The Hon. Galahad started. His monocle fell from his eye, and he screwed it in again thoughtfully. There was a concerned and disapproving look on his face. He shook his head gravely.

'Going about under a false name? Bad. I don't like that.'

'Cor!'

'It never pays. Honestly, it doesn't. Sooner or later you're bound to be found out, and then you get it all the hotter from the judge. I remember saying that to Stiffy Vokes in the year ninety-nine, when he was sneaking about London calling himself Orlando Maltravers in the empty hope of baffling the bookies after a bad City and Suburban. And he, unlike you, had had the elementary sense to put on a false beard. Stinker, old chap,' said the Hon. Galahad kindly, 'is it worth while? Can this do anything but postpone the inevitable end? Why not go back and face the music like a man? Or, if the thing's too bad for that, at least look in at some good theatrical costumier's and buy some blond whiskers. What is it they are after you for?'

Lord Tilbury was beginning to wonder if even a volume of Reminiscences which would rock England was worth the price he was paying.

'I call myself Tilbury,' he said between set teeth, 'because in a recent Honours List I received a peerage, and Tilbury was the title I selected.'

Light flooded in upon the Hon. Galahad's darkness.

'Oh, you're *Lord* Tilbury?'

'I am.'

'What on earth did they make you a lord for, Stinker?' asked the Hon. Galahad in frank amazement.

Lord Tilbury was telling himself that he must be strong.

'I happen to occupy a position of some slight

importance in the newspaper world. I am the proprietor of a concern whose name may be familiar to you – the Mammoth Publishing Company.'

'Mammoth?'

'Mammoth.'

'Don't tell me,' said the Hon. Galahad. 'Let me think. Why, aren't the Mammoth the people I sold that book of mine to?'

'They are.'

'Stinker – I mean Pyke – I mean Tilbury,' said the Hon. Galahad regretfully, 'I'm sorry about that. Yes, by Jove, I am. I've let you down, haven't I? I see now why you've come here. You want me to reconsider. Well, I'm afraid you've had your journey for nothing, Stinker, old man. I won't let that book be published.'

'But . . .'

'No. I can't argue. I won't do it.'

'But, good heavens! . . .'

'I know, I know. But I won't. I have reasons.'

'Reasons?'

'Private and sentimental reasons.'

'But it's outrageous. It's unheard of. You signed the contract. You were satisfied with the terms we proposed . . .'

'It's got nothing to do with the terms.'

'And you can't pretend that you are not in a position to deliver the book. There it is on your desk, finished.'

The Hon. Galahad took up the manuscript with something of the tenderness of a mother dandling her first-born. He stared at it, sighed, stared at it again, sighed once more. His heart was aching.

The more he reread it, the more of a tragedy did it seem to him that this lovely thing should not be given to the world. It was such dashed good stuff. Yes, if he did say it himself, such dashed good stuff. Faithfully and well he had toiled at his great task of erecting a lasting memorial to an epoch in London's history which, if ever an epoch did, deserved its Homer or its Gibbon, and he had done it, by George! Jolly good, ripping good stuff.

And no one would ever read the dashed thing.

'A book like this is never finished,' he said. 'I could go on adding to it for the rest of my life.'

He sighed again. Then he brightened. The suppression of his masterpiece was the price of Dolly's daughter's happiness. If it brought happiness to Dolly's daughter, there was nothing to regret, nothing to sigh about at all.

All the same, he did wish that his brother Clarence could have been of tougher fibre and better able, without assistance, to cope with the females of the family.

He put the manuscript away in a drawer.

'But it's finished,' he said, 'as far as any chance of its ever getting into print is concerned. It will never be published.'

'But . . .'

'No, Stinker, that's final. I'm sorry. Don't imagine I don't see your side of it. I know I've treated you badly, and I quite realize how justified you are in blinding and stiffing . . .'

'I am not blinding and stiffing. I flatter myself that I have – under extreme provocation – succeeded in keeping this discussion on an amicable footing. I merely say . . .'

'It's no use your saying anything, Stinker.'

'Don't call me . . .'

'I can't possibly explain the situation to you. It would take too long. But you can rest assured that nothing you can say will make the slightest difference. I won't publish.'

There was a pregnant silence. Lord Tilbury's gaze, which had fastened itself, like that of a Pekingese on coffee-sugar, upon the drawer into which he had seen the manuscript disappear, shifted to the man who stood between him and it. He stared at the Hon. Galahad wistfully, as if yearning for that side of beef which had once proved so irresistible a weapon in the hand of Plug Basham.

The fever passed. The battle-light died out of his eyes. He rose stiffly.

'In that case I will bid you good afternoon.'

'You're not going?'

'I am going.'

The Hon. Galahad was distressed.

'I wish you wouldn't take it like this. Why get stuffy, Stinker? Sit down. Have a chat. Stay on and join us for a bite of dinner.'

Lord Tilbury gulped.

'Dinner!'

A harmless word, but on his lips it somehow managed to acquire the sound of a rich Elizabethan oath – the sort of thing Ben Jonson, in his cups, might have flung at Beaumont and Fletcher.

'Dinner!' said Tilbury. 'Cor!'

There are moments in life when only sharp physical action can heal the wounded spirit. Just as a native of India, stung by a scorpion, will seek to relieve his agony by running, so now did Lord Tilbury, fresh from this scene with one who seemed to him well fitted to be classified as a human scorpion, desire to calm himself with a brisk cross-country walk. Reaching the broad front steps and seeing before him the station taxi, he was conscious of a feeling amounting almost to nausea at the thought of climbing into its mildew-scented interior and riding back to the Emsworth Arms.

He produced money, thrust it upon the surprised Robinson, mumbled unintelligently and, turning abruptly, began to stump off in a westerly direction. Robinson, having pursued him with a solid, silent, Shropshire stare till he had vanished behind a shrubbery, threw in his clutch and drove pensively homewards.

Lord Tilbury stumped on, busy with his thoughts.

At first chaotic, these began gradually to take shape.

His mind returned to that project which he had conceived while standing alone in the small library. A single object seemed to be imprinted on his retina – that desk in which the Hon. Galahad had placed his manuscript.

He yearned for direct action against that desk.

Like all reformed buccaneers, he put up a good case for himself in extenuation of this resurgence of the Old Adam. To take that manuscript, he argued, would merely be to take that which was rightfully his. He had a legal claim to it. The contract had been signed and witnessed. Payment in advance had changed hands. Normally, no doubt, as between author and publisher, the author would have wrapped his work in brown paper, stuck stamps on it, and posted it. But if the eccentric fellow preferred to leave it in a desk for the publisher to come and fetch it, the thing still remained a legitimate business transaction.

And how simple the looting of that desk would be, he felt, if only he were staying in the house. From the careless, casual way in which the Hon. Galahad had put the manuscript in that drawer he had received a strong impression that he would not even bother to lock it. Anybody staying in the house . . .

Bitter remorse swept over Lord Tilbury as he strode broodingly through the heat-hushed grounds of Blandings Castle. He saw now what a mistake he had made in taking that proud, offended attitude with the Hon. Galahad. If only he had played his cards properly, taken the thing with a smile, accepted that invitation to dinner and gone on playing his cards properly, he would almost certainly before nightfall have been asked to move his belongings from the Emsworth Arms and come and stay at the Castle. And then . . .

Of all sad words of tongue or pen, the saddest are these: It might have been. Groaning in spirit, Lord Tilbury walked on. And suddenly as he walked there came to his nostrils the only scent in the world which could have diverted his mind from that which weighed it.

He had smelt a pig.

To those superficially acquainted with them, it would have seemed incredible that George, Viscount Tilbury, and Clarence, Earl of Emsworth, could have possessed a single taste in common. The souls of the two men, one would have said, lay poles apart. And yet such was the remarkable fact. Widely though their temperaments differed in every other respect, they were both pig-minded. In his little country place in Buckinghamshire, whither he was wont to retire for recuperating over the week-ends, Lord Tilbury kept pigs. He not only kept pigs, but loved and was proud of them. And anything to do with pigs, such as a grunt, a gollop, or, as in this case, a smell, touched an immediate chord in him.

So now he came out of his reverie with a start, to find that his aimless wanderings had brought him to within potato-peel throw of a handsomely appointed sty.

And in this sty stood a pig of such quality as he had never seen before.

The afternoon, as has been said, was overcast. An unwholesome blight, like a premature twilight, had fallen upon the world. But it needed more than a little poorness of visibility to hide the Empress. Sunshine would have brought out her opulent curves more starkly, perhaps, but even seen through this grey murk she was quite impressive enough to draw Lord Tilbury to her as with a lasso. He hurried forward and stood gazing breathlessly.

His initial reaction to the spectacle was a feeling of sick envy, a horrible, aching covetousness. That was the effect the first view of Empress of Blandings always had on visiting fanciers. They came, saw, gasped, and went away unhappy, discontented men, ever after to move

through life bemused and yearning for they knew not
what, like men kissed by goddesses in dreams. Until this
moment Lord Tilbury had looked on his own
Buckingham Big Boy as a considerable pig. He felt now
with a pang that it would be an insult to this supreme
animal before him even to think of Buckingham Big Boy
in her presence.

The Empress, after a single brief but courteous glance
at this newcomer, had returned to the business which
had been occupying her at the moment of Lord Tilbury's
arrival. She pressed her nose against the lowest rail of
the sty and snuffled moodily. And Lord Tilbury, looking
down, saw that a portion of her afternoon meal, in the
shape of an appetising potato, had been dislodged from
the main *couvert* and had rolled out of bounds. It was
this that was causing the silver medallist's distress and
despondency. Like all prize pigs who take their career
seriously, Empress of Blandings hated to miss anything
that might be eaten and converted into firm flesh.

Lord Tilbury's pig-loving heart was touched. Envy left
him, swept away on the tide of a nobler emotion. All
that was best and humanest in him came to the surface.
He clicked his tongue sympathetically. His build made
it unpleasant for him to stoop, but he did not hesitate.
At the cost of a momentary feeling of suffocation, he
secured the potato. And he was on the point of dropping
it into the Empress's upturned mouth, when there
occurred a startling interruption.

Hot breath fanned his cheek. A hoarse voice in his ear
said 'Ur!!' A sinewy hand closed vice-like about his
wrist. Another attached itself to his collar. And, jerked
violently away, he found himself looking into the
accusing eyes of a tall, thin, scraggy man in overalls.

It was the time of day when most of Nature's
children take the afternoon sleep. But Jas. Pirbright had
not slept. His employer had instructed him to lurk, and
he had been lurking ever since lunch. Sooner or later,

Lord Emsworth had told him, quoting that
second-sighted man, the Hon. Galahad Threepwood,
there would come sneaking to the Empress's sty a
mysterious stranger. And here he was, complete with
poison-potato, and Pirbright had got him. The Pirbrights,
like the Canadian Mounted Police, always got their
man.

'Gur!' said Jas. Pirbright, which is Shropshire for 'You
come along with me and I'll shut you up somewhere
while I go and inform his lordship of what has occurred.'

Monty Bodkin, meanwhile, after parting from Sue on the
roof, had been making his way slowly and pensively
through the grounds in the direction of the Empress's
headquarters. It was his intention to look in on the
noble animal and try to do himself a bit of good by
fraternizing with it.

He was not hurrying. The afternoon was too hot for
that. Shropshire had become a Turkish bath. The sky
seemed to press down like a poultice. Butterflies had
ceased to flutter, and as he dragged himself along it was
only the younger and more sprightly rabbits that had the
energy to move out of his path.

Yet even had the air been nipping and eager, it is
probable that he would still have loitered, for his
mind was heavy with care. He didn't like the look of
things.

No, mused Monty, he didn't like the look of things at
all. Sheridan once write of 'a damned disinheriting
countenance', and if Monty had ever read Sheridan he
would have felt that he had found the perfect description
for the face of the ninth Earl of Emsworth as seen across
the table in the big library or peering out from behind
trees. Not even in that interview with Lord Tilbury in
his office at the Mammoth had he been surer that he
was associating with a man who proposed very shortly
to dispense with his services. The sack, it seemed to

him, was hovering in the air. Almost he could hear the beating of its wings.

He came droopingly to the paddock where the Empress resided. There was a sort of potting-shed place just inside the gate, and here he halted, using its surface to ignite the match which was to light the cigarette he so sorely needed.

Yes, he felt, as he stood smoking there, if he had any power of reading faces, any skill whatever in interpreting the language of the human eye, his latest employer was on the eve of administering the bum's rush. It seemed to him that even now he could hear his voice, crying 'Get out! Get out!'

And then, as the sound persisted, he became aware that it was no dream voice that spoke, but an actual living voice; that it proceeded from the shed against which he was leaning; and that what it was saying was not 'Get out!' but 'Let me out!'

He was both startled and intrigued. For a moment, his mind toyed with the thought of spectres. Then he reflected, and very reasonably, that a ghost that had only to walk a quarter of a mile to find one of the oldest castles in England at its disposal would scarcely waste its time haunting potting-sheds. There was a small window close to where he stood. Emboldened, he put his face to it.

'Are you there?' he asked.

It was a fair question, for the interior of the shed was of an Egyptian blackness. Nevertheless, it appeared to annoy the captive. An explosive 'Cor!' came hurtling through the air, and Monty leaped a full two inches. The thing seemed incredible, but if a fellow was to trust the evidence of his senses this unseen acquaintance was none other than –

'I say,' he gasped, 'that isn't Lord Tilbury, by any chance, is it?'

'Who are you?'

'Bodkin speaking. Bodkin, M. Monty Bodkin. You remember old Monty?'

It was plain that Lord Tilbury did, for he spoke with a familiar vigour.

'Then let me out, you miserable imbecile. What are you wasting time for?'

Monty was groping at the door.

'Right-ho,' he said. 'In one moment. There's a sort of wooden gadget that needs a bit of shifting. All right. Done it. Out you pop. Upsy-daisy!'

And with these words of encouragement he removed the staple, and Lord Tilbury emerged, snorting.

'Yes, but I say –!' pleaded Monty, after a few moments, anxious, like Goethe, for more light. This was one of the weirdest and most mysterious things that he had encountered in his puff, and it was apparently his companion's intention merely to stand and snort about it.

Lord Tilbury found speech.

'It's an outrage!'

'What is?'

'I shall have the fellow severely punished.'

'What fellow?'

'I shall see Lord Emsworth about it immediately.'

'About what?'

Briefly and with emotion Lord Tilbury told his tale.

'I kept explaining to the man that if he had any doubts as to my social standing your uncle, Sir Gregory Parsloe, who I believe lives in this neighbourhood, would vouch for me . . .'

Monty, who had been listening with a growing understanding, checking up each point in the narrative with a sagacious nod, felt compelled at this juncture to interrupt.

'My sainted aunt!' he cried. 'You say you offered the porker a spud? And then this chap grabbed you? And then you told him you were a friend of my Uncle

Gregory? And now you're going to the Castle to lodge a complaint with Old Man River? Don't do it!' said Monty urgently, 'don't do it. Don't go anywhere near the Castle, or they'll have you in irons before you can say "Eh, what?" You aren't on to the secret history of this place. There are wheels within wheels. Old Emsworth thinks Uncle Gregory is trying to assassinate his pig. You are caught in the act of giving it potatoes and announce that you are a pal of his. Why, dash it, they'll ship you off to Devil's Island without a trial.'

Lord Tilbury stared, thinking once again how much he disliked this young man.

'What are you drivelling about?'

'Not drivelling. It's quite reasonable. Look at it from their point of view. If this pig drops out of the betting, my uncle's entry will win the silver medal at the show in a canter. Can you blame this fellow Pirbright for looking a bit cross-eyed at a chap who comes creeping in and administering surreptitious potatoes and then gives Uncle Gregory as a reference? He probably thought that potato contained some little-known Asiatic poison.'

'I never heard of anything so absurd.'

'Well, that's Life,' argued Monty. 'And, in any case, you can't get away from it that you're trespassing. Isn't there some law about being allowed to shoot trespassers on sight? Or is it burglars? No, I'm a liar. It's stray dogs when you catch them worrying sheep. Still, coming back to it, you *are* trespassing.'

'I am doing nothing of the kind. I have been paying a call at the Castle.'

The conversation had reached just the point towards which Monty had been hoping to direct it.

'Why? Now we're on to the thing that's been baffling me. What were you doing in these parts at all? Why have you come here? Always glad to see you, of course,' said Monty courteously.

Lord Tilbury appeared to resent this courtesy. And,

indeed, it had smacked a little of the gracious seigneur making some uncouth intruder free of his estates.

'May I ask what you are doing here yourself?'

'Me?'

'If, as you say, Lord Emsworth is on such bad terms with Sir Gregory Parsloe, I should have thought that he would have objected to his nephew walking in his grounds.'

'Ah, but, you see, I'm his secretary.'

'Why should the fact you are your uncle's secretary –?'

'Not my uncle's. Old Emsworth's. Pronouns are the devil, aren't they? You start saying "he" and "his" and are breezing gaily along, and you suddenly find you've got everything all mixed up. That's Life, too, if you look at it in the right way. No, I'm not my uncle's secretary. He hasn't got a secretary. I'm old Emsworth's. I secured the post within twenty-four hours of your slinging me out of *Tiny Tots*. Oh, yes, indeed,' said Monty, with airy nonchalance, 'I very soon managed to get another job. Dear me, yes. A good man isn't long getting snapped up.'

'You are Lord Emsworth's secretary?' Lord Tilbury seemed to have difficulty in assimilating the information. 'You are living at the Castle? You mean that you are actually living – residing at Blandings Castle?'

Monty, thinking swiftly, decided that that airy nonchalance of his had been a mistake. Well meant, but a blunder. The sounder policy here would be manly frankness. He believed in taking at the flood that tide in the affairs of men which, when so taken, leads on to fortune. It was imperative that he secure another situation before Lord Emsworth should apply the boot; and he could scarcely hope to find a more propitious occasion for approaching this particular employer of labour than when he had just released him from a smelly potting-shed.

He replied, accordingly, that for the nonce such was indeed the case.

'But only,' he went on candidly, 'for the nonce. I don't mind telling you that I expect a shake-up shortly. I anticipate that before long I shall find myself once more at liberty. Nothing actually said, mind you, but all the signs pointing that way. So if by any chance you are feeling that we might make a fresh start together – if you are willing to let the dead past bury its dead – if, in a word, you would consider overlooking that little unpleasantness we had and taking me back into the fold, I, on my side, can guarantee quick delivery. I should be able to report for duty almost immediately, with a heart for any fate.'

Upon most men listening to this eloquent appeal there might have crept a certain impatience. Lord Tilbury, however, listened to it as though to some grand sweet song. Like Napoleon, he had had some lucky breaks in his time, but he could not recall one luckier than this – that he should have found in this young man before him a man who at one and the same time was living at Blandings Castle and wanted favours from him. There could have been no more ideal combination.

'So you wish to return to Tilbury House?'

'Definitely.'

'You shall.'

'Good egg!'

'Provided –'

'Oh, golly! Is there a catch?'

Lord Tilbury had fallen into a frowning silence. Now that the moment had arrived for putting into words the lawless scheme that was in his mind, he found a difficulty in selecting the words into which to put it.

'Provided what?' said Monty. 'If you mean provided I exert the most watchful vigilance to prevent any more dubious matter creeping into the columns of *Tiny Tots*, have no uneasiness. Since the recent painful episode, I have become a changed man and am now thoroughly attuned to the aims and ideals of *Tiny Tots*. You can restore my hand to the tiller without a qualm.'

'It has nothing to do with *Tiny Tots*.' Lord Tilbury paused again. 'There is something I wish you to do for me.'

'A pleasure. Give it a name. Even unto half of my kingdom, I mean to say.'

'I . . . That is . . . well, here is the position in a nutshell. Lord Emsworth's brother, Galahad Threepwood, has written his Reminiscences.'

'I know. I'll bet they're good, too. They would sell like hot cakes. Just the sort of book to fill a long-felt want. Grab it, is my advice.'

'That,' said Lord Tilbury, relieved at the swiftness with which the conversation had arrived at the vital issue, 'is precisely what I want to do.'

'Well, I'll tell you the procedure,' said Monty helpfully. 'You get a contract drawn up, and then you charge in on old Gally with your cheque-book . . .'

'The contract already exists. Mr Threepwood signed it some time ago, giving the Mammoth all rights to his book. He has now changed his mind and refuses to deliver the manuscript.'

'Good Lord! Why?'

'I do not know why.'

'But the silly ass will be losing a packet.'

'No doubt. His decision not to publish means also the loss of a considerable sum of money to myself. And so, I consider that, the contract having been signed, I am legally entitled to the possession of the manuscript, I – er – I intend – well, in short, I intend to take possession of it.'

'You don't mean pinch it?'

'That, crudely, is what I mean.'

'I say, you do live, don't you? But how?'

'Ah, there I would have to have the assistance of somebody who was actually in the house.'

A bizarre idea occurred to Monty.

'You aren't suggesting that you want *me* to pinch it?'

'Precisely.'

'Well, lord-love-a-duck!' said Monty.

He stared in honest amazement.

'It would be the simplest of tasks,' went on Lord Tilbury insinuatingly. 'The manuscript is in the desk of a small room which I imagine is a sort of annexe to the library. The drawer in which it is placed is not, unless I am very much mistaken, locked – and even if locked it can readily be opened. You say you are anxious to return to my employment. So . . . well, think it over, my dear boy.'

Monty was plucking feebly at the lapel of his coat. This was new stuff to him. What with being invited to become a sort of Napoleon of Crime and hearing himself addressed as Lord Tilbury's dear boy, his head was swimming.

Lord Tilbury, a judge of men, was aware that there are minds which adjust themselves less readily than others to new ideas. He was well content to allow an interval of time for this to sink in.

'I can assure you that if you come to me with that manuscript, I shall only be too delighted to restore you to your old position at Tilbury House.'

Monty's aspect became a little less like that of a village idiot who has just been struck by a thunderbolt. A certain animation crept into his eye.

'You will?'

'I will.'

'For a year certain?'

'A year?'

'It must be for a year, positively guaranteed. You may remember me speaking about those wheels.'

In spite of his anxiety to enrol this young man as his

accomplice and set him to work as soon as possible, Lord Tilbury was conscious of a certain hesitation. Most employers of labour would have felt the same in his position. A year is a long time to have a Monty Bodkin on one's hands, and Lord Tilbury had been consoling himself with the reflection that, once the manuscript was in his possession, he could get rid of him in about a week.

'A year?' he said dubiously.

'Or twelve months,' said Monty, making a concession.

Lord Tilbury sighed. Apparently the thing had to be done.

'Very well.'

'You will take me on for a solid year?'

'If you make that stipulation.'

'You will be prepared to sign a letter – an agreement – a document to that effect, if I draw it up?'

'Yes.'

'Then it's a deal. Shake hands on it.'

Lord Tilbury preferred to omit this symbolic gesture.

'Kindly put the thing through as soon as possible,' he said coldly. 'I have no wish to remain indefinitely at a rustic inn.'

'Oh, I'll snap into it. What rustic inn, by the way? I ought to have your address.'

'The Emsworth Arms.'

'I know it well. Try their beer with a spot of gin in it. Warms the cockles. All right, then. Expect me there very shortly, with manuscript under arm.'

'Good-bye, then, for the present.'

'Toodle-oo till we meet again,' said Monty cordially.

He watched Lord Tilbury disappear, then resumed his walk, immersed in roseate daydreams.

This, he reflected, was a bit of all right. There were no traces in his mind now of the scruples and timidity which had given him that slightly sandbagged feeling when this proposition had first been sprung upon him.

He felt bold and resolute. He intended to secure that manuscript if he had to use a meat-axe.

In the shimmering heat-mist that lay along the grass it seemed to him that he could see the lovely face of Gertrude Butterwick gazing at him with gentle encouragement, as if she were endeavouring to suggest that he could count on her support and approval in this enterprise. Almost he could have fancied that the ripple of a lonely little breeze which had lost its way in the alder bushes was her silver voice whispering 'Go to it!'

Writers are creatures of moods. Too often the merest twiddle of the tap is enough to stop the flow of inspiration. It was so with the Hon. Galahad Threepwood. His recent unpleasant scene with that acquaintance of his youth, the erstwhile Stinker Pyke, had been brief in actual count of time, but it had left him in a frame of mind uncongenial to the resumption of his literary work. He was a kindly man, and it irked him to be disobliging even to the Stinker Pykes of this world.

To send poor Stinker off with a flea in his ear was not, of course, the same as rebuffing, say, dear old Plug Basham or good old Freddie Potts, but it was quite enough to upset a man who always liked to do the decent thing by everyone and hated to say No to the meanest of God's creatures. After Lord Tilbury's departure the Hon. Galahad allowed the manuscript of his lifework to remain in its drawer. With no heart for further polishing and pruning, he heaved a rueful sigh, selected a detective novel from his shelf, and left the room.

Having paused in the hall to ring the bell and instruct Beach, who answered it, to bring him a whisky and soda out on to the lawn, he made his way to his favourite retreat beneath the big cedar.

'Oh, and Beach,' he said when the butler arrived with

clinking tray, 'sorry to trouble you, but I wonder if you'd mind leaping up to the small library and fetching me my reading glasses. I forgot them. You'll find them on the desk.'

'No trouble at all, Mr Galahad,' said the butler affably. 'Is there anything else you require?'

'You haven't seen Miss Brown anywhere?'

'No, Mr Galahad. Miss Brown was taking the air on the terrace shortly after luncheon, but I have not seen her since.'

'All right, then. Just the reading glasses.'

Addressing himself to the task of restoring his ruffled nerves, the Hon. Galahad had swallowed perhaps a third of the contents of the long tumbler when he observed the butler returning.

'What on earth have you got there, Beach?' he asked, for the other seemed heavily laden for a man who had been sent to fetch a pair of tortoiseshell-rimmed spectacles. 'That's not my manuscript?'

'Yes, Mr Galahad.'

'Take it back,' said the author, with pardonable peevishness. 'I don't want it. Good Lord, I came out here to forget it.'

He broke off, mystified. A strange, pop-eyed expression had manifested itself on the butler's face, and his swelling waistcoat was beginning to quiver faintly. The Hon. Galahad watched these phenomena with interest and curiosity.

'What are you waggling your tummy at me for, Beach?'

'I am uneasy, Mr Galahad.'

'You shouldn't wear flannel vests, then, in weather like this.'

'Mentally uneasy, sir.'

'What about?'

'The safety of this book of yours, Mr Galahad.' The butler lowered his voice. 'May I inform you, sir, of what occurred a few moments ago when I proceeded to the small library to find your glasses?'

'What?'

'Just as I was about to enter I heard movements within.'

'You did?' The Hon. Galahad clicked his tongue. 'I wish to goodness people would keep out of that room. They know I use it as my private study.'

'Precisely, Mr Galahad. Nobody has any business there while you are in residence at the Castle. That is an understood thing. And it was for that reason that I immediately found myself entertaining suspicions.'

'Eh? Suspicions? How do you mean?'

'That some person was attempting to purloin the material which you have written, sir.'

'What!'

'Yes, Mr Galahad. And I was right. I paused for an instant,' said the butler impressively, 'and then flung the door open sharply and without warning. Sir, there was Mr Pilbeam standing with his hand in the open drawer.'

'Pilbeam?'

'Yes, Mr Galahad.'

'Good gad!'

'Yes, Mr Galahad.'

'What did you say?'

'Nothing, Mr Galahad. I looked.'

'What did *he* say?'

'Nothing, Mr Galahad. He smiled.'

'Smiled?'

'In a weak, guilty manner.'

'And then?'

'Still without speaking, I proceeded to the desk, secured the written material, and started to leave the room. At the door I paused and gave him a cold glance. I then withdrew.'

'Splendid, Beach!'

'Thank you, Mr Galahad.'

'You're sure he was trying to steal the thing?'

'The papers were actually in his grasp, sir.'

'He couldn't have been just looking for notepaper or something?'

A man of Beach's build could not look like Sherlock Holmes listening to fatuous theories from Doctor Watson, nor could a man of his position, conversing with a social superior, answer as Holmes would have done. The word 'Tush!' may have trembled on his lips, but it got no farther.

'No, sir,' he said briefly.

'But his motive? What possible motive could this extraordinary little perisher have for wanting to steal my book?'

A certain embarrassment seemed to grip Beach. He hesitated.

'Might I take the liberty, Mr Galahad?'

'Don't talk rot, Beach. Liberty? I never heard such nonsense. Why, we've known each other since we were kids of forty.'

'Thank you, Mr Galahad. Then, if I may speak freely, I should like to recapitulate briefly the peculiar circumstances connected with this book. In the first place, may I say that I am aware of its extreme importance as a factor in the affairs of Mr Ronald and Miss Brown?'

The Hon. Galahad gave a little jump. He had always known the butler as a man who kept his eyes open and his ears pricked up and informed himself sooner or later of most things that happened at the Castle, but he had not realized that his secret service system was quite so efficient as this.

'In order to overcome the opposition of her ladyship to the union of Mr Ronald and Miss Brown, you expressed your willingness to refrain from giving this volume of Reminiscences into the printer's hands – her ladyship being hostile to its publication owing to the fact that in her opinion its contents might give offence to many of her friends – notably Sir Gregory Parsloe. Am I not correct, Mr Galahad?'

'Quite right.'

'Your motive in making this concession being that you were apprehensive lest, without this check upon her actions, her ladyship might possibly persuade his lordship to refuse to countenance the match?'

'"Possibly" is good. You needn't be coy, Beach. This meeting is tiled. No reporters present. We can take our hair down and tell each other our right names. What you actually mean is that my brother Clarence is as weak as water, and that if it wasn't for this book of mine there would be nothing to stop my sister Constance nagging him into a state where he would agree to forbid a dozen weddings just for the sake of peace and quiet.'

'Exactly, Mr Galahad. I would not have ventured to put the matter into precisely those words myself, but since you have done so I feel free to point out that, the circumstances being as you have outlined, it would be very agreeable to her ladyship were this manuscript to be stolen and destroyed.'

The Hon. Galahad sat up, electrified.

'Beach, you've hit it! That fellow Pilbeam was working for Connie!'

'The evidence would certainly appear to point in that direction, Mr Galahad.'

'Probably Parsloe's sitting in with them.'

'I feel convinced of it, Mr Galahad. I may mention that on the night of our last dinner-party her ladyship instructed me with considerable agitation to summon Sir Gregory to the Castle by telephone for an urgent conference. Her ladyship and Sir Gregory were closeted in the library for some little time, and then Sir Gregory emerged, obviously labouring under considerable excitement, and a few moments later I observed him talking to Mr Pilbeam very earnestly in a secluded corner of the hall.'

'Giving him his riding orders!'

'Precisely, Mr Galahad. Plotting. The significance of the incident eluded me at the time, but I am now convinced that that was what was transpiring.'

The Hon. Galahad rose.

'Beach,' he observed with emotion, 'I've said it before, and I say it again – you're worth your weight in gold. You've saved the situation. You have preserved the happiness of two young lives, Beach.'

'It is very kind of you to say so, sir.'

'I do say so. It's no use our kidding ourselves. With that manuscript out of the way, those two wouldn't have a dog's chance of getting married. I know Clarence. Capital fellow – nobody I'm fonder of in the world – but constitutionally incapable of standing up against arguing women. We must take steps immediately to ensure the safety of this manuscript, Beach.'

'I was about to suggest, Mr Galahad, that it might be advisable if in future you were to lock the drawer in which you keep it.'

The Hon. Galahad shook his head.

'That's no good. You don't suppose a determined woman like my sister Constance, aided and abetted by this ghastly little weasel of a detective, is going to be stopped by a locked drawer? No, we must think of something better than that. I've got it. You must take the thing, Beach, and keep it in some safe place. In your pantry, for instance.'

'But, Mr Galahad!'

'Now what?'

'Suppose her ladyship were to learn that the papers were in my possession and were to request me to hand them to her? It would precipitate a situation of considerable delicacy were I to meet such a demand with a flat refusal.'

665

'How on earth is she to know you've got it? She doesn't ever drop into your pantry for a chat, does she?'

'Certainly not, Mr Galahad,' said the butler, shuddering at the horrid vision the words called up.

'And at night you could sleep with it under your pillow. No risk of Lady Constance coming to tuck you up in bed, what?'

This time Beach's emotion was such that he could merely shudder silently.

'It's the only plan,' said the Hon. Galahad with decision. 'I don't want any argument. You take this manuscript and you put it away somewhere where it'll be safe. Be a man, Beach.'

'Very good, Mr Galahad.'

'Do it now.'

'Very good, Mr Galahad.'

'And naturally, not a word to a soul.'

'Very good, Mr Galahad.'

Beach walked slowly away across the lawn. His head was bowed, his heart heavy. It was a moment when a butler of spirit should have worn something of the gallant air of a soldier commissioned to carry dispatches through the enemy's lines. Beach did not look like that. He resembled far more nearly in his general demeanour one of those unfortunate gentlemen in railway station waiting-rooms who, having injudiciously consented at four-thirty to hold a baby for a strange woman, look at the clock and see that it is now six-fifteen and no relief in sight.

Dusk was closing down on the forbidding day. Sue, looking out over her battlements, became conscious of an added touch of the sinister in the view beneath her. It was the hour when ghouls are abroad, and there seemed no reason why such ghouls should not decide to pay a visit to this roof on which she stood. She came to the conclusion that she had been here long enough. Eerie little noises were chuckling through the world, and somewhere in the distance an owl had begun to utter its ominous cry. She yearned for her cosy bedroom, with the lights turned on and something to read till dressing for dinner-time.

It was very dark on the stone stairs, and they rang unpleasantly under her feet. Nevertheless, though considering it probable that at any moment an icy hand would come out from nowhere and touch her face, she braved the descent.

Her relief as her groping fingers touched the comforting solidity of the door was short-lived. It gave way a moment later to the helpless panic of the human being trapped. The door was locked. She scurried back up the stairs on to the roof, where at least there was light to help her cope with this disaster.

She remembered now. Half an hour before, a footman had come up and hauled down the flag which during the day floated over Blandings Castle. He had not seen her, and it had not occurred to her to reveal her presence. But she wished now that she had done so, for, supposing the roof empty, he had evidently completed his evening ritual by locking up.

Something brushed against Sue's cheek. It was not actually a ghoul, but it was a bat, and bats are bad enough in the gloaming of a haunted day. She uttered a sharp scream – and, doing so, discovered that she had unwittingly hit upon the correct procedure for girls marooned on roofs.

She hurried to the battlements and began calling 'Hi!' – in a small, hushed voice at first, for nothing sounds sillier than the word 'Hi!' when thrown into the void with no definite objective; then more loudly. Presently, warming to her work, she was producing quite a respectable volume of sound. So respectable that Ronnie Fish, smoking moodily in the garden, became aware that there were voices in the night, and, after listening for a few moments, gathered that they proceeded from the castle roof.

He made his way to the path that skirted the walls.

'Who's that?'

'Oh, Ronnie!'

For two days and two nights grey doubts and black cares had been gnawing at the vitals of Ronald Fish. The poison had not ceased to work in his veins. For two days and two nights he had been thinking of Sue and of Monty Bodkin. Every time he thought of Sue it was agony. And every time his reluctant mind turned to the contemplation of Monty Bodkin it was anguish. But at the sound of that voice his heart gave an involuntary leap. She might have transferred her affections to Monty Bodkin, but her voice still remained the most musical sound on earth.

'Ronnie, I can't get down.'

'Are you on the roof?'

'Yes. And they've locked the door.'

'I'll get the key.'

And at long last she heard the clang of the lock, and he appeared at the head of the stairs.

His manner, she noted with distress, was still Eton, still Cambridge. Nobody could have been politer.

'Nuisance, getting locked in like that.'

'Yes.'

'Been up here long?'

'All the afternoon.'

'Nice place on a fine day.'

'I suppose so.'

'Though hot.'

'Yes.'

There was a pause. The heavy air pressed down upon them. In the garden the owl was still hooting.

'When did you get back?' asked Sue.

'About an hour ago.'

'I didn't hear you.'

'I didn't come to the front. I went straight round to the stables. Dropped mother at the Vicarage.'

'Yes?'

'She wanted to have a talk with the vicar.'

'I see.'

'You've not met the vicar, have you?'

'Not yet.'

'His name's Fosberry.'

'Oh?'

Silence fell again. Ronnie's eyes were roaming about the roof. He took a step forward, stooped, and picked up something. It was a slouch hat.

He hummed a little under his breath.

'Monty been up here with you?'

'Yes.'

Ronnie hummed another bar or two.

'Nice chap,' he said. 'Let's go down, shall we?'

8

If you turn to the right on leaving the main gates of
Blandings Castle and follow the road for a matter of two
miles, you will find yourself approaching the little town
of Market Blandings. There it stands dreaming the
centuries away, a jewel in a green heart of Shropshire. In
all England there is no sweeter spot. Artists who come
to paint its old grey houses and fishermen who angle for
bream in its lazy river are united on this point. The idea
that the place could possibly be rendered more pleasing
to the eye is one at which they would scoff – and have
scoffed many a night over the pipes and tankards at the
Emsworth Arms.

And yet, on the afternoon following the events just
recorded, this miracle occurred. The quiet charm of this
ancient High Street was suddenly intensified by the
appearance of a godlike man in a bowler hat, who came
out of an old-world tobacco shop. It was Beach, the
butler. With the object of disciplining his ample figure,
he had walked down from the Castle to buy cigarettes.
He now stood on the pavement, bracing himself to the
task of walking back.

This athletic feat was not looking quite so good to
him as it had done three-quarters of an hour ago in his
pantry. That long two-mile hike had taxed his powers of
endurance. Moreover, this was no weather for
Marathons. If yesterday had been oppressive, today was a
scorcher. Angry clouds were banking themselves in a
copper-coloured sky. No breath of air stirred the trees.
The pavement gave out almost visible waves of heat,
and over everything there seemed to brood a sort of

sulphurous gloom. If they were not in for a
thunderstorm, and a snorter of a thunderstorm, before
nightfall, Beach was very much mistaken. He removed
his hat, produced a handkerchief, mopped his brow,
replaced the hat, replaced the handkerchief, and said
'Woof!' Disciplining the figure is all very well, but there
are limits. An urgent desire for beer swept over Beach.

He could scarcely have been more fortunately
situated for the purpose of gratifying this wish. The ideal
towards which the City Fathers of all English country
towns strive is to provide a public-house for each
individual inhabitant; and those of Market Blandings
had not been supine in this matter. From where Beach
stood, he could see no fewer than six such
establishments. The fact that he chose the Emsworth
Arms must not be taken to indicate that he had
anything against the Wheatsheaf, the Waggoner's Rest,
the Beetle and Wedge, the Stitch in Time, and the Jolly
Cricketers. It was simply that it happened to be closest.

Nevertheless, it was a sound choice. The advice one
would give to every young man starting life is, on
arriving in Market Blandings on a warm afternoon, to go
to the Emsworth Arms. Good stuff may be bought there,
and of all the admirable hostelries in the town it
possesses the largest and shadiest garden. Green and
inviting, dotted about with rustic tables and snug
summerhouses, it stretches all the way down to the
banks of the river; so that the happy drinker, already
pleasantly in need of beer, may acquire a new and deeper
thirst from watching family parties toil past in
row-boats. On a really sultry day a single father,
labouring at the oars of a craft loaded down below the
Plimsoll mark by a wife, a wife's sister, a cousin by
marriage, four children, a dog, and a picnic basket, has
sometimes led to such a rush of business at the
Emsworth Arms that seasoned barmaids have staggered
beneath the strain.

It was to one of these summerhouses that Beach now took his tankard. He generally went there when circumstances caused him to visit the Emsworth Arms, for as a man with a certain position to keep up he preferred privacy when refreshing himself. It was not as if he had been some irresponsible young second footman who could just go and squash in with the boys in the back room. This particular summerhouse was at the far end of the garden, hidden from the eye of the profane by a belt of bushes.

Thither, accordingly, Beach made his way. There was nobody in the summerhouse, but he did not enter it, having a horror of earwigs and suspecting their presence in the thatch of the roof. Instead, he dragged a wicker chair to the table which stood at the back of it, and, sinking into this, puffed and sipped and thought. And the more he thought, the less did he like what he thought about.

As a rule, when members of the Family showed their confidence in him by canvassing his assistance in any little matter, Beach was both proud and pleased. His motto was 'Service'. But he could not conceal it from himself that the Family had a tendency at times to go a little too far.

The historic case of this, of course, had been when Mr Ronald, having stolen the Empress and hidden her in a disused keeper's cottage in the West Wood, had prevailed upon him to assist in feeding her. His present commission was not as fearsome an ordeal as that, but nevertheless he could not but feel that the Hon. Galahad, in appointing him the custodian of so vitally important an object as the manuscript of his book of Reminiscences, had exceeded the limits of what a man should ask a butler to do. The responsibility, he considered, was one which no butler, however desirous of giving satisfaction, should have been called upon to undertake.

The thought of all that hung upon his vigilance unnerved him. And he had been brooding on it with growing uneasiness for perhaps five minutes, when the sound of feet shuffling on wood told him that he had no longer got his favourite oasis to himself. An individual or individuals had come into the summerhouse.

'We can talk here,' said a voice, and a seat creaked as if a heavy body had lowered itself upon it.

And such was, indeed, the case. It was Lord Tilbury who had just sat down, and his was one of the heaviest bodies in Fleet Street.

When, a few minutes before, meditating in the lounge of the Emsworth Arms, he had beheld Monty Bodkin enter through the front door, Lord Tilbury's first thought had been for some quiet retreat where they could confer in solitude. He could see that the young man had much to say, and he had no desire to have him say it with half a dozen inquisitive Shropshire lads within easy earshot.

Great minds think alike. Beach, intent on an unobtrusive glass of beer, and Lord Tilbury, loath to have intimate private matters discussed in an hotel lounge, had both come to the conclusion that true solitude was best to be obtained at the bottom of the garden. Silencing his young friend, accordingly, with an imperious gesture his lordship had led the way to this remote summerhouse.

'Well,' he said, having seated himself. 'What is it?' It seemed to Beach, who had settled himself comfortably in his chair and was preparing to listen to the conversation with something of the air of a nonchalant dramatic critic watching the curtain go up, that that voice was vaguely familiar. He had a feeling that he had heard it before, but could not remember where or when. He had no difficulty, however, in recognizing the one which now spoke in answer. Monty Bodkin's vocal delivery, when his soul was at all deeply disturbed, was individual and peculiar, containing something of the

673

tonal quality of a bleating sheep combined with a
suggestion of a barking prairie wolf.

'What is it? I like that!'

Monty's soul at this moment was very deeply
disturbed. Since breakfast-time that morning, this young
man, like Sir Gregory Parsloe, had run what is known as
the gamut of the emotions. A pictorial record of his
hopes and despairs would have looked like a fever chart.

He had begun, over the coffee and kippers, by feeling
gay and buoyant. It seemed to him that Fortune – good
old Fortune – had amazingly decently put him on to a
red-hot thing. All he had to do, in order to ensure the
year's employment which would enable him to win
Gertrude Butterwick, was to nip into the small library
and lift the manuscript out of the desk in which, Lord
Tilbury had assured him, it reposed.

Feeling absolutely in the pink, accordingly, and
nipping as planned, he had fallen, like Lucifer, from
heaven to hell. The bally thing was not there. Fortune,
in a word, had been pulling his leg.

And here was this old ass before him saying 'What is
it?'

'Yes, I like that!' he repeated. 'That's rich! Oh, very
fruity, indeed.'

Lord Tilbury, as we have said, had never been very
fond of Monty. In his present peculiar mood he found
himself liking him less than ever.

'What is it you wish to see me about?' he asked, with
testy curtness.

'What do you think I want to see you about?' replied
Monty shrilly. 'About that dashed manuscript of Gally's
that you told me to pinch, of course,' he said with a
bitter laugh, and Beach, having given a single shuddering
start like a harpooned whale, sat rigid in his chair, his
gooseberry eyes bulging; the beer frozen, as one might
say, on his lips.

Nor was Lord Tilbury unmoved. No plotter likes to

have his accomplices bellowing important secrets as if
they were calling coals.

'Sh!'

'Oh, nobody can hear us.'

'Nevertheless, kindly do not shout. Where is the
manuscript? Have you got it?'

'Of course I've not got it.'

Lord Tilbury was feeling dismally that he might have
expected this. He saw how foolish he had been to place
so delicate a commission in the hands of a popinjay. Of
all classes of the community, popinjays, when it comes
to carrying out delicate commissions, are the most
inept. Search History's pages from end to end, reflected
Lord Tilbury, and you will not find one instance of a
popinjay doing anything successfully except eat, sleep,
and master the new dance steps.

'It's a bit thick . . .' bellowed Monty.

'Sh!'

'It's a bit thick,' repeated Monty, sinking his voice to
a conspiratorial growl. 'Raising hopes only to cast them
to the ground is the way I look at it. What did you want
to get me all worked up for by telling me the thing was
in that desk?'

'Is it not?' said Lord Tilbury, staggered.

'Not a trace of it.'

'You cannot have looked properly.'

'Looked properly!'

'Sh!'

'Of course I looked properly. I left no stone unturned. I
explored every avenue.'

'But I saw Threepwood put it there.'

'Says you.'

'Don't say "says you". I tell you I saw him with my
own eyes place the manuscript in the top right-hand
drawer of the desk.'

'Well, he must have moved it. It's not there now.'

'Then it is somewhere else.'

675

'I shouldn't wonder. But where?'

'You could easily have found out.'

'Oh, yeah?'

'Don't say "Oh, yeah".'

'Well, what *can* I say, dash it? First you keep yowling "Shush" every time I open my mouth. Then you tell me not to say, "Says you". And now you beef at my remarking "Oh, yeah". I suppose what you'd really like,' said Monty, and it was plain to the listening ear that he was deeply moved, 'would be for me to buy a flannel dressing-gown and a spade and become a ruddy Trappist monk.'

This spirited outburst led to a certain amount of rather confused debate. Lord Tilbury said that he did not propose to have young popinjays taking that tone with him; while Monty, on his side, wished to be informed who Lord Tilbury was calling a popinjay. Lord Tilbury then said that Monty was a bungler, and Monty said, Well, dash it, Lord Tilbury had told him to be a burglar, and Lord Tilbury said he had not said 'burglar', he had said 'bungler', and Monty said, What did he mean, bungler, and Lord Tilbury explained that by the expression 'bungler', he had intended to signify a wretched, feckless, blundering, incompetent imbecile. He added that an infant of six could have found the manuscript, and Monty, in a striking passage, was making a firm offer to give any bloodhound in England a shilling if it could do better than he had done, when the argument stopped as abruptly as it had started. Childish voices had begun to prattle close at hand and it was evident that one of those picnic parties from the river was approaching.

'Cor!' said Lord Tilbury, rather in the manner of the moping owl in Gray's 'Elegy' under similar provocation.

One of the childish voices spoke.

'Pa, there's someone here.'

Another followed.

'Ma, there's someone here.'

The deeper note of a male adult made itself heard.

'Emily, there's someone here.'

And then the voice of a female adult.

'Oh dear. What a shame! There's someone here.'

The conspirators appeared to be men who could take a tactful hint when they heard one. There came to Beach's ears the sound of moving bodies. And presently, from the fact that the summerhouse seemed to have become occupied by a troupe of performing elephants, he gathered that the occupation had been carried through according to plan.

He sat on for some minutes; then, hurrying to the inn, asked leave of the landlord to use his telephone in order to summon Robinson and his station taxi. His mind was made up. He would not know an easy moment until he was back in his pantry, on guard. The station taxi would run into money, for Robinson, like all monopolists, drove a hard bargain; but if it would get him to the Castle before Monty it would be half a crown well spent.

'Robinson's taxi's outside now, Mr Beach,' said the landlord, tickled by the coincidence. 'A gentleman phoned for it only two minutes ago. Going up to the Castle himself he is. Maybe he'd give you a lift. You can catch him if you run.'

Beach did not run. Even if his figure had permitted such a feat, his sense of his position would have forbidden it. But he walked quite rapidly, and was enabled to leave the front door just as Monty was bidding farewell to a short, stout man in whom he recognized the Lord Tilbury who had called at the Castle on the previous day to see Mr Galahad. So it was he who had been egging young Mr Bodkin on to bungle!

For an instant, this discovery shocked the butler so much that he could hardly speak. That Baronets like Sir Gregory Parsloe should be employing minions to steal

important papers had been a severe enough blow. That
Peers should stoop to the same low conduct made the
foundations of his world rock. Then came a restorative
thought. This Lord Tilbury, he reminded himself, was
no doubt a recent creation. One cannot expect too high a
standard of ethics from the uncouth (*hoi polloni*) who
crash into Birthday Honours lists.

He found speech.

'Oh, Mr Bodkin. Pardon me, sir.'

Monty turned.

'Why, hullo, Beach.'

'Would it be a liberty, sir, if I were to request
permission to share this vehicle with you?'

'Rather not. Lots of room for all. What are you doing
in these parts, Beach? Slaking the old thirst, eh?
Drinking-bouts in the tap-room, yes?'

'I walked down from the Castle to purchase cigarettes
at the tobacconist's, sir,' replied Beach with dignity.
'And as the afternoon heat proved somewhat trying . . .'

'I know, I know,' said Monty sympathetically. 'Well,
leap in, my dear old stag at eve.'

At any other moment Beach would have been
offended at such a mode of address and would have
shown it in his manner. But just as he was about to draw
himself up with a cold stare he chanced to catch sight of
Lord Tilbury, who had retreated to the shadow of the
inn wall.

On his marriage to the daughter of Donaldson's
Dog-biscuits, of Long Island City, NY, and his
subsequent departure for America, the Hon. Freddie
Threepwood, Lord Emsworth's younger son, who had
assembled in the days of his bachelorhood what was
pretty generally recognized as the finest collection of
mystery thrillers in Shropshire, had bequeathed his
library to Beach; and the latter in his hours of leisure had
been making something of a study of the literature of
Crime of late.

Lord Tilbury, brooding there with folded arms, reminded him of The Man With The Twisted Eyebrows in *The Casterbridge Horror*.

Shuddering strongly, Beach climbed into the cab.

When two careworn men, one of whom has just discovered that the other has criminal tendencies, take a drive together on a baking afternoon, conversation does not run trippingly. Monty was thinking out plans and schemes; and Beach, in the intervals of recoiling with horror from this desperado, was wondering why the latter had called him a stag at eve. Silence, accordingly, soon fell upon the station taxi and lasted till it drew up at the front door of the Castle. Here Monty alighted, and the taxi took Beach round to the back door. As he got out and handed Robinson his fare, the butler was conscious of an unwilling respect for the fiendish cunning of the criminal mind – which, having offered you a lift in a cab, gets out first and leaves you to pay for it.

He hastened to his pantry. Reason told him that the manuscript must still be in the drawer where he had placed it, but he did not breathe easily until he had seen it with his own eyes. He took it out and, having done so, paused irresolutely. It was stuffy in the pantry and he longed to be in the open air, in that favourite seat of his near the laurel bush outside the back door. And yet he could not relax with any satisfaction there, separated from his precious charge.

There is always a way. A few moments later he perceived that all anxiety might be obviated if he took the manuscript with him. He did so. Then, reclining in his deck-chair, he lit one of the cigarettes which it had cost him such labour to procure, and gave himself up to thought.

His moonlike face was drawn and grave. The situation, he realized, was becoming too complex for comfort.

The views of butlers who have been given important papers to guard and find that there are persons on the premises who wish to steal them are always clear-cut and definite. Broadly speaking, a butler in such a position can bear up with a reasonable amount of fortitude against the menace of one gang of would-be thieves. He may not like it, but he can set his teeth and endure. Add a second gang, however, and the thing seems to pass beyond his control.

Beach's researches in the library bequeathed to him by the Hon. Freddie Threepwood had left him extremely sensitive on the subject of Gangs. In most of the volumes in that library Gangs played an important part, and he had come to fear and dislike them. And here in Blandings Castle, groping about and liable at any moment to focus their malign attention on himself, were two Gangs – the Parsloe and the Tilbury. It made a butler think a bit.

To divert his mind, he began to read the manuscript. Being of an inquisitive nature, he had always wanted to do so, and this seemed an admirable opportunity. Opening the pages at random, therefore, and finding himself in the middle of Chapter Six ('Nightclubs of the Nineties'), he plunged into a droll anecdote about the Bishop of Bangor when an undergraduate at Oxford, and despite his cares was soon chuckling softly, like some vast kettle coming to the boil.

It was at this moment that Percy Pilbeam, who had been smoking cigarettes in the stable yard, came sauntering round the corner.

The stable yard had been a favourite haunt of Percy Pilbeam's ever since his arrival at the Castle. A keen motor-cyclist, he liked talking to Voules, the chauffeur, about valves and plugs and things. And, in addition to this, he found the place soothing because it was out of the orbit of the sisters and nephews of his host. You did

not meet Lady Constance Keeble there, you did not meet
Lady Julia Fish there, and you did not meet Lady Julia
Fish's son Ronald there; and for Percy Pilbeam that was
sufficient to make any spot Paradise enow.

He was also attracted to the stable-yard because he
found it a good place to think in.

He had been thinking a great deal these last two days.
A self-respecting private investigator is always loath to
admit that he is baffled, but baffled was just what
Pilbeam had been ever since a second visit to the small
library had informed him that the manuscript which he
had been commissioned to remove was no longer in its
desk. Like Monty, he felt at a loss.

It was all very well, he felt sourly, for that Keeble
woman to say in her impatient, duchess-talking-to-a-
worm way that it must be somewhere and that she was
simply amazed that he had not found it. The point was
that it might be anywhere. No doubt if he had a Scotland
Yard search-warrant, a troupe of African witch-doctors
and unlimited time at his disposal he could find it. But
he hadn't.

A well-defined dislike of Lady Constance Keeble had
been germinating in Percy Pilbeam since the first
moment they had met. He was brooding upon that
unpleasant supercilious manner of hers as he turned the
corner now. And he had just come to the conclusion, as
he always came on these occasions, that what she
needed was a thoroughly good ticking off, when he was
suddenly jerked out of his daydreams by the sound of a
huge, reverberating, explosive laugh; and looking up
with a start, espied protruding over the top of a
deck-chair a few feet before him an eggshaped head
which he recognized as that of Beach, the butler.

We left Beach, it will be remembered, chuckling softly.
And for a few minutes soft chuckles had contented him.
But in a book of the nature of the Hon. Galahad

Threepwood's Reminiscences the student is sure sooner or later to come upon some high spot, some supreme expression of the writer's art which demands a more emphatic tribute. What Beach was reading now was the story of Sir Gregory Parsloe-Parsloe and the prawns.

'HA... HOR... HOO!' he roared.

Pilbeam stood spellbound. His had not been a wide experience of butlers, and he could not recall ever before having heard a butler laugh – let alone laugh in this extraordinary fashion, casting dignity to the winds and apparently without a thought for his high blood-pressure and the stability of his waistcoat buttons. As soon as the first numbing shock had passed away, an intense curiosity seized him. He drew near, marvelling. On tiptoe he stole behind the chair, agog to see what it could be that had caused this unprecedented outburst.

The next moment he found himself gazing upon the manuscript of the Hon. Galahad's Reminiscences.

He recognized it instantly. Ever since that attempt upon it which this same butler had foiled, its shape and aspect had been graven upon his memory. And even if that straggling handwriting had not been familiar to him, the two lines which he read before uttering an involuntary cry would have told him what it was flickered before his eyes.

'Oof!' said Pilbeam unable to check himself.

Beach gave a convulsive start, turned, and, looking up, beheld within six inches of his eyes the face of the leading executive of the sinister Parsloe Gang.

'Oof!' he exclaimed in his turn, and the deck-chair, as if in sympathy, also made an oof-like sound. Then, cracking under the strain, it spread itself out upon the ground.

Even under the most favourable conditions, the situation would have been one of embarrassment. The peculiar circumstances rendered it cataclysmic. Pilbeam, who had never seen a butler take a toss out of a deck-chair before, stood robbed of speech; while Beach, his heart palpitating dangerously, sat equally silent. He was frozen with horror. That the enemy should have succeeded in tracking him down already seemed to him to argue a cunning that transcended the human.

Rising with the manuscript clutched to the small of his back, if his back could be said to have a small, he began to retreat slowly towards the house. Continuing to recoil, he bumped into stonework, and with an infinite relief found that he was within leaping distance of the back door. With a last, lingering look, of a nature which a sensitive snake would have resented, he shot in, leaving Pilbeam staring like one in a dream.

Almost exactly at the instant when he reached the haven of his pantry, Monty Bodkin, taking a thoughtful stroll on the terrace, suddenly remembered with a start of shame and remorse that he had left Beach to pay that cab fare.

One points at Monty Bodkin with a good deal of pride. Most young men in his position would either have dismissed the matter with a careless 'What of it?' or possibly even the still more ignoble reflection that a bit of luck had put them half a crown up; or else would have made a mental note to slip the fellow the money at some vague future date. For in the matter of Debts the young man of today wavers between straight repudiation and a moratorium.

But in a lax age Monty Bodkin had his code. To him this obligation was a blot on the Bodkin escutcheon which had to be wiped off immediately.

And so it came about that Beach, panting from his recent clash with the Parsloe Gang and in his dazed condition not having heard the door open, became suddenly aware of emotional breathing in the vicinity of his left ear and discovered that the right-hand man of the Tilbury Gang had now invaded his fastness.

It was a moment which would have tried the *morale*

of the hero of a Secret Service novel. It made Beach feel
like a rabbit with not one stoat but a whole platoon of
stoats on its track. He had been sitting, relaxed. He now
rose like a rocket and, snatching up the manuscript in
the old familiar manner, stood holding it to his heaving
chest.

Monty, who, like Pilbeam, had reacted strongly to the
wholly unforeseen discovery of the precious object in
the butler's possession, was the first to recover from the
shock.

'What ho!' he said. 'Afraid I startled you, what?'

Beach continued to pant.

'I came to give you the money for that cab.'

Beach, though reluctant to take even one hand off the
manuscript, was not proof against half-crowns.
Cautiously extending a palm, he accepted the coin,
thrust it into his pocket, and restored his grasp to the
papers almost in a single movement.

'Must have given you a jump. Sorry. Ought to have
blown my horn.'

There was a pause.

'I see you've got that book of Mr Galahad's there,' said
Monty, with a rather overdone carelessness.

To Beach it seemed more than rather overdone. He
had been manoeuvring with the open door as his
objective, and he now took a shuffling step in that
direction.

'Pretty good, I should imagine? Now, there's a thing,'
said Monty, 'that I'd very much like to read.'

Beach had now reached the door, and the thought of
having a clear way to safety behind him did something
to restore his composure. That trapped feeling had left
him, and in its stead had come a stern, righteous wrath.
He stared at Monty, breathing heavily. A sort of glaze
had come over his eyes, causing them to resemble two
pools of cold gravy.

'You couldn't lend it to me, I suppose?'

'No, sir.'

'No?'

'No, sir.'

'You won't?'

'No, sir.'

There was a pause. Monty coughed. Beach, with an inward shudder, felt that he had never heard anything so roopy and so villainous. He was surprised at Monty. A nice, respectable young gentleman he had always considered him. He could only suppose that he had been getting into bad company since those early days when he had been a popular visitor at the Castle.

'I'd give a good deal to read that thing, Beach.'

'Indeed, sir?'

'Ten quid, in fact.'

'Indeed, sir?'

'Or, rather, twenty.'

'Indeed, sir?'

'And when I say twenty,' explained Monty, 'I mean, of course, twenty-five.'

The sophisticated modern world has, one fears, a little lost its taste for the type of scene, so admired of an older generation, where Virtue, drawing itself up to its full height, scorns to be tempted by gold. Yet even the most hard-boiled and cynical could scarcely have failed to be thrilled had they beheld Beach now. He looked like something out of a symbolic group of statuary – Good Citizenship Refusing To Accept A Bribe From Big Business Interests in Connection With The Contract For The New Inter-Urban Tramway System, or something of that kind. His eyes were hard, his waistcoat quivered, and when he spoke it was with a formal frigidity.

'I regret to say, sir, that I am not in a position to fall in with your wishes.'

And with a last stare, of about the same calibre as the

last stare which he had directed at Percy Pilbeam, he
moved in good order to the Housekeeper's Room,
leaving Monty plunged in thought.

Too often, when a man of Monty Bodkin's mental
powers is plunged in thought, nothing happens at all.
The machinery just whirs for a while, and that is the end
of it. But on the present occasion this was not so. Love is
the great driving force, and now it was as if Gertrude
Butterwick had her dainty foot on the accelerator of his
brain, whacking it up to unprecedented m.p.h. The
result was that after about two minutes of intense
concentration, during which he felt several times as if
the top of his head were coming off, an idea suddenly
shot out of the welter like a cork from the Old Faithful
geyser.

It was obvious that, with Beach turning so
unaccountably spiky as he had done, he could
accomplish nothing further by his own efforts. He must
put the matter into the hands of a competent agent. And
the chap to apply to was beyond a question this bird
Pilbeam.

Pilbeam, he reasoned, was a private detective. The job
to be done, therefore, would be right up his street: for
stealing things must surely be one of the commonplaces
of a private detective's daily life. From what he could
remember of his reading, they were always being called
upon to steal things – compromising letters, Admiralty
Plans, Maharajah's rubies, and what not. No doubt the
fellow would be only too glad of the commission.

He went in search of him, and found him lying back
in an arm-chair in the smoking-room. He had the tips of
his fingers together, Monty noted approvingly. Always a
good sign.

'I say, Pilbeam,' he said, 'are you in the market at the
moment for a bit of stealthy stuff?'

'Pardon?'

'If so, I've got a job for you.'

'A job?'

Like Monty, Pilbeam had been thinking tensely, and what with the strain on his brain and the warmth of the weather, was not feeling so bright as he usually did.

'You *are* a detective?' said Monty anxiously. 'You weren't just pulling my leg about that, were you?'

'Certainly I am a detective. I think I have one of my cards here.'

Monty inspected the grubby piece of pasteboard, and all anxiety left him. Argus Inquiry Agency. You couldn't get round that. Secrecy and Discretion Guaranteed. Better still. A telegraphic code address, too – Pilgus, Piccy, London. Most convincing.

'Topping,' he said. 'Well, then, coming back to it, I can put business in your way.'

'You wish to make use of my professional services?'

'If you're open for a spot of work at this juncture, I do. Of course, if you're simply down here taking a well-earned rest . . .'

'Not at all. I shall be glad to render you any assistance that is in my power. Perhaps you will tell me the facts.'

Monty was a little doubtful about the procedure. He had never engaged a private detective before.

'Do you want to know my name?'

'Isn't your name Bodkin?' said Pilbeam surprised.

'Oh, yes. Rather. Definitely. Only in all the stories I've read the chap who comes to the detective always starts off with a long yarn about what his name is and where he lives and who left him his money, and so forth. Save a lot of time if we can cut all that.'

'All I require are the facts.'

Monty hesitated again.

'It sounds so dashed silly,' he said coyly.

'I beg your pardon?'

'Well, bizarre, if you prefer the expression. Nobody could say it wasn't. Bizarre is the word that absolutely

springs to the lips. It's about that book of Gally
Threepwood's.'

Pilbeam gave a little jump.

'Oh?'

'Yes. You knew he had written a book?'

'Quite.'

'Well . . .' Monty giggled '. . . I suppose you'll think I'm
a silly ass, but I want to get hold of it.'

Pilbeam was silent for a moment. He had not known
that he had a rival in the field, and was none too pleased
to hear it.

'You do think I'm a silly ass?'

'Not at all,' said Pilbeam, recovering himself. 'No
doubt you have your reasons?'

It had just occurred to him, so far from being a
disconcerting piece of news, what he had heard was
really tidings of great joy. He supposed, mistakenly, that
Monty, who no doubt had many friends in high places,
had been asked by one of them to take advantage of his
being at the Castle to destroy the book. England, he
knew, was full of men besides Sir Gregory Parsloe who
wanted those Reminiscences destroyed.

The situation now began to look very good to Percy
Pilbeam. He had only to secure that manuscript and he
would be in the delightful position of having two
markets in which to sell it. Competition is the soul of
Trade. The one thing a man of affairs wants, when he
has come into possession of something valuable, is to
have people bidding against one another for it.

'Oh, I have my reasons all right,' said Monty. 'But it's
a long story. Do you mind if we just leave it at this, that
there are wheels within wheels?'

'Just as you please.'

'The thing is, a certain bloke – whom I will not
specify – has asked me to get hold of this manuscript –
for reasons into which I need not go – and . . . well, there
you are.'

688

'Quite,' said Pilbeam, satisfied that the position was exactly as he had supposed.

Monty proceeded with more confidence.

'Well, that's that, then. Now we get down to it. I've just found out that the chap who's got the thing is – '

'Beach,' said Pilbeam.

Monty was astounded.

'You knew that?'

'Certainly.'

'But how on earth – ?'

'Oh, well,' said Pilbeam carelessly, as one who has his methods.

Monty was now more convinced that he had come to the right shop. This man was uncanny. 'Beach,' he said. Just like that. Might have been a mind-reader.

'Yes, that's the strength of it,' he went on as soon as he had ceased marvelling. 'That's where the snag lies. Beach has got it and is hanging on to it like a limpet. He won't let me lay a finger on the thing. So the problem, as I see it . . . You don't mind me outlining the problem as I see it? . . .'

Pilbeam waved a courteous hand.

'Well, then, the problem, as I see it,' said Monty, 'is, how the hell is one to get it away from the blighter?'

'Quite.'

'That is, as you might say, the nub?'

'Quite.'

'Have you any ideas on the subject?'

'Oh, yes.'

'Such as – ?'

'Ah, well,' said Pilbeam, a little stiffly.

Monty was all apologies.

'I see, I see,' he said. 'Naturally you don't want to blow the gaff prematurely. Shouldn't have asked. Sorry. But I can leave the matter in your hands with every confidence, as I believe the expression is?'

'Quite.'

689

'He might let you borrow the thing to read?'

'At any rate, I have no doubt that I shall find a way of getting it into my possession.'

Monty eyed him admiringly. Externally, Percy Pilbeam was not precisely his idea of a detective. Not quite enough of that cold, hawk-faced stuff, and a bit too much brilliantine on the hair. But as far as brain was concerned he was undoubtedly the goods.

'I bet you will,' he said. 'You can't run a business like yours without knowing a thing or two. I expect you've pinched things before.'

'I have occasionally been commissioned to recover papers, and so forth, of value,' said Pilbeam guardedly.

'Well, consider yourself jolly well commissioned now,' said Monty.

9

Safe in the Housekeeper's Room, Beach sat gazing out of the window at the lowering sky. His chest was still rising and falling like a troubled ocean.

Too hot, felt Beach, too hot. Things were becoming too hot altogether.

His whole mind was obsessed by an instant urge to get rid of these papers, the guardianship of which had become so hazardous a matter. The chase was growing too strenuous for a man of regular habits who liked a quiet life.

Nearly everything in this world cuts both ways. A fall from a deck-chair, for instance, is – physically – a painful experience. Against its obvious drawbacks, however, must be set the fact that it does render the subject nimbler mentally. It shakes up the brain. To the circumstance of his having so recently come down with a bump on his spacious trousers-seat must be attributed the swiftness with which Beach now got an idea that seemed to him to solve everything.

He saw the way out. He would hand this manuscript over to Mr Ronald. There was its logical custodian. Mr Ronald was the person most interested in its safety. He was, moreover, a young man. And the more he mused on the whole unpleasant affair, the more firmly did Beach come to the conclusion that the foiling of the Parsloe Gang and the Tilbury Gang was young man's work.

It would be necessary, of course, to apply to the Hon. Galahad for permission to take the step. If you went behind his back and acted on your own initiative after he had given you instructions, Mr Galahad could be quite as bad as any gang. Years of association with London's toughest citizens had given him a breadth of vocabulary which was not lightly to be faced. Beach had no intention of drawing upon himself the lightnings of that Pelican-Club trained tongue. As soon as he felt sufficiently restored to move, he went in search of the Hon. Galahad and found him in the small library.

'Might I speak to you, Mr Galahad?'

'Say on, Beach.'

Clearly and well the butler told his tale. He recounted the scene at the Emsworth Arms, the subsequent invasion of his pantry by the man Bodkin, the proffered bribe. The Hon. Galahad listened with fire smouldering behind his monocle.

'The young toad!' he cried. 'Monty Bodkin. A fellow I've practically nursed in my bosom. Why, I can remember, when he was a boy at Eton, taking him aside as he was going back to school one time and urging him to put his shirt on Whistling Rufus for the Cesarewitch.'

'Indeed, sir?'

'And he notified me subsequently that, thanks to my kindly advice, he had cleaned up to the extent of eleven shillings – in addition to a bag of bananas, two strawberry ice-creams, and a three-cornered Cape of Good Hope stamp at a hundred to sixteen from a schoolmate who was making a book. And this is how he repays me!' said the Hon. Galahad, looking like King Lear. 'Isn't there such a thing as gratitude in the world?'

He expressed his disgust with a wide, passionate gesture. The butler, with his nice instinct for class distinctions, expressed his with one a little less wide and not quite so passionate. These callisthenics seemed to relieve them both, for when the conversation was resumed it was on a calmer note.

'I might have known,' said the Hon. Galahad, 'that a fellow like Stinker Pyke . . . what does he call himself now, Beach?'

'Lord Tilbury, Mr Galahad.'

'I might have known that a fellow like Lord Tilbury wouldn't give up the struggle after one rebuff. You don't make a large fortune by knuckling under to rebuffs, Beach.'

'Very true, Mr Galahad.'

'I suppose old Stinker has been up against this sort of thing before. He knows the procedure. The first thing he would do, after I had turned him down, would be to set spies and agents to work. Well, I don't see what there is to be done except employ renewed vigilance, like Clarence with his pig.'

Beach coughed.

'I was thinking, Mr Galahad, that if I were to hand the documents over to Mr Ronald . . .'

'You think that would be safer?'

'Considerably safer, sir. Now that Mr Pilbeam is aware that they are in my possession, I am momentarily apprehensive lest her ladyship approach me with a direct request that I deliver them into her hands.'

'Beach! Are you afraid of my sister Constance?'

'Yes, sir.'

The Hon. Galahad reflected.

'Well, I see what you mean. It would be difficult for you. You couldn't very well tell her to go and put her head in a bag.'

'No, sir.'

'All right, then. Give the thing to Mr Ronald.'

'Thank you very much, Mr Galahad.'

Infinitely relieved, Beach allowed his gaze, hitherto concentrated on his companion, to travel to the window.

'Storm looks like breaking at last, sir.'

'Yes.'

The Hon. Galahad also looked out of the window. It was plain that Nature in all her awful majesty was about to let herself go. On the opposite side of the valley there shot jaggedly across the sky a flash of lightning. Thunder

693

growled, and raindrops began to splash against the pane.

'That fool's going to get wet,' he said.

Beach followed his pointing finger. Into the scene below a figure had come, walking rapidly. His interview with Percy Pilbeam had left Monty in that exhilarated frame of mind which demands strenuous exercise. Where Lord Tilbury, on a previous occasion, had walked because his heart was heavy, Monty walked because his heart was light. Pilbeam had filled him with the utmost confidence. He did not know how or when, but he felt that Pilbeam would find a way.

So now he strode briskly across the park, regardless of the fact that the weather was uncertain.

'Mr Bodkin, sir.'

'So it is, the young reptile. He'll get soaked.'

'Yes, sir.'

There was quiet satisfaction in the butler's voice. It was even possible, he was reflecting, that this young man might be struck by lightning. If so, it was all right with Beach. As far as he was concerned, Nature's awful majesty could go the limit. He only wished that Pilbeam, too, were being exposed to the fury of the elements. He viewed members of gangs in rather an Old Testament spirit, and believed in their getting treated rough.

Ronnie was in his bedroom. When the heart is aching, there are few better refuges than a country-house bedroom. A man may smoke and think there, undisturbed.

Beach, tracking him down a few minutes later, found him well disposed to the arrangement he had come to suggest. He made no difficulties about accepting custody of the manuscript. Indeed, it seemed to Beach that he was scarcely interested. Listless was the word that occurred to the butler, and he put it down to the weather. He took his departure with feelings resembling

those of the man who got rid of the Bottle Imp; and
Ronnie, having thrown the manuscript into a drawer,
resumed his seat and began thinking of Sue once more.

Sue! . . .

It wasn't that he blamed her. If she loved Monty
Bodkin – well, that was that. You couldn't blame a girl
for preferring one fellow to another.

All that stuff his mother had been saying about her
being the typical chorus-girl fluttering from affair to
affair was, of course, just a lot of pernicious bilge. Sue
wasn't like that. She was as straight as they make 'em. It
was simply that she had been dazzled by this blasted
lissom Monty and couldn't help herself.

You were always reading about that sort of thing in
novels. Girl gets engaged to bloke, thinking at the
moment that he is what the doctor ordered. Then runs
into second bloke and discovers in a sort of flash that
she has picked the wrong one. No doubt, on that trip of
hers to London she had happened to meet Monty
accidentally in Piccadilly or somewhere and the thing
had come on her like a thunderbolt.

It was what he had been expecting all along, of
course. He had told her so himself. It stood to reason, he
meant, that a terrific girl like her – a girl who practically
stood alone, as you might say – was bound sooner or
later to come across someone capable of cutting out a
bally pink-faced midget who, except for getting a
feather-weight Boxing Blue at Cambridge, had never
done a thing to justify his existence.

Yes, that was about what it all boiled down to, felt
Ronnie. He rose and went to the window. For some time
now, in a subconscious sort of way, he had been dimly
aware that there was something rummy going on
outside.

He found himself looking out upon a changed world.
The storm was now at its height. Torrents of rain were
coursing down the glass. Thunder was booming,

lightning flashing. A hissing, howling, roaring, devastated world. A world that seemed to fit in neatly with his stormy emotions.

Sue! . . .

Yesterday on the roof. Finding that hat and realizing that she and Monty had been up there together all the afternoon. He flattered himself that she couldn't possibly have detected anything from his manner – no, he had worn the good old mask all right – but there had been a moment, before he got hold of himself, when he had understood how those chaps you read about in the papers who run amok and slay two get that way.

Yes, reason might tell him that it was perfectly natural for Sue to be in love with Monty Bodkin, but nothing was going to make him like it.

The storm seemed to be conking out a bit. The thunder had rolled away into the distance. The lightning flashes had lost much of their zip. Even the rain showed a disposition to cheese it. What had been a Niagara was now little more than a drizzle. And suddenly, watery and faint, there gleamed on the drenched stone of the terrace, a ray of sunshine.

It grew. Blue spread over the sky. Across the valley there was a rainbow. Ronnie opened the window and a wave of cool, sweet-smelling air poured into the room.

He leaned out, sniffing. And abruptly he became aware that the heavy depression of the last two days had left him. The thunderstorm had wrought its customary miracle. He felt like a man recovered from a fever. It was as if the whole world had suddenly been purged of gloom. A magic change had come over everything.

Birds were singing in the shrubberies below, and for twopence Ronnie could have sung himself.

Why, dash it, he felt, he had been making a fat-headed fuss about absolutely nothing. He saw it all now. What had given him that extraordinary notion that Sue was in love with Monty was simply the foul weather. Of course there was nothing between them really. That lunch could easily be explained. So could that afternoon together on the roof. Everything could easily be explained in this best of all possible worlds.

And scarcely had he reached this conclusion when he perceived on the drive below him a draggled figure. It was Monty Bodkin, home from his ramble. He leaned farther out of the window, overflowing with the milk of human kindness.

'Hullo,' he said.

Monty looked up.

'Hullo.'

'You're wet.'

'Yes.'

'By Jove, you *are* wet!' said Ronnie. It hurt him to think that this brave new world could contain a fellow human being in such a soluble condition. 'You'd better go and change.'

'Yes.'

'Into something dry.'

Monty nodded, scattering water like a public fountain. He brushed the tangle of hair out of his eyes, and squelched on his way.

It was perhaps two minutes later that Ronnie, still aching with compassion, remembered that on the shelf above his wash-stand he had a bottle of excellent embrocation.

When once a man has reacted from a mood of abysmal depression, there is no knowing how far he will go in the opposite direction. In a normal frame of mind, Ronnie would probably have dismissed the moistness of Monty from his thoughts as soon as the other had left him. But now, in the grip of this strange feeling of universal benevolence, he felt that those few words of sympathy had not been enough. He wanted to do something practical, something constructive that would help to

ward off the nasty cold in the head which this man
might so easily catch as the result of his total
immersion. And, as we say, he remembered that bottle
of embrocation.

It was Riggs's Golden Balm, in the large (or
seven-and-sixpenny) size, and he knew, not only from
the advertisements, which were very frank about it, but
also from personal trial, that it communicated an
immediate warm glow to the entire system, averting
catarrh, chills, rheumatism, sciatica, stiffness of the
joints, and lumbago, and in addition imparted a
delightful sensation of *bien-être*, toning up and
renovating the muscular tissues. And if ever a fellow
stood in need of warm glows and tonings up, it was
Monty.

Seizing the bottle, he hurried off on his errand of
mercy. He found Monty in his room, stripped to the
waist, rubbing himself vigorously with a rough towel.

'I say,' he said, 'I don't know if you know this stuff!
You might like to try it. It communicates a warm
glow.'

Monty, the towel draped about him like a shawl,
examined the bottle with interest. He sloshed it
tentatively. This consideration touched him.

'Dashed good of you.'

'Not a bit.'

'You're sure it's not for horses?'

'Horses?'

'Some of these embrocations are. You rub them well
in, and then you take another look at the directions and
you see "For horses only", or words to that effect, and
then you suffer the tortures of the damned for about half
an hour, feeling as if you had been having a dip in
vitriol.'

'Oh, no. This stuff's all right. I use it myself.'

'Then have at it!' said Monty, relieved.

He poured some of the fluid into the palm of his hand

and expanded his torso. And, as he did so, Ronnie Fish
uttered a quick, sharp exclamation.

Monty looked up, surprised. His benefactor had
turned a vivid vermilion and was staring at him in a
marked manner.

'Eh?' he said, puzzled.

Ronnie did not speak immediately. He appeared to be
engaged in swallowing some hard, jagged substance.

'On your chest,' he said at length, in a strange,
toneless voice.

'Eh?'

Eton and Cambridge came to Ronnie's aid. Outwardly
calm, he swallowed again, picked a piece of fluff off his
left sleeve, and cleared his throat.

'There's something on your chest.'

He paused.

'It looks like "Sue".'

He paused again.

' "Sue",' he said casually, 'with a heart round it.'

The hard jagged substance seemed to have transferred
itself to Monty's throat. There was a brief silence while
he disposed of it.

He was blaming himself. Rummy, he reflected
ruefully, how when you saw a thing day after day for a
couple of years or so it ceased to make any impression
on what he rather fancied was called the retina. This
heart-encircled 'Sue', this pink and ultramarine tribute
to a long-vanished love, which in a gush of romantic
fervour he had caused to be graven on his skin in the
early days of their engagement, might during the last
eighteen months just as well not have been there for all
the notice he had taken of it. He had practically
forgotten that it was still in existence.

It was a moment for quick thinking.

'Not "Sue",' he said. 'SUE. – Sarah Ursula Ebbsmith.'

'What!'

'Sarah Ursula Ebbsmith,' repeated Monty firmly. 'Girl

I used to be engaged to. She died. Pneumonia. Very sad. Don't let's talk of it.'

There was a long pause. Ronnie moved to the door. His feelings were almost too deep for words, but he managed a couple.

'Well, bung-o!'

The door closed behind him.

Sue had watched the storm from the broad window-seat of the library.

Her feelings were mixed. As a spectacle she enjoyed it, for she was fond of thunderstorms. The only thing that spoiled it for her was the knowledge that Monty was out in it. She had seen him cross the terrace in an outwardbound direction just as it began to break. The poor lamb, she felt, must be getting soaked.

Her first act, accordingly, when the rain stopped and that sea of blue began to spread itself over the sky, was to go out on to the balcony and scan the horizon, like Sister Ann, for signs of him. She was thus enabled to witness his return and to hear the brief exchange of remarks between him and Ronnie.

'Hullo.'

'Hullo.'

'You're wet.'

'Yes.'

'By Jove, you *are* wet. You'd better go and change.'

'Yes.'

'Into something dry.'

Considered as dialogue, not, perhaps, on the highest level. Reading it through, one sees that it lacks a certain something. But the noblest effort of a great dramatist could not have stirred Sue more. It seemed to her, as she listened, that a great weight had rolled off her heart.

It was the way Ronnie had spoken that impressed and thrilled. The kindly, considerate tone. The cheerful cordiality. For two days it had been as though some sullen changeling had taken his place; and now, if one could judge from the genial ring of his voice, the old Ronnie was back again.

She stood on the balcony, drinking in the fragrant air. It was astonishing what a change that healing storm had brought about. Shropshire, which yesterday had been so depressing a spectacle, was now an earthly Paradise. The lake glittered. The river shone. The spinneys were their friendly selves again. Rabbits were darting about in the park with all the old carefree abandon, and as far as the eye could reach there were contented cows.

She left the room, humming a little tune. Eventually, she would seek out Monty and make inquiries after his well-being, but her immediate desire was to find Ronnie.

The click of billiard-balls arrested her attention as she came to the foot of the stairs. Gally, probably, playing a solitary hundred up; but he might be able to tell her where Ronnie was. His voice during that conversation with Monty had seemed to come from one of the passage windows.

She opened the door, and Ronnie, sprawled over the table, looked up at her.

That tattoo-mark had settled things for Ronnie. It had swept away in an instant all the gay optimism brought by the passing of the storm. With a heart like lead, he had groped his way downstairs. The open door of the billiard-room had seemed to offer a means of diverting his thoughts temporarily, and he had gone in and begun to practise sombre cannons. For even if a man is leaden-hearted there is no harm in his brushing up his near-the-cushion game a bit. Indeed, it is an intelligent thing to do, for if the girl he loves loves another his life is obviously going to be pretty much of a blank for the next fifty years or so, and he will have to fall back for solace on his ambitions. One of Ronnie's ambitions was some day to make a flukeless break of thirty.

'Hullo,' he said politely, straightening himself and

701

standing with cue at rest. Eton and Cambridge stood at his elbow, to help him through this ordeal.

No sense of impending disaster came to Sue. To her, this man was still the sort of modern Cheeryble Brother whom she had heard chatting so gaily out of the window.

'Oh, Ronnie,' she said, 'you can't stay indoors on an evening like this. It's simply lovely out.'

'Oh, yes?' said Eton.

'Perfectly wonderful.'

'Oh, yes?' said Cambridge.

Something seemed to stab at Sue's heart. Her eyes widened. A numbing thought had begun to frame itself. Could it be that that sunny geniality which she had so recently observed playing upon Monty Bodkin like a fountain was to be withheld from her?

But she persevered.

'Let's go for a drive in your car.'

'I don't think I will, thanks.'

'Then let's take a boat out on the lake.'

'Not for me, thanks.'

'Or the court might be dry enough for tennis by now.'

'I shouldn't think so.'

'Well, then, come for a walk.'

'Oh, for God's sake,' said Ronnie, 'let me alone!'

They stared at one another. Ronnie's eyes were hot and miserable. But they did not look hot and miserable to Sue. She read in them only the dislike, the sullen, trapped dislike of a man tied to a girl for whom he has ceased to feel any affection, so that merely to speak to her is an affliction to his nerves. She drew a deep breath, and walked to the window.

'Sorry,' said Ronnie gruffly. 'Shouldn't have said that.'

'I'm glad you did,' said Sue. 'It's better to come right out with these things.'

She traced little circles with her finger on the glass. A heavy silence filled the room.

'I think we might as well chuck it, don't you?' she said.

'Just as you say,' said Ronnie.

'All right,' said Sue.

She moved to the door. He hurried forward and opened it for her. Polite to the last.

Up in his bedroom, meanwhile, anointing his chest with Riggs's Golden Balm, Monty Bodkin had suddenly become amazingly cheerful.

'Tiddly-iddly-om, pom-POM,' he chanted, as blithely as any thrush in the shubbery below.

A great idea had just come to him.

It was the embrocation that had done the trick. As he stood there enjoying the immediate warm glow and the delightful sensation of *bien-être*, it was as if his brain, as well as his muscular tissues, had been toned up and renovated. This bottle of embrocation, it suddenly occurred to him, was more than a mere three or four fluid ounces of stuff that smelled like a miasmic swamp – it was a symbol. If Ronnie was taking the trouble to bring him bottles of embrocation, it must mean that all was well between them; that that odd coldness had ceased to be; that his dear old pal, in a word, was once more a dear old pal. And if a man is a dear old pal, it stands to reason that he will be delighted to do a fellow a good turn.

The good turn Monty wanted Ronnie to do for him now was to go to Beach and use his influence with that obdurate butler to persuade him to cough up that manuscript.

It was not that Monty had lost faith in Pilbeam. No doubt, if given time, Pilbeam, exercising his subtle craft, would be able to secure the thing all right. But why go to all that trouble when you could take a short cut and work the wheeze quite simply without any fuss? Besides, there was the fellow's fee to be considered.

These sleuths probably came pretty high, and a penny
saved is a penny earned.

A room-to-room search brought him to where the
Last of the Fishes was once more practising cannons.
He approached him with all the happy confidence of a
child entering the presence of a rich and indulgent
uncle.

For Monty Bodkin was no mind-reader. He had
detected no change in his friend's manner at the end of
their recent interview. It had been awkward for a
moment, no doubt, that business of the tattoo-mark, but
he felt that his quick thinking had passed off a tricky
situation pretty neatly, satisfactorily lulling all possible
suspicions.

'I say, Ronnie, old lad,' he said, 'I wonder if you could
spare me a moment of your valuable time?'

Ronnie laid the cue down carefully. For all that he
had now resigned himself to the fact that Sue preferred
this man to him, he was conscious of a well-defined
desire to bat him over the head with the butt end.
White-hot knives were gashing Ronnie Fish's soul, and
he could not but feel a very vivid distaste for the man
responsible for his raw misery.

'Well?' he said.

It seemed to Monty that his friend was a bit on the
chilly side, not quite the effervescing chum of the dear
old embrocation days, but he carried on with only a
momentary twinge of concern.

'Tell me, old man, how do you stand with Beach?'

'With Beach? How do you mean?'

'Well, does he feel pretty feudal where you're
concerned? Would he, in fine, be inclined to stretch a
point to oblige the young master?'

Ronnie stared bleakly. He had been prepared to be
civil to this man who had wrecked his life, but he was
dashed if he was going to spend the evening listening to
him talking drip.

'What is all this bilge?' he demanded sourly. 'Come to the point.'

'Oh, I'm coming to the point.'

'Well, be quick.'

'I will, I will. Here, then, is the gist or nub. Beach has got something I badly want, and he refuses to disgorge. And I thought that perhaps if you went to him and did the Young Squire a bit – exerting your influence, I mean to say, and rather throwing your weight about generally – he might prove more . . . what's the word . . . beginning with an A . . . amenable.'

Ronnie glowered wearily.

'I can't understand a damn thing you're talking about.'

'Well, in a nutshell, Beach has got that book of old Gally's and I can't get him to let me have it.'

'Why do you want it?'

Monty decided, as he had done when talking with Lord Tilbury by the potting-shed, that manly frankness was the only policy.

'You know all about that book?'

'Yes.'

'That Gally won't let it be published, I mean?'

'Yes.'

'And that he had signed a contract for it with the Mammoth Publishing Company?'

'No. I didn't know that.'

'Well, he did. And his backing out has rendered poor old Pop Tilbury, the boss of same, as sick as mud. Well, naturally, I mean to say, Old Tilbury had got serial rights and book rights and American rights and every other kind of rights including the Scandinavian, and you know what a packet there is in any literary effort that really dishes the dirt about the blue-gored. I should say, taking it one way and another, he stands to lose in the neighbourhood of twenty thousand quid if Gally sticks to his resolve not to publish. And so, to cut a long story s., old man, this Tilbury is so anxious to get hold of the manuscript that he states specifically that if I can snitch it for him he will take me back into his employment – from which, as I dare say you know, I was recently booted out.'

'I thought you resigned.'

Monty smiled sadly.

'That may be the story going the round of the clubs,' he said, 'but as a matter of actual fact I was booted out. There was a spot of technical trouble which wouldn't interest you and into which I will not go. Suffice it to say that we did not see eye to eye as regarded the conduct of the Uncle Woggly to his Chicks department, and my services were dispensed with. So now you get the run of the scenario. The thing is a straight issue. Let me grab this MS and turn it in to the Big Chief, and I start working again at Tilbury House.'

'What do you want to do that for?'

'It's imperative. I must have a job.'

'I should have thought that you would have been happy enough here.'

'Ah, but I'm liable to get the sack here at any moment.'

'Too bad.'

'Quite bad enough,' agreed Monty. 'But it'll be all right if you can induce Beach to give up that manuscript, I shall then secure a long-term contract with old Tilbury and be in a posish to marry the girl I love.'

A strong convulsion shook Ronnie Fish. This, he considered, was pretty raw. A nice thing, taking a fellow's girl away from him and then coming to him to ask him to help him marry her. He had credited the other with more delicacy.

'You will, eh?' he said, after a pause to master his emotion.

'Positively. It's all fixed up.'

'Who is she?' asked Ronnie sardonically. 'Sarah Ursula Ebbsmith?'

'Eh? Oh, ah,' said Monty hastily. He had forgotten for the moment. 'No, not poor dear Sarah. Oh, no, no, no. She's dead. Tuberculosis. Very sad.'

'You told me it was pneumonia.'

'No, tuberculosis.'

'I see.'

'This is a new one. Girl named Gertrude Butterwick.'

Misunderstandings being always unfortunate, it was a pity, firstly, that Monty should have paused for a reverent second before uttering that sacred name and, secondly, that the girl of his dreams should have possessed a name which, one has to admit, sounded a little thin. In certain moods, a man whose mind is biased simply does not believe that there is such a name as Gertrude Butterwick. To Ronnie, noting that second's hesitation, it was just one this man had made up on the spur of the moment, even he not having the face to tell Sue's fiancé, as he supposed him still to be, that he wanted his assistance in taking Sue from him.

'Gertrude Butterwick, eh?'

'That's right.'

'Fond of her?'

'My dear chap!'

'And I suppose she's crazy about you?'

'Oh, deeply enamoured.'

Ronnie felt suddenly listless. What, he asked himself, did it matter, anyway? What did anything matter now?

Every man is tempted at times by the great gesture. This temptation had just come overwhelmingly upon Ronnie Fish. From the other's words he had become confirmed in his suspicion that somehow or other Monty since their last meeting must have lost all his money. Otherwise, why should jobs at Tilbury House be of such importance to him?

Unless he got that job at Tilbury House, he would not be able to marry Sue. And unless he, Ronnie Fish, helped him, he would not get it.

The Sidney Carton spirit descended upon Ronnie – with this difference, that where Sidney, if one remembers correctly, was rather pleased about the whole thing he himself felt bitter and defiant.

Monty had taken Sue from him. Sue had gone to Monty without a pang. All right, then. All jolly right. He would show them he didn't care. He would let them see the stuff Fishes were made of.

'Listen,' he said. 'There's no need to worry about Beach. He hasn't got that manuscript.'

'Oh, yes, he has. I saw him reading . . .'

'He gave it to me,' said Ronnie. He picked up his cue and shaped at the spot ball. 'You'll find it in the chest of drawers in my room. Take the damned thing if you want it.'

Monty gasped. No Israelite caught in a sudden manna-shower in mid-desert could have felt a greater mixture of surprise and gratification.

'My dear old man!' he began effusively.

Ronnie did not speak. He was practising cannons.

IO

The passing of the storm had left the Hon. Galahad
Threepwood at rather a loose end. He was not quite sure
where he wanted to go or what he wanted to do. His
favourite lawn, he knew, would be too wet to walk on,
his favourite deck-chair too wet to sit in. The whole
world out of doors, in fact, for all that the sun was
shining so brightly, was much too moist and dripping to
attract a man with his feline dislike of dampness.

After Beach had left him, he had remained for a while
in the small library. Then, tiring of that, he had
wandered aimlessly about the house, winding as many
clocks as he could find. He was, and always had been, a
great clock-winder. Eventually, he had drifted to the
hall, and was now lounging on a settee there in the hope
that, if he lounged long enough, somebody would come
along with whom he might chat till it was time to dress
for dinner. He always found this part of the evening a
little depressing.

Up to the present, he had had no luck. Monty Bodkin
had come downstairs, but after Beach's revelations he
had no wish to do anything but glower sternly at Monty.
Without attempting to draw him into conversation,
though he had just remembered a thirty-year-old
Limerick which he would have liked to recite to
someone, he watched him go into the billiard-room,
where the opening showed a glimpse of Ronnie
practising cannons. Presently, he had come out again
and gone upstairs, followed as before by that stern
eye.

'Young toad!' muttered the Hon. Galahad severely.

He was shocked at Monty, and disappointed in him.
He wished he had never given him that tip on the
Cesarewitch.

Soon after this, Pilbeam had appeared, smiled weakly,
and gone into the smoking-room. Here, again, there was
nothing for the Hon. Galahad to work on. He had no
desire to tell Limericks to Pilbeam. Apart from the fact
that the fellow was conspiring with his sister Constance
to steal his manuscript, he did not like the detective.
Brought up in a sterner school of hairdressing, he
disapproved of these modern young men who went
about with their fungoid growth in sticky ridges.

It began to look to him as if in the matter of society
he had but two choices open. Clarence, who would have
appreciated that Limerick once he could have been
induced to bring his mind to bear upon it, was
presumably down at the sty making eyes at that pig of
his; and Sue, the person he really wanted to talk to,
seemed to have disappeared off the face of the earth. As
far as he could see, he was reduced to the alternatives of
going into the billiard-room and joining Ronnie, and of
stepping up to the drawing-room and having a word with
his sister Constance, who at this hour would no doubt
be taking tea there. He was just about to adopt this
second course, for he rather wanted a straight talk with
Constance about that Pilbeam matter, when Sue came
in from the garden.

Immediately, the idea of tackling Connie left him. He
could do that at his leisure, and he was in the mood now
for something pleasanter than a brother-and-sister
dog-fight. Sue's bright personality was just the tonic he
needed at this lowering point in the day's progress. He
would be unable to tell her the Limerick, it not being
that sort of Limerick, but at any rate they could talk of
this and that.

He called to her, and she came over to where he sat. It
was dim in the hall, but it struck him that she was not

looking quite herself. The elasticity seemed to have gone out of her walk, that jaunty suppleness which he had always admired so in Dolly. But possibly this was merely his imagination. He was always inclined to read a fictitious sombreness into things when the shadows began to creep over the world and it was still too early for a cocktail.

'Well, young woman.'

'Hullo, Gally.'

'What have you been doing with yourself?'

'I was walking on the terrace.'

'Get your feet wet?'

'I don't think so. Perhaps I had better go up and change my shoes, though.'

The Hon. Galahad would have none of this. He pulled her down on to the settee beside him.

'Amuse me,' he said. 'I'm bored.'

'Poor Gally. I'm sorry.'

'This,' said the Hon. Galahad, 'is the hour of the day that searches a man out. It makes him examine his soul. And I don't want to examine my soul. I expect the thing looks like an old boot. So, as I say, amuse me, child. Sing to me. Dance before me. Ask me riddles.'

'I'm afraid . . .'

The Hon. Galahad gave her a sharp glance through his monocle. It was as he had suspected. This girl was not festive.

'Anything the matter?'

'Oh, no.'

'Sure?'

'Quite.'

'Cigarette?'

'No, thanks.'

'Shall I turn on the radio? There may be a lecture on Newts.'

'No, don't.'

'There *is* something the matter?'

'There isn't, really.'

The Hon. Galahad frowned. Then a possible solution occurred to him.

'I suppose it's the heat.'

'It was hot, wasn't it? It's better now.'

'You're under the weather.'

'I am a little.'

'Thunderstorms often upset people. Are you afraid of thunder?'

'Oh, no.'

'Lots of girls are. I knew one once who, whenever there was a thunderstorm, used to fling her arms round the neck of the nearest man, hugging and kissing him till it was all over. Purely nervous reaction, of course, but you should have seen the young fellows flocking round as soon as the sky began to get a little overcast. Gladys, her name was. Gladys Twistleton. Beautiful girl with large, melting eyes. Married a fellow in the Blues called Harringay. I'm told that the way he used to clear the drawing-room during the early years of their married life at the first suspicion of a rumble was a sight to be seen and remembered.'

The Hon. Galahad had brightened. Like all confirmed raconteurs, he took on new life when the anecdotes started to come briskly.

'Talking of thunder,' he said, 'did I ever tell you the story of Puffy Benger and the thunderstorm?'

'I don't think so.'

'It was one time when Plug Basham and I and a couple of other fellows had gone to stay with him in a cottage he had down in Somersetshire, for a bit of fishing. Puffy, I ought to tell you, was one of those chaps who are always drawing the long bow. Charming man, but a shocking liar. He had a niece he was always bragging about. His niece could do this, and his niece could do that. She was one of these business girls – must have been about the first of them – and he was very proud of her. And one day when we had been driven indoors by a thunderstorm and were sitting round yarning, he happened to mention that she was the quickest typist in England.'

Sue was leaning forward with her chin in her hands.

'Well, we said "Oh, yes!" and "Fancy!" and so on – the fellow was our host – and there the thing would have ended, no doubt, only Puffy, who could never let anything alone, went on to say that this girl's proficiency as a typist had had a most remarkable effect on her piano-playing. It wasn't that it had improved it – it had always been perfect – but it had speeded it up quite a good deal. "In fact," said Puffy, "you won't believe this, but it's true, she can now play Chopin's Funeral March in forty-eight seconds!"

'This was a bit too much for us, of course. "Not forty-eight seconds?" said somebody. "Forty-eight seconds," insisted Puffy firmly. He said he had frequently timed her on his stop-watch. And then Plug Basham, who was always an outspoken sort of chap, took the licence of an old friend to tell Puffy he was the biggest liar in the country, not even excluding Dogface Weeks, the then champion of the Pelican Club. "It isn't safe sitting in the same house with you during a thunderstorm," said Plug. "Why isn't it safe sitting in the same house with me during a thunderstorm?" said Puffy. "Because at any moment," said Plug, "the Almighty is liable to strike it with lightning. That's why it isn't safe." "Listen," said Puffy, a good deal worked up, "If my niece Myrtle can't play Chopin's Funeral March in forty-eight seconds, I hope this house *will* be struck by lightning this very minute." And by what I have always thought rather an odd coincidence, it was. There was a sort of sheet of fire and a fearful crash, and the next thing I saw was Puffy crawling out from under the table. He seemed more aggrieved than frightened, I remember. He gave one reproachful look up at the ceiling, and then he said in a peevish sort of voice, "You do take a chap so dashed literally!"'

He paused.

'Yes?' said Sue.

Most raconteurs would have found the observation a little dampening. The Hon. Galahad was no exception.

'How do you mean, yes?' he asked, with something of the querulousness exhibited on that other occasion by Puffy Benger.

'Oh, I'm sorry,' said Sue with a start. 'I'm afraid . . . What were you saying, Gally?'

The Hon. Galahad took her chin firmly, and, tilting her face up, stared accusingly into her eyes.

'Now, then,' he said, 'no more of this nonsense about there being nothing the matter. What's the trouble?'

'Oh, Gally!' said Sue.

'Good God!' cried the Hon. Galahad, stricken with the cold horror that comes upon a man who finds he is holding the chin of a crying girl.

It was a stern, hard-faced Galahad Threepwood who entered the billiard-room some ten minutes later. His hair seemed to bristle, his black-rimmed monocle to shoot forth flame.

'Ah, there you are!' he observed, as he closed the door.

Ronnie looked up wanly. Since the departure of Monty Bodkin, he had been sitting hunched up in a corner, staring at nothing.

'Hullo,' he said.

Despite the fact that his own company had been the reverse of enjoyable, he did not welcome his uncle's arrival. He was fond of the Hon. Galahad, but at the moment had no wish for his society. What a man on the rack wants is solitude. He supposed that the other had come to suggest a friendly game of snooker, and the mere thought of playing friendly games of snooker with anyone made him feel sick.

'I was just off,' he said, to nip this project in the bud.

The Hon. Galahad swelled like a little turkey-cock. His monocle was now a perfect searchlight.

'Just off be damned!' he snorted. 'You sit down and listen to me. Just off, indeed! You can go off when I've finished talking to you, and not before.'

Ronnie abandoned the snooker theory. Plainly it did not cover the facts. His moroseness had become tinged with bewilderment. It was many years since he had beheld his good-natured relative in a mood like this. It seemed to bring back the tang of the brave old days of chimney-stacks and whangees. He could think of nothing in his recent conduct that could have caused so impressive an upheaval.

'Now, then,' said the Hon. Galahad, 'what's all this?'

'That's just what I was going to ask,' said Ronnie. 'What *is* all this?'

'Don't pretend you don't know.'

'But I don't know.'

'It's no good taking that attitude.' The Hon. Galahad jerked his thumb at the door. 'I've just been talking to young Sue out there.'

A thin coating of ice seemed to creep over Ronald Fish.

'Oh, yes?' he said politely.

'She's crying.'

'Oh, yes?' said Ronnie, still politely, but with those white-hot knives at work on his soul again. His mind was divided against itself. Part of it was pointing out passionately that it was ghastly to think of Sue in tears. The other part was raising its eyebrows and shooting its cuffs and observing with a sneer that it was blowed if it could see what *she* had to cry about.

'Crying, I tell you! Crying her dashed eyes out!'

'Oh, yes?'

The Hon. Galahad Threepwood was himself an Old Etonian, and in his time had frequently had occasion to

715

employ the Eton manner to the undoing of his
fellow-men. There were grey-haired bookies and elderly
card-sharps going about London to this day, who still felt
an occasional twinge, as of an old wound, when they
recalled the agony of seeing him stare at them as Ronnie
was staring and of hearing him say 'Oh, yes?' as Ronnie
was saying it now. But this did not make his nephew's
attitude any the easier for him to endure. The whole
point of the Eton manner, as of a shotgun, is that you
have to be at the right end of it.

He brought his fist down on the billiard-table with a
thump.

'So you're not interested, eh? You don't care? Well, let
me tell you,' said the Hon. Galahad, once more
maltreating the billiard-table, 'that I do care. That girl's
mother was the only woman I ever loved, and I don't
propose to have her daughter's happiness ruined by any
sawn-off young half-portion with a face like a strawberry
ice who takes the notion into his beastly turnip of a
head to play fast and loose with her. Understand that!'

There were so many ramifications to this insult that
Ronnie was compelled to take them in rotation.

'I can't help it if my face is like a strawberry ice,' he
said, electing to begin with that one.

'It ought to be much more like a strawberry ice. You
ought to be blushing yourself sick.'

'And when,' said Ronnie, feeling on safe ground here,
'you talk about sawn-off half-portions, may I point out
that I'm about an inch taller than you are?'

'Rot!' said the Hon. Galahad, stung.

'I am.'

'You're certainly not.'

'Measure you against the wall,' insisted Ronnie.

'I'll do nothing of the sort. And what the devil,'
demanded the Hon. Galahad, suddenly aware that the
main issue of debate was becoming shelved, 'has that got
to do with it? You may be a giraffe, for all I care. The

point I am endeavouring to make is that you are
breaking this girl's heart, and I'm not going to have it.
She tells me your engagement is off.'

'Quite right.'

Once more the Hon. Galahad smote the green cloth.

'You'll smash that table,' said Ronnie.

There flashed into the Hon. Galahad's mind the story
of how old Beefy Muspratt, with some assistance,
actually had smashed a billiard-table in the year
ninety-eight; and such is the urge of the raconteur's
ruling passion that he almost stopped to tell it. Then he
recovered himself.

'Curse the table!' he cried. 'I didn't come here to talk
about tables. I came to tell you that, if you care to know
what a calm, unprejudiced observer thinks of you, you're
an infernal young snob . . . and a hound . . .'

'What!'

'. . . and a worm,' went on the Hon. Galahad, as pink
himself now as any pink-faced nephew. 'Do you think I
can't see what's happened? If you want to know, Sue
told me herself. Told me in so many words, out there in
the hall just now. You're such a wambling, spineless,
invertebrate jellyfish that you've let your mother talk
you into breaking off this engagement. You've allowed
her to persuade you that that poor child isn't good
enough for you.'

'What!'

'As if Dolly Henderson's daughter wasn't good enough
for the finest man in the kingdom – let alone a . . .'

On the brink of becoming a little personal again, the
Hon. Galahad found himself interrupted. This time it
was Ronnie who had thumped the table.

'Don't talk such absolute dashed nonsense!'
thundered Ronnie. 'You don't suppose I broke off the
engagement, do you? Sue broke it off herself.'

'Yes, because she could see that you wanted to get out
of it and, being the splendid girl she is, wasn't going to

717

cheapen herself by hanging on to a man who was obviously dying to be rid of her.'

'I like that! Dying to be rid of her! I . . . I . . . Why, damn it!'

'You aren't telling me you're still fond of her?'

'What do you mean, still? And what do you mean, fond of her? Fond of her! My God!'

The Hon. Galahad was astounded.

'Then what on earth have you been going about for these last few days like a spavined frog? Treating her as if . . .'

His manner softened. He began to see daylight. He could not lay his hand gently on his nephew's shoulder, for they were at opposite sides of a regulation-sized billiard-table. But he infused a gentle hand-laying into his voice.

'I see it all! You were worrying about something else; is that it? Or was it the heat? Anyhow, for some reason you allowed yourself to be odd in your manner. My dear boy, when you get to my age you'll know better than to take chances like that. Never be odd in your manner with a woman. Don't you realize that, even under the best of conditions, there's practically nothing that won't make a sensitive, highly strung girl break off her engagement? If she doesn't like her new hat . . . or if her stocking starts a ladder . . . or if she comes down late to breakfast and finds all the scrambled eggs are finished. It's like servants giving notice. I had a man back in the nineties – Spatchett, his name was – who used to give me notice every time he backed a horse that didn't finish in the first three. Why, he gave me notice once purely and simply because his wife's sister had had a baby. I never paid any attention to it. I knew it was just a form of emotional expression. Where you or I would have lit a cigarette, Spatchett gave notice. And it's the same with women. No doubt Sue saw you brooding and assumed that love was dead. Well, this has certainly eased my mind, Ronnie, my dear boy. I'll go and explain things to her at once.'

'Half a minute, Uncle Gally.'

'Eh?'

Pausing half-way to the door, the Hon. Galahad saw that a peculiar expression had come into his nephew's face. An expression a little like that of a young Hindu fakir who, having settled himself on his first bed of spikes, is beginning to wish that he had chosen one of the easier religions.

'I'm afraid it isn't quite so simple as that,' said Ronnie.

The Hon. Galahad drew in the slack of his monocle, which in the recent excitement had fallen from his eye. He screwed the thing into place, and surveyed his nephew inquiringly.

'What do you mean?'

'You've got it all wrong. Sue doesn't love me.'

'Nonsense!'

'It isn't nonsense. She's in love with Monty Bodkin.'

'What!'

'It's all settled between them that they're going to get married.'

'I never heard such . . .'

'Oh, it's perfectly true,' said Ronnie, his mouth twisting. 'I'm not blaming her. Nobody's fault. Just one of those things. Still, there it is. She's crazy about him. She went up to London to meet him the moment I was out of the place, just because she couldn't keep away from him. She got him to apply for Hugo's job as Uncle Clarence's secretary, just because she was so keen to have him here. She was up on the roof with him all yesterday afternoon. And . . .' Ronnie had to pause for a moment here to control his voice '. . . he's got her name tattooed on his chest, with a heart round it.'

'You don't mean that?'

'I saw it myself.'

'Well, I'm dashed! Hurts like sin, that sort of thing. I haven't heard of anybody having a girl's name tattooed on him since the year ninety-nine, when Jack Bellamy-Johnstone . . .'

Ronnie held up a restraining hand.

'Not now, uncle, if you don't mind.'

'Most amusing story,' said the Hon. Galahad, wistfully.

'Later on, what?'

'Well, yes, perhaps you're right,' admitted the Hon. Galahad. 'I suppose you're not in the mood for stories. It was simply that poor old Jack fell in love with a girl named Esmeralda Parkinson-Willoughby and had the whole thing tattooed on his wishbone, and the wounds had scarcely healed when they quarrelled and he got engaged to another girl called May Todd. So if he had only waited . . . However, as you say, that is neither here nor there. Ronnie, my dear boy,' said the Hon. Galahad, 'this beats me. I had always looked on you as a pretty average sort of young poop, but never, never would I have imagined that you could have allowed yourself to believe all that drivel . . .'

'Drivel!'

'Perfect drivel. You've got hold of the wrong end of the stick entirely. Suppose Sue did go to London . . .'

'There's no supposition about it. My mother saw her and Monty lunching together at the Berkeley.'

'She would. Dashed Nosey Parker. Sorry, my boy. Forgot she was your mother. Still, she was my sister before you were ever born or thought of, and I hope a man can call his own sister a Nosey Parker. What did she tell you?'

'She said . . .'

'All right. Never mind. I can guess. No doubt she's been filling you up with all sorts of stories. Well, now you can hear the truth. Young Sue had nothing whatever to do with Monty Bodkin coming here. The first she

720

heard of his having been taken on as Clarence's secretary was from me, and the news absolutely bowled her over. I can see her now, looking at me like a dying duck and saying here was a nice bit of fruit-box because she had once, when a mere child, been engaged to the fellow . . .'

'What!'

'Certainly. Years ago. Before she ever met you. Only lasted a week or two, as far as I can gather, and she was glad to get out of it. But there the fact was. She had been engaged to him, and he was coming here, and if he wasn't tipped off to keep the thing dark he would be sure to say something tactless about the old days, and that would upset you, because you were such a blasted jealous half-wit, always ready to make heavy weather about nothing. She asked me what she ought to do. I gave her the only possible advice. I told her to rush up to London before you got back, get hold of Monty, and tell him to keep his mouth shut. Which she did. That is how she came to be in London that day, and that is why she was lunching with him. So there you are. The whole thing, you observe, done from start to finish in the kindliest spirit of altruism, with no other motive than to preserve your peace of mind. Perhaps this will be a lesson to you in future not to give way to jealousy, which I have always said and always shall say is one of the dashed silliest . . .'

Ronnie was staring, perplexed in the extreme.

'Is this true?'

'Of course it's true. If you can't see by this time that Sue is a girl in a million – pure gold – and that you've been treating her abominably . . .'

'But she was up on the roof with him.'

The childishness of this seemed to nettle the Hon. Galahad. He uttered a sound which was rather like Lord Tilbury's 'Cor!'

'Why shouldn't she be up on the roof with him? Must people be in love with one another just because they are up on roofs together? I was up on that roof with you once, but if you thought I was in love with you you must have been singularly obtuse. It's been a grief to me for years that you were so nippy round that chimney-stack. Sue in love with young Bodkin, indeed! Why, Monty Bodkin is engaged himself. She told me so. To a girl named Gertrude Butterwick. Butterwick,' said the Hon. Galahad musingly. 'I used to know several Butterwicks. I wonder if she would be any relation to old Legs Butterwick, who used to paint his face with red spots to make duns who called at his rooms think he'd got smallpox.'

A shuddering groan burst from the lips of Ronnie Fish.

'Oh, gosh, what a fool I've made of myself!'

'You have.'

'I'm a hound and a cad.'

'You are.'

'I ought to be kicked.'

'You ought.'

'Of all the . . .'

'Hold it,' urged the Hon. Galahad. 'Don't waste all this on me. Tell it to Sue. I'll fetch her.'

He darted from the room, to return a moment later, dragging the girl behind him.

'Now!' he said authoritatively. 'Do your stuff. Tie yourself in knots at her feet, and ask her to kick you in the face. Grovel before her on your wretched stomach. Roll about the floor and bark. And while you're doing it I'll be stepping up to the drawing-room and having a word with your mother and my sister Constance.'

A stern, resolute look came into the Hon. Galahad's face.

'I'll spoil their tea and shrimps!' he said.

In the drawing-room, however, when he arrived there after taking the stairs three at a time in that juvenile way of his which gout-crippled contemporaries so resented, he found only his sister Julia. She was seated in an armchair, smoking a cigarette and reading an illustrated weekly paper. The tea which he had hoped to spoil was in the process of being cleared away by Beach and a footman.

She looked contented, and she was feeling contented. Ronnie's growing gloom during the past two days had not escaped her. In a mood to be genial to everybody, even to one on whom she had always looked as the Family Blot, she welcomed the Hon. Galahad with a pleasant nod.

'You're late, if you've come for tea,' she said.

'Tea!' snorted the Hon. Galahad.

He stood fuming until the door closed.

'Now, then, Julia,' he said, 'I want a word with you.'

Lady Julia raised her shapely eyebrows.

'My dear Galahad! This is very menacing and ominous. Is something the matter?'

'You know what's the matter. Where's Connie?'

'Gone to answer the telephone, I believe.'

'Well, you'll do to start with.'

'Galahad, really!'

'Put down that paper.'

'Oh, very well.'

The Hon. Galahad strode to the hearthrug and stood with his back to the empty fire-place. Racial instinct made him feel more authoritative in that position. He frowned forbiddingly.

'Julia, you make me sick.'

'Indeed? Why is that?'

'What the devil do you mean by trying to poison young Ronnie's mind against Sue Brown?'

'Really, Galahad!'

'Do you deny that that is what you have been doing ever since you got here?'

'I may have pointed out to him once or twice the

723

inadvisability of marrying a girl who appears to be in love with another man. If this be treason, make the most of it. Surely it's a tenable theory?'

'You think she's in love with young Bodkin?'

'Apparently.'

'If you will step down to the billiard-room,' said the Hon. Galahad, 'I think you may possibly alter your opinion.'

Something of Lady Julia's self-confidence left her.

'What do you mean?'

'Touching,' said the Hon. Galahad unctuously. 'That's what it was. Touching. It nearly made me cry. I never saw a more united couple. All their doubts and misunderstandings cleared away . . .'

'What!'

'Locked in each other's arms, weeping on each other's chests . . . you ought to go down and have a look, Julia. You'll be in plenty of time. It's evidently going to be one of those non-stop performances. Well, anyway, that's the first thing I came up here to tell you. You have been taking a lot of trouble to ruin this girl's happiness these last few days, and now you are getting official intimation that you haven't succeeded. They are all right, those two. Sweethearts still is the term.'

The Hon. Galahad spread his coat-tails to the invisible blaze and resumed.

'The other thing I came to say is that there must be no more of this nonsense. If you have objections to young Ronnie marrying Sue, don't mention them to him. It worries him and makes him moody, and that worries Sue and makes her unhappy, and that worries me and spoils my day. You understand?'

Lady Julia was shaken, but she had not lost her spirit.

'I'm afraid you must make up your mind to having your days spoiled, Galahad.'

'You don't mean that even after this you intend to keep making a pest of yourself?'

'You put these things so badly. What you are trying to say, I imagine is, do I still intend to give my child a mother's advice? Certainly I do. A boy's best friend is his mother, don't you sometimes think? Ronnie, handicapped by being virtually half-witted, may not have seen fit to take my advice as yet; but if in the old days you ever had a moment to spare from your life-work of being thrown out of shady night-clubs and were able to look in at the Adelphi Theatre, you may remember the expression "A time will come!"'

The Hon. Galahad stared at this indomitable woman with something that was almost admiration.

'Well, I'm dashed!'

'Are you?'

'You always were a tough nut, Julia.'

'Thank you.'

'Always. Even as a child. It used to interest me in those days to watch you gradually dawning on the latest governess. I could have read her thoughts in her face, poor devil. First, she would meet Connie and you could almost hear her saying to herself "Hullo! A vicious specimen this one." And then you would come along, all wide, innocent blue eyes and flaxen curls, and she would feel a great wave of relief and fling her arms round you; thinking "Well, here's one that's all right, thank God!" Little knowing that she had just come up against the stoniest-hearted, beastliest-natured, and generally most poisonous young human rattlesnake in all Shropshire.'

Lady Julia seemed genuinely pleased at this tribute. She laughed musically.

'You are silly, Galahad.'

The Hon. Galahad adjusted his monocle.

'So your hat is still in the ring, eh?'

'Still there, my dear.'

'But what have you got against young Sue?'

'I don't like chorus-girls as daughters-in-law.'

'But, great heavens above, Julia, surely you can see

that Sue isn't the sort of girl you mean when you say "chorus-girls" in that beastly sniffy way?'

'You can't expect me to classify and tabulate chorus-girls. I haven't your experience. They're all chorus-girls to me.'

'There are moments, Julia,' said the Hon. Galahad meditatively, 'when I should like to drown you in a bucket.'

'A butt of malmsey would have been more in your line, I should have thought.'

'Your attitude about young Sue infuriates me. Can't you see the girl's a nice girl . . . a sweet girl . . . and a lady, if it comes to that.'

'Tell me, Gally,' said Lady Julia, 'just as a matter of interest, *is* she your daughter?'

The Hon. Galahad bristled.

'She is not. Her father was a man in the Irish Guards, named Cotterleigh. He and Dolly were married when I was in South Africa.'

He stood for a moment, his mind in the past.

'Fellow told me about it quite casually one day when I was having a drink in a Johannesburg bar,' he said with a far-off look in his eyes. ' "I see that girl Dolly Henderson who used to be at the Tivoli has got married," he said. Out of a blue sky . . .'

Lady Julia took up her paper.

'Well, if you have no further observations of interest to make . . .'

The Hon. Galahad came back to the present.

'Oh, I have.'

'Please hurry, then.'

'I have something to say which I fancy will interest you very much.'

'That will make a nice change.'

The Hon. Galahad paused a moment. His sister took advantage of the fact to interject a question.

'It isn't by any chance that, if this marriage of

Ronnie's is stopped, you will publish those
Reminiscences of yours, is it?'

'It is.'

Lady Julia gave another of her jolly laughs.

'My dear man, I had all that days ago from Constance.
And my flesh didn't even creep a bit. It seems to agitate
Connie tremendously but speaking for myself I haven't
the slightest objection to you publishing a dozen books
of Reminiscences. It will be nice to think of you making
some money at last, and as for the writhings of the
nobility and gentry . . .'

'Julia,' said the Hon. Galahad, 'one moment.'

He eyed her intently. She returned his gaze with an
air of faintly bored inquiry.

'Well?'

'You are the relict of the late Major-General Sir Miles
Fish, CBE, late of the Brigade of Guards.'

'I have never denied it.'

'Let us speak for awhile,' said the Hon. Galahad
gently, 'of the late Major-General Sir Miles Fish.'

Slowly a look of horror crept into Lady Julia's blue
eyes. Slowly she rose from the chair in which she had
been reclining. A hideous suspicion had come into her
mind.

'When Miles Fish married you,' said the Hon.
Galahad, 'he was a respectable – even a stodgily
respectable – Colonel. I remember your saying the first
time you met him that you thought him slow. Believe
me, Julia, when I knew dear old Fishy Fish as a young
subaltern, while you were still poisoning governesses'
lives at Blandings Castle, he was quite the reverse of
slow. His jolly rapidity was the talk of London.'

She stared at him, aghast. Her whole outlook on life,
as one might say, had been revolutionized. Hitherto, her
attitude towards the famous Reminiscences had been, as
it were, airy . . . detached . . . academic is perhaps the
word one wants. The thought of the consternation

727

which they would spread among her friends had amused her. But then she had naturally supposed that this man would have exercised a decent reticence about the pasts of his own flesh and blood.

'Galahad! You haven't . . . ?'

The historian was pointing a finger at her, like some finger of doom.

'Who rode a bicycle down Piccadilly in sky-blue underclothing in the late summer of '97?'

'Galahad!'

'Who, returning to his rooms in the early morning of New Year's Day, 1902, mistook the coal-scuttle for a mad dog and tried to shoot it with the fire-tongs?'

'Galahad!'

'Who . . .'

He broke off. Lady Constance had come into the room.

'Ah, Connie,' he said genially. 'I've just been having a chat with Julia. Get her to tell you all about it. I must be going down and seeing how the young folks are getting on.'

He paused at the door.

'Supplementary material,' he said, focusing his monocle on Lady Julia, 'will be found in Chapters Three, Eleven, Sixteen, Seventeen, and Twenty-one, especially Chapter Twenty-one.'

With a final beam, he passed jauntily from the room and began to descend the stairs.

In the billiard-room, the scene which he had rightly described as touching was still in progress. He wished he could take a snapshot of it to show to his sister Julia.

'That's right, my boy,' he said cordially. 'Capital!'

Ronnie detached himself and began to straighten his tie. He had not heard the door open.

'Oh, hullo, Uncle Gally,' he said. 'You here?'

Sue ran to the Hon. Galahad and kissed him.

'I shouldn't,' said the gratified but cautious man.
'He'll be getting jealous of me next.'

'There is no need,' said Ronnie with dignity, 'to rub it
in.'

'Well, I won't, then. Merely contenting myself with
remarking that of all the young poops I ever met . . .'

'He is not a poop!' said Sue.

'My dear,' insisted the Hon. Galahad, 'I was brought
up among poops. I spent my formative years among
poops. I have been a member of clubs which consisted
exclusively of poops. You will allow me to recognize a
poop when I see one. Moreover, we won't argue the
point. What I want to talk about now is that manuscript
of mine.'

A wordless cry broke from Ronnie's lips.

'Poop or no poop,' proceeded the Hon. Galahad, 'he
has got to guard that manuscript with his life. Because if
ever there were two women who would descend to the
level of the beasts of the field to lay their hooks on
it . . .'

'Uncle Gally!'

'Ronnie, darling,' cried Sue, 'what is it?'

She might well have asked. The young man's eyes
were fixed in a ghastly stare. His usually immaculate
hair was disordered where he had thrust a fevered hand
through it. Even his waistcoat seemed ruffled.

'. . . they are your mother and Lady Constance,'
proceeded the Hon. Galahad, who was never an easy
man to interrupt. 'And here's something that will
surprise you. Young Monty Bodkin is after the thing,
too. Young Bodkin has turned out to be an A1 snake in
the grass, I'm sorry to say. He's under orders from the
man who runs the firm that was going to publish my
book to pinch it and take it to him – Lord Tilbury. I used
to know him years ago as Stinker Pyke. Why they ever
made young Stinker a peer . . .'

'Uncle Gally!'

A little testily the Hon. Galahad allowed the stream of his eloquence to be diverted at last.

'Well, what is it?'

A sort of frozen calm, the calm of utter despair, had come upon Ronnie Fish.

'Monty Bodkin was in here just now,' he said. 'He wanted that manuscript. I told him where it was. And he went off to get it.'

11

No joy in the world is ever quite perfect. *Surgit*, as the old Roman said, *aliquid amari*. Monty Bodkin, having removed the manuscript from Ronnie's chest of drawers and gloated over it and taken it to his room and, after gloating over it again, deposited it in a safe place there, found his ecstasy a little dimmed by the thought of the awkward interview with Percy Pilbeam which now faced him. He was a young man who shrank from embarrassing scenes, and it seemed to him that this one threatened to be extremely embarrassing. Pilbeam, he realized, would have every excuse for being as sore as a gumboil.

Look at the thing squarely, he meant to say. A private detective has his feelings. He resents being made a silly ass of. If you commission him to do something, and then buzz off and do it yourself, pique inevitably supervenes. Suppose Sherlock Holmes, for instance, had sweated himself to the bone to recover the Naval Plans or something, and then the Admiralty authorities had come along and observed casually, 'Oh, I say, you know those Naval Plans, old man? Well, don't bother about them. We've just gone and snitched them ourselves.' Pretty sick the poor old human bloodhound would have felt, no doubt. And pretty sick in similar circumstances Monty anticipated that Percy Pilbeam was going to feel. He did not like the job of breaking the news at all.

However, it had to be done. He found the proprietor of the Argus (Pilgus, Piccy, London) in the smoking-room, massaging his moustache, and with some trepidation proceeded to edge into the agenda.

'Oh, there you are, Pilbeam. I say . . .'

The investigator looked up. It increased Monty's feeling of guilt to note that he had evidently been thinking frightfully hard. He had a sort of boiled look.

'Ah, Bodkin, I was just coming to find you. I have been thinking . . .'

Monty's tender heart bled for the fellow, but he supposed it was kindest to let him have it on the chin without preamble.

'I know you have, my poor old sleuth,' he said. 'I can see it in your eye. Well, I've got a bit of bad news for you, I'm afraid. What I came to tell you was to switch off the brain-power. Stop scheming. Put the mind back into neutral. I'm taking you off the case.'

'Eh?'

'I'm sorry, but there it is. You see, what with one thing and another, I've been and got that manuscript myself.'

'What!'

'Yes.'

There was a long pause.

'Well, that's fine,' said Pilbeam. 'I hope you have hidden it carefully?'

'Oh, yes. It's shoved away under the bed in my room. Right up against the wall.'

'Well, that's fine,' said Pilbeam.

His attitude occasioned Monty much relief. He had braced himself up to endure reproaches, to wince beneath recriminations. It seemed to him extraordinarily decent of the man to take it like this. He was dashed, indeed, if he could remember ever having met anyone who, under such provocation, had been so extraordinarily decent.

'What are you going to do with it?' asked Pilbeam.

'I'm taking it down to the Emsworth Arms to a fellow of the name of Tilbury.'

'Not Lord Tilbury?'

'That's right,' said Monty, surprised. 'Do you know him?'

'Before I opened the Argus, I was editor of *Society Spice.*'

'No, really? Fancy that. Before he booted me out, I was assistant editor of *Tiny Tots*. It seems to bring us very close together, what?'

'But why does Lord Tilbury want it?'

'Well, you see, he has a contract with Gally for the book, and when Gally refused to publish he saw himself losing the dickens of a lot of money. Naturally he wants it.'

'I see. He ought to give you a pretty big reward.'

'Oh, I'm not asking him for money. I've got lots of money. What I want is a job. He promised to take me back on *Tiny Tots* if I would get the thing for him.'

'You are leaving here, then?'

Monty chuckled amusedly.

'You bet I'm leaving here. I expect the sack any moment. I'd have got it yesterday, all right,' said Monty, with another chuckle, 'if old Emsworth had happened to come along when I was working on the door of that potting-shed.'

'What was that?'

'Rather amusing. I found old Tilbury locked up in a species of shed yesterday afternoon. Apparently he had been caught in conversation with that pig of the old boy's, offering it potatoes and so forth, and was suspected of trying to poison the animal. So they shut him up in this shed, and I came along and let him out. Just imagine how quick I should be leaving if Emsworth knew that I was the chap who flung wide the gates.'

'My word, yes!' said Pilbeam, laughing genially.

'He'd throw me out in a second.'

'He certainly would.'

'Rummy, his attitude about that pig,' said Monty

musingly. 'A few years ago, he used to be crazy about pumpkins. I suppose, if you really face the facts, he's the sort of chap who has to be practically off his rocker about something. Yesterday, pumpkins. Today, pigs. Tomorrow, rabbits. This time next year, roosters or rhododendrons.'

'I suppose so,' said Pilbeam. 'And when are you thinking of taking this manuscript to Lord Tilbury?'

'Right away.'

'I wouldn't do that,' said Pilbeam, shaking his head. 'No, I don't think I would advise you to do that. You want to wait till everybody's dressing for dinner. Suppose you were to run into Threepwood.'

'I never thought of that.'

'Or Lady Constance.'

'Lady Constance?'

'I happen to know that she is trying to get that manuscript. She wants to destroy it.'

'I say! You certainly find things out, don't you?'

'Oh, one keeps one's ears open.'

'I suppose you've got to, if you're a detective. Well, I do seem properly trapped in the den of the Secret Nine, what? I'd better not make a move till dressing for dinner-time, as you say. I'm glad you gave me that tip. Thanks.'

'Don't mention it,' said Pilbeam.

He rose.

'You off?' said Monty.

'Yes. I've just remembered there is something I want to speak to Lord Emsworth about. You don't know where he is, do you?'

'Sorry, no. The ninth doesn't confide in me much.'

'I suppose he's in the pigsty.'

'You can tell him by his hat,' said Monty automatically. 'Yes, I imagine he would be. Anything special you wanted to see him about?'

'Just something he asked me to find out for him.'

'In your professional capacity, do you mean? Pilgus, Piccy, London?'

'Yes.'

'Is he employing your services, then?'

'Oh, yes. That's why I'm here.'

'I see,' said Monty.

This made him feel much easier in his mind. If Pilbeam was drawing a nice bit of cash from old Simon Legree, it put a different complexion on everything. Naturally, in that case, he wouldn't so much mind being done out of the Bodkin fee.

Still, he did feel that the fellow had behaved most extraordinarily decently.

Lord Emsworth was not actually in the pigsty, but he was quite near it. It took more than a thunderstorm to drive him from the Empress's side. A vague idea that he was getting a little wet had caused him to take shelter in the potting-shed during the worst of the downpour, but he was now out and about again. When Pilbeam arrived, he was standing by the rails in earnest conversation with Pirbright. He welcomed the detective warmly.

'You're just the man I was wanting to see, my dear Pilbeam,' he said. 'Pirbright and I have been discussing the question of moving the Empress to a new sty. I say Yes, Pirbright says No. One sees his point, of course. I quite see your point, my dear Pirbright. Pirbright's point,' explained Lord Emsworth, 'is that she is used to this sty and moving her to a strange one might upset her and put her off her feed.'

'Quite,' said Pilbeam, profoundly uninterested.

'On the other hand,' proceeded Lord Emsworth, 'we know that there is this sinister cabal against her well-being. Attempts have already been made to nobble her, as I believe the term is. They may be made again. And my view is that this sty here is in far too lonely and remote a spot for safety. God bless my soul,' said Lord

Emsworth, deeply moved, 'in a place like this, a quarter
of a mile away from anywhere, Parsloe could walk in
during the night and do her a mischief without so much
as taking the cigar out of his mouth. Where I was
thinking of moving her, Pirbright would be within call
at any moment. It's near his cottage. At the slightest
sign of anything wrong, he could jump out of bed and
hurry to the rescue.'

It was possibly this very thought that had induced the
pig-man to say 'Nur' as earnestly as he had done. He was
a man who liked to get his sleep. He shook his head
now, and a rather bleak look came into his gnarled face.

'Well, there is the position, my dear Pilbeam. What do
you advise?'

It seemed to the detective that the sooner he gave his
decision the sooner the unprofitable discussion would be
ended. He was completely indifferent about the whole
thing. Officially at the castle to help guard the Empress,
his heart had never been in that noble task. Pigs bored
him.

'I'd move her,' he said.

'You really feel that?'

'Quite.'

A mild triumph shone from Lord Emsworth's
pince-nez.

'There you have an expert opinion, Pirbright,' he said.
'Mr Pilbeam knows. If Mr Pilbeam says Move her, she
must certainly be moved. Do it as soon as possible.'

'Yur, m'lord,' said the pig-man despondently.

'And now, Lord Emsworth,' said Pilbeam, 'can I have a
word with you?'

'Certainly, my dear fellow, certainly. But before you
do so I have something very important to tell you. I
want to hear what you make of it. Let me mention that
first, and then you can tell me whatever it is that you
have come to talk about. You won't forget whatever it is
that you have come to talk about?'

'Oh, no.'

'I frequently do. I intend to tell somebody something, and something happens to prevent my doing so immediately, and when I am able to tell it to them I find I have forgotten it. My sister Constance has often been very vehement about it. I recollect her once comparing my mind to a sieve. I thought it rather clever. She meant that it was full of holes, you understand, as I believe sieves are. That was on the occasion when –'

Pilbeam had not had the pleasure of the ninth Earl's acquaintance long, but he had had it long enough to know that, unless firmly braked, he was capable of trickling on like this indefinitely.

'What was it you wished to tell me, Lord Emsworth?' he said.

'Eh? Ah, yes, quite so, my dear fellow. You want to hear that very important fact that I was going to put before you. Well, I would like you to throw your mind back, my dear Pilbeam, to yesterday. Yesterday evening. I wonder if you remember my mentioning to you the extraordinary mystery of that man getting out of the potting-shed?'

'Certainly.'

'The facts –'

'I know.'

'The facts –'

'I remember them.'

'The facts,' proceeded Lord Emsworth evenly, 'are as follows. In pursuance of my instructions, Pirbright was lurking near this sty yesterday afternoon, and what should he see but a ruffianly-looking fellow trying to poison my pig with a potato. He crept up and caught him in the act, and then shut him in that shed over there, intending to come back after he had informed me of the matter and hale him to justice. I should mention that, after placing the fellow in the shed, he carefully secured the door with a stout wooden staple.'

737

'Quite. I . . .'

'It seemed out of the question that he could effect an
escape – I am speaking of the fellow, not of Pirbright –
and you may imagine his astonishment, therefore – I am
speaking of Pirbright, not of the fellow – when, on
returning, he discovered that that is just what had
occurred. The door of the shed was open, and he – I am
once more speaking of the fellow – was gone. He had
completely disappeared, my dear Pilbeam. And here is
the very significant thing I wanted to tell you. Just
before you came up I got Pirbright to shut me in the
shed and secure the door with the staple, and I found it
impossible – quite impossible, my dear fellow, to release
myself from within. I tried and tried and tried, but no, I
couldn't do it. Now, what does that suggest to you,
Pilbeam?' asked Lord Emsworth, peering over his
pince-nez.

'Somebody must have let him out.'

'Exactly. Undoubtedly. Beyond a question. Who it
was, of course, we shall never know.'

'I have found out who it was.'

Lord Emsworth was staggered. He had always known
in a nebulous sort of way that detectives were gifted
beyond the ordinary with the power to pierce the
inscrutable, but this was the first time he had actually
watched them at it.

'You have found out who it was?' he gasped.

'I have.'

'Pirbright, Mr Pilbeam has found out who it was.'

'Ur, m'lord.'

'Already! Isn't that amazing, Pirbright?'

'Yur, m'lord.'

'I wouldn't have thought it could have been done in
the time. Would you, Pirbright?'

'Nur, m'lord.'

'Well, well, well!' said Lord Emsworth. 'That is the

most extraordinary . . . Ah, I knew there was something I
wanted to ask you . . . Who was it?'

'Bodkin.'

'Bodkin!'

'Your secretary, young Bodkin,' said Pilbeam.

'I knew it!' Lord Emsworth shook a fist skywards, and
his voice, as always in moments of emotion, became
high and reedy. 'I knew it! I suspected the fellow all
along. I was convinced that he was an accomplice of
Parsloe's. I'll dismiss him,' cried Lord Emsworth, almost
achieving an A in alt. 'He shall go at the end of the
month.'

'It would be safer to get him off the place at once.'

'Of course it would, my dear fellow. You are quite
right. He shall be turned out immediately. Where is he? I
must see him. I will go to him instantly.'

'Better let me send him to you out here. More
dignified. Don't go to him. Let him come to you.'

'I see what you mean.'

'You wait here, and I'll go and tell him you wish to
see him.'

'My dear fellow, I don't want to put you to all that
trouble.'

'No trouble,' Pilbeam assured him. 'A pleasure.'

It is one of the distinguishing characteristics of your
man of the world that he can keep his poise even under
the most trying of conditions. Beyond a sort of whistling
gasp and a sharp 'God give me strength!' the Hon.
Galahad Threepwood displayed no emotion at Ronnie's
sensational announcement.

He did, however, gaze at his nephew as if the latter
had been a defaulting bookmaker.

'Are you crazy?' he said.

It was a question which Ronnie found difficult to
answer. Even to himself, as he now told it, the story of

that great gesture of his sounded more than a little imbecile. The best, indeed, that you could really say of the great gesture, he could not help feeling, was that, like so many rash acts, it had seemed a good idea at the time. He was bright scarlet and had had occasion to straighten his tie not once but many times before he reached the end of the tale. And not even the fact that Sue, with womanly sympathy, put her arm through his and kissed him was able to bring real consolation. To his inflamed senses that kiss seemed so exactly the sort of kiss a mother might have given her idiot child.

'You see what I mean, I mean to say,' he concluded lamely. 'I thought Sue had finished with me, so there didn't seem any point in holding on to the thing any longer, and Monty said he wanted it, and so . . . well, there you are.'

'You can't blame the poor angel,' said Sue.

'I can,' said the Hon. Galahad. He moved to the fireplace and pressed the bell. 'It would surprise you how easily I could blame the poor angel. And if there was time I would. But we haven't a moment to waste. We must get hold of young Monty without a second's delay and choke the thing out of him. We'll have no nonsense. I am an elderly man, past my prime, but I am willing and ready to sit on his head while you, Ronnie, kick him in the ribs. We'll soon make him – Ah, Beach.'

The door had opened.

'You rang, Mr Galahad?'

'I want to see Mr Bodkin, Beach. At once.'

'Mr Bodkin has left, sir.'

'Left!' cried the Hon. Galahad.

'Left!' shouted Ronnie.

'Left!' squeaked Sue.

'It is possible that he may still be in his bedchamber, packing the last of his effects,' said the butler, 'but I was instructed some little while ago that he was leaving the Castle immediately. There has been trouble, sir, between Mr Bodkin and his lordship. I am unable to inform you as to what precisely eventuated, but . . .'

A cry like that of a tiger leaping on its prey interrupted him. Through the open door the Hon. Galahad had espied a lissom form crossing the hall. He was outside in a flash, confronting it.

'You there! You bloodstained Bodkin!'

'Oh, hullo.'

The Hon. Galahad, as his opening words had perhaps sufficiently indicated, had not come for any mere exchange of courtesies.

'Never mind the "Oh, hullo." I want that manuscript of mine, young Bodkin, and I want it at once, so make it slippy, you sheep-faced young exile from Hell. If it's on your person, disgorge it. If it's in your suitcase, unpack it. And Ronnie here and I will be standing over you while you do it.'

There was an infinite sadness in Monty Bodkin's gaze. He looked like a male Mona Lisa.

'I haven't got your bally manuscript.'

'Don't lie to me, young Bodkin.'

'I'm not lying. Pilbeam's got it.'

'Pilbeam!'

Monty's voice trembled with intense feeling.

'I told the foul, double-crossing little blister where it was, like a silly chump, and he went off and squealed to Lord Emsworth about my letting old Tilbury out of the potting-shed, and Lord Emsworth sent for me and fired me, and while I was out of the way, being fired, he nipped up to my room and sneaked the thing.'

'Where is he? Where is this Pilbeam?'

'Ah,' said Monty, 'I'd like to know myself. Well, good-bye, all. I'm off to the Emsworth Arms.'

He strode sombrely out of the front door and down the steps. A cough sounded behind the Hon. Galahad.

'Would there be anything further, sir?'

The Hon. Galahad drew a deep breath.

'No thank you, Beach,' he said. 'I think that perhaps this will be enough to be getting on with.'

12

At the moment when Monty Bodkin and the Hon. Galahad Threepwood, two minds with but a single thought, were wondering where he was and wishing they could have a word with him, Percy Pilbeam, the manuscript under his arm, had just emerged furtively from the back of the Castle. He did not wish to have anything to do with front doors. Directly he had crawled out from under Monty's bed, dragging his treasure trove after him, he had dusted his fingers and made for the servants' staircase. This had led him through twisting by-ways to a vast echoing stone passage, and from that to the back door was but a step. He had not encountered so much as a housemaid.

In his bearing, as he hurried along the path that skirted the kitchen garden – in the oily smirk beneath his repellent moustache, in the jaunty tilt of his snub nose, even in the terraced sweep of the brilliantine swamps of his corrugated hair – there was the look of a man who is congratulating himself on a neat bit of work. Brains, reflected Percy Pilbeam – that was what you needed in this life. Brains and the ability to seize your opportunity when it was offered to you.

He had a long walk before him. It was his intention, in order to avoid meeting any interested party, to make a wide circle round the outskirts of Lord Emsworth's domain and strike the road to Market Blandings near Matchingham. There, no doubt, he would be able to get a lift to the Emsworth Arms. Then, having seen Lord Tilbury and arrived at some satisfactory financial arrangement with him, he proposed to take the next train to London. He had his whole plan of campaign neatly mapped out.

The one thing he had not allowed for was a sudden change in the weather. When he had left the Castle, the sun had been shining; but now it was blotted out by a dark rack of clouds. Apparently some minor storm, late for the big event, had come hurrying up and intended to hold a private demonstration of its own. There was a tentative rumble over the hills, and a raindrop splashed on his face. Before he had reached the end of the kitchen garden, quite a respectable deluge was falling.

Pilbeam, like the Hon. Galahad, hated getting wet. He looked about him for shelter, and perceived standing by itself in a small paddock not far away a squat building of red brick and timber. A man not used to country life, he had no idea what it was supposed to be, but it had a stout tiled roof beneath which he could keep dry, so he hastened thither, arriving just in time, for a moment later the world had become a shower-bath. He retreated farther into his nook and sat down on some straw.

In such a situation, the only method of passing the time is to think. Pilbeam thought. And as he did so he began to revise that scheme of his of taking the manuscript straight to Lord Tilbury.

It was a scheme which he had adopted as seeming to be the only one open to him. He would vastly have preferred his original idea of holding an auction sale, with Lord Tilbury and Lady Constance Keeble raising each other's bids; but until now the fatal objection to that course had seemed to him to be that there was no safe place where he could store the goods till the auction sale was over.

A visitor at a country house with something to hide is a good deal restricted in his choice of *caches*. He is, indeed, more or less driven back to his bedroom. And a bedroom, as had been proved in the case of Monty Bodkin, is very far from being a safe-deposit. From the

744

inception of their acquaintance, Pilbeam had been greatly impressed by Lady Constance's strong personality. A woman of action, he considered, if ever there was one. If she knew that he had the manuscript and deduced that it was hidden in his bedroom, he could see her acting very swiftly. She would have the thing in her hands in half an hour.

But suppose he were to hide it in some such place as that in which he was now sitting. Things would be very different then.

He glanced round the dim interior, and felt that he was on the right track. This building was a deserted building. It did not appear to be used for anything. Presumably no one ever came here. And even if someone did happen to wander in, it would be a simple matter to hide the manuscript . . . under this straw, for instance.

He rose and thrust the papers under the straw. He eyed the straw appraisingly. It had as innocent a look as any straw he had ever seen.

A shaft of sunlight played in the doorway. The brief storm was over. Well content, Percy Pilbeam came out and started to walk back to the Castle.

Beach met him in the hall.

'Her ladyship is expressing a desire to see you, sir,' said Beach, regarding him with restrained horror and loathing. The recent exchange of remarks between Monty Bodkin and the Hon. Galahad in his presence had confirmed the butler in his view that of all the human serpents that ever wriggled their way into a respectable castle this private investigator was the worst. Knowing what the manuscript of the Reminiscences meant to Mr Ronald and his betrothed, Beach, had he been younger and slimmer and in better condition and not a butler, could – for two pins – have taken Percy Pilbeam's unpleasant neck in his hands and twisted it into a lover's knot.

His physique and his circumstances being as they

were, he merely delivered the message he had been instructed to deliver. As far as any hostile demonstration was concerned, he had to be content with letting his lip curl.

Percy Pilbeam, however, was feeling far too pleased with himself to be daunted by butlers' curling lips. On the present occasion, moreover, he was not aware that the other's lip *was* curling. He had noted the facial spasm, but attributed it to a tickling nose.

'Lady Constance?'

'Yes, sir. Her ladyship is in the drawing-room, awaiting you.'

What the proprietor of Riggs's Golden Balm embrocation would have described as the delightful sensation of *bien-être* began to leave Pilbeam. He stood there looking thoughtful. He twisted his moustache uneasily.

Now that the moment had actually arrived for confronting Lady Constance Keeble and informing her that he was proposing to double-cross her and hold her up and extract large sums of money from her, he felt unpleasantly weak about the knees.

'H'm!' said Percy Pilbeam.

And then suddenly he remembered that nature in her infinite wisdom has provided a sovereign specific against these Lady Constance Keebles.

'Well, then, I'll tell you what,' he said, inspired. 'Bring me a large bottle of champagne, and I'll look into the matter.'

Beach withdrew to execute the commission. His demeanour, as he passed from the hall, was downcast. There in a nutshell, he was feeling, you had the tragedy of a butler's life. His not to reason why; his not to discriminate between the deserving and the undeserving; his but to go and bring bottles of champagne to marcelled-haired snakes to whom he would greatly have preferred to supply straight cyanide.

The eternal conflict between duty and personal inclination, with duty, because one was a conscientious worker and took one's profession reverently, winning hands down.

Her sister Julia's report of her conversation with the Hon. Galahad, retailed to her immediately, upon the latter's departure, had strengthened Lady Constance Keeble's already firm view that something had got to be done without any more of what she forcefully described as dilly-dallying.

The fact that it was now three days since the task of securing the manuscript had been placed in Percy Pilbeam's hands and that he had to all appearances accomplished absolutely nothing seemed to her to argue dilly-dallying of the worst kind, if not actual shilly-shallying. She could not understand why Sir Gregory Parsloe seemed to entertain so high an opinion of this young man's abilities. So far as she had been able to ascertain, they were non-existent, and she said as much to Lady Julia, who agreed with her.

It was, therefore, to no warm-hearted assembly of personal admirers that Pilbeam some quarter of an hour later proceeded to betake himself. If his specific had acted a little less rapidly, he might have been frozen to the bone by the cold wave of aristocratic disapproval which poured over him as he entered the drawing-room. As it was, the sight of Lady Constance, staring haughtily from a high-backed chair like Cleopatra about to get down to brass tacks with an Ethiopian slave, merely entertained him. He thought she looked quaint. He was feeling just the slightest bit dizzy, but extraordinarily debonair. If Lady Constance at that moment had proposed a little part-singing, he would have fallen in with the suggestion eagerly.

'You want to see me, Beach says,' he observed, slurring the honoured name a little.

'Sit down, Mr Pilbeam.'

The detective was glad to do so. Spiritually, he was at the peak of his form, but as regards his legs there appeared to be some slight engine trouble.

'Now then, Mr Pilbeam, about that book.'

'Quite,' said Pilbeam, smiling benignly. This, he was feeling, was just the sort of thing he enjoyed – a cosy chat on current literature with cultured women. He was about to say so, when his eye, wandering to the wall, caught that of the fourth Countess – Emilia Jane, 1747–1815 – and so humorous did her aspect seem to him that he lay back in his chair, laughing immoderately.

'Mr Pilbeam!'

Before the detective had time to explain that his mirth had been caused by the fact that the fourth Countess looked exactly like Buster Keaton, Lady Constance had gone on speaking. She spoke well and vigorously.

'I cannot understand, Mr Pilbeam, what you have been doing all this time. You know perfectly well the vital importance of getting my brother's book into our hands. The whole thing has been clearly explained to you both by Sir Gregory Parsloe and myself. And yet you appear to have done nothing whatever about it. Sir Gregory told me you were enterprising. You seem to me to have about as much enterprise as a . . .'

She paused to search her mind for fauna of an admittedly unenterprising outlook on life, and Lady Julia, who had been listening with approval, supplied the word 'slug'. The agitation which Lady Julia Fish had betrayed in the presence of her brother Galahad had passed. She had become her cool, sardonic self again. She was watching Pilbeam with a brightly interested eye, trying to diagnose the strangeness which she sensed in his manner.

'Exactly,' said Lady Constance, welcoming the suggestion. 'As much enterprise as a slug.'

'Less,' said Lady Julia.

'Yes, less,' agreed Lady Constance.

'Much less,' said Lady Julia. 'I've seen some quite nippy slugs.'

Pilbeam's amiability waned a little. He frowned. His mind was not at its clearest, but it seemed to him that a derogatory remark had been passed.

The Pilbeams had always been a clan to stand up for themselves. Treat them right and, if it suited their convenience, they would treat you right. But try to come it over them, and they could be very terrible. It was a Pilbeam – Ernest William of Mon Abri, Kitchener Road, East Dulwich – who sued his next-door neighbour, George Dobson, of The Elms, for throwing snails over the fence into his back garden. Another Pilbeam – Claude – once refused to give up his hat and umbrella at the Hornibrook Natural History Museum, Sydenham Hill. P. Frobisher was no unworthy kin of these sturdy fighters.

'Did you call me a slug?' he asked sternly.

'In a purely Pickwickian sense,' said Lady Julia.

'Ah,' said Pilbeam, his affability returning. 'That's different.'

Lady Constance resumed the speech for the prosecution.

'You have had three whole days in which to do something, and you have not even found out where the manuscript is.'

Pilbeam smiled roguishly.

'Oh, haven't I?'

'Well, have you?'

'Yes, I have.'

'Then why in the name of goodness, Mr Pilbeam,' said Lady Constance, 'did you not tell us? And why don't you do something about it? Where is it, then? You said it was not in my brother's desk. Did he give it to somebody else?'

'He gave it to Beash.'

'Beash?' Lady Constance seemed at a loss. 'Beash?'

'Reading between the lines,' said Lady Julia, 'I think he means Beach.'

Lady Constance uttered an exclamation which was almost a battle cry. This was better than she had hoped. She felt a complete confidence in her ability to impose her will upon the domestic staff.

'Beach?' Her eyes lit up. 'I will see Beach at once.'

Pilbeam chuckled heartily.

'You may see him,' he said, 'but a fat lot of good that's going to do you. A fat, fat, fat lot of good.'

Lady Julia had completed her diagnosis.

'Forgive the personal question, Mr Pilbeam,' she said, 'but are you slightly intoxicated?'

'Yes,' said Pilbeam sunnily.

'I thought so.'

Lady Constance was less intrigued by the detective's physical condition than the mystical obscurity of his speech.

'What do you mean?'

'A little blotto,' explained Pilbeam. 'I've just had a bollerer champagne, and, what's more, I had it on an empty stomach.'

'Are you interested in Mr Pilbeam's stomach, Constance?'

'I am not.'

'Nor I,' said Lady Julia. 'Let us waive your stomach, Mr Pilbeam, and get back to the point. Why will it do us a fat lot of good seeing Beach?'

'Because he hasn't got it.'

'You seemed to suggest that he had.'

'So he had. But he hasn't. He gave it to Ronnie.'

'My son, do you mean?'

'That's right. I always think of him as Ronnie.'

'How sweet of you.'

'He tried to break my neck once,' said Pilbeam, throwing out the information for what it was worth.

'And of course that forms a bond, doesn't it?' said Lady Julia sympathetically. 'So now Ronnie has the manuscript?'

'No, he hasn't.'

'But you said he had.'

'I said he had, and he had, but he hasn't. He gave it to Bonty Modkin.'

'Oh, the man's impossible,' cried Lady Constance.

Pilbeam looked about him, but could see no man. Some mistake, probably.

'What is the good of wasting any more time on a person in his condition? Can't you see he's just maundering?'

'Wait a minute, Connie. I may be wrong, but I think something will soon emerge from the fumes. Everybody seems to have been handing Galahad's great work to somebody else. A little patient inquiry, and he may discover to whom Mr Bodkin handed it.'

Pilbeam laughed a ringing laugh.

'"Handed it" is good. Oh, very good, indeed. Considering that I had to crawl under his bed to get it.'

'What!'

'Gave my head a nasty bump, too, on the woodwork.'

'Do you mean to say, Mr Pilbeam, that all this time we've been talking *you* have got my brother's manuscript?'

'I told you something would emerge, Connie.'

'Yes, Connie,' said Pilbeam, 'I have.'

'Then why in the name of goodness could you not have said so from the first? Where is it?'

'Ah, that's telling,' said Pilbeam, wagging a playful finger.

'Mr Pilbeam,' said Lady Constance, with all the Cleopatrine haughtiness at her command, 'I insist on knowing what you have done with it. Kindly let us have no more of this nonsense.'

She could not have taken a more unfortunate

attitude. The detective's resemblance to a roguish, if slightly inebriated, pixie vanished and in its place came pique, mortification, resentment, anger and defiance. His beady little eyes hardened, and from them there peeped out the fighting spirit of that Albert Edward Pilbeam who once refused to pay a fine and did seven days in Brixton jail for failing to abate a smoky chimney.

'Oh?' he said. 'Oh? It's like that, is it? Let me tell you, Connie, that I don't like your tone. Insist, indeed! A nice way to talk. I've got that manuscript hidden away somewhere where you won't find it, let me inform you. And it's going to stay there till I take it to Tilbury . . .'

'What *is* he talking about?' asked Lady Constance despairingly. Tilbury to her suggested merely a small town in Essex. She had a vague recollection that Queen Elizabeth had once held a review there or something.

But Lady Julia, with her special knowledge of Tilburies, had become suddenly grave.

'Wait,' she said. 'This is beginning to look a little sticky. I wouldn't take it to Lord Tilbury, Mr Pilbeam, really I wouldn't. I'm sure, if we only talk it over sensibly, we can come to some arrangement.'

Pilbeam, who had risen and was now tacking uncertainly towards the door, waved a hand and clutched at a table to restore his balance.

'Too late,' he said. 'Too late for that. Been insulted. Don't like Connie's tone. I was going to sit and let you bid against each other, but too late, too late, too late, because I've been insulted. No further discussion. Tilbury gets it. He's waiting for it at the Emsworth Arms. Well, good-by-ee,' said Percy Pilbeam, and was gone.

Lady Constance turned to her sister for enlightenment.

'But I don't understand, Julia. What did he mean! Who is this Lord Tilbury?'

'Only the proprietor of the publishing concern with

whom Gally signed his contract, my angel. Nothing
more than that.'

'You mean,' cried Lady Constance, aghast, 'that if the
manuscript gets into his hands, he will publish it?'

'That's it.'

'I won't allow him to. I'll get an injunction.'

'How can you? He'll stand on the contract.'

'Do you mean, then, that nothing can be done?'

'All I can suggest is that you telephone to Sir Gregory
Parsloe and get him over. Tell him to come to dinner.
He seems to have some influence with that little fiend.
He may be able to talk him round. Though I doubt
it. He's in a nasty mood. I rather wish sometimes,
Connie,' said Lady Julia meditatively, 'that you were a
little less of the *grande dame*. It's wonderful to watch
you in action, I admit – one seems to hear the bugles
blowing for the Crusades and the tramp of the mailed
feet of a hundred steel-clad ancestors – but there's no
getting away from it that you do put people's backs up a
bit.'

Down at the Emsworth Arms, a servitor informed Lord
Tilbury that he was wanted on the telephone. He walked
to the instrument broodingly. The Bodkin popinjay, he
presumed, that broken reed on which he had foolishly
supposed that it would be possible to lean. He prepared
to be a little terse with Monty.

Ever since his interview with Monty in the garden of
the Emsworth Arms, Lord Tilbury had found his
thoughts turning wistfully to the one man of his
acquaintance who could have been relied upon to put
through this commission of his. During the years when
P. Frobisher Pilbeam had worked on his staff as editor of
Society Spice Lord Tilbury had never actually asked him
to steal anything, but he had no doubt at all that, if
adequately paid, Percy would have sprung to the task.
And now that he had blossomed out as a private

investigator it was probable that he would spring to it with an even greater readiness. All that afternoon Lord Tilbury had been wondering whether the solution of the whole thing would not be to send Pilbeam a wire, telling him to come at once.

What deterred him was the reflection that it would be impossible to get him into the Castle. You cannot insert private inquiry agents in country-houses as if you were slipping ferrets down a rabbit-hole. This it was that had made him abandon the roseate dream. And it was the fact that he had been compelled to abandon it that lent additional asperity to his manner as he now took up the receiver.

'Yes?' he said curtly. 'Well?'

A rollicking voice nearly cracked his ear-drum.

'Hullo, there, Tilbury! This is Pilbeam.'

Lord Tilbury's eyes seemed to shoot out suddenly, like a snail's. This was the most amazing coincidence he had ever experienced. More a miracle, he felt with some awe, than a mere coincidence.

'Speaking from Blandings Castle, Tilbury.'

'What!'

The receiver shook in Lord Tilbury's hands. Was this what was known as the direct answer to prayer? Or – taking the gloomier view – was he undergoing some aural hallucination?

'Speaking from Blandings Castle, Tilbury,' repeated the voice. 'You don't mind me calling you Tilbury, do you, Tilbury?' it added solicitously. 'I'm a bit tight.'

'Pilbeam!' Lord Tilbury's voice shook. 'Did I really understand you to say that you were speaking from Blandings Castle?'

'Quite.'

A man capable of building up the Mammoth Publishing Company is not a man who wastes time in unnecessary questions. Others might have asked

Pilbeam how he had got there, but not Lord Tilbury. He could do all that later.

'Pilbeam,' he said, 'this is providential! Kindly come to me here as soon as possible. There is something I wish you to do for me. Most urgent.'

'A commission?'

'Yes, a commission.'

'And what,' inquired the voice, playfully, yet with a certain metallic note, 'is there in it for me?'

Lord Tilbury thought rapidly.

'A hundred pounds.'

A hideous noise sent his head jerking back. It was apparently a derisive laugh. When it was repeated more softly a moment later, he recognized it as such.

'Two hundred, Pilbeam.'

'Listen, Tilbury. I know what it is you want me to do. Oh, yes, I know. Something to do with a certain book . . .'

'Yes, yes.'

'Then let me tell you, Tilbury, that I've been offered five hundred in another quarter, and can easily work it up to the level thousand. But, seeing it's you, I won't sting you for more than that. Think on your feet, Tilbury. One thousand is the figure.'

Lord Tilbury thought on his feet. There were few men in England whom the prospect of parting with a thousand pounds afflicted with a greater sensation of nausea, but he could speculate in order to accumulate. And in the present case, what was a mere thousand? A sprat to catch a whale.

'Very well.'

'It's a deal?'

'Yes, I agree.'

'Right!' said the voice, with renewed cheeriness. 'Be in after dinner tonight. I'll bring the thing down with me.'

'What!'

'I say I'll bring the you-know-what to you after dinner

tonight. And now *a river*-whatever-it-is, Tilbury, old cock. *Au revoir*, Tilbury. I'm feeling rather funny, and I think I'll get a bit of sleep. Ay tank I go home, Tilbury. Pip-pip!'

There was a click at the other end of the wire. Pilbeam had hung up.

Fingers tried the handle of Pilbeam's bedroom door. A fist banged on the panel. The detective looked up frowningly from the bed on which he lay. He had been on the point of sinking into a troubled doze.

'Who's that?'

'Open this door and I'll show you who it is.'

'Is that old Gally?'

'Damn your impudence!'

'What do you want?'

'A little talk with you, young man.'

'Go away, old Gally,' said Pilbeam. 'Don't want any little talks. Trying to get to sleep, old Gally. Tell 'em I shan't be down to dinner. Feeling funny.'

'You'll feel funnier if I can get in.'

'Ah, but you can't get in,' Pilbeam pointed out.

And, laughing softly to himself at the wit and cleverness of the retort, he sank back on the pillows and closed his eyes again. The handle rattled once more. The door creaked as a weight was pressed against it. Then there was silence, broken shortly by a rhythmic snoring.

Percy Pilbeam slept.

13

Darkness had fallen on Blandings Castle, the soft, caressing darkness that closes in like a velvet curtain at the end of a summer day. Now slept the crimson petal and the white. Owls hooted in the shadows. Bushes rustled as the small creatures of the night went about their mysterious business. The scent of the wet earth mingled with the fragrance of stock and of wallflower. Bats wheeled against the starlit sky, and moths blundered in and out of the shaft of golden light that shone from the window of the dining-room. It was the hour when men forget their troubles about the friendly board.

But troubles like those now weighing upon the inmates of Blandings Castle are not to be purged by meat and drink. The soup had come and gone. The fish had come and gone. The entrée had come and was going. But still there hung over the table a foglike pall of gloom. Of all those silent diners, not one but had his hidden care. Even Lord Emsworth, who was not easily depressed, found his meal entirely spoiled by the fact that it was being shared by Sir Gregory Parsloe-Parsloe.

As for Sir Gregory himself, the news communicated to him over the telephone by Lady Constance Keeble an hour before had been enough to ruin a dozen dinners. His might have been, as his whilom playmate, the Hon. Galahad Threepwood, had made so abundantly clear in Chapters Four, Seven, Eleven, Eighteen, and Twenty-four of his immortal work, a frivolous youth, but in his late fifties he was taking life extremely seriously. Very earnest was his wish to represent the

Unionist party as their Member for Bridgeford and Shifley Parliamentary Division of Shropshire: and if Pilbeam fulfilled his threat of taking that infernal manuscript to Lord Tilbury, his chances of doing so would be simply *nil*. He knew that local committee. Once let the story of the prawns appear in print, and they would drop him like a hot brick.

He had come tonight to reason with Pilbeam, to plead with Pilbeam, to appeal to Pilbeam's better feelings, if such existed. And, dash it, there was no Pilbeam to be reasoned with, to be pleaded with, or to be appealed to.

Where *was* the dam' feller?

The same question was torturing Lady Constance. Where was Pilbeam? Could he have gone straight to Lord Tilbury after taking his zigzag departure from the drawing-room?

It was Lord Emsworth who put the question into words. For some moments he had been staring down the table over the top of his crooked pince-nez in a puzzled manner like that of a cat trying to run over the muster-roll of its kittens.

'Beach!'

'M'lord?' said that careworn man hollowly. Foxes were gnawing at Beach's vitals, too.

'Beach, I can't see Mr Pilbeam. Can you see Mr Pilbeam, Beach? He doesn't seem to be here.'

'Mr Pilbeam is in his bedchamber, m'lord. He informed the footman who knocked at the door with his hot water that he would not be among those present at dinner, m'lord, owing to a headache.'

The Hon. Galahad endorsed this.

'I knocked at his door just before the dressing gong went, and he said he wanted to go to sleep.'

'You didn't go in?'

'No.'

'You should have gone in, Galahad. The poor fellow may be feeling unwell.'

'Not so unwell as he would have felt if I could have got in.'

'You think you would have made his headache worse?'

'A good deal worse,' said the Hon. Galahad, taking a salted almond and giving it a hard look through his monocle.

The news that Pilbeam was on a bed of sickness acted on three members of the party rather as the recent rain had acted on the parched earth. Lady Constance seemed to expand like a refreshed flower. Lady Julia did the same. Sir Gregory Parsloe, in addition to expanding, gave such a sharp sigh of relief that he blew a candle out. Three pairs of eyes exchanged glances. There was the same message of cheer in each of them. If Pilbeam had not taken the irrevocable step, those eyes said, all might yet be well.

'God bless my soul,' said Lord Emsworth solicitously. 'I hope he isn't really bad. These infernal thunderstorms are enough to give anyone a headache. I had a slight headache myself before dinner. I'll run up and see the poor chap as soon as we've finished here My goodness, I don't want Pilbeam on the sick list now, of all times,' said Lord Emsworth, with a glance at Sir Gregory so full of meaning that the latter, who was lifting his wine-glass to his lips, shied like a startled horse and spilled half its contents.

'Why now, particularly?' asked Lady Julia.

'Never mind,' said Lord Emsworth darkly.

'I only asked,' said Lady Julia, 'because I, personally, consider that all times are good times for Mr Pilbeam to have headaches. Not to mention botts, glanders, quartan ague, frog in the throat and the Black Death.'

A soft, sibilant sound, like gas escaping from a pipe, came from the shadows by the sideboard. It was Beach expressing, as far as butlerine etiquette would permit him to express, his adhesion to this sentiment.

Lord Emsworth, on the other hand, showed annoyance.

'I wish you wouldn't say such things, Julia.'

'On the spur of the moment I couldn't think of anything worse.'

'Don't you like Pilbeam?'

'My dear Clarence, don't be fantastic. Nobody *likes* Mr Pilbeam. There are people who do not actually put poison in his soup, but that is as far as you can go.'

'I disagree with you,' said Lord Emsworth warmly. 'I regard him as a capital fellow, capital. And most useful, let me tell you. Attempts are being made,' said Lord Emsworth, once more sniping Sir Gregory with a penetrating eye, 'by certain parties whom I will not name, to injure my pig. Pilbeam is helping me thwart them. Thanks to his advice, I have now put my pig where the parties to whom I allude will not find it quite so easy to get at her. Let me tell you that I think very highly of Pilbeam. I've a good mind to send him up half a bottle of champagne.'

'Making the perfect example of carrying coals to Newcastle.'

'Eh?'

'Oh, nothing. 'Twas but a passing jest.'

'Champagne is good for headaches,' argued Lord Emsworth. 'It might make all the difference to Pilbeam.'

'Are we to spend the whole of dinner talking of Mr Pilbeam and his headache?' demanded Lady Constance imperiously. 'I am sick and tired of Mr Pilbeam. And I don't want to hear any more of that pig of yours, Clarence. For goodness' sake let us discuss some reasonable topic.'

This bright invitation having had the not unnatural effect of killing the conversation completely, dinner proceeded in an unbroken silence. Only once did one of the revellers venture a remark. As Beach and his assistants removed the plates which had contained fruit

salad and substituted others designed for dessert, Lady
Julia raised her glass.

'To the body upstairs – I hope,' she said.

Percy Pilbeam, however, was not actually dead. At the
precise moment of Lady Julia's toast, almost as if he
were answering a cue, he sat up on his bed and stared
muzzily about him. The fact that the room was now in
darkness made it difficult for him to find his bearings
immediately, and for perhaps half a minute he sat
wondering where he was. Then memory returned, and
with it an opening-and-shutting sensation in the region
of the temples which made him regret that he had gone
on sleeping. Even if he had had the Black Death to
which Lady Julia had so feelingly alluded, he could not
have felt very much worse.

There are heads which are proof against
over-indulgence in champagne. That of the Hon.
Galahad Threepwood is one that springs to the mind.
Pilbeam's, however, did not belong to this favoured
class. For a while he sat there, wincing at each fresh
wave of agony; then, levering himself up, he switched on
the light and hobbled to the wash-stand, where he
proceeded to drink deeply out of the water-jug. This
done, he filled the basin and started to give himself
first-aid treatment.

Presently, a little restored, he returned to the bed and
sat down again. Endeavouring to recall the events which
had led up to the tragedy, he found that he could do so
only sketchily. One fact alone stood out clearly in his
recollection – to wit, that in some way which he could
not quite remember he had been insulted by Lady
Constance Keeble. A great bitterness against Lady
Constance began to burgeon within Percy Pilbeam, and
it was not long before he reached the decision that, cost
what it might, she must be scored off. There would be
no auction sale. As soon as he felt physically capable of

moving, he would take that manuscript to Lord Tilbury at the Emsworth Arms.

At this point in his meditations the house was blown up by a bomb. Or, what amounted to much the same thing as far as the effect on his nervous system was concerned, there was a knock at the door.

'May I come in, my dear fellow?'

Pilbeam recognized the voice. He could not be rude to his only friend at Blandings Castle. He swallowed his heart again, and unlocked the door.

'Ah! Sitting up, I see. Feeling a little better, eh? We all missed you at dinner,' said Lord Emsworth, beginning to potter about the room as he pottered about all rooms which he honoured with his presence. 'We wondered what had become of you. My sister Julia, if I remember rightly, speculated as to the possibility of your having got the Black Death. What put the idea into her head, I can't imagine. Absurd, of course. People don't get the Black Death nowadays. I've never heard of anyone getting the Black Death. In fact,' said Lord Emsworth, with a burst of confidence, dropping into the fireplace the hair-brush which he had been attempting to balance on the comb, 'I don't believe I know what the Black Death *is*.'

A sense of being in hell stole over Percy Pilbeam. What with the clatter of that brush, which had set his head aching again, and his host's conversation, which threatened to make it ache still more, he was sore beset.

'No doubt all that has happened,' proceeded Lord Emsworth, moving the soap-dish a little to the left, the water-bottle a little to the right, a chair a little nearer the door, and another chair a little nearer the window, 'is that that thunderstorm gave you a headache. And I was wondering, my dear fellow, if a breath of fresh air might not do you good. Fresh air is often good for headaches. I am on my way to have a look at the

Empress, and it crossed my mind that you might care to
come with me. It is a beautiful night. There is a lovely
moon, and I have an electric torch.'

Here, Lord Emsworth, pausing from tapping the
mirror with a buttonhook, produced from his pocket the
torch in question and sent a dazzling ray shooting into
his companion's inflamed eyes.

The action decided Pilbeam. To remain longer in the
confined space of a bedroom with this man would be to
subject his sanity to too severe a test. He said he would
be delighted to come and take a look at the Empress.

Out on the gravel drive he began to feel a little better. As
Lord Emsworth had said, it was a beautiful night.
Pilbeam was essentially a creature of the city, with
urban tastes, but even he could appreciate the sweet
serenity of the grounds of Blandings Castle under that
gracious moon. So restored did he feel by the time they
had gone a hundred yards or so that he even ventured on
a remark.

'Aren't we,' he asked, 'going the wrong way?'

'What's that, my dear fellow?' said Lord Emsworth,
wrenching his mind from the torch, which he was
flashing on and off like a child with a new toy. 'What did
you say?'

'Don't you get to the sty by crossing the terrace?'

'Ah, but you've forgotten, my dear Pilbeam. Acting on
your advice, we moved her to the new one just before
dinner. You recollect advising us to move her from her
old sty?'

'Of course. Quite. Yes, I remember.'

'Pirbright didn't like it. I could tell that by the strange
noises he made at the back of his throat. He has some
idea that she will feel restless and unhappy away from
her old home. But I was particularly careful to wait and
see that she was comfortably settled in, and I could
detect no signs of restlessness whatever. She proceeded

to eat her evening meal with every indication of enjoyment.'

'Good,' said Pilbeam, feeling distrait.

'Eh?'

'I said "Good".'

'Oh, "Good"? Yes, quite so. Yes, very good. I feel most pleased about it. As I pointed out to Pirbright, the risk of leaving her in her old quarters was far too great to be taken. Why, my dear Pilbeam, do you know that my sister Constance had actually invited that man Parsloe to dinner tonight? Oh, yes, there he was, at dinner with us. No doubt he had persuaded her to invite him, thinking that, having got into the place, he would be able to find an opportunity during the evening of slipping away and going down to the sty and doing the poor animal a mischief. A nice surprise he's going to get when he finds the sty empty. He won't know what to make of it. He'll be nonplussed.'

Here Lord Emsworth paused to chuckle. Pilbeam, though not amused, contrived to emit on his side something that might have passed as a mirthful echo.

'This new sty,' proceeded Lord Emsworth, having switched the torch on and off six times, 'is an altogether more suitable place. As a matter of fact, I had it built specially for the Empress in the spring, but owing to Pirbright's obstinacy I never moved her there. I don't know if you know these Shropshire fellows at all, Pilbeam, but they can be as obstinate as Scotsmen. I have a Scots head gardener, Angus McAllister, and he is intensely obstinate. Like a mule. I must tell you some time about the trouble I had with him regarding hollyhocks. But Pirbright can be fully as stubborn when he gets an idea into his head. I reasoned with him. I said, "Pirbright, this sty is a new sty, with all the latest improvements. It is up to date, in keeping with the trend of modern thought, and, what is more – and this I consider very important – it adjoins the kitchen garden . . ." '

He broke off. A sound beside him in the darkness had touched his kindly heart.

'Is your head hurting you again, my dear fellow?'

But the bubbling cry which had proceeded from Percy Pilbeam had not been caused by pain in the head.

'The kitchen garden?' he gasped.

'Yes. And that is most convenient, you see, because Pirbright's cottage is so close. No doubt you have seen the place if you have ever strolled round by the kitchen garden. It is made of stout red brick and timber, with a good tiled roof . . . In fact,' said Lord Emsworth, flashing his torch, 'here it is. And there,' he went on with satisfaction, 'is the Empress, still feeding away without a care in the world. I told Pirbright he was all wrong.'

The Empress might have been without a care in the world, but Percy Pilbeam was very far from sharing that ideal state. He leaned on the rail of the sty and groaned in spirit.

In the light of the electric torch, Empress of Blandings made a singularly attractive, even a fascinating, picture. She had her noble head well down and with a rending, golluping sound was tucking into a late supper. Her curly little tail wiggled incessantly, and ever and anon a sort of sensuous quiver would pass along her Zeppelin-like body. But Percy Pilbeam was in no frame of mind to admire the rare and the beautiful. He was trying to adjust himself to this utterly unforeseen disaster.

He had only himself to blame – that was what made it all the more bitter. If he had not so casually given his casting vote in favour of shifting this infernal pig to new quarters, he would not now have been faced by a problem which every moment seemed to become more difficult of solution.

For Pilbeam was afraid of pigs. He seemed to

remember having read somewhere that if you go into a pig's sty and the pig doesn't know you it comes for you like a tiger and chews you to ribbons. Greedy though he was for Lord Tilbury's gold, something told him that never, no matter how glittering the reward, would he be able to bring himself to go into that sty in quest of the manuscript, guarded as it now was by this ravening beast. The Prodigal Son might have mixed with these animals on a clubby basis, but Percy Pilbeam knew himself to be incapable of imitating him.

How long he would have stood there, savouring the bitterness of defeat, one cannot say. Left to himself, probably quite a considerable time. But his reverie had scarcely begun when it was shattered by a cry at his elbow.

'God bless my soul!'

It seemed to Pilbeam for an instant that he had come unstuck. He clutched the rail, quivering in every limb.

'What on earth's the matter?' he demanded, far more brusquely than a guest should have done of his host.

An agitation almost equal to his own was causing the torch to wobble in Lord Emsworth's hands.

'God bless my soul, what's that she's eating? Pirbright! Pirbright! Can you see what she's eating, Pilbeam, my dear fellow? Pirbright! Pirbright! Can it be *paper*?'

With a febrile swoop Lord Emsworth bent through the rails. He came up again, breathing heavily. The light of the torch came and went like a heliograph upon something which he held in his hand.

Galloping feet sounded in the night.

'Pirbright!'

'Yur, m'lord?'

'Pirbright, have you been giving the Empress paper?'

'Nur, m'lord.'

'Well, that's what she's eating. Great chunks of it.'

'Ur, m'lord?' said the pig-man, marvelling.

'I assure you, yes. Paper. Look! Well, God bless my
soul,' cried Lord Emsworth, at last steadying the torch,
'I'm dashed if it isn't that book of my brother Galahad's!'

14

At about the moment when Lord Emsworth had knocked at Percy Pilbeam's door to inquire after his health and make his kindly suggestion of a breath of fresh air, his sister Lady Constance Keeble, his sister Lady Julia Fish, and his neighbour and guest Sir Gregory Parsloe-Parsloe were gathered together in the drawing-room, talking things over and endeavouring to come to some agreement as to the best method of handling the situation which had arisen.

The tone of the meeting had been a little stormy from the very outset. Owing to the suddenness of his summons to the Castle and the difficulty of explaining things over the telephone, all that Sir Gregory had known till now was the bare fact that Pilbeam had obtained possession of the manuscript and was proposing to deliver it to Lord Tilbury. Informed over the coffee cups by Lady Julia that the whole disaster was to be attributed to her sister Constance's tactless handling of the fellow, he had drawn his breath in sharply, gazed at Lady Constance in a reproachful manner, and started clicking his tongue.

Any knowledgeable person could have guessed what would happen after that. No woman of spirit can sit calmly and have a man click his tongue at her. No hostess, on the other hand, can be openly rude to a guest. Seeking an outlet for her emotions, Lady Constance had begun to quarrel with Lady Julia. And as Lady Julia, always fond of a family row, had borne her end of the encounter briskly, before he knew where he was Sir Gregory became aware that he had sown the wind and was reaping the whirlwind.

We mention these things to explain why it happened that there was a certain delay before GHQ took the obvious step of trying to establish communication with Percy Pilbeam. More than a quarter of an hour had elapsed before Sir Gregory was able to still the tumult of battle with these arresting words:

'But, I say, dash it all, don't you think we ought to see the feller?'

They acted like magic. Angry passions were chained. Good things about to be said were corked up and stored away for use on some future occasion. The bell was rung for Beach. Beach was dispatched to Pilbeam's room with instructions to desire him to be so good as to step down to the drawing-room for a moment. And the end of it all was that Beach returned and announced that Mr Pilbeam was not there.

Consternation reigned.

'Not there?' cried Lady Constance.

'Not *there*?' cried Lady Julia.

'But he must be there,' protested Sir Gregory. 'Fellow goes to his room with a headache to lie down and have a sleep,' he proceeded, arguing closely. 'Stands to reason he must be there.'

'You can't have knocked loudly enough, Beach,' said Lady Constance.

'Go up and knock again,' said Lady Julia.

'Hit the dashed door a good hard bang,' said Sir Gregory.

Beach's demeanour was respectful but unsympathetic.

'Receiving no response to my knocking, m'lady, I took the liberty of entering the room. It was empty.'

'Empty?'

'Empty!'

'You mean,' said Sir Gregory, who liked to get these things straight, 'there wasn't anybody *in* the room?'

Beach inclined his head.

'The bedchamber was unoccupied,' he assented.

'He may be in the smoking-room,' suggested Lady Constance.

'Or the billiard-room,' said Lady Julia.

'Having a bath,' cried Sir Gregory, inspired. 'Fellow with a headache might quite easily go and have a bath. Do his headache good.'

'I visited the smoking-room and the billiard-room, m'lady. The door of the bathroom on Mr Pilbeam's floor was open, revealing emptiness within. I am inclined to think, m'lady,' said Beach, 'that the gentleman has gone for a walk.'

The awful words produced a throbbing silence. Only too well could these three visualize the direction in which, if he had taken a walk, Percy Pilbeam would have taken it.

'Thank you, Beach,' said Lady Constance dully.

The butler bowed and withdrew. The silence continued unbroken. Sir Gregory walked heavily to the window and stood looking out into the night. It almost seemed to him that across that starry sky he could see written in letters of flame the story of the prawns.

Lady Constance gave a shuddering sigh.

'We shan't have a friend left!'

Lady Julia lit a cigarette.

'Poor old Miles! Bang goes *his* reputation!'

Sir Gregory turned from the window.

'Those Local Committee chaps will give the nomination to old Billing now, I suppose.' His Regency-buck face twisted with injured wrath. 'Why the devil need the feller have been in such a hurry? Why couldn't he at least have let me *talk* to him? I brought my cheque-book with me specially. He knows I'd have given him five hundred pounds. I'll bet he won't get that

from this Tilbury of his. I've met Tilbury. I've heard
stories about him. Mean man. Tight with his money.
Pilbeam'll be lucky if he gets a couple of hundred out of
him.'

'A pity you put his back up like that, Connie,' said
Lady Julia suavely. 'I don't suppose now he cares about
the money so much. What he wants is to be nasty.'

'What I think a pity,' retorted Lady Constance, with
the splendid Keeble spirit, 'is that Sir Gregory ever
mentioned the matter to a man like this Pilbeam. He
might have known that he was not to be trusted.'

'Exactly,' said Lady Julia. 'An insane thing to
do.'

This unexpected alliance disconcerted Sir Gregory
Parsloe. He spluttered.

'Well, I had had dealings with the fellow before on a
. . . on a private matter, and had found him alert and
enterprising. I just went and engaged him naturally, as
you would engage anyone to do something. It never
occurred to me that he wasn't to be trusted.'

'Not even after you saw that moustache?' said Lady
Julia. 'Well, there's just one gleam of comfort in this
business, Connie. We shall now be able to talk to
Clarence and put a stop to any nonsense of his giving
Ronnie his money.'

'That's true,' said Lady Constance, brightening a
little.

As she spoke, the door opened and Percy Pilbeam
came in.

Everybody, as the poet so well says, is loved by
someone, and it is to be supposed, therefore, that
somewhere in the world there were faces that lit up
when even Percy Pilbeam entered the room. But never,
not even by his mother, if he had a mother, nor by some
warm-hearted aunt, if he had a warm-hearted aunt,
could he have been more rapturously received than he
was received now by Lady Constance Keeble, by Lady

Julia Fish, and by Sir Gregory Parsloe-Parsloe, Bart, of
Matchingham Hall, Salop. Santa Claus himself would
have had a less enthusiastic welcome.

'Mr Pilbeam!'

'Mr *Pilbeam*!'

'Pilbeam, my *dear* chap!'

'Come in, Mr Pilbeam!'

'Sit down, Mr Pilbeam!'

'Pilbeam, my dear fellow, a chair.'

'How is your headache, Mr Pilbeam?'

'Are you feeling better, Mr Pilbeam?'

'Pilbeam, old man, I have a cigar here which I think
you will appreciate.'

The investigator looked from one to the other with
growing bewilderment. Though an investigator, he could
not deduce what had caused this exuberance. He had
come to the room expecting a sticky ten minutes, and
had forced himself to face it because business was
business and, now that that ghastly pig had transferred
almost the entire manuscript of the Hon. Galahad's
Reminiscences to its loathsome inside, it was from the
group before him alone that he could anticipate anything
in the nature of a cash settlement.

'Thanks,' he said, accepting the chair.

'Thanks,' he said, taking the cigar.

'Thanks,' he said, in response to the inquiries after his
health. 'No, it isn't so bad now.'

'That's good,' said Sir Gregory heartily.

'Splendid,' said Lady Constance.

'Capital,' said Lady Julia.

These paeans of joy concluded, there occurred that
momentary hush which always comes over any
gathering or assembly when business is about to be
discussed. Pilbeam's eyes were flickering warily from
face to face. He had got to do some expert bluffing, and
was bracing himself to the task.

'I came about – that thing,' he said, at length.

'Exactly, exactly, exactly,' cried Sir Gregory. 'You've been thinking it over and . . .'

'I'm afraid I was a little abrupt, Mr Pilbeam,' said Lady Constance winningly, 'when we had our last little talk. I was feeling rather upset. The weather, I suppose.'

'You did say you had your cheque-book with you, Sir Gregory?' said Lady Julia.

'Certainly, certainly. Here it is.'

There came into Pilbeam's eyes the gleam which always came into them when he saw cheque-books.

'Well, I've done it,' he said, in what he tried to make a cheery, big-hearted manner.

'Done it?' cried Lady Constance, appalled. The words conveyed to her a meaning different from that intended by their speaker. 'You don't mean you have taken . . . ?'

'You wanted that manuscript destroyed, didn't you?' said Pilbeam. 'Well, I've done it.'

'What?'

'I've destroyed it. Torn it up. As a matter of fact, I've burned it. So . . .' said Pilbeam, and cut his remarks off short on the word, filling out the hiatus with a meaning glance at the cheque-book. He licked his lips nervously as he did so. He was well aware that the conference had now arrived at what Monty Bodkin would have called the nub.

The committee of three evidently felt the same. There was another silence – an awkward silence this time, pulsing with embarrassment and doubt. It is always so embarrassing for well-bred people to tell a fellow human being that they do not believe him. Moreover, any intimation on the part of these particular well-bred people that they thought this man was lying to them would most certainly wound that sensitiveness of his which it was so dangerous to wound.

On the other hand, could they pay out large sums of money to a man with a moustache like that, purely on the off-chance that he might for once be telling the

truth? The committee paused on the horns of a
dilemma.

'Ha h'r'm'ph!' said Sir Gregory, rather neatly
summing up the sentiment of the meeting.

Percy Pilbeam displayed an unforeseen amiability in
this delicate situation.

'Of course, I don't expect you to take my word for it,'
he said. 'Naturally you want some sort of proof. Well,
here's a bit of the thing which I saved to show you. The
rest is a pile of ashes.'

From his breast pocket he produced a tattered
fragment of paper and handed it to Sir Gregory. Sir
Gregory, after wincing with some violence, for by an odd
chance the fragment happened to deal with the story of
the prawns, passed it to Lady Constance. Lady
Constance looked at it, and gave it to Lady Julia. The
tension relaxed.

'It is not quite what we intended,' said Lady
Constance. 'Naturally we expected you to bring the
manuscript to us, so that we could destroy it with our
own hands. Still . . .'

'Comes to the same thing,' argued Pilbeam.

'Yes, I suppose it does not really matter.'

Glances flitted to and fro like butterflies. Sir Gregory
looked at Lady Constance, seeking guidance. Lady
Constance silently consulted Lady Julia. Lady Julia gave
a quick nod. Sir Gregory having noted it and looked at
Lady Constance again and received a nod from her, went
to the writing-table and became busy with pen and ink.

Chattiness ensued. Something of the atmosphere of a
Board Room at the conclusion of an important meeting
had crept into the air.

'I am sure we are all very much obliged to you,' said
Lady Constance.

'But tell me, Mr Pilbeam,' said Lady Julia, 'what
caused this sudden change of heart?'

'Pardon?'

'Well, when you left us before dinner, you seemed so determined to . . .'

'Oh, Clarence!' cried Lady Constance, with the exasperation which the head of the family's entry into a room so often caused her. He would, she felt, choose this moment to come in and potter.

But for once in his life Lord Emsworth was in no pottering mood. The tempestuous manner of his irruption should have told Lady Constance that. His demeanour and the tone of his remarks now enabled her to perceive it. Quite plainly, something had occurred to stir him out of his usual dreamy calm.

'Who moves my books?' he demanded fiercely.

'What books?'

'I keep a little book of telephone numbers on the table in the library, and it's gone. Ha,' said Lord Emsworth. 'Beach would know.'

He leaped to the fireplace and pressed the bell.

'You'll break your neck if you go springing about like that on this parquet floor,' observed Lady Julia languidly. 'Why skip ye so, ye high hills?'

Lord Emsworth returned to the centre of the room. He was glaring in what his sister Constance considered an extremely uppish manner. He seemed to her to have got quite above himself.

'Do go away, Clarence,' she said. 'We are talking about something important.'

'And so am I talking about something important. Once and for all, I insist on having my personal belongings respected. I will not have my things moved. My little book of telephone numbers has gone. I suppose you've got it, Connie. Took it to look up some number or other and couldn't be bothered to put it back. Tchah!' said Lord Emsworth.

'I have not got your wretched little book,' said Lady Constance wearily. 'What do you want it for?'

'I want to ring up that fellow.'

'What fellow?'

'That fellow what's-his-name. The vet. It's a matter of life and death. And I've forgotten his number.'

'What do you want the vet. for?' asked Lady Julia. 'Are you ill?'

Lord Emsworth stared.

'What do I want the vet. for? When the Empress has been eating that paper?'

'What paper does the Empress take in?' said Lady Julia. 'I've often wondered. Something sound and conservative, I suppose. Probably the *Morning Post*.'

'What *are* you talking about, Clarence?' said Lady Constance.

'Why, about the Empress eating that book of Galahad's, of course. Hasn't Pilbeam told you?'

'What!'

'Certainly. Went to her sty just now and found her finishing the last chapters. How the thing got there is more than I can tell you. Ink and paper! Probably poisonous. Ha, Beach!'

'M'lord?'

'Beach, what is that vet.'s telephone number? You know what I mean. The telephone number of what's-his-name, the vet.'

'Matchingham 2–2–1, m'lord.'

'Then get him quickly and put him through to the library. Tell him my pig has just eaten the complete manuscript of my brother Galahad's Reminiscences.'

And, so saying, Lord Emsworth made a dart for the door. Finding Beach in the way, he sprang nimbly to the right. The butler also moved to the right. Lord Emsworth dashed to the left. So did Beach. From above the mantelpiece the portrait of the sixth Earl looked down approvingly on these rhythmical manoeuvres. He, too, had been fond of the minuet in his day.

'Beach!' cried Lord Emsworth, passionate appeal in his voice.

'M'lord?'

'Stand still, man. You aren't a jumping bean.'

'I beg your lordship's pardon. I miscalculated the direction in which your lordship was intending to proceed.'

This delay at such a time had robbed Lord Emsworth of the last vestiges of prudence and self-control. On the polished floor of the drawing-room only a professional acrobat could have executed without disaster the bound which he now gave. There was a slithering crash, and he came to a halt against a china-cabinet, rubbing his left ankle.

'I told you you would come a purler,' said Lady Julia, with the satisfaction of a Cassandra, one of whose prophecies has at last been fulfilled. 'Hurt yourself?'

'I think I've twisted my ankle. Beach, help me to the library.'

'Very good, m'lord.'

'Ronnie has some embrocation, I believe,' said Lady Julia.

'I don't want embrocation,' snarled the wounded man, as he hopped from the room on the butler's supporting arm. 'I want a doctor. Beach, as soon as you've got the vet., get a doctor.'

'Very good, m'lord.'

The door closed. And, as it did so, Lady Constance, her lips set and her eyes gleaming with a fierce light, walked to where Sir Gregory stood gaping, took the cheque from his fingers, and tore it across.

A passionate cry rang through the room. It came from the lips of Percy Pilbeam.

'Hi!'

Lady Constance gave him one of the Keeble looks.

'Surely, Mr Pilbeam, you do not expect to be paid for having done nothing? Your instructions were to deliver the manuscript to myself or to Sir Gregory. You have not done so. The agreement is, therefore, null and void.'

'Spoken like a man, Connie,' said Lady Julia, with approval.

The investigator was staring helplessly.

'But the thing's destroyed.'

'Not by you.'

'Certainly not,' said Sir Gregory, with animation. He could follow an argument as well as the next man. 'Not by you at all. Eaten by that pig.'

'Just an Act of God,' put in Lady Julia.

'Exactly,' agreed Sir Gregory. 'A very good way of putting it. Act of God. No obligation on our part to pay you a penny.'

'But . . .'

'I am sorry, Mr Pilbeam,' said Lady Constance, becoming queenly. 'I see no reason to discuss the matter further.'

'Especially,' said Lady Julia, 'as we have a very urgent matter to discuss with Clarence, Connie.'

'Why, of course. I was forgetting that.'

'I wasn't,' said Lady Julia. 'You will forgive us for leaving you, Sir Gregory?'

Sir Gregory Parsloe was looking like a Regency buck who has just won a fortune on the turn of a card at Wattier's.

'By all means, Lady Julia. Certainly. As a matter of fact, I think I'll be getting along.'

'I'll order your car.'

'Don't bother,' said Sir Gregory. 'Don't need a car. Going to walk. The relief of knowing that infernal book isn't hanging over my head any longer . . . phew! I think I'll walk ten miles.'

His eye fell on the tattered fragment of paper on the table. He gathered it up, tore it in half, and put the pieces in his pocket. Then, with the contented air of a man out of whose life stories of prawns have gone for ever, he strode briskly to the door.

Percy Pilbeam continued to sit where he was, looking like a devastated area.

15

While these events were in progress at Blandings Castle, there sat in the coffee-room of the Emsworth Arms in Market Blandings a young man eating turbot. It was the second course of a belated dinner which he was making under the reproachful eye of a large, pale, spotted waiter who had hoped to be off duty half an hour ago.

The first thing anyone entering the coffee-room would have noticed, apart from the ozone-like smell of cold beef, beer, pickles, cabbage, gravy soup, boiled potatoes and very old cheese which characterizes coffee-rooms all England over, would have been this young man's extraordinary gloom. He seemed to have looked on life and seen its hollowness. And so he had. Monty Bodkin – for this decayed wreck was he – was in the depths. It is fortunate that the quality of country hotel turbot is such that you do not notice much difference when it turns to ashes in your mouth, for this is what Monty's turbot was doing now.

He had never, he realized, been exactly what you might call sanguine when making his way to the Emsworth Arms to plead with Lord Tilbury to act like a sportsman and a gentleman. All the ruling of the form-book, he knew, was against him. And yet he had nursed, despite the whisperings of Reason, a sort of thin, sickly hope. This hope the proprietor of the Mammoth had slain dead within five minutes of his arrival.

When Monty had claimed consideration on the ground that it was through no fault of his own that he was not charging in, manuscript in hand, Lord Tilbury had remained mute and stony. When he had gone on to

779

point out that Pilbeam could not have got the thing but for him, Lord Tilbury had uttered a sharp, sneering snort. And when, as happened a little farther on in the scene, Monty had called his former employer a fat, double-crossing wart-hog, the latter had terminated the interview by walking away with his hands under his coat-tails.

So Monty dined broodingly, his heart bowed down with weight of woe. Silence reigned in the coffee-room, broken only by the breathing of the waiter, a man who would have done well to put himself in the hands of some good tonsil specialist.

Optimist though he was by nature, Monty Bodkin could not conceal it from himself that the future looked black. Unless the senior partner of Butterwick, Mandelbaum and Price relented – a hundred to one shot – or Gertrude Butterwick jettisoned her sturdy middle-class prejudices and decided to defy her father's wishes – call this one eighty-eight to three – that wedded bliss of which he had dreamed could never be his. It was an unpleasant thought for a man to have to face, and one well calculated to turn to ashes the finest portion of turbot ever boiled, let alone the rather obscene-looking mixture of bones and eyeballs and black macintosh which the chef of the Emsworth Arms had allotted to him.

Roast mutton succeeded the turbot and became ashes in its turn, as did the potatoes and brussels sprouts which accompanied it. The tapioca pudding, owing to an accident in the kitchen, was mostly ashes already. Monty gave it one look, then flung down his napkin with a Byronic gesture and, declining the waiter's half-hearted suggestion of a glass of port and a bit of Stilton, dragged himself downstairs and out into the garden.

Pacing the wet grass, he found his mind turning to thoughts of revenge. He was a kindly and good-tempered young man as a general rule, but conduct like that of Percy Pilbeam and Lord Tilbury seemed to him simply to clamour for reprisals. And it embittered him still further to discover at the end of ten minutes that he was totally without ideas on the subject. For all he could do about it, he was regretfully forced to conclude, these wicked men were apparently going to prosper like a couple of bay trees.

In these circumstances there was only one thing that could heal the spirit, viz. to go in and write a long, loving letter of appeal to Gertrude Butterwick, urging her to follow the dictates of her heart and come and spring round with him to the registrar's or Gretna Green or somewhere. With this end in view, he proceeded to the writing-room, where he hoped to be able to devote himself to the task in solitude.

The writing-room of the Emsworth Arms, as of most English rural hotels, was a small, stuffy, melancholy apartment, badly-lit and very much in need of new wallpaper. But it was not its meagre dimensions nor its closeness nor its dimness nor the shabbiness of its walls that depressed Monty as he entered. What gave him that grey feeling was the sight of Lord Tilbury seated in one of the two rickety armchairs.

Lord Tilbury was smoking an excellent cigar, and until that moment had been feeling quietly happy. His interview with Bodkin M. before dinner had relieved his mind of a rather sinister doubt which had been weighing on it. Until Monty had informed him of what had occurred, he had been oppressed by a speculation as to whether the voice which had spoken to him on the telephone had been the voice of Pilbeam or merely that of the alcoholic refreshment of which Pilbeam was so admittedly full. Had he, in short, really got the manuscript? Or had his statement to that effect been the mere inebriated babbling of an investigator who had just been investigating Lord Emsworth's cellar? Monty had

made it clear that the former and more agreeable theory
was the correct one, and Lord Tilbury was now awaiting
the detective's arrival in a frame of mind that blended
well with an excellent cigar.

The intrusion of a young man of whom he hoped he
had seen the last ruffled his placid mood.

'I have nothing more to say,' he observed irritably. 'I
have told you my decision, and I see nothing to be
gained by further discussion.'

Monty raised his eyebrows coldly.

'I have no desire to speak to you, my good man,' he
said loftily. 'I came in here to write a letter.'

'Then go and write it somewhere else. I am expecting
a visitor.'

It had been Monty's intention to ignore the fellow
and carry on with the job in hand without deigning to
bestow another look on him. But having gone to the
desk and discovered that it contained no notepaper, no
pen, not a single envelope, and in the inkpot only about
a quarter of an inch of curious sediment that looked like
black honey, he changed his mind.

He toyed for an instant with the idea of taking one of
the magazines which lay on the table and sitting down
in the other armchair and spoiling the old blighter's
evening; but as those magazines were last-year copies of
the *Hotel Keepers Register* and *Licensed Victuallers
Gazette* he abandoned the project. With a quiet look of
scorn and a meaning sniff he left the room and wandered
out into the garden again.

And barely had he strolled down to the river and
smoked two cigarettes and thrown a bit of stick at a
water-rat and strolled back and thrown another bit of
stick at a noise in the bushes, when the significance of
Lord Tilbury's concluding remark suddenly flashed upon
him.

If Lord Tilbury was expecting a visitor, that visitor
obviously must be Pilbeam. And if Pilbeam was coming

to the Emsworth Arms to see Lord Tilbury, equally obviously he must be bringing the manuscript with him.

Very well, then, where did one go from there? One went, he perceived, straight to this arresting conclusion – that there the two blisters would be in that writing-room with the manuscript between them, thus offering a perfect sitter of a chance to any man of enterprise who cared to dash in and be a little rough.

A bright confidence filled Monty Bodkin. He felt himself capable of taking on ten Tilburies and a dozen Pilbeams. All he had to do was bide his time and then rush in and snatch the thing. And when he had got it and was dangling it before his eyes, would Lord Tilbury take a slightly different attitude? Would he adopt a somewhat different tone? Would he be likely to reopen the whole matter, approaching it from another angle? The answer was definitely in the affirmative.

But first to spy out the land. He remembered that the window of the writing-room had been open a few inches at the bottom. He tiptoed across the grass with infinite caution. And just as he had reached his objective a voice spoke inside the room.

'You hid it? But are you sure it is safe?'

Monty leaned against the wall, holding his breath. He felt like the owner of a home-made radio who has accidentally got San Francisco.

The Pilbeam who had borrowed Voules' motor-bicycle and ridden down to the Emsworth Arms and now faced Lord Tilbury in the writing-room of that hostelry was a very different Pilbeam from the gay telephoner of before dinner. The telephoning Pilbeam had been a man who gave free rein to a jovial exuberance, knowing himself to be sitting on top of the world. The writing-room Pilbeam was a taut and anxious gambler, staking his all on one last throw.

After that painful scene in the drawing-room, it had

taken the detective perhaps ten minutes to realize that, though all seemed lost, there did still remain just one chance of saving the day. If he were salesman enough to dispose of that manuscript to Lord Tilbury, sight unseen, without being compelled to mention that it was no longer – except in a greatly transmuted state inside Empress of Blandings – in existence, all would be well.

There might possibly be a little coldness on the other's side next time they met, for Lord Tilbury, he knew, was one of those men who rather readily take umbrage on discovering that they have paid a thousand pounds for nothing, but he was used to people being cold to him and could put up with that.

So here he was, making his last throw.

'You hid it?' said Lord Tilbury, after the detective in a brief opening speech had explained that he had not come to deliver the goods in person. 'But are you sure it is quite safe?'

'Oh, quite.'

'But why did you not bring it with you?'

'Too risky. You don't know what that house is like. There's Lady Constance after the thing and Gally Threepwood after the thing and Ronnie Fish and . . . well, as I said to Monty Bodkin this afternoon, a fellow trying to smuggle that manuscript out of the place is rather like a chap in a detective story trapped in the den of the Secret Nine.'

A little gasp of indignation forced itself from Monty's outraged lips. This, he felt, was just that little bit that is too much. He had been modestly proud of that crack about the Secret Nine. Not content with pinching his manuscripts, this dastardly detective was pinching his nifties. It was enough to make a fellow chafe, and Monty chafed a good deal.

'I see,' said Lord Tilbury. 'Yes, I see what you mean. But if you hid it in your bedroom . . .'

'I didn't.'

'Then where?'

The crucial moment had arrived, and Pilbeam braced himself to cope with it.

'Ah!' he said. 'I think, perhaps, before I tell you that, we had better just get the business end of the thing settled, eh? If you have your cheque-book handy . . .'

'But, my dear Pilbeam, surely you do not expect me to pay before . . . ?'

'Quite,' said the detective, and held his breath. His stake was on the board and the wheel had begun to spin.

It seemed to Monty that Lord Tilbury also must be holding his breath, for there followed a long silence. When he did speak, his tone was that of a man who has been wounded.

'Well, really, Pilbeam! I think you might trust me.'

' "Trust nobody" is the Pilbeam family motto,' replied the detective with a return of what might be called his telephone manner.

'But how am I to know . . . ?'

'*You've* got to trust *me*,' said Pilbeam brightly. 'Of course,' he went on, 'if you don't like that way of doing business, well, in that case, I suppose the deal falls through. No hard feelings on either side. I simply go back to the Castle and take the matter up with Sir Gregory Parsloe and Lady Constance. They want that manuscript just as much as you do, though, of course, their reasons aren't the same as yours. They want to destroy it. Parsloe's original offer was five hundred pounds, but I shall have no difficulty in making him improve on that . . .'

'Five hundred pounds is a great deal of money,' said Lord Tilbury, as if he were having a tooth out.

'It's not nearly as much as a thousand,' replied Pilbeam, as if he were a light-hearted dentist. 'And you agreed to that on the telephone.'

'Yes, but then I assumed that you would be bringing . . .'

'Well, take it or leave it, Tilbury, take it or leave it,' said the detective, and from the little crackling splutter which followed the words Monty deduced that he was doing what we are so strongly advised to do when we wish to appear nonchalant, lighting a cigarette. 'Good!' he said a moment later. 'I think you're wise. Make it open, if you don't mind.'

There was a pause. The heavy breathing that came through the window could only be that of a parsimonious man occupied in writing a cheque for a thousand pounds. It is a type of breathing which it is impossible to mistake, though in some respects it closely resembles the sound of a strong man's death agony.

'There!'

'Thanks.'

'And now – ?'

'Well, I'll tell you,' said Pilbeam. 'It's like this. I didn't dare hide the thing in the house, so I put it carefully away in a disused pigsty near the kitchen garden. Wait. If you'll lend me your fountain pen, I'll draw you a map. See, here's the wall of the kitchen garden. You go along it, and on your left you will see this sty in a little paddock. You can't mistake it. It's the only building there. You go in and under the straw, where I'm putting this cross, is the manuscript. That's clear?'

'Quite clear.'

'You think you will be able to find it all right?'

'Perfectly easily.'

'Good. Well, now, there's just one other thing. The merest trifle, but you want to be prepared for it. I said this pigsty was disused, and when I put the manuscript in it so it was. But since then they've gone and shifted that pig of Lord Emsworth's there, the animal they call the Empress of Blandings.'

'What?'

'I thought I had better mention it, as otherwise it might have given you a surprise when you got there.'

The momentary spasm of justifiable indignation which had attacked Lord Tilbury on hearing this piece of information left him. In its place came, oddly enough, a distinct relief. In some curious way the statement had removed from his mind a doubt which had been lingering there. It made Pilbeam's story seem circumstantial.

'That is quite all right,' he said as cheerfully as could be expected of a man of his views on parting with money so soon after the writing of a thousand-pound cheque. 'That will cause no difficulty.'

'You think you can cope with this pig?'

'Certainly. I am not afraid of pigs. Pigs like me.'

At these words, Monty found his respect for a breed of animal which he had always rather admired waning a good deal. No animal of the right sort, he felt, could like Lord Tilbury.

'Then that's fine,' said Pilbeam. 'I'd start at once if I were you. Are you going to walk?'

'Yes.'

'You'll need a torch.'

'No doubt I can borrow one from the landlord of this inn.'

'Good. Then everything's all right.'

There came to Monty's ears the sound of the opening and closing of a door. Lord Tilbury had apparently left to begin the business of the night. For a moment Monty thought that Pilbeam must have left, too, but after a brief silence there came through the window a muttered oath, and, peeping in, he saw that the detective was leaning over the writing-desk. The ejaculation had presumably been occasioned by his discovery that there was no paper, no envelope, no pen, and only what a dreamer could have described as ink.

And such, indeed, was the case. Percy Pilbeam was a man who believed in prompt action. He intended to dispatch that cheque to his bank without delay.

He rang the bell.

'I want some ink,' Monty heard him say. 'And a pen and some paper and an envelope.'

He had placed the cheque on the desk before making the discovery of its lack of stationery. He now picked it up and stood looking at it lovingly.

He was well pleased with himself. It was a far, far better thing that he had done than he had ever done, felt Pilbeam. He wondered how many men there were who would have snatched victory out of defeat like that. He reached for his unpleasant moustache and gave it a complacent tug.

And, as he did so, over his shoulder there came groping a hand. The cheque was twitched from his grasp. And, turning, he perceived Monty Bodkin.

'Hell!' cried Pilbeam, aghast.

Monty did not reply. Actions speak louder than words. With a severe look, he tore the cheque in two pieces, then in four, then in eight, then in sixteen, then in thirty-two. Then, finding himself unable to bring the score up to sixty-four, he moved to the fireplace and, still with that austere expression on his face, dropped them in the grate like a shower of confetti.

After that first anguished cry Pilbeam had not spoken. He stood watching the tragedy with a frozen stare. It seemed to him that he had spent most of his later life looking at people tearing up cheques made out to himself. For one brief instant the battling spirit of the Pilbeams urged him to attack this man with tooth and claw, but the impulse faded. The Pilbeams might be brave, but they were not rash. Monty was some eight inches taller than himself, some twenty pounds heavier, and in addition to this had a nasty look in his eye.

He accepted the ruling of Destiny. In silence he

watched Monty leave the room. The door closed. Percy Pilbeam was alone with his thoughts.

Monty strolled into the lounge of the Emsworth Arms. It was empty, but presently Lord Tilbury appeared, hatted, booted, and ready for the long trail. Monty eyed him sardonically. He proposed very shortly to put a stick of dynamite under this Lord Tilbury.

'Going out?' he said.

'I am taking a walk, yes.'

'God bless you!' said Monty.

He followed Lord Tilbury with his eye. Shortly he was going to follow him in actual fact. But that could wait. He knew that he could give that stout, stumpy man five minutes' start and still be at the tryst before him. And in the meantime there was grim work to be done.

He went to the telephone and rang up Blandings Castle.

'I want to speak to Lord Emsworth,' he said, in one of those gruff assumed voices that sound like a bull-frog with catarrh.

'I will put you through to his lordship,' replied the more melodious voice of Beach.

'Do so,' said Monty, sinking an octave. 'The matter is urgent.'

16

Lord Emsworth had taken his twisted ankle to the
library and was lying with it on one of the
leather-covered settees. The doctor had come and gone,
leaving instructions for the application of hot
fomentations and announcing that the patient was out
of danger. And as the pain had now entirely disappeared
it might have been supposed that the ninth Earl's mind
would have been at rest.

This, however, was far from being the case. Not only
was he anxiously awaiting the veterinary surgeon's
report on the paper-filled Empress, which was enough to
agitate any man ill accustomed to bear up calmly under
suspense, but to add to his mental discomfort, his two
sisters, the Lady Constance Keeble and the Lady Julia
Fish, had gathered about his sick-bed and were driving
him half mad with some nonsense about his nephew
Ronald's money.

However, for some time he had been adopting the
statesmanlike policy of saying 'Eh?' 'Yes?' 'Oh, ah?' and
'God bless my soul' at fairly regular intervals, and this
had given him leisure to devote his mind to the things
that really mattered.

Paper . . . Ink . . . Wasn't ink a highly corrosive acid or
something? And could even the stoutest pig thrive on
corrosive acids? Thus Lord Emsworth when his thoughts
took a gloomy trend.

But there were optimistic gleams among the grey. He
recalled the time when the Empress, mistaking his
carelessly dropped cigar for something on the bill of fare,
had swallowed it with every indication of enjoyment

and had been none the worse next day. Also Pirbright's Sunday hat. There was another case that seemed to make for hopefulness. True, she had consumed only a mouthful or two of that, but to remain in excellent health and spirits after eating even a portion of the sort of hat that Pirbright wore on Sundays argued a constitution well above the average. Reviewing these alimentary feats of the past, Lord Emsworth was able to endure.

But he wished that Beach would return and put an end to this awful suspense. The butler had been dispatched with the vet. to the sty to bring back his report, and should have been here long ago. Lord Emsworth found himself yearning for Beach's society as poets of a former age used to yearn for that of gazelles and Arab steeds.

It was at this tense moment in the affairs of the master of Blandings that Monty's telephone call came through.

'Lord Emsworth?' said a deep, odd voice.

'Lord Emsworth speaking.'

'I have reason to believe, Lord Emsworth . . .'

'Wait!' cried the ninth Earl. 'Wait a moment. Hold the line.' He turned. 'Well, Beach, well?'

'The veterinary surgeon reports, m'lord, that there is no occasion for alarm.'

'She's all right?'

'Quite, m'lord. No occasion for anxiety whatsoever.'

A deep sigh of relief shook Lord Emsworth.

'Eh?' said the voice at the other end of the wire, not knowing quite what to make of it.

'Oh, excuse me. I was just speaking to my butler about my pig. Extremely sorry to have kept you waiting, but it was most urgent. You were saying – ?'

'I have reason to believe, Lord Emsworth, that an attack is to be made upon your pig tonight.'

Lord Emsworth uttered a sharp, gargling sound.

'What!'

'Yes.'

'You don't mean that?'

'Yes.'

'Oh, do hurry, Clarence,' said Lady Constance, who wished to get on with the business of the evening. 'Who is it? Tell him to ring up later.'

Lord Emsworth waved her down imperiously, and continued to bark into the telephone's mouthpiece like a sea-lion.

'Tonight?'

'Yes.'

'What time tonight?'

'Any time now.'

'What!'

('Oh, Clarence, do stop saying "What" and ring off.')

'Yes, almost immediately.'

'Are you sure?'

'Yes.'

'God bless my soul! What a ghastly thing! Well, I am infinitely obliged to you, my dear fellow . . . By the way, who are you?'

'A Well-wisher.'

'What?'

('Oh, Clar-*ence!*')

'A Well-wisher.'

'Fisher?'

'Wisher.'

'Disher? Beach,' cried Lord Emsworth, as a click from afar told him that the man of mystery had hung up, 'a Mr A. L. Fisher or Disher – I did not quite catch the name – says that an attack is to be made upon the Empress tonight.'

'Indeed, m'lord?'

'Almost immediately.'

'Indeed, m'lord?'

'Don't keep saying "Indeed, m'lord", as if I were telling you it was a fine day! Can't you realize the frightful – ? And you, Connie,' said Lord Emsworth, who was now in thoroughly berserk mood, turning on his sister like a stringy tiger, 'stop sniffing like that!'

'Really, Clarence!'

'Beach, go and bring Pirbright here.'

'He shall do nothing of the kind,' said Lady Constance sharply.

'The idea of bringing Pirbright into the library!'

It was not often that Beach found himself in agreement with the chatelaine of Blandings, but he could not but support her attitude now. Like all butlers, he held definite views on the sanctity of the home and frowned upon attempts on the part of the outside staff to enter it – especially when, like Pirbright, they smelt so very strongly of pigs. Five minutes of that richly scented man in the library, felt Beach, and you would have to send the place to the cleaner's.

'Perhaps if I were to convey a message to Pirbright from your lordship?' he suggested tactfully.

Lord Emsworth, though dangerously excited, could still listen to the voice of Reason. It was not the thought of the pig-man's aroma that made him change his mind – the library, in his opinion, would have been improved by a whiff of bouquet de Pirbright – but that deep, grave voice had said that the attack was to take place almost immediately, and in that case it would be madness to remove the garrison from its post even for an instant.

'Yes,' he said. 'A very good idea. Much better. Yes, capital. Excellent. Thank you, Beach.'

'Not at all, m'lord.'

'Go at once to Pirbright and tell him what I have told you, and say that he is to remain in hiding near the sty and spring out at the right moment and catch this fellow.'

'Very good, m'lord.'

'He had better strike him over the head with a stout stick.'

'Very good, m'lord.'

'So we shall wind up the evening with a nice murder,' said Lady Julia.

'Eh?'

'Don't pay any attention to me, of course. If you like to incite pig-men to brain people with sticks, it's none of my affair. But I should have thought you were taking a chance.'

Lord Emsworth seemed impressed.

'You think he might injure Parsloe fatally?'

'Parsloe!' Lady Constance's voice caused a statuette of the young David prophesying before Saul to quiver on its base. 'Are you off your head, Clarence?'

'No, I'm not,' replied Lord Emsworth manfully. 'What's the use of pretending that you don't know as well as I do that it's Parsloe who is making this attempt tonight? The way you let that fellow pull the wool over your eyes, Constance, amazes me. What do you think he wheedled you into inviting him to dinner for? So that he could be on the premises and have easy access to the Empress, of course. I'll bet you find he has sneaked off while you were not looking.'

'Clarence!'

'Well, where is he? Produce Parsloe! Show me Parsloe!'

'Sir Gregory left the house a few minutes ago. He wished to take a walk.'

'Take a walk!' This time it was Lord Emsworth's voice that rocked the young David. 'Beach, there isn't a moment to lose! Hurry, man, hurry! Run to Pirbright and say that the blow may fall at any moment.'

'Very good, m'lord. And in the matter of the stick – ?'

'Tell him to use his own judgement.'

Lord Emsworth sank back on his settee. His mental condition resembled that of a warrior who, crippled by

wounds, must stay in his tent while the battle is joined
without. He snorted restlessly. His place was by
Pirbright's side, and he could not get there. He put his
foot to the floor and tentatively leaned his weight upon
it but a facial contortion and a sharp 'Ouch!' showed
that there was no hope. Pirbright, that strong shield of
defence, must be left to deal with this matter alone.

'I'm sure everything will be quite all right, Clarence,'
said Lady Julia, who believed in the methods of
diplomacy, silencing with a little gesture her sister
Constance, who did not.

'You really feel that?' said Lord Emsworth eagerly.

'Of course. You can trust Pirbright to see that nothing
happens.'

'Yes. A good fellow, Pirbright.'

'I expect that when Sir Gregory sees him,' said Lady
Julia, with a steady, quelling glance at her sister, who
was once more sniffing in rather a marked manner, 'he
will run away.'

'Pirbright will?' said Lord Emsworth, starting.

'No, Sir Gregory will. There is nothing for you to
worry about at all. Just lie back and relax.'

'Bless my soul, you're a great comfort, Julia.'

'I try to be,' said Lady Julia virtuously.

'You've made me feel easier in my mind.'

'Splendid,' said Lady Julia, and with another little
gesture she indicated to Lady Constance that the subject
was now calmed and that she could proceed.

Lady Constance gave her a masonic glance of
understanding.

'Julia is quite right,' she said. 'There is no need for you
to worry.'

'Well, if you think that, too . . .' said Lord Emsworth,
beginning to achieve something like that delightful
feeling of *bien-être*.

'I do, decidedly. You can dismiss the whole thing from
your mind and give me your attention again.'

'My attention? What do you want my attention for?'

'We were speaking,' said Lady Constance, 'of this money of Ronald's and the criminal folly of allowing him to have it in order that he may make a marriage of which Julia and I both disapprove so very strongly.'

'Oh, that?' said Lord Emsworth, the glow beginning to fade.

He looked at the door wistfully, feeling how easy a task it would have been, but for this ankle of his, to disappear through it like an eel and not let himself be cornered again before bedtime.

Cornered, however, he was. He leaned back against the cushions and women's voices began to beat upon him like rain upon a roof.

Down at the Emsworth Arms, Monty Bodkin had just decided to make a small alteration in the plan of action which he had outlined for himself. It had been his original intention, it may be recalled, to follow Lord Tilbury to the trap which he had prepared for him, so that, lurking in the background – probably with folded arms, certainly with a bitter sneer of triumph on his lips – he might have the gratification of witnessing his downfall. But when, wearying of the Wisher-Fisher-Disher controversy, he hung up the receiver and left the telephone booth, he found this project looking less attractive to him.

A man who is by nature a light baritone cannot conduct a conversation for any length of time in a deep bass without acquiring a parched and burning throat. Monty came out of the booth feeling as if his had been roughly sandpapered, and the thought of that two and a half mile walk to the Castle and its little brother, the two and a half mile walk back, intimidated him. The more he thought of it, the less worth while did it seem to him to go to all that fearful sweat simply in order to see the scruff of Lord Tilbury's neck grasped by a pig-man. Far better, he felt, to toddle along to the bar-parlour and there, over a soothing tankard, follow the scene with the eye of imagination.

Thither, accordingly, he made his way, and presently, seated in a corner with a stoup of the right stuff before him, was lubricating his tortured vocal chords and exchanging desultory chit-chat with the barmaid.

For himself, gripped as he still was by that melancholy which torments those who have loved and lost, Monty would have preferred to be allowed to meditate in silence. But as he happened to be the only customer in the place at the moment, the barmaid, a matronly lady in black satin with a bird's nest of gold hair on her head, was able to give him her full attention, and her social sense urged her to converse. On such occasions she very rightly regarded herself as a hostess.

They spoke, accordingly, of the weather, touching on such aspects of it as the heat before the storm, the coolness after the storm, the violence of the storm, its possible effect on the crops and what always happened to the barmaid's digestive organs when there was thunder. It was after she had finished a rather lengthy description (one which would, perhaps, have interested a physician more than a layman) of what she had suffered earlier in the summer through rashly eating cucumber during a storm that Monty happened to mention that he had been caught in the downpour.

'Not reely?' said the barmaid. 'What, were you out in it?'

'Absolutely,' said Monty. 'I got properly soaked.'

'But what a silly you must be, if you'll excuse me saying so,' observed the barmaid, 'not to have took shelter in a shop or somewhere. Or were you taking one of those country hikes?'

'I was in the park. Up at Blandings.'

'Oh, are you up at the Castle?' said the barmaid, interested.

'I was then,' said Monty, with reserve.

The barmaid polished a glass.

'There's a great to-do up there,' she said. 'I expect you've heard?'

'A to-do?'

'About his lordship's pig. Eating all that paper.'

'Eh?'

'Oh, you haven't heard?' said the barmaid, gratified. 'Oh, yes, his lordship is terribly upset. I had it from Mr Webber, the vet., who stepped in for a quick one on his way up there. He'd just been phoned for, extremely urgent. About half an hour ago, it was.'

'Paper?'

'That's what Mr Webber said. Some book his lordship's brother had been writing, he said, and somehow, he said, it had got into this pig's sty, and the pig had eaten it. That's what he said. Though how a book could have got into a pigsty, is more than I can tell you.'

The barmaid broke off to attend to a customer who came in for a stout-and-mild, and Monty was able to wrestle in silence with this extraordinary piece of news.

So that was why Pilbeam had been so urgent in demanding cash in advance! From the confused welter of Monty's thoughts there emerged a clear realization that there must be a lot of hidden good in Percy Pilbeam that he had overlooked. A man with the resource and initiative to extract a thousand pounds from Lord Tilbury for a piece of property which he knew to be in the process of being digested by a pig was surely a man of whom one wished to see more, a fellow one would like to know better. As he reviewed that scene in the writing-room and remembered the confidence with which the detective had stated his terms, the gallant nonchalance of that take-it-or-leave-it of his which had sent Lord Tilbury scrambling for his cheque-book,

something very like a warm affection for Percy Pilbeam
began to burgeon in Monty. He did his hair in a pretty
gruesome way, and there was no question but that that
moustache of his was a bit above the odds –
nevertheless, he definitely felt that he would like to
fraternize with the man.

He saw now – what had puzzled him before – why
that cheque-tearing stuff had gone so big. At the
moment of the cheque's destruction, Monty, like Ronnie
Fish on another occasion, had intended merely the great
gesture. Even while his fingers were busy, he was feeling
that he was accomplishing little of practical value,
because all the fellow had to do was to go and get
another cheque from Lord Tilbury. But this news put an
entirely different aspect on the matter. Obviously, Lord
Tilbury would not do any more cheque-writing now.
The great gesture had landed Pilbeam squarely in the
soup, he realized, and, oddly enough, he felt remorseful.

He could now see the thing from Pilbeam's point of
view. With a sum like a thousand pounds at stake, could
the fellow be blamed for stooping to some fairly raw
work? Was he not almost justified in going a bit near the
knuckle in his methods? Absolutely, felt Monty as he
supped his tankard.

What with this dawning of the big, broad outlook and
the excellence of the Emsworth Arms draught ale, he
began to be conscious of an almost maudlin change in
his attitude towards the investigator. Anyone who could
send Lord Tilbury two and a half miles on a fool's errand
was Monty's friend. More like a brother the detective
now seemed than the tripe-hound he had once supposed
him.

At this moment, just as he was at his mellowest, the
man in person came into the bar-parlour.

'Good evening, sir,' said the barmaid in her spacious
way. As with so many barmaids, there was always
a suggestion in her manner of being somebody who

was bestowing the Freedom of the City on someone.

'Evening,' said Pilbeam.

He caught sight of Monty in his corner, and frowned. If Monty had begun to warm to him, it was plain that he was nowhere near warming to Monty. He eyed him sourly. His intention had apparently been to consume liquid refreshment in the bar-parlour, but the sight of the person who had so recently impaired his finances made him change his mind. One does not drink in an atmosphere poisoned by a man who has just robbed one of a thousand pounds.

'I want a double whisky,' said Pilbeam. 'Send it into the writing-room, will you?'

He stalked out. The barmaid, whose manner during their brief conversation had shown impressment, jerked a rather awed thumb at the door.

'See that feller?' she said. 'Know who he is? Mr Voules, the chauffeur up at the Castle, was telling me. He runs a big detective agency in London. Employs hundreds and hundreds of skilled assistants, Mr Voules says. Sort of spider, if you get my meaning, sitting in his web and directing the movement of his skilled assistants.'

'Good gosh!' cried Monty.

'Yes,' said the barmaid, pleased at his emotion. She polished a glass with something of an air.

But Monty's emotion had been caused by something of which she was not aware. Where she beheld a good-gosher who good-goshed from sheer astonishment at her sensational information, this young man's good-goshing had not been due to surprise. It was that bit about the skilled assistants that had wrenched the ejaculation from Monty's lips. Those two words had given him the idea of a lifetime.

Thirty seconds later he was in the writing-room, the detective looking up at him like a startled basilisk.

'I know, I know,' said Monty, rightly interpreting the

message in his eye. 'But I've got a bit of business to talk over. I can do you a spot of good, Pilbeam.'

It would be too much to say that the investigator's eye melted. It still looked like that of a basilisk. But at these words it became that of a basilisk which reserves its judgement.

'Well?' he said.

Monty perpended.

'It's a little difficult to know where to begin.'

'As far as I'm concerned,' said Pilbeam, his feelings momentarily overcoming his business instinct, 'you can begin by getting out of here and breaking your ruddy neck.'

Monty waved a pacific hand.

'No, no,' he urged. 'Don't talk like that. The wrong attitude, old soul. Not the right tone at all.'

At this moment there entered a lad in shirt-sleeves bearing the investigator's double whisky. The interruption served to enable Monty to marshal his thoughts. When the lad had withdrawn, he began to speak fluently and with ease.

'It's like this, my dear old chap,' he said, paying no heed to an odd noise which proceeded from his companion, who appeared not to like being called his dear old chap. 'I seem to recollect mentioning to you this afternoon that as far as my affairs were concerned there were wheels within wheels. Well, there are. Not long ago I became betrothed to a girl, and her ass of a father won't let me marry her unless I get a job and hold it down for a year. And, dash it, my every effort to do so seems to prove null and void, if null and void is the expression I want. No,' said Monty, gently corrective, 'it isn't a bit of luck for the girl. It's very tough on the girl. She loves me madly. On the other hand, being a sort of throwback to the Victorian age, she won't go against her old dad's wishes. So I've got to have that job. I tried being assistant editor of *Tiny Tots*. No good. The boot. I

became secretary to old Emsworth. Again no good. Once
more the boot. And this is the idea that struck me just
now, listening to the conversation of that female who
works the beer-engine out there. You run a detective
agency. You employ hundreds of skilled assistants. Well,
come on now, be a sport. Employ me!'

The only reason why Percy Pilbeam did not at this
point interject a blistering comment on the proposal
thus put before him was that three such comments
entered his mind simultaneously, and in the effort to
decide which was the most blistering he drank some
whisky the wrong way. Before he had finished choking,
Monty had gone on to speak further. And what he went
on to say was so amazing, so arresting, that the
investigator found himself choking again.

'There's a thousand quid in it for you.'

Percy Pilbeam at last contrived to clear his vocal
chords.

'A thousand quid?'

'Oh, I've got packets of money,' said Monty,
misreading the look in those watering eyes and taking it
for incredulity. 'I'm simply ill with the stuff. If money
had been the trouble, there never would have been any
trouble, if you follow what I mean. That hasn't been the
difficulty. What's been the difficulty has been the
extraordinary mental attitude of J. G. Butterwick. He
insists . . .'

An astonishing change had come over the demeanour
of P. Frobisher Pilbeam. One has seen much the same
thing, of course, in the film of Jekyll and Hyde, but on a
much less impressive scale. His scowling face had
melted into a face that glowed as if lit by some inner
lantern. Aesthetically, he looked equally unpleasant
whether scowling or smiling, but Monty was far from
being in the frame of mind to regard him from the
austere standpoint of a judge in a Beauty Competition.
He saw the smile, and his heart leaped within him.

Pilbeam had still to wrestle with his emotions for a moment before he could speak.

'You'll pay a thousand pounds to come into my Agency?'

'That exact figure.'

'For a thousand pounds,' said Pilbeam simply, 'you can be a partner, if you like.'

'But I don't like,' said Monty urgently. 'You're missing the idea. This has got to be a job. I want to be a skilled assistant.'

'You shall be.'

'For a year?'

'For ten years, if you want to.'

Monty sat down. There was in the simple action something of the triumph and exhaustion of the winner of a Marathon race. He stared in silence for a moment at a framed advertisement of Sigbee's Soda ('It Sizzles') which was assisting the wallpaper to impart to the room that note of hideousness at which hotel-keepers strive.

'Butterwick's her name,' he said at length. 'Gertrude Butterwick.'

'Yes?' said Pilbeam. 'Where's your cheque-book?'

'Her eyes,' said Monty, 'are greyish. And yet, at the same time, blueish.'

'I bet they are,' said Pilbeam. 'In one of your pockets, perhaps?'

'About her hair,' said Monty. 'Some people might call it brown. Chestnut has always seemed to me a closer description. She's tallish, but not too tall. Her mouth . . .'

'I'll tell you,' said Pilbeam. 'Let me get a sheet of paper.'

'You want me to draw you a picture of her?' said Monty, a little doubtfully.

'I want you to write a cheque for me.'

'Oh, ah, yes, I see what you mean. My cheque-book's upstairs in my suitcase.'

'Then come along,' said Pilbeam buoyantly, 'and I'll help you unpack.'

Beach sat in his pantry, sipping brandy. And if ever a butler was entitled to a glass of brandy, that butler, he felt, was himself. He rolled the stuff round his tongue, finding a certain comfort in the fiery sting of it.

His heart was heavy. It was a kindly heart, and from the very first it had been deeply stirred by the stormy romance of Mr Ronald and his young lady. He wished that life were as the writers of the detective stories, to which he had become so addicted, portrayed it. In those, no matter what obstacles Fate might interpose in the shape of gangs, shots in the night, underground cellars, sinister Chinamen, poisoned asparagus and cobras down the chimney, the hero always got his girl. In the present case Beach could see no such happy ending. The significance of the presence in the library of Lady Constance Keeble and Lady Julia Fish had not escaped him. He feared that it meant the worst.

Eighteen years of close association with Clarence, Earl of Emsworth, had left the butler with a very fair estimate of his overlord's character. He wished well to everyone – Beach knew that. But where viewpoints clashed and arguments began, a passionate desire for peace at any price would undoubtedly lead him to decide in favour of whoever argued loudest. And eighteen years of close association with Lady Constance Keeble told Beach who, on the present occasion, that would be.

He saw no hope. Sighing despondently, he helped himself to another glass of brandy. Usually at this hour he drank port. But port to him was a symbol. He never touched it till dinner was over and the coffee served, and it signified that the responsibilities of his office were at an end and that until the morrow should bring its new cares and duties his soul was at rest. Port tonight would have been quite unsuitable.

Sighing again and about to start sipping once more, he became aware that he was no longer alone. Mr Ronald had entered the room.

'Don't get up, Beach,' said Ronnie.

He sat down on the table. His face had a pinkness deeper than its wont. There was a repressed excitement in his manner. The butler was reminded of that other occasion, ten days ago, when this young man had come into his pantry looking much the same as he was looking now and, having announced that he intended to steal his lordship's pig, had proceeded to cajole him into becoming his accomplice and helping him to feed the animal. The weighing machine in the servants' bathroom had informed Beach that he had lost three pounds in two days over that little affair.

'Bad show, this, Beach.'

Beach stirred mountainously. Solicitude shone from his prominent eyes. It has already been mentioned that Beach in the drawing-room and Beach in his pantry were different entities. He was now in his pantry, where he could cast off the official mask and be the man with whom a younger Ronnie had once played bears on this very floor.

'Extremely, Mr Ronald. Then you have heard?'

'Heard?'

'The unfortunate news.'

'You were there when I heard it. In the hall.'

The butler rolled his eyes, to indicate that there was something much more Stop Press than that.

'The Empress has eaten Mr Galahad's book, Mr Ronald.'

'What!'

'Yes, sir. Somebody apparently left it in her sty, and she was devouring the last of it when his lordship found her.'

'Pilbeam!'

'So one would be disposed to imagine, Mr Ronald. No doubt he had employed the sty as a hiding-place.'

'And it's gone?'

'Quite gone, Mr Ronald.'

'And Aunt Constance knows about it?'

'I fear so, Mr Ronald.'

Ronnie's face became a little pinker.

'Well, it doesn't make much odds. There was never any chance of recovering it from Pilbeam. That's why I . . . I think I could do with a spot of that brandy, Beach.'

'Certainly, sir. I will get you a glass. Why you . . . you were saying, Mr Ronald?'

'Oh, just a sort of decision I came to. This is good stuff, Beach.'

'Yes, sir.'

'A sort of decision,' said Ronnie, sipping pensively. 'I don't know if you noticed that I was a bit quiet at dinner?'

'You did strike me as somewhat silent, Mr Ronald.'

'I was thinking.'

'I see, sir.'

'Thinking,' repeated Ronnie. 'Doing a bit of avenue-exploring. I came to this decision with the fish.'

'Indeed, sir?'

'Yes. And I think it will work, too.'

Ronnie swung his legs for a while without speaking.

'Have you ever been in love, Beach?'

'In my younger days, Mr Ronald. It never came to anything.'

'Love's a rummy thing, Beach.'

'Very true, sir.'

'Sort of keys you up, if you understand me. Makes you feel you'd stick at nothing. Take any chance. To win the girl you love, I mean.'

'Quite so, sir.'

'Go through fire and water, as you might say. Brave every peril.'

'No doubt, sir.'

'Got another dollop of that brandy, Beach?'

'Yes, sir.'

'Well, there it is,' said Ronnie, emptying his glass and holding it out for fresh supplies. 'Half-way through the fish course I made up my mind. Now that that manuscript has gone, I'm up against it. At any moment Aunt Constance will be at Uncle Clarence, telling him not to give me my money.'

The butler coughed commiseratingly.

'I rather fancy, Mr Ronald, that her ladyship was in the act of doing so when I entered the library not long ago.'

'Then by this time she has probably clicked?'

'I very much fear so, Mr Ronald.'

'Right!' said Ronnie briskly. 'Then there's nothing left but strong measures. The time has come to act, Beach.'

'Sir?'

'I'm going to steal that pig.'

'What, *again*, Mr Ronald?'

Ronnie eyed him affectionately.

'Ah, you remember that other time, then?'

'Remember it, Mr Ronald? Why, it was only ten days ago.'

'So it was. It seems years. Not that I can't recall every detail of it. I haven't forgotten how staunchly you stood by me then, Beach. You were splendid.'

'Thank you, sir.'

'Wonderful! Marvellous!' continued Ronnie in an exalted voice. 'I doubt if there has ever been anybody who came out of an affair better than you did out of that one. A sportsman to the finger-tips, that's what you showed yourself. And don't,' said Ronnie earnestly, 'think that I didn't notice it, either. I appreciated it very much, Beach.'

'It is very kind of you to say so, sir,' said the butler, his head swimming a little.

'You're a fellow a fellow can rely on.'

'Thank you, sir.'

'Through thick and thin.'

'Thank you, sir.'

'When I got this idea of stealing the Empress this second time, Miss Brown said to me, "Oh, but you can't ask Beach to help you again." And I said, "Of course I can. Apart from the fact that Beach and I have been pals for eighteen years, he's devoted to you." And she said, "Is he?" and I said, "You bet he is. There's nothing in the world Beach wouldn't do for you." And she said, "The darling!" Just like that. And you should have seen the look in her eyes as she said it, Beach. They went all soft and dreamy. I believe if you had been there at the moment she would have kissed you. And I shall be greatly surprised,' said Ronnie, with the air of one offering a treat to a deserving child, 'if, when everything is over and you've been as staunch as you were before and chipped in and done your bit again, as you did then, she doesn't do it.'

All through this moving address the butler had been shaking and rumbling in a manner which would have reminded an eyewitness irresistibly of a volcano on the point of finding self-expression. His eyes had bulged, and his breathing was coming in little puffs.

'But, Mr Ronald!'

'I knew you would be pleased, Beach.'

'But, Mr Ronald!'

Ronnie eyed him sharply.

'Don't tell me you're thinking of backing out?'

'But, sir!'

'You can't at the last moment like this, after all our plans have been made. It would upset everything. I can't act without you. You wouldn't let me down, Beach?'

'But, sir, the risk!'

'Risk? Nonsense.'

'But, Mr Ronald, his lordship was notified on the telephone in my presence not half an hour ago that an attempt was to be made upon the Empress tonight. I have only just returned from seeing Pirbright and conveying his lordship's instructions to him to be on his guard.'

'Well, that's fine. Don't you see how this fits in with our plans? Pirbright will be waiting for this chap. He will catch him. And then what will he do, Beach? He will march him off to Uncle Clarence, leaving the coast absolutely clear. While he's gone we nip in and collar the animal without the slightest danger of inconvenience.'

The butler puffed silently.

'Think what it means, Beach! My happiness! Miss Brown's happiness! You aren't going to go through the rest of your life kicking yourself at the thought that a little zeal, a little of the pull-together spirit on your part would have meant happiness for Miss Brown?'

'But if I were detected, sir, my position would be so extremely equivocal.'

'How can you be detected? Pirbright won't be there. Nobody will be there. I only need your help for about five minutes. This isn't like the last time. I'm not planning to hide the Empress somewhere and feed her. This is the real, straight kidnapping stuff. Just five minutes of your time, Beach, just five little minutes and you can come back here and forget all about it.'

Strong tremors continued to shake the butler's massive frame.

'Really only five minutes, Mr Ronald?' he said pleadingly.

'Ten at the outside. I forgot to tell you, Beach, that one of the things Miss Brown said about you was that you reminded her of her father. Oh, yes, and that you had such kind eyes.'

The butler's mouth opened. Lava might have been expected to flow from it, for his resemblance to a volcano had now become exceptionally close. But it was not lava that emerged. What did so was a strangled croak. This was followed by a remark which Ronnie did not catch.

'Eh?'

'I said "Very good," Mr Ronald,' said Beach, looking as if he were facing a firing squad.

'You'll do it?'

'Yes, Mr Ronald.'

'Beach,' said Ronnie with emotion, 'when I'm a millionaire, as I expect to be a few years after I've put my money in that motor business, the first thing I shall do is to come to this pantry with a purse of gold. Two purses of gold. Dash it, a keg of gold. I'll roll it in and knock off the lid and tell you to wade in and help yourself.'

'Thank you, Mr Ronald.'

'Don't thank *me*, Beach. You're the fellow who's entitled to all the gratitude that's going. And, talking of going, shall we be? There isn't a moment to lose. Shift ho, yes?'

'Very good, Mr Ronald,' said the butler in a strange, deep, rumbling voice, not unlike that of Mr A. L. Disher on the telephone.

17

Lady Julia Fish gave a little yawn and moved towards the
door. For ten minutes she had been listening to her sister
Constance express her views on the subject under
discussion, and she was not a woman who accepted
contentedly a thinking role in any scene in which she
took part. If Connie had a fault – and off-hand she could
name a dozen – it was that she tended to elbow her
associates out of the picture at times like this. Standing
by and acting as a silent audience bored Lady Julia.

'Well, if anybody wants me,' she said, 'they'll find me
in the drawing-room.'

'Are you going, Julia?'

'There doesn't seem much for me to do round here. I
feel that I am leaving the thing in competent hands. You
speak for me. The voice is the voice of Constance, but
you can take the sentiments, Clarence, as representing
the views of a syndicate.'

Lord Emsworth watched her go without much sense
of consolation. It is better, perhaps, to have one woman
rather than two women making your life an inferno, but
not so much better as to cause an elderly gentleman of
quiet tastes to rejoice to any very marked extent.

'Now, listen, Clarence . . .'

Lord Emsworth stifled a moan, and tried – a task
which the deaf adder of Scripture apparently found so
easy – to hear nothing and give his mind to the things
that really mattered.

He shifted restlessly on his settee. Surely soon there
ought to be news from the Front. By this time, if Mr

Disher was to be believed, the assault should have been made and, one hoped, rolled back by the devoted Pirbright.

Musing on Pirbright, Lord Emsworth became a little calmer. A capital fellow, he told himself, just the chap to handle the emergency which had arisen. Not much of a conversationalist, perhaps; scarcely the companion one would choose for a long railway journey; a little on the 'Ur' and 'Yur' side; but then who wanted a lively and epigrammatic pig-man? The point about Pirbright was that, if silent, he had that quality which so proverbially goes with silence – strength.

The door opened.

'Well, Beach?' said Lady Constance with queenly displeasure, for nobody likes to be interrupted in moments of oratory. 'What is it?'

Lord Emsworth sat up expectantly.

'Well, Beach, well?'

A close observer, which his lordship was not, would have seen that the butler had recently passed through some soul-searing experience. His was never a rosy face, but now it wore a pallor beyond the normal. His eyes were round and glassy, his breathing laboured. He looked like a butler who has just been brought into sharp contact with the facts of life.

'Everything is quite satisfactory, m'lord.'

'Pirbright caught the fellow?'

'Yes, m'lord.'

'Did he tell you what happened?'

'I was an eye-witness of the proceedings, m'lord.'

'Well? Well?'

'Oh, Clarence, must we really have all this now?'

'What? What? What? Of course we must have it now. God bless my soul! Yes, Beach?'

'The facts, m'lord, are as follows. In pursuance of your lordship's instructions, Pirbright had placed himself in concealment in the vicinity of the animal's sty, and from this post of vantage proceeded to keep a keen watch.'

'What were you doing there?'

The butler hesitated.

'I had come to lend assistance, m'lord, should it be required.'

'Splendid, Beach. Well?'

'My cooperation, however, was not found to be necessary. The man arrived . . .'

'Parsloe?'

('Clarence!')

'No, m'lord. Not Sir Gregory.'

'Ah, an accomplice.'

('Oh, Clarence!')

'No doubt, m'lord. The man arrived and came to the rails of the sty, where he remained for a moment . . .'

'Nerving himself! Nerving himself to his frightful task.'

'He seemed to be manipulating an electric torch, m'lord.'

'And then – ?'

'Pirbright sprang out and overpowered him.'

'Excellent! And where is the fellow now?'

'Temporarily incarcerated in the coal-cellar, m'lord.'

'Bring him to me at once.'

'Clarence, do we want this man, whoever he is, in here?'

'Yes, we do want him in here.'

Beach coughed.

'I should mention, m'lord, that he is considerably soiled. In order to overpower him, Pirbright was compelled to throw him face downwards and rest his weight upon him, and the ground in the neighbourhood of the sty had been somewhat softened by the heavy rain.'

'Never mind. I want to see him.'

'Very good, m'lord.'

The interval between the butler's retirement and reappearance was spent by Lady Constance in sniffing indignantly and by Lord Emsworth in congratulating himself that a sense of civic duty and a lively apprehension of what his sister would say if he resigned that office had kept him a Justice of the Peace. Representing, as he did, the majesty of the Law, he was in a position to deal summarily with this criminal. He would have to look it up in the book of instructions, of course, but he rather fancied he could give the chap fourteen days without moving from this settee.

The door had opened again.

'The miscreant, m'lord,' announced Beach.

With a final sniff, Lady Constance dissociated herself from the affair by withdrawing into a corner and opening a photograph album. There was a scuffling of feet, and the prisoner at the bar entered, trailing like clouds of glory Stokes, first footman, attached to his right arm, and Thomas, second footman, clinging like a limpet to his left.

'Good God!' cried Lord Emsworth, startled out of his judicial calm. 'What a horrible-looking brute!'

Lord Tilbury, though resenting the description keenly, would have been compelled, had he been able at the moment to look in a mirror, to recognize its essential justice. Beau Brummel himself could not have remained spruce after lying in four inches of mud with a six-foot pigman on top of him. Pirbright was a man who believed that a thing well begun is half done, and his first act had been to thrust Lord Tilbury's face firmly below the surface and keep it there.

A sudden idea struck Lord Emsworth.

'Beach!'

'Did Pirbright say if this was the same fellow he shut up in the shed yesterday?'

'Yes, m'lord.'

'It is?'

'Yes, m'lord.'

'God bless my soul!' cried Lord Emsworth.

This pertinacity appalled him. It showed how dangerous the chap was. None of that business here of the burned child dreading the potting-shed. No sooner was this fellow out of that mess than back he came for a second pop, as malignant as ever. The quicker he was put safely away behind the bars of Market Blandings' picturesque little prison, the better, felt Lord Emsworth.

He was interrupted in this meditation by a voice proceeding from behind the mud.

'Lord Emsworth, I wish to speak to you alone.'

'Well, you dashed well can't speak to me alone,' replied his lordship with decision. 'Think I'm going to allow myself to be left alone with a fellow like you? Beach!'

'M'lord?'

'Take that thingummajig,' said Lord Emsworth, indicating the young David prophesying before Saul, 'and if he so much as stirs hit him a good hard bang with it.'

'Very good, m'lord.'

'Now, then, what's your name?'

'I refuse to tell you my name unless you will let me speak to you alone.'

Lord Emsworth's gaze hardened.

'You notice how he keeps wanting to get me alone, Beach.'

'Yes, m'lord.'

'Suspicious.'

'Yes, m'lord.'

'Stand by with that thing.'

'Very good, m'lord,' said the butler, taking a firmer grip on David's left leg.

'Hallo,' said a voice. 'What's all this? Ah, Connie, I thought I should find you here.'

Lord Emsworth, peering through his pince-nez,

perceived that his brother Galahad had entered the room. With him was that little girl of Ronald's. At the sight of her Lord Emsworth found his righteous wrath tinged with a certain embarrassment.

'Don't come in here now, Galahad, there's a good fellow,' he begged. 'I'm busy.'

'Good God! What on earth's that?' cried the Hon. Galahad, his monocle leaping from his eye as he suddenly caught sight of the mass of alluvial deposits which was Lord Tilbury.

'It's a horrible chap Pirbright found sneaking into the Empress's sty,' explained Lord Emsworth. 'Parsloe's accomplice, whom you warned me about. I'm just going to give him fourteen days.'

This frank statement of policy decided Lord Tilbury. For the second time that day he thought on his feet. Passionately though he desired to preserve his incognito, he did not wish to do so at the expense of two weeks in jail.

'Threepwood,' he cried, 'tell this old fool who I am.'

The Hon. Galahad had recovered his monocle.

'But, my dear chap,' he protested, staring through it, 'I don't know who you are. You look like one of those Sons of Toil Buried by Tons of Soil I once saw in a headline. Are you somebody I've met?' He peered more closely and uttered an astonished cry. 'Stinker! Is it really you, my poor old Stinker, hidden away under all that real estate? I can explain all this, Clarence. I think first, perhaps, though, it would be as well to clear the court. Pop off, Beach, for a moment, if you don't mind.'

'Very good, Mr Galahad,' said Beach, with the disappointed air of a man who is being thrown out of a theatre just as the curtain is going up. He put down the young David and, collecting eyes like a hostess at a dinner-party, led Thomas and Stokes from the room.

'Is it safe, Galahad?' said Lord Ermsworth dubiously.

'Oh, Stinker – Pyke, I mean – Tilbury, that is to say, is quite harmless.'

'What did you say his name was?'

'Tilbury. Lord Tilbury.'

'*Lord* Tilbury?' said Lord Emsworth, gaping.

'Yes. Apparently they've made old Stinker a peer.'

'Then what was he doing trying to kill my pig?' asked Lord Emsworth, perplexed, for he had a high opinion of the moral purity of the House of Lords.

'He wasn't trying to kill your blasted pig. You came after that manuscript of mine, eh, Stinker?'

'I did,' said Lord Tilbury stiffly. 'I consider that I have a legal right to it.'

'Yes, we went into all that before, I remember. But abandon all hope, Stinker. There isn't any manuscript. The pig's eaten it.'

'What!'

'Yes. So unless you care to publish the pig . . .'

There was too much mud on Lord Tilbury's face to admit of any play of expression, but the sudden rigidity of his body told how shrewdly the blow had gone home.

'Oh!' he said at length.

'I'm afraid so,' said the Hon. Galahad sympathetically.

'If you will excuse me,' said Lord Tilbury, 'I will return to the Emsworth Arms.'

The Hon. Galahad took his soiled arm.

'My dear old chap! You can't possibly go to any pub looking like that. Beach will show you to the bathroom. Beach!'

'Sir?' said the butler, manifesting himself with the celerity of one who has never been far from the keyhole.

'Take Lord Tilbury to the bathroom, and then telephone to the Emsworth Arms to send up his things. He will be staying the night. Several nights. In fact, indefinitely. Yes, yes, Stinker, I insist. Dash it, man, we haven't seen one another for twenty-five years. I want a long yarn with you about the old days.'

For an instant it seemed as if the proud spirit of the Pykes was to flame in revolt. Lord Tilbury definitely drew himself up. But he was not the man he had been. Every man, moreover, has his price. That of the proprietor of the Mammoth Publishing Company at this moment was a hot bath with plenty of soap, a sprinkling of bath-salts, and well-warmed towels.

'Kind of you,' he said gruffly.

Like the mountain reluctantly deciding to come to Mahomet, he followed Beach from the room.

'And now, Connie,' said the Hon. Galahad, 'you can put that book down and come and join the party.'

Lady Constance moved with dignified step from her corner.

'I suppose,' said the Hon. Galahad, eyeing her unfraternally, 'you've been nagging and bullying poor old Clarence till he doesn't know where he is?'

'I have been giving Clarence my views.'

'You would. I suppose the poor devil's half off his head.'

'Clarence has been listening very patiently and attentively,' said Lady Constance. 'I think he understands what is the right thing for him to do in this matter – a matter which I must say I would prefer to discuss, if we are going to discuss it, in private.'

'You mean you don't want Sue here?'

'I should imagine that Miss Brown would find it less embarrassing not to be present.'

'Well, I do want her here,' said the Hon. Galahad. 'I brought her specially. To show her to you, Clarence.'

'Eh?' said Lord Emsworth, jumping. He had been dreaming of pigs.

'To show her to you, I said. I want you to take a look at this little girl, Clarence. Get those dashed pince-nez of yours straight and examine her steadily and carefully. What do you think of her?'

818

'Charming, charming,' said Lord Emsworth courteously.

'Isn't she just the very girl any sensible man would choose for his nephew's wife?'

'My dear Galahad!' said Lady Constance.

'Well?'

'I cannot see what all this is leading to. I imagine that nobody is disputing the fact that Miss Brown is a pretty girl.'

'Pretty girl be dashed! I'm not talking about her being a pretty girl. I'm talking of what anybody with half an eye ought to be able to see when he takes one look at her – that she's all right. Just as her mother was all right. Her mother was the sweetest, straightest, squarest, honestest, jolliest thing that ever lived. And Sue's the same. Any man who marries Sue is in luck. Damn it all, the way you women have been going on about him, one would think young Ronnie was the Prince of Wales or something. Who *is* Ronnie, dash it? My nephew. Well, look at me. Do you mean to assert that a fellow handicapped by an uncle like me isn't jolly lucky to get *any* girl to marry him?'

This sentiment so exactly chimed in with her own views that for once in her masterful life Lady Constance had nothing to say. She seemed vaguely to suspect a fallacy somewhere, but before she could investigate it her brother had gone on speaking.

'Clarence,' he said, 'take that infernal glassy look out of your eyes and listen to me. I realize that you hold the situation in your hands. You can't have been hearing Connie talk for any length of time without knowing that. This little girl's happiness depends entirely on what you make up your woolly, wobbly mind to do. Nobody is more alive than myself to the fact that young Ronnie, like all members of this family, is worth about twopence a week in the open market. He's got to have capital behind him.'

'Which he won't have.'

'Which he will have, if Clarence is the man I take him for. Clarence, wake up!'

'I'm awake, my dear fellow, I'm awake,' said Lord Emsworth.

'Well, then, does Ronnie get his money or doesn't he?'

Lord Emsworth looked like a hunted stag. He fiddled nervously with his pince-nez.

'Connie seems to think . . .'

'I know what Connie thinks, and when we're alone I'll tell you what I think of Connie.'

'If you are simply going to be abusive, Galahad . . .'

'Nothing of the kind. Abusive be dashed! I am taking great pains to avoid anything in the remotest degree personal or offensive. I consider you a snob and a mischief-maker, but you may be quite sure I shall not dream of saying so . . .'

'How very kind of you.'

'. . . until I am at liberty to confide it to Clarence in private. Well, Clarence?'

'Eh? What? Yes, my dear fellow?'

'It's a simple issue. Are you going to do the square thing or are you not?'

'Well, I'll tell you, Galahad. The view Connie takes . . .'

'Oh, damn Connie!'

'Galahad!'

'Yes, I repeat it. Damn Connie! Forget Connie. Drive it into your head that the view Connie takes doesn't amount to a row of beans.'

'Indeed! Really! Well, allow me to tell *you*, Galahad . . .'

'I won't allow you to tell me a thing.'

'I insist on speaking.'

'I won't listen.'

'Galahad!'

'May I say something?' said Sue.

She spoke in a small, deprecating voice, but if it had been a bellow it could scarcely have produced a greater effect. Lord Emsworth, in particular, who had forgotten that she was there, leaped on his settee like a gaffed trout.

'It's only this,' said Sue, in the silence. 'I'm awfully sorry to upset everybody, but Ronnie and I are motoring to London tonight, and we're going to get married tomorrow.'

'What!'

'Yes,' said Sue. 'You see, there's been so much trouble and misunderstanding and everything's so difficult as it is at present that we talked it over and came to the conclusion that the only safe thing is to be married. Then we feel that everything will be all right.'

Lady Constance turned majestically to the head of the family.

'Do you hear this, Clarence?'

'What do you mean, do I hear it?' said Lord Emsworth with that weak testiness which always came upon him when family warfare centred about his person. 'Of course I hear it. Do you think I'm deaf?'

'Well, I hope you will show a little firmness for once in your life.'

'Firmness?'

'Exert your authority. Forbid this.'

'How the devil can I forbid it? This is a free country, isn't it? People have a perfect right to motor to London if they want to, haven't they?'

'You know quite well what I mean. If you are firm about not letting Ronald have his money, he can do nothing.'

The Hon. Galahad seemed regretfully to be of this opinion, too.

'My dear child,' he said, 'I don't want to damp you, but what on earth are you going to live on?'

'I think that when he hears everything, Lord Emsworth will give Ronnie his money.'

'Eh?'

'That's what Ronnie thinks. He thinks that when Lord Emsworth knows that he has got the Empress . . .'

Lord Emsworth rose up like a rising pheasant.

'What! What? What's that? Got her? How do you mean, got her?'

'He took her out of her sty just now,' explained Sue, 'and put her in the dicky of his car.'

Even in his anguish Lord Emsworth had to stop to inquire into this seemingly superhuman feat.

'What! How on earth could anyone put the Empress in the dicky of a car?'

'Exactly,' said Lady Constance. 'Surely even you, Clarence, can see that this is simply ridiculous . . .'

'Oh, no,' said Sue. 'It was quite easy, really. Ronnie pulled – and a friend of his pushed.'

'Of course,' said the Hon. Galahad, the expert. 'What you're forgetting, Clarence, what you've overlooked is the fact that the Empress has a ring through her nose, which facilitates moving her from spot to spot. When Puffy Benger and I stole old Wivenhoe's pig the night of the Bachelors' Ball at Hammer's Easton in ninety-five, we had to get her up three flights of stairs before we could put her in Plug Basham's bedroom . . .'

'What Ronnie says he thinks he'll do,' proceeded Sue, 'is to take the Empress joy-riding . . .'

'Joy-riding!' cried Lord Emsworth, appalled.

'Only if you won't give him his money, of course. If you really don't feel you can, he says he's going to drive her all over England . . .'

'What an admirable idea!' said the Hon. Galahad with approval. 'I see what you mean. Birmingham today, Edinburgh tomorrow, Brighton the day after. Sort of circular tour. See the country a bit, what?'

'Yes.'

'He ought to take in Skegness. Skegness is so bracing.'

'I must tell him.'

Lord Emsworth was fighting to preserve what little sanity he had.

'I don't believe it,' he cried.

'Ronnie thought you might not. He felt that you would probably want to see for yourself. So he's waiting down there on the drive, just outside the window.'

It was not at a time like this that Lord Emsworth would allow a trifle like an injured ankle to impede him. He sprang acrobatically from the settee and hopped to the window.

From the dicky of the car immediately below it the mild face of the Empress peered up at him, silvered by the moonlight. He uttered a fearful cry.

'Ronald!'

His nephew, seated at the wheel, glanced up, tooted the horn with a sort of respectful regret, threw in his clutch, and passed on into the shadows. The tail-light of the car shone redly as it halted some fifty yards down the drive.

'I'm afraid it's no good shouting at him,' said Sue.

'Of course it isn't,' agreed the Hon. Galahad heartily. 'What you want to do, Clarence, is to stop all this nonsense and give a formal promise before witnesses to cough up that money, and then write a cheque for a thousand or two for honeymoon expenses.'

'That was what Ronnie suggested,' said Sue. 'And then Pirbright could go and take the Empress back to bed.'

'Clarence!' began Lady Constance.

But Lord Emsworth in his travail was proof against any number of 'Clarence's!' He had hopped to the desk and with feverish fingers was fumbling in the top drawer.

'Clarence, you are not to do this!'

'I certainly am going to do it,' said Lord Emsworth, testing a pen with his thumb.

'Does this miserable pig mean more to you than your nephew's whole future?'

'Of course it does,' said Lord Emsworth, surprised at the foolish question. 'Besides, what's wrong with his future? His future's all right. He's going to marry this nice little girl here; I've forgotten her name. She'll look after him.'

'Bravely spoken, Clarence,' said the Hon. Galahad approvingly.

'The right spirit.'

'Well, in that case . . .'

'Don't go, Connie,' urged the Hon. Galahad. 'We may need you as a witness or something. In any case, surely you can't tear yourself away from a happy scene like this? Why, dash it, it's like that thing of Kipling's . . . how does it go . . . ?

'We left them all in couples a-dancing on the decks,
We left the lovers loving and the parents signing
    cheques,
In endless English comfort, by County folk caressed,
We steered the old three-decker . . .'

The door slammed.

'". . . to the Islands of the Blest,"' concluded the Hon. Galahad. 'Write clearly, Clarence, on one side of the paper, and don't forget to sign your name, as you usually do. The date is August the fourteenth.'

18

The red tail-light of the two-seater turned the corner of
the drive and vanished in the night. The Hon. Galahad
polished his monocle thoughtfully, replaced it in his eye,
and stood for some moments gazing at the spot where it
had disappeared. The storm had left the air sweet and
fresh. The moon rode gallantly in a cloudless sky. The
night was very still, so still that even the lightest
footstep on the gravel would have made itself heard. The
one which now attracted the Hon. Galahad's attention
was not light. It was the emphatic, crunching thump of a
man of substance.

He turned.

'Beach?'

'Yes, Mr Galahad.'

'What are you doing out at this time of night?'

'I thought that I would pay a visit to the sty, sir, and
ascertain that the Empress had taken no harm from her
disturbed evening.'

'Remorse, eh?'

'Sir?'

'Guilty conscience. It was you who did the pushing,
wasn't it, Beach?'

'Yes, sir. We discussed the matter, and Mr Ronald was
of opinion that on account of my superior weight I
would be more effective than himself in that capacity.'
A note of anxiety crept into the butler's voice. 'You will
treat this, Mr Galahad, as purely confidential, I trust?'

'Of course.'

'Thank you, sir. It would jeopardize my position, I

fear, were his lordship to learn of what I had done. I saw
Mr Ronald and the young lady go off, Mr Galahad.'

'You did? I didn't see you.'

'I had taken up a position some little distance away,
sir.'

'You ought to have come and said good-bye.'

'I had already taken leave of the young couple, sir.
They visited me in my pantry.'

'So they ought. You have fought the good fight, Beach.
I hope they kissed you.'

'The young lady did, sir.'

There was a soft note in the butler's fruity voice. He
drew up the toe of his left shoe and rather coyly
scratched his right calf with it.

'She did, eh? "Jenny kissed me when we met, jumping
from the chair she sat in." I'm full of poetry tonight,
Beach. The moon, I suppose.'

'Very possibly, sir. I fear Mr Ronald and the young
lady will have a long and tedious journey.'

'Long. Not tedious.'

'It is a great distance to drive, sir.'

'Not when you're young.'

'No, sir. Would it be taking a liberty, Mr Galahad, if I
were to inquire if Mr Ronald's financial position has
been satisfactorily stabilized? When I saw him, the
matter was still in the balance.'

'Oh, quite. And did you find the Empress pretty
fit?'

'Quite, Mr Galahad.'

'Then everything's all right. These things generally
work themselves out fairly well, Beach.'

'Very true, sir.'

There was a pause. The butler lowered his voice
confidentially.

'Did her ladyship express any comment on the affair,
Mr Galahad?'

'Which ladyship?'

'I was alluding to Lady Julia, sir.'

'Oh, Julia? Beach,' said the Hon. Galahad, 'there are the seeds of greatness in that woman. I'll give you three guesses what she said and did.'

'I could not hazard a conjecture, sir.'

'She said "Well, well!" and lit a cigarette.'

'Indeed, sir?'

'You never knew her as a child, did you, Beach?'

'No, sir. Her ladyship must have been in the late twenties when I entered his lordship's employment.'

'I saw her bite a governess once.'

'Indeed, sir?'

'In two places. And with just that serene, angelic look on her face which she wore just now. A great woman, Beach.'

'I have always had the greatest respect for her ladyship, Mr Galahad.'

'And I'm inclined to think that young Ronnie, in spite of looking like a minor jockey with scarlatina, must have inherited some of her greatness. Tonight has opened my eyes, Beach. I begin to understand what Sue sees in him. Stealing that pig, Beach. Shows character. And snatching her up like this and whisking her off to London. There's more in young Ronnie than I suspected. I think he'll make the girl happy.'

'I am convinced of it, sir.'

'Well, he'd better, or I'll skin him. Did you ever see Dolly Henderson, Beach?'

'On several occasions, sir, when I was in service in London. I frequently went to the Tivoli and the Oxford in those days.'

'This girl's very like her, don't you think?'

'Extremely, Mr Galahad.'

The Hon. Galahad looked out over the moon-flooded garden. In the distance there sounded faintly the splashing of the little waterfall that dropped over fern-crusted rocks into the lake.

'Well, good night, Beach.'
'Good night, Mr Galahad.'

Empress of Blandings stirred in her sleep and opened an eye. She thought she had heard the rustle of a cabbage-leaf, and she was always ready for cabbage-leaves, no matter how advanced the hour. Something came bowling across the straw, driven by the night breeze.

It was not a cabbage-leaf, only a sheet of paper with writing on it, but she ate it with no sense of disappointment. She was a philosopher and could take things as they came. Tomorrow was another day, and there would be cabbage-leaves in the morning.

The Empress turned on her side and closed her eyes with a contented little sigh. The moon beamed down upon her noble form. It looked like a silver medal.

The P G Wodehouse Society (UK)

The P G Wodehouse Society (UK) was formed in 1997 and exists to promote the enjoyment of the works of the greatest humorist of the twentieth century.

The Society publishes a quarterly magazine, *Wooster Sauce*, which features articles, reviews, archive material and current news. It also publishes an occasional newsletter in the *By The Way* series which relates a single matter of Wodehousean interest. Members are rewarded in their second and subsequent years by receiving a specially produced text of a Wodehouse magazine story which has never been collected into one of his books.

A variety of Society events are arranged for members including regular meetings at a London club, a golf day, a cricket match, a Society dinner, and walks round Bertie Wooster's London. Meetings are also arranged in other parts of the country.

Membership enquiries

Membership of the Society is available to applicants from all parts of the world. The cost of a year's membership in 1998 was £15. Enquiries and requests for an application form should be addressed in writing to the Membership Secretary, Christine Hewitt, at 26 Radcliffe Road, Croydon, Surrey CRO 5QE, or write to the Editor of *Wooster Sauce*, Tony Ring, at 34 Longfield, Great Missenden, Bucks HP16 OEG.

You can visit their website at:
http://www.eclipse.co.uk/wodehouse

PENGUIN ONLINE

READ MORE IN PENGUIN

In every corner of the world, on every subject under the sun, Penguin represents quality and variety – the very best in publishing today.

For complete information about books available from Penguin – including Puffins, Penguin Classics and Arkana – and how to order them, write to us at the appropriate address below. Please note that for copyright reasons the selection of books varies from country to country.

In the United Kingdom: Please write to *Dept. EP, Penguin Books Ltd, Bath Road, Harmondsworth, West Drayton, Middlesex UB7 ODA*

In the United States: Please write to *Consumer Sales, Penguin Putnam Inc., P.O. Box 12289 Dept. B, Newark, New Jersey 07101-5289.* VISA and MasterCard holders call 1-800-788-6262 to order Penguin titles

In Canada: Please write to *Penguin Books Canada Ltd, 10 Alcorn Avenue, Suite 300, Toronto, Ontario M4V 3B2*

In Australia: Please write to *Penguin Books Australia Ltd, P.O. Box 257, Ringwood, Victoria 3134*

In New Zealand: Please write to *Penguin Books (NZ) Ltd, Private Bag 102902, North Shore Mail Centre, Auckland 10*

In India: Please write to *Penguin Books India Pvt Ltd, 11 Community Centre, Panchsheel Park, New Delhi 110017*

In the Netherlands: Please write to *Penguin Books Netherlands bv, Postbus 3507, NL-1001 AH Amsterdam*

In Germany: Please write to *Penguin Books Deutschland GmbH, Metzlerstrasse 26, 60594 Frankfurt am Main*

In Spain: Please write to *Penguin Books S. A., Bravo Murillo 19, 1° B, 28015 Madrid*

In Italy: Please write to *Penguin Italia s.r.l., Via Benedetto Croce 2, 20094 Corsico, Milano*

In France: Please write to *Penguin France, Le Carré Wilson, 62 rue Benjamin Baillaud, 31500 Toulouse*

In Japan: Please write to *Penguin Books Japan Ltd, Kaneko Building, 2-3-25 Koraku, Bunkyo-Ku, Tokyo 112*

In South Africa: Please write to *Penguin Books South Africa (Pty) Ltd, Private Bag X14, Parkview, 2122 Johannesburg*

MORE P. G. WODEHOUSE IN PENGUIN 🐧

'The funniest writer ever to put words on paper' Hugh Laurie

SHORT STORIES

Blandings Castle

'A collection of short snorts between the solid orgies' was how P.G. Wodehouse regarded these stories, which range from the Blandings of Lord Emsworth to the Hollywood of the Mulliners.

Lord Emsworth and Others

Nine delicious stories which include the disgraceful affair of the crime wave at Blandings, extracts from the unsteady career of Ukridge and more tales from Mr Mulliner and from the Oldest Member at the golf club.

The Man with Two Left Feet

Consider the case of Henry Pitfield Rice, Detective. Or the King of Coney Island, the Super-Fan, or, of course, Henry Wallace Mills, of the two left feet. Consider any or all of these twelve vintage cases of good eggs and decent chaps entangled in snares of young love . . .

The Pothunters and Other School Stories

Wodehouse won the first of his many laurels with these school stories where, in the daily round of prefects, fags, dorms and cricket, he creates a gloriously absurd and immortal world which never palls.

Eggs, Beans and Crumpets

'*Eggs, Beans and Crumpets* was the first Wodehouse I ever read and it changed my life . . . I devoured it and read, must have been, fifty other Wodehouse over the next couple of years' Ben Elton, *Booked*

MORE P. G. WODEHOUSE IN PENGUIN ⓟ

'Witty and effortlessly fluid. His books are laugh-out-loud funny'
Arabella Weir

LIFE AT BLANDINGS

A selection:

'For Wodehouse there has been no fall of Man ... the gardens of
Blandings Castle are the original gardens from which we are all exiled'
Evelyn Waugh

The tranquil idyll of life at Blandings is once again shattered by
scrapes and skulduggery, mishaps and mix-ups in:

Galahad at Blandings

A major mix-up at the Castle, in which Gally introduces yet another
impostor to Lord Emsworth's residence, and the Empress of Blandings somehow gets drunk in her sty.

A Pelican at Blandings

Lovers and thieves gather at Blandings: Lord Emsworth wants them
all to go away. To cap it all, the Empress has refused a potato.
Galahad, last of the Pelicans, flies to the rescue.

Sunset at Blandings

This, the last unfinished chronicle of Blandings, includes a treasure
trove of detailed notes on the final stages of the plot, enabling us to
observe the Master at work.

Lord Emsworth Acts for the Best
The Collected Blandings Short Stories

Brought together in one volume for the first time and introduced by
Frank Muir, these immortal stories show that Blandings is a place
where anything can happen ...

MORE P. G. WODEHOUSE IN PENGUIN 🐧

'What can one say about Wodehouse? He exhausts superlatives'
Stephen Fry, Mail on Sunday

LIFE AT BLANDINGS

Omnibus editions, also published in separate volumes:

Imperial Blandings
Full Moon • Pigs Have Wings • Service with a Smile

Perfect happiness for Lord Emsworth is to listen to the contented night breathing of his medal-winning pig. But so often there is a snake in his Garden of Eden, a crumpled leaf in his bed of roses, a grain of sand in his spiritual spinach. For Blandings is regarded by his sisters as a suitable repository for young women engaged to impecunious suitors. Worse still a bad baronet and a devious Duke attempt some funny business with the ancestral porker. But usually the Hon. Galahad Threepwood or Lord Ickham can bring sweetness and light back into the rose garden and save Lord Emsworth's bacon for him – to *almost* everyone's satisfaction . . .

Uncle Fred
Uncle Fred in the Springtime • Uncle Dynamite • Cocktail Time

Amid kidnappings, jewel-thefts, *amours*, and comedy galore, Frederick, fifth Earl of Ickenham, spreads sweetness and light. Without him, Beefy Bastable, QC, might never have penned his alarming bestseller, *Cocktail Time*; and Lord Emsworth's beloved pig, the Empress, would undoubtedly have been abducted from Blandings. Worst of all, the Earl's myopic nephew Pongo would have breezed past the sweetest girl in the world, and be hitched eternally to the truly ghastly Hermione Bostock.